THE VIKING PORTABLE LIBRARY
Nineteenth-Century Russian Reader

George Gibian, who has taught at Smith College and the University of California at Berkeley, is presently the Goldwin Smith Professor of Russian and Comparative Literature at Cornell University. He received his Ph.D. from Harvard and has had a Senior Fellowship in the National Endowment for the Humanities and a Guggenheim Fellowship. His publications include *Tolstoy and Shakespeare, The Interval of Freedom: Soviet Russian Literature During the Thaw, The Man in the Black Coat: Russia's Literature of the Absurd,* and the Norton Critical Editions of *Crime and Punishment, Anna Karenina, War and Peace,* and *Dead Souls.*

Each volume in The Viking Portable Library either presents a representative selection from the works of a single outstanding writer or offers a comprehensive anthology on a special subject. Averaging 700 pages in length and designed for compactness and readability, these books fill a need not met by other compilations. All are edited by distinguished authorities, who have written introductory essays and included much other helpful material.

The Portable

Nineteenth-Century Russian Reader

Edited by

GEORGE GIBIAN

PENGUIN BOOKS

PENGUIN BOOKS
Published by the Penguin Group
Penguin Group (USA) Inc., 375 Hudson Street, New York, New York 10014, U.S.A.
Penguin Group (Canada), 90 Eglinton Avenue East, Suite 700, Toronto,
Ontario, Canada M4P 2Y3 (a division of Pearson Penguin Canada Inc.)
Penguin Books Ltd, 80 Strand, London WC2R 0RL, England
Penguin Ireland, 25 St Stephen's Green, Dublin 2, Ireland
(a division of Penguin Books Ltd)
Penguin Group (Australia), 250 Camberwell Road, Camberwell,
Victoria 3124, Australia (a division of Pearson Australia Group Pty Ltd)
Penguin Books India Pvt Ltd, 11 Community Centre, Panchsheel Park,
New Delhi – 110 017, India
Penguin Group (NZ), 67 Apollo Drive, Rosedale, North Shore 0632, New Zealand
(a division of Pearson New Zealand Ltd)
Penguin Books (South Africa) (Pty) Ltd, 24 Sturdee Avenue, Rosebank,
Johannesburg 2196, South Africa

Penguin Books Ltd, Registered Offices: 80 Strand, London WC2R 0RL, England

First published in Penguin Books 1993

20

Copyright © Viking Penguin, a division of Penguin Books USA Inc., 1993
All rights reserved

Pages 643–644 constitute an extension of this copyright page.

LIBRARY OF CONGRESS CATALOGING IN PUBLICATION DATA
The portable nineteenth-century Russian reader/ edited by George Gibian.
p. cm.
ISBN 978-0-14-015103-9
1. Russian literature—19th century—Translations into English.
I. Gibian, George.   II. Title: Portable 19th century Russian reader.
PG3213.P66   1993
891.7'08'003—dc20   92–39863

Printed in the United States of America
Set in Sabon
Designed by Cheryl L. Cipriani

CONTENTS

NOTE: Names of translators are indicated in italics

INTRODUCTION BY GEORGE GIBIAN   ix
CHRONOLOGY BY GEORGE GIBIAN   xvii

ALEKSANDR PUSHKIN

Seclusion (*Walter Arndt*)   4
Epigram on A. A. Davydova (*Walter Arndt*)   4
Winter Evening (*Vladimir Nabokov*)   5
To . . . (*Walter Arndt*)   6
Arion (*Walter Arndt*)   6
Remembrance (*Walter Arndt*)   7
The dreary day is spent (*Walter Arndt*)   7
I loved you (*Walter Arndt*)   8
The Bronze Horseman (*Walter Arndt*)   8
Exegi Monumentum (*Vladimir Nabokov*)   21
The Shot (*Gillon R. Aitken*)   22

ALEKSANDR GRIBOYEDOV

The Trouble with Reason (*Frank R. Reeve*)   35

MIKHAIL LERMONTOV

My Native Land (*Vladimir Nabokov*)   131
Farewell (*Vladimir Nabokov*)   132
From the Author's Introduction to *A Hero of Our Time*   132
    (*George Gibian*)

Preface to *Pechorin's Diary* (*George Gibian*)   133
Princess Mary (*Vladimir Nabokov with Dmitri   133
    Nabokov*)

NIKOLAY GOGOL

The Overcoat (*Bernard Guilbert Guerney*)   202
Easter Sunday (from *Selected Passages*)   232
    (*George Gibian*)
In Praise of Russian Peasants (from *Dead Souls*, vol. 2)   236
    (*Jesse Zeldin*)
On the Character of the Russians (*George Gibian*)   237
The Controversy over Gogol's *Selected Passages*:
    Vissarion Belinsky, Letter to Gogol (*George Gibian*)   237
    Apollon Grigoryev, on Gogol (*George Gibian*)   239
    Aleksandr Blok, on Gogol and Grigoryev (*George   240
    Gibian*)
    Vladimir Kniazhnin, on Grigoryev (*George Gibian*)   240

SERGEY AKSAKOV

Mikhail Maximovich Kurolesov (from *The Family   242
    Chronicle*) (*M. C. Beverley*)

FYODOR TYUTCHEV

Tears   276
Summer Nightfall   277
Appeasement   277
Silentium!   278
The Abyss   278
Human Tears   279
Last Love (*all by Vladimir Nabokov*)   279
Is Russia Distinct from the West? (*George Gibian*)   280

KAROLINA PAVLOVA

From *A Double Life*   282
Strange, the Way We Met (*both by Barbara Heldt*)   291

IVAN GONCHAROV

Oblomov's Dream (*David Magarshack*)   295

Contents

.

15

IVAN TURGENEV

First Love (*Ivy and Tatiana Litvinov, revised by George Gibian*) — 336

On Belinsky (*David Magarshack*) — 390

On the Russian Language (*George Gibian*) — 391

ALEKSANDR HERZEN

Recollections of Russian Intellectuals—1830s and 1860s (from *My Past and Thoughts*) (*Leo Navrozov*) — 393

RUSSIAN FOLK PROVERBS

(*George Gibian*) — 401

KOZMA PRUTKOV

The Fruits of Reflection: Thoughts and Aphorisms (*George Gibian*) — 406

A Memory of Bygone Days (*Barbara Heldt*) — 409

FYODOR DOSTOYEVSKY

The Grand Inquisitor (from *The Brothers Karamazov*) (*Richard Pevear and Larissa Volokhonsky*) — 413

On the Mission of Russia (*George Gibian*) — 433

On Russian Distinctiveness and Universality (from a speech on Pushkin) (*George Gibian*) — 433

LEO TOLSTOY

The Death of Ivan Ilych (*Aylmer Maude*) — 440

Master and Man (*S. Rapoport and John C. Kenworthy, revised by George Gibian*) — 489

How Literature Teaches Us about Moral and Psychological Life (*George Gibian*) — 529

ANTON CHEKHOV

The Lady with the Dog (*Ivy Litvinov*) — 534

Uncle Vanya (*David Magarshack*) — 549

MIKHAIL SALTYKOV-SHCHEDRIN

The Story of How One Russian Peasant Fed Two Russian Generals (*George Gibian*)   609

MAKSIM GORKY

Twenty-Six Men and One Girl (*Bernard Isaacs, revised by George Gibian*)   618

VLADIMIR SOLOVYOV

Lectures on Godmanhood (*George L. Kline*)   631

SUGGESTIONS FOR FURTHER READING   639

INTRODUCTION

RUSSIAN AUTHORS were almost unknown outside of Russia as late as the middle of the nineteenth century. But by the end of World War I, Dostoyevsky, Tolstoy, Gogol, Pushkin, Turgenev, Chekhov, and Gorky had become household names in the West, and writers from Hemingway to Gide and Hesse were learning their craft by closely studying the art of those Russian literary giants.

Modern Russian literature emerged seemingly out of nowhere around 1825 and was fully developed by the 1840s. Though many works of Russian literature had been produced since the Middle Ages, some excellent and many very interesting and historically valuable, none had yet become part of the treasure house of the greatest achievements of European literary culture, comparable to the work of Dante, Shakespeare, Molière, or Goethe. Then suddenly Pushkin, Lermontov, Gogol, and others appeared, and—after a delay in some countries amounting to one generation, in others to two or three—their splendid works overwhelmed readers in many parts of the world.

Literature in Russia played a far broader role than in other societies. While Winston Churchill's *History of the English-Speaking Peoples* does not even list Shakespeare in its index, it would be unimaginable for a history of the Russian people not to give a lion's share of attention to the country's great writers. They were an artistic, spiritual, and social force. Russian readers (and censors and opponents) looked to the great novelists, poets, and playwrights for plots, characters, and ideas expressive of the chief issues of their age.

Characters like Chekhov's Lady with the Dog, Tolstoy's Ivan Ilych Golovkin, Gogol's Akakii Akakiievich and his overcoat, Pushkin's Bronze Horseman, Goncharov's Oblomov, Dostoyevsky's Grand Inquisitor, and others have entered the Russian collective consciousness.

Russians shape and fill their minds with their literary works. They look to them for their models, for lessons about themselves and their country. We, too, can learn about their culture from their writings and become better able to understand Russians—both our contemporaries and those of past centuries.

Isaiah Berlin has spoken of the vast "bill of indictment which Russian literature has been drafting against Russian life." But Russian writing was not always a critique, an accusation. It was also a rich and varied literature that celebrated many aspects of life and that sought to create a sense of Russian national identity.

Few other outlets existed in Russia for expressing one's view of the life of individuals and of society. What the Russians called the "eternal questions" or the "cursed questions"—the questions of good and evil and the purpose of life presented in Dostoyevsky's *Brothers Karamazov*, for example—were the staple of Russian literary works, not of church sermons or debates in Parliament.

What are some of the outstanding qualities of Russian literature (and, necessarily, Russian culture and social psychology)? One of them is intensity. Russian writing tends to the extreme—to that which is piercing, strong, fervent, untrammeled. The favorite biblical passage of Dostoyevsky, found in the Book of Revelation—"I would thou wert either cold or hot. If you are lukewarm, I shall spew you out"—typifies one characteristic mind-set: the famous Russian "maximalism." Those imbued with this cultural preference share a broad soul, largeness, and magnanimity, while disdaining pettiness, carefulness (called "accuracy"), penny-pinching, and legalism as mere "formalism."

The Russian tendency toward going to extremes is often combined with a high level of moral fervor, such as is exhibited in the characters of Dostoyevsky and Tolstoy. Hence the tendency to succumb to the lure of utopias—religious-social, Bolshevik, or nationalistic. Self-sacrifice is attractive, but for what cause? We see many examples of this push toward, and beyond, the limit, from Lermontov's Pechorin and Pushkin's Silvio onward. Ideas and systems imported from the West (where they may be circumscribed and limited by local traditions and habits of moderation) quickly grew and exploded in Russia, leading people to act upon blueprint utopias. Gogol's *Easter Sunday* and Dostoyevsky's "Grand Inquisitor" section from *The Brothers Karamazov* represent this Russian tendency.

There was little inclination toward closed forms in Russian literature, toward contrived, carefully crafted works. On the contrary, nineteenth-century Russian writers were attracted toward openness and freedom. Critics and literary historians have described nineteenth-century Russian literature as an attempt to burst through Western genres: to amalgamate, to broaden, to loosen or abolish the restrictions of literary modes, to move to mixed, original, and more fluid structures.

We often encounter multiple, conflicting visions and voices. For example, Gogol in his *Selected Passages* created many voices—of the warning Jeremiah, of the eulogist, of the preacher. From scourging what is corrupt in the world of his own time, he turns to the voice of the celebrator of what *could* be a new reality. In "Exegi Monumentum," Pushkin speaks with a prophet's voice, but elsewhere he assumes numerous other personae. The voices of Russian authors can range from the quiet, intimate narration of Turgenev and Chekhov to the zeal of a Dostoyevsky or the satirical tone of Saltykov-Shchedrin.

Russian writers also possessed subtle perceptiveness in psychological analysis and skill in portraiture of characters. They presented the human individual personality as fluid, psychology as dynamic. Long before Freud, Lawrence, Gide, and Hesse, they recognized human nature to be complex, deep, contradictory, unstable, changeable. Chekhov, Turgenev, and Tolstoy were each masters of psychological insight.

Russian culture tends to downgrade the intellect, theories, and abstractions. It finds significance in the aptly chosen detail and in representations of a variety of nuances of human feeling. Compassion is an especially prized emotion in Russia. (Prisoners were called "the pitiable ones"—*zhalkie* and *goremychnye*—in the vernacular.) Spontaneous emotion and intuition are valued above reason.

Interest in the individual, a talent for catching the essence of an idiosyncratic human being, may be the most appealing quality of Russian authors. Their literature is focused on individuals and the narratives that encapsulate them. As the narrator of Herzen's *Who Is to Blame?* explains just before launching into the life story of a minor figure in the novel,

> There is nothing on earth more individual and more diversified than the biographies of ordinary people, especially where no two people ever share the same idea, where each person develops in his own way without either looking back or worrying about where it will lead. . . . For this reason I never avoid biographical digressions. They reveal the full splendor of the universe. The reader who so wishes may skip over these episodes, but in doing so he will miss the essence of the story.

Other authors besides Herzen preferred narratives to discursive, abstract interpretations of life, and prized stories of individual human fates even if they were digressions from the main plot of their works. A foreign reader may well follow the Russian view that when we seek to know Russian reality, narratives lead us nearer our goal than abstract systems.

One important and often neglected fact of Russian history is that there were two very distinct types of Russian culture: the oral (folk) and the educated (literate). The "people" (*narod*) lived within a traditional culture, and the educated in a very different, Westernized milieu. The people's subliterate culture had its own folk medicine, folk sayings, folktales, songs, customs, riddles, superstitions, religious beliefs (pre-Christian as well as Russian Orthodox and those of Old Believer and other sects), various social organizations, and, most important, its own values and attitudes about everything surrounding their life.

The people also exerted an influence over their educated superiors (and not merely the other way around). They served as nannies to the children of the gentry, worked for them in the house and in the fields, sometimes bore them illegitimate children, and could at times become the object of a cult—the worship, almost a deification, of "the people" by the writers and intelligentsia. Sacralizing of the simple people was performed largely unconsciously, at other times quite overtly—by Gogol, Dostoyevsky, and Tyutchev, among others. Gogol, for example, felt that love of Russian songs, enthusiasm for fast travel on the highways, and the people's malleability, instinctive astuteness, and capacity for a utopian vision were indications of a distinctive, transcendent quality. The selection of proverbs in this anthology represents down-to-earth expressions of popular opinion about distinctive "Russianness." (As will be seen, the works by Goncharov, Aksakov, Saltykov-Shchedrin, and others also incorporate proverbs and folk beliefs.)

Another element in the literature being considered here—one often not given sufficient attention—is the Russia-oriented tradition, which can be contrasted with the mainstream tradition of progressive, Westernized, rationalistic opinion. Western writers and students (also for the most part adherents of progressive, rationalistic worldviews) have tended to follow the lead of nineteenth- and twentieth-century Russian critics and literary historians of the progressivist camp, who install these so-called liberal traditions as the dominant or even sole representation of Russian culture. Yet the other tradition—stressing unique

Russian qualities—also existed and was very important, even if despised and disregarded by its opponents. And by no means did all of it degenerate into its several xenophobic, chauvinistic, or imperialistic manifestations. We can trace this Russia-oriented tradition from Gogol and Grigoryev to Dostoyevsky and Blok.

At the turn of the century a remarkable revival of Russian spiritual, religious, and sometimes mystical interests took place. (Eventually it was stamped out by the Bolshevik Revolution, but it began its second rebirth in the late 1980s.) Believing that Russia cannot be understood without paying some attention to this current of opinion, I have tried to rescue a sampling of some such writings from the silent treatment they often suffered—in Gogol, Grigoryev, and Solovyov.

Russian literature is indeed rich in deep, philosophical, moody, and even gloomy writing. But there is as well a vibrant body of humorous writing, too often slighted in both Russian and Western discussions and anthologies—not for ideological reasons, but because the academic guardians of culture, both Eastern and Western, put a high value on earnestness and are sometimes even downright ashamed of plain fun and comedy. But humor (even if irreverent or blasphemous), parodies, and nonsense are very much present in nineteenth-century Russian culture, as represented in this volume with the selections from the nonsense and absurd works attributed to a (fictitious) Kozma Prutkov.

Students of Russian culture and social psychology—such as the Tartu scholar Yuri Lotman, the linguist and anthropologist Vyacheslav Ivanov, and others—have shown that the propensity for distinguishing one's own identity from the other—universal among humans—is stronger in Russian culture than in most other nations. Nineteenth-century Russian thinkers concerned with their country's mission in history invariably compared Russia with Western Europe: How was Russia different? How different should it be? Did it have similarities with Asia—or was it really somewhere in between, a Eurasian culture? Should it have its own institutions, or should it try to adopt "advanced" European forms? Solutions to these questions varied greatly. The Slavophiles and Russophiles supported more distinctiveness— "nativism"—while the Westernizers favored borrowing and learning from Germany, France, and England.

Russian culture also tends to alternate between long periods of passivism and brief, violent rebellions. Their folktale character Ivan will sleep warming himself atop the stove for seven years, then awaken, get drunk, swing his ax around indiscriminately, and finally relapse again into quiet sleep. Such, at least, is one Russian self-image or myth.

Russian culture in the nineteenth century was also still very much in touch with pre-Christian myths (Mother Earth and other chthonic folk attitudes), as well as Christian, Orthodox beliefs and rituals.

Russian writers suffered from a double handcuffing and strait-jacketing—not merely by the czarist regime and its censors, but also by their own equally intolerant colleagues among the intelligentsia, with their unequivocal insistence on complete loyalty and agreement, and no divergence of opinion in private life.

Russian culture had and continues to have a very strong communal emphasis, even herdishness (*stadnost'* in Pasternak's *Doctor Zhivago*). All is to be shared within one's own circle of intimate friends. It is suffocating yet atavistically attractive to others, to Westerners, to belong to such a close, sharing community. It gives one a feeling of warmth and intimacy, of a tight group huddling together. Russians are comforted by being thus archaically close, confiding, and reminiscing. (Confession and reminiscence are frequent and favorite literary forms.) And Russians expect others to behave the same way, making great demands on others' friendship and generosity. There is little sense of privacy.

When such intimacy is absent, Russians suffer from anomie, atomization, alienation. When Dostoyevsky was living in Germany, he missed Russia, yearned for Russian warmth, and described his homesickness by saying he felt like a slice of bread cut away from its loaf. Russian culture encourages its members to look for a warm coat—the image applied by Gorky to Tolstoy (about whom he said that he sought a religious belief in order "to make himself a warm coat against the fear of death"). So the Russians tend to seek a "warm coat" against the fear of loneliness and isolation—and they seek it in their intimate circles of trusted friends, various political and social utopias, ideological paradises, and vodka (which has been described as the one true religion of the Russians). They may therefore also seek the comfort of unanimity à la the Grand Inquisitor—against the alienation of a modern, technological, rational, Western bourgeois culture.

Westerners living in Russia are often attracted to a temporary spell of diving into this Russian togetherness, this bear hug of Russian embrace. Yet they also realize they could never live like that permanently, but would go crazy, suffocated by the constant, demanding intimacy.

And then there is the Russians' love affair with their own language—the deification of Russian itself. Gogol apostrophizes the Russian language in his novel *Dead Souls*. Turgenev's eulogy of the

Russian language is learned by heart by Russian schoolchildren. It would be difficult to find a Russian writer who has not somewhere given rhapsodic expressions of love for the beauties of his or her language. The Russians' language is very much a key component of their sense of identity.

Why is there only one woman author in this anthology of the best of nineteenth-century Russian literature? Women writers began to emerge in number soon after 1900—with the great poets Anna Akhmatova and Marina Tsvetayeva, among others. And in the second half of the twentieth century women authors may even be said to dominate some parts of the literary scene, particularly drama and the short story. But in the nineteenth century only Karolina Pavlova was especially prominent; there was no Russian Jane Austen or George Eliot or George Sand. (In folk culture, on the other hand, women were prominent as creators of folk stories and songs and as performers; there were many famous *skazitel'nitsy*, women storytellers.)

A final paradox: Russian literature is very much locally rooted, focused on the topical internal Russian situation—and yet its appeal is universal, from Japan to the United States, Argentina to Norway. With their exceptional skill and focus in choosing the telling social detail, Russian writers also give us powerful psychological insights of general application.

In prose narratives there were two principal traditions. The major tradition of clear, transparent prose went from Pushkin and Turgenev to Tolstoy and Chekhov; the second tradition, that of decorative or ornamental prose calling attention to the medium of its narration, went from Gogol to Leskov and various twentieth-century writers. The following prefaces to individual contributors give more information about the place of each in Russian literary history.

Russian literature has a unique magnetism. It has charm, it is engrossing. Specific as to time and place, it is also eminently universal. Reading it leads us into the heart of a strange, fascinating, sometimes bizarre country. Immersing ourselves in Russian literature is the best, perhaps the only way for us (and for the Russians themselves) to feel the essence of the special qualities of Russian culture, of the distinctiveness of Russia.

CHRONOLOGY

POLITICAL AND SOCIAL HISTORY	LITERATURE
seventh to twelfth centuries Emergence of separate East Slavic linguistic group; development of Russian-Ukrainian state beginning in ninth century	
988 Baptism of Vladimir, Grand Prince of Kiev, and entry of Byzantine Christianity into Kiev	
	late twelfth century The Igor Tale composed
1237–1480 The Tartar Yoke: Mongolian conquest and domination of Russia	
sixteenth to seventeenth centuries Rise of Muscovy	
1613 Election of Michael Romanov as czar	
1645–1676 Reign of Alexis	
	1682 Archpriest Avvakum, author of first Russian autobiography, *Life Written by Himself*, burned at stake for heresy
1689–1725 Reign of Peter the Great: Extensive reforms aimed at modernizing Russia; construction of St. Petersburg	

POLITICAL AND SOCIAL HISTORY	LITERATURE
1762–1796 Reign of Catherine the Great	
	1791 Birth of Aksakov
	1795 Birth of Griboyedov
1801–1825 Reign of Alexander I: Some reform measures attempted	
	1803 Birth of Tyutchev
	1807 Birth of Karolina Pavlova
	1809 Birth of Gogol
	1811 Birth of Belinsky
1812–1814 Fatherland War against Napoleon: Moscow burned; defeat of French Grande Armée	*1812* Birth of Goncharov Birth of Herzen
	1814 Birth of Lermontov
	1818 Birth of Turgenev
	1821 Birth of Dostoyevsky
	1822–1824 Griboyedov writes *Trouble with Reason*
1825 Decembrist uprising thwarted	
1825–1855 Reign of Nicholas I: Introduction of repressive laws and institutions	
1826 Supreme Censorship Council established	*1826* Birth of Saltykov-Shchedrin
	1828 Birth of Tolstoy
	1829 Griboyedov killed in Persia

POLITICAL AND SOCIAL HISTORY	LITERATURE
1830 Growth of Third Section (secret police)	
1830–1831 First Polish uprising suppressed	
	1831 Pushkin's *The Shot* published
1832 First codification of laws of the Russian empire	
	1836 Pushkin's *Bronze Horseman* published
	1837 Pushkin killed in duel
	1840 Lermontov writes *Princess Mary*
	1841 Lermontov killed in duel
	1842 Publication of Gogol's *Overcoat* and *Dead Souls*
	1847 Belinsky writes his *Letter to Gogol*
1848 Revolutions break out in Europe; Nicholas establishes the Committee on Censorship	*1848* Pavlova writes *A Double Life* Death of Belinsky
	1849 Goncharov publishes *Oblomov's Dream*, which would later (1859) be included as part of complete *Oblomov*
	1849–1858 Dostoyevsky exiled in Siberia
	1852 Death of Gogol Herzen settles in England, starts Russian free press

POLITICAL AND SOCIAL HISTORY	LITERATURE
1853–1856 Crimean War: Russia defeated by English and French	*1853* Birth of Solovyov
1855–1881 Reign of Alexander II: Institution of new reform measures	
1856–1862 Liberalization of censorship	*1856* Publication of Aksakov's *Family Chronicle*
	1859 Death of Aksakov
	1860 Turgenev writes *First Love* Birth of Chekhov
1861 Emancipation of serfs	
	1860–1861 Turgenev writes *Fathers and Sons*
1863 Second Polish uprising suppressed	
1864 Reforms of local government: *zemstvos* (committees) to supervise roads, education, public health	*1864* Dostoyevsky writes *Notes from the Underground*
1865–1905 Preventive and punitive censorship imposed after unsuccessful assassination attempt	*1865–1866* Dostoyevsky writes *Crime and Punishment* *1865–1869* Publication of Tolstoy's *War and Peace*
	1868 Birth of Gorky
	1870 Death of Herzen
1870s Growth of revolutionary movements led by university students	*1872–1876* Publication of Saltykov-Shchedrin's *Golovlyovs*
	1873–1877 Tolstoy writes *Anna Karenina* Death of Tyutchev

POLITICAL AND SOCIAL HISTORY	LITERATURE

1877–1878 War with Turkey

1880 Birth of Blok
Dostoyevsky publishes *The Brothers Karamazov*
Dostoyevsky delivers speech at Pushkin Festival

1881 Alexander II assassinated

1881 Death of Dostoyevsky

1881–1894 Reign of Alexander III: Reactionary measures aimed at suppressing revolutionaries

1883 Death of Turgenev

1886 Tolstoy writes *The Death of Ivan Ilych*

1889 Death of Saltykov-Shchedrin

1891 Death of Goncharov

1893 Death of Karolina Pavlova

1894–1917 Reign of Nicholas II

1896 Widespread strikes

1899 Chekhov writes *The Lady with a Dog*

1900 Death of Solovyov
First production of Chekhov's *Uncle Vanya*

1901 Chekhov writes *The Three Sisters*

1902 Gorky writes *The Lower Depths*

POLITICAL AND
SOCIAL HISTORY

LITERATURE

1903 Chekhov writes *The Cherry Orchard*

1904–1905 Russo–Japanese War: Russia badly defeated

1904 Death of Chekhov

1905 First Russian revolution fails after some initial reforms are attempted

1910 Death of Tolstoy

1914–1917 Russian involvement in World War I

1917 February Revolution: abdication of czar; provisional government established October Revolution: Bolsheviks under Lenin seize power

1921 Death of Blok

1936 Death of Gorky

The Portable

Nineteenth-Century
Russian Reader

ALEKSANDR PUSHKIN

IF IT WERE POSSIBLE TO TAKE a public-opinion poll to find out whom most people outside of Russia believe to be the most widely known and best Russian writer, then the vote might well go to Dostoyevsky —or perhaps Tolstoy or Chekhov. But inside Russia, there could be little doubt about the outcome of such a poll: it is Pushkin whom the Russians consider their best, their national poet. He has become embedded in the Russian consciousness—with his characters, lines, images, attitudes, and rhythms.

Aleksandr Pushkin (1799–1837) was born in Moscow to a landowning family that traced its ancestry to ancient Russian nobility. It is of some interest that his ancestry was one-eighth African. One of his forebears on his mother's side was an Ethiopian boy presented as a gift—in the bizarre manner of the eighteenth century—by the pasha of Turkey to Peter the Great. Later this same person became a Russian military officer and married into the Russian aristocracy. Pushkin prided himself on his African ancestry and, with a glee that may seem naive or even embarrassing, often attributed his sensuality (and the attraction he felt this exercised on Russian women) to his African origin.

Pushkin attended a special boarding school, the Lyceum, organized at the czar's summer residence to educate pupils whom the government hoped to prepare for future government service. He soon stood out as an unusually gifted as well as boisterous young poet. His verses in praise of freedom were punished by a form of house arrest in his country home, a circumstance which may have saved him from participating in the failed December 1825 uprising in St. Petersburg. (Some of his friends who took part in the Decembrist plot suffered severe punishment.) Pushkin was eventually permitted to return to St. Petersburg, where he married a young society beauty. The czar, wishing Pushkin's wife to adorn social events, appointed the poet to a somewhat humiliating junior court post. His marriage brought him pain and jealousy and finally led to his death at the age of thirty-seven: he was shot in a duel caused by malicious intriguers who mocked him for allegedly being cuckolded by his wife.

Despite the fact that thousands of teachers have taught his works to millions of Russian schoolchildren, Pushkin still remains the most beloved writer in the Russian language. During his rather short life, he wrote in all the literary forms of his time—short plays, a historical drama (Boris Godunov), historical novels, short stories, lyrical poems, other poems of all possible kinds, a long novel in verse (Yevgeny Onegin), engrossing personal letters (more than seven hundred), literary criticism, and many other works that cannot be easily pigeonholed into one or another of the recognized literary genres or subgenres.

If one had to single out the foremost quality of Pushkin's writing, it would be that of being "golden"—his lines seem easy, just right, natural. Like Mozart, he appears to have been a natural genius, a poet endowed with the gift of creating masterpieces merely by the easy touch. In fact, of course, Pushkin worked very hard to achieve his artistry, but he strove to make it all seem incredibly light and effortless.

Pushkin was at the center of the Russian "Golden Age." William M. Todd, one of the foremost Western scholars on the period, wrote of this epoch that the "hope-filled first decades of the nineteenth century—especially the years between the defeat of Napoleon and the crushing of the Decembrist uprising (from 1814–25)—remain in the popular consciousness as an unprecedented and subsequently unrepeated time of cultural plenitude, grace, harmony, humor, and elegance." The achievements of later writers were more serious and more tortured.

Pushkin's short poems were written over a span of thirty years, and from the earliest juvenilia straight through to the end they exhibit incredible variety. A witty and irreverent epigram may be followed by a reflective religious poem, a satire by an appreciation of nature, a sad love poem by a philosophical one, a rousing political libertarian poem by naughty or downright pornographic verses.

According to William M. Todd, Pushkin's works were the first Russian texts that adequately came to grips with the cultural patterns set in conflict by the Westernization of Russia begun during the eighteenth century. His works are virtuousolike dialogues with conventions that explore the ways in which worldviews are conditioned by literary and cultural stereotypes. They question the extent to which these literary stereotypes are adequate for perceiving experience, and they move *the world of art closer to the world of cultural and physical experience.*

Pushkin, though esteemed as a Russian national poet, has qualities that are unlike many of those considered typically Russian. He is not extreme, not prone to excess, not chiefly absorbed in metaphysics and politics. It is a myth that he created the modern Russian literary language. His language was that of the enlightened Westernized gentry. Later, Russian literature became Germanized, metaphysical, romantic. It went on to absorb many academic and philosophical styles alien to Pushkin, whose syntax, in Todd's view, "has a spare, Voltairean quality that has hardly become the norm." (It is ironic that Dostoyevsky should have praised Pushkin so highly when they are so different in spirit and style.)

Pushkin in all his guises and metamorphoses, with all his diversity, is always capable of self-restraint. He felt tremendous love for the human life of this earth, rather than what Montaigne called the supercelestial or subterranean. But he did write poems of regret and melancholy, very earnest, committed poems. Many of his poems refer to political matters of the day. "Arion," for example, refers to the crushed Decembrist uprising of 1825, with which he sympathized.

The Bronze Horseman (1833) is based on a real flood in St. Petersburg, the city built in the early eighteenth century to replace Moscow as capital of Peter the Great's empire; situated in desolate bogland in the Gulf of Finland, the new city represented a supreme engineering achievement, the triumph of man over nature. In his poem Pushkin balances two poles. First, he expresses admiration for imperial achievement: the assertion, through willpower, of creation, of city and empire building. But he also conveys the opposite pole, the price to be paid: the pitiable destruction of the "little" people caught between the sweep of rebellious nature—the flood—and the current of ordinary life in a city decreed by the empire builder.

Like one of the last of the great nineteenth-century authors, Chekhov, Pushkin does not come out as a thundering judge, as the indicter. He merely poses the problem for our contemplation. Numerous critics and philosophers have been debating what the thrust of the poem is —and whether there is any thrust at all. Seemingly unaffected by this scholarly debate, generations of Russian readers continue to be enthralled by the poem's magical imagery and verse.

Yevgeny Onegin, too long to include here, is the fountainhead of the Russian novel. Though written in verse, it nevertheless began the line of the Russian sociopsychological novel that was to culminate in Tolstoy's Anna Karenina *and Dostoyevsky's* The Brothers Karamazov.

Pushkin's short prose is chiseled and lean. Pushkin believed that prose should be written at least as well as verse, and he illustrated this belief in a number of works—most notably in the five Belkin tales, told by various narrators and collected by the fictional Belkin. The Shot, included here, is one of these. It conveys an individual's passionate monomania within highly conventionalized military etiquette. It is a drama of intense concentration—on revenge—in the most highly conventionalized world: that of formal dueling. The action is projected against the background of the social stratifications and codes of a small garrison town. The Shot pits an individual's obsession against the formal rules of early nineteenth-century Russian military honor. The sense of extreme passion is further enhanced by the controlled, hard-edged voice in which the story is narrated.

SECLUSION

Blessed he who in secluded leisure,
Far from the numskull's brazen ways,
Between hard work and slothful pleasure,
Old thoughts, new hopes, divides his days;
Whose friends by kindly fate were chosen
So as to save him, lucky pup,
Both from the bore that sends you dozing,
And from the boor that wakes you up.

(1819)

EPIGRAM ON A. A. DAVYDOVA*

One had Aglaya by attraction
Of raven curls and martial stance,
One for his money (no objection),
A third because he was from France,
Cleon by dint of being clever,
Damis for tender songs galore;
But, my Aglaya, say, whatever
Did your own husband have you for?

(1822)

* Aglaya Davydova, née Duchesse de Grammont, the promiscuous wife of General Aleksandr Davydov (the southern Decembrist's brother), whose favors Pushkin also enjoyed briefly. [Walter Arndt]

WINTER EVENING

Storm has set the heavens scowling,
Whirling gusty blizzards wild,
Now they are like beasts a-growling,
Now a-wailing like a child;
Now along the brittle thatches
They will scud with rustling sound,
Now against the window latches
Like belated wanderers pound.

Our frail hut is glum and sullen,
Dim with twilight and with care.
Why, dear granny, have you fallen
Silent by the window there?
Has the gale's insistent prodding
Made your drowsing senses numb,
Are you lulled to gentle nodding
By the whirling spindle's hum?

Let us drink for grief, let's drown it,
Comrade of my wretched youth,
Where's the jar? Pour out and down it,
Wine will make us less uncouth.
Sing me of the tomtit hatching
Safe beyond the ocean blue,
Sing about the maiden fetching
Water at the morning dew.

Storm has set the heavens scowling,
Whirling gusty blizzards wild,
Now they sound like beasts a-growling,
Now a-wailing like a child.
Let us drink for grief, let's drown it,
Comrade of my wretched youth,
Where's the jar? Pour out and down it,
Wine will make us less uncouth.

(1825)

TO . . .

I recollect that wondrous meeting,
That instant I encountered you,
When like an apparition fleeting,
Like beauty's spirit, past you flew.

Long since, when hopeless grief distressed me,
When noise and turmoil vexed, it seemed
Your voice still tenderly caressed me,
Your dear face sought me as I dreamed.

Years passed; their stormy gusts confounded
And swept away old dreams apace.
I had forgotten how you sounded,
Forgot the heaven of your face.

In exiled gloom and isolation
My quiet days meandered on,
The thrill of awe and inspiration,
And life, and tears, and love, were gone.

My soul awoke from inanition,
And I encountered you anew,
And like a fleeting apparition,
Like beauty's spirit, past you flew.

My pulses bound in exultation,
And in my heart once more unfold
The sense of awe and inspiration,
The life, the tears, the love of old.

                                              (1825)

ARION

We sailed in numerous company.
A few of us drew fast the sheeting,
The rest with mighty oar were beating
The brine; while, calm on slumbrous sea,
Our skillful helmsman clasped the rudder

To guide the laden vessel's thrust,
And I, at ease in carefree trust,
I sang to them . . . A sudden gust
Swept down and set the deep ashudder,
And crew and helmsman, all were lost!—
I only, secret singer, tossed
Upon the coast by seas in torment,
I sing my anthems as before,
And by a boulder on the shore
Dry in the sun my sodden garment.

(1827)

REMEMBRANCE

When for us mortal men the noisy day is stilled,
    And, the mute spaces of the town
With half-transparent nightly shadow filled,
    Sleep, daily toil's reward, drifts down,
Then is it that for me the gloom and quiet breed
    Long hours of agonized prostration;
On my nocturnal languor more intently feed
    The asps of mortal desolation;
Then fancies seethe at will, and the despondent mind
    Groans with excess of grim reflection;
Relentless Memory will wordlessly unwind
    Her long, long scroll for my inspection;
With loathing I peruse the record of my years,
    I execrate, I quail and falter,
I utter bitter plaints, and hotly flow my tears,
    But those sad lines I cannot alter.

(1828)

The dreary day is spent, and dreary night has soon
In leaden-colored draperies the heavens shrouded,
And over firry groves has risen all beclouded
A wan and spectral moon;
All these in me a mood of dark unease engender . . .
Up yonder far the moon ascends in splendor,
There is the air with sunset warmth replete,

There would the ocean like a sumptuous sheet
Beneath a sapphire sky enfold us . . .
This is the time, I know, she walks the mountain brow
Toward the strand besieged by surging, plunging shoulders,
There, at the foot of hallowed boulders
Forlornly and alone she must be sitting now . . .
Alone . . . no one to weep before her, none to languish,
No one to kiss her knees in rapt, oblivious anguish . . .
Alone . . . and no one's lips she suffers to be pressed
Upon her shoulders, her moist lips, her snowy breast,
No one is worthy of the heaven in her arms . . .
You surely are alone . . . in tears . . . then I am calm.
But if . . .

(1828)

I loved you: and the feeling, why deceive you,
May not be quite extinct within me yet;
But do not let it any longer grieve you;
I would not ever have you grieve or fret.
I loved you not with words or hope, but merely
By turns with bashful and with jealous pain;
I loved you as devotedly, as dearly
As may God grant you to be loved again.

(1829)

THE BRONZE HORSEMAN: A Tale of Petersburg

The occurrence described in this narrative is based on truth. The details of the flood are drawn from journals of the time. The curious may consult the account composed by V. N. Berkh. [Pushkin's Note]

PROLOGUE

Upon a shore of desolate waves
Stood *he*, with lofty musings grave,
And gazed afar. Before him spreading
Rolled the broad river, empty save
For one lone skiff stream-downward heading.

Strewn on the marshy, moss-grown bank,
Rare huts, the Finn's poor shelter, shrank,
Black smudges from the fog protruding;
Beyond, dark forest ramparts drank
The shrouded sun's rays and stood brooding
And murmuring all about.
He thought;
"Here, Swede, beware—soon by our labor
Here a new city shall be wrought,
Defiance to the haughty neighbor.
Here we at Nature's own behest
Shall break a window to the West,
Stand planted on the ocean level;
Here flags of foreign nations all
By waters new to them will call,
And unencumbered we shall revel."

A century passed, and there shone forth
From swamps and gloomy forest prison,
Crown gem and marvel of the North,
The proud young city newly risen.
Where Finnish fisherman before,
Harsh Nature's wretched waif, was plying,
Forlorn upon that shallow shore,
His trade, with brittle net-gear trying
Uncharted tides—now bustling banks
Stand serried in well-ordered ranks
Of palaces and towers; converging
From the four corners of the earth,
Sails press to seek the opulent berth,
To anchorage in squadrons merging;
Neva is cased in granite clean,
Atop its waters bridges hover,
Between its channels, gardens cover
The river isles with darkling green.
Outshone, old Moscow had to render
The younger sister pride of place,
As by a new queen's fresh-blown splendor
In purple fades Her Dowager Grace.

I love thee, Peter's own creation,
I love thy stern and comely face,

Neva's majestic perfluctation,
Her bankments' granite carapace,
The patterns laced by iron railing,
And of thy meditative night
The lucent dusk, the moonless paling;
When in my room I read and write
Lampless, and street on street stand dreaming,
Vast luminous gulfs, and, slimly gleaming,
The Admiralty's needle bright;
And rather than let darkness smother
The lustrous heavens' golden light,
One twilight glow speeds on the other
To grant but half an hour to night.

I love thy winter's fierce embraces
That leave the air all chilled and hushed,
The sleighs by broad Neva, girls' faces
More brightly than the roses flushed,
The ballroom's sparkle, noise, and chatter,
And at the bachelor rendezvous
The foaming beakers' hiss and spatter,
The flaming punch's flickering blue.
I love the verve of drilling duty
Upon the playing fields of Mars,*
Where troops of riflemen and horse
Turn massed precision into beauty,
Where laureled flags in tatters stream
Above formations finely junctured,
And brazen helmets sway and gleam,
In storied battles scarred and punctured.
I love, war-queen, thy fortress pieces
In smoke and thunder booming forth
When the imperial spouse increases
The sovereign lineage of the North,
Or when their muzzles roar in token
Of one more Russian victory,
Or scenting spring, Neva with glee,
Her ice-blue armor newly broken,
In sparkling floes runs out to sea.

* The parade grounds of St. Petersburg are called Mars Field.

Thrive, Peter's city, flaunt thy beauty,
Stand like unshaken Russia fast,
Till floods and storms from chafing duty
May turn to peace with thee at last;
The very tides of Finland's deep
Their long-pent rancor then may bury,
And cease with feckless spite to harry
Czar Peter's everlasting sleep.

There was a time—our memories keep
Its horrors ever fresh and near us . . .
Of this a tale now suffer me
To tell before you, gentle hearers.
A grievous story it will be.

PART ONE

Through Peter's darkened city rolled
November's breath of autumn cold.
Neva, her clamorous waters splashing
Against the crest of either dike,
Tossed in her shapely ramparts, like
A patient on his sickbed thrashing.
Already dark it was and late;
A rainstorm pressed its angry spate
At windowpanes, with moaning driven
By dismal winds. Just then was seen
Back from a friend's house young Yevgeny—
(A pleasant name that we have given
The hero of our tale; what's more,
My pen was friends with it before.)
His surname may go unrecorded;
Though once, who knows but it was lauded
In native lore, its luster keen
Blazed by the pen of Karamzin,*
By now the world and rumor held
No trace of it. Our hero dwelled

* Allusion to Karamzin's monumental *History of the Russian State.*

In poor Kolomna,* humbly serving
Some office, found the great unnerving,
And cared for neither buried kin
Nor legend-woven origin.

And so tonight Yevgeny had wandered
Back home, slipped off his cloak, undressed,
Composed himself, but found no rest,
As ill at ease he lay and pondered.
What were his thoughts? That he was poor,
And by his labor must secure
A portion of esteem and treasure;
That God might well have eased his pains
With wits and cash; that men of leisure,
Endowed with luck if not with brains,
Could idly leave him at a distance,
And lead so carefree an existence!
He thought that in the post he held
He had attained but two years' rating;
That still the storm was not abating,
And that the banked-up river swelled
Still more—and since by now they surely
Had struck the bridges down securely,
He and Parasha must, he knew,
Be parted for a day or two.
And poetlike, Yevgeny, exhaling
A sigh, fell musing on his lot:

"Get married? I? And, yet, why not?
Of course, it won't be easy sailing,
But what of that? I'm young and strong,
Content to labor hard and long,
I'll build us soon, if not tomorrow,
A simple nest for sweet repose
And keep Parasha free of sorrow,
And in a year or two, who knows,
I may obtain a snug position,
And it shall be Parasha's mission
To tend and rear our children . . . yes,

* Then an outlying suburb of St. Petersburg.

So we will live, and so forever
Will be as one, till death us sever,
And grandsons lay us both to rest . . ."
Thus ran his reverie. Yet sadly
He wished that night the wind would still
Its mournful wail, the rain less madly
Be rattling at the windowsill.
At last his eyelids, heavy-laden
Droop into slumber . . . soon away
The night's tempestuous gloom is fading
And washes into pallid day . . .
Disastrous day! Neva all night
Has seaward strained, in hopeless muster
Of strength against the gale's wild bluster,
But now at last must yield the fight.

From morning, throngs of people line
The banks and marvel at the fountains
Of spray, the foam-tipped rolling mountains
Thrust up by the envenomed brine;
For now Neva, her flow arrested
By the relentless sea-wind's force,
Reared up in fury, backward-crested,
And drowned the islands in her course.
The storm more fiercely yet upsoaring,
Neva, engorged, with swell and roaring
As from a caldron's swirl released,
Abruptly like a frenzied beast
Leaped on the city. At her onrush
All scattered, every place was swept
An instant void, swift waters crept
Into the deeply hollowed basements,
Canals rose gushing to the casements,
There streamed Petropolis, foam-laced,
Like Triton foundered to the waist.

Beset! Besieged! The vile surf charges
Through window frames like thieves, loose barges
Dash in the panes, stern forward wrenched.
Street-hawkers' trays, their covers drenched,
Smashed cabins, roofing, rafters reeling,

The stock-in-trade of thrifty dealing,
The wretched gain of misery pale,
Whole bridges loosened by the gale,
Coffins unearthed, in horrid welter
Float down the streets.
In stricken gloom
All see God's wrath and bide their doom.
Alas! All founders, food and shelter!
Where now to turn?
That fateful year
Our famed late sovereign still was sitting
On Russia's throne—he sadly here
Upon his balcony did appear
And owned: "For czars there is no pitting
Their power against the Lord's." His mien
All grief, he sat and contemplated
The fell disaster's desolate scene.
Into the squares to lakes dilated,
Debouched, like riverbeds inflated,
What had been streets. The palace stood
Like a lone cliff the waters riding.
The Czar spoke out: and where they could,
By roadways near and distant gliding,
Upon their stormy path propelled,
The Emperor's generals went speeding
To save the people, who, unheeding
With fear, were drowning where they dwelled.

That night, where on Czar Peter's square
A corner-house* new risen there
Had lately on its high porch shown—
One paw raised, as in live defiance—
A marble pair of guardian lions:
Astride upon the beast of stone
There sat, his arms crossed tight, alone,
Unmoving, deathly pale of feature,
Yevgeny. He was afraid, poor creature,
Not for himself. He did not hear
The evil breakers crest and rear,
His soles with greedy lashes seeking,

* The new edifice of the Ministry of War.

Nor feel the rain splash in his face,
Nor yet the gale with boisterous shrieking
Tear off his hat. Impaled in space,
His eyes held fast a distant border
And there in frozen anguish gazed.
There, mountainous, in wild disorder
From depths of chaos skyward raised,
Huge waves were towering and gloating,
There howled the storm and played with floating
Wreckage . . . God, God! Just there should be,
Set hard upon the inland sea,
Close, ah, too close to that mad billow,
A fence unpainted, and a willow,
And a frail hut: there dwelt those two,
Her mother and she, his bride bespoken,
Long dreamed-of . . . or was all he knew
A dream, naught but an empty token
All life, a wraith and no more worth,
But Heaven's mockery at Earth?

And he, as by a spell enfolded,
By irons to the marble bolted,
Could not descend; all within sight
Was an unending watery blight.
And o'er Neva all spray-ensheeted,
Its back to where Yevgeny still clung,
There towered immobile, undefeated,
Upon its bronzen charger seated,
The Idol with its arm outflung.

PART TWO

With rack and ruin satiated,
Neva, her wanton frenzy spent,
At last drew back her element—
By her own tumult still elated—
And nonchalantly abdicated
Her plunder. Thus a highwayman
Comes bursting with his vicious clan
Into some village, wrecking, slashing,
Destroying, robbing—shrieks and gnashing

Of teeth, alarms, oaths, outrage, roar—
Then, heavily with booty weighted,
Fearing pursuers, enervated,
The band of robbers homeward pour
And strew the wayside with their plunder.

The waters fell, and as thereunder
Dry footing showed, Yevgeny, heartsore,
Benumbed with sorrow, fear, and wonder,
Made headlong for the riverside,
Close on the barely ebbing tide.
For still Neva, high triumph breathing,
Sent angry billows upward seething
As from live coals beneath her course,
And still the whitecaps heaved and slanted,
And heavily the river panted
As will a battle-winded horse.
Yevgeny looks round: a boat on station!
He greets it like a revelation,
Calls to the wherryman—and he,
With daring unconcern, is willing
To take him for a quarter-shilling
Across that formidable sea.

And long he struggled hard to counter
The turmoil with his practiced strength;
Time after time their craft, aflounder
Between banked waves, seemed sure to founder
With its rash crew—until at length
They reached the shore.

Yevgeny, fear-stricken,
Runs down the long-familiar lane,
By long-dear places, looks—in vain:
Unknowable, a sight to sicken
The heart, all stares in disarray,
This flung aside, that swept away,
Here half-uprooted cabins listed,
There others lay all crushed and twisted,
Still others stood misplaced—all round,
Strewn as upon a battleground,
Were scattered corpses. Barely living,

Yevgeny flies onward arrow-straight,
Worn out with terror and misgiving,
Onward to where he knows his fate
Awaits him with a secret message,
As it might be a sealed dispatch.
Here is the suburb now, the passage
Down to the bay, and here the thatch . . .
But what is this?

He stopped, confounded.
Retraced his steps and once more rounded
That corner . . . stared . . . half raised a hand:
Here is the place where it should stand,
Here is the willow. There, remember,
The gate stood—razed, no doubt. And where,
Where is the house? Distraught and somber,
He paces back and forward there,
Talks to himself aloud, soon after
Bursts out abruptly into laughter
And slaps his forehead.

Night sank down
Upon the horror-shaken town;
But few found sleep, in every dwelling
They sat up telling and retelling
About the day just past.

Dawn's ray
From pallid banks of weary gray
Gleamed down upon the silent city
And found of yesterday's alarm
No trace. The purple cloak* of pity
Already covered recent harm
And all returned to former calm.
Down streets rewon for old endeavor
Men walk as callously as ever,
The morning's civil service troops,
Emerged from their nocturnal coops,
Are off to work. Cool tradesmen labor

---

* This is assumed to refer either to imperial charity or to the calm dawn, or ambiguously to both.

To open cellar, vault, and store,
Robbed by Neva the night before,
The sooner to surcharge their neighbor
For their grave loss. They carted off
Boats from the courtyards.

(Count Khvostov,
A poet whom Parnassus nurses,
Lamented in immortal verses
The blight Neva had left behind.)
My pitiful Yevgeny, though—evil
His lot; alas, his clouded mind
Could not withstand the brute upheaval
Just wrought on it. The clash and strain
Of flood and storm forever thundered
Upon his ear; his thoughts a train
Of horrors, wordlessly he wandered;
Some secret vision seemed to chill
His mind. A week—a month—and still
Astray from home he roved and pondered.
As for the homestead he forsook,
The landlord let his vacant nook
To some poor poet. Yevgeny never
Returned to claim it back, nor took
His left possessions. Growing ever
More alien to the world, he strayed
All day on foot till nightfall led him
Down to the wharves to sleep. He made
His meals of morsels people fed him
Through windows. His poor clothing frayed
And moldered off him. Wicked urchins
Threw pebbles at his back. The searching
Coachwhips not seldom struck him when,
As often now, he would be lurching
Uncertain of his course; but then
He did not feel it for the pain
Of some loud anguish in his brain.
Thus he wore on his luckless span,
A moot thing, neither beast nor man,
Who knew if this world's child, or whether
A caller from the next.

He slept
One night by the Neva. The weather
Was autumn-bent. An ill wind swept
The river. Sullen swells had crept
Up banks and steps with splash and rumble,
As a petitioner might grumble
Unheard outside the judge's gate.
Yevgeny woke up. The light was failing,
The rain dripped, and the wind was wailing
And traded through the darkness late
Sad echoes with the watchman's hailing . . .

Yevgeny sprang up, appeared to waken
To those remembered terrors; shaken,
He hurried off at random, then
Came to a sudden stop; again
Uncertainly his glances shifted
All round, wild panic marked his face.
Above him the great mansion lifted
Its columns. On the terrace-space,
One paw raised as in live defiance,
Stood sentinel those guardian lions,
And high above those rails, as if
Of altitude and darkness blended,
There rode in bronze, one arm extended,
The Idol on its granite cliff.

Yevgeny's heart shrank. His mind unclouding
In dread, he knew the place again
Where the great flood had sported then,
Where those rapacious waves were crowding
And round about him raged and spun—
That square, the lions, and him—the one
Who, bronzen countenance upslanted
Into the dusk aloft, sat still,
The one by whose portentous will
The city by the sea was planted . . .
How awesome in the gloom he rides!
What thought upon his brow resides!
His charger with what fiery mettle,
His form with what dark strength endowed!

Where will you gallop, charger proud,
Where next your plunging hoofbeats settle?
Oh, Destiny's great potentate!
Was it not thus, a towering idol
Hard by the chasm, with iron bridle
You reared up Russia to her fate?

The piteous madman fell to prowling
About the statue's granite berth,
And furtively with savage scowling
He eyed the lord of half the earth.
His breath congealed in him, he pressed
His brow against the chilly railing,
A blur of darkness overveiling
His eyes; a flame shot through his breast
And made his blood seethe. Grimly lowering,
He faced the haughty image towering
On high, and fingers clawed, teeth clenched,
As if by some black spirit wrenched,
He hissed, spite shaking him: "Up there,
Great wonder-worker you, beware! . . ."
And then abruptly wheeled to race
Away full tilt. The dread czar's face,
With instantaneous fury burning,
It seemed to him, was slowly turning . . .
Across these empty spaces bound,
Behind his back he heard resound,
Like thunderclouds in rumbling anger,
The deep reverberating clangor
Of pounding hoofs that shook the ground.
And in the moonlight's pallid glamour
Rides high upon his charging brute,
One hand stretched out, 'mid echoing clamor
The Bronze Horseman in pursuit.
And all through that long night, no matter
What road the frantic wretch might take,
There still would pound with ponderous clatter
The Bronze Horseman in his wake.

And ever since, when in his erring
He chanced upon that square again,
They saw a sick confusion blurring

His features. One hand swiftly then
Flew to his breast, as if containing
The anguished heart's affrighted straining;
His worn-out cap he then would raise,
Cast to the ground a troubled gaze
And slink aside.

A little island
Lies off the coast. There now and then
A stray belated fisherman
Will beach his net at dusk and, silent,
Cook his poor supper by the shore,
Or, on his Sunday recreation
A boating clerk might rest his oar
By that bleak isle. There no green thing
Will grow; and there the inundation
Had washed up in its frolicking
A frail old cottage. It lay stranded
Above the tide like weathered brush,
Until last spring a barge was landed
To haul it off. It was all crushed
And bare. Against the threshold carried,
Here lay asprawl my luckless knave,
And here in charity they buried
The chill corpse in a pauper's grave.
                    (1833)

EXEGI MONUMENTUM

No hands have wrought my monument; no weeds
will hide the nation's footpath to its site.
Czar Alexander's column it exceeds
        in splendid insubmissive height.

Not all of me is dust. Within my song,
safe from the worm, my spirit will survive,
and my sublunar fame will dwell as long
        as there is one last bard alive.

Throughout great Rus' my echoes will extend,
and all will name me, all tongues in her use:

the Slavs' proud heir, the Finn, the Kalmuk, friend
    of steppes, the yet untamed Tungus.

And to the people long shall I be dear
because kind feelings did my lyre extoll,
invoking freedom in an age of fear,
    and mercy for the broken soul.

Obey thy God, and never mind, O Muse,
the laurels or the stings: make it thy rule
to be unstirred by praise as by abuse,
    and do not contradict the fool.

                                             (1836)

THE SHOT

CHAPTER ONE

We fought a duel.
                                            Baratynsky

I swore to kill him—rightfully, in a duel.
(I owed him one shot.)
                                            Marlynsky

We were stationed in the small town of ***. The life of an army officer
is known to all. In the morning, drill and riding school; dinner with
the regimental commander or at some Jewish inn; punch and cards in
the evening. There was not a single house open to us in ***—nor a
single marriageable young lady. We used to meet in one another's
rooms, where there was nothing to look at but each other's uniforms.
    There was only one man in our society who was not a soldier. He
was about thirty-five, and we looked upon him as being quite old. His
experience gave him many advantages over us, and his habitual mo-
roseness, his stern temper, and his malicious tongue created a strong
impression on our young minds. Some sort of mystery surrounded his
fate; it appeared that he was a Russian, and yet he had a foreign name.
At one time or other he had served in the Hussars, and with success
even; nobody knew the reasons that had prompted him to resign his
commission and settle down in a wretched little town, where he lived
at the same time poorly and extravagantly, always going about on foot

in a black threadbare frock coat, and yet keeping open house for all the officers in our regiment. Admittedly, his dinners consisted only of two or three courses, and were prepared by an ex-soldier, but the champagne flowed like water. Nobody knew what his circumstances were, or what his income was, and nobody dared to inquire about them. He had a good collection of books, mostly military histories and novels. He was always willing to lend these, and he never asked for them back; similarly, he never returned to its owner a book that he had borrowed. His main occupation was pistol shooting. The walls of his room were riddled with bullet holes, and were like a honeycomb in appearance. His rich collection of pistols was the only luxury in the wretched mud-walled cottage in which he lived. The skill which he had acquired with this weapon was incredible, and if he had proposed shooting a pear from off somebody's forage cap, there was not a single man in our regiment who would have had any doubts about allowing his head to be used for such a purpose. Conversation among us frequently turned to dueling; Silvio (as I propose to call him) never took any part in it. When asked whether he had ever fought a duel, he replied dryly that he had, but entered into no details, and it was evident that such questions were disagreeable to him. We came to the conclusion that there lay on his conscience the memory of some unfortunate victim of his terrifying skill. It certainly never entered our heads to suspect him of anything like cowardice. There are some people whose appearance alone forbids such suspicions. But then an event took place that astonished us all.

One day about ten of our officers were dining at Silvio's. We drank about as much as usual—that is, a very great deal. After dinner we asked our host to keep bank for us. For a long time he refused, for he rarely played cards; at last, however, he ordered the cards to be brought, and pouring about fifty ten-rouble pieces onto the table, he sat down to deal. We gathered around him, and the game began. It was Silvio's custom to maintain absolute silence while he played, neither arguing nor entering into any explanations. If the player happened to make a miscalculation, Silvio either paid up the difference immediately or recorded the surplus. We were all aware of this and made no attempt to interfere with his habit. But among us was an officer only recently transferred to the regiment. While playing, this officer absentmindedly doubled the stake in error. Silvio took up the chalk and, as was his habit, corrected the score. The officer, thinking that Silvio had made a mistake, began to explain. Silvio continued to deal in silence. The officer, losing patience, picked up the brush and rubbed out what he considered to be a mistake. Silvio took up the chalk and again righted the score. The officer, heated by the wine, the gambling, and the laughter of his comrades, considered himself cruelly insulted, and in his rage he seized a brass candlestick from the table and hurled it at Silvio, who only just managed to avoid the impact of it. We were greatly upset. Silvio rose, white with anger and, his eyes gleaming, he said:

"Sir, be so good as to leave, and thank God that this happened in my house."

None of us had the slightest doubt as to what would follow, and we already looked upon our new comrade as a dead man. The officer went out, saying that he was ready to answer for the insult at the convenience of the gentleman in control of the bank. We continued to play for a few more minutes, but feeling that our host was no longer in the mood for a game, we withdrew one by one, discussing the probable vacancy that would shortly be occurring in the regiment as we made for our respective rooms.

At riding school the following day we were already asking one another whether the unfortunate lieutenant was still alive, when he suddenly appeared among us; we put the same question to him. He replied that as yet he had heard nothing from Silvio. We were astonished by this. We went to see Silvio and found him firing shot after shot at an ace which had been pasted to the gate. He received us as usual, making no mention of the incident of the previous evening. Three days went by, and the lieutenant was still alive. Was it possible that Silvio was not proposing to fight? we asked ourselves in amazement. Silvio did not fight. He contented himself with a very slight apology and made peace with the lieutenant.

This lowered him greatly in the eyes of the young men. Lack of courage is the last thing to be forgiven by young people, who as a rule regard valor as the foremost of human virtues, and as an excuse for every conceivable sin. However, little by little, the affair was forgotten, and Silvio regained his former influence.

I alone could not feel the same about him. By nature a romantic, I had been more attached than the others to the man whose life was such a mystery, and whom I regarded as the hero of some strange tale. He liked me; at least, it was with me alone that he would drop his usual sharp tone and converse on various topics with a simple and unusual charm. But after that unfortunate evening, the thought that he had not voluntarily wiped out the stain on his honor never left me, and prevented me from treating him as I had done before. I was ashamed to meet his eyes. Silvio was too intelligent and experienced not to notice this and to guess its cause. It seemed to grieve him. At least, on one or two occasions I noticed in him a desire to explain matters to me; but I avoided such opportunities, and Silvio gave up the attempt. Thenceforward I saw him only in the company of my comrades, and our former private talks ceased.

The distractions of the capital prevent its inhabitants from having any conception of many sensations that are familiar to the inhabitants of villages or small towns, such as, for example, that of waiting for the day on which the mail arrives. On Tuesdays and Fridays our regimental office was always filled with officers, expecting money, letters, or newspapers. Letters were usually unsealed on the spot and items of news exchanged, so that the office always presented a very lively scene. Silvio, whose letters were sent through the regiment, was usually to be found there. One day he was handed a letter the seal of which he tore away with an air of the greatest impatience. His eyes shone as he read swiftly through the contents. The officers, each concerned with his own letters, noticed nothing.

"Gentlemen," he said to them, "circumstances demand my instant departure; I must leave tonight. I trust you will not refuse to dine with me for the last time. I shall expect you," he continued, addressing me. "You must come!"

With these words he hastened out of the office; the rest of us, after agreeing to meet at Silvio's, each went his own way.

I arrived at Silvio's house at the appointed time and found almost the entire regiment there. His possessions were already packed; nothing remained but the bare, bullet-riddled walls. We sat down at the table; our host was in exceedingly good spirits, and his gaiety quickly spread to the rest of us. Corks popped unendingly, the wine in our glasses foamed and hissed, and with the utmost warmth we wished our departing host a good journey and every success. It was late in the evening when we rose from the table. We fetched our caps, and Silvio bade farewell to each of us as we went out; just as I was about to leave, he took me by the arm and stopped me.

"I must talk to you," he said softly.

I stayed behind.

The guests had all gone; the two of us were alone; we sat down opposite one another and lit our pipes in silence. Silvio seemed greatly preoccupied; all traces of his spasmodic gaiety had vanished. The grim pallor of his face, his shining eyes, and the thick smoke issuing from his mouth gave his face a truly diabolical appearance. Several minutes passed; at last, Silvio broke the silence.

"Perhaps we shall never see each other again," he said. "Before we part, I should like to talk to you. You may have noticed that I don't really care what other people think of me, but I like you, and it would pain me to leave you with a false impression in your mind."

He stopped and began to refill his pipe; I was silent, my eyes downcast.

"You thought it strange," he continued, "that I did not demand satisfaction from that drunken madcap R**. You will agree that with choice of weapons I held his life in my hands, and that my own was scarcely in danger at all. I could ascribe my moderation to magnanimity alone, but I will not lie to you. If I could have punished R** without endangering my own life in any way, I should never have pardoned him."

I looked at Silvio in astonishment. Such a confession completely dumbfounded me. Silvio continued:

"Yes, it's true—but I have no right to risk my life; six years ago I received a slap in the face, and my enemy is still alive."

My curiosity was strongly aroused.

"And you didn't fight him?" I asked. "Perhaps circumstances separated you?"

"I did fight him," answered Silvio, "and I'll show you a souvenir of our duel."

Silvio rose from his chair and drew from a cardboard box an embroidered red cap with a gold tassel (what the French call a *bonnet de police*); he put it on; a bullet had penetrated it about two inches above the forehead.

"You know already," continued Silvio, "that I served in the *** Hussar regiment. And you understand my temperament: in all things I am accustomed to taking the lead—this has been a passion with me since my youth. Riotousness was the fashion in our day, and in the army I was the biggest fire-eater of them all. We used to boast of our drunkenness, and I once outdrank the famous Burtsov, about whom Denis Davydov wrote two songs. Duels were constant occurrences in our regiment; in all of them I was either a second or an active participant. While my regimental commanders, who were continually changing, looked upon me as a necessary evil, my comrades worshiped me.

"I was calmly (or not so calmly!) enjoying my reputation when a rich young man from a distinguished family (I won't mention the name) joined up with the regiment. Never in my life have I met anyone so blessed or so brilliant. Imagine for yourself—youth, intelligence, good looks, boundless gaiety, reckless courage, a great name, an inexhaustible supply of money—imagine all these, and you can understand the effect he was bound to have on us. My supremacy was shaken. Attracted by my reputation, he began to seek my friendship, but I received him coldly, and without any regret he held aloof from me. I conceived a hatred for him. His successes in the regiment and in the society of ladies drove me to utter desperation. I attempted to seek a quarrel with him; to my epigrams he replied with epigrams which always struck me as more spontaneous and more cutting than mine, and which of course were incomparably more amusing; he jested, I bore malice. Finally, however, at a ball given by a Polish landowner, seeing him as the object of all the ladies' attention, and in particular that of the hostess, with whom I was having an affair, I went up to him and whispered some vulgarity in his ear. He flared up and struck me in the face. Our hands flew to our swords; ladies fainted; we were separated, and that very night we went out to fight a duel.

"Dawn was breaking. I stood at the appointed spot with my three seconds. I awaited my opponent with indescribable impatience. It was spring and the sun was already beginning to make itself felt. I saw him in the distance. He was on foot, his uniform coat draped over his sword, accompanied by one second. We went to meet him. He approached, holding his cap, which was full of cherries, in his hand. The seconds measured out twelve paces. I was to shoot first, but I was so shaken by fury that I could not rely on the steadiness of my hand, and so, in order to give myself time to calm down, I yielded first shot to him; my opponent, however, would not agree to this. We decided to draw lots; the winning number fell to him, ever fortune's favorite. He took aim and his bullet went through my cap. It was my turn. At last his life was in my hands. I looked at him keenly, trying to detect if only the slightest shadow of uneasiness in him. He stood in range of my pistol, selecting ripe cherries from his cap and spitting out the stones so that they almost fell at my feet. His indifference infuriated me.

" 'What's the use,' I thought, 'of depriving him of his life when he sets no value upon it?' A malicious thought flashed through my mind. I lowered my pistol.

" 'You do not seem to be in the mood to die,' I said to him; 'perhaps you would like to finish your breakfast; I would hate to disturb you.'

" 'You would not be disturbing me in the least,' he replied. 'Have the goodness to fire . . . or, just as you please . . . the shot is yours; I shall always be at your service.'

"I turned to my seconds, informed them that I had no intention of shooting at that moment, and with that the duel ended.

"I resigned my commission and retired to this small town. Since that time, not a day has passed without my thinking of revenge. And now my hour has come. . . ."

Silvio took the letter that he had received that morning out of his pocket and handed it to me to read. Someone (it seemed to be his business agent) had written to him from Moscow with the news that a "certain person" had announced his engagement to a young and beautiful girl.

"You will guess who that 'certain person' is," said Silvio. "I am going to Moscow. We will see whether he regards death with the same indifference on the eve of his wedding as when he regarded it over a capful of cherries!"

With these words Silvio rose, threw his cap on the floor, and began to walk up and down the room like a caged tiger. I had listened to him in silence, agitated by strange, conflicting emotions.

A servant entered and announced that the horses were ready. Silvio grasped my hand tightly; we embraced. He got into the carriage, in which had been put two trunks, one containing his pistols, and the other his personal belongings. We bade each other farewell once more, and the horses galloped off.

CHAPTER TWO

Several years passed, and domestic circumstances forced me to settle in a poor little village in the district of N**. Occupied with the management of my estate, I never ceased to sigh for my former noisy and carefree life. The hardest thing of all was having to accustom myself to spending the spring and winter evenings in complete solitude. I managed somehow or other to pass the time until dinner, conversing with the village elder, driving around to see how the work was going, or visiting some new project on the estate; but as soon as dusk began to fall, I had not the least idea of what to do with myself. The contents of the small collection of books I had unearthed from the cupboards and storeroom I already knew by heart. All the stories that the housekeeper, Kirillovna, could remember had been related to me over and over again. The songs of the women depressed me. I tried drinking unsweetened liqueurs, but they made my head ache; moreover, I confess that I was afraid of the possibility of sheer melancholy making a drunkard out of me—and of all types of drunkenness that is the most inveterate, and I have seen many examples of it in this district. I had no near neighbors, apart from two or three such wretches, whose conversation consisted for the most part of hiccups and sighs. Solitude was preferable to their company.

Four versts away from my house was the rich estate of Countess B**, but, besides the steward, nobody lived there. The countess had visited her estate only once, during the first year of her marriage, and had not stayed much longer than a month then. However, during the second spring of my seclusion, the rumor went around that the countess and her husband were going to visit their estate in the summer. And indeed they arrived at the beginning of June.

The arrival of a rich neighbor is an important event in the lives of country dwellers. The landowners and their household servants talk about it for two months before the occurrence and three years after. As far as it concerned me, I confess that the news of the arrival of a young and beautiful neighbor had a powerful effect upon me; I burned with impatience to see her, and the first Sunday after her arrival I set off after dinner to the village of ***, in order to introduce myself to Their Excellencies as their nearest neighbor and most humble servant.

The footman led me into the count's study and then departed to announce me. The spacious study was furnished with the greatest possible luxury; bookcases, each surmounted by a bronze bust, stood against the walls; a large looking glass hung above the marble fireplace; the floor was covered with green cloth, over which carpets were scattered. Unaccustomed to such luxury in my modest quarters, and for so long shut away from the opulence of other people, I began to feel nervous, and awaited the appearance of the count with some trepidation, as a suppliant from the provinces awaits the arrival of a minister. The doors were opened, and a very handsome man of about thirty-two entered the room. The count approached me with an open and friendly air. I tried to recover my composure, and was on the point of introducing myself when he anticipated me. We sat down. His conversation, which was frank and agreeable, soon allayed my nervousness; I was just beginning to feel myself again, when the countess suddenly entered, and I became more confused than ever before. She was indeed beautiful. The count introduced me; I wished to seem at my ease, but the more nonchalant I tried to appear, the more awkward I felt. In order to give me time to recover myself and to become accustomed to a new acquaintanceship, they began to talk to each other, treating me as a good neighbor and without ceremony. Meanwhile, I began to walk up and down the room, looking at the books and pictures. I am no judge of pictures, but there was one that attracted my attention. It portrayed some view or other in Switzerland, but it was not the painting that struck me so much as the fact that two bullets had been shot through it, one immediately above the other.

"That was a good shot," I said, turning to the count.

"Yes," he replied, "a very remarkable shot. Do you shoot well?" he continued.

"Tolerably well," I replied, glad that the conversation had at last turned on a subject that was close to my heart. "I can hit a card at thirty paces—that, with a pistol that I'm much used to, of course."

"Really?" said the countess, with a look of the greatest interest. "And you, my dear, could you hit a card at thirty paces?"

"We'll try it out and see one day," replied the count. "In my day, I used to be quite a good shot, but it's four years now since I've held a pistol in my hand."

"Oh," I remarked, "in that case I'll bet Your Excellency couldn't hit a card at twenty paces. Pistol shooting demands daily practice; I know that from experience. I was reckoned one of the best shots in our regiment. But once it happened that I didn't handle a pistol for a whole month, since mine were being repaired. And what do you think, Your Excellency? The first time I shot again after that I missed a bottle four times running at twenty-five paces. Our captain, a witty and amusing fellow, happened to be there and he said to me: 'It's clear that your hand cannot bring itself to hit a bottle, my friend!' No, Your Excellency, you must not neglect to practice, or you'll quickly lose your skill. The best shot I ever met used to practice at least three times a day. It was as much a habit with him as drinking a couple of glasses of vodka every evening."

The count and countess were pleased that I had begun to talk.

"And what sort of a shot was he?" the count asked me.

"I'll tell you how good he was, Your Excellency. If he saw a fly settle on the wall—you smile, Countess, but I swear to God it's true —if he saw a fly, he would shout out: 'Kuzka, my pistol!' Kuzka would fetch him a loaded pistol, and bang!—the fly would be crushed against the wall."

"Amazing!" exclaimed the count. "And what was his name?"

"Silvio, Your Excellency."

"Silvio!" cried the count, jumping up from his chair. "You knew Silvio?"

"Indeed, Your Excellency, we were close friends; he was taken into our regiment like a brother officer. But it's five years since I've heard anything of him. Your Excellency knew him as well then?"

"I knew him, I knew him very well. Did he ever tell you of a certain very strange incident in his life?"

"Does Your Excellency refer to the occasion on which he was struck in the face by some rake or other at a ball?"

"Did he ever tell you who that rake was?"

"No, Your Excellency, he did not. . . . Oh! Your Excellency," I continued, guessing the truth, "forgive me. . . . I did not know. . . . Could it have been you?"

"It was," replied the count with a look of great distress; "and that picture with the bullet holes is a souvenir of our last meeting. . . ."

"Oh, my dear," said the countess. "Don't talk about it, for heaven's sake; it would be too terrible for me to listen to."

"No," rejoined the count, "I will relate everything; he knows how I insulted his friend; he should know how Silvio avenged himself."

The count pushed a chair toward me, and with the liveliest possible interest I listened to the following story:

"Five years ago I got married. The honeymoon was spent here, in this village. It is to this house that I owe the happiest moments of my life, and also one of my most painful memories.

"One evening we were out riding together. My wife's horse became restless, and feeling some alarm, she gave the reins to me and went home on foot. I rode on in front. I saw a traveling carriage in the courtyard, and was told that a man was waiting for me in my study, and that he had refused to give his name, merely stating that he had business with me. I went into this room and in the twilight I saw a man, unshaven and covered in dust, standing by the fireplace—just there. I approached him, trying to remember his features.

" 'You do not recognize me, Count?' he asked in a shaking voice.

" 'Silvio!' I cried, and I confess I felt as if my hair were standing up on end.

" 'Exactly,' he continued. 'I owe you one shot. I have come for it. Are you ready?'

"A pistol protruded from his side pocket. I measured out twelve paces and stood in the corner over there, beseeching him to be quick and fire before my wife returned. He hesitated, and asked for a light. Candles were brought in. I closed the door, gave orders that nobody should enter the room, and again besought him to fire. He drew out his pistol and took aim. . . . I counted the seconds. . . . I thought of her. . . . A terrible minute passed. Silvio lowered his hand.

" 'I'm sorry,' he said, 'that my pistol is not loaded with cherry stones—bullets are so heavy. It seems to me that this is not a duel, but murder; I am not accustomed to aiming at an unarmed man. Let us begin again; we shall cast lots to see who should fire first.'

"My head went round. . . . I think I made some objection. . . . Eventually we loaded another pistol; two pieces of paper were folded; he placed them in the cap—the same that I had once pierced with my shot; I again drew the lucky number.

" 'You're devilish lucky, Count,' he said with a smile that I shall never forget.

"I cannot understand what was the matter with me, or how he forced me to do it . . . but I fired and hit that picture there."

The count pointed at the picture with the bullet holes; his face was burning like fire; the countess was paler than her own handkerchief. I was unable to hold back an exclamation.

"I fired," continued the count, "and thank God I missed. Then Silvio—he was terrible to behold at that moment—began to take aim at me. Suddenly the door opened, and Masha rushed in, and with a shriek threw herself on my shoulder. Her presence restored to me all my courage.

" 'My dear,' I said to her, 'surely you can see we're joking? How frightened you look! Go and find yourself a drink of water and then come back again; I should like to introduce my old friend and comrade to you.'

"Masha still did not believe me.

" 'Tell me, is it true what my husband says?' she asked, turning to the terrible Silvio. 'Is it true that you're both only joking?'

" 'He is always joking, Countess,' replied Silvio; 'he once struck me in the face for a joke, he shot through my cap for a joke, and just now he missed his aim for a joke; now it's my turn to feel in the mood for a joke. . . .'

"With these words he made as if to take aim again—in front of her! Masha threw herself at his feet.

" 'Get up, Masha, for shame!' I cried in a frenzy; 'and you, sir, will you cease to make fun of an unfortunate woman? Are you going to fire or not?'

" 'No, I'm not going to fire,' Silvio replied. 'I am satisfied. I have seen your alarm, your confusion; I forced you to shoot at me, and that is enough. You will remember me. I commit you to your conscience.'

"Here he turned to go, but stopping in the doorway, he glanced at the picture through which my bullet had passed, shot at it almost without aiming, and then vanished. My wife had fainted; the servants, not daring to stop him, looked at him in horror. He went out into the porch, called to his coachman, and had gone before I had time to collect my senses."

The count was silent. And thus it was that I discovered the end of the story, whose beginning had once impressed me so deeply. I never met its hero again. It is said that Silvio commanded a detachment of Hetairists* at the time of the revolt of Alexandros Ypsilantis, and was killed at the battle of Skulyany.

(*1830*)

---

* Greek soldiers who fought against the Turks in their war of independence (1820–1827).

ALEKSANDR GRIBOYEDOV

ALEKSANDR GRIBOYEDOV (1795–1829) entered Moscow University at the age of eleven, served in the military during the war with Napoleon in 1812, and then became a diplomat in the Ministry of Foreign Affairs. A friend of some of the young liberals and revolutionaries who participated in the Decembrist uprising of 1825, Griboyedov was arrested and imprisoned in St. Petersburg for several months. When released, he returned to diplomatic work in a higher rank. (Thus he came to know from personal experience what it was like to be prosecuted by the military and civil bureaucracy, as well as to be within it and working for it.)

Griboyedov's dramatic death came while serving in Tehran as a Russian envoy to Persia in 1829. A war between Russia and Persia ended with a settlement resented by the latter. Griboyedov had been in charge of the negotiations on the Russian side; it was he who delivered the text of the treaty to the Czar in St. Petersburg in 1828. When he returned to Tehran as minister to Persia, anti-Russian feelings ran high. A Persian mob, worked up into a frenzy, stormed the Russian Embassy, believing that an Armenian eunuch from the harem of the Persian shah was being sheltered there, and tore to pieces every Russian they could find. Griboyedov was among those killed.

Griboyedov wrote the play for which he is best known, The Trouble with Reason, mainly in 1823 and 1824. The play circulated only in manuscript, but it was read by many, and it was also recited and commented on widely. Two incomplete, censored acts were finally published in 1825, a still incomplete text in 1833, and the entire text only in the early 1860s.

The play captures the spirit of criticism and rebellion of its age. There was desire for change, combined with a sense of hopeless con-

finement within a repressive, rigid, traditional society. Numerous phrases from the play entered the everyday Russian language as part of the common stock of proverbs and commonly quoted epigrams. According to one count, sixty such epigrams coined by Griboyedov had become part of the Russian language by the end of the nineteenth century.

The translation following by the poet Frank Reeve was made by him expressly for this volume, and it is being printed here for the first time.

The language of the drama is pithy, lively, witty, poignant—brilliant. The verse—rhymed free iambics—varies in number of feet per line from one to thirteen syllables. More than half the lines are regular alexandrines (twelve-syllable lines with a regular caesura.)

The hero, Chatsky, is an angry young man. He scourges the members of society with whom he comes into contact; he is laughed at, declared mad, then ignored. In the end, his efforts hopeless, he flees.

Griboyedov's play is highly mannered. It is taut, focused, sharply pointed—a perfect vehicle for the depiction of the lot of an outsider and the expression of his resentment. This is the birth of the famous Russian "superfluous man," whom we see further developed in the works of Lermontov, Turgenev, and many other writers. He is the disappointed Russian who has traveled abroad and cannot stand the condition of things at home. It is a perfect presentation of an eloquent would-be reformer's frustration in trying to attack social conditions— corruption, sloth, the immobility of society. The status quo is presented as a fortification, a pillbox. Chatsky gets nowhere, but he manages to attack in beautiful language: he is the champion of invective.

At times compared to Molière's Misanthrope and Shakespeare's Thersites and Timon of Athens, Chatsky is the ancestor of the Russian outsider, the critic, the rejected one.

THE TROUBLE WITH REASON

A Comedy in Four Acts in Verse

CHARACTERS

PAVEL AFANASYEVICH FAMUSOV, *manager of a government office*

SOFYA PAVLOVNA, *his daughter*

LIZA, *a maid*

ALEKSEY STEPANOVICH MOLCHALIN, *Famusov's secretary, resident in the house*

ALEKSANDR ANDREYEVICH CHATSKY

COLONEL SERGEY SERGEYEVICH SKALOZUB

NATALYA DMITRIYEVNA GORICH, *a young lady*

PLATON MIKHAILOVICH GORICH, *her husband*

PRINCE TUGOUKHOVSKY *and*

THE PRINCESS, *his wife, with their six daughters: Zizi, Mimi, and four others*

COUNTESS KHRYUMIN, *grandmother, and*

COUNTESS KHRYUMIN, *granddaughter*

ANTON ANTONOVICH ZAGORETSKY

OLD LADY KHLYOSTOV, *Famusov's wife's sister*

MR. N.

MR. D.

REPETILOV

PETRUSHKA *and several servants with speaking roles*

Many guests of every description and their footmen

FAMUSOV's stewards

The action takes place in Famusov's house in Moscow.

A NOTE ON SOME OF THE NAMES

FÁMUSOV *From the Latin* fama *(rumor) or* famosus *(well known). A fictitious character with characteristics drawn from Griboyedov's uncle.*

SÓFYA PÁVLOVNA *A typical, classical heroine's name.*

MOLCHÁLIN *From* molchat', molchanie, molchalivy *(to keep silent, silence, taciturn).*

CHÁTSKY *In one manuscript* Chadsky, *suggesting derivation from* chad *(fumes, dazedness).*

SKALOZÚB *From* skalit' zuby *(to grin; literally, to show one's teeth).*

TUGOÚKHOVSKY *From* tugo *(taut) and* ukho *(ear), as in the phrase* tugoi na ukho *(hard of hearing).*

KHRYÚMIN *A suggestive combination of* khryukat' *(to grunt) and* ugryúmy *(sullen).*

ZAGORÉTSKY *From* zagoret', zagoret'sya *(to bake in the sun, to catch fire, to light up, to be eager).*

KHLYÓSTOV *From* khlyostky *(trenchant). A portrait of Natalya Dmitriyevna Ofrosimova, portrayed in* War and Peace *as Akhrosimova.*

REPETÍLOV *From the Latin* repeto, repetere *(to revisit, the repeat) and* Shatilov, *prototype of the character and a contemporary of Griboyedov's.*

GÓRE OT UMÁ *The Russian title, literally* Grief from Intelligence *or, as it has often been translated,* Woe from Wit. Gore *means "grief, sorrow, woe, misfortune, trouble." It occurs in such phrases as* na svoë gore *(to one's sorrow),* gore v tom, chto *(the trouble is that) and* gore emu *(woe unto him).* Um *means "mind, intellect, wit, intelligence, wisdom, reason." It occurs in many colloquial and ironic phrases, such as* vzyat'sya za um *(to come to one's senses),* byt' na ume *(to be on one's mind),* ot bol'shogo uma *(in one's infinite wisdom), and* soyti s uma *(to go mad).*

ACT I

The living room, with a grandfather's clock; a door on the right leads to SOFYA's *room, from which come the sounds of a piano and a flute that then fall silent.* LIZA *is asleep in the middle of the room, stretched out on the armchairs.*
It is morning. Daylight is breaking.

LIZA *(Suddenly awakes, gets up, looks around)*
It's getting light! How fast the night went by!
Asked her if I could go to bed;
"My friend's expected. Keep watch," she said,
"so long as you don't tumble off the chair."
Now I hardly closed my eyes
and it's daybreak. So—
(Knocks on SOFYA's *door)*

You people there,
Hey! Sofya Pavlovna, beware!
Your tête-à-tête's gone past the night.
Madam, can't you hear?
Aleksey Stepanich!—Nothing gives them a fright!
     (Moves back from the door)
Now like a bolt from up above,
her father'll probably come in!
What it is to serve a debutante in love!
     (Returns to the door)
You've got to go. It's morning. —What?

                    SOFYA'S VOICE
What time is it?

                         LIZA
Everybody's up.

                    SOFYA *(From her room)*
What time is it?

                         LIZA
Seven, eight, and nine.

                    SOFYA *(Still from there)*
No, it isn't.

                         LIZA
Ah, curse Cupid's line!
They hear but won't believe their ears.
What'll I do to make it clear?
I'll change the clock, though I know that I'll get scolded.
I'll make it chime.
     (She climbs on a chair, moves the hand, and the clock strikes and chimes. FAMUSOV enters)
Oh! Sir!

                        FAMUSOV
Your sir; yes, sir.
     (Stops the chiming)
What a naughty little girl you are.
I couldn't imagine who was making such a stir!
First sounded like a flute; then more like a piano;
besides, Sofya can't be up and around now.

LIZA

No, sir, accidentally I—

FAMUSOV

Accidentally—that's why I've got to keep an eye
on you. What's up your sleeve?
    (Presses close to her and makes advances)
Cute girl, little pesky filly!

LIZA

Pest yourself, making faces makes you look silly!

FAMUSOV

So modest, but not a thing behind
it—just the mischief of an empty mind.

LIZA

The empty-headed one is you.
Don't forget, you're getting old—

FAMUSOV

Not yet.

LIZA

If someone comes, what'll we do?

FAMUSOV

Who's going to come?
Isn't Sofya asleep?

LIZA

She's now taking a snooze.

FAMUSOV

Just now?! Last night?

LIZA

She read the whole night through.

FAMUSOV

What whims and fancies are the rage these days!

LIZA

Locked in her room, she reads aloud in French.

FAMUSOV

Tell her there's no sense ruining her eyes;
besides, reading's nothing to boast about:

French books may keep her up all night,
but Russian ones knock me out.

LIZA

As soon as she's up, I will.
Please leave lest you wake her; she may be sleeping still.

FAMUSOV

Me, wake her? Why, you started up the clock
as loud as an orchestra throughout the block.

LIZA (As loudly as possible)

Oh, stop that, sir!

FAMUSOV (Puts his hand over her mouth)

Save us, how you shout.
You losing your senses?

LIZA

I hope it isn't one of those—

FAMUSOV

Those what?

LIZA

It's time you learned, sir—you're not a child—
girls' morning sleep is so refined
that if a door squeaks or you just whisper your intentions,
they hear it all—

FAMUSOV

That's all your invention.

SOFYA'S VOICE

Hey, Liza!

FAMUSOV (Hastily)

Shhh!
    (Tiptoes out of the room)

LIZA (Alone)

Gone. Oh, it's best to avoid the upper class.
With them you never know what you'll be in for next.
More than all the griefs with which we're vexed,
Lord, help their anger and their love to pass.
    (SOFYA enters with a candle, MOLCHALIN following)

SOFYA

Liza, what's gotten into you?
You're making so much noise!

LIZA

So, parting's hard?
Closeted all night, but still that's not enough?

SOFYA

Ah, it's morning after all!
   (Blows the candle out)
Come dawn, come grief. How quick the nights.

LIZA

Don't expect me to sympathize with your plight.
Your old man came in, I figured I was as good as dead;
put on an act for him—I forget what lies I said—
but why are you standing there? Sir, a parting bow,
then go. Everything's upset now.
Look what time it is. Look out the window:
everybody's tending to his business.
And in the house they're sweeping, beating, cleaning, scouring.

SOFYA

Happy people never count the hours.

LIZA

You don't have to if you don't want to,
but I'm the one who has to account for you.

SOFYA *(To* MOLCHALIN*)*

Go now. Somehow we'll live through one more boring day.

LIZA

Good-bye, sir, hands off, and on your way.
   (Parts them. In the doorway MOLCHALIN *bumps into* FAMUSOV*)*

FAMUSOV

What a surprise! Molchalin, m'boy, is it you?

MOLCHALIN

Aye, sir.

FAMUSOV

But why precisely here? and at this hour?
And Sofya dear! Good morning, gentle Sofya!

What made you rise so early? what worries or what motives?
And how did you two chance to come together?

SOFYA

It was only a moment ago that he entered—

MOLCHALIN

From taking a walk.

FAMUSOV

Dear friend, when you want to take a walk
can't you find a back street farther off?
And, madam, scarcely have you gotten up
than you're with a man! A young man, too! What a thing for a girl
to do!
All night she reads things that have been made up,
and now we see what are the results.
It's all because we have Kuznetsky Street
and the French forever with their fashions and their arts,
who devastate our pockets and our hearts.
May the Great Creator soon liberate
us from their fancy hats and bonnets and pins and fops
and all the book and pastry shops!

SOFYA

Excuse me, Father, I feel rather faint.
This sudden fright has taken away my breath.
You ran in so briskly and so nimbly
that I'm all confused.

FAMUSOV

Thankee humbly, humbly,
says I caught her unprepared!
came in too quick! made her scared!
Sofya Pavlovna, I'm upset myself. All day
I run around like mad every which way,
carrying out the duties of my position,
with everyone trying to get me to approve some requisition!
Did I expect this new situation? that I'd be deceived—

SOFYA *(In tears)*

By whom, Father?

FAMUSOV

Now I'm being accused
of always being unfairly furious.

Stop crying; I'm being serious.
Wasn't everything always done
to bring you up right from the day you were born?
After your dear mother died, it was my pleasure
to hire Madame Rosier to replace her.
I made that treasure of a lady your governess—
so smart she was, so quiet, with such scruples—
though one thing doesn't go with all the rest—
for a raise of an extra five hundred rubles
she let some other people lure her away.
There's something else I meant to say.
Indeed, you need no other model
when the one before you is your father.
Take a good look: I don't boast about my figure,
although I'm hale and hearty, have reached my silver age,
a widower, and free, the master of my fate,
well known for my ascetic nature—

LIZA

Permit me, sir—

FAMUSOV

Not a peep out of you!
A terrible time! No one knows what to do!
Everyone's too clever for their breeches,
especially our daughters, and we've gone along.
All these foreign languages!
We take the hoboes in as tutors or pay for lessons
to teach our daughters all, all, all!—
how to dance and sing and sigh and flatter
as if marrying them off to clowns is all that matters.
You, stranger, what do you want? What are you here for, sir?
I took you in as an orphan, made you part of my family,
got you officer's rank, made you my secretary—
your transfer to Moscow came through the weight I carry—
if it wasn't for me, you'd still be rotting out in Tver.

SOFYA

Your anger makes no sense to me at all.
He lives here in our house, O grave misfortune!
He simply got mixed up in the hall.

FAMUSOV

Mixed up, or mixed things up himself?
And you both here? That's no accident. And quite unseemly.

SOFYA

Well, let me explain what really happened.
When you and Liza were here not long ago,
your voice terrified me extremely,
and I dashed in here to be safe from harm.

FAMUSOV

Why, she's laying the whole fuss at my door.
My voice caused them inopportune alarm!

SOFYA

When you toss and turn, a whisper seems an uproar.
Let me tell you my dream; then you'll understand.

FAMUSOV

What happened?

SOFYA

Want me to tell you?

FAMUSOV

Of course.
 (Sits down)

SOFYA

All right—you see—at first
a field of flowers—I search
some herb,
but now I can't remember which.
Suddenly a lovely man—one of those
we feel on first sight we've known forever—
is right beside me—generously polite, and smart, too,
but humble. You know, a man who was born poor—

FAMUSOV

Oh, heavens, dear, don't make it harder.
A poor man can't become your partner.

SOFYA

Then the whole thing vanished—field and sky.
We're in a darkened room. Like a miracle
the parquet parts—and you come scrambling

up from below, death-pale, your hair on end!
Creatures neither beast nor human
with a clap of thunder fling the doors open,
hurl us apart—and torment the man who was beside me.
I feel he's dearer than any treasure
and try to reach him—you drag me off sideways
followed by the groaning and howling and hissing mockery of the
monsters!
He shouts after us!
I wake up. Somebody's saying something.
Your voice it was—but why so early?
I dash in here—and here I find you two.

FAMUSOV

A bad dream, surely, the way I see it,
with all things in it, if it's true—
demons, and love, and fear, and flowers.
Now, my good man, what about you?

MOLCHALIN

I heard your voice.

FAMUSOV

How amusing.
My voice is something they're obsessed with, listen to
so carefully they have a predawn convocation.
You hurried when you heard my voice? But why? Explain it.

MOLCHALIN

The things to sign, sir.

FAMUSOV

That's all we needed.
Heaven help us, why this sudden feeling
we have to get the paperwork done?
    (Rises)
Well, Sonyushka, I'll leave you alone.
Some dreams are strange, but waking life is stranger.
You were looking for an herb
but came across a friend in danger.
Get all this nonsense out of your head.
What's miraculous can't be reasoned about.
Go, lie down; go back to sleep.

(To MOLCHALIN)
Come; we'll get those papers sorted out.

MOLCHALIN

I brought them only to report
they need to be corrected here and there before
being passed on—contradictions to be clarified—

FAMUSOV

Of one thing only, sir, am I terrified:
that most of them will end up in a pile.
If you had your way, one correction's all it'd take.
As for me, whatever sense it makes,
my way wrong or right,
once it's signed it's out of sight.
     (Exits with MOLCHALIN, *letting him go first)*

LIZA

Isn't this some holiday! What fun and laughter!
Not really, though; this isn't a laughing matter;
you start to faint; your heart stops beating;
a sin's no problem, but gossip's cheating.

SOFYA

What does gossip matter? Let them all criticize,
but Father's actions make you realize
he always was impetuous and restless,
indefatigable and breathless,
but now—what do you think?

LIZA

I don't trust hearsay.
Perhaps he'll lock you up—lucky if that means me, too—
because otherwise, God save us, what'll you do
if he sends me and Molchalin and everybody else away?

SOFYA

Think how happiness is independent!
Some awful things just disappear;
When sad nothings can't be brought to bear,
we're lost in music, and time seems half suspended,
as if Fate were watching over us,
and we had no worries and no doubts—
though trouble lurks around the corner.

LIZA

That's what I said. You never pay attention
to all the things that I point out,
and then you have problems.
How could you want a better fortune-teller?
I've always said this affair won't come to anything
no matter when.
Your old man's like all the Moscow men:
He wants a son-in-law who's already rich and famous—
though some famous men aren't rich, just between us—
one who has enough
to live real well and offer lots of balls,
like, for example, Colonel Skalozub,
whose pockets are well lined and who aims to be a general.

SOFYA

And so, so nice! I'm just beside myself
hearing tales of battles and of armies of relief.
He hasn't said a smart thing all his life.
I'd rather drown than have to be his wife.

LIZA

You're right, he *is* a talker, and a stupid one at that.
But whether you're thinking of soldier or civilian,
who's half so sensitive and gay and witty
as Aleksandr Andreyevich Chatsky?
I'm not saying this to make you embarrassed—
I know you can't bring back the past—
but I remember—

SOFYA

What? How good he was
at making fun of everybody else?
He chatted, joked; I found him entertaining.
Laughter fits in any place.

LIZA

That's all? Come on! Who's fooling who?
The tears streamed down as he, poor man, was leaving you.
"Why are you weeping, sir? Live and be merry."
And he says to me, "Liza, I know the cost.
Who can say what I'll find on my return,
and how much will be, perhaps, forever lost?"
Poor soul, I think he sensed that three years later—

SOFYA

Careful, don't take undue liberties with me.
Perhaps I did behave in a very foolish way—
I admit it and regret it—but what did I betray?—
or whom?—to be reproached for infidelity?
Chatsky and I, you're right, were brought up side by side.
The daily habit of being inseparably together
bound us in friendship through all the changes of childhood weather,
but then he went away, apparently at our place bored
and seldom came to see us anymore.
Later he came back, pretending to be lovelorn,
so demanding and trouble-laden!
Witty, quick, with a ready phrase,
among friends spending his happiest days
and getting an exaggerated opinion of who he was.
Then the travel passion overwhelmed him. Tell me,
if a person really loves somebody,
why look for wit and reason and go so far?

LIZA

Where, in fact? So far away?
Took the cure at a Caucasian spa, they say,
and not because he was sick, I bet, but bored.

SOFYA

And I bet happy anywhere people are absurd.
The man I love isn't like that.
Molchalin's always ready to put other people first.
How he hates vulgarity! How modestly
and shyly a whole long night goes by with such a man!
I mean, we're sitting there, outdoors it's getting lighter,
and what do you think we're doing?

LIZA

God knows,
m'lady, I doubt I should inquire.

SOFYA

He presses my hand against his heart
and sighs from the depths of his soul
without a word too free—and thus the night goes by
hand in hand, me always in his eye.
You're laughing! How dare you! What possible excuse
did I give you for such laughter?!

LIZA

Me, ma'am? I just remembered about your aunt,
when the young Frenchman ran off from her house.
Poor dear, wanted her sorrow dead and
buried but couldn't make it;
forgot to blacken her hair to fake it,
so three days later turned gray-headed.
(Continues laughing)

SOFYA *(Annoyed)*

And that's how afterward I'll be talked about.

LIZA

I'm sorry, truly, as God's holy.
I hoped a silly laugh or two
would help to cheer you up some.
(A SERVANT enters, followed by CHATSKY)

SERVANT

Aleksandr Andreyevich Chatsky has come.
(Exits)

CHATSKY

Daybreak—you're on your feet! and I, prostrate before them.
(Fervently kisses her hand)
Come, embrace me! Didn't expect me? What do you say?
Glad to see me? No? Turn your head this way!
Surprised? That's all? Some welcome home!
As if it weren't a week that I was gone;
as if yesterday we two together
had bored each other half to death.
Not a shred of love! and oh so refined!
while I dashed heedless on, out of breath,
some five and forty hours without a wink,
across five hundred miles through wind and storm,
often lost completely, falling countless times—
heroic deeds get some reward!

SOFYA

Ah! Chatsky, I'm delighted to see you.

CHATSKY

You are? Well, at last!
Though, who sincerely is delighted in this sort of way?
It seems to me, when all's said and done,

that of those who might have cared how I drove
servants and horses through bitter weather, I'm the only one.

LIZA

Why, sir, had you been here outside the door,
honest to God, not five minutes ago,
how we were recalling the things you did— So,
madam, it's your turn to have the floor.

SOFYA

We always have, not only now.
You have nothing to reproach me for.
Whoever happens by, or drops in
by chance, whatever, a stranger from afar,
I always ask, even of a sailor,
hasn't he somewhere run across you in a coach?

CHATSKY

Let's assume that's so.
Blessed is the man of faith; the world's his home.
My Lord, it's hard to believe I'm here again
in Moscow! In your house! And how you've changed!
Where has time gone? that innocent age
when on long evenings you and I
played hide-and-seek here, there, everywhere
loudly among the tables and the chairs;
then your father'd enter with your mother to play piquet;
we'd huddle in a darkened corner as if done for,
remember? Trembling lest the table squeak, a door—

SOFYA

Childish games!

CHATSKY

Indeed; but now
at seventeen you've blossomed beautifully,
inimitably, as you yourself well know,
and therefore still are modest, don't seek a social life.
You're not in love? I beg you to reply
without a second thought—enough confusion.

SOFYA

If there's anyone such rapid questions
and such prying looks ever might confuse—

CHATSKY

Oh, heavens, what should astonish me but you?
What's new in Moscow, now that I'm home?
Last night there was a ball; tomorrow there'll be two.
The lucky man's engaged; the unlucky got left alone:
everything's the same; in all the albums, the same poems.*

SOFYA

Hounded into Moscow! By traveling, disencharmed!
So, where's it better?

CHATSKY

Wherever we aren't.
So, how's your father? Still the faithful old-line member
of the English Club† until his dying day?
Your uncle already packed up with his lifetime's work?
And—what's his name—is he a Greek or Turk?—‡
the swarthy man with legs like a crane—
I don't think I ever knew his name—
but wherever you go you'll find him there
in the salon or the dining-room chairs.
And what of the three boulevard beauties
who for fifty years have made it their duty
to stay young? They have a million female relatives, thanks to whom
they'll be related to all Europe soon.
And what about our shining glory?
His forehead reads: Stage and Story;
his house is all in green like a woodland grove;
he's as fat as a barrel; his actors, as thin as staves.
Remember how at that ball we two together
discovered in a secret room behind the screens
a man trilling like a nightingale,
a winter singer of summer weather?
And what about your tubercular relative
who hates all books but got himself a chair

* Young people often kept an album, a sort of combination journal and autograph book, in which they and their friends wrote poems and other personal matter.
† A fashionable Moscow club patterned after those in London.
‡ The "Turk or Greek" and the "shining glory" amateur theatrical producer seem to refer to living contemporaries. Some rich gentlemen had private theaters and troupes of serf actors. Often, rooms were extensively decorated with trees, plants, and pastoral scenes.

on the Scholarly Committee* and made everybody swear
they do not now and never will know how to read and write?
Fate wills that I must cross their paths again!
I'm fed up with their ways, but what man has no faults?
After you've been traveling, and you get home, then
the home fires of our native land smell good and sweet!†

SOFYA

I must get you together with my aunt
so you can make a complete list of complaints.

CHATSKY

How is your aunt? still the debutante Athena?
still lady-in-waiting to Empress Katerina?
she still training orphan girls and pugs?
Speaking of education, have they pulled the rug
from under any change, so that they still
try gathering teachers by regiment and brigade
as many as they can and all underpaid?
Not that we're scientifically behind:
in Russia, under threat of a huge fine
we've been ordered to confer
on everyone the title of historical geographer!
Our leader—remember his pointed cap, his workman's smock,
his index finger, all the signs of learning
that so alarmed our timid little minds
that early on we became accustomed to believe
we can't be saved without the Germans?
What about Guillaumé, the Frenchman, the empty-headed fool?
He married yet?

SOFYA

To whom?

CHATSKY

Oh, maybe, by the way,
to some Princess Pulkheriya Andrevna, say?

* The *Uchony komitet* was set up in 1817 to exercise ideological control over all
scholarly activity. Under the Ministry of Ecclestical Affairs and National Education,
it had broad censorship powers.
† The quoted line dates back to the *Odyssey* and to the Latin proverb *Et fumus
patriae est dulcis*. It served as epigraph for the journal *The Russian Museum* and
was quoted by a number of turn-of-the-century poets, notably by Derzhavin in his
poem "The Harp."

SOFYA

A dancing master! Out of the question!

CHATSKY

Why not, he's a partner, too.
We're required to have an estate and a solid position,
but Guillaumé! That's certainly the tone today
at all the formal balls and parish holidays!
And isn't there still that strange linguistic combination
of high-toned French and street expressions?

SOFYA

A language mixture?

CHATSKY

Two in one—that's what people do.

SOFYA

How complicated to make one from two, like you.

CHATSKY

At least it's not inflated.
So that's the news! Elated
by seeing you, I've taken advantage
of the moment and talked a lot, but aren't there times
when I'm even stupider than Molchalin? Where's he now?
Is it true he still hasn't broken his silent vow?
Used to be he'd see sheet notes of the latest songs
and badger friends to have them copied down.
But he ought to make out rather well:
these days they advance who don't speak but spell.

SOFYA *(Aside)*

Not a man but a serpent!
    (Aloud and constrainedly)
Let me ask you this:
Has it ever happened that you—jokingly, perhaps—or sadly—
or by mistake—said something good about somebody?
I don't mean now, but back in childhood maybe?

CHATSKY

When everything's so soft? and tender? and immature?
Why look back so far? Here's a deed good to mention:
making the harness bells resound
day and night across vast empty fields of snow,

I broke my neck to get to you—and found
you stiff and pompous, indifferent, all outward show!
A half hour I've put up with your being unfriendly!
A face that could be the saintliest nun's!
And nevertheless I love you blindly—
      (A moment's silence)
Listen, do my words really seem as sharp as pins?
And always doing somebody else in?
If so, then head and heart work apart.
Once I laugh at some foolishness
I put it behind me and forget the rest.
Try me by fire: I'll walk in as to dinner. See if I won't.

SOFYA

Well, fine, if you burn—but what if you don't?
      (FAMUSOV enters)

FAMUSOV

Now here's another.

SOFYA

Oh, Father, the dream came true.
      (Exits)

FAMUSOV *(In a low voice, after her)*
That damned dream.
      (CHATSKY eyes the door through which SOFYA exited)
What a thing for you to do!
Three whole years you don't send two words,
and then you drop in like out of the clouds!
      (They embrace)
Welcome, welcome, welcome, friend, hello.
So, go ahead: I bet you're ready to show
and tell a grand gathering of information.
Sit down there now. Wind up and let go.
      (They sit down)

CHATSKY *(Absentmindedly)*
How beautiful Sofya Pavlovna has become!

FAMUSOV

You young men seem to have no other duty
but to keep track of young girls' beauty.
She said something by the way, and you,
carried away with hope, I bet, have been struck dumb.

CHATSKY

No, hope has never been too kind to me.

FAMUSOV

"The dream came true"—you overheard her softly say,
and so you thought—

CHATSKY

Not I. No way.

FAMUSOV

Who did she dream of? What's it mean really?

CHATSKY

I'm no interpreter of dreams.

FAMUSOV

Don't believe her; it's silly.

CHATSKY

I believe my own two eyes.
I've never met in all my life, I swear,
anyone who can compare.

FAMUSOV

A one-track mind. Rather, tell me where
you were and what you saw. You were gone so long!
Where have you just come from?

CHATSKY

How can I start!
I meant to go around the world
but didn't cover a hundredth part.
　(*Quickly rises*)
Excuse me. I came to call on you in such a hurry
that I didn't stop at home. Good-bye! In an hour
I'll come back and tell you all—on my word!
I'll tell you first, then you can tell everyone what you've heard.
　(*In the doorway*)
So beautiful!
　(*Exits*)

FAMUSOV (*Alone*)

Which one of the two?
"Oh, Father, the dream came true!"
Says it so everyone can hear her!

My fault, my fault! I didn't have to detour!
Recently Molchalin has given me cause to wonder.
Now out of the frying pan into the fire!
He's a beggar, but this one's a dandy,
known as a wastrel and terror to the world.
What a job it is, O Heavenly Creator,
to be the father of a grown-up girl!
    (Exits)

ACT II

FAMUSOV

Petrushka, you're always in new livery
with your elbows showing through. Bring the calendar over.
And don't give it a sacristan's delivery
but read it meaningfully and deep and slowly.
One moment. On the page for entering appointments
opposite next week put down:
*To Praskovya Fyodorovna's house
invited on Tuesday to eat trout.*
How wondrous strange the world's created!
Philosophizing makes the mind a mess;
one day you fast, the next you're feted;
three hours' dining takes three days to digest.
Note that on that day— No, don't.
On Thursday invited to an interment.
O humankind, I fear you have forgot
that each alone must crawl into the little box
where nobody may stand or sit.
But whoever'd like to leave a good memory behind
by leading an exemplary life, consider this:
the late-departed was an honored chamberlain
who left his key as legacy to his son.*
Rich he was, and rich his wife;
set children, grandchildren up in life,
then passed away, deeply mourned by us now—
Kuzma Petrovich, may he rest in peace!

* A gold key embroidered on the back of the chamberlain's dress uniform signified his right of access to the czar's chambers. [A *kammerger* (Russian, from the German *kammerherr*) was a courtier with a role similar to the chamberlain's in England.]

What bigwigs live and die in Moscow!
Make a note: on Thursday, what with this and that,
or perhaps on Friday, or Saturday perhaps,
Must attend the christening at the doctor's widow's.
She hasn't had the child yet, but
I figure any day she will now.
   (CHATSKY *and a* SERVANT *enter*)
Ah, Aleksandr Andreyevich, come in, pull up a chair.

CHATSKY

Are you busy?

FAMUSOV *(To the* SERVANT*)*

You may go.
   (The SERVANT *exits)*
Just jotting down some things to keep in mind.
A thing forgotten can trip you from behind.

CHATSKY

For some reason you seem depressed.
Is anything wrong? Is this a bad time to come?
Or has some misfortune happened
to Sofya Pavlovna herself?
I see worry written on your face.

FAMUSOV

Ah, friend, you've made a perfect guess.
I *am* depressed. A man as old as me
can't gaily dance and bend the knee!

CHATSKY

Nobody's inviting you.
I merely wondered if you'd tell
me if Sofya Pavlovna's, perhaps, unwell?

FAMUSOV

Phew, Lord save us! Five thousand times
he sings the same old tune!
First, Sofya Pavlovna's more beautiful than the moon;
now, Sofya Pavlovna's got some disease.
Honestly, seeing her, were you pleased?
You've been round the world—time to settle down?

CHATSKY

Why do you ask?

FAMUSOV

Might be wise to ask my opinion,
for she and I are more or less related;
at least, for years people have treated
me as her father—with reason why.

CHATSKY

Suppose I asked for her hand; how'd you reply?

FAMUSOV

I'd reply that, first, don't be capricious,
run your estate to make it worth the while,
but most importantly, go into public service.

CHATSKY

I'd glady serve, but I sicken at being servile.

FAMUSOV

That's my point! You're too proud, all of you!
You ought to ask, What did your fathers do?
You ought to learn by copying your elders—
me, for example, or my late uncle
Maksim Petrovich. He didn't eat off silver
but off gold; had a hundred servants waiting on him;
bedecked with medals; drove a four-in-hand;
and what a court, the court he served forever,
not like of late,
but the court of Catherine the Great.
In those days, all were men of stature—great, solid men—
bow greetings to them, they wouldn't even nod.
A nobleman was different back then,
drank differently and dined on different food.
My uncle, say—not like your prince or count not—
his countenance grave, his mien and manner proud.
When he had to show his loyalty
he bowed as low as anyone:
one court reception day he chanced to stumble,
down he went and nearly broke his crown;
the old man moaned and wheezed;
the empress, seeing his mistake, was pleased
to laugh; and so what did he do then?
Stood up, straightened out, began bowing lower than ever—
and fell again—intentionally, of course—

lots more laughter—so, down he went once more.
Ho, what do you think of that? I think it very clever.
Landed hurt, got up safe and sound.
Afterward was anyone more sought for whist?
Who always heard a welcome word around the court?
Maksim Petrovich. Who received all honor first?
Maksim Petrovich. Fact!
Who made promotions? gave out pensions?
Maksim Petrovich. You men today, match that!

CHATSKY

Indeed, you may say—and heave a sigh—
when you compare the present period
with olden times gone by
that the world seems to have gotten stupid.
The tradition's there, but accepting it is hard.
He was then most praised who most often bent his neck
not in a frontal attack in war
but pounding the floor with his forehead in peace.
The needy were neglected, left in the dirt in place;
people higher up were webbed with flattery like lace.
A straightforward age of submissiveness and fear,
all beneath a mask of devotion to the crown—
I'm not referring to the uncle you spoke of,
whose ashes we'll duly leave alone—
though I might inquire who these days, suddenly
seized by a fit of servility like a fool
to be the butt of everybody's laughter,
would bravely sacrifice his skull?
Back then, a man his own age, or some
old man falling apart in his antique skin,
seeing a somersault like that,
would have said, I bet, "Oh, if only I could have a turn!"
Though there always are flatterers who press their luck,
now ridicule scares them off and shame keeps them in check.
Wisely the sovereigns grant them less and less.

FAMUSOV

Oh, my God, he's a Carbonarist!*

* A member of a secret political society first established in Naples around 1811
with the aim of founding a republic. The movement later spread to other countries,
notably France.

CHATSKY

No, the world's no longer what it was.

FAMUSOV

A dangerous man!

CHATSKY

Each man breathes more freely
and doesn't rush to join the regiment of clowns.

FAMUSOV

The things he says! Talks like it's being written down!

CHATSKY

Stares at the ceiling in a patron's house,
where he speaks little, shuffles and sups,
holds someone's chair, picks a kerchief up.

FAMUSOV

He's advocating liberty straight out!

CHATSKY

Some men travel; some stay home on their estates—*

FAMUSOV

He doesn't even recognize the state!

CHATSKY

They serve a cause and not a patron—

FAMUSOV

I'd make sure such gentlemen were forbidden
from getting within gunshot of the capitals.†

CHATSKY

I'll let you go after all—

FAMUSOV

No patience, no strength left, alas.

CHATSKY

I spared no pains in giving the past
a going over; now I yield to you
to redress the balance,

* A man who left his estate to travel was presumed to be radical.
† From 1713 until [after the Bolshevik Revolution of 1917], St. Petersburg was the
seat of the government, but both Moscow, long the center of Muscovy, and St.
Petersburg were considered capital cities.

even adding to the present day
past faults you take away.

FAMUSOV

I don't want to know you; I can't stand depravity.

CHATSKY

I've had my say.

FAMUSOV

I've closed my ears.

CHATSKY

Against what? I won't offend them.

FAMUSOV *(Speaking in a patter)*

They knock around the world, waste their youthful years,
come home—how can they know the right and proper way!

CHATSKY

I've finished—

FAMUSOV

Please—no more today.

CHATSKY

I've no wish to prolong the debate.

FAMUSOV

Let me go in peace before it's too late!—
    (A SERVANT *enters)*

SERVANT

Colonel Skalozub.

FAMUSOV *(Hearing and noticing nothing)*

It's into court you'll be hauled
as sure as winter follows fall.

CHATSKY

Someone has come to pay you a call.

FAMUSOV

I'm not listening; you'll be arrested!

CHATSKY

Your footman's trying to talk.

FAMUSOV

Not listening—arrested! arrested!

CHATSKY

Turn around; you're being called.

FAMUSOV *(Turns)*

What? Appalled? Indeed, it's Sodom and Gomorrah.

SERVANT

Colonel Skalozub. Shall I show him in?

FAMUSOV *(Rises)*

Asses! How many times must I say the same thing?
Show him, call him, beg him in. Say what a pleasure
it is to receive him. Get going—psht, psht—hurry.
   (The SERVANT *exits)*
Pu-lease, good sir, when he comes, take it easy.
He's a very famous man, respectable,
who already has amassed a pile of medals.
Young for his rank—which is enviable—
any day now he'll be a general.
Pu-lease, sir, when he comes in behave discreetly—
Ah, Aleksandr Andreyich, I feel it in my bones!
He calls upon me almost weekly—
you know I receive whoever comes—
but in Moscow people exaggerate by thirty-thirds,
as if he were going to marry Sofyushka. Absurd!
Maybe he'd be sincerely glad to,
but I myself don't see any need to
give my daughter away tomorrow or today.
After all, she's young. Though it's as the good Lord wills.
So, pu-lease don't argue with him up and down,
and drop your crazy, wild ideas.
Not here yet? Where could he have gone?
Went to catch me in the other wing, must be.
   (Hastily exits)

CHATSKY

How he fumes and fusses! What energy!
As for Sofya? Isn't this a suitor out and out?
How long I've been treated like someone they don't want to know
about!
How can she not be here?

Who's this Skalozub? The father raves and cheers,
and maybe not the father alone—
Oh, farewell to love declares the man
who goes away for three long years.
    (FAMUSOV *and* SKALOZUB *enter*)

                FAMUSOV
Sergey Sergeyich, come in, come in.
It's warmer here; make yourself at home.
We'll warm you up—you're chilled to the bone—
I'll just open up this draft again.

              SKALOZUB *(In a deep bass)*
Why should you yourself reach in there?
It makes me feel bad, as a frank and candid officer.

                FAMUSOV
How can't I lift a little finger for a friend,
dear Sergey Sergeyich!
Set down your hat, take off your sword,
there's the sofa, stretch out any way you please.

                SKALOZUB
As you wish, if only to be seated.
    (*All three sit,* CHATSKY *a ways off*)

                FAMUSOV
I say, my friend, I better not forget
to bring up the fact that we're related
though distantly—no inheritance to split—
you had no idea—me, too—
it's your cousin I have to thank for this information—
what sort of relation is Nastasya Nikolavna to you?

                SKALOZUB
Can't say as I know, sir, sorry;
we never were in the same rotation.

                FAMUSOV
Sergey Sergeyich, that's unlike you!
Indeed, I'm on all fours before any relative I meet;
I'll find her at the bottom of the sea.
Why, very few serving under me aren't related in this life;
they're mostly my sister's children, or of the sister of my wife.
Molchalin alone isn't part of the family,

which accounts for his having so much efficiency.
You know, when you put someone up for a little medal or position,
how can you not oblige your family by your decision?
Indeed, your cousin's a friend of mine and has often said
that you've showered many service benefits on his head.

SKALOZUB

In '13 both my cousin and I distinguished ourselves
in the Thirtieth Chasseurs, and then in the Forty-fifth.*

FAMUSOV

Happy is the man who has that sort of son!
And in a bow, I bet, a little medal that he won?†

SKALOZUB

For August third, for holding firmly in the trench;
he got one with a ribbon; I, one around my neck.‡

FAMUSOV

What an amiable man, your cousin, and, I own,
a very dashing, marvelous man about town.

SKALOZUB

But now he has picked up some whole new life design.
Slated to advance, he suddenly resigned
and in the country started reading books.

FAMUSOV

That's what youth is! Reading! And then you're cooked!
But you've been orderly and meticulous—
now long a colonel though not so long in service.

SKALOZUB

I've had good fortune, say, in who've been at my side—
some openings were opportune,
some senior officers retired,
while others, see, were shot and died.

FAMUSOV

God above is great the way He grants His favors!

* These regiments were in reserve throughout the war.
† D. P. Costello, the editor of an annotated edition of the play, published in Letch-
worth, Herts, England, by Prideaux Press, 1977, points out that "the badge of
Russian orders of the first class was a star and a broad ribbon; that of orders of
the intermediate classes was a cross worn at the opening of the collar; of the lowest
class, a cross suspended from a ribbon tied in a bow and worn on the breast."
‡ On August 3, 1813, a truce was in effect on all fronts.

SKALOZUB

Some men have had much better luck· than I, however—just in our
own Fifteenth Division, to call a spade a spade,
for example, the general commanding our brigade.

FAMUSOV

Oh, heavens, what good fortune haven't you yet savored?

SKALOZUB

No complaints—I haven't been passed over—
but to get my regiment for two years I was led round by the nose.

FAMUSOV

Competing for a regiment?
Although, of course, in everything else
everyone's far behind you.

SKALOZUB

No, you'll find seniors to me in the corps. Mind you,
I've been in only since 1809.
Oh, there are many avenues by which one may advance,
and like a true philosopher I study them all the time—
if only to be a general by my inheritance.

FAMUSOV

And brilliantly you study; God grant you health
and a general's epaulets—which having,
why postpone till later in life
the question of a general's wife?

SKALOZUB

Get married? That's something I might do.

FAMUSOV

Well, so? There are sisters, nieces, daughters, too—
Moscow has no end of lovely brides—
and why?—because each year they multiply.
Ah, friend, admit no matter how you scour
the world you'll find no capital like ours.

SKALOZUB

So far ahead the distance can't be measured.

FAMUSOV

In taste, friend, in excellence of manner—
in everything, its special laws.

Take, for example, the old tradition still among us
that a son's accepted according to his father.
He may be feeble, not up to much, but if, as an heirloom,
he has a couple of thousand family serfs
he's a groom.
Another may be livelier, or even arrogant,
or maybe known for being very clever,
but no family'll accept him. That shouldn't surprise you ever.
It's only here, you know, that nobility's still honored.
And that's not all—take our custom of bread and salt*
according to which we receive whoever comes to call.
The door's wide open for uninvited guests,
especially those more foreign than the rest;
whether he's an honest man or sinner
makes no difference to us—everyone gets dinner.
Take a glance from head to foot, you'll see
each Muscovite bears a mark as special as can be.
Just consider our young people if you please,
our young men, our grandsons, and our sons:
We discipline them hard, but you'll see in every case
by age fifteen they teach their teachers how to get things done!
You wonder about our old folks? When a passion seizes them,
they come to a decision as fair as a verdict and as firm.
They're old-line gentry, see, so nobody impresses them,
and sometimes the way they talk about the government†
you'd think would lead to trouble—if anyone overheard.
Not that they're innovators—far from it, Lord
have mercy on us—not a bit. But they'll bicker and bray
over one thing or another, or nothing even oftener,
and argue and shout and finally go their separate ways.
Oh, they're as smart as retired chancellors!
Let me tell you, maybe the time hasn't come,
but without them nothing'll ever get done.
And our ladies? Let anyone try to get a hold on them!
Judges of everything everywhere, they have no judges over them.
When they rise in protest playing cards,
you need God's patience—I know; I was married before.
Send them to lead the troops along the front!

* Symbols of hospitality, bread and salt were given to entering guests.
† The lines that follow characterize the "cantankerous spirit of opposition" of the
English Club and the degree to which the political air in the period preceding the
Decembrist coup seemed filled with conspiracy.

Have them take their places on the Senate floor!
Irina Vlasevna! Lukeriya Alekseyevna!
Tatya Yurevna! Pulkheriya Andreyevna!
But the daughers now—who looks on them will really bow—
His Majesty the Prussian king was here,*
and he marveled not at the young ladies' aims or faces
but at their demeanor and their moral graces.
And he was right—could anyone be more well brought up?
How skillfully they doll themselves in taffetas
and velvet thats and thises and little veils;
never say a word directly but with a dimple,
and sing you French love songs, in which
they bring out all the upper notes, and simply
faint at the sight of an officer's tunic
merely because they're so patriotic.
No, I mean it: no matter how you scour
the world you'll find no capital like ours.

SKALOZUB

I remain an adherent
of the view that the fire greatly helped improve its appearance.†

FAMUSOV

Don't bring that up; everybody yacks about it.
Since then, the sidewalks and the roads,
the houses—the whole city's been done over new.

CHATSKY

The houses, new; the prejudices, old.
Be glad that neither time
nor taste nor fire'll wipe them out.

FAMUSOV *(To* CHATSKY*)*

Knot your kerchief to remind you;
I asked you to keep quiet—not too big a favor.
    (To SKALOZUB*)*
If you please, sir. This is Chatsky, a friend and neighbor,
the late Andrey Ilyich's boy;
He doesn't work for the government—he sees
no point in—but if he wanted, he'd do it very wisely.
It's a shame, a shame, because he's a bright young man

---

* Frederick Wilhelm III visited Moscow in the summer of 1818.
† After the fire of 1812, Moscow was thoroughly and rapidly rebuilt.

who writes and translates very nicely.
Can't help but feeling sorry that so intelligent—

CHATSKY

Is there no one else for whom you can feel sorry?
I find even your praise very annoying.

FAMUSOV

I'm not the only one. That's what everybody's saying.

CHATSKY

And who's this everybody? They're such antiques
that a free life is an intolerable idea;
they dig their judgments out of newspapers discarded
in the days of the Ochakov siege and the conquest of the Crimea.*
Always ready to pick and pull,
they chant the same old verse,
not noticing about themselves
that whatever's older's worse.
Where are the fathers of our fatherland who are
the models you insist we must acknowledge?
Surely not these who by robbery made themselves rich?
Who got around the law through family and acquaintance?
Who then erected magnificent palatial mansions
where life stretches out in feasting and wild extravagance?
Where foreign comers can't resurrect—for all they try—
the most ignoble features of a way of life gone by?†
Who in Moscow, by the way, hasn't had
his fill of dinners, suppers, dances?
Surely the man, when I was scarcely out of diapers,
you, for some reason still unclear to me,
took me dutifully to see?
That old Nestor of the no-good nobility‡
surrounded by a crowd of servants
who always did their best by him and many times
had saved his life and honor and kept him from drunken crimes—

* A Turkish fortress at the mouth of the Onepr, Ochakov was captured by the
Russians under Suvorov in 1788. Russia annexed the Crimea in 1783.
† After the Revolution of 1789, many Frenchmen who sought restoration of the old
ways emigrated to Russia, where they were mostly hangers-on in upper-class families,
or tutors.
‡ Probably a reference to L. D. Izmailov, a general and extremely rich landowner,
who was infamous for his terrible abuse of his serfs.

whom he suddenly exchanged one day for three coursing hounds!
Or that other one, who, to amuse himself
for his serf ballet, sent many wagons round
to gather chidren wrenched from their families?!
His mind sunk deeply in his Zephyrs and his Cupids,
he made all Moscow marvel at their grace and beauty!
But his creditors weren't half so stupid—
the Cupids and the Zephyrs to make the sum
were sold off one by one.*
Those are the men who lived to have gray hair!
These are the men whom, for lack of others, we must admire!
These are our harshest critics, who sit in the judgment chair!
Let one young man today aspire
to live his life without any self-promotion,
not looking for advancement or any set position,
his mind on scholarship, on really wanting to know,
or maybe one in whom there burns a sacred passion
for creative work that's beautiful and noble,
and they'll cry out: Robbery! Fire!
and treat him as subversive—and impractical!—
The uniform! It's all the uniform! Once handsome
and embroidered, in the old days it covered up
faintheartedness and impoverished reason.
And we're to follow in their steps!
Why, wives and daughters, too, go crazy over it!
How long ago did I forswear my soft spot for it?
Though that's a childishness I'll not fall into now,
who then didn't go along with the crowd?
Whenever any guardsmen or members of the court
arrived here on their way somewhere,
"Hurrah!" all the women would shout
and toss their bonnets in the air!

                         FAMUSOV *(To himself)*
He's about to cause me lots of grief.
     (Aloud)
Sergey Sergeyich, I'm going to leave;
come to my study, where I'll be waiting.
     (Exits)

---

* Probably a reference to Prince A. N. Golitsyn, who so loved theatrical performances
that he squandered a huge fortune on them and died in poverty. To sell serfs singly,
unattached to land, was made an abuse by the State Council in 1820.

SKALOZUB

I liked the way in your appraisal
you artfully touched upon
Moscow's bias toward favorite sons,
the guard in general, guardsmen and the grenadiers.
Their gold embroidery draws attention like shining suns.
Have we First Army men ever lagged behind? No sir!
Everything so trim, and all the waists so tight,
and with a list of officers
who speak French fluently—at least, some might.
    (SOFYA *and* LIZA *enter*)

SOFYA *(Runs to the window)*
Oh, my God! He fell! He killed himself!
    (She faints)

CHATSKY

Who's that?
Who did?

SKALOZUB

Who's in trouble?

CHATSKY

She's petrified!

SKALOZUB

But who? What's up?

CHATSKY

Hit himself on what?

SKALOZUB

Maybe our old man took a slide?

LIZA *(Fussing around her young lady)*
When your number comes, that's fate, no matter how you beg:
Molchalin, set to ride, placed foot in stirrup, mounted;
the horse rose on its hind legs
and threw Molchalin on his head.

SKALOZUB

Yanked hard on the reins. That's no way to ride.
Better see how he landed—on his chest or on his side.
    (Exits)

CHATSKY

How can I help her? Tell me quick.

LIZA

There's a pitcher of water inside the door.
    (CHATSKY *runs and brings it back. The lines that follow are spoken softly until the moment that* SOFYA *comes to*)
Pour a glass.

CHATSKY

I did.
Undo her corset—that's the trick—
rub vinegar on her temples—
sprinkle some water—look!
She's breathing more freely. Can
we give her more air?

LIZA

Here's a fan.

CHATSKY

Look out in the street:
Molchalin's up and on his feet!
There was nothing to be alarmed about.

LIZA

Indeed, sir, debutantes are filled with dread:
they can't stand idly by and watch
when people go falling on their heads.

CHATSKY

Sprinkle some more water on her.
Like that. Some more. Some more.

SOFYA *(With a deep sigh)*

Who's here? Where am I?
It all seems like a dream.
    (Hurriedly and at full voice)
Where is he? How is he? Tell me, tell me.

CHATSKY

I don't care if he breaks his neck;
he almost was the death of you.

SOFYA

Murderous you with your indifference!
I can't stand to listen or to look!

CHATSKY

You wish me, for his sake, to rack myself?

SOFYA

Run out there and stay there and see if you can't help.

CHATSKY

So you'd be left alone, with nobody to help?

SOFYA

What can you do for me?
Indeed, other people's problems are what you find amusing.
If your father killed himself you wouldn't care.
    (To LIZA*)*
Come, let's go. Hurry.

LIZA *(Taking her aside)*

Think a minute! What's the use?
He's alive and well. Just look out there.
    (SOFYA *pokes her head out the window*)

CHATSKY

Turmoil! Fainting! Haste! Raw anger! Fear!
You only can feel things like that
when you lose the friend you've held most dear.

SOFYA

They're coming in. He can't lift his arm.

CHATSKY

I wish we'd both got hurt—

LIZA

And stuck together?*

SOFYA

No, leave it a wish—don't go further.
    (Enter SKALOZUB *and* MOLCHALIN *with his arm bandaged)*

---

* Liza's line (in the original, *dlya kompanii*, "to keep him company") came from
P. A. Vyazemsky, who in his journals noted that in the first version, "Chatsky said,
'I wish I had gotten hurt with him to keep him company.' I pointed out that it was
out of place for Chatsky, deeply in love, to use the trite phrase 'to keep him company,'
which would be better assigned to the servant Liza. Griboyedov did so."

SKALOZUB

Arisen and unharmed, his arm
but lightly bruised;
the whole thing was a false alarm.

MOLCHALIN

For heaven's sake, forgive my frightening you to death.

SKALOZUB

Damn! I had no idea that this would cause
you any irritation. You came running in
half out of your mind—we gasped and shuddered—you fainted—and
then—
what then? why, your fear was wholly false.

SOFYA *(Without looking at anyone)*

Ah, I clearly see there was no basis for it,
but still it makes me shake and shiver.

CHATSKY *(To himself)*

Say nothing to Molchalin.

SOFYA

One thing I'll say about myself, however—
I'm not a coward. Sometimes, for example,
the carriage breaks down, and then they fix it, and I'm
ready to go galloping on;
but the littlest thing that happens to others makes me waver,
although it may not even make a difference,
although I may not even know them—that's not the point.

CHATSKY *(To himself)*

She's asking him to pardon her
for feeling sorry for someone once!

SKALOZUB

Let me tell you something that happened.
There's a Princess Lasov here in the capital,
a horsewoman and widow but you never hear
stories of her having many cavaliers.
The other day she smashed herself to bits—
her groom wasn't supporting her—his wits woolgathering—
and anyway she's awkward, according to report,
so now she's missing a rib
and looking for a husband for support.

SOFYA

Ah, Aleksandr Andreyich, there!
Now be magnanimous indeed!
You're so involved whenever your friends are in need.

CHATSKY

Surely I just now showed I am
the way I superdiligently tried
by sprinkling this and rubbing that—
I don't know who for, but I brought you back to life.
(Picks up his hat and exits)

SOFYA

Will you call on us this evening?

SKALOZUB

How early?

SOFYA

Sooner rather than later. Some family friends
are coming for dancing to the piano.
Because we're in mourning we can't have a formal party.

SKALOZUB

I will. But now I promised to see your father.
My compliments.

SOFYA

Good-bye.

SKALOZUB *(Shaking* MOLCHALIN's *hand)*

Your servant, sir.
(Exits)

SOFYA

Molchalin! How did my wits ever stay together!
You know, don't you, how dear your life's to me.
Why take a chance with it, and so carelessly?
Tell me, what happened to your arm?
Shouldn't you have some drops? And peace and quiet?
Or go see the doctor? We mustn't leave anything out.

MOLCHALIN

Since I bound it with a kerchief it hasn't hurt.

LIZA

It's all a lot of nonsense, that's what I bet.
And you wouldn't wear a bandage if it didn't look so hep;
but what isn't nonsense is you won't escape the fame:
just you wait—Chatsky'll make a mockery of your name.
And Skalozub, once he begins to gossip,
will tell about the fainting in a hundred different ways;
He's no mean joker, either—who doesn't joke these days!

SOFYA

What do I care for either of them?
I love whom I want to; if I want to, I'll tell.
Molchalin! didn't I perfectly keep my self-control?
You came in—I didn't say a thing—
I·didn't breathe as long as they were here,
or question you, or even look.

MOLCHALIN

Oh, Sofya Pavlovna, you're much too outspoken and frank.

SOFYA

How can I suddenly decide to hold things back?
I was ready to leap out the window to you.
What's everyone else to me? those two? the universe?
Ridiculous? Let them mock! A nuisance? Let them curse.

MOLCHALIN

Let's hope that such outspokenness does us no damage.

SOFYA

You think you really will be challenged to a duel?

MOLCHALIN

Ah, evil tongues are more frightening than a pistol's hammer.

LIZA

They're in there with your old man now,
so what if you bounced through the door
just like that, a big smile on your face—
When people tell us what we want to hear
how readily we believe our ears!
And Aleksandr Andreyich—be sure
to let yourself go in telling tales
about the olden days and the tricks you played.

A little smile and a couple of words,
and a man in love will act absurd.

MOLCHALIN

I don't presume to advise on this.
(Kisses her hand)

SOFYA

You both wish it? I'll go make small talk through my tears.
I'm afraid I won't be able to keep up the pretense.
Why oh why did God bring Chatsky here!
(Exits)

MOLCHALIN

You creature bright and gay! so lively, you!

LIZA

Please let me go; you and m'lady are already two.

MOLCHALIN

What a lovely little face on you!
How I love you passionately!

LIZA

And the young lady?

MOLCHALIN

Ooo,
that's from duty, you—
(Tries to embrace her)

LIZA

From nothing to do today.
Please take your hands away!

MOLCHALIN

I have three lovely little things:
a dressing table worked with wondrous skill—
a little mirror on the outside, and another, in—
fretwork all around, and done in gilt;
a little cushion with a pearl design:
a mother-of-pearl brush and comb
with needle case and little scissors—oh so precious!
and little pearls ground into white ceruse!
There's red pomade for lips and for any other use,
and little perfume vials—mignonette and jasmine—

LIZA

You know I won't be tempted by how much I might make.
So, instead, tell me why
you're modest with the lady but with the maid, a rake?

MOLCHALIN

Today I'm ill, I daren't take off my bandage;
come dine with me and stay a while, too;
I'll reveal everything to you.
   (Exits through the side door)
   (SOFYA enters)

SOFYA

I went to Father's study—not a soul.
Today I'm ill, I won't go in to dinner.
Let Molchalin know, and please tell
him to come see me in my chamber.
   (She exits to her room)

LIZA

Whew! What the people here can be!
She's after him; he's after me,
and me—I guess I'm the only one who's scared to do it—
And yet how can I not love the pantry man Petrushka?

ACT III

CHATSKY

I'll wait until she comes and make her tell
who's the one she cares for—Molchalin or Skalozub?
Molchalin used to be such a dupe,
a creature pitiful as well—
can he have gotten smarter? And the other—
his croaky, creaky voice, like a bassoon, half smothered,
a constellation of mazurkas and maneuvers!
Love plays blind man's buff over and over,
while I—
   (SOFYA enters)
You're here? I'm very pleased.
I hoped for this.

SOFYA *(To herself)*

The timing couldn't be worse.

CHATSKY

Surely you weren't looking for me?

SOFYA

Surely I wasn't.

CHATSKY

Would you, perhaps, inform me—
though, if inconvenient, don't feel pressed—
who do you love?

SOFYA

Good God, he's like all the rest.

CHATSKY

Who do you care for more?

SOFYA

Lots, lots—my relatives—

CHATSKY

All more than me?

SOFYA

Some.

CHATSKY

So, what should I expect when all's said and done?
A noose around my neck to strike your funny bone?

SOFYA

You want to know the truth in just two words?
If anyone behaves the least bit strange
your merriment finds the range
and you have a witticism set to hurl,
while you yourself—

CHATSKY

Myself? Ridiculous, am I not?

SOFYA

Yes! Your cutting voice, your quick, hot
look—your idiosyncrasies are endless,
though bringing thunder on oneself is far from useless.

CHATSKY

Who isn't odd? Who'd prove the rule?
Whoever's like the pack of fools—
Molchalin, for example—

SOFYA

I've heard your examples before.
It's clear you're ready to vent your spleen on everyone,
so I—not to interfere—am going out that door.

CHATSKY *(Restraining her)*

Stop!
    (Aside)
For once in my life I'll dissemble.
    (Aloud)
Let's stop all this debate.
I was wrong about Molchalin; I take it back;
he's not at all what he was three years ago perhaps.
Earth has such underlying changes of season,
of tendencies and climates, of moral laws and reasons.
Some important people once reputed to be fools—
one's an army man; one's a rotten poet;
one's—I'm afraid to name them, but all the world knows who
and says, especially in recent years,
they've become clever in every way.
Suppose Molchalin has a quick, bold mind and spirit,
but does he have the passion, fervor, and commitment
which would make the whole world—except for you—
seem vanity and worthless clay?
Is the beating of his heart
quickened by his love of you?
Are you in all his thoughts? In his innermost soul
is his only wish your happiness?
Myself I feel it, although I can't express it,
and I wouldn't wish on my worst enemy
what now roils and rages in me and drives me wild.
But he? He never speaks and hangs his head.
Sure he's quiet; nobody like that is frisky;
God knows, maybe there's some secret there.
God knows what you've decided to attribute to him,
things that have never even crossed his mind.
Perhaps, because of your attraction,

you've assigned him all your virtuous reactions.
It's certainly not his fault; it's a hundred times more yours.
No, no! Assume he's smart and getting smarter by the hour,
but is he worthy of you? That's what you must ask.
So that I may bear my loss more collectedly and calmly,
give me, as one who grew up with you side by side,
who's equally a friend and brother,
the chance to be convinced he is.
And then
I'll be able to be careful not to lose my mind.
I'll travel far away to let things cool, grow cold,
no longer think of love but learn to roam the world,
forgetful of myself while having a good time.

SOFYA *(To herself)*

Unwittingly I've made him lose his mind!
   (Aloud)
Why dissemble?
Just now Molchalin might have lost his arm,
and I felt very involved in the whole thing.
But you, who at that moment happened
to be here, didn't bother to examine
whether you could be kind to others without thinking—
though, maybe, there's some truth in what you've hinted,
and I passionately rise in his defense.
Why have—I speak the truth; the truth is blunt—
such a loose, intemperate tongue?
Such a condescending attitude?
No mercy for the most submissive? Why? Why?
If someone happens to mention his name,
down come your barbs and snide remarks like hail.
Mocking, always mocking—we've had enough of that!

CHATSKY

My lord, am I really one of those
whose aim in life is looking down his nose?
I feel like laughing when I meet people who're absurd,
but usually with them I'm bored.

SOFYA

And wrongly. All of this applies to others.
Molchalin could hardly be a one to bore you
if you two had a chance to get closer.

CHATSKY *(Fervently)*
And why did you get to know him all that closely?

SOFYA
I didn't try; it was God did it.
Just look—he's made friends with everybody in the house.
He's worked for Father three years now,
who often unreasonably causes a row,
and he disarms him by remaining silent
and forgives him out of natural kindness.
And by the way,
he could find ways to be amused,
but no, he never oversteps his elders' bounds.
We laugh and sport around,
but gay or sad, he'll sit with them all day long,
playing—

CHATSKY
Playing all day!
Silent when he's being scolded!
    (Aside)
She doesn't respect him.

SOFYA
Of course he doesn't have that steel-trap mind
which, for some, is genius but for others, plague,
which is quick and brilliant but soon is tiresome,
which curses everybody on the spot,
so everybody'll talk about it, like it or not.
Is that the kind of mind that makes a family happy?

CHATSKY
Does all of this come down to satire and morality?
    (Aside)
She doesn't care a whit for him.

SOFYA
But after all he has
marvelous characteristics—compliant, modest, meek,
never a shadow of worry on his face
and in his heart no thought of a breach of peace.
He doesn't cut down people he doesn't know,
and that's the reason I love him so.

CHATSKY *(Aside)*
She's fooling! She doesn't.
  (Aloud)
Let me relieve you of having to
finish the portrait of Molchalin.
But Skalozub? Now, there's a sight!
Stands behind the army like a rock,
a hero by the way he stands
erect, his expression and his voice—

SOFYA
Not in my book.

CHATSKY
No? Who can guess what goes on inside you?
  (LIZA enters)

LIZA *(Whispering)*
Madam, Aleksey Stepanich is right
behind me coming to see you.

SOFYA
Excuse me, I must leave immediately.

CHATSKY
Where to?

SOFYA
The hairdresser's.

CHATSKY
Don't.

SOFYA
The irons'll get cold.

CHATSKY
Let them.

SOFYA
I can't; we're having guests tonight.

CHATSKY
Oh, never mind, I'm left with my puzzlement again.
However, let me stealthily look in
your room once more for a minute or two.
The walls, the air—it was all so pleasant!

Recollections of the things that won't return
warm me inside, make me feel alive and easy!
I won't be long. I'll go in—a minute—no more than two—
and then—just think—as a member of the English Club
I'll sacrifice entire days to reporting on
Molchalin's mind and the kind heart of Skalozub.
    (SOFYA *shrugs, exits to her room,* LIZA *behind her, and locks the door.)*

                            CHATSKY
Sofya! Is Molchalin really the one she's picked?
Why not husband? He may not be so smart,
but merely having children
has never been an art.
Obliging, very modest, a little color in his face—
    (MOLCHALIN *enters)*
Here he comes on tiptoe, with not too much to say;
by what black magic did he manage to worm his way?
    (Addresses him)
Aleksey Stepanich, you and I
haven't yet exchanged two words.
Well, what's life like for you these days?
No troubles now? No cause for grief?

                            MOLCHALIN
Like always, sir.

                            CHATSKY
How was "always," then?

                            MOLCHALIN
From day to day, one day like another.

                            CHATSKY
From cards to pen? and back to cards again?
The hour set for both the flood and ebb?

                            MOLCHALIN
For my efforts and compilations,
since joining the archival staff
I've received three decorations.

                            CHATSKY
Cajoled respect and noble rank?

MOLCHALIN

No, sir; talents differ—

CHATSKY

Yours is?—

MOLCHALIN

Two, sir:
Moderation and preciseness.

CHATSKY

Most wonderful a pair! worthy of all the rest.

MOLCHALIN

Were you not promoted for official unsuccess?

CHATSKY

People make promotions,
and people sometimes have wrong notions.

MOLCHALIN

How surprised we were!

CHATSKY

What were you surprised about?

MOLCHALIN

We felt sorry for you.

CHATSKY

Wasted effort.

MOLCHALIN

Back from Petersburg, Tatyana Yurevna
was saying something about how
you had ministerial connections
but then broke off—

CHATSKY

How does that involve her?

MOLCHALIN

Tatyana Yurevna!

CHATSKY

I don't know her.

MOLCHALIN

Tatyana Yurevna!!

CHATSKY

I've never met her in my life.
She's cantankerous, I've heard.

MOLCHALIN

Who do you mean?
Tatyana Yurevna!!! Why, sir, she's famous—and besides,
every man of rank and power
is her friend or related to her.
You ought to call on Tatyana Yurevna once at least.

CHATSKY

What for?

MOLCHALIN

Well, very often there
we find favors of which we have been unaware.

CHATSKY

I often call on women, but that's not the reason why.

MOLCHALIN

How sophisticated! How kind, how plain, how nice!
You can't give balls more lavish
from Christmas up to Lent
and summer parties at her dacha.
What about joining us in Moscow in the service?
Getting decorations and really enjoying life?

CHATSKY

When it's time for business, I set foolish things aside;
When it's time to be silly, I, too, play the fool;
there's a host of experts at confounding these
two lines of work, but don't count me among them, please.

MOLCHALIN

Excuse me, though I see nothing criminal about it.
Take Foma Fomich himself—you know him, don't you?

CHATSKY

What of it?

MOLCHALIN

Under three ministers he was department head,
got transferred here.

CHATSKY

Some merit!
One of the stupidest and most superficial!

MOLCHALIN

You don't mean it! The way he writes is our example!
Have you read him?

CHATSKY

Rubbish I don't read,
especially exemplary.

MOLCHALIN

On the contrary, I had occasion to read it with great pleasure,
though I'm not creative—

CHATSKY

Quite obviously.

MOLCHALIN

I don't really dare to put my opinions forth.

CHATSKY

But why keep them secretly?

MOLCHALIN

At my age one mustn't dare
express his opinion anywhere.

CHATSKY

Heaven help us, you and I are grown up;
why are only other men's opinions sacred?

MOLCHALIN

But, you know, one must depend on others.

CHATSKY

Why do you say "must"?

MOLCHALIN

We're not so important.

CHATSKY *(Almost aloud)*

The lover—with such emotions and such a heart!
Why, the deceitful lady was treating me to farce!

(SERVANTS *enter. Evening. All the doors open wide except the door
to* SOFYA's *bedroom. A series of brightly lit rooms and bustling*
SERVANTS *leads into the distance. One of them speaks.)*

BUTLER

Hey, Filka, Fomka, keep it moving!
Card tables, chalk, the brushes and the candles!
    (He knocks on SOFYA's *door)*
Quick, tell our mistress, Lizaveta, that Natalya Dmitriyevna
and her husband have arrived and another coach
has pulled up to the porch.
    (They all exit, leaving CHATSKY *alone.* NATALYA DMITRIYEVNA, *a
young lady, enters)*

NATALYA DMITRIYEVNA

Am I mistaken? Exactly like him—the face—
Oh, Aleksandr Andreyevich, is it you?

CHATSKY

You're looking skeptically from head to foot.
Have three years really made such a difference?

NATALYA DMITRIYEVNA

I supposed you far away from Moscow.
Long back?

CHATSKY

Arrived today.

NATALYA DMITRIYEVNA

For long?

CHATSKY

Can't say.
One look at you, though, and who wouldn't be amazed?
Fuller than before, terrifically pretty,
you look younger, fresher;
there's fire, color, laughter, playfulness in all your features.

NATALYA DMITRIYEVNA

I'm married.

CHATSKY

You should have said so first!

NATALYA DMITRIYEVNA

My husband's a delightful husband—here he comes.
I'll introduce you—may I?

CHATSKY

Please.

NATALYA DMITRIYEVNA

I know ahead of time
you'll like him. Cast a glance and be the judge.

CHATSKY

I believe you; he's your husband.

NATALYA DMITRIYEVNA

Oh, no, that's not why.
For his character and intelligence, in his own right.
Platon Mikhailich is my one and only, priceless!
A military man, he's now retired;
And everyone who used to know him in those days
says that with his courage and his talent
if he had continued in the service
of course he'd be the Moscow commandant.
    (PLATON MIKHAILOVICH *enters*)
Here's my Platon Mikhailich.

CHATSKY

Good Lord!
Old friend—we've known each other for years—how's that for fate!

PLATON MIKHAILOVICH

Hello, dear Chatsky!

CHATSKY

Platon, good man, how great.
You get the medal of merit—you've done things perfectly.

PLATON MIKHAILOVICH

Dear friend, as you see—
a Muscovite wed happily.

CHATSKY

The barracks noise behind you, comrades-in-arms forgot?
Contented now and lazy?

PLATON MIKHAILOVICH

No, there still is lots
to do, like practicing the A-minor duet
on the flute.

CHATSKY

The one you were practicing some five years back?
Well, constancy in a husband is the most valued attribute.

PLATON MIKHAILOVICH

When you get married, friend, remember me.
Out of boredom you'll be whistling the same tune.

CHATSKY

Boredom? You mean you already pay her tribute?

NATALYA DMITRIYEVNA

My Platon Mikhailich likes doing different things,
which aren't available now, like instructions and inspections
and dressage—so, some mornings he's a little bored.

CHATSKY

But who, dear friend, has issued you such orders?
Back to the regiment! You'll get a troop. You junior officer or staff?

NATALYA DMITRIYEVNA

My Platon Mikhailich's health is on and off.

CHATSKY

Poor health?! For long? That true?

NATALYA DMITRIYEVNA

A lot of rheumatism, and headaches, too.

CHATSKY

To the country, to a warmer place. More exercise.
Go riding more. In summer the country's paradise.

NATALYA DMITRIYEVNA

Platon Mikhailich loves the city,
loves Moscow. Wasting his days in the backwoods would be a pity.

CHATSKY

Moscow, and the city? You've donned a strange hat!
Remember how things were?

PLATON MIKHAILOVICH

Aye, friend, these days things aren't like that.

NATALYA DMITRIYEVNA

Ah, my little sweetie!
It's so chilly here you'll catch your death,
but you've opened up your coat and undone your vest.

PLATON MIKHAILOVICH

These days, friend, I'm not the man—

NATALYA DMITRIYEVNA

An itsy-bitsy entreaty,
sweetheart, to quickly button up.

PLATON MIKHAILOVICH *(Coldly)*

At once.

NATALYA DMITRIYEVNA

And move away from the door.
There's a draft blowing on your back.

PLATON MIKHAILOVICH

These days, friend, I'm not the man—

NATALYA DMITRIYEVNA

Angel, for God's sake,
move a little farther from the door.

PLATON MIKHAILOVICH *(Eyes looking up)*

Oh, Mother!

CHATSKY

Well, as God is our judge—
though you didn't take much time to become a different man.
Wasn't it toward the end of last year only
we were in the regiment? Scarcely dawn,
foot in stirrup, and you'd be off on a swift stallion,
the autumn wind howling at your back or in your face.

PLATON MIKHAILOVICH *(With a sigh)*

Ah, dear friend, what a grand life that really was.

(PRINCE TUGOUKHOVSKY, *the* OLD PRINCESS, *and their* SIX
DAUGHTERS *enter*)

NATALYA DMITRIYEVNA *(In a light voice)*

Prince Peter Ilyich! Princess! My lord!
Princess Zizi! Mimi!

(*A loud exchange of kisses, after which they sit down and examine
each other from head to foot.*)

FIRST PRINCESS

That line's the latest fashion!

SECOND PRINCESS

What lovely little pleats!

FIRST PRINCESS
Fringe all along the border.

NATALYA DMITRIYEVNA
That's nothing; you should see my French shawl made of satin!

THIRD PRINCESS
What an *écharpe* my cousin gave me!

FOURTH PRINCESS
Oh, yes—real barege.

FIFTH PRINCESS
Oh, just lovely!

SIXTH PRINCESS
Oh, so dear.

OLD PRINCESS
Sssh! Who's that in the corner there, who bowed when we came in?

NATALYA DMITRIYEVNA
A visitor, Chatsky.

OLD PRINCESS
Re-tir-ed?

NATALYA DMITRIYEVNA
Yes, he was traveling, not long ago returned.

OLD PRINCESS
A ba-che-lor?

NATALYA DMITRIYEVNA
Unmarried, yes.

OLD PRINCESS
Prince, Prince, come here quick.

PRINCE *(Turning his ear trumpet toward her)*
O-hm!

OLD PRINCESS
Invite Natalya Dmitriyevna's friend
to our house Thursday evening—that's him there!

PRINCE
Ee-hm!

(The PRINCE *goes off, weaves in and out around* CHATSKY, *and keeps clearing his throat)*

OLD PRINCESS

With children you have to face it:
the ball's for them, but their father has to get things prepared—
dancing partners have become so scarce!
He's a kammer-junker?*

NATALYA DMITRIYEVNA

No.

OLD PRINCESS

But ri-ich?

NATALYA DMITRIYEVNA

Oh, no!

OLD PRINCESS *(As loudly as she can)*

Prince, come back! Prince!
    (The COUNTESSES KHRYUMIN, GRANDMOTHER *and* GRAND-
DAUGHTER, *enter)*

GRANDDAUGHTER

Ah, grand'maman! Nobody ever comes so early!
We're the first!
    (Disappears into the next room)

OLD PRINCESS

What an insult!
I was first, and she pretends we're nobody!
Malicious thing, old maid all her life, God help her.

GRANDDAUGHTER *(Returning, looks at* CHATSKY *through her lorgnette)*
Monsieur Chatsky, you're in Moscow! Nothing about you changed?

CHATSKY

Why should I be different?

GRANDDAUGHTER

No marriage was arranged?

CHATSKY

Who's there for me to marry?

* A court rank just below kammerherr (chamberlain); Pushkin was a kammer-junker.

GRANDDAUGHTER

Who not when you're abroad?
So many of our men get married there
without a second thought and thereby make us related
to couturiers and milliners.

CHATSKY

Unlucky men, why must we bear reproach
from ladies copying modistes?
Is it because we've dared prefer
the originals to the copyists?
  (Many other guests enter, including ZAGORETSKY. *Men come in,
bow, step aside, move from room to room, and so on.* SOFYA *comes
out from hers, and everyone goes to meet her)*

GRANDDAUGHTER

*Eh! bon soir! vous voilà! Jamais trop diligente.
Vous nous donnez toujours le plaisir de l'attente.*

ZAGORETSKY

Do you have a ticket to the theater tomorrow night?

SOFYA

No.

ZAGORETSKY

Allow me to hand you this; another man would have
but vainly tried to please you; though
where I didn't dash:
at the box office, all gone;
the producer—he's a friend of mine—
at six this morning also declined.
By evening nobody could get one—all sold out.
This one, that one—I knocked them flat—
then finally snatched this ticket by sheer force
from a sickly old acquaintance
who's famous for always staying home;
so, let him stay at home in peace.

SOFYA

I'm doubly grateful for the ticket
and all you did to get it.
  (Some more people come in, and simultaneously ZAGORETSKY *joins
the men)*

ZAGORETSKY

Platon Mikhailich—

PLATON MIKHAILOVICH

Go away!
Go join the women, lie, pull the wool over their eyes.
I can tell such truthful stories about you
worse than any lie. Here's someone
    (*To* CHATSKY)
I want you to meet!
How to refer to people like him more courteously?
More kindly? He's a man about town,
an outright swindler, cheat, and clown—
Anton Antonich Zagoretsky.
Be careful around him—he passes on things of every sort—
and don't sit down to cards—he'll sell you short.

ZAGORETSKY

Original! and peevish, but minus any malice.

CHATSKY

It'd be silly for you to be offended,
Besides honesty, there's a host of joys and comforts—
Here you're damned; next place, praise and thanks are blended.

ZAGORETSKY

Oh, no, my friend! Our custom is
to damn and welcome everywhere.
    (ZAGORETSKY *gets lost in the crowd.* KHLYOSTOV *comes forward*)

KHLYOSTOV

You think it's easy for me at sixty-five
to drag myself to your place, niece? It's torture!
More than an hour from Pokrovka*—hardly alive—
Night's madness, the End of the World!
To cheer me up I brought along
my little black girl and my doggy.
See that they get something to eat, some supper
leftovers or something, dearie.
Princess, how do you do!
    (*She sits down*)
So, Sofyushka, dear,
what a Negro servant girl I have!

* A street in Moscow.

Curly-headed! hunchbacked! fierce!
Shrieks and scratches like a cat!
And so black! and so scary!
Hard to believe God created such a tribe!
A very demon; in the maids' room waiting;
want me to call her?

SOFYA

No, thank you, later.

KHLYOSTOV

Can you imagine, they exhibit them like animals—
I've heard that there—some Turkish city—
you know who got her for me, don't you?
Anton Antonich Zagoretsky.
(ZAGORETSKY *steps forward*)
A paltry liar, a gambler, and a thief.
(ZAGORETSKY *disappears*)
I was on the verge of locking him out of the house, but he's
a master at obliging: he got two little Negroes
at the trade fair for me and my sister Praskovya.
Bought them, he says, but I bet he swindled them at cards.
What a nice little present for me, God bless his heart.

CHATSKY (*Laughing loudly to* PLATON MIKHAILOVICH)
That kind of praise won't make him strong and well,
and Zagoretsky himself couldn't keep up and failed.

KHLYOSTOV

Who's that cheerful man? What sort of work he do?

SOFYA

That one? Chatsky.

KHLYOSTOV

And what amused him so?
What's he glad about? What's funny?
Making fun of old age is shameful.
I remember—you often danced with him when you were a child,
I used to box his ears, but that was much too mild.
(FAMUSOV *enters*)

FAMUSOV (*In a loud voice*)
Still waiting for Prince Peter Ilyich,
and here's the prince already! And I was in my study.

Where's Skalozub, Sergey Sergeyich?
Not here—not here yet. He's certainly outstanding—
Sergey Sergeyich Skalozub.

KHLYOSTOV
Lord save us, he deafened me—louder than a tuba!
(SKALOZUB enters, followed by MOLCHALIN)

FAMUSOV
Sergey Sergeyich, you're late.
And we waited, waited, waited.
(Leads him to KHLYOSTOV)
My sister-in-law, to whom we have conveyed
many things in your praise.*

KHLYOSTOV *(Seated)*
You were here before—in some regiment—the grenadiers?

SKALOZUB *(In his bass voice)*
In His Highness's—you surely have in mind—
Novozemlyansky Musketeers.

KHLYOSTOV
I'm no hand at telling regiments apart.

SKALOZUB
There are little signs on the uniforms—
the piping on the dress coats, the shoulder straps, the tabs.

FAMUSOV
Come, my friend, this way. I promise to amuse
you the way we play whist. And you, too, Prince, please!
(He leads SKALOZUB and the PRINCE out)

KHLYOSTOV *(To SOFYA)*
Whew! That was close! I just barely did escape the noose!
Your father really is dim-witted:
He's gone for this daredevil hook, line, and sinker,
and whether we like it or not, makes sure he's introduced.

* In Russian, *nevéstushka (nevéstka)*, "his brother's wife." Khlyostov (being a
woman, in Russian, Khlyostova) is his wife's sister, or *svoyáchenitsa*. It was an old
Moscow custom to give relatives in one's presence a closer relationship than they
actually had.

MOLCHALIN *(Handing her a card)*
I have set your foursome up—*Monsieur Coq*,
Foma Fomich, and I.

KHLYOSTOV

Thank you, dear heart.
 (Rises)

MOLCHALIN
Your spitz is so adorable—and no bigger than
a thimble! And such a silky coat on the little man!

KHLYOSTOV

Thank you, dear boy.
 (She exits, followed by MOLCHALIN *and many others.* CHATSKY,
SOFYA, *and several others come forward, then continue to disperse)*

CHATSKY
Well, we chased the clouds away—

SOFYA

Why can't we continue?

CHATSKY

Did I give you a scare?
My intention was to praise the way he pacified
the very upset guest.

SOFYA
But would have ended spewing spite.

CHATSKY
Shall I tell you what I thought?
Old ladies are an angry lot;
A good thing it was that at that moment there stood
a faithful servant like a lightning rod.
Molchalin! Who else can settle things so well!
He knows when to pet a lapdog,
when to palm a note card off—
he's Zagoretsky's legatee!
Besides the qualities that recently you cited,
aren't there many you forgot? Right?
 (Exits)

SOFYA *(To herself)*

Oh, that man always makes
me terribly upset! He's so pleased
to sting and humiliate. So envious, proud, and bad!

MR. N. *(Coming up to her)*

You're lost in thought.

SOFYA

About Chatsky.

MR. N.

Did you think that he had changed a lot?

SOFYA

He's not in his right mind.

MR. N.

You mean, he's really mad?

SOFYA *(After a pause)*

Not really—

MR. N.

But, you mean, there are indications?

SOFYA *(Staring at him)*

I think so.

MR. N.

Hard to believe, at his age!

SOFYA

Can't be helped!
   (Aside)
He's ready to accept it!
Ah, Chatsky, you like to line them up as fools in rows?
Now try it on yourself—see how it goes.
   (Exits)

MR. N.

Out of his mind. So she thinks. There you have it!
Something to it? Must be. Where could she have got it?
   (MR. D. enters)
Have you heard?

MR. D.

What?

MR. N.

About Chatsky?

MR. D.

What about him?

MR. N.

He's gone mad!

MR. D.

Nonsense.

MR. N.

I'm just repeating what others say.

MR. D.

But you're pleased to spread it?

MR. N.

I'll go find out. Somebody, I bet, must know for sure.
  (Exits)
Believe a gossip!
Picks up rubbish and right away repeats it!
  (ZAGORETSKY enters)
You know the news about Chatsky?

ZAGORETSKY

What's that?

MR. D.

He's gone mad!

ZAGORETSKY

Oh, I do; I heard that, I remember.
How couldn't I know? We have the precise event to go by,
when his swindler of an uncle locked him up with madmen,
seized him, put him in a madhouse, and set him on a chain.

MR. D.

Heaven help us, he was standing in this room just now.

ZAGORETSKY

That means they must have let him out.

MR. D.

Well, dear friend, no need of newspapers with you.
I think I'll go and spread my wings,

and ask around. But meanwhile—sssh!—don't tell a soul.
   (He exits)

ZAGORETSKY

Which Chatsky is it? The name's terribly familiar.
There was a Chatsky I once used to know.
   (The countess's GRANDDAUGHTER *enters)*
Have you heard about him?

GRANDDAUGHTER

About whom?

ZAGORETSKY

About Chatsky. He was just now in this room.

GRANDDAUGHTER

Indeed,
I was talking to him.

ZAGORETSKY

Then let me wish you Godspeed—
he's out of his mind.

GRANDDAUGHTER

What?

ZAGORETSKY

Truly, he's gone mad.

GRANDDAUGHTER

Imagine that; I noticed it myself.
You took the words right out of my mouth, want to bet?
   (The Countess's GRANDMOTHER *enters)*
Ah! *grand'maman*, here's the most amazing miracle yet!
You haven't heard the local calamity?
Listen. It's wonderful! It's so awfully cute!

GRANDMOTHER

My dear, my ears are stuffed;
speak louder—

GRANDDAUGHTER

I haven't a minute!
   (Points to ZAGORETSKY*)*
Il vous dira toute l'histoire—

I'll go ask—
    (*Exits*)

                    GRANDMOTHER
What? What? Now maype there's a fire?

                    ZAGORETSKY
No, no; Chatsky was the cause of all this turmoil.

                    GRANDMOTHER
What, Chatsky? Somepody put him in jail?

                    ZAGORETSKY
Fell in the mountains, nearly broke his neck, has turned into a madman.

                    GRANDMOTHER
Henh? Joined the Freemason sect? Became a Mohammedan?*

                    ZAGORETSKY
She'll never get it.
    (*Exits*)

                    GRANDMOTHER
Anton Antonich! Oh,
he's off, too. They're all scared. Look at him go!
    (PRINCE TUGOUKHOVSKY *enters*)
Prince, Prince! Oh, that's the prince at palls can't preathe,
Prince, you've heard?

                    PRINCE
Ah-hm?

                    GRANDMOTHER
Can't hear a word indeed!
Maybe you saw if the police chief was here—and his men as well?

                    PRINCE
Eh-hm?

                    GRANDMOTHER
Prince, who took Chatsky off to jail?

* Freemasonry was outlawed in Russia in 1822.

PRINCE

Ee-hm?

GRANDMOTHER

A soldier's pack and broadsword—
an ordinary private, no joke! And left the church!*

PRINCE

Oo-hm?

GRANDMOTHER

True! Turned Mohammedan!
Ah, the cursed Voltairean!
What? Hunh? Deaf, my dear? Get your trumpet.
Deafness is a serious defect.

(KHLYOSTOV, SOFYA, MOLCHALIN, PLATON MIKHAILOVICH, NA-
TALYA DMITRIYEVNA, *the countess's* GRANDDAUGHTER, *the* PRINCESS
with [*the six*] DAUGHTERS, ZAGORETSKY, SKALOZUB [*enter*], *followed
by* FAMUSOV *and many others*)

KHLYOSTOV

He's gone mad! Put that in your pipe!
So nimbly, too! All in a trice!
You hear about it, Sofya?

PLATON MIKHAILOVICH

Who announced it first?

NATALYA DMITRIYEVNA

Ah, my friend, we all did!

PLATON MIKHAILOVICH

Then willy-nilly all
believe, but, still, I doubt it.

FAMUSOV (*Entering*)

What's that? Chatsky?
What do you doubt? I was the first! I found out!
For months I've been astounded that no one locked him up!
Start in on authority, God knows the things he'll say!
Start to bow a little, or all the way to the floor,
when, say, presented to the czar,
and you'll be called a rogue and knave.

* In this period, a Russian Orthodox could not leave his faith. When found guilty
by a court of law, nobles and men of "high society" were frequently sentenced to
military service in the ranks.

KHLYOSTOV

Also, he's easily amused.
I dropped a word or two—he broke out in guffaws.

MOLCHALIN

He advised me to quit Moscow, stop serving in the archives.

GRANDDAUGHTER

And me he thought to call a modiste—the gall!

NATALYA DMITRIYEVNA

He told my husband he should take up country life.

ZAGORETSKY

Mad on all counts!

GRANDDAUGHTER

I could see it in his eyes.

FAMUSOV

Takes after his mother, after Anna Aleksevna.
That late-lamented lady lost her mind eight times.

KHLYOSTOV

Such marvelous events are always coming about!
At his age, to go off his rocker!
I bet he drank too much.

PRINCESS

Oh, surely.

GRANDDAUGHTER

Without a doubt.

KHLYOSTOV

Sucked champagne in by the glass.

NATALYA DMITRIYEVNA

By the bottle—the very biggest.

ZAGORETSKY *(Fervently)*

No, sir—by the forty-bucket cask!

FAMUSOV

There you have it! What a shame
when a man carries drink too far!
But study—that's the plague; learning—that's the reason

that nowadays as never before
so many madmen have sprung up, and mad opinions.

KHLYOSTOV

You really will go crazy from all these thats and thises—
the boarding schools, and day schools, lycées—and all what-is-its—
and those Landmap Mutual Education Systems.*

PRINCESS

Now, in Petersburg they have
a pe-da-go-gic institute, I think it's called,
where they practice church dissension and unbelief.†
the professors do! A relative of ours went there,
came out—and should have gone to work in a pharmacy!
He runs away from women—even runs from me!
Has no respect for rank! He's a chemist and a botanist—
Prince Fyodor, my nephew, that is.

SKALOZUB

I have good news for you: there is a general report
that a proposal has been made for lycées, schools, and pensions,
whereby teaching will be done the Russian way—right! left!
and books will be set aside for very special occasions.

FAMUSOV

Sergei Sergeyevich, no! To nip evil in the bud
all books must be collected—and burned.

ZAGORETSKY *(Meekly)*

Nay, sirs, there are books and books. But if, quite strictly speaking,
I were made the censor now,
I'd go after fables. Oh, fables will be the death of me!
Those endless mockeries of lions and of eagles!

---

* The *Obshchestvo uchilishch vzaimnogo obucheniya* was established in 1819, patterned after the free elementary school monitorial system of Joseph Lancaster (1778–
1838) in which abler students helped the less able. Many Russian supporters were
members of secret, because illegal, political societies. V. F. Rayevsky, the Decembrist,
arrested in 1822, was accused of propagandizing among the military in conjunction
with his teaching in a Lancaster school. Popular among liberals, the system was
regarded by the government and by conservatives as a breeding ground of subversive
ideas. Khlyostov uses, instead of the adjective *lankastersky*, the adjective *land-
kartchnyi*, which means "map."
† Among suspect institutions were the Nobles' Boarding School of Moscow University, the center at Tsarskoye Selo, and the Petersburg Pedagogical Institute, where
in 1821 four professors were accused of "open rejection of Scripture and Christianity
and continued attempts to undermine the authority of the state." They were fired.

Say what you think,
they're animals, but in every manner, kings.

KHLYOSTOV
Kind friends, once somebody has lost his mind,
it's all the same whether from books or wine.
I'm sorry for Chatsky.
In a Christian way, you know—faith, hope, and pity's worth.
He was a witty man and had three hundred serfs.

FAMUSOV
Four.

KHLYOSTOV
Good sir, three.

FAMUSOV
Four hundred.

KHLYOSTOV
No, no! Three.

FAMUSOV
In my date-book calendar—

KHLYOSTOV
Calendars always lie.

FAMUSOV
It says four hundred. Oh, she's screaming for a debate!

KHLYOSTOV
No! Three! You think I don't know about other people's estates!

FAMUSOV
Four hundred, please accept the fact.

KHLYOSTOV
No! Three hundred, three, three, three.
(CHATSKY *enters*)

NATALYA DMITRIYEVNA
Here he is.

GRANDDAUGHTER
Sssh!

EVERYONE

Sssh!
(They all back away from him.)

KHLYOSTOV

What if, from the madness in his eyes,
he decides to have a duel and demands some satisfaction?

FAMUSOV

O Lord, have mercy on us sinners!
(Cautiously)
Dear, good man, you're not at all yourself.
You're unwell. Let me feel your pulse. You need to rest.

CHATSKY

True, I'm worn out, a million crampings
in my breast from friends' embraces,
in my feet from shuffling, in my ears from ooh-and-aahing,
but worst, in my head from all the empty commonplaces.
(Goes up to SOFYA)
Some troubling sadness seems to have compressed my soul,
and I feel lost among these many people here.
No, Moscow's not for me.

KHLYOSTOV

And see, that's Moscow's fault.

FAMUSOV

Get away from him!
(Makes a sign to SOFYA)
Sofya! Ah, not looking.

SOFYA *(To* CHATSKY)

Tell us what upsets you so.

CHATSKY

Back there, I had a casual encounter:
pulling on the heartstrings, a Frenchman from Bordeaux
gathered people in a sort of round
and told about his getting set to go
to the barbarians in Russia, tearful and afraid.
He arrived—and found no end of kindness.
He never heard a Russian word, nor saw
a Russian face. As if he had stayed home with friends.
It's his own province. Consider: every evening

here he feels as if he were a little king—
the ladies have the same understanding, the same attire.
He's delighted, but not we.
He stopped. Then everybody
moaned and groaned and sighed.
"Ah, France! The best land in the world!" cried
two young sister princesses who had memorized
the lesson repeated constantly throughout their childhood.
Where can one hide from princesses?
I, from a distance, expressed my wishes—
humble, to be sure, but said aloud—
that the Lord would rout this adulterated spirit
of blind, pointless, servile imitation;
that He would drop a spark in somebody who cared
who could, by word and deed,
restrain us—as by strong reins in his hands—
from sickly longing for the ways of someone's else's land.
Call me, if you want, an Old Believer.*
Our North for me is now a hundred times debased
since it gave everything away for this foreign face—
its customs, language, and its sacrosanct traditions,
even its majestic dress for something like
the motley of a jester—
behind, a tail; in front, some kind of cut
that makes no sense and defies the elements;
faces without charm; tight, little gestures;
chins ridiculous, clean-shaved and swart!
Like the hair and dresses, the minds are short!†
Ah, if we've been born to copy everything,
at least we ought to borrow from the Chinaman
some of his sage ignorance of foreigners.
Will we someday arise from under fashion's power?
So that our wise and valiant people
won't mistake us—at least, by the way we speak—for Germans?
"How can you pretend what's European is parallel
to what's national? That's very odd!
How would you translate *madame* and *mademoiselle*?
Not simply 'madam'!" somebody beside me muttered.

* An Old Believer was a member of a dissident sect, which refused to support church reform in the seventeenth century; the term came to refer loosely to an old-fashioned conservative.
† The proverb is: *A woman's hair is long, but her mind is short.*

Everyone laughed. Of course, I sensed
that the laughter was at my expense.
" 'Madam'! Ha! ha! ha! ha! Splendidious!"
" 'Madam'! Ha! ha! ha! ha! Hideous!"
Cursing life and what men say,
I got a crushing answer ready,
but everybody went away.
That happened to me then—and earlier.
Petersburg or Moscow—in Russia, the fact is
that someone from the city of Bordeaux
has but to open his mouth to have the pleasure
of being showered with princesses' treasures.
In Petersburg, and Moscow, too,
who's against false faces, mannerisms, florid speech,
whose head may hold an idea or two—
or more than a jot of common sense—
and who's bold enough publicly to brook—
Look—

(He looks around. Everyone is whirling around in a waltz with
great enthusiasm. The older people have withdrawn to the card tables)

ACT IV

The front hall of FAMUSOV's *house. A wide staircase leads down*
from the second floor; many side rooms on the mezzanine open on to
it. Downstairs stage right, a doorway leads to the front porch and the
porter's lodge. MOLCHALIN's *room is at the same depth stage left.*

Night. The lights are dim. Some footmen bustle about, some sleep,
while waiting for their masters.

The countess's GRANDMOTHER *and the countess's* GRAND-
DAUGHTER *enter, preceded by their* FOOTMAN.

FOOTMAN
Countess Khryumin's carriage.

GRANDDAUGHTER *(While she is being bundled up)*
So much for that ball! And Famusov! Who he invited!
Some sort of otherworldly freaks!
Nobody to dance with—or even talk politely.

GRANDMOTHER
Let's go, poor girl. I can't truly bear another minute.
Someday they'll take me from pall to grave and put me in it.

(They drive off. PLATON MIKHAILOVICH *and* NATALYA DMI-
TRIYEVNA *[enter].* A FOOTMAN *takes care of them; another* FOOTMAN
in the doorway shouts:)

FOOTMAN

The Gorich carriage.

NATALYA DMITRIYEVNA

Angel mine, love of my life,
Priceless sweetie, Poposh,* why are you depressed?
    (Kisses his forehead)
Admit it—the Famusovs' parties are among the best.

PLATON MIKHAILOVICH

Natasha, darling, balls put me to sleep. So,
I'm mortally loath to have to go,
but I don't refuse. Your faithful workman,
I keep my post past midnight, often
pleasing you despite my sadness,
obeying your command to dance.

NATALYA DMITRIYEVNA

You're making a very unprofessional pretense.
Your mortal passion is to pass yourself off as being old.
    (Exits with the FOOTMAN*)*

PLATON MIKHAILOVICH *(Coolly)*

A ball's all right; it's being captured that really galls.
And who compels us to get married?!
I guess some lives are set from the beginning—

FOOTMAN *(From the porch)*

The madam's in the carriage, sir, and getting angry.

PLATON MIKHAILOVICH *(With a sigh)*

Coming, coming.
    (Drives away. CHATSKY *[enters] behind his* FOOTMAN*)*

CHATSKY

Call to them to bring it quickly.
    (The FOOTMAN *exits)*
And so another day has gone—
and with it, all the ghosts, the fumes

* A Frenchified diminutive of Platon.

and smoke of all the hopes with which my heart was filled.
What was I waiting for? or expecting to find?
Was there any joy in meeting? Who showed real concern?
A shout! Delight! Embrace!—All vain.
Sitting back in a simple carriage
on a road across a vast, unrolling plain,
where everything you see ahead
shimmers brightly, blue and varied,
you ride an hour, then another, then all day;
in high spirits you reach your lodging—then on all sides
you see one flat, dead, empty steppe roll far away.
The more you think about it, the more you're overwhelmed.
    (The FOOTMAN *returns)*
Ready?

FOOTMAN

The coachman, sir, is nowhere yet in sight.

CHATSKY

Go find him, then. I refuse to spend the night.
    (The FOOTMAN *exits again.* REPETILOV *dashes in from the porch,*
falls flat on his face in the doorway, and picks himself up)

REPETILOV

Damn! I slipped!—Lord in heaven!
Let me clear my eyes. My friend, where did you come from?
My dearest friend! Most wonderful friend! *mon cher!*
Of course, I've had mocking comments so many times
that I'm stupid, superstitious, and full of hot air,
that I have forebodings of everything, keep seeing signs;
but let me now explain how I,
while rushing here, somehow foreknew
that—crash!—I'd catch my toe and fly
flat on the floor in front of you.
Go ahead and laugh at me.
Say Repetilov's simple, that Repetilov lies,
but there's in me a longing for you, like a disease,
a sort of love—a passion, really—
a readiness to stake my life
that in all the world you'll never find a friend like me,
so good and faithful, truly.
May I lose my children and my wife,
may ostracism be my lot,

may I perish on this spot,
and God in heaven strike me full—

CHATSKY

Cut the bull.

REPETILOV

You dislike me—sure—that's natural enough.
With others I take it as it comes;
with you I'm never bold and tough—
I'm pitiful, ridiculous, untrained, and dumb.

CHATSKY

What a strange sort of put-down!

REPETILOV

Curse me. Myself, I curse the day that I was born.
When I consider what I've done to kill the time—
by the way, what time is it?

CHATSKY

Time to go to bed.
Ready to dance, now that you've arrived
you can turn around instead.

REPETILOV

What does *ball* signify? A place where we, dear friend,
are chained in manners until dawn, can't throw off the yoke.
Have you read about it? There's a book—

CHATSKY

Have you? What puzzles me no end
is, are you really Repetilov?

REPETILOV

I'm a vandal, say.
That's a name that I deserve
because the people that I served
were hollow, and I dined and danced my life away!
I ignored my children! I deceived my wife!
I gambled, lost, had a guardianship decreed!*
I kept a ballerina! In fact, not just one
but three!

---

* A roundabout way of saying that, by the czar's *ukaz*, surveillance was established over him.

I drank like a fish, and often didn't sleep a week!
I flouted everything—the laws, my faith, my spirit!

CHATSKY

Listen! Lie, but know the limits.
That's enough to make a man despair.

REPETILOV

Congratulate me, for now I know the cleverest
people! I don't roam from pillar to post till dawn.

CHATSKY

What about tonight?

REPETILOV

What does one signify? It doesn't count.
But ask me where I've been.

CHATSKY

That's not hard to guess.
Your club, I bet.

REPETILOV

The English. My confession begins by saying
I left a very noisy meeting—
puh-lease breathe not a word; I promised secrecy—
we have a society and hold our secret meetings
Thursdays. It's a union of the most secret sort—*

CHATSKY

Mustn't you be careful?
Like that? In the club?

REPETILOV

Precisely.

CHATSKY

What an extraordinary way
to get your secrets and yourselves tossed out!

REPETILOV

No reason for you to be concerned.
We speak up loudly—no one ever understands.

* This passage parodies the "secret societies" of the time. Pushkin's antisociety
society *Arzamas*, to which Griboyedov was unsympathetic, was itself such a parody
and met on Thursday. Among the Decembrists there was such discussion of introducing constitutional government with houses (chambers) of representatives and
trial by jury.

When the talk turns to separate chambers and jury trials,
to Byron, and, in general, important topics,
I most often listen without opening my mouth.
It's beyond me, friend, and I can feel I'm stupid.
Ah, Alexandre! You're the one we couldn't do without.
Listen, dearest friend, do me a tiny favor:
Let's now go—since, after all, we're on our way—
the people that I'll introduce
you to! You'll see they're not at all like me, God's truth.
What people, *mon cher!* The cream of our educated youth!

CHATSKY

God help them—and you, too. Where would I gallop in the dead
of night? And what for? No, home—I want to go to bed.

REPETILOV

Oh, stop it! Who sleeps these days? Come, come: no more preludes!
Decide. We—our group—contains decisive people,
a dozen brilliant hotheads!
We yell and shout—you'd think there were a hundred!

CHATSKY

What makes you carry on so wildly?

REPETILOV

We're always rather noisy.

CHATSKY

That's not putting it too mildly?

REPETILOV

This isn't the place now to explain, and I haven't time,
but it has to do with the government,
something which hasn't yet developed,
and can't of a sudden.
What people, *mon cher!* Without further ado or other stories,
I'll tell you who: first of all, Prince Grigory!
What a real eccentric! Makes us die from laughter!
Always with the English, has an English temper,
speaks through clenched teeth in the English manner,
and just like them is shorn for law and order.*

---

* In Russian, *obstrizhen dlya poryadka*. Applied to a serf, it meant that he had had his hair cropped after having been caught as a runaway. To have a foreign haircut was equated with looking like a runaway serf.

You don't know him? Oh, you must get to meet him.
Another's Evdokim Vorkulov.
You've never heard him sing? Oh, wonder of wonders!
Listen especially to how
he does his favorite piece:
"A! non lasciar mi, no, no, no!"*
We have two brothers, too:
Levon and Borinka, wonderful young men!
It's hard to know where to begin.
If you give the order to include a genius,
we have Ippolit Markelych Udushev!
Have you read anything he's written?
Just a scrap. You'll be smitten,
my friend, because he doesn't write just nothing.
People like him should be whipped
and handed down the sentence: write, write, write.
However, in the journals you can always find
a "fragment" or a "view" or "little something"
by him—covering everything, by the way.
He knows everything. We're saving him for a rainy day.
But our star and brains, unmatched in any quarter,
I don't need to name—you'll recognize his portrait:†
By night a robber and duelist,
once exiled to Kamchatka, he returned as an Aleut,
He's a roundly underhanded thief,
but no smart man these days can help but be a cheat.
However, when he talks of grand integrity
some demon takes possession of him,
his eyes get bloodshot, his face takes fire,
he starts to weep, and so do we.
Those are our people—are there any like them? Hardly.
Among them, I'm, of course, only mediocre,
somewhat out of date, lazy—the mere thought's awful!
On the other hand, when, putting my modest mind to work,

---

* From Dido's aria in Act II of Baldassare Galuppi's opera *Didone abbandonata*.
Catherine the Great invited Galuppi from Venice to Russia in 1766–1768. His operas
were warmly received, and he influenced Russian church music.
† The "portrait" is of Count Fyodor Yevanovich Tolstoy (1782–1846), a distant
relative of Lev Nikolayevich. He led a wild life, spent some time in the Aleutians
and the Russian colonies in America (he was nicknamed "The American"), sailed
to Kamchatka, and returned to St. Petersburg across Siberia on foot. He was a
distinguished soldier, a notorious cardsharp, a scandalous duelist (he killed eleven
men) and a friend of the leading intellectual and literary figures of his day.

I join them, I'm not there an hour
before, suddenly, unexpectedly, I drop a pun.
Others pick up this idea of mine, then six of us slap
a comedy together, and six more add the music,
and then when it's presented, all the others clap.
Laugh, my friend, but such pleasure's very pleasant.
God didn't endow me with any special talent,
but He gave me a good heart—that's why people think I'm nice.
They don't mind my lies—

FOOTMAN *(At the entrance)*

The Skalozub carriage.

REPETILOV

Whose?
(SKALOZUB comes down the stairs. REPETILOV goes to meet him)
Ah! Skalozub, my dear,
stop there! Where to? Embrace a friend.
(Smothers him in an embrace)

CHATSKY

There must be someplace I can hide!
(Enters the vestibule)

REPETILOV *(To SKALOZUB)*

Some time ago the rumors died,
about your setting off to serve your regiment again.
You know each other?
(Looks around for CHATSKY)
Obstinate! Galloped off!
No matter. Here I've found you by surprise,
and you must come with me right now—no alibis!
There's a host of people at Prince Grigory's,
some forty of us—maybe more—
and so much wit and clever talk
all night long—and no one's bored!
First of all, they're trying to kill us with champagne,*
and secondly they're teaching stuff
that you and I, of course, could never even think up.

SKALOZUB

Spare me. You won't fool me with your learning. Summon
others together, and, if you need one,

---

* The Russian is *napoyat shampanskim nauboi*, which is a play on the phrase *otkarmlivat' na uboi*, "to fatten [animals] for slaughter."

I'll give Prince Grigory and you
a sergeant-major to play Voltaire.
He'll line you up three abreast—
one peep, and—blink!—he'll have you at rest.

REPETILOV

The service always on your mind! *Mon cher*, take me:
I, too, would have climbed the ranks but had a lot
of failures—more than anyone, maybe.
I served the government back when
a cabinet post seemed sure for Baron Von Klotz,
and for me,
a son-in-lawship.
So, straight without a second thought
I joined him and his wife at playing reversi.
God save us, what a huge amount
went to the two of them from me!
He lived on the Fontanka; I built a house there, too,
an expensive one with columns! It was huge!
I wed his daughter finally, extending thanks,
but for dowry I got a fig, and no advance in rank.
He was German; so what was the use?
He was afraid, see, of being accused
of nepotism and being weak-kneed!
He was afraid—may he rot in hell—but did that help me?
His secretaries all are boors, all bought with money,
little men, scribbling creatures,
self-made aristocrats, self-inflated—
just look them up in the registry.
Hell! Service, rank, and medals are the soul's ordeals;
as Aleksey Lakhmotyev has wonderfully expressed,
radical medicines are now everywhere in need
because the stomach can't digest.

(*He stops, having seen that* ZAGORETSKY *has replaced* SKALOZUB,
who has meanwhile driven away)

ZAGORETSKY

Please continue. I sincerely want to let you know
that I, like you, am committed to the liberal cause!
And since I'm candid, a man who boldly speaks his mind,
how much—how very much—I've lost!

REPETILOV *(Disappointedly)*
Without a sound, everyone withdraws:
one's barely out of sight before the next is gone.
Chatsky suddenly disappeared, then Skalozub.

ZAGORETSKY
What do you think of Chatsky?

REPETILOV
He's not stupid.
Our paths just crossed; we chatted happily away;
presenting light comedy was seriously discussed;
You know, comedy's the thing! The rest's not worth the fuss.
He and I—we have—the exact same tastes.

ZAGORETSKY
Talking with him, didn't you find
he has unfortunately lost his mind?

REPETILOV
Stuff and nonsense!

ZAGORETSKY
It's what everyone maintains.

REPETILOV
Mere lies.

ZAGORETSKY
Ask them.

REPETILOV
Water on their brains.

ZAGORETSKY
What luck—here's Prince Peter Ilyich,
the Princess, and their daughters.

REPETILOV
Wild goose chase.
   (The PRINCE, the PRINCESS, and their six DAUGHTERS enter. A few moments later, KHLYOSTOV comes down the stairs. MOLCHALIN escorts her on his arm. FOOTMEN bustle about.)

ZAGORETSKY
Princesses, I beg you, give us your opinion.
Is Chatsky mad or isn't he?

FIRST PRINCESS
Is there anywhere any skepticism?

SECOND PRINCESS
It's something that the whole world sees.

THIRD PRINCESS
The Dryanskys, the Khvorovs, the Varlyanskys, and the Skachkovs—

FOURTH PRINCESS
Who thinks that that's latest news? That's all old stuff.

FIFTH PRINCESS
Does someone doubt it?

ZAGORETSKY
He doesn't believe it.

SIXTH PRINCESS
You!

ALL TOGETHER
M'sieu Repetilov! You! M'sieu Repetilov! You don't mean it!
How can you go against the grain!
Why *you*? Ridiculous! For shame!

REPETILOV *(Puts his hands over his ears)*
My fault—I had no idea that this is so well known.

THE OLD PRINCESS
Not only known, but to talk to him you risk your own;
should have been locked up long ago.
To hear him say his little finger's
the smartest, even smarter than Prince Peter!
I think he's just a Jacobin, that
Chatsky of yours! Let's go. Prince, you might take
Katish or Zizi, and I'll go in the coach for six.

KHLYOSTOV *(From the staircase)*
Princess, the card-game stake.

THE OLD PRINCESS
On account, my dear.

ALL *(Each to the others)*
Good-bye.
    (The PRINCELY FAMILY *drives off, and* ZAGORETSKY *also)*

REPETILOV

Lord, what a fix!
Amfisa Nilovna! Ah! Poor Chatsky! What next!
What's noble reason worth! The effort that we make!
Tell me, why in this world do we try and try?

KHLYOSTOV

So God decreed for him; besides,
they'll treat him—and most likely work a cure.
But you, dear old acquaintance, are incurable for sure.
What a time you chose to arrive!—
Molchalin, there's your tiny quarters.
Don't see me to my carriage, no. Go on. God bless you.
  (MOLCHALIN *goes into his room*)
Good-bye, my friend. It's time you stopped sowing your wild oats.
  (*She drives away*)

REPETILOV (*With his* FOOTMAN)

What's the place to head for now?
The light of dawn is in the air.
Come, put me in my carriage
and take me anywhere.
  (*He drives away. The last light goes out*)

CHATSKY (*Comes out of the vestibule*)

What's going on? Did I really hear what I think I heard?
Not ridicule but outright malice. What wondrous words,
what sort of black and secret magic
do they use with one voice to repeat such stuff about me?
For some it even seems to be a triumph;
others seem sympathetic—
If only one could see inside:
which is worse, their tongue or heart?
Who made this work of art!
The idiots took it on faith, then passed it on;
at once, the old ladies sounded the alarm;
and there you have the general opinion!
And there you have the homeland—by coming back today,
I see that I'll grow tired of it very soon.
But Sofya—has she heard? Surely she was told,
but she's not the kind of person—whether or not it made sense—
to amuse herself explicitly at my expense.
No matter it's me or someone else;

she honestly doesn't care for anyone at all.
So, why the fainting, the loss of consciousness, the frenzy?
Indulgence of the nerves, a whimsy—
a little thing upsets them, and a little calms them down—
I took to indicate real passions. Hardly that:
certainly she'd have passed out just the same
if anybody had stepped on
the tail of a little dog or cat.

SOFYA *(On the second floor, carrying a candle)*
That you, Molchalin?
(The door begins to close quickly, but remains ajar)

CHATSKY
It's her! Herself! Some sign?
Oh, my head's burning, the blood's roaring through my chest!
She appeared! No more. Was it nothing but her ghost?
Have I really lost my mind?
Though I'm ready and waiting for anything unusual,
here was not a ghost but one setting up a rendezvous.
Why should I fool myself? I heard her call
Molchalin. And there's his room off the hall.

HIS FOOTMAN *(From the porch)*
Your car—

CHATSKY
Sssh!
(Pushes him out)
I'll stay here and not shut an eye
until the morning. If one must drink one's grief,
best do it at one go,
because trouble isn't gotten round by going slow.
The door's opening.
(He hides behind a column. LIZA [enters] with a candle)

LIZA
It's terrible! I'm scared to death.
In the empty hall! in the dead of night! the spirits out—
never mind what the living are about.
My young lady, my tormentor, God help her.
And Chatsky like a cross to bear—
She thought she saw him, seems, somewhere here downstairs.
(Looks around)

Indeed, a lot he wants to wander around the hall!
I bet he's long gone instead,
saved the loving for tomorrow,
and home now in bed.
But I've been ordered to wake up the apple of her heart.
    (Knocks on MOLCHALIN's *door)*
Hello there, sir. You're asked to wake up, please.
The young lady's hailing you, it's the young lady calls.
And hurry, so you don't get caught.
    *(*CHATSKY *[remains] behind the column.* MOLCHALIN *[enters], stretches, and yawns.* SOFYA *steals down the stairs)*
You're hard as stone, sir; you're cold as ice.

MOLCHALIN

Ah, Liza, did you come on your own?

LIZA

From my lady, sir.

MOLCHALIN

Who would guess
that the blush of love hasn't yet
danced in these little veins and cheeks?
Is all you want to be your lady's go-between?

LIZA

You men who go a-seeking brides
shouldn't yawn and be so lazy;
Kind and comely is he who's hungry
and never sleepy before he marries.

MOLCHALIN

Marries? Marry whom?

LIZA

Not my young lady?

MOLCHALIN

Who said!
There's lots to hope for up ahead.
We'll make time pass without a wedding.

LIZA

What are you saying, sir! Who else
do we intend to be her husband?

MOLCHALIN

No idea. Sometimes I start to tremble so
and get cold feet at the very thought
that Pavel Afanasych someday
will catch us and drive me away
and damn me. What else? Shall I open up my heart?
I don't see a thing to envy in Sofya Pavlovna.
God grant her a long and prosperous life; she loved
Chatsky once upon a time;
she'll fall out of love with me like that.
My little angel, I might wish I felt
for her even half of what I feel for you,
but no matter how I memorize my lines
or get ready to be tender, I meet her and turn cold.

SOFYA *(Aside)*

How mean! How low!

CHATSKY *(Behind the column)*

The dog!

LIZA

You're not ashamed?

MOLCHALIN

My father left me this advice:
First of all, please everyone without exception—
the man whose place you happen to live in,
the manager of the office you work in,
his servant who keeps your clothing clean,
the doorman, the yardman—to avoid all trouble—
and the yardman's dog, so it's always gentle.

LIZA

Indeed, sir, you have a great responsibility!

MOLCHALIN

And so I adopt the appearance of a lover
to satisfy the daughter of a man—

LIZA

Who gives you food and drink
and sometimes raises you in rank?
Let's go now; we talked enough.

MOLCHALIN

Let's go share the love of our lamenting beauty.
Come, I want to hug you from the fullness of my heart.
        (LIZA *does not yield*)
How come she isn't you!
        (*Starts to go;* SOFYA *does not let him*)

   SOFYA (*Almost whispers, speaks the whole scene in an undertone*)
Go no farther. I've heard more than I can take,
you awful person! How ashamed I am—and for these walls.

MOLCHALIN

What! Sofya Pavlovna—

SOFYA

Not a word, for God's sake.
Silence! I'll decide it all.

   MOLCHALIN (*Falls to his knees.* SOFYA *pushes him away*)
Oh, remember! Don't be angry; look—

SOFYA

I don't remember a thing—don't pester me.
Oh, memories! How like a pointed knife they are!

   MOLCHALIN (*Crawling at her feet*)
Forgive me!

SOFYA

Don't behave like a dog; get up.
I don't want a reply. What your reply will be I know.
You'll lie—

MOLCHALIN

Do me the great favor—

SOFYA

No. No. No.

MOLCHALIN

I was only joking, and whatever it was I said about—

SOFYA

Stop this minute, I'm telling you,
or I'll wake the whole house with a shout
and ruin both myself and you.
        (MOLCHALIN *rises*)

From this moment on, it's as if I never knew you.
Don't think you'll get reproaches, tears
or complaints from me—you're unworthy.
See to it that you're not still in this house at dawn,
and may I never hear of you ever again.

MOLCHALIN

As you wish.

SOFYA

Otherwise I'll tell
Father the whole truth, out of spite.
You know, I don't set great store on myself.
Go now. Wait! Take delight
in the fact that during our meetings in the midnight quiet
you were much more timid in your manner than in daylight hours,
or when others are around, or than you really are.
There's less impudence in you than deviousness of heart.
Myself, I'm very glad I found all this out at night.
No reproachful witnesses are watching me to point
a finger, as earlier today when I fainted
and Chatsky was there—

CHATSKY (Rushes between them)

He's here, you hypocrite!

LIZA and SOFYA

Oh! Oh!
    (LIZA *drops her candle in fright.* MOLCHALIN *sneaks off to his room*)

CHATSKY

Hurry up and faint: now it's the thing to do.
At least, the excuse is better than it was before.
The solution to the riddle now in view,
look who it was I yielded to!
I don't know how I held my rage inside.
I looked, I saw, and didn't believe my eyes!
But the darling in whose name
she forgot both an old friend and her woman's shame
has hid behind his door, afraid of being called
to account. Ah, how can we make sense of fate?

It's the persecutor of the heart, a plague!
Molchalins live in bliss around the world.

SOFYA *(Completely in tears)*

Don't continue. I blame myself from beginning to end.
But who could have thought he'd be so insidious!

LIZA

Crash! Bang! Oh, my God! Here comes the entire house!
Your father's going to thank you a lot.

(FAMUSOV *and a crowd of servants with candles enter)*

FAMUSOV

This way! Hurry! Follow me!
Fetch more candles! Lanterns, too!
What spirits of the house? These faces are familiar.
Sofya Pavlovna, shame on you!
You shameless girl! Where? With who? Exactly like
her mother, my dear-departed wife.
Just turn my back on my better half, and time and again
she'd be away somewhere with men!
Have you no fear of God? How did he entice you?
You're the one who said that he was mad!
Stupidity and blindness got me; I've been had
by this whole plot, which he helped form and grow,
with all our guests. Oh, why am I being punished so?

CHATSKY *(To SOFYA)*

So, I'm obliged to you for the flight of fancy, too?

FAMUSOV

My friend, don't try your tricks, I won't be fooled,
even if you two pretend to fight.
You, Filka, you're a block of wood,
a lazy jackass I promoted to be porter
who's not aware of anything and gets nothing right.
Where were you? Where'd you go?
How come you didn't lock the hall?
How come you didn't check? How come you heard no sound?
Hard labor's what you get, Siberian exile,*
willing to betray me for a kopek.
You, little busybody, look what your mischief did,

---

* Landowners had the right to punish their serfs by sending them to hard labor or
to exile in Siberia.

Kuznetsky Street, new dresses, and the latest fads.
That's where you learned to make acquaintance with new lovers,
but wait, I'll straighten you out yet:
to a country cottage, if you please, to feed the chickens.
And you, my dear, my daughter, I won't leave you out, either:
be patient for another day or two—
you'll not remain in Moscow—no society for you—
but far from swashbucklers and pants
in Saratov at your country aunt's,
where you can grieve to your heart's content
sitting at your lacework and reading about the saints.
You, sir, I ask as plain as day,
never present yourself by highway or by byway.
And such was the final figure that you cut
that now to anyone our door will be tight shut.
I'll do all I can, I will, to sound the alarm;
I'll make an effort everywhere in town
and shout out to everybody who you are.
I'll take it to the Senate, the cabinet, and the czar!

CHATSKY *(After a brief pause)*
It makes no sense— My fault, if you will—
I hear the words but don't understand—
as if they're trying to explain everything to me,
but I'm confused, expecting something still.
   (Ardently)
I was blind! Whom did I hope to get my labors' long reward from?
I rushed! I flew! I trembled! I thought happiness at hand.
On whom did I so passionately, humbly squander
words both delicate and fond?
But you! O Lord in heaven! Who did you select?
When I think about the one that you preferred!
Why did you lure me on by keeping up my hope?
Why didn't you simply give me the word
that you had turned the whole past into ridicule?!
That even your memory of the feelings
that once moved our hearts in common had grown cold,
feelings which no distance cooled in me,
no diversions, and no change of scene.
I lived and breathed them all day long and every day!
If you had said you found my suddenly arriving,
my appearance, words, or actions offensive in any way,

I'd have immediately broken off relations
and, before saying farewell to you forever,
wouldn't have bothered to nail down
who this person is you think so nice.
   (Derisively)
On second thought, you and he'll be reconciled:
that means destroying yourself—what for?
Think a moment: you can always show your care
for him, swaddle him, and send him, like a child,
on errands. To remain a boy—to wait upon his wife—
this is a Moscow man's idea of the noble life.
Well, enough. I pride myself on breaking off with you.
And you, sir father, who care so much about position,
I wish you blissfully ignorant dormition.
From me you'll get no threats to wed or woo.
A man without a social flaw
will turn up, a toady and a hard ass,
in all his qualities at last
just like his future father-in-law.
So! I've completely sobered up.
Away with the visions before my eyes—the veil has fallen.
Now I might as well let out
all my spleen and all my spite
on father and on daughter
and on the idiotic lover
and on society the whole world over.
Who I was with! Where I got cast up by fate!
A mob of rushing, swearing torturers who betray
each other's love, who pursue their selfish hates,
whose silly stories never end—
simpletons who connive, dimwits who can't think straight,
sinister old women, old men
gone senile over things they made up that make no sense.
A man who can spend a day with you—you're right!—
breathing the same air you're breathing
and keeping his senses and his reason,
will pass unharmed through death by fire.
Away from Moscow! I won't take this road again.
I'm off—I won't look back—to see if in some part
of the wide world there's a corner for an outraged heart.
My carriage, now, my carriage!
   (He drives off)

FAMUSOV *(To* SOFYA*)*
What do you make of that? Didn't you see he's mad?
Tell me truthfully, now—
out of his mind! What a lot of rubbish he spewed!
"Toady!" "Ass!" "Father-in-law!" And so hard on Moscow!
And you've resolved to put me in my grave?
Isn't my life sad enough already?
Ah, my Lord, my Lord, what will Princess
Mary Alekseevna say?

                                                        (1823–1825)

MIKHAIL LERMONTOV

IN HIS BRIEF LIFE MIKHAIL LERMONTOV (1814–1841) *accomplished two important cultural firsts: he brought into Russia full-blown Romantic, Byronic poetry (with all its attendant attitudes as well as conventions of diction and theme); and he wrote* A Hero of Our Time *(1840), a remarkable novel composed of a cycle of stories loosely linked through the character of its main hero, Pechorin. This was the first of many Russian works whose goal was to create a "type" of the Russian literary hero meant to be expressive and characteristic of his entire epoch.*

His name derived from that of a Scottish ancestor (Learmount), Lermontov suffered through several unhappy love affairs in his late teens and while studying at the University of Moscow. He became an officer in the Hussars in 1834 and later distinguished himself at the Battle of the Valerik River. He first achieved fame and recognition as a poet in 1837 with his poem on the death of Pushkin, "The Death of a Poet" (like his great predecessor, Lermontov would himself be killed in a duel). It was a poem of reverence for Pushkin, but it was also an attack against fashionable government circles. He was arrested as a result and transferred to military service in the Caucasus. He loved romantic scenery, and he found in the Caucasus Russia's romantic and poetic geographic myth par excellence. His outstanding works were all written here in these last four years of his life.

Lermontov's poetry at its best (in about twenty poems) is very moving and passionate. The poem "My Native Land" played a large role in the construction of an important body of myths and images within the Russian set of perceptions of what constitutes a distinctive Russian identity. The discernment of typically Russian qualities in the poor, rural, peasant population and the country landscapes became a frequent motif of Russian discussions and representations of "Russianness"—in contrast to the official, demonstrative, military-aristocratic governmental representations.

Lermontov was a born attacker. He indicted, blamed, and railed. His targets were the court circles, the nobility, but also the imperfections and griefs of life in general. Besides his lyrics, he also wrote several long narrative poems (including the immensely popular Demon) and five plays.

Princess Mary (and the other stories in Lermontov's 1840 prose masterpiece, A Hero of Our Time) introduced several innovations to the Russian literary repertoire. One is psychological: the lengthy and detailed expoundings of Pechorin's inner world. If we compare Pechorin with Pushkin's Silvio, we see the contrast between Pushkin's aesthetic spareness and Lermontov's expansive and probing presentations of detailed psychological portraits. (Pushkin's Yevgeny Onegin had already done this in the form of a novel in verse.) A Hero of Our Time presents a self-absorbed hero who wallows in his self-centeredness and isolation. There are both internal and external portraits (the self-revelation comes through the vehicle of the diary form.) The tone is ironic, cynical, stringent. There is contempt for established opinion and an assertion of intense individualism (with much self-consciousness).

The last paragraph of Princess Mary is a good illustration of Lermontov's heroes' predilection for and pride in melancholy, loneliness, sadness, being different, exceptional, isolated. As Vladimir Nabokov has pointed out, although Lermontov claims Pechorin is typical and derived from Russian reality, his antecedents are clearly literary and European (in the creations of Goethe, Rousseau, Constant, Byron, and other Romantic writers).

Along with Pushkin's Onegin and Griboyedov's Chatsky, Lermontov's creation of Pechorin marks one of the earliest instances in Russian literature of the "Superfluous Man"—a character type whom Turgenev would later popularize in his story The Diary of a Superfluous Man.

Throughout modern Russian Literature, the "Superfluous Man" reappears as a character who has not found his niche, an outsider, either a rebel without cause or a rebel with a very good cause. He can be someone who is ready to do battle to reform society, to struggle against oppression, injustice, and the backwardness of Russia—and is unable to do so because of the sheer power and inertia of his opponents. Or he may be a second type—a character who fails not through the fault of his surroundings, but because he himself is weak, or irresolute, or too soft. Between these two extremes there fall a variety of hybrid "superfluous men"—all flawed characters struggling against a likewise flawed but all-powerful establishment.

From Griboyedov's Chatsky and Pushkin's Onegin, through Lermontov's Pechorin, Turgenev's Rudin, and Goncharov's Oblomov, these "superfluous men" stretch all the way to Doctor Zhivago in Pasternak's novel, and they have been recognized by readers for generations as a Russian type, in literature and in actual life.

The Byronic coldness, disillusionment, the toying with those who surround one, struck a chord in Russian society and literature of the 1840s. Lermontov marks an important stage in nascent Russian prose and in Russian self-awareness.

MY NATIVE LAND

If I do love my land, strangely I love it:
'tis something reason cannot cure.
Glories of war I do not covet,
but neither peace proud and secure,
nor the mysterious past and dim romances
can spur my soul to pleasant fancies.

And still I love thee—why I hardly know:
I love thy fields so coldly meditative,
native dark swaying woods and native
rivers that sea-like foam and flow.

In a clattering cart I love to travel
on country roads: watching the rising star,
yearning for sheltered sleep, my eyes unravel
the trembling lights of sad hamlets afar.

I also love the smoke of burning stubble,
vans huddled in the prairie night;
corn on a hill crowned with the double
grace of twin birches gleaming white.

Few are the ones who feel the pleasure
of seeing barns bursting with grain and hay,
well-thatched cottage-roofs made to measure
and shutters carved and windows gay.

And when the evening dew is glistening,
long may I hear the festive sound
of rustic dancers stamping, whistling
with drunkards clamoring around.

(1841)

FAREWELL

Farewell! Nevermore shall we meet,
we shall never touch hands—so farewell!
Your heart is now free, but in none
will it ever be happy to dwell.

•   •   •

One moment together we came:
time eternal is nothing to this!
All senses we suddenly drained,
burned all in the flame of one kiss.
Farewell! And be wise, do not grieve:
our love was too short for regret,
and hard as we found it to part
harder still would it be if we met.

(1832)

FROM THE AUTHOR'S INTRODUCTION TO
A HERO OF OUR TIME

A Hero of Our Time, gentlemen, is indeed a portrait, but not of a single individual. It is the portrait composed of all the vices of our generation in their fullest development. You will tell me again that no man can be as bad as all this; and I shall tell you that since you have believed in the possibility of so many tragic and romantic villains having existed, why can you not believe in the reality of Pechorin? If you have admired fictions far more frightful and horrible, why does this character, even as a fiction, not find mercy with you? Is it not perhaps because there is more truth in this character than you would like there to be?

You will say that morality gains nothing from this. I beg your pardon. People have been fed enough sweets, which have given them indigestion. They need bitter medicine, caustic truth. However, do not think that the author of this book ever had the proud dream of becoming a reformer of mankind's vices. God defend him from such benightedness! He merely found it amusing to draw modern man such as he understood him to be, such as he had met him—all too frequently, unfortunately, for him and you. Suffice it that the disease has been pointed out; only God knows how to cure it.

(1840)

PREFACE TO PECHORIN'S DIARY

I heard not long ago that Pechorin had died on his return journey from Persia. The news made me very glad, for it gave me the right to publish these notes. I took advantage of this opportunity to sign my name to another man's work. God grant that readers do not reproach me for such an innocent forgery. . . .

While reading these notes, I became persuaded of the sincerity of this man who so mercilessly revealed his own faults and vices. The history of a human soul, even the meanest one, can hardly be less curious or less instructive than the history of a whole nation—especially when it is the result of self-examination on the part of a mature mind, and when it is written without the ambitious desire to provoke sympathy or amazement. Rousseau's *Confessions* had this defect, that he wrote them to be read to his friends. . . .

(1840)

PRINCESS MARY NATURE

May 11th

Yesterday, I arrived in Pyatigorsk and rented lodgings on the outskirts of the town, at its highest point, at the foot of Mount Mashuk: when there is a thunderstorm, the clouds will descend down to my roof. At five this morning, when I opened the window, my room was filled with the perfume of flowers growing in the modest front garden. The branches of cherry trees in bloom look into my window, and the wind occasionally strews my desk with their white petals. The view on three sides is marvelous: to the west, the five-peaked Besh Tau looms blue like "the last thundercloud of a tempest dispersed"; to the north, Mount Mashuk rises like a shaggy Persian fur cap and closes off all that part of the horizon; to the east, the outlook is gayer; right below me, lies the varicolored, neat, brand-new little town, the medicinal springs babble, and so does the multilingual crowd; and, beyond the town, amphitheatrical mountains pile up, ever bluer and mistier, while on the edge of the horizon there stretches a silver range of snowy summits, beginning with Mount Kazbek, and ending with the bicephalous Mount Elbruz. It is gay to live in such country! A kind of joyful feeling permeates all my veins. The air is pure and fresh, like the kiss of a child, the sun is bright, the sky is blue—what more, it seems, could one wish? Who, here, needs passions, desires, regrets? However, it is time. I shall go to the Elizabeth Spring: there, I am told, the entire spa society gathers in the morning.

Upon descending into the center of town, I followed the boulevard where I came across several melancholy groups that were slowly going uphill. These were mostly families of landowners from the steppe provinces: this could be inferred immediately from the worn-out, old-fashioned frock coats of the husbands and the elaborate attires of the wives and daughters. Obviously they had already taken stock of all the young men at the waters for they looked at me with tender curiosity. The St. Petersburg cut of my military surtout misled them, but soon, recognizing the epaulets of a mere army officer, they turned away in disgust.

The wives of the local officials, the hostesses of the waters, so to speak, were more favorably disposed; they have lorgnettes, they pay less attention to uniforms, they are used to encountering in the Caucasus an ardent heart under a numbered army button, and a cultivated mind under a white army cap. These ladies are very charming, and remain charming for a long time! Every year, their admirers are replaced by new ones, and herein, perhaps, lies the secret of their indefatigable amiability. As I climbed the narrow path leading to the Elizabeth Spring, I overtook a bunch of men, some civilian, some military, who, as I afterward learned, make up a special class of people among those hoping for the action of the waters. They drink—but not water, they walk little, they flirt only in passing, they gamble and complain of ennui. They are dandies: as they dip their wicker-encased glasses into the well of sulphurous water, they assume academic poses: the civilians wear pale-blue neckerchiefs, the military men allow ruffles to show above their coat-collars. They profess a profound contempt for provincial houses and sigh after the capitals' aristocratic salons where they are not admitted.

At last, there was the well. Near it, on the terrace, a small redroofed structure was built to house the bath, and a little further, there was the gallery where one walked when it rained. Several wounded officers sat on a bench, their crutches drawn up, looking pale and sad. Several ladies walked briskly back and forth on the terrace awaiting the action of the waters. Among them there were two or three pretty faces. In the avenues of vines that cover the slope of Mount Mashuk, one could glimpse now and then the variegated bonnets of ladies partial to shared isolation, since I would always notice, near such a bonnet, either a military cap or one of those round civilian hats that are so ugly. On a steep cliff where the pavilion termed The Aeolian Harp is built, the lovers of scenery perched and trained a telescope on Mount Elbruz: among them were two tutors with their charges, who had come to have their scrofula treated.

I had stopped out of breath on the edge of the hill and, leaning against the corner of the bathhouse, had begun to survey the picturesque landscape, when suddenly I heard a familiar voice behind me:

"Pechorin! Have you been here long?"

I turned around: it was Grushnitsky! We embraced. I had made his acquaintance in a detachment on active duty. He had been wounded by a bullet in the leg and had left for the waters about a week before me.

Grushnitsky is a cadet. He has been in the service only one year; he wears, following a peculiar kind of foppishness, a soldier's thick coat. He has a soldier's St. George's Cross. He is well built, swarthy, and black-haired; judging by his appearance, one might give him twenty-five years of age, although he is hardly twenty-one. He throws his head back when he speaks, and keeps twirling his mustache with his left hand since he uses his right for leaning on his crutch. His speech is rapid and ornate; he is one of those people who, for every occasion in life, have ready-made pompous phrases, whom unadorned beauty does not move, and who solemnly drape themselves in extraordinary emotions, exalted passions, and exceptional sufferings. To produce an effect is rapture to them; romantic provincial ladies go crazy over them. With age they become either peaceful landowners, or drunkards; sometimes, both. Their souls often possess many good qualities, but not an ounce of poetry. Grushnitsky's passion was to declaim; he bombarded you with words as soon as the talk transcended the circle of everyday notions: I have never been able to argue with him. He does not answer your objections, he does not listen to you. The moment you stop, he launches upon a long tirade apparently having some connection with what you have said, but actually being only a continuation of his own discourse.

He is fairly witty; his epigrams are frequently amusing, but they are neither to the point nor venomous; he will never kill anyone with a single word; he does not know people and their vulnerable spots, since all his life he has been occupied with his own self. His object is to become the hero of a novel. So often has he tried to convince others that he is a being not made for this world and doomed to suffer in secret, that he has almost succeeded in convincing himself of it. That is why he wears, so proudly, that thick soldier's coat of his. I have seen through him, and that is why he dislikes me, although outwardly we are on the friendliest of terms. Grushnitsky has the reputation of an exceptionally brave man. I have seen him in action: he brandishes his sword, he yells, he rushes forward with closed eyes. Somehow, this is not Russian courage!

I don't like him either: I feel that one day we shall meet on a narrow path, and one of us will fare ill.

His coming to the Caucasus is likewise a consequence of his fanatic romanticism. I am sure that on the eve of his departure from the family country seat, he told some pretty neighbor, with a gloomy air, that he was going to the Caucasus not merely to serve there, but that he was seeking death because . . . and here, probably, he would cover his eyes with his hand and continue thus: "No, you must not know this! Your pure soul would shudder! And what for? What am I to you? Would you understand me? . . ." and so forth.

He told me himself that the reason which impelled him to join the K. regiment would remain an eternal secret between him and heaven.

Yet during those moments when he casts off the tragic cloak, Grushnitsky is quite pleasant and amusing. I am curious to see him with women: that is when, I suppose, he really tries hard!

We met like old chums. I began to question him about life at the spa and its noteworthy people.

"Our life here is rather prosaic," he said with a sigh. "Those who drink the waters in the morning are insipid like all invalids, and those who drink wine in the evening are unbearable like all healthy people. Feminine society exists, but there is little comfort therein: these ladies play whist, dress badly and speak dreadful French! From Moscow this year, there is only Princess Ligovskoy with her daughter, but I am not acquainted with them. My soldier's coat is like a seal of rejection. The sympathy that it arouses is as painful as charity."

At that moment, two ladies walked past us in the direction of the well: one was elderly, the other young and graceful. Their bonnets prevented me from getting a good look at their faces, but they were dressed according to the strict rules of the best taste: there was nothing superfluous. The younger one wore a pearl-gray dress closed at the throat, a light silk fichu twined around her supple neck, shoes, *couleur puce*, so pleasingly constricted at the ankle of her spare little foot, that even one uninitiated into the mysteries of beauty would have certainly uttered an exclamation, if only of surprise. Her light, yet noble, gait had something virginal about it that escaped definition, but was comprehensible to the gaze. As she walked past us, there emanated from her that ineffable fragrance which breathes sometimes from a beloved woman's letter.

"That's Princess Ligovskoy," said Grushnitsky, "and with her is her daughter, Mary, as she calls her after the English fashion. They have been here only three days."

"And yet you already know her name?"

"Yes, I happened to hear it," he answered flushing. "I confess, I do not wish to meet them. Those proud aristocrats look upon us army men as savages. And what do they care whether or not there is a mind under a numbered regimental cap and a heart under a thick army coat?"

"Poor coat," I said with a smile. "And who is the gentleman going up to them and so helpfully offering them tumblers?"

"Oh, that's the Moscow dandy Raevich. He is a gamester: it can be seen at once by the huge, golden watch chain that winds across his sky-blue waistcoat. And what a thick walking stick—like Robinson Crusoe's; and his beard and haircut *à la moujik* are also characteristic."

"You are embittered against the whole of humanity?"

"And there is a good reason for that."

"Oh, really?"

At this point the ladies moved away from the well and came level with us. Grushnitsky had time to assume a dramatic attitude with the help of his crutch, and loudly answered me in French:

"Mon cher, je hais les hommes pour ne pas les mépriser, car autrement la vie serait une farce trop dégoûtante."

The pretty young princess turned her head and bestowed a long curious glance upon the orator. The expression of this glance was very indefinite, but it was not derisive, a fact on which I inwardly congratulated him with all my heart.

"This Princess Mary is extremely pretty," I said to him. "She has such velvety eyes—yes, velvety is the word for them. I advise you to appropriate this term when you speak of her eyes: the upper and lower lashes are so long, that the pupils do not reflect the rays of the sun. I like this kind of lusterless eyes: they are so soft, they seem to stroke you. However, this seems to be the only nice thing about her face. And her teeth, are they white? This is very important! Pity she did not smile at your pompous phrase."

"You talk of a pretty woman as of an English horse," said Grushnitsky with indignation.

"*Mon cher*," I answered trying to copy his manner, "*je méprise les femmes pour ne pas les aimer, car autrement la vie serait un mélodrame trop ridicule.*"

I turned and walked away from him. For about half an hour, I strolled along the viny avenues, the limestone ledges, and the bushes hanging between them. It was getting hot, and I decided to hurry home. When passing the sulphurous spring, I stopped at the covered walk to draw a deep breath in its shade, and this provided me with the opportunity to witness a rather curious scene. This is how the actors were placed. The elderly princess and the Moscow dandy sat on a bench in the covered walk, and both seemed to be engrossed in serious conversation. The young princess, probably having finished her last glass of water, strolled pensively near the well. Grushnitsky stood right beside it; there was no one else on the terrace.

I drew closer and hid behind a corner of the walk. At this moment, Grushnitsky dropped his glass upon the sand and tried hard to bend down in order to pick it up. His injured leg hampered him. Poor fellow! How he exerted himself while leaning on his crutch, but all in vain. His expressive face reflected real pain.

Princess Mary saw it all even better than I. Lighter than a little bird, she skipped up to him, bent down, picked up the glass, and handed it to him with a movement full of inexpressible charm. Then she blushed dreadfully, glanced back at the covered walk, but having convinced herself that her mamma had seen nothing, appeared at once to regain her composure. When Grushnitsky opened his mouth to thank her, she was already far away. A minute later, she left the gallery with her mother and the dandy, but as she passed by Grushnitsky, she assumed a most formal and dignified air, she did not even turn her head, did not even take notice of the passionate glance with which he followed her for a long time until she reached the bottom of the hill and disappeared beyond the young lindens of the boulevard. Presently, however, her bonnet could be glimpsed crossing the street; she hurried through the gate of one of the best houses in Pyatigorsk. Her mother walked in after her, and at the gate gave Raevich a parting nod.

Only then did the poor passionate cadet notice my presence.

"Did you see?" he said, firmly gripping me by the hand. "A very angel!"

"Why?" I asked, with an air of the most genuine naïveté.

"Didn't you see?"

"I did: she picked up your glass. Had an attendant been around, he would have done the same thing, and with even more alacrity since he would be hoping for a tip. However, one can quite understand that she felt sorry for you: you made such an awful face when you shifted your weight onto your wounded leg."

"And you did not feel at all touched looking at her at the moment her soul shone in her face?"

"No."

I lied, but I wanted to infuriate him. Contradiction is, with me, an innate passion; my entire life has been nothing but a chain of sad and frustrating contradictions to heart or reason. The presence of an enthusiast envelops me with midwinter frost, and I think that frequent commerce with an inert phlegmatic individual would have made of me a passionate dreamer. I further confess that a nasty but familiar sensation, at that moment, skimmed over my heart. This sensation was envy: I boldly say "envy" because I am used to being frank with myself in everything, and it is doubtful if there can be found a young man who, upon meeting a pretty woman who has riveted his idle attention and has suddenly given obvious preference to another man equally unknown to her, it is doubtful, let me repeat, that there can be found a young man (provided, of course, that he has lived in the *grand monde* and is accustomed to indulge his vanity), who would not be unpleasantly struck by this.

In silence, Grushnitsky and I descended the hill and walked along the boulevard past the windows of the house into which our charmer had vanished. She was sitting at the window. Grushnitsky jerked me by the arm, and threw upon her one of those blurrily tender glances which have so little effect upon women. I trained my lorgnette on her and noticed that his glance made her smile, and that my insolent lorgnette angered her in no uncertain way. And how, indeed, does a Caucasian army officer dare to train his quizzing-glass on a young princess from Moscow?

May 13th

This morning my doctor friend called on me: his surname is Werner, but he is Russian. Why should this be surprising? I used to know an Ivanov who was German.

Werner is a remarkable man in many respects. He is a skeptic and a materialist, like almost all medical men, but he is also a poet, and this I mean seriously. He is a poet in all his actions, and frequently in his utterings, although in all his life he never wrote two lines of verse. He has studied all the live strings of the human heart in the same way as one studies the veins of a dead body, but he has never learned how to put his knowledge to profit: thus sometimes an excellent anatomist may not know how to cure a fever. Ordinarily, Werner made unobtrusive fun of his patients, but once I saw him cry over a dying soldier. He was poor; he dreamt of becoming a millionaire but would never have taken one additional step for the sake of money. He told me once that he would rather do a favor for an enemy than for a friend, because in the latter case it would mean selling charity, whereas hatred only grows in proportion to an enemy's generosity. He had a caustic tongue: under the label of his epigram, many a kindly man acquired the reputation of a vulgarian and a fool. His competitors, envious resort doctors, once spread the rumor that he drew cartoons of his patients—the patients became infuriated—and almost all refused to be treated by him. His friends, that is to say, all the really decent people serving in the Caucasus, tried in vain to restore his fallen credit.

His appearance was of the kind that, at first glance, impresses one unfavorably but attracts one later, when the eye has learned to decipher in irregular features the imprint of a dependable and lofty soul. Examples are known of women falling madly in love with such people and of not exchanging their ugly exterior for the beauty of the freshest and rosiest Endymions. Women must be given their due: they have a flair for spiritual beauty. This may be why men like Werner are so passionately fond of women.

Werner was of small stature, thin and frail like a child. One of his legs was shorter than the other, as in the case of Byron; in proportion to his body, his head seemed enormous; he cropped his hair; the bumps of his skull, thus revealed, would have amazed a phrenologist by their bizarre interplay of contradictory inclinations. His small black eyes, never at rest, tried to penetrate your mind. His dress revealed taste and tidiness; his lean, wiry, small hands sported light-yellow gloves. His frock coat, neckcloth and waistcoat were always black. The younger men dubbed him Mephistopheles. He pretended to resent this nickname, but, in point of fact, it flattered his vanity. We soon came to understand each other and became pals—for I am not capable of true friendship. One of the two friends is always the slave of the other, although, often, neither of the two admits this to himself. I can be nobody's slave, while to assume command in such cases is tiresome work because it has to be combined with deceit. I, moreover, am supplied with lackeys and money. We became pals in the following way: I first met Werner in the town of S——, among a numerous and noisy group of young men. Toward the end of the evening, the conversation took a philosophic and metaphysical turn; convictions were discussed; everyone was convinced of something or other.

"As for me, I am convinced of only one thing," said the doctor.

"Of what?" I asked, wishing to learn the opinion of this man who up to now had been silent.

"Of the fact," he answered, "that, sooner or later, one fine morning, I shall die."

"I'm better off than you," I said. "I've one more conviction besides yours, namely that one miserable evening I had the misfortune to be born."

Everybody found that we were talking nonsense, but, really, not one of them said anything more intelligent than that. Henceforth, we distinguished each other in the crowd. We would often see each other and discuss, together, with great seriousness, abstract matters, until we noticed that we were gulling each other. Then, after looking meaningly into each other's eyes, we began to laugh as Roman augurs did, according to Cicero, and having had our fill of mirth, we would separate well-content with our evening.

. I was lying on the divan, with eyes directed at the ceiling and hands clasped under my head, when Werner entered my room. He sat down in an armchair, placed his cane in a corner, yawned, and declared that it was getting hot out of doors. I answered that the flies were bothering me, and we both fell silent.

"Observe, my dear doctor," said I, "that without fools, the world would be a very dull place. . . . Consider: here we are, two intelligent people; we know beforehand that one can argue endlessly about anything, and therefore we do not argue; we know almost all the secret thoughts of each other; one word is a whole story for us; we see the kernel of our every emotion through a triple shell. Sad things seem to us funny, funny things seem to us melancholy, and generally we are, to tell the truth, rather indifferent to everything except our own selves. Thus, between us there can be no exchange of feelings and thoughts: we know everything about each other that we wish to know, and we do not wish to know anything more. There remains only one solution: telling the news. So tell me some piece of news."

Tired by my long speech, I closed my eyes and yawned.

He answered, after a moment's thought: "Nevertheless, your drivel contains an idea."

"Two ideas," I answered.

"Tell me one, and I'll tell you the other."

"All right, you start!" said I, continuing to examine the ceiling and inwardly smiling.

"You'd like to learn some details about some resort guest, and I have already an inkling as to the subject of your concern, because there have already been inquiries about you in that quarter."

"Doctor! It is definitely impossible for us to converse: we read in each other's souls."

"Now, the other idea . . ."

"Here is the other idea: I wanted to make you relate something or other—in the first place, because to listen is less fatiguing; in the second place, because a listener cannot give himself away; in the third place, because one can discover another's secret; and in the fourth place, because such intelligent people as you prefer an audience to a storyteller. Now, to business! What did the old Princess Ligovskoy say to you about me?"

"You are quite sure that it was the old princess and not the young one?"

"I'm absolutely sure."

"Why?"

"Because the young princess asked about Grushnitsky."

"You've a great talent for putting two and two together. The young princess said she was sure that that young man in the soldier's coat had been degraded to the ranks for a duel."

"I hope you left her under this pleasant delusion."

"Naturally."

"We have the beginning of a plot!" I cried in delight. "The denouement of this comedy will be our concern. Fate is obviously taking care of my not being bored."

"I have a presentiment," said the doctor, "that poor Grushnitsky is going to be your victim. . . ."

"Go on with your story, Doctor."

"The old princess said that your face was familiar to her. I observed to her that no doubt she had met you in Petersburg, at some fashionable reception. I told her your name. The name was known to her. I believe your escapade caused a big sensation there. The old princess started to tell of your exploits, adding her own remarks to what was probably society gossip. Her daughter listened with curiosity. In her imagination, you became the hero of a novel in the latest fashion. I did not contradict the old lady, though I was aware she was talking nonsense."

"My worthy friend!" said I, extending my hand to him. The doctor shook it with feeling, and continued:

"If you wish, I'll introduce you. . . ."

"Mercy!" said I, raising my hands. "Does one introduce heroes? They never meet their beloved other than in the act of saving her from certain death."

"And so you really intend to flirt with the young princess?"

"On the contrary, quite on the contrary! Doctor, at last I triumph: you do not understand me! This, however, saddens me, doctor," I went on, after a moment of silence. "I never disclose my secrets myself, but I am awfully fond of having them divined, because that way I can always repudiate them if necessary. But come, you must describe to me the mamma and the daughter. What sort of people are they?"

"Well, in the first place, the mother is a woman of forty-five," answered Werner. "Her digestion is excellent, but there is something wrong with her blood; there are red blotches on her cheeks. She has spent the latter half of her life in Moscow, and there, in retirement, has grown fat. She likes risqué anecdotes and sometimes, when her daughter is not in the room, says improper things herself. She announced to me that her daughter was as innocent as a dove. What do I care? I was on the point of replying that she need not worry, I would not tell anybody. The mother is being treated for rheumatism, and what the daughter's complaint is, goodness knows. I told them both to drink two glasses of oxysulphuric water daily, and take a diluted bath twice a week. The old princess, it seems, is not used to command; she has great respect for the intelligence and the knowledge of her daughter, who has read Byron in English and knows algebra. It seems that in Moscow young ladies have taken to higher education, and, by Jove, it's a good thing! Our men, generally speaking, are so boorish that to coquet with them must be unbearable for any intelligent woman. The old princess is very fond of young men; the young princess looks at them with a certain contempt—a Moscow habit! In Moscow, all they enjoy is the company of forty-year-old wags."

"And you, Doctor, have you been in Moscow?"

"Yes, I had a fair amount of practice there."

"Go on with your story."

"Well, I seem to have told you everything . . . Oh yes! One more thing: the young princess seems fond of discussing sentiments, passions, and so forth. She spent one winter in Petersburg, and did not like it, especially the society there: probably she was given a cool reception."

"You saw no one at their house today?"

"On the contrary, there was one adjutant, one stiff-looking guardsman, and a lady who has recently arrived, a relative of the princess by marriage, a very pretty woman but a very sick one, it seems . . . Didn't you chance to meet her at the well? She's of medium height, a blonde, with regular features, her complexion is consumptive, and she has a little black mole on her right cheek. Her face struck me by its expressiveness."

"A little mole!" I muttered through my teeth. "Really?"

The doctor looked at me and said solemnly, placing his hand on my heart: "She is someone you know! . . ." My heart, indeed, was beating faster than usual.

"It is now your turn to triumph," I said, "but I rely on you; you will not betray me. I have not seen her yet, but I am sure that I recognize, from your depiction, a certain woman whom I loved in the old days. Don't tell her a word about me; should she ask, give a bad account of me."

"As you please!" said Werner with a shrug.

When he left, a dreadful sadness constrained my heart. Was it fate that was bringing us together again in the Caucasus, or had she come here on purpose, knowing she would meet me? And how would we meet? And, anyway, was it she? Presentiments never deceive me. There is no man in the world over whom the past gains such power as it does over me. Every reminder of a past sorrow or joy painfully strikes my soul and extracts from it the same old sounds. . . . I am stupidly made, I forget nothing . . . nothing!

After dinner, around six, I went out onto the boulevard: there was a crowd there; the princess sat with her daughter on a bench, surrounded by young men who vied in paying attention to them. I sat down on another bench some way off, stopped two officers of the D. regiment whom I knew, and began telling them something; apparently, it was amusing, because they began laughing like mad. Curiosity attracted to me some of those who surrounded the young princess; little by little, they all abandoned her and joined my group. I never ceased talking; my stories were clever to the point of stupidity, my raillery, directed at the freaks who passed by, was wicked to the point of frenzy. I went on entertaining my audience till sunset. Several times, the young princess and her mother passed by me, arm in arm, accompanied by a little old man with a limp; several times her glance, falling upon me, expressed vexation while striving to express indifference.

"What has he been telling you?" she inquired of one of the young men who had returned to her out of politeness. "Surely, a very entertaining story . . . his exploits in battles?" She said this rather loudly and probably with the intention of pin-pricking me. "Aha," I thought, "you are angry in earnest, my dear princess; just wait, there is more to come!"

Grushnitsky watched her like a beast of prey and never took his eyes off her: I bet that tomorrow he will beg somebody to introduce him to her mother. She will be very pleased, because she is bored.

his goals/ intentions are shrouded in mystery   *opague*

                                                                        May 16th

During the last two days, my affairs have advanced tremendously. The young princess definitely hates me: people have already reported to me two or three epigrams aimed at me, fairly caustic, but at the same time very flattering. She finds it awfully strange that I, who am used to high society and am on such intimate terms with her Petersburg female cousins and aunts, do not try to make her acquaintance. Every day, we run into each other at the well or on the boulevard; I do my best to lure away her admirers, brilliant adjutants, pallid Moscovites and others—and almost always, I succeed. I have always hated to entertain guests at my house. Now, my place is full every day; people dine, sup, play cards, and, alas, my champagne triumphs over the power of her magnetic young eyes!

Yesterday, I saw her in Chelahov's store: she was bargaining for a wonderful Persian rug. The young princess kept begging her mamma not to be stingy; that rug would be such an adornment for her dressing room! I offered forty roubles more and outbid her; for this I was rewarded by a glance in which glittered the most exquisite rage. About dinner time, I purposely ordered my Circassian horse to be covered with that rug and led past her windows. Werner was with them at the time, and told me that the effect of that scene was most dramatic. The young princess wants to preach a crusade against me: I have even noticed that already two adjutants in her presence greet me very dryly, although they dine at my house every day.

Grushnitsky has assumed a mysterious air: he walks with his hands behind his back and does not seem to recognize anybody; his leg has suddenly got well, he hardly limps at all. He has found the occasion to enter into conversation with the old princess and to pay a compliment to her daughter. The latter is apparently none too choosy, for since then she has been acknowledging his salute with the prettiest of smiles.

"You are sure you do not wish to make the acquaintance of the Ligovskoys?" he said to me yesterday.

"Quite sure."

"Oh come! Theirs is the pleasantest house at the spa! All the best society here. . . ."

"My friend, I am dreadfully sick of the best society which is not here. And you . . . do you go there?"

"Not yet. I have talked to the young princess a couple of times, and more. It is kind of embarrassing to fish for an invitation, you know, though it is done here. . . . It would have been another matter, if I wore epaulets. . . ."

"Oh come! You are much more intriguing this way! You simply don't know how to take advantage of your lucky situation. In the eyes of any sentimental young lady, your soldier's coat is bound to make a hero of you, a martyr."

Grushnitsky smiled smugly.

"What nonsense!" he said.

"I'm sure," I went on, "that the young princess is already in love with you."

He blushed to the ears, and puffed out his chest.

O vanity! you are the lever by means of which Archimedes wished to lift the earth!

"You always joke!" he said, feigning to be cross. "In the first place, she knows me so little as yet."

"Women love only those whom they do not know."

"But I have no pretension whatever to make her fond of me, I simply want to gain access to a pleasant house, and it would have been quite absurd if I had any hopes . . . Now you people, for example, are another matter; you St. Petersburg lady-killers, you have only to look . . . and women melt. . . . By the way, Pechorin, do you know what the young princess said about you?"

"Really? Has she already started to speak to you about me?"

"Wait—there is nothing to be glad about. The other day I entered into conversation with her at the well, by chance. Her third word was: 'Who is that gentleman with that unpleasant oppressive gaze? He was with you when . . .' She blushed and did not want to name the day, remembering her charming gesture. 'You don't have to mention the day,' I replied to her, 'it will always remain in my memory.' Pechorin, my friend! I do not congratulate you; you are on her black list. And this, indeed, is regrettable because my Mary is a very charming girl!"

It should be noted that Grushnitsky is one of those people who, when speaking of a woman whom they hardly know, call her *my Mary, my Sophie*, if she has had the fortune to catch their fancy.

I assumed a serious air and replied to him:

"Yes, she is not bad. . . . But beware, Grushnitsky! Russian young ladies, for the most part, nourish themselves on platonic love, without admixing to it any thought of marriage: now, platonic love is the most troublesome kind. The young princess seems to be one of those women who want to be amused: if she is bored in your presence for two minutes together, you are irretrievably lost. Your silence must excite her curiosity, your talk should never entirely satisfy it; you must disturb her every minute. She will disregard convention, publicly, a dozen times for your sake, and will call it a sacrifice, and, in order to reward herself for it, she will begin to torment you. and after that she will simply say that she cannot stand you. Unless you gain some ascendency over her, even her first kiss will not entitle you to a second: she will have her fill of flirting with you, and in two years or so she will marry a monster out of submissiveness to her mother, and will start persuading herself that she is miserable, that she loved only one man, meaning you, but that Heaven had not wished to unite her with him because he wore a soldier's coat, although under that thick gray coat there beat a passionate and noble heart. . . ."

Grushnitsky hit the table with his fist and started to pace up and down the room.

I inwardly roared with laughter, and even smiled once or twice, but fortunately he did not notice.

It is clear that he is in love, for he has become even more credulous than before: there even appeared on his finger, a nielloed, silver ring of local production. It looked suspicious to me. I began to examine it, and what would you think? . . . The name *Mary* was engraved in minuscule letters on the inside, and next to it was the day of the month when she picked up the famous glass. I concealed my discovery. I do not wish to force a confession from him, I want him to choose me for a confidant himself—and it is then that I shall enjoy myself! . . .

Today I rose late; when I reached the well, there was already nobody there. It was getting hot; furry white clouds were rapidly scudding from the snowy mountains with the promise of a thunderstorm; the top of Mount Mashuk smoked like an extinguished torch; around it there coiled and slithered, like snakes, gray shreds of cloud, which had been delayed in their surge and seemed to have caught in its thorny brush. The air was pervaded with electricity. I plunged into a viny avenue that led to a grotto; I was sad. I kept thinking of that young woman with the little birthmark on her cheek of whom the doctor had been talking. Why was she here? And was it she? And why did I think it was she? And why was I even so sure of it? Were there not many

women with little moles on their cheeks! Meditating in this fashion, I
came close to the grotto. As I looked in, I saw in the cool shade of its
vault, on a stone bench, a seated woman, wearing a straw hat, a black
shawl wrapped around her shoulders, her head sunken on her breast:
the hat screened her face. I was on the point of turning back, so as not
to disturb her revery, when she looked up at me.

"Vera!" I cried involuntarily.

She started and grew pale.

"I knew that you were here," she said.

I sat down near her and took her hand. A long-forgotten thrill ran
through my veins at the sound of that dear voice: she looked into my
eyes with her deep and calm eyes; they expressed distrust and something
akin to reproachfulness.

"We have not seen each other for a long time," I said.

"Yes, a long time, and we have both changed in many ways!"

"So this means that you do not love me any more? . . ."

"I am married! . . ." she said.

"Again? Several years ago, however, the same reason existed, and
yet . . ."

She snatched her hand out of mine. And her cheeks flamed.

"Perhaps you love your second husband. . . ."

She did not answer and turned away.

"Or is he very jealous?"

Silence.

"Well? He is young, handsome, he is, in particular, rich, no doubt,
and you are afraid . . ." I glanced at her and was shocked: her face
expressed profound despair, tears sparkled in her eyes.

"Tell me," she whispered at last, "do you find it very amusing to
torture me? I ought to hate you. Ever since we have known each other,
you gave me nothing but sufferings. . . ." Her voice trembled; she
leaned toward me to lay her head on my breast.

"Perhaps," I thought, "this is exactly why you loved me: one
forgets joys, one never forgets sorrows. . . ."

I embraced her warmly, and thus we remained for a long time. At
last our lips came close together and merged in an ardent rapturous
kiss; her hands were as cold as ice, her brow was burning. Between
us, started one of those conversations which have no sense on paper,
which cannot be repeated and which one cannot even retain in one's
mind: the meaning of sounds replaces and enhances the meaning of
words, as in the Italian opera.

She definitely does not wish that I meet her husband, that little
old gentleman with the limp whom I glimpsed on the boulevard: she

married him for the sake of her son. He is rich and suffers from rheumatism. I did not allow myself a single jibe at him: she respects him as a father—and will deceive him as a husband. What a bizarre thing, the human heart in general, and a woman's heart in particular!

Vera's husband, Semyon Vasilyevich G——v, is a distant relation of Princess Ligovskoy. He lives near her: Vera often visits the old princess. I gave her my word that I would get acquainted with the Ligovskoys and court the young princess in order to divert attention from Vera. In this way, my plans have not been upset in the least, and I shall have a merry time. . . .

Merry time! Yes, I have already passed that stage of the soul's life when one seeks only happiness, when the heart feels the need to love someone strongly and passionately. At present, all I wish is to be loved, and that by very few: it even seems to me that I would be content with one permanent attachment, a pitiful habit of the heart!

One thing has always struck me as strange: I never became the slave of the women I loved; on the contrary, I have always gained unconquerable power over their will and heart, with no effort at all. Why is it so? Is it because I never treasured anything too much, while they incessantly feared to let me slip out of their hands? Or is it the magnetic influence of a strong organism? Or did I simply never succeed in encountering a woman with a stubborn will of her own?

I must admit that, indeed, I never cared for women with wills of their own; it is not their department.

True, I remember now—once, only once did I love a strong-willed woman, whom I could never conquer. We parted enemies—but even so, perhaps, had our meeting occurred five years later, we would have parted differently.

Vera is ill, very ill, although she will not admit it: I fear she may have consumption, or that disease which is called *fièvre lente*, a completely non-Russian disease, for which there is no name in our language.

The thunderstorm caught us in the grotto and detained us there for an extra half hour. She did not make me swear that I would be true to her, did not ask if I had loved other women since we had parted. She entrusted herself to me again with the same unconcern as before —and I will not deceive her. She is the only woman on earth whom I could not bear to deceive. I know that we shall soon part again— perhaps, forever; that each of us will go his separate way, graveward. But her memory will remain inviolable in my soul: I have always repeated this to her, and she believes me, although she says she does not.

At last, we separated: for a long time, I followed her with my gaze until her hat disappeared behind the shrubs and cliffs. My heart pain-

So he's using Vera in a way already

fully contracted as after the first parting. Oh, how that feeling gladdened me! Could it be that youth with its beneficial storms wants to return to me again, or is it merely its farewell glance—a last gift to its memory? And yet it's absurd to think that in appearance I am still a boy: my face is pale but still fresh-complexioned, my limbs are supple and svelte, my thick hair curls, my eyes sparkle, my blood is ebullient.

When I returned home, I got on my horse and galloped out into the steppe. I love to gallop on a spirited horse through tall grass, against the wind of the wilderness; avidly do I swallow the redolent air and direct my gaze into the blue remoteness, trying to distinguish the nebulous outlines of objects that become, every minute, clearer and clearer. Whatever sorrow may burden my heart, whatever anxiety may oppress my mind, everything is dispersed in a moment: the soul feels easy, bodily fatigue vanquishes mental worry. There is no feminine gaze that I would not forget at the sight of mountains covered with curly vegetation, and illuminated by the southern sun, at the sight of the blue sky, or at the sound of a torrent that falls from crag to crag.

I think that the Cossacks yawning on the top of their watchtowers, upon seeing me galloping without need or goal, were for a long time tormented by this riddle, for I am sure they must have taken me for a Circassian because of my dress. Indeed, I have been told that when riding in Circassian garb, I look more like a Kabardan than many a Kabardan. And, in point of fact, as regards that noble battle garb, I am an absolute dandy: not one bit of superfluous braid; costly arms in plain setting; the fur of the cap neither too long nor too short; leggings and boots fitted with the utmost exactitude; a white *beshmet*; a dark-brown *cherkeska*. I have studied, for a long time, the mountain peoples' style of riding: there is no better way of flattering my vanity than to acknowledge my skill in riding a horse in the Caucasian fashion. I keep four horses: one for myself, three for pals, so as not to feel dull while ranging the fields alone: they take my horses with alacrity, and never ride with me. It was already six in the evening, when I remembered that it was time to dine. My horse was worn out; I came out onto the road which led from Pyatigorsk to the German settlement where the spa society frequently went for picnics. The road ran winding among bushes, and descending into small ravines where noisy creeks flowed under the shelter of tall grasses; all around rose an amphitheater of blue masses—Besh Tau, Snake Mountain, Iron Mountain and Bald Mountain. Upon descending into one of these ravines, called *balkas* in the local dialect, I stopped to water my horse. At that moment, there appeared on the road a noisy and resplendent cavalcade, the ladies in black or light-blue riding habits, and the gentlemen in costumes rep-

he thinks a lot about him
What others think about him

resenting a mixture of Circassian and Nizhni-Novgorodan: Grushnitsky rode in front with Princess Mary.

Ladies at Caucasian spas still believe in the possibility of Circassian attacks in broad daylight: presumably, this is why Grushnitsky had hung a sword and a brace of pistols onto his soldier's coat. He was rather absurd in this heroic attire. A tall shrub hid me from them, but through its foliage I could see everything and could guess from the expressions on their faces that the conversation was sentimental. Finally, they drew close to the declivity; Grushnitsky took the princess's horse by the bridle, and then I heard the end of their conversation:

"And you wish to remain for the rest of your life in the Caucasus?" the princess was saying.

"What is Russia to me?" answered her companion, "a country where thousands of people will look on me with contempt because they are richer than I am—whereas here—here this thick soldier's coat has not prevented me from making your acquaintance. . . ."

"On the contrary . . ." said the princess, blushing.

Grushnitsky's face portrayed pleasure. He went on:

"My life here will flow by noisily, unnoticeably, and rapidly under the bullets of the savages, and if God would send me, every year, one radiant feminine glance, one glance similar to the one . . ."

At this point they came level with me; I struck my horse with my riding crop and rode out from behind the bush. . . .

"*Mon Dieu, un Circassien!* . . ." cried the princess in terror.

In order to dissuade her completely, I answered in French, bowing slightly:

"*Ne craignez rien, madame—je ne suis pas plus dangereux que votre cavalier.*"*

She was embarrassed—but why? Because of her mistake, or because my answer seemed insolent to her? I would have liked my second supposition to be the correct one. Grushnitsky cast a look of displeasure at me.

Late this evening, that is to say around eleven, I went for a stroll in the linden avenue of the boulevard. The town was asleep: only in some windows lights could be glimpsed. On three sides, there loomed the black crest of cliffs, offshoots of Mount Mashuk, on the summit of which an ominous little cloud was lying. The moon was rising in the east; afar glittered the silvery rim of snow-covered mountains. The cries of the sentries alternated with the sound of the hot springs, which had been given free flow for the night. At times, the sonorous stamp

---

* "Do not be afraid, madame; I am not more dangerous than your cavalier."

of a horse was heard in the street, accompanied by the creaking of a
Nogay wagon and a mournful Tatar song. I sat down on a bench and
became lost in thought. I felt the need of pouring out my thoughts in
friendly talk—but with whom? What was Vera doing now, I wondered.
I would have paid dearly to press her hand at that moment.

Suddenly I heard quick irregular steps—Grushnitsky, no doubt.
So it was!

"Where do you come from?"

"From Princess Ligovskoy," he said very importantly. "How Mary
can sing!"

"Do you know what?" I said to him, "I bet she does not know
that you are a cadet; she thinks you have been degraded to the ranks."

"Perhaps! What do I care?" he said absently.

"Oh, I just happened to mention it."

"Do you know, you made her dreadfully angry today? She found
it an unheard-of insolence. I had a lot of trouble convincing her that
you are too well brought up and that you know the *grand monde* too
well to have had any intention of insulting her: she says that you have
an impudent gaze and that, no doubt, you have the highest opinion of
yourself."

"She is not mistaken. . . . Perhaps you would like to stand up for
her?"

"I regret that I do not have that right yet. . . ."

"Oh, oh!" I thought, "I see he already has hopes."

"Well, so much the worse for you," Grushnitsky continued, "it
would be difficult for you to make their acquaintance now; and that's
a pity! It is one of the most pleasant houses that I know of."

I smiled inwardly.

"The most pleasant house for me is now my own," I said yawning,
and got up to go.

"But first confess, you repent?"

"What nonsense! If I choose, I shall be at the old princess's house
tomorrow evening. . . ."

"We shall see. . . ."

"And even, to oblige you, I shall flirt with the young princess. . . ."

"Yes, if she is willing to speak to you. . . ."

"I shall only wait for the moment when your conversation begins
to bore her. . . . Good-bye."

"And I shall go roaming; I could never fall asleep now. . . . Look,
let's better go to the restaurant, there is gambling there. . . . Tonight
I require strong sensations. . . ."

"I wish you bad luck."
I went home.

May 21st

Almost a week has passed, and I still have not made the acquaintance of the Ligovskoys. I am waiting for a convenient occasion. Grushnitsky, like a shadow, follows the young princess everywhere; their conversations are endless: when will he begin to bore her at last? Her mother does not pay any attention to this because he is not an "eligible" young man. That's the logic of mothers for you! I have observed two or three tender glances—an end must be put to it.

Yesterday, Vera appeared for the first time at the well. Since our meeting in the grotto, she has not been out of the house. We dipped our glasses simultaneously and, bending, she said to me in a whisper:

"You don't want to get acquainted with the Ligovskoys? It's the only place where we could see each other."

A reproach! How dull! But I have deserved it. . . .

Apropos, tomorrow there is a subscription dance in the ballroom of the restaurant, and I am going to dance the mazurka with the young princess.

May 22nd

The restaurant's ballroom was transformed into that of the Club of the Nobility. By nine o'clock, everybody had arrived. The old princess and her daughter were among the last to appear: many ladies looked at her with envy and ill will because Princess Mary dresses with taste. Those ladies who regard themselves as the aristocrats of the place concealed their envy and attached themselves to her. What can you do? Where there is feminine society, there will appear at once a higher and a lower circle. Outside the window, in a crowd of people, stood Grushnitsky, pressing his face to the windowpane and never taking his eyes off his goddess: as she passed by, she gave him a hardly perceptible nod. He beamed like the sun. The dancing began with a polonaise; then the band began to play a waltz. Spurs tinkled, coat tails flew up and whirled.

I stood behind a stout lady: her head was crowned with pink plumes; the luxuriance of her dress recalled the times of farthingales, and the variegation of her rough skin, the happy era of black taffeta patches. The largest wart on her neck was concealed by the clasp of a necklace. She was saying to her dancing partner, a captain of dragoons:

"That young Princess Ligovskoy is an intolerable little thing! Fancy, she bumped into me and never apologized, but in addition turned around and looked at me through her lorgnette. . . . *C'est impayable!* . . . And what is she so proud of? She ought to be taught a lesson. . . ."

"No trouble in getting that done," answered the obliging captain, and went into the next room.

I immediately went up to the young princess and engaged her for the waltz, taking advantage of the easy local customs which allow one to dance with ladies to whom one has not been introduced.

She could hardly force herself not to smile and not to hide her triumph: she managed, however, rather soon to assume a completely indifferent and even severe air. She nonchalantly dropped her hand on my shoulder, slightly inclined her pretty head to one side—and off we went. I do not know a waist more voluptuous and supple! Her fresh breath touched my face; sometimes a curl that had become separated in the whirl of the waltz from its fellows, would brush my burning cheek. I made three turns (she waltzes amazingly well). She was out of breath, her eyes were dim, her half-opened lips could hardly murmur the obligatory "Merci, monsieur."

After several moments of silence, I said to her, assuming a most submissive air:

"I hear, Princess, that despite my being completely unknown to you, I have already had the misfortune to earn your displeasure . . . that you've found me insolent. . . . Can this be true?"

"And now you would like to confirm me in this opinion?" she replied with an ironic little grimace, which incidentally was very becoming to her mobile features.

"If I had the insolence to offend you in any way, then allow me to have the still greater insolence to beg your pardon. And truly, I would wish very much to prove to you that you are mistaken about me."

"You will find this rather difficult."

"Why so?"

"Because you do not come to our house, and these balls will probably not take place very often."

"This means," I thought, "that their door is closed to me forever."

"Do you know, Princess," I said with some vexation, "one should never turn down a repentant criminal: out of sheer despair he may become twice as criminal as before, and then . . ."

Laughter and whispering among the people around us made me

turn and interrupt my sentence. A few steps away from me stood a group of men, and among them was the captain of dragoons who had declared hostile intentions against the charming young princess. He was particularly satisfied with something; he rubbed his hands, he laughed and exchanged winks with his companions. Suddenly out of their midst emerged a person in a dresscoat, with a long mustache and a florid face, and he directed his unsteady steps straight toward the young princess: he was drunk. Having come to a stop in front of the disconcerted princess, and clasping his hands behind his back, he fixed her with his bleary, gray eyes and uttered in a hoarse, treble voice:

"Permetay . . . oh, what's the use of that! . . . I simply engage you for the mazurka. . . ."

"What do you want?" she uttered in a trembling voice, as she cast around her an imploring glance. Alas! her mother was far away, and in her vicinity she could see none of the gentlemen she knew. One adjutant, I think, witnessed it all, but hid behind the crowd so as not to be involved in a row.

"Well?" said the drunk, winking at the captain of dragoons, who was encouraging him with signs, "don't you want to? Here I am again requesting the honor of engaging you *pour mazurque*. . . . You think, perhaps, that I am drunk? That does not matter! One is much freer that way, I can assure you."

I saw that she was about to swoon from fear and indignation.

I went up to the drunk, took him rather firmly by the arm and looking steadily into his eyes, asked him to go away, because, I added, the princess had long ago promised to dance the mazurka with me.

"Well, nothing to be done! . . . Some other time!" he said with a laugh, and went off to join his abashed companions, who immediately led him away into the other room.

I was rewarded by a deep, wonderful glance.

The princess went up to her mother and told her everything: the latter sought me out in the crowd and thanked me. She informed me that she used to know my mother and was on friendly terms with half a dozen of my aunts.

"I do not know how it happened that we have not met before now," she added, "but you must admit that you alone are to blame for this; you shun everybody: I have never seen anything like it. I hope that the atmosphere of my drawing room will dissipate your spleen. . . . Am I right?"

I said to her one of those phrases which everyone should have in store for such occasions.

The quadrilles dragged on for a terribly long time.

At last, the mazurka resounded from the upper balcony. The young princess and I seated ourselves.

Never once did I allude either to the tipsy man, or to my former behavior, or to Grushnitsky. The impression that the unpleasant scene had made upon her gradually dissipated. Her pretty face bloomed, she joked very charmingly, her conversation was witty, without any pretention to wit, it was lively and free; her observations were sometimes profound. I gave her to understand, by means of a very involved sentence, that I had long been attracted to her. She inclined her young head and colored slightly.

"You're a bizarre person!" she presently said, raising upon me her velvety eyes and laughing in a constrained way.

"I did not wish to make your acquaintance," I continued, "because you were surrounded by too dense a crowd of admirers, and I was afraid of getting completely lost in it."

"Your fears were unfounded: all of them are most dull. . . ."

"All! Are you sure you mean all?"

She looked at me intently, as if trying to recall something, then she slightly blushed again, and finally uttered resolutely: *"All!"*

"Including even my friend Grushnitsky?"

"Why, is he your friend?" she said, revealing some doubt.

"Yes."

"He does not enter, of course, into the category of dull people."

"Rather the category of unfortunate ones," I said laughing.

"Of course! You find it funny? I wish you were in his place."

"Well, I used to be a cadet myself and indeed it was the very best time of my life!"

"But is he a cadet? . . ." she said quickly, and then added: "I thought that . . ."

"What is it you thought?"

"Nothing! . . . Who is that lady?"

Here the conversation took another direction, and did not return to that subject any more.

The mazurka came to an end, and we parted—until our next meeting. The ladies left. I went to have supper and ran into Werner.

"Aha!" he said, "so that's the way you are! Didn't you intend not to make the princess's acquaintance in any other way than by saving her from certain death?"

"I did better," I answered him, "I saved her from fainting at a ball. . . ."

"How's that? Tell me. . . ."

"No, try and guess—you, who can guess all things in the world!"

Around seven tonight, I was out strolling on the boulevard. Grush-nitsky, on seeing me in the distance, came up to me: a kind of absurd exaltation shone in his eyes. He gripped my hand and said in a tragic voice:

"I thank you, Pechorin. . . . You understand me?"

"No; but whatever it is, it is not worth gratitude," I answered, having indeed no charitable action on my conscience.

"But what about last night? You can't have forgotten? . . . Mary told me everything. . . ."

"Do you two have everything in common now? Even gratitude?"

"Look," said Grushnitsky very importantly, "please do not make fun of my love, if you wish to remain my pal. . . . You see, I love her to distraction. And I think, I hope, that she loves me too. . . . I have a favor to ask of you. You are going to visit them tonight: promise me to observe everything. I know you are experienced in these matters, you know women better than I do. . . . Women! Women! Who will understand them? Their smiles contradict their glances, their words promise and lure, while the sound of their voices drives us away. One minute they comprehend and divine our most secret thought, and the next, they do not understand the clearest hints. Take the young princess, for instance, yesterday her eyes blazed with passion when they rested upon me, today they are dull and cold. . . ."

"This, perhaps, is due to the effect of the waters," I answered.

"You see in everything the nasty side . . . you materialist," he added contemptuously. "Let us switch, however, to another matter." And pleased with this poor pun, he cheered up.

Around half past eight, we went together to the princess's house.

Walking past Vera's windows, I saw her at the window. We threw each other a fleeting glance. She entered the Ligovskoys' drawing room soon after us. The old princess introduced me to her as to a relation of hers. Tea was being served; there were many visitors; the conversation was general. I endeavored to ingratiate myself with the old princess; I jested, I made her laugh heartily several times: the young princess also wanted to laugh more than once, but she restrained herself so as not to depart from the role she had assumed. She finds that a languorous air suits her, and perhaps she does not err. Grushnitsky was apparently very glad that my gaiety did not infect her.

After tea, we all went into the music room.

"Are you pleased with my obedience, Vera?" I said as I passed her.

She threw me a glance full of love and gratitude. I am now used to those glances, but there was a time when they made my bliss. The old princess had her daughter sit down at the piano: everyone was asking her to sing something. I kept silent and, taking advantage of the hubbub, I drew away toward a window with Vera, who wanted to tell me something very important for both of us. It turned out to be nonsense. *throwaway comments, diminutive*

Meanwhile, my indifference was annoying to the young princess, as I could conjecture by a single angry, blazing glance. . . . Oh, I understand wonderfully that kind of conversation, mute but expressive, brief but forcible! . . .

She started to sing: her voice is not bad, but she sings poorly. I did not listen, however. In compensation, Grushnitsky, with his elbows on the piano, facing her, devoured her with his eyes and every minute kept saying under his breath: *"Charmant! Délicieux!"*

"Listen," Vera was saying to me, "I do not want you to meet my husband, but you must, without fail, please the old princess. It is easy for you; you can achieve anything you want. We shall see each other only here. . . ."

"Only here? . . ."

She colored and went on: "You know that I am your slave; I never was able to resist you . . . and for this I shall be punished. You will cease to love me. I wish, at least, to save my reputation . . . not for my own sake: you know that very well! Oh, I beseech you, do not torment me as before with empty doubts and feigned coldness. I shall die soon, perhaps. I feel myself getting weaker every day . . . and, in spite of that, I cannot think of a future life, I think only of you. . . . You men do not understand the delights of a glance, of a handshake . . . while I, I swear to you, I, when listening to your voice, I experience such deep, strange bliss that the most ardent kisses could not replace it.

Meanwhile Princess Mary had stopped singing. A murmur of praise sounded around her. I went up to her after all the other guests and said something to her about her voice, rather casually.

She made a grimace, protruding her lower lip, and curtsied in a very mocking manner.

"It is all the more flattering to me," she said, "since you did not listen to me at all; but then, perhaps, you do not like music?"

"On the contrary . . . particularly after dinner."

"Grushnitsky is right in saying that you have most prosaic tastes. . . . And I see that you like music in a gastronomic way."

"You are wrong again. I am far from being a gourmet: my digestion is exceedingly bad. But music after dinner puts one to sleep, and sleep after dinner is good for one's health. Consequently, I like music from a medical point of view. In the evening, on the contrary, it irritates my nerves too much; my mood becomes either too melancholy, or too gay. Both are exhausting, when there is no positive cause to be sad or to be joyful, and, moreover, melancholy at a social gathering is absurd, while immoderate gaiety is improper. . . ."

She did not hear me out, moved away, sat down next to Grushnitsky, and there started between them some kind of sentimental conversation. The young princess, it seemed, replied rather absently and irrelevantly to his wise pronouncements, though she tried to show that she listened to him with attention, for now and then he would glance at her with surprise, trying to guess the reason for the inward agitation that expressed itself now and then in her restless glance.

But I have found you out, my dear princess. Beware! You want to repay me in my own coin, to prick my vanity—you will not succeed. And if you declare war on me, I shall be merciless.

In the course of the evening, I tried several times, on purpose, to join their conversation, but she countered my remarks rather dryly, and, with feigned annoyance, I finally moved away. The young princess triumphed; Grushnitsky, likewise. Have your triumph, my friends, hurry—you won't triumph long! What is to be done? I have a presentiment. . . . Whenever I become acquainted with a woman, I always guess without fail, whether she will fall in love with me or not.

I spent the rest of the evening at Vera's side and talked of old times to my heart's content. What does she love me for so much—I really don't know; particularly since she is the only woman who has completely understood me with all my petty weaknesses and wicked passions. Can evil possibly be so attractive?

Grushnitsky and I left together: when we got outside, he put his arm through mine and said after a long silence:

"Well, what do you think?"

"That you are a fool," I wanted to answer, but restrained myself, and merely shrugged my shoulders.

May 29th

During all these days, I never once departed from my system. The young princess begins to like my conversation. I told her some of the strange occurrences in my life, and she begins to see in me an extraordinary person. I laugh at everything in the world, especially at feelings:

this is beginning to frighten her. In my presence she does not dare to launch upon sentimental debates with Grushnitsky, and has several times already replied to his sallies with a mocking smile; but every time that Grushnitsky comes up to her, I assume a humble air and leave them alone together. The first time she was glad of it or tried to make it seem so; the second time she became cross with me; the third time she became cross with Grushnitsky.

"You have very little vanity!" she said to me yesterday. "Why do you think that I have more fun with Grushnitsky?"

I answered that I was sacrificing to a pal's happiness, my own pleasure.

"And mine," she added.

I looked at her intently and assumed a serious air. After this, I did not say another word to her all day. In the evening, she was pensive; this morning, at the well, she was more pensive still. When I went up to her, she was absently listening to Grushnitsky, who, it seems, was being rhapsodical about nature; but as soon as she saw me, she began to laugh (very much *mal à propos*), pretending not to notice me. I walked off some distance and stealthily watched her: she turned away from her interlocutor and yawned twice. Decidedly, Grushnitsky has begun to bore her. I shall not speak to her for two more days.

insane levels of manipulation

June 3rd

I often wonder, why I do so stubbornly try to gain the love of a little maiden whom I do not wish to seduce, and whom I shall never marry? Why this feminine coquetry? Vera loves me more than Princess Mary will ever love anyone: if she had seemed to me to be an unconquerable belle, then perhaps I might have been fascinated by the difficulty of the enterprise.

But it is nothing of the sort! Consequently, this is not that restless need for love that torments us in the first years of youth, and drives us from one woman to another, until we find one who cannot abide us: and here begins our constancy—that true, infinite passion, which can be mathematically expressed by means of a line falling from a given point into space: the secret of that infinity lies solely in the impossibility of reaching a goal, that is to say, reaching the end.

Why then do I take all this trouble? Because I envy Grushnitsky? Poor thing! He has not earned it at all. Or is it the outcome of that nasty but unconquerable feeling which urges us to destroy the sweet delusions of a fellow man, in order to have the petty satisfaction of saying to him, when he asks in despair, what is it he should believe:

"My friend, the same thing happened to me, and still, you see, I dine, I sup, I sleep in perfect peace, and hope to be able to die without cries and tears."

And then again . . . there is boundless delight in the possession of a young, barely unfolded soul! It is like a flower whose best fragrance emanates to meet the first ray of the sun. It should be plucked that very minute and after inhaling one's fill of it, one should throw it away on the road: perchance, someone will pick it up! I feel in myself this insatiable avidity, which engulfs everything met on the way. I look upon the sufferings and joys of others only in relation to myself as on the food sustaining the strength of my soul. I am no longer capable myself of frenzy under the influence of passion: ambition with me has been suppressed by circumstances, but it has manifested itself in another form, since ambition is nothing else than thirst for power, and my main pleasure—which is to subjugate to my will all that surrounds me, and to excite the emotions of love, devotion, and fear in relation to me— is it not the main sign and greatest triumph of power? To be to some-body the cause of sufferings and joys, without having any positive right to it—is this not the sweetest possible nourishment for our pride? And what is happiness? Sated pride. If I considered myself to be better and more powerful than anyone in the world, I would be happy; if every-body loved me, I would find in myself infinite sources of love. Evil begets evil: the first ache gives us an idea of the pleasure of tormenting another. The idea of evil cannot enter a person's head without his wanting to apply it to reality: ideas are organic creations. Someone has said that their very birth endows them with a form, and this form is action; he in whose head more ideas have been born is more active than others. This is why a genius chained to an office desk must die or go mad, exactly as a powerfully built man, whose life is sedentary and whose behavior is virtuous, dies of apoplexy.

The passions are nothing else but ideas in their first phase of development; they are an attribute of the youth of the heart; and he is a fool who thinks he will be agitated by them all his life. Many a calm river begins as a turbulent waterfall, yet none hurtles and foams all the way to the sea. But that calm is often the sign of great, though concealed, strength; the plenitude and depth of feelings and thoughts does not tolerate frantic surgings; the soul, while experiencing pain or pleasure, gives itself a strict account of everything and becomes con-vinced that so it must be; it knows that without storms, a constantly torrid sun will wither it; it becomes penetrated with its own life, it fondles and punishes itself, as if it were a beloved child. Only in this supreme state of self-knowledge can a man evaluate divine justice.

On re-reading this page, I notice that I have strayed far from my subject . . . But what does it matter? . . . I write this journal for myself and, consequently, anything that I may toss into it will become, in time, for me, a precious memory. *oh so its a journal*

↳ interesting

Grushnitsky came and threw himself on my neck: he had been promoted to an officer's rank. We had some champagne. Dr. Werner dropped in soon after him.

"I do not congratulate you," he said to Grushnitsky.

"Why?"

"Because a soldier's coat is very becoming to you, and you must admit that an infantry army officer's uniform, made in this watering place, will not give you any glamor. You see, up to now you were an exception, while now you will come under the general rule."

"Talk on, talk on, Doctor! You will not prevent me from being delighted. He does not know," added Grushnitsky, whispering into my ear: "what hopes these epaulets give me. . . . Ah . . . epaulets, epaulets! Your little stars are guiding stars. No! I'm entirely happy now."

"Are you coming with us for that walk to The Hollow?" I asked him.

"I? For nothing in the world shall I show myself to the young princess till my uniform is ready."

"Do you wish me to announce the glad news to her?"

"No, please do not tell her. . . . I want to surprise her. . . ."

"By the way, tell me, how are you getting on with her?"

He lost countenance and grew pensive: he wanted to boast and lie, but he was ashamed to do so, and yet it would have been mortifying to admit the truth.

"What do you think, does she love you?"

"Love me? Come, Pechorin, what notions you do have! . . . How could this happen so fast? . . . Even if she does love one, a decent woman would not tell. . . ."

"Fine! And probably, according to you, a decent man should also keep silent about his passion?"

"Ah, my good fellow! There is a way of doing things; there is much that is not said, but guessed. . . ."

"That's true. . . . However, the love that is read in the eyes does not bind a woman to anything, whereas words . . . Take care, Grushnitsky, she is fooling you."

"She? . . ." he answered, raising his eyes to Heaven and smiling complacently: "I pity you, Pechorin!"

He left.

In the evening, a numerous party set out on foot for The Hollow.

In the opinion of local scientists, that "hollow" is nothing else than an extinguished crater: it is situated on a slope of Mount Mashuk, less than a mile from town. To it leads a narrow trail, among bushes and cliffs. As we went up the mountain, I offered the young princess my arm, and she never abandoned it during the entire walk.

Our conversation began with gossip: I passed in review our acquaintances, both present and absent: first, I brought out their comic traits, and then their evil ones. My bile began to stir. I started in jest and finished in frank waspishness. At first it amused her, then frightened her.

"You are a dangerous man!" she said to me. "I would sooner find myself in a wood under a murderer's knife than be the victim of your sharp tongue. . . . I ask you seriously, when it occurs to you to talk badly about me, better take a knife and cut my throat: I don't think you will find it very difficult."

"Do I look like a murderer?"

"You are worse. . . ."

I thought a moment, and then said, assuming a deeply touched air:

"Yes, such was my lot since my very childhood! Everybody read in my face the signs of bad inclinations which were not there, but they were supposed to be there—and so they came into existence. I was modest—they accused me of being crafty: I became secretive. I felt deeply good and evil—nobody caressed me, everybody offended me: I became rancorous. I was gloomy—other children were merry and talkative. I felt myself superior to them—but was considered inferior: I became envious. I was ready to love the whole world—none understood me: and I learned to hate. My colorless youth was spent in a struggle with myself and with the world. Fearing mockery, I buried my best feelings at the bottom of my heart: there they died. I spoke the truth —I was not believed: I began to deceive. When I got to know well the fashionable world and the mechanism of society, I became skilled in the science of life, and saw how others were happy without that skill, enjoying, at no cost to themselves, all those advantages which I so indefatigably pursued. And then in my breast despair was born—not that despair which is cured with the pistol's muzzle, but cold, helpless despair, concealed under amiability and a good-natured smile. I became a moral cripple. One half of my soul did not exist; it had withered away, it had evaporated, it had died. I cut it off and threw it away— while the other half stirred and lived, at the service of everybody. And this nobody noticed, because nobody knew that its dead half had ever existed; but now you have aroused its memory in me, and I have read to you its epitaph. To many people, all epitaphs, in general, seem ridiculous, but not so to me; especially when I recall what lies beneath them. However, I do not ask you to share my views; if my outburst seems to you ridiculous, please, laugh: I warn you, that it will not distress me in any way."

At that moment, I met her eyes: tears danced in them; her arm, leaning on mine, trembled, her cheeks glowed; she was sorry for me! Compassion—an emotion to which all women so easily submit—had sunk its claws into her inexperienced heart. During the whole walk she was absent-minded, did not coquet with anyone—and that is a great sign!

We reached The Hollow: the ladies left their escorts, but she did not abandon my arm. The witticisms of the local dandies did not amuse her; the steepness of the precipice near which she stood did not frighten her, while the other young ladies squealed and closed their eyes.

On the way back, I did not renew our melancholy conversation, but to my trivial questions and jokes she replied briefly and absently.

"Have you ever loved?" I asked her at last.

She glanced at me intently, shook her head and again became lost in thought: it was evident that she wanted to say something, but she did not know how to begin. Her breast heaved. . . . What would you—a muslin sleeve is little protection, and an electric spark ran from my wrist to hers. Almost all passions start thus; and we often deceive ourselves greatly in thinking that a woman loves us for our physical or moral qualities. Of course, they prepare and incline their hearts for the reception of the sacred fire: nonetheless, it is the first contact that decides the matter.

"Don't you think I was very amiable today?" said the young princess to me, with a forced smile when we returned from the excursion.

We parted.

She is displeased with herself; she accuses herself of having treated me coldly . . . Oh, this is the first, the main triumph!

Tomorrow she will want to recompense me. I know it all by heart—that is what is so boring.

Today, I saw Vera. She has exhausted me with her jealousy. The young princess, it seems, took it into her head to confide the secrets of the heart to Vera: not a very fortunate choice, one must admit!

"I can guess to what it all tends," Vera kept saying to me. "Better tell me now, plainly, that you love her."

"But if I don't?"

"Then why pursue her, disturb her, excite her imagination? Oh, I know you well! Listen, if you want me to believe you, then come next week to Kislovodsk: we are going there after tomorrow. The Ligovskoys remain here for a little while longer. Rent an apartment nearby. We shall be living in the big house near the spring, on the mezzanine floor, Princess Ligovskoy will be on the first floor, and next door, there is a house belonging to the same proprietor, which is not yet occupied. . . . Will you come?"

I promised, and on the same day sent a messenger to rent those lodgings.

Grushnitsky came to see me at six in the evening, and announced that his uniform would be ready on the morrow, just in time for the ball.

"At last I shall dance with her the whole evening. . . . What a chance to talk!" he added.

"When is that ball?"

"Why, tomorrow! Didn't you know? A big festival. And the local authorities have undertaken to arrange it. . . ."

"Let's go for a walk on the boulevard."

"Not for anything, in this horrid coat. . . ."

"What, have you ceased liking it?"

I went alone and, upon meeting Princess Mary, asked her to dance the mazurka with me. She seemed surprised and pleased.

"I thought you danced only out of necessity, as last time," she said, smiling very prettily.

It seems she does not notice at all Grushnitsky's absence.

"Tomorrow you will be agreeably surprised," I said to her.

"What will that be?"

"It's a secret. . . . You will discover it for yourself at the ball."

I finished the evening at the old princess's: there were no visitors except Vera and a very entertaining old gentleman. I was in high spirits, I improvised all kinds of extraordinary stories: the young princess sat opposite me and listened to my tosh with such deep, tense, even tender attention that I felt ashamed of myself. What had become of her vi-

finally

vacity, her coquetry, her whims, her arrogant mien, scornful smile, abstracted gaze?

Vera noticed it all: deep melancholy expressed itself on her sickly face: she sat in shadow, near the window, sunk in an ample armchair. . . . I felt sorry for her.

Then I related the whole dramatic story of our acquaintanceship, of our love—naturally, concealing it under invented names.

So vividly did I picture my tenderness, my anxiety, my transports, in such an advantageous light did I present her actions, her character, that, willy-nilly, she had to forgive me my flirtation with the princess.

She got up, came over to us, became animated . . . and only at two in the morning did we remember that the doctor's order was to go to bed at eleven.

June 5th

Half an hour before the ball, Grushnitsky appeared before me in the full splendor of an infantry army officer's uniform. To the third button, he had attached a bronze chainlet from which hung a double lorgnette; epaulets of incredible size were turned upward like the wings of a cupid; his boots squeaked; in his left hand, he held a pair of brown kid gloves and his cap, and with his right he kept fluffing up, every moment, his shock of hair, which was waved in small curls. Self-satisfaction and, at the same time, a certain lack of assurance were expressed in his countenance: his festive exterior, his proud gait, would have made me burst out laughing, had that been in accordance with my plans.

He threw his cap and gloves onto the table and began to pull down the skirts of his coat and to preen himself before the mirror: a huge black neckcloth that was wound over a tremendously high stiffener, the bristles of which propped up his chin, showed half an inch above his collar. He thought this was not enough: he pulled it up, till it reached his ears. This laborious task—for the collar of his uniform was very tight and uncomfortable—caused the blood to rush to his face.

"I'm told you have been flirting terribly with my princess these days?" he said rather casually, and without looking at me.

"It's not for us, oafs, to drink tea!" I answered him, repeating the favorite saying of one of the most dashing rakes of the past, of whom Pushkin once sang.

"Tell me, how does the coat fit me? Oh, that confounded Jew! . . . How it cuts me under the arms! . . . Have you got any perfume?"

"Good gracious, do you need any more? You simply reek of rose pomade, as it is."

"No matter. Give it here."

He poured out half of the vial between neck and neckcloth, onto his pocket handkerchief, and upon his sleeves.

"Are you going to dance?" he asked.

"I don't think so."

"I'm afraid that I shall have to begin the mazurka with the princess, and I hardly know one figure of it."

"Have you asked her for the mazurka?"

"Not yet. . . ."

"Look out, you might be forestalled. . . ."

"That's right!" he said, clapping a hand to his forehead. "Goodbye . . . I'm going to wait for her at the entrance door." He seized his cap and ran off.

Half an hour later, I also set out. The streets were dark and deserted; around the club, or tavern—whichever you choose to call it—the crowd was dense; the windows shone; the sounds of the military band were brought to me by the evening breeze. I walked slowly; I felt sad . . . "Is it possible," I thought, "that my only function on earth is to ruin other people's hopes? Ever since I have lived and acted, fate has always seemed to bring me in at the denouement of other people's dramas, as if none could either die or despair without me! I am the indispensable persona in the fifth act; involuntarily, I play the miserable part of the executioner or the traitor. What could be fate's purpose in this? Might it not be that it had designated me to become the author of bourgeois tragedies and family novels, or the collaborator of some purveyor of stories for the "Library for Reading"? How should one know? How many people, in the beginning of life, think they will finish it as Alexander the Great or Lord Byron, and instead, retain for the whole of their existence, the rank of titulary counsellor?

Upon coming into the ballroom, I hid in the crowd of men and began to make my observations. Grushnitsky stood next to the young princess and was saying something to her with great animation: she listened to him absentmindedly, kept glancing this way and that, putting her fan to her lips. Her face expressed impatience, her eyes sought around for someone: I softly approached from behind, in order to overhear their conversation.

"You torment me, Princess," Grushnitsky was saying. "You have changed tremendously since I last saw you. . . ."

"You too have changed," she answered, casting upon him a swift glance, in which he failed to discern secret mockery.

"I? I have changed? . . . Oh, never! You know that it is impossible! He who has once seen you, will carry with him, forever, your divine image."

"Stop, please. . . ."

"Why then will you not listen now to what only recently, and so often, you listened with favor?"

"Because I do not like repetition," she answered laughing.

"Oh, I've made a bitter mistake! . . . I thought, in my folly, that at least these epaulets would give me the right to hope . . . No, it would have been better for me had I remained all my life in that miserable soldier's coat to which, maybe, I owed your attention."

"Indeed, that coat suited you much better. . . ."

At this point I came up and bowed to the young princess: she blushed slightly and said quickly:

"Am I not right, Monsieur Pechorin, that the gray soldier's coat was much more becoming to Monsieur Grushnitsky?"

"I disagree with you," I replied. "In this uniform, he looks even more youthful."

Grushnitsky could not bear this blow: like all youths, he professes to be an old man; he thinks that deep traces of passions replace the imprint of years. He cast on me a furious glance, stamped his foot and walked away.

"Now confess," I said to the young princess, "that despite his having always been very absurd, still, quite recently, you thought him interesting . . . in his gray coat?"

She dropped her eyes and did not answer.

All evening Grushnitsky pursued the young princess, either dancing with her or being her *vis-à-vis;* he devoured her with his eyes, sighed and pestered her with entreaties and reproaches. After the third quadrille, she already detested him.

"I did not expect this of you," he said, coming up to me and taking me by the arm.

"What, exactly?"

"You are dancing the mazurka with her, aren't you?" he asked in a solemn voice. "She confessed to me. . . ."

"Well, what of it? Is it a secret?"

"Naturally . . . I should have expected this from a frivolous girl, from a flirt . . . But I'll have my revenge!"

"Blame your soldier's coat or your officer's epaulets, but why blame her? Is it her fault that you no longer appeal to her?"

"Why then give me hopes?"

"Why then did you hope? I can understand people who desire something and strive for it; but who wants to hope?"

"You have won your bet, though not quite," he said with a wrathful smile.

The mazurka began. Grushnitsky kept choosing nobody but the princess, the other men chose her continuously: it was obviously a conspiracy against me. So much the better. She wants to talk to me, they prevent her—she will want it twice as much.

Once or twice, I pressed her hand: the second time, she snatched it away, without saying a word.

"I shall sleep badly tonight," she said to me, when the mazurka was over.

"It's Grushnitsky's fault."

"Oh no!" And her face became so pensive, so sad, that I promised myself to kiss her hand, without fail, that evening.

People began to leave. As I handed the princess into her carriage, I rapidly pressed her small hand to my lips. It was dark, and no one could see it.

I re-entered the ballroom, well content with myself.

At a long table, young men were having supper, and among them was Grushnitsky. When I came in, they all fell silent: evidently, they had been talking about me. Many are ill-disposed toward me since the last ball, especially the captain of dragoons, and now, it seems, an inimical gang is actually being organized against me, under the leadership of Grushnitsky. He had such a proud and courageous air.

I am very glad; I love my enemies, although not in a Christian sense: they amuse me, they quicken my pulses. To be always on the lookout, to intercept every glance, to catch the meaning of every word, to guess intentions, to thwart plots, to pretend to be fooled, and suddenly, with one push, to upset the entire enormous and elaborate structure of cunning and scheming—that is what I call life.

During the supper Grushnitsky kept whispering and exchanging winks with the captain of dragoons.

June 6th

This morning, Vera left for Kislovodsk with her husband. I met their coach as I was on my way to Princess Ligovskoy. Vera nodded to me: there was reproach in her glance.

Whose fault is it? Why does she not want to give me the chance

to see her alone? Love, like fire, goes out without fuel. Perchance
jealousy will accomplish what my entreaties could not.

I stayed at the princess's an hour by the clock. Mary did not appear;
she was ill. In the evening she was not on the boulevard. The newly
organized gang, armed with lorgnettes, has assumed a truly threatening
appearance. I am glad that the princess is ill: they might have done
something insolent in regard to her. Grushnitsky's hair was all awry
and he looked desperate: I think he is really distressed. His vanity, in
particular, is injured; but, oddly enough, there are people who are
ludicrous even in their despair!

On coming home, I noticed a lack of something. *I have not seen
her! She is ill!* Can it be that I have really fallen in love? . . . What
nonsense!

June 7th

At eleven in the morning—the hour at which the old Princess Ligovskoy
is usually sweating it out in the Ermolov bathhouse—I was walking
past her house. The young princess was sitting pensively at the window.
When she saw me, she rose abruptly.

I entered the vestibule, none of the servants were there, and without
being announced, taking advantage of the local customs, I made my
way into the drawing room.

A dull pallor was spread over the princess's pretty face. She stood
at the piano, leaning with one hand on the back of an armchair: that
hand trembled ever so slightly. I quietly went up to her and said:

"You are angry with me?"

She raised upon me a languid, deep gaze and shook her head; her
lips wanted to utter something, and could not; her eyes filled with tears;
she sank into the armchair and covered her face with her hand.

"What is the matter with you?" I said, taking her hand.

"You do not respect me! . . . Oh, leave me alone!"

I made a few steps. . . . She straightened herself up in her chair;
her eyes glittered.

I stopped, with my hand on the door handle, and said:

"Forgive me, Princess, I have acted like a madman. . . . This will
not happen again: I will see to it. . . . Why must you know what, up
to now, has been taking place in my soul? You will never learn it, and
so much the better for you. Adieu."

As I went out, I believe I heard her crying.

Till evening, I roamed on foot about the outskirts of Mount Ma-

shuk, got terribly tired and, on coming home, threw myself on my bed
in utter exhaustion.

Werner dropped in.

"Is it true," he asked, "that you are going to marry the young
Princess Ligovskoy?"

"Why?"

"The whole town says so; all my patients are preoccupied with
this important news: that's the kind of people patients are; they know
everything!"

"Grushnitsky's tricks," I thought to myself.

"In order to prove to you, Doctor, that these rumors are false, let
me inform you in secret that tomorrow I am moving to Kislovodsk."

"And the Ligovskoys, too?"

"No; they remain here for another week."

"So you are not marrying her?"

"Doctor, Doctor! Look at me: do I resemble a fiancé, or anything
of the kind?"

"I do not say it. . . . But you know there are cases," he added with
a cunning smile, "in which an honorable man is obliged to marry, and
there are mammas who do not at least avert such cases. Therefore, I
advise you as a pal to be more careful. Here at the spa the atmosphere
is most dangerous: I have seen so many fine, young men, worthy of a
better lot, who have gone straight from here to the altar. Would you
believe it, there has even been an attempt to have me marry! Namely,
on the part of a provincial mamma whose daughter was very pale. I
had had the misfortune to tell her that her daughter's face would regain
its color after marriage. Then, with tears of gratitude, she offered me
her daughter's hand and their entire fortune—fifty serfs, I believe. But
I answered that I was incapable of marriage."

Werner left, fully convinced that he had put me on my guard.

From his words, I note that various nasty rumors have already
been spread in town about the young princess and me. Grushnitsky
will have to pay for this!

June 10th

I have been here, in Kislovodsk, three days already. Every day I see
Vera at the well and at the promenade. In the morning, upon awakening, I sit down by the window and train my lorgnette on her balcony:
she is already long since dressed and awaits the prearranged signal: we
meet, as if by chance, in the garden, which descends from our houses

to the well. The vivifying mountain air has brought back her color and strength. It is not for nothing that Narzan is termed "The Fountain of Mightiness." The local inhabitants maintain that the air of Kislovodsk disposes one romantically, that here comes the denouement of all the love affairs that ever were started at the foot of Mount Mashuk. And, indeed, everything here breathes seclusion; everything here is mysterious—the dense canopies of linden avenues that bend over the torrent which, as it noisily and foamily falls from ledge to ledge, cuts for itself a path between the verdant mountains; and the gorges filled with gloom and silence that branch out from here in all directions; and the freshness of the aromatic air, laden with the emanations of tall southern grasses and white acacias; and the constant deliciously somniferous babble of cool brooks which, meeting at the far end of the valley, join in a friendly race and, at last, fall into the Podkumok River. On this side the gorge widens and turns into a green glen; a dusty road meanders through it. Every time I look at it, I keep imagining that a close carriage comes there, and from the window of the carriage, there peers out a rosy little face. Many coaches have, by now, passed on that road, but never that one. The suburb beyond the fort has grown populous: in the restaurant, built on a bluff a few steps from my dwelling, lights begin to flicker in the evenings through a double row of poplars; noise and the clinking of glasses resound there till late at night.

Nowhere is there consumed so much Kahetian wine and mineral water as here.

> To mix these two pursuits, a lot of men
> Are eager—I'm not one of them.

Grushnitsky with his gang, every day, carouses at the tavern, and hardly nods to me.

He arrived only yesterday, and has already managed to quarrel with three old men who wanted to take their baths before him: definitely—misfortunes develop in him a martial spirit.

June 11th

They have come at last. I was sitting by the window when I heard the rattle of their coach: my heart quivered. . . . What is it then? Could it be that I am in love? . . . I am so stupidly made that this could be expected from me.

I have dined at their house. The old princess looks at me very

tenderly and does not leave her daughter's side. . . . That's bad! On
the other hand, Vera is jealous of the young princess—this is a nice
state of things I have brought about! What will not a woman do in
order to vex a rival? I remember one woman who fell in love with me,
because I was in love with another. There is nothing more paradoxical
than a woman's mind: it is difficult to convince women of anything;
you have to bring them to a point where they will convince their own
selves. The sequence of proofs by means of which they overcome their
prejudices, is very original: to learn their dialectic, one must overturn
in one's mind all the school rules of logic. Here, for instance, is the
normal method:

That man loves me; but I am married: consequently, I must not
love him.

Now for the feminine method:

I must not love him for I am married; but he loves me—consequently . . .

Here come several dots, for reason does not say anything more,
and what speaks mainly, is the tongue, the eyes, and in their wake, the
heart, if the latter exists.

What if these notes should ever fall under a woman's eyes? "Slander!" she will cry with indignation.

Ever since poets have been writing and women reading them (for
which they should receive the deepest gratitude), they have been called
angels so many times, that in the simplicity of their souls, they have
actually believed this compliment, forgetting that the same poets
dubbed Nero a demigod, for money.   he has been though

It is not I who should speak of women with such spite—I, who
love nothing in the world save them—I, who have always been ready
to sacrifice to them peace of mind, ambition, life. But then, it is not in
a fit of annoyance and offended vanity that I try to tear from them
that magic veil, through which only an experienced gaze penetrates.
No, all that I am saying about them is only a result of

> The mind's cold observations,
> The mournful comments of the heart.

Women ought to desire that all men know them as well as I do,
because I love them a hundred times better, ever since I stopped fearing
them and comprehended their little weaknesses.

Apropos, the other day Werner compared women to the enchanted
forest of which Tasso tells in his "Jerusalem Liberated": "Only come
near," said Werner: "and mercy, what horrors will come flying at you

from every side: Duty, Pride, Propriety, Public Opinion, Mockery, Scorn . . . All you have to do is not look and walk straight on: little by little, the monsters disappear and before you there opens a serene and sunny meadow, in the midst of which, green myrtle blooms. On the other hand, woe to you if, at the first steps, your heart fails you and you look back!"

June 12th

This evening has been rich in events. Within two miles of Kislovodsk, in a canyon through which flows the Podkumok River, there is a cliff, called The Ring. This is a gateway formed by nature; it rises from a high hill, and through it the setting sun throws its last flaming glance on the world. A large cavalcade set out thither to view the sunset through that window of stone. None of us, to say the truth, was thinking of sunsets. I was riding by the young princess's side: on our way home, the Podkumok River had to be forded. The shallowest mountain streams are dangerous, especially because their bottom is an absolute kaleidoscope: every day it changes from the pressure of the waves. Where yesterday there was a stone, today there is a hole. I took the princess's horse by the bridle and led it down into the water, which was no more than knee-deep: we started to advance slowly in an oblique direction against the current. It is well known that when fording rapid streams, one should not look at the water, for otherwise one immediately gets dizzy. I forgot to warn Princess Mary of this.

We were already in midstream, where the current was swiftest, when she suddenly swayed in her saddle. "I feel faint!" she said in a weak voice. I quickly bent toward her and wound my arm around her supple waist.

"Look up!" I whispered to her. "It is nothing, only don't be afraid; I'm with you."

She felt better; she wanted to free herself from my arm, but I wound it still tighter around her tender, soft body; my cheek almost touched her cheek; flame emanated from it.

"What are you doing to me? . . . Good God! . . ."

I paid no attention to her tremor and confusion, and my lips touched her tender cheek; she gave a start but said nothing. We were riding behind: nobody saw. When we got out onto the bank, everybody started off at a trot. The young princess held her horse in; I stayed by her. It could be seen that my silence worried her, but I swore not to

like w/ the hand kiss

say a word—out of curiosity. I wanted to see how she would extricate
herself from this embarrassing situation.

"Either you despise me, or love me very much!" she said at last,
in a voice in which there were tears. "Perhaps you want to laugh at
me, to trouble my soul, and then leave me. . . . It would be so base,
so mean, that the mere supposition . . . Oh no! Isn't it true," she added
in a tone of tender trust, "isn't it true that there is nothing in me that
would preclude respect? Your insolent action . . . I must, I must forgive
it you, because I allowed it. . . . Answer, do speak, I want to hear your
voice! . . ."

In the last words, there was such feminine impatience that I could
not help smiling. Fortunately, it was beginning to get dark. . . . I did
not answer anything.

"You are silent?" she went on. "Perhaps you wish me to be the
first to say that I love you."

I was silent.

"Do you wish it?" she went on, quickly turning toward me. In
the determination of her gaze and voice, there was something
frightening.

"What for?" I answered shrugging my shoulders.

She gave her horse a cut of the whip and set off at all speed along
the narrow dangerous road. It happened so fast, that I hardly managed
to overtake her, and when I did, she had already joined the rest of the
party. All the way home she talked and laughed incessantly. In her
movements there was something feverish; not once did she glance at
me. Everybody noticed this unusual gaiety. And the old princess inwardly rejoiced, as she looked at her daughter; yet her daughter was
merely having a nervous fit. She will spend a sleepless night and will
weep. This thought gives me boundless delight: there are moments
when I understand the vampire. . . . And to think that I am reputed
to be a jolly good fellow and try to earn that appellation!

Having dismounted, the ladies went to the old princess's. I was
excited and galloped off into the mountains to dissipate the thoughts
that crowded in my head. The dewy evening breathed delicious coolness. The moon was rising from behind the dark summits. Every step
of my unshod horse produced a hollow echo in the silence of the gorges.
At the cascade, I watered my steed, avidly inhaled, a couple of times,
the fresh air of the southern night, and started back. I rode through
the suburb. The lights were beginning to go out in the windows; the
sentries on the rampart of the fort, and the Cossacks in outlying pickets,
exchanged long-drawn calls.

In one of the houses of the suburb, which stood on the edge of a ravine, I noticed an extraordinary illumination: at times there resounded discordant talk and cries, indicating that an officers' banquet was in progress. I dismounted and stole up to the window: an improperly closed shutter allowed me to see the revelers and to make out their words. They were speaking about me.

The captain of dragoons, flushed with wine, struck the table with his fist, demanding attention.

"Gentlemen!" he said, "this is really impossible! Pechorin must be taught a lesson! These fledglings from Petersburg always give themselves airs, till you hit them on the nose! He thinks that he alone has lived in the world of fashion, just because he always has clean gloves and well-polished boots."

"And what an arrogant smile! Yet I'm sure he is a coward—yes, a coward!"

"I think so too," said Grushnitsky. "He likes to jest his way out. I once said to him such things, for which another would have hacked me to pieces then and there, but Pechorin gave it all a humorous interpretation. I, naturally, did not call him out, because it was up to him. Moreover, I did not want to get entangled. . . ."

"Grushnitsky is mad at him because he took away the young princess from him," said someone.

"What a notion! As a matter of fact, I did flirt slightly with her, but gave it up at once, because I do not want to marry, and it is not in my rules to compromise a young girl."

"Yes, I assure you that he is a first-rate coward—that is to say, Pechorin, and not Grushnitsky. Oh, Grushnitsky is a capital fellow, and moreover, he is a true friend of mine!" said the captain of dragoons. "Gentlemen! Nobody here stands up for him? Nobody? All the better! Would you like to test his courage? You might find it entertaining."

"We would like to; but how?"

"Well, listen, Grushnitsky is particularly angry with him—he gets the main part! He will pick some kind of silly quarrel with him and challenge Pechorin to a duel. . . . Now wait a bit, here comes the point. . . . He will challenge him to a duel—good! All this—the challenge, the preparations, the conditions—will be as solemn and terrible as possible—I shall see to that. I shall be your second, my poor friend! Good! But now, here is the hitch: we shall not put any balls into the pistols. I here answer for it that Pechorin will funk it—I shall have them face each other at six paces distance, by Jove! Do you agree, gentlemen?"

"A capital plan! We agree! Why not?" sounded from all sides.

"And you, Grushnitsky?"

In a tremor of eagerness, I awaited Grushnitsky's reply. Cold fury possessed me at the thought that, had it not been for chance, I might have become the laughing stock of those fools. If Grushnitsky had refused, I would have thrown myself upon his neck. But after a short silence, he rose from his chair, offered his hand to the captain and said very pompously: "All right, I agree."

It would be difficult to describe the delight of the whole honorable company. *and this what he wanted*

I returned home, agitated by two different emotions. The first was sadness. "What do they all hate me for?" I thought. "What for? Have I offended anybody? No. Could it be that I belong to the number of those people whose appearance alone is sufficient to produce ill will?" And I felt a venomous rancor gradually filling my soul. "Take care, Mr. Grushnitsky!" I kept saying, as I paced to and fro in my room. "I am not to be trifled with like this. You may have to pay dearly for the approval of your stupid cronies. I am not a plaything for you!"

I did not sleep all night. By morning, I was as yellow as a wild orange.

In the morning, I met the young princess at the well.

"Are you ill?" she said, looking at me intently.

"I did not sleep all night."

"Nor did I. . . . I accused you . . . perhaps, wrongly? But explain your behavior, I may forgive you everything."

"Everything?"

"Everything. . . . Only tell me the truth . . . and hurry. . . . I have thought a lot, trying to explain, to justify your conduct: perhaps, you are afraid of obstacles on the part of my family. . . . It does not matter. When they hear of it . . . (her voice trembled) my entreaties will convince them. . . . Or is it your own situation? . . . But I want you to know that I can sacrifice anything for the one I love. . . . Oh, answer quick . . . have pity. . . . You do not despise me, do you?"

She grasped my hand.

The old princess was walking in front of us with Vera's husband, and did not see anything, but we might have been seen by the promenading patients, of all inquisitive people the most inquisitive gossipers, and I quickly freed my hand from her passionate grasp.

"I shall tell you the whole truth," I replied to the princess, "I shall neither justify myself, nor explain my actions. I do not love you."

Her lips paled slightly.

"Leave me," she said almost inaudibly.

I shrugged my shoulders, turned, and walked away.

June 14th

I sometimes despise myself. . . . Is this not why I despise others? . . . I
have become incapable of noble impulses. I am afraid of appearing
laughable to myself. Another man in my place would offer the young
princess *son coeur et sa fortune;* but over me the word "marry" has
some kind of magic power. However much I may love a woman, if
she only lets me feel that I must marry her—farewell to love! My heart
turns to stone, and nothing can warm it again. I am ready to make
any sacrifice except this one. I may set my life upon a card twenty
times, and even my honor—but I will not sell my freedom. Why do I
treasure it so? What good is it to me? What do I prepare myself for?
What do I expect from the future? . . . Indeed, nothing whatever. It is
a kind of innate fear, an ineffable presentiment. Aren't there people
who have an unaccountable fear of spiders, cockroaches, mice? Shall
I confess? When I was still a child, an old woman told my fortune to
my mother. She predicted of me "death from a wicked wife." It made
a deep impression upon me then: in my soul was born an insuperable
aversion to marriage. Yet something tells me that her prediction will
come true, at least, I shall do my best to have it come true as late as
possible.

June 15th

Yesterday there arrived here the conjurer Apfelbaum. On the door of
the restaurant, there appeared a long *affiche,* informing the esteemed
public that the above-named, wonderful conjurer, acrobat, chemist,
and optician, would have the honor to give a superb performance at
eight tonight, in the reception hall of the Club of the Nobility (in other
words, the restaurant); admission two roubles, fifty.

Everybody intends to go to see the wonderful conjurer: even Princess Ligovskoy, despite the fact that her daughter is ill, took a ticket
for herself.

Today after dinner, I passed under Vera's windows. She was sitting
on the balcony alone. A billet fell at my feet:

"Tonight, around half past nine, come to me by the main staircase.
My husband has gone to Pyatigorsk and will return only tomorrow
morning. My footmen and maidservants will not be in the house: I
have distributed tickets to all of them, as well as to the princess's
servants. I await you. Come without fail."

"Aha!" I thought, "at last I am having my way after all."

At eight, I went to see the conjurer. The spectators assembled shortly before nine: the performance began. In the back rows of chairs, I recognized the lackeys and the maids of Vera and the princess. Everybody was here. Grushnitsky sat in the front row, with his lorgnette. The conjurer turned to him every time he needed a pocket handkerchief, a watch, a ring, and so forth.

Grushnitsky does not greet me since some time ago, and tonight, once or twice, he glanced at me rather insolently. All this shall be remembered when the time comes to settle our accounts.

Shortly before ten, I rose and left.

It was pitch dark outside. Heavy, cold clouds lay on the summits of the surrounding mountains; only now and then a dying breeze soughed in the crests of the poplars around the restaurant. There was a crowd of people outside the windows. I descended the hill and, turning into the gateway, accelerated my pace. Suddenly it seemed to me that someone was walking behind me. I stopped and looked about me. Nothing could be distinguished in the darkness; however, I took the precaution to go around the house as if I were taking a stroll. As I passed under the windows of the young princess, I again heard steps behind me. A man wrapped up in a military cloak ran past me. This alarmed me: however, I stole up to the porch and swiftly ran up the dark stairs. The door opened, a small hand grasped my hand.

"No one saw you?" said Vera in a whisper, pressing herself to me.

"No one."

"Now do you believe that I love you? Oh! For a long time I wavered, for a long time I was tormented. . . . But you make of me all you want." *again*

Her heart was beating violently, her hands were as cold as ice. There began the reproaches of jealousy, plaints: she demanded of me that I confess to her all, saying she would bear, with submission, my unfaithfulness, since all she desired was my happiness. I did not quite believe this, but I calmed her with vows, promises, and so forth.

"So you are not going to marry Mary? You don't love her? And she thinks . . . do you know, she is madly in love with you, the poor thing!"

Around two o'clock in the morning, I opened the window and, having tied two shawls together, let myself down from the upper balcony to the lower one, holding onto a pillar. In the young princess's room, a light was still burning. Something urged me toward that window. The curtain was not completely drawn, and I could cast a curious glance into the interior of the room. Mary was sitting on her bed, her hands folded in her lap; her abundant hair was gathered under a night cap fringed with lace; a large crimson kerchief covered her slender white shoulders; her small feet hid in variegated Persian slippers. She sat motionless, her head sunk onto her breast; before her, on a little table, a book was opened, but her eyes, motionless and full of ineffable sadness, seemed, for a hundredth time, to skim over the same page, while her thoughts were far away.

At this moment, somebody stirred behind a bush. I jumped down from the balcony onto the turf. An invisible hand seized me by the shoulder.

"Aha!" said a rough voice, "you're caught! . . . I'll teach you to visit young princesses at night! . . ."

"Hold him tight!" cried somebody else, springing from behind a corner.

They were Grushnitsky and the captain of dragoons.

I struck the latter upon the head with my fist, knocked him down, and dashed into the shrubbery. All the paths of the garden which covered the sloping ground in front of our houses were known to me.

"Thieves! Help!" they cried. A gun shot rang out; a smoking wad fell almost at my feet.

A minute later, I was already in my room; I undressed and lay down. Hardly had my valet locked the door, than Grushnitsky and the captain began to knock.

"Pechorin! Are you asleep? Are you there?" the captain cried.

"I am asleep," I answered crossly.

"Get up! . . . Thieves . . . Circassians . . ."

"I have a cold," I answered, "I'm afraid to catch a chill."

They left. I should not have answered them: they would have gone on looking for me in the garden for another hour. In the meantime, the alarm became terrific. A Cossack came, at full speed, from the fort. There was a universal stir: they started to look for Circassians in every bush—and, naturally, found nothing. But many people, probably, remained firmly convinced that, had the garrison revealed more courage and promptness, at least a score of pillagers would have remained lying about.

June 16th

This morning, at the well, there was nothing but talk about the night raid of the Circassians. Having drunk the prescribed number of glasses

of the Narzan water, and having walked the length of the long linden
avenue ten times or so, I met Vera's husband, who had just arrived
from Pyatigorsk. He took my arm, and we went to the restaurant to
have lunch. He was terribly anxious about his wife. "How frightened
she was last night," he kept saying, "and to think it should have happened precisely during my absence." We sat down to lunch near a door
which led to the corner room, where a dozen young people were assembled, including Grushnitsky. For a second time, destiny provided
me with the chance to overhear a conversation, which was to decide
his fate. He could not see me and, consequently, I could not suspect
him of a deliberate purpose; but this only increased his guilt in my
eyes.

"Could it have really been the Circassians?" someone said. "Did
anybody see them?"

"I shall tell you the whole story," answered Grushnitsky, "but
please do not give me away. This is how it was. Last night, a man,
whom I shall not name to you, came to me and told me that shortly
before ten he saw someone steal into the house where the Ligovskoys
live. I should mention to you that the old princess was here, and the
young princess was at home. So he and I betook ourselves under their
windows to waylay the lucky fellow."

I must confess that I was alarmed, although my interlocutor was
very busy with his luncheon. He might have heard things that would
be disagreeable to him, if Grushnitsky had inadvertently guessed the
truth; but being blinded by jealousy, the latter did not suspect it.

"Well, you see," Grushnitsky went on, "we set out, taking a gun
with us, loaded with a blank cartridge—just to frighten him. Till two
o'clock, we waited in the garden. Finally—God knows where he appeared from, certainly not from the window, because it was never
opened, but presumably he came out through the glass door which is
behind the pillar—finally, as I say, we saw someone come down from
the balcony. . . . How do you like the princess's behavior, eh? Well, I
must say, those Moscow misses are something! After that, what would
you believe? We wanted to seize him, but he freed himself and, like a
hare, dashed into the bushes. It was then I took a shot at him."

A murmur of incredulity resounded around Grushnitsky.

"You do not believe me?" he continued. "I give you my honest
and honorable word that all this is the very truth, and in proof, if you
wish it, I shall name the gentleman."

"Tell us, tell us who he is!" resounded from all sides.

"Pechorin," answered Grushnitsky.

At this moment, he raised his eyes—I was standing in the door opposite him—he flushed dreadfully. I went up to him and said slowly and distinctly:

"I regret very much that I entered after you had already given your word of honor in support of the vilest slander. My presence would have saved you from extra knavery."

Grushnitsky jumped up from his seat and was about to flare up.

"I beg you," I continued, in the same tone of voice, "I beg you to retract your words at once: you know very well that it is an invention. I do not think that a woman's indifference to your brilliant qualities merits so awful a vengeance. Think well. By affirming your opinion, you lose your right to the name of a gentleman, and you risk your life."

Grushnitsky stood before me, with lowered eyes, in violent agitation. But the struggle between conscience and vanity did not last long. The captain of dragoons, who was sitting next to him, nudged him with his elbow: he started and quickly replied to me, without raising his eyes:

"Sir, when I say something, I mean it, and am ready to repeat it. I am not afraid of your threats, and am prepared for anything."

"This last you have already proved," I answered coldly and, taking the captain of dragoons by the arm, I left the room.

"What is it you want?" asked the captain.

"You are a friend of Grushnitsky and will probably be his second?"

The captain bowed with great importance.

"You have guessed," he answered. "I am even obliged to be his second, because the insult inflicted upon him refers also to me. I was with him last night," he added, straightening his stooping shoulders.

"Ah! So it was you that I hit so awkwardly on the head?"

He turned yellow, turned blue; concealed malevolence was expressed in his face.

"I shall have the honor to send you my second today," I added with a very polite bow, pretending not to pay any attention to his rage.

On the porch of the restaurant, I came across Vera's husband. Apparently, he had been waiting for me.

He grasped my hand with an emotion resembling enthusiasm.

"Noble young man," he said with tears in his eyes, "I heard it all. What a scoundrel! What lack of gratitude! Who will want to admit them into a decent house after that! Thank God I have no daughters! But you will be rewarded by her for whom you risk your life. You may rely on my discretion for the time being," he went on. "I have been young myself, and have served in the military service: I know one should not interfere in these matters. Good-bye."

Poor thing! He rejoices he has no daughters.

I went straight to Werner, found him at home and told him everything—my relations with Vera and with the young princess, and the conversation I had overheard, from which I had learned the intention those gentlemen had of making a fool of me by forcing me to fight a duel with pistols loaded with blanks. But now the matter was going beyond a joke: they, probably, had not expected such an outcome.

The doctor agreed to be my second; I gave him some instructions concerning the terms of the duel. He was to insist on the affair remaining as secret as possible because, although I am ready to brave death any time, I am not at all disposed to ruin, forever, my future career in this world.

After this I went home. An hour later, the doctor returned from his expedition.

"There is, indeed, a plot against you," he said. "I found at Grushnitsky's the captain of dragoons and yet another gentleman, whose name I do not remember. For a moment I stopped in the vestibule to take off my rubbers. They were making a lot of noise and arguing. 'For nothing in the world shall I agree,' Grushnitsky was saying. 'He insulted me in public: before that, things were entirely different.' 'What business is this of yours?' answered the captain. 'I take everything upon myself. I was a second in five duels, and you may be sure I know how to arrange it. I have planned it all. Only please do not interfere. It won't do any harm to scare the fellow. But why expose oneself to danger if one can avoid it? . . .' At this moment, I entered. They were suddenly silent. Our negotiations lasted a considerable time. Finally, we decided the matter in the following way: within three miles from here there is a desolate gorge; they will drive there tomorrow at four in the morning, and we shall set out half an hour after them; you will shoot at each other at six paces—Grushnitsky himself demanded this. The one who is killed is to be put down to the Circassians. Now, here are my suspicions: they, that is to say the seconds, have apparently altered somewhat their former plan and want to load, with a bullet, only Grushnitsky's pistol. This slightly resembles murder, but in time of war, and especially Asiatic war, trickery is allowed. However, Grushnitsky seems to be a little nobler than his companions. What do you think, should we show them that we have found them out?"

"Not for anything on earth, Doctor! Rest assured, I shall not fall in their trap."

"What then do you want to do?"

"That's my secret."

"See that you don't get caught. . . . Remember, the distance is six paces!"

"Doctor, I expect you tomorrow at four: the horses will be ready. . . . Good-bye."

Till evening I remained at home, locked up in my room. A footman came with an invitation from the old princess—I had him told that I was ill.

he seems to be losing the cool & calm

Two o'clock in the morning . . . Sleep does not come. . . . Yet I ought to have some sleep so that my hand does not shake tomorrow. Anyway, it would be difficult to miss at six paces. Ah, Mr. Grushnitsky! Your mystification will not come off. . . . We shall exchange parts: it is now I who will search your pale face for signs of secret fear. Why did you designate yourself those fatal six paces? You think that I shall present my forehead to you without arguing. . . . But we shall cast lots . . . and then . . . then . . . what if his luck outweighs mine? What if my star at last betrays me? . . . It would hardly be strange, it has so long served my whims faithfully. There is no more constancy in heaven than there is on earth.

Well, what of it? If I am to die, I'll die! The loss to the world will not be large and, anyway, I myself am sufficiently bored. I am like a man who yawns at a ball and does not drive home to sleep, only because his carriage is not yet there. But now the carriage is ready . . . good-bye! . . .

I scan my whole past in memory and involuntarily wonder: why did I live, for what purpose was I born? . . . And yet that purpose must have existed, and my destination must have been a lofty one, for I feel, in my soul, boundless strength. But I did not divine that destination, I became enticed by the lure of hollow and thankless passions. From their crucible, I emerged as hard and cold as iron, but lost forever the ardor of noble yearnings—the best blossom of life. And since then, how many times I have played the part of an axe in the hands of fate! As an executioner's tool, I would fall upon the head of doomed victims, often without malice, always without regret. My love brought happiness to none, because I never gave up anything for the sake of those whom I loved. I loved for myself, for my proper pleasure; I merely satisfied a bizarre need of my heart, avidly consuming their sentiments, their tenderness, their joys and sufferings—and never could I have my fill. Thus a man, tormented by hunger and fatigue, goes to sleep and sees before him rich viands and sparkling wines; he devours with delight the airy gifts of fancy, and he seems to feel relief; but as soon as he awakes—the vision vanishes. He is left with redoubled hunger and despair!

And, perhaps tomorrow, I shall die! . . . And there will not remain, on earth, a single creature that would have understood me completely. Some deem me worse, others better than I actually am. Some will say he was a good fellow; others will say he was a scoundrel. Both this and that will be false. After this, is it worth the trouble to live? And yet one lives—out of curiosity. One keeps expecting something new. . . . Absurd and vexatious!

he is cold & calculating again

It is now a month and a half already that I have been in the fort of N——. Maksim Maksimich is out hunting. I am alone, I am sitting at the window. Gray clouds have shut off the mountains to their base: through the mist, the sun looks like a yellow blur. It is cold: the wind whistles and shakes the shutters. . . . How dull! . . . I am going to continue my journal, which has been interrupted by so many strange events.

I read over the last page: how funny!—I expected to die: it was impossible. I had not yet drained the cup of sufferings, and I now feel that I still have many years to live.

How clearly and sharply the past has crystallized in my memory! Time has not erased one line, one shade!

I remember that, during the night before the duel, I did not sleep one minute. I could not write long: a secret restlessness had taken possession of me. For an hour or so, I paced the room, then I sat down and opened a novel by Walter Scott which lay on my table: it was *The Scottish Puritans*. At first I read with an effort, but then I lost myself in it, carried away by the magic fantasy. Could it be that, in the next world, the Scottish bard is not paid for every glad minute that his book gives?

Dawn came at last. My nerves had quieted down. I looked at myself in the mirror: a dull pallor was spread over my face, which bore the traces of painful insomnia; but the eyes, although surrounded by brown shadows, glittered proudly and inflexibly. I was satisfied with myself.

After having ordered the horses to be saddled, I dressed and ran down to the bathhouse. As I immersed myself in the cold ebullience of Narzan water, I felt the forces of my body and soul return. I emerged from the bath, refreshed and braced up, as if I were about to go to a ball. Try to say after this that the soul is not dependent on the body!

Upon returning home, I found the doctor there. He wore gray riding breeches, a Caucasian overcoat and a Circassian cap. I burst out laughing at the sight of his small figure under that huge shaggy cap: his face is anything but that of a warrior, and on this occasion it looked longer than ever.

"Why are you so sad, Doctor?" I said to him. "Haven't you seen people off on their way to the next world with the greatest indifference, a hundred times before? You should imagine that I have bilious fever. I may get well, and again, I may die; both are in the natural order of things. Try to see in me a patient afflicted with an illness that is still unknown to you—and then your curiosity will be roused to the highest pitch. By watching me you can now make several important physiological observations. Isn't the expectation of violent death, after all, a genuine illness?"

This thought impressed the doctor and he cheered up.

We got on our horses. Werner clutched at the bridle with both hands, and we set off. In a twinkle we had galloped past the fort by way of the suburb, and entered the gorge along which the road wound, half-choked with tall grasses, and constantly crossed and recrossed by a loud brook, which had to be forded, to the great dismay of the doctor, for every time his horse stopped in the water.

I do not remember a bluer and fresher morning. The sun had just appeared from behind the green summits, and the merging of the first warmth of its rays with the waning coolness of the night pervaded all one's senses with a kind of delicious languor. The glad beam of the young day had not yet penetrated into the gorge; it gilded only the tops of the cliffs that hung on both sides above us. The dense-foliaged bushes, growing in the deep crevices, asperged us with a silver rain at the least breath of wind. I remember that on this occasion, more than ever before, I was in love with nature. How curiously I examined every dewdrop that trembled upon a broad vine leaf and reflected a million iridescent rays! How avidly my gaze tried to penetrate into the hazy distance! There, the road was becoming narrower, the cliffs were growing bluer and more awesome, and finally, they seemed to blend in an impenetrable wall. We rode in silence.

"Have you made your will?" Werner suddenly asked.

"No."

"And what if you are killed?"

"My heirs will turn up of themselves."

"Do you mean you have not got any friends to whom you would wish to send a last farewell?"

I shook my head.

"Do you mean there is not one woman in the world to whom you would want to leave something in remembrance?"

"Do you want me, Doctor," I answered him, "to open my soul to you? . . . You see, I have outlived those years when people die uttering the name of their beloved and bequeathing a tuft of pomaded or unpomaded hair to a friend. When I think of near and possible death, I am thinking of myself only: some people don't do even that. Friends who, tomorrow, will forget me or, worse, will saddle me with goodness knows what fictions; women who, while embracing another, will laugh at me so as not to make him jealous of a dead man—what do I care for them all! Out of life's storm I carried only a few ideas— and not one feeling. For a long time now, I have been living not with the heart, but with the head. I weigh and analyze my own passions and actions with stern curiosity, but without participation. Within me there are two persons: one of them lives in the full sense of the word, the other cogitates and judges him. The first will, perhaps, in an hour's time, take leave of you and the world forever, while the other . . . what about the other? . . . Look, Doctor, do you see on that cliff on the right three black figures? These are our adversaries, I believe."

We set off at a trot.

In the bushes at the foot of the cliff, three horses were tied. We tied our horses there too, and clambered up a narrow path to a flat ledge, where Grushnitsky was awaiting us with the captain of dragoons and his other second, whose name and patronymic were Ivan Igna- tyevich. I never learned his surname.

"We have been expecting you for a long time," the captain of dragoons said with an ironic smile.

I took out my watch and showed it to him.

He apologized, saying that his was fast.

For several moments there was an awkward silence: at last, the doctor broke it by addressing himself to Grushnitsky:

"It seems to me," he said, "that both parties having shown their readiness to fight, and having thus satisfied the demands of honor, you might, gentlemen, talk matters over and close the affair amicably."

"I'm willing," I said.

The captain gave Grushnitsky a wink, and he, thinking that I was scared, assumed a proud air, although up to then a dull pallor had been spread over his cheeks. For the first time since we had come, he raised his eyes to look at me; but in his glance there was some kind of perturbation betraying an inner struggle.

"Explain your terms," he said, "and whatever I can do for you, you may be assured . . ."

"Here are my terms: this very day you will publicly retract your slander and will apologize to me."

"Sir, I am amazed that you dare offer such things to me!"

"What else could I offer you?"

"We shall fight."

I shrugged my shoulders.

"As you please; but consider—one of us will certainly be killed."

"My wish is that it may be you."

"And I'm convinced of the opposite."

He lost countenance, colored, then burst into forced laughter.

The captain took his arm and led him aside: for a long time, they whispered together. I had arrived in a fairly peaceable state of mind, but all this was beginning to annoy me.

The doctor came up to me.

"Listen," he said with obvious anxiety, "you must have forgotten about their plot. I do not know how to load a pistol, but in the present case . . . You are a strange fellow! Tell them that you are aware of their intention, and they will not dare . . . What is the sense of this? They'll bring you down like a bird."

"Please don't worry, Doctor, and wait a bit. . . . I shall arrange everything in such a way that on their side there will be no advantage whatever. Let them hugger-mugger a little."

"Gentlemen! This is becoming tiresome," I said in a loud voice. "If we are to fight, let us fight: you had plenty of time to talk it over yesterday."

"We are ready," answered the captain. "To your places, gentlemen! Doctor, have the kindness to measure off six paces."

"To your places!" repeated Ivan Ignatyevich, in a squeaky voice.

"Allow me!" I said. "There is one further condition. Since we are going to fight to the death, we should do everything possible to keep the matter secret and to avoid our seconds being held responsible. Do you agree?"

"We completely agree."

"Well, this is what I have thought up. Do you see at the summit of that sheer cliff on the right, a narrow bit of flat ground? There is a drop of about three hundred feet or more from there; below, there are sharp rocks. Each of us will take his stand on the very edge of the shelf, and in this way even a light wound will be fatal. This must be in keeping with your desire for you stipulated yourself, a distance of six paces. The one who is wounded will inevitably topple down and will be dashed to pieces; the doctor will take out the bullet, and then it should be very easy to ascribe this sudden death to an unfortunate leap. We shall draw lots to decide who is to shoot first. Let me inform you, in conclusion, that otherwise I will not fight."

"Have it your way!" said the captain after glancing meaningfully at Grushnitsky, who nodded in sign of consent. His face kept changing every minute. I had placed him in an awkward position. Had we fought under ordinary conditions, he might have aimed at my leg, wounded me lightly and satisfied, in this way, his thirst for revenge, without burdening his conscience too heavily. But now he had either to discharge his pistol into the air, or become a murderer, or lastly, abandon his vile plan and expose himself to equal danger with me. At this moment, I would not have wished to be in his place. He led the captain aside and began to say something to him with great heat. I saw his livid lips tremble, but the captain turned away from him with a contemptuous smile. "You're a fool!" he said to Grushnitsky, rather loudly, "you do not understand anything! Let us go, gentlemen!"

A narrow trail led up the precipice between the bushes; broken rocks formed the precarious steps of this natural staircase: holding onto bushes, we started to climb up. Grushnitsky was in front, behind him were his seconds, and after them came the doctor and I.

"I am amazed at you," said the doctor, giving my hand a strong squeeze. "Let me feel your pulse!... Oho! it's feverish!... But nothing shows in your face.... Only your eyes shine brighter than usual."

Suddenly, small stones noisily rolled down to our feet. What was it? Grushnitsky had stumbled. The branch which he had grasped broke and he would have slid down on his back, had not his seconds supported him.

"Take care!" I cried to him. "Don't fall beforehand: it's a bad omen. Remember Julius Caesar!"

Presently we reached the top of the jutting cliff: its flat surface was covered with fine sand, as if made especially for a duel. All around, melting in the golden mist of the morning, mountain summits teemed like an innumerable herd, and to the south Mount Elbruz raised its white mass, the last link in the chain of icy crests among which wispy clouds, which had blown from the east, were already roaming. I went to the edge of the natural platform and looked down: my head almost began to turn. Down below it was dark and cold as in the tomb; mossgrown jags of rocks, cast down by storm and time, were awaiting their prey.

The platform on which we were to fight presented an almost regular triangle. Six paces were measured off from the jutting angle and it was decided that he who would have to face first his foe's fire, should stand at the very apex, with his back to the chasm. If he were not killed, the principals were to change places.

I decided to give Grushnitsky every advantage; I wished to test

him. A spark of magnanimity might awaken in his soul—and then
everything would turn out for the best; but vanity and weakness of
character were to triumph! . . . I wished to give myself the full right
to show him no quarter, if fate spared me. Who has not concluded
similar agreements with his conscience?

"Spin the coin, Doctor!" said the captain.

The doctor took out of his pocket a silver coin and held it up.

"Tails!" cried Grushnitsky hurriedly, like a man who has been
suddenly awakened by a friendly nudge.

"Heads!" I said.

The coin soared up and fell with a tinkle; everyone rushed toward
it.

"You're lucky," I said to Grushnitsky, "you are to fire first! But
remember that if you do not kill me, I shall not miss—I give you my
word of honor."

He colored; he was ashamed to kill an unarmed man. I was looking
at him intently; for a moment it seemed to me that he would throw
himself at my feet, begging for forgiveness, but who could own having
such a villainous design? . . . Only one recourse remained to him—to
fire in the air. I was sure he would fire in the air! Only one thing could
interfere with it: the thought that I should demand another duel.

"It is time!" the doctor whispered to me, pulling my sleeve. "If
you do not tell them now that we know their intentions, all is lost.
Look, he is already loading. . . . If you do not say anything, I myself
shall. . . ."

"Not for anything in the world, Doctor!" I replied, holding him
back by the arm. "You would spoil everything. You gave me your word
not to interfere. . . . What does it matter to you? Perhaps, I wish to be
killed. . . ."

He glanced at me with surprise.

"Oh, that's different! . . . Only do not bring complaints against
me in the next world."

In the meantime, the captain had loaded his pistols; he handed
one to Grushnitsky, whispering something to him with a smile; the
other he handed to me.

I took my stand at the apex of the platform, bracing my left foot
firmly against the rock and leaning forward a little, so as not to fall
backward in the case of a light wound.

Grushnitsky stationed himself opposite me and at a given signal
began to raise his pistol. His knees shook. He was aiming straight at
my forehead.

Ineffable fury flared up in my breast.

Suddenly, he lowered the muzzle of his pistol and, going as white as a sheet, turned toward his second:

"I can't," he said in a hollow voice.

"Coward!" answered the captain.

The shot rang out. The bullet grazed my knee. Involuntarily, I took several steps forward so as to get away, as soon as possible, from the brink.

"Well, friend Grushnitsky, it's a pity you've missed!" said the captain. "Now it's your turn, take your stand! Embrace me first: we shall not see each other again!" They embraced; the captain could hardly keep himself from laughing. "Have no fear," he added, with a sly glance at Grushnitsky. "All's nonsense on earth! . . . Nature is a ninny, fate is a henny, and life is a penny!"

After this tragic phrase, delivered with appropriate dignity, he withdrew to his place. Ivan Ignatyevich, with tears, likewise embraced Grushnitsky, and now he was left alone facing me. To this day I try to explain to myself what kind of feeling was boiling then in my breast. It was the irritation of injured vanity, and contempt, and wrath which arose at the thought that this man, now looking at me with such confidence and such calm insolence, had tried, two minutes before, without exposing himself to any danger, to kill me like a dog, for if I had been wounded in the leg a little more severely, I would have certainly fallen off the cliff.

For several moments, I kept looking intently into his face, striving to discern the slightest trace of repentance. But it seemed to me that he was withholding a smile.

"I advise you to say your prayers before dying," I then said to him.

"Do not worry about my soul more than you do about your own. One thing I ask of you: shoot quickly."

"And you do not retract your slander? You do not ask my pardon? Think well: does not your conscience say something to you?"

"Mr. Pechorin!" cried the captain of dragoons, "you are not here to hear confession, allow me to tell you. . . . Let us finish quickly, otherwise somebody may come driving through the gorge and see us."

"All right. Doctor, come over to me."

The doctor came. Poor doctor! He was paler than Grushnitsky had been ten minutes before.

I spaced on purpose the following words, pronouncing them loudly and distinctly, the way a death sentence is pronounced:

"Doctor, these gentlemen, no doubt in their hurry, forgot to place a bullet in my pistol. Please, load it again—and properly!"

"This cannot be!" the captain was shouting, "it cannot be! I loaded both pistols: perhaps, the ball rolled out of yours. . . . That is not my fault! And you have no right to reload . . . no right whatsoever. It is utterly against the rules; I shall not permit it. . . ."

"All right!" I said to the captain. "If so, you and I will have a duel on the same conditions."

He faltered.

Grushnitsky stood, his head sunk on his breast, embarrassed and gloomy.

"Leave them alone!" he finally said to the captain who wanted to snatch my pistol out of the doctor's hands. "You know very well yourself that they are right."

In vain did the captain make various signs to him. Grushnitsky would not even look.

Meanwhile, the doctor had loaded the pistol, and now handed it to me.

Upon seeing this, the captain spat and stamped his foot.

"Brother, you *are* a fool!" he said. "A vulgar fool! . . . Since you've relied upon me, you should obey me in everything. . . . Serve you right! Perish like a fly . . ." He turned away and, as he walked off, he muttered: "And still it is utterly against the rules."

"Grushnitsky!" I said. "There is still time: retract your slander and I shall forgive you everything. You did not succeed in fooling me, and my self-esteem is satisfied. Remember, we were friends once. . . ."

His face blazed, his eyes glittered.

"Shoot!" he answered. "I despise myself and hate you. If you do not kill me, I shall cut your throat in a dark alley. There is no room in this world for the two of us. . . ."

I fired. . . .

When the smoke dispersed, Grushnitsky was not on the ledge. Only dust in a light column still revolved on the brink of the precipice.

All cried out in one voice.

"*Finita la commedia!*" I said to the doctor.

He did not answer and turned away in horror.

I shrugged my shoulders and bowed to Grushnitsky's seconds as I took leave of them.

On my way down the trail, I noticed, among the crevices of the cliffs, Grushnitsky's blood-stained body. Involuntarily, I shut my eyes.

I untied my horse and set out for home at a walk: a stone lay on my heart. The sun seemed to me without luster; its rays did not warm me.

Before reaching the suburb, I turned off to the right, down the gorge. The sight of a human being would have been burdensome to me. I wanted to be alone. With slack reins, my head sunk on my breast, I rode a long while; at last, I found myself in a spot that was completely unknown to me. I turned my horse around and began to look for the road; the sun was already setting when I reached Kislovodsk, exhausted, on an exhausted horse.

My valet told me that Werner had called, and handed me two notes: one from Werner himself, the other . . . from Vera.

I unsealed the first one; it contained the following message:

"Everything has been arranged as well as possible: the body has been brought back in a disfigured condition, the bullet has been extracted from the breast. Everybody believes that his death had been caused by an accident; only the commandant, to whom your quarrel was probably known, shook his head, but said nothing. There are no proofs against you whatsoever, and you can sleep in peace . . . if you can. . . . Good-bye."

For a long time, I could not make myself open the second note. . . . What could she tell me? . . . A heavy presentiment agitated my soul.

Here it is, this letter, whose every word is indelibly graven in my memory:

"I write to you with the complete certitude that we shall never see each other again. Several years ago, when parting with you, I thought the same; but Heaven chose to try me a second time. I did not withstand this trial: my weak heart submitted again to the familiar voice. You will not despise me for this, will you? This letter is going to be both a farewell and a confession: I feel obliged to tell you all that has accumulated in my heart ever since it loved you. I shall not blame you— you treated me as any other man would have done; you loved me as your property, as a source of joys, agitations and sorrows, which mutually replaced one another and without which life would have been dull and monotonous. This I understood from the first; but you were unhappy, and I sacrificed myself, hoping that some day you would appreciate my sacrifice, that some day you would understand my deep tenderness, not depending on any circumstances. Since then much time has passed. I penetrated into all the secrets of your soul . . . and realized that my hope had been a vain one. It made me bitterly sad! But my love had grown one with my soul; it became darker, but did not go out.

"We part forever; yet you may be sure that I shall never love another: my soul has spent upon you all its treasures, its tears and hopes. She, who has loved you once, cannot look without a certain

contempt on other men, not because you are better than they—oh,
no!—but because there is something special about your nature, peculiar
to you alone, something proud and mysterious. In your voice, whatever
you may be saying, there is unconquerable power. None is able to
desire so incessantly to be loved; in none is evil so attractive; the gaze
of none promises so much bliss; none knows better to use his advantages; and none can be so genuinely unhappy as you, because none
tries so hard to convince himself of the contrary.

"I must now explain to you the reason for my hurried departure:
it will seem to you of little importance, since it concerns me alone.

"This morning, my husband came into my room and related your
quarrel with Grushnitsky. Evidently, I looked terribly upset, for he
looked long and intently into my eyes. I nearly fainted at the thought
that you must fight today and that I was the cause of it: it seemed to
me that I would go mad. . . . But now that I can reason, I feel sure
that your life will be spared: it is impossible that you should die without
me, impossible! My husband paced the room for a long time. I do not
know what he was saying to me, I do not remember what I answered
him. . . . No doubt, I told him that I loved you. . . . I only remember
that toward the end of our conversation, he insulted me with a dreadful
word and went out. I heard him order the coach to be got ready. . . .
I have now been sitting at the window for three hours, awaiting your
return. . . . But you are alive, you cannot die! . . . The coach is almost
ready. . . . Farewell, farewell . . . I perish—but what does it matter?
If I could be sure that you will always remember me—I don't say, love
me—no, only remember. . . . Farewell. . . . Somebody is coming. . , .
I must hide this letter. . . .

"You do not love Mary, do you? You will not marry her? Listen,
you must make this sacrifice to me: for you I have lost everything in
the world. . . ."

Like a madman, I rushed out onto the porch, jumped on my
Circassian horse which was being promenaded in the yard, and galloped
off, at full speed, on the road to Pyatigorsk. Unmercifully I urged my
exhausted steed, which, snorting and all covered with foam, carried
me swiftly along the stony road.

The sun had already hidden in a black cloud that rested on the
ridge of the western mountains; it had become dark and damp in the
gorge. The Podkumok River roared dully and monotonously as it made
its way over stones. I galloped on, breathless with impatience. The
thought of arriving in Pyatigorsk too late to find her, beat like a hammer
on my heart. To see her for one minute, one more minute, say good-
bye to her, press her hand . . . I prayed, cursed, wept, laughed. . . .

No, nothing can express my anxiety, my despair! Faced by the possibility of losing Vera forever, I felt that she had become dearer to me
than anything in the world—dearer than life, honor, happiness! God
knows what strange, mad plans swarmed in my head. . . . And meanwhile I continued to gallop, urging my horse mercilessly. And presently,
I began to notice that my steed was breathing more heavily; once or
twice he had already stumbled on level ground. Three miles remained
to Essentuki, a Cossack settlement where I might be able to change
horses.

Everything would have been saved had my horse's strength lasted
for another ten minutes! But suddenly, as we emerged from a small
ravine at the end of the defile where there was a sharp turn, he crashed
onto the ground. I nimbly jumped off, tried to make him get up, tugged
at the bridle—in vain. A hardly audible moan escaped through his
clenched teeth; a few minutes later he was dead. I remained alone in
the steppe, my last hope gone; I tried to proceed on foot—my legs
gave way under me. Worn out by the agitations of the day and by
insomnia, I fell on the wet grass and began crying like a child.

And for a long time, I lay motionless and cried bitterly, not attempting to hold back the tears and sobs. I thought my chest would
burst; all my firmness, all my coolness vanished like smoke; my soul
wilted, my reason was mute and if, at that moment, anyone had seen
me, he would have turned away in contempt.

When the night dew and the mountain breeze had cooled my
burning head, and my thoughts had regained their usual order, I realized
that to pursue perished happiness was useless and senseless. What was
it that I still needed? To see her? What for? Was not everything ended
between us? One bitter farewell kiss would not enrich my memories,
and after it, we would only find it harder to part.

Yet it pleases me that I am capable of weeping. It may have been
due, however, to upset nerves, to a sleepless night, to a couple of
minutes spent facing the muzzle of a pistol, and to an empty stomach.

Everything is for the best! That new torment produced in me, to
use military parlance, a fortunate diversion. Tears are wholesome, and
then, probably, if I had not gone for that ride, and had not been
compelled to walk ten miles home, that night, too, sleep would not
have come to close my eyes.

I returned to Kislovodsk at five in the morning, threw myself on
my bed and slept the sleep of Napoleon after Waterloo.

When I awoke it was already dark outside. I seated myself at the
open window, unbuttoned my Caucasian overcoat, and the mountain
breeze cooled my breast, which had not yet been appeased by the heavy

---

sleep of exhaustion. Far away, beyond the river, through the tops of the dense limes sheltering it, there flickered lights in the buildings of the fort and of the suburb. Around the house, all was quiet. The princess's house was in darkness.

The doctor came in; his brow was furrowed; contrary to his custom, he did not give me his hand.

"Where do you come from, Doctor?"

"From the Princess Ligovskoy. Her daughter is ill—a nervous breakdown.... However, that is not the matter, but this: the authorities are suspicious, and, although nothing can be proved positively, I would nevertheless advise you to be more careful. The princess told me today that she knows you fought a duel over her daughter. She learned it all from that little old man—what's his name? He witnessed your clash with Grushnitsky at the restaurant. I came to warn you. Good-bye. I suppose we shan't see each other again: you will be transferred somewhere."

On the threshold, he stopped. He would have liked to shake my hand, and had I displayed to him the slightest desire for it, he would have thrown himself on my neck; but I remained as cold as stone—and he left.

That's the human being for you! They are all like that: they know beforehand all the bad sides of an action. They help you, they advise you, they even approve of it, perceiving the impossibility of a different course—and afterward they wash their hands of it, and turn away indignantly from him who had the courage to take upon himself the entire burden of responsibility. They are all like that, even the kindest, even the most intelligent ones.

On the following morning, upon receiving from the higher authorities the order to proceed to the fort of N——, I called on the old princess to say good-bye.

She was surprised when, to her question, whether I had not anything particularly important to tell her, I answered that I wished her happiness and so forth.

"As to me, I must talk to you very seriously."

I sat down in silence.

It was obvious she did not know how to begin. Her face turned purple, her plump fingers drummed upon the table; at last, she began thus, in a halting voice:

"Listen, Monsieur Pechorin, I believe you are a gentleman."

I bowed.

"I am even convinced of it," she went on, "although your behavior is somewhat ambiguous; but you may have reasons which I do not know, and it is those reasons that you now must confide to me. You have defended my daughter from slander; you fought a duel for her—consequently, risked your life. Do not reply. I know you will not admit it, because Grushnitsky is dead." (She crossed herself.) "God will forgive him, and He will forgive you, too, I hope! . . . That does not concern me. . . . I dare not condemn you, since my daughter, though innocently, was the cause of it. She told me everything—I think, everything. You declared your love to her . . . she confessed her love to you." (Here the princess sighed heavily.) "But she is ill, and I am certain that it is no ordinary illness! A secret sorrow is killing her; she does not admit it, but I am certain that you are its cause. . . . Listen, you may think, perhaps, that I am looking for rank, for huge riches. Undeceive yourself! I seek only my daughter's happiness. Your present situation is not enviable, but it can improve: you are a man of means. My daughter loves you; she has been brought up in such a way that she will make her husband's happiness. I am rich, she is my only child. . . . Tell me, what holds you back? . . . You see, I should not have been saying all this to you, but I rely on your heart, on your honor. . . . Remember, I have but one daughter . . . one. . . ."

She began to cry.

"Princess," I said, "it is impossible for me to answer you. Allow me to talk to your daughter alone."

"Never!" she exclaimed, rising from her chair in great agitation.

"As you please," I answered, preparing to go.

She lapsed into thought, made me a sign to wait, and left the room.

Five minutes passed; my heart was beating violently, but my thoughts were calm, my head cool. No matter how hard I searched my breast for one spark of love for the charming Mary, my efforts were in vain.

Presently the door opened, and she came in. Good Lord! How she had altered since I saw her last—and had that been so very long ago?

On reaching the middle of the room, she swayed; I jumped up, gave her my arm and led her to an armchair.

I stood facing her. For a long time we were silent. Her great eyes, filled with ineffable sadness, seemed to seek in my eyes something resembling hope; her pale lips vainly tried to smile; her delicate hands, folded in her lap, were so thin and diaphanous, that I felt sorry for her.

"Princess," I said, "you know that I laughed at you? You must despise me."

A feverish rosiness appeared on her cheeks.

I went on: "Consequently, you cannot love me. . . ."

She turned away, rested her elbow on a table, covered her eyes with her hand, and it seemed to me that tears glistened in them.

"Oh God!" she uttered almost inaudibly.

This was becoming unbearable: another minute, and I would have fallen at her feet.

"So you see for yourself," I said, in as firm a voice as I could and with a strained smile, "you see for yourself that I cannot marry you. Even if you wished it now, you would soon regret it. My talk with your mother obliged me to have it out with you, so frankly and so roughly. I hope she is under a delusion: it will be easy for you to undeceive her. You see, I am playing, in your eyes, a most miserable and odious part, and even this I admit—this is all I'm able to do for you. However unfavorable the opinion you may have of me, I submit to it. You see, I am base in regard to you. Am I not right that even if you loved me, from this moment on you despise me?"

She turned to me as pale as marble; only her eyes glittered marvelously.

"I hate you," she said.

I thanked her, bowed respectfully and left.

An hour later, an express *troika* was rushing me away from Kislovodsk. A few miles before reaching Essentuki, I recognized, by the roadside, the carcass of my gallant steed. The saddle had been removed, probably by some passing Cossack and, instead of the saddle, there were two ravens perched on the dead beast's back. I sighed and turned away.

And now here, in this dull fort, I often scan the past in thought, and wonder why I had not wanted to tread that path, which fate had opened for me, where quiet joys and peace of mind awaited me? No, I would not have got used to such an existence! I am like a sailor born and bred on the deck of a pirate brig. His soul is used to storms and battles, and, when cast out on the shore, he feels bored and oppressed, no matter how the shady grove lures him, no matter how the peaceful sun shines on him. All day long he haunts the sand of the shore, hearkens to the monotonous murmur of the surf and peers into the misty distance. Will there not appear, glimpsed on the pale line separating the blue main from the gray cloudlets, the longed-for sail, at first like the wing of a sea gull, but gradually separating itself from the foam of the breakers and, at a smooth clip, nearing the desolate quay?

(1840)

NIKOLAY GOGOL

*THE CONTEMPORARIES OF NIKOLAY GOGOL (1809–1852) regarded
him as the most Russian writer of all. Turgenev said of him, "Gogol
was more than a writer to us: he revealed us to ourselves. . . . One
has to be Russian to feel this. Even the most acute minds among
foreigners saw Gogol only as a humorist in the English manner. They
failed to see his historic significance."*

*Gogol was born into a small landowner's family in Ukraine. He
was one of twelve children, of whom five survived. This unparalleled
master of the Russian language was sickly all his life, or a
hypochondriac—probably both. As a schoolboy and young man, he
showed great interest in poetry, painting, and theater. His strange behavior earned him the nickname "the mysterious dwarf" from his
schoolmates. Gogol was a voracious reader and educated himself by
indiscriminately devouring masses of odd assortments of books and
tracts. In 1828 he moved to the capital, St. Petersburg, and in the next
eight years wrote* The Wedding *and* The Inspector General, *satirical
and comic masterpieces, which belong to the short list of the Russian
dramas known to almost all Russians. He wrote stories based on
Ukrainian folklore and local color, and later the so-called Petersburg
stories, fantastic narratives, of which "The Overcoat" is one.*

*Between 1836 and 1848, he traveled and lived mainly in Europe.
He returned to Russia only twice during that period. While he resided
in Italy, he wrote, besides other works, his great paradoxical novel,*
Dead Souls, *an epic of Russian provincial life, detailing the adventures
and misadventures of Chichikov, a con artist who buys up titles to
deceased serfs in order to use them for shady financial dealings. Gogol
filled his novel with a gallery of amazing provincial characters, using
these grotesque portraits to satirize the status quo, yet also to afford*

glimpses of a potentially heroic and glorious Russia, one hinted at in spirited Russian song and in zestful travel along the highways of the country. It is a novel of collapse and corruption, of failures in the real world, suffused in laughter, and suggesting that a redemption, a regeneration, might nevertheless be possible.

The remaining years of his life he spent attempting to write a second and possibly third part of Dead Souls. *He was melancholy and ill. Never married, he was afraid of women, whom he either idealized or regarded as dangerous, destructive demons. Gogol's spiritual self-education grew increasingly important to him. He read much devotional literature and works by the church fathers, and associated with religious teachers. He wrote a slim volume,* Meditations on the Divine Liturgy, *which was published only many years after his death. His* Selected Passages from a Correspondence with Friends *expressed his deep and at times unrealistic or arrogant religious fervor. He was a remarkable and strange man of great naïveté, who enjoyed the firm friendship of a number of the outstanding people of his age.*

He went to Jerusalem on a pilgrimage, but was disappointed in its lack of effect on himself. After a long illness aggravated by bizarre medical treatments, during which he starved himself and burned manuscripts of his unpublished works, he died in 1852.

This enigmatic eccentric, who was both a comic genius and a man of superterrestrial spiritual strivings and visions, a magician and juggler with the Russian language, came to be venerated as the first great Russian storyteller and dramatist.

The saying has become established in Russian literary tradition that "we have all come out from under Gogol's overcoat." While there is no agreement either on who first said it or on what exactly it means, Gogol's story "The Overcoat" perhaps best illustrates the twin effects—entertainment and mystification—that are his trademark.

On one hand the story stirs the reader's compassion. Particularly in the 1840s and 1850s and again during the Communist period of Russian history, "The Overcoat" was read as the best of the innumerable early nineteenth-century stories intended to arouse pity for the lowly, unjustly treated clerks of the vast imperial civil service. On the other hand, the story has been regarded chiefly as a masterpiece of literary nonsense, of the absurd, of fantasy, and of humor.

The story takes place in Gogol's St. Petersburg, which Donald Fanger, in his superb book The Creation of Nikolai Gogol, *has called "an image of an unnatural and malevolent capital." Writes Fanger, "A meek, puppet-like clerk is set on the road to a minimal kind of manhood, robbed of the possession which triggered the change in him . . .*

[the tale] raises questions: of ethical spiritual values, love, humility, fellow feeling, Christian brotherhood, of what is significant in life (and art). . . . Neither fellow feeling nor indifference are adequate" toward such insignificant people as the little clerk-victim Akakii.

The story mixes tones and illustrates Gogol's aesthetic of striking effects—exaggeration, incoherence, spinning off into the space of endless elaboration. "The Overcoat" is full of astonishing details such as the toenail of the tailor Petrovich or the pigs living in private houses. But there is also the pitiful pathos of Akakii Akakiievich's pleas for understanding and compassion.

The narrator frustrates expectations of the reader, sidetracking him often—and switching from the tone of a chatty author to a pitying one, and then on to a ghost story. He combines pathos, satire, and playfulness, and supplies a solid dose of the so-called realistic elements—humble clerks, a tailor and his wife, rank distinctions, and so forth. The world he creates is absurd and the characters bizarre. The ornamental curlicues of style combine with sociopsychological elements.

This ornamental style, a subcategory of Russian fiction, grew into a firm family tree and continues to spread (in the early Dostoyevsky, Leskov, Remizov, Babel, Olesha, Sinyavsky, Nabokov, and others.)

Mystification played a large role in Gogol's life as well as in his works. Fanger has termed this paradoxical creature of contradictions "an artist-monk, a Christian-satirist, an ascetic and humorist, a martyr of the exalted ideal and the unsolved riddle." Vladimir Nabokov called "The Overcoat" "a grotesque and grim nightmare making black holes in the dim pattern of life." In response to his publisher's request to supply a plot summary of "The Overcoat," Nabokov wrote that the story went "like that—mumble, mumble, lyrical wave, mumble, lyrical wave, mumble, lyrical wave, mumble, fantastic climax, mumble, mumble, and back into the chaos from which they all derived. His work is a phenomenon of language, not of ideas . . . not concerned with pitying the underdog or cursing the upper dog."

Gogol's contradictory, perplexing, infuriating Russian tendencies are pronounced in the infuriating and perplexing Selected Passages from a Correspondence with Friends. *The passage on Easter Sunday included here expresses Gogol's yearning and vision, his sense of a gap between things as they are and as they could be. He ranges—in the same breath—from indictment of Russia as it is to a praise of Russia as potentially the greatest, most saintly country. He is propelled into an ecstatic faith that the Russians are the most Christian and saintly people not in spite of being so fallen, so depraved, but almost because of it.*

This "flux of attitudes and tendencies," as Donald Fanger calls it, these "sights and sounds" are "the raw material of an unborn national self-consciousness"—or at least, of one important part of it.

Gogol believed that Russia, as it had come to be constituted, was the worst possible fallen society, but he also believed that it could be redeemed by a process of regeneration. This belief in the power of the teacher's and writer's word led him to a touching, perhaps ludicrous confidence in his ability to persuade his readers to take the path toward self-transformation. The response to his Selected Passages set the terms of the discourse throughout nineteenth-century Russian intellectual history.

The passage from the influential critic Vissarion Belinsky's letter to Gogol is the main document of the attitude that carried the day with the Russian radical intelligentsia: the refutation of Gogol's religious ideology. That letter gave voice to what became the ruling, accepted view of Gogol, in Russia and abroad. But there was a rivulet of pro-Gogolian followers—a positive legacy. The passages included here by Grigoriev, Blok, and Kniazhnin, represent this other, pro-Gogol current. These express persistent strains in the Russian sensibility, toward which we should not adopt an ostrichlike attitude, even if the majority of nineteenth-century Russian intellectuals, and almost all twentieth-century Russian and Western observers, did shut their eyes to it. The Gogol-Grigoriev-Blok penchant or extreme addiction for seeing both how potentially marvelous Russia could be and how sordid and no-account it is in actuality plays a very important part in the utopian saga of the Russian mind.

THE OVERCOAT

In the Bureau of . . . but it might be better not to mention the bureau by its precise name. There is nothing more touchy than all these bureaus, regiments, chancelleries of every sort, and, in a word, every sort of person belonging to the administrative classes. Nowadays every civilian, even, considers all of society insulted in his own person. Quite recently, so they say, a petition came through from a certain captain of rural police in some town or other (I can't recall its name), in which he explained clearly that the whole social structure was headed for ruin and that his sacred name was actually being taken entirely in vain, and, in proof, he documented his petition with the enormous tome of some romantic work or other wherein, every ten pages or so, a captain of rural police appeared—in some passages even in an out-and-out drunken state. And so, to avoid any and all unpleasantnesses, we'd better call the bureau in question *a certain bureau*. And so, in *a certain bureau* there served *a certain clerk*—a clerk whom one could hardly style very remarkable: quite low of stature, somewhat pockmarked, somewhat rusty-hued of hair, even somewhat purblind, at first glance; rather bald at the temples, with wrinkles along both cheeks, and his face of that complexion which is usually called hemorrhoidal. Well, what would you? It's the Petersburg climate that's to blame. As far as his rank is concerned (for among us the rank must be made known first of all), why, he was what they call a perpetual titular councilor —a rank which, as everybody knows, various writers who have a praiseworthy wont of throwing their weight about among those who are in no position to hit back have twitted and exercised their keen wits against often and long. This clerk's family name was Bashmachkin. It's quite evident, by the very name, that it sprang from *bashmak* or shoe, but at what time, just when, and how it sprang from a shoe— of that nothing is known. For not only this clerk's father but his grandfather and even his brother-in-law, and absolutely all the Bashmachkins, walked about in boots, merely resoling them three times a year.

His name and patronymic were Akakii Akakiievich. It may, perhaps, strike the reader as somewhat odd and out of the way, but the reader may rest assured that the author has not gone out of his way at all to find it, but that certain circumstances had come about of themselves in such fashion that there was absolutely no way of giving him any other name. And the precise way this came about was as follows. Akakii Akakiievich was born—unless my memory plays me false—on the night of the twenty-third of March. His late mother, a government clerk's wife, and a very good woman, was all set to christen her child, all fit and proper. She was still lying in bed, facing the door, while on her right stood the godfather, a most excellent man by the name of Ivan Ivanovich Eroshkin, who had charge of some department or other in a certain administrative office, and the godmother, the wife of the precinct police officer, a woman of rare virtues, by the name of Arina Semenovna Byelobrushkina. The mother was offered the choice of any one of three names: Mokii, Sossii—or the child could even be given the name of that great martyr, Hozdavat. "No," the late lamented had reflected, "what sort of names are these?" In order to please her they opened the calendar at another place—and the result was again three names: Triphilii, Dula, and Varahasii. "What a visitation!" said the elderly woman. "What names all these be! To tell you the truth, I've never even heard the likes of them. If it were at least Baradat or

Baruch, but why do Triphilii and Varahasii have to crop up?" They turned over another page—and came up with Pavsikahii and Vahtissii. "Well, I can see now," said the mother, "that such is evidently his fate. In that case it would be better if he were called after his father. His father was an Akakii—let the son be an Akakii also." And that's how Akakii Akakiievich came to be Akakii Akakiievich.

The child was baptized, during which rite he began to bawl and made terrible faces as if anticipating that it would be his lot to become a perpetual titular councilor. And so that's the way it had all come about. We have brought the matter up so that the reader might see for himself that all this had come about through sheer inevitability and it had been utterly impossible to bestow any other name upon Akakii Akakiievich.

When, at precisely what time, he entered the bureau, and who gave him the berth, were things which no one could recall. No matter how many directors and his superiors of one sort of another came and went, he was always to be seen in the one and the same spot, in the same posture, in the very same post, always the same clerk of correspondence, so that subsequently people became convinced that he evidently had come into the world just the way he was, all done and set, in a uniform frock and bald at the temples. No respect whatsoever was shown him in the bureau. The porters not only didn't jump up from their places whenever he happened to pass by, but didn't even as much as glance at him, as if nothing more than a common housefly had passed through the reception hall. His superiors treated him with a certain chill despotism. Some assistant or other of some head of a department would simply shove papers under his nose, without as much as saying "Transcribe these," or "Here's a rather pretty, interesting little case," or any of those small pleasantries that are current in well-conducted administrative institutions. And he would take the work, merely glancing at the paper, without looking up to see who had put it down before him and whether that person had the right to do so; he took it and right then and there went to work on it. The young clerks made fun of him and sharpened their wits at his expense, to whatever extent their quill-driving wittiness sufficed, retailing in his very presence the various stories made up about him; they said of his landlady, a crone of seventy, that she beat him, and asked him when their wedding would take place; they scattered torn paper over his head, maintaining it was snow.

But not a word did Akakii Akakiievich say in answer to all this, as if there were actually nobody before him. It did not even affect his work: in the midst of all these annoyances he did not make a single clerical error. Only when the jest was past all bearing, when they jostled his arm, hindering him from doing his work, would he say: "Leave me alone! Why do you pick on me?" And there was something odd about his words and in the voice with which he uttered them. In that voice could be heard something that moved one to pity—so much so that one young man, a recent entrant, who, following the example of the others, had permitted himself to make fun of Akakii Akakiievich, stopped suddenly, as if pierced to the quick, and from that time on everything seemed to change in his eyes and appeared in a different light. Some sort of preternatural force seemed to repel him from the companions he had made, having taken them for decent, sociable people. And for a long time afterward, in the very midst of his most cheerful moments, the little squat clerk would appear before him, with the small bald patches on each side of his forehead, and he would hear his heart-piercing words "Leave me alone! Why do you pick on me?" And in these heart-piercing words he caught the ringing sound of others: "I am your brother." And the poor young man would cover his eyes with his hand, and many a time in his life thereafter did he shudder, seeing how much inhumanity there is in man, how much hidden ferocious coarseness lurks in refined, cultured worldliness and, O God! even in that very man whom the world holds to be noble and honorable. . . .

It is doubtful if you could find anywhere a man whose life lay so much in his work. It would hardly do to say that he worked with zeal; no, it was a labor of love. Thus, in this transcription of his, he visioned some sort of diversified and pleasant world all its own. His face expressed delight; certain letters were favorites of his and whenever he came across them he would be beside himself with rapture: he'd chuckle, and wink, and help things along by working his lips, so that it seemed as if one could read on his face every letter his quill was outlining. If rewards had been meted out to him commensurately with his zeal, he might have, to his astonishment, actually found himself among the state councilors; but, as none other than those wits, his own co-workers, expressed it, all he'd worked himself up to was a button in a buttonhole too wide, and piles in his backside.

However, it would not be quite correct to say that absolutely no attention was paid him. One director, being a kindly man and wishing to reward him for his long service, gave orders that some work of a more important nature than the usual transcription be assigned to him; to be precise, he was told to make a certain referral to another administrative department out of a docket already prepared; the matter consisted, all in all, of changing the main title as well as some pronouns here and there from the first person singular to the third person singular.

This made so much work for him that he was all of a sweat, kept mopping his forehead, and finally said: "No, better let me transcribe something." Thenceforth they left him to his transcription for all time. Outside of this transcription, it seemed, nothing existed for him.

He gave no thought whatsoever to his dress; the uniform frock coat on him wasn't the prescribed green at all, but rather of some rusty-flour hue. His collar was very tight and very low, so that his neck, even though it wasn't a long one, seemed extraordinarily long emerging therefrom, like those gypsum kittens with nodding heads which certain outlanders balance by the dozen atop their heads and peddle throughout Russia. And, always, something was bound to stick to his coat: a wisp of hay or some bit of thread; in addition to that, he had a peculiar knack whenever he walked through the streets of getting under some window at the precise moment when garbage of every sort was being thrown out of it, and for that reason always bore off on his hat watermelon and cantaloupe rinds and other such trifles. Not once in all his life had he ever turned his attention to the everyday things and doings out in the street—something, as everybody knows, that is always watched with eager interest by Akakii Akakiievich's confrere, the young government clerk, the penetration of whose lively gaze is so extensive that he will even take in somebody on the opposite sidewalk who has ripped loose his trouser strap—a thing that never fails to evoke a sly smile on the young clerk's face. But even if Akakii Akakiievich did look at anything, he saw thereon nothing but his own neatly, evenly penned lines of script, and only when some horse's nose, bobbing up from no one knew where, would be placed on his shoulder and let a whole gust of wind in his face through its nostrils, would he notice that he was not in the middle of a line of script but, rather, in the middle of the roadway.

On coming home he would immediately sit down at the table, gulp down his cabbage soup, and bolt a piece of veal with onions, without noticing in the least the taste of either, eating everything together with the flies and whatever else God may have sent at that particular time of the year. On perceiving that his belly was beginning to bulge, he'd get up from the table, take out a small bottle of ink, and transcribe the papers he had brought home. If there was no homework, he would deliberately, for his own edification, make a copy of some paper for himself, especially if the document was remarkable not for its beauty of style but merely addressed to some new or important person.

Even at those hours when the gray sky of Petersburg becomes entirely extinguished and all the pettifogging tribe has eaten its fill and

finished dinner, each as best he could, in accordance with the salary
he receives and his own bent, when everybody has already rested up
after the scraping of quills in various departments, the running around,
the unavoidable cares about their own affairs and the affairs of others,
and all that which restless man sets himself as a task voluntarily and
to an even greater extent than necessary—at a time when the petty
bureaucrats hasten to devote whatever time remained to enjoyment:
he who was of the more lively sort hastening to the theater; another
for a saunter through the streets, devoting the time to an inspection of
certain pretty little hats; still another to some evening party, to spend
that time in paying compliments to some comely young lady, the star
of a small bureaucratic circle; a fourth (and this happened most frequently of all) simply going to call on a confrere in a flat up three or
four flights of stairs, consisting of two small rooms with an entry and
a kitchen and one or two attempts at the latest improvements—a ker-
osene lamp instead of candles, or some other elegant little thing that
had cost many sacrifices, such as going without dinners or good
times—in short, even at the time when all the petty bureaucrats scatter
through the small apartments of their friends for a session of dummy
whist, sipping tea out of tumblers and nibbling at cheap zwieback,
drawing deep at their pipes, the stems thereof as long as walking sticks,
retailing, during the shuffling and dealing, some bit of gossip or other
from high society that had reached them at long last (something which
no Russian, under any circumstances, and of whatever estate he be,
can ever deny himself), or even, when there was nothing whatsoever
to talk about, retelling the eternal chestnut of the commandant to whom
people came to say that the tail of the horse on the Falconet monument
had been docked—in short, even at the time when every soul yearns
to be diverted, Akakii Akakiievich did not give himself up to any
diversion. No man could claim having ever seen him at any evening
gathering. Having had his sweet fill of quill-driving, he would lie down
to sleep, smiling at the thought of the next day: just what would God
send him on the morrow?

Such was the peaceful course of life of a man who, with a yearly
salary of four hundred, knew how to be content with his lot, and that
course might even have continued to a ripe old age had it not been for
sundry calamities, such as are strewn along the path of life, not only
of titular, but even privy, actual, court, and all other sorts of councilors,
even those who never give any counsel to anybody nor ever accept any
counsel from others for themselves.

There is, in Petersburg, a formidable foe of all those whose salary
runs to four hundred a year or thereabouts. This foe is none other than

our northern frost—even though, by the bye, they do say that it's the
most healthful thing for you. At nine in the morning, precisely at that
hour when the streets are thronged with those on their way to sundry
bureaus, it begins dealing out such powerful and penetrating fillips to
all noses, without any discrimination, that the poor bureaucrats absolutely do not know how to hide them. At this time, when even those
who fill the higher posts feel their foreheads aching because of the frost
and the tears come to their eyes, the poor titular councilors are sometimes utterly defenseless. The sole salvation, if one's overcoat is of the
thinnest, lies in dashing, as quickly as possible, through five or six
blocks and then stamping one's feet for a long time in the porter's
room, until the faculties and gifts for administrative duties, which have
been frozen on the way, are thus thawed out at last.

For some time Akakii Akakiievich had begun to notice that the
cold was somehow penetrating his back and shoulders with especial
ferocity, despite the fact that he tried to run the required distance as
quickly as possible. It occurred to him, at last, that there might be some
defects about his overcoat. After looking it over rather thoroughly at
home he discovered that in two or three places—in the back and at
the shoulders, to be exact—it had become no better than the coarsest
of sacking; the cloth was rubbed to such an extent that one could see
through it, and the lining had crept apart. The reader must be informed
that Akakii Akakiievich's overcoat, too, was a butt for the jokes of the
petty bureaucrats; it had been deprived of the honorable name of an
overcoat, even, and dubbed a negligee. And, really, it was of a rather
queer cut; its collar grew smaller with every year, inasmuch as it was
utilized to supplement the other parts of the garment. This supplementing was not at all a compliment to the skill of the tailor, and the
effect really was baggy and unsightly.

Perceiving what the matter was, Akakii Akakiievich decided that
the overcoat would have to go to Petrovich the tailor, who lived somewhere up four flights of backstairs and who, despite a squint-eye and
pockmarks all over his face, did quite well at repairing bureaucratic as
well as all other trousers and coats—of course, be it understood, when
he was in a sober state and not hatching some nonsartorial scheme in
his head. One shouldn't, really, mention this tailor at great length, but
since there is already a precedent for each character in a tale being
clearly defined, there's no help for it, and so let's trot out Petrovich as
well. In the beginning he had been called simply Grigory and had been
the serf of some squire or other; he had begun calling himself Petrovich
only after obtaining his freedom papers and taking to drinking rather
hard on any and every holiday—at first on the red-letter ones and then,

without any discrimination, on all those designated by the church: wherever there was a little cross marking the day on the calendar. In this respect he was loyal to the customs of our grandsires and, when bickering with his wife, would call her a worldly woman and a German Frau. And, since we've already been inadvertent enough to mention his wife, it will be necessary to say a word or two about her as well; but, regrettably, little was known about her—unless, perhaps, the fact that Petrovich had a wife, or that she even wore a house cap and not a kerchief; but as for beauty, it appears that she could hardly boast of any; at least the soldiers in the guards were the only ones with hardihood enough to bend down for a peep under her cap, twitching their mustachios as they did so and emitting a certain peculiar sound.

As he clambered up the staircase that led to Petrovich—the staircase, to render it its just due, was dripping all over from water and slops and thoroughly permeated with that alcoholic odor which makes the eyes smart and is, as everybody knows, unfailingly present on all the backstairs of all the houses in Petersburg—as he clambered up this staircase Akakii Akakiievich was already conjecturing how stiff Petrovich's asking price would be and mentally determined not to give him more than two rubles. The door was open, because the mistress of the place, being busy preparing some fish, had filled the kitchen with so much smoke that one actually couldn't see the very cockroaches for it. Akakii Akakiievich made his way through the kitchen, unperceived even by the mistress herself, and at last entered the room wherein he beheld Petrovich, sitting on a wide table of unpainted deal with his feet tucked in under him like a Turkish pasha. His feet, as is the wont of tailors seated at their work, were bare, and the first thing that struck one's eyes was the big toe of one, very familiar to Akakii Akakiievich, with some sort of deformed nail, as thick and strong as a turtle's shell. About Petrovich's neck were loops of silk and cotton thread, while some sort of ragged garment was lying on his knees. For the last three minutes he had been trying to put a thread through the eye of a needle, couldn't hit the mark, and because of that was very wroth against the darkness of the room and even the thread itself, grumbling under his breath: "She won't go through, the heathen! You've spoiled my heart's blood, you damned good-for-nothing!"

Akakii Akakiievich felt upset because he had come at just the moment when Petrovich was very angry; he liked to give in his work when the latter was already under the influence or, as his wife put it, "He's already full of rotgut, the one-eyed devil!" In such a state Petrovich usually gave in willingly and agreed to everything; he even bowed and was grateful every time. Afterward, true enough, his wife would come around and complain weepily that, now, her husband had been drunk and for that reason had taken on the work too cheaply; but all you had to do was to tack on another ten kopecks—and the thing was in the bag. But now, it seemed, Petrovich was in a sober state, and for that reason on his high horse, hard to win over, and bent on boosting his prices to the devil knows what heights. Akakii Akakiievich surmised this and, as the saying goes, was all set to make backtracks, but the deal had already been started. Petrovich puckered up his one good eye against him very fixedly and Akakii Akakiievich involuntarily said, "Greetings, Petrovich!" "Greetings to you, sir," said Petrovich, and looked askance at Akakii Akakiievich's hands, wishing to see what sort of booty the other bore.

"Well, now, I've come to see you, now, Petrovich!"

Akakii Akakiievich, the reader must be informed, explained himself for the most part in prepositions, adverbs, and such verbal oddments as had absolutely no significance. But if the matter was exceedingly difficult, he actually had a way of not finishing his phrase at all, so that, quite frequently, beginning his speech with such words as "This, really, is perfectly, you know—" he would have nothing at all to follow up with, and he himself would be likely to forget the matter, thinking that he had already said everything in full.

"Well, just what is it?" asked Petrovich, and at the same time, with his one good eye, surveyed the entire garment, beginning with the collar and going on to the sleeves, the back, the coat skirts, and the buttonholes, for it was all very familiar to him, inasmuch as it was all his own handiwork. That's a way all tailors have; it's the first thing a tailor will do on meeting you.

"Why, what I'm after, now, Petrovich . . . the overcoat, now, the cloth . . . there, you see, in all the other places it's strong as can be . . . it's gotten a trifle dusty and only seems to be old, but it's really new, there's only one spot . . . a little sort of . . . in the back . . . and also one shoulder, a trifle rubbed through—and this shoulder, too, a trifle—do you see? Not a lot of work, really—"

Petrovich took up the negligee, spread it out over the table as a preliminary, examined it for a long time, shook his head, and then groped with his hand on the window sill for a round snuffbox with the portrait of some general or other on its lid—just which one nobody could tell, inasmuch as the place occupied by the face had been holed through with a finger and then pasted over with a small square of paper. After duly taking tobacco, Petrovich held the negligee taut in his hands and scrutinized it against the light, and again shook his head; after this he turned it with the lining up and again shook his head, again took off the lid with the general's face pasted over with paper and, having fully loaded both nostrils with snuff, covered the snuffbox, put it away, and, at long last, gave his verdict:

"No, there's no fixin' this thing: your wardrobe's in a bad way!"

Akakii Akakiievich's heart skipped a beat at these words.

"But why not, Petrovich?" he asked, almost in the imploring voice of a child. "All that ails it, now . . . it's rubbed through at the shoulders. Surely you must have some small scraps of cloth or other—"

"Why, yes, one could find the scraps—the scraps will turn up," said Petrovich. "Only there's no sewing them on: the whole thing's all rotten: touch a needle to it—and it just crawls apart on you."

"Well, let it crawl—and you just slap a patch right onto it."

"Yes, but.there's nothing to slap them little patches onto; there ain't nothing for the patch to take hold on—there's been far too much wear. It's cloth in name only, but if a gust of wind was to blow on it, it would scatter."

"Well, now, you just fix it up. That, really, now . . . how can it be?"

"No," said Petrovich decisively, "there ain't a thing to be done. The whole thing's in a bad way. You'd better, when the cold winter spell comes, make footcloths out of it, because stockings ain't so warm. It's them Germans that invented them stockings, so's to rake in more money for themselves. (Petrovich loved to needle the Germans whenever the chance turned up.) But as for that there overcoat, it looks like you'll have to make yourself a new one."

At the word *new* a mist swam before Akakii Akakiievich's eyes and everything in the room became a jumble. All he could see clearly was the general on the lid of Petrovich's snuffbox, his face pasted over with a scrap of paper.

"A new one? But how?" he asked, still as if he were in a dream. "Why, I have no money for that."

"Yes, a new one," said Petrovich with a heathenish imperturbability.

"Well, if there's no getting out of it, how much, now—"

"You mean, how much it would cost?"

"Yes."

"Why, you'd have to cough up three fifties and a bit over," pronounced Petrovich, and significantly pursed up his lips at this. He was very fond of strong effects, was fond of somehow nonplusing somebody, utterly and suddenly, and then eyeing his victim sidelong, to see what sort of wry face the nonplusee would pull after his words.

"A hundred and fifty for an overcoat!" poor Akakii Akakiievich cried out—cried out perhaps for the first time since he was born, for he was always distinguished for his low voice.

"Yes, sir!" said Petrovich. "And what an overcoat, at that! If you put a marten collar on it and add a silk-lined hood it might stand you even two hundred."

"Petrovich, please!" Akakii Akakiievich was saying in an imploring voice, without grasping and without even trying to grasp the words uttered by Petrovich and all his effects. "Fix it somehow or other, now, so's it may do a little longer, at least—"

"Why, no, that'll be only having the work go to waste and spending your money for nothing," said Petrovich, and after these words Akakii Akakiievich walked out annihilated. But Petrovich, after his departure, remained as he was for a long time, with meaningfully pursed lips and without resuming his work, satisfied with neither having lowered himself nor having betrayed the sartorial art.

Out in the street, Akakii Akakiievich walked along like a somnambulist. "What a business, now, what a business," he kept saying to himself. "Really, I never even thought that it, now . . . would turn out like that. . . ." And then, after a pause, added: "So that's it! That's how it's turned out after all! Really, now, I couldn't even suppose that it . . . like that, now—" This was followed by another long pause, after which he uttered aloud: "So that's how it is! This, really, now, is something that's beyond all, now, expectation . . . well, I never! What a fix, now!"

Having said this, instead of heading for home, he started off in an entirely different direction without himself suspecting it. On the way a chimney sweep caught him square with his whole sooty side and covered all his shoulder with soot; enough quicklime to cover his entire hat tumbled down on him from the top of a building under construction. He noticed nothing of all this and only later, when he ran up against a policeman near his sentry box (who, having placed his halberd near him, was shaking some tobacco out of a paper cornucopia on to his callused palm), did Akakii Akakiievich come a little to himself, and that only because the policeman said: "What's the idea of shoving your face right into mine? Ain't the sidewalk big enough for you?" This made him look about him and turn homeward.

Only here did he begin to pull his wits together; he perceived his situation in its clear and real light; he started talking to himself no longer in snatches but reasoningly and frankly, as with a judicious friend with whom one might discuss a matter most heartfelt and intimate. "Well, no," said Akakii Akakiievich, "there's no use reasoning with Petrovich now; he's, now, that way. . . . His wife had a chance

to give him a drubbing, it looks like. No, it'll be better if I come to
him on a Sunday morning; after Saturday night's good time he'll be
squinting his eye and very sleepy, so he'll have to have a hair of the
dog that bit him, but his wife won't give him any money, now, and
just then I'll up with ten kopecks or so and into his hand with it—so
he'll be more reasonable to talk with, like, and the overcoat will then
be sort of . . ."

That was the way Akakii Akakiievich reasoned things out to himself, bolstering up his spirits. And, having bided his time till the next
Sunday and spied from afar that Petrovich's wife was going off somewhere out of the house, he went straight up to him. Petrovich, sure
enough, was squinting his eye hard after the Saturday night before,
kept his head bowed down to the floor, and was ever so sleepy; but,
for all that, as soon as he learned what was up, it was as though the
devil himself nudged him.

"Can't be done," said he. "You'll have to order a new overcoat."

Akakii Akakiievich thrust a ten-kopeck coin on him right then
and there.

"I'm grateful to you, sir; I'll have a little something to get me
strength back and will drink to your health," said Petrovich, "but as
for your overcoat, please don't fret about it; it's of no earthly use
anymore. As for a new overcoat, I'll tailor a glorious one for you; I'll
see to that."

Just the same, Akakii Akakiievich started babbling again about
fixing the old one, but Petrovich simply would not listen to him and
said: "Yes, I'll tailor a new one for you without fail; you may rely on
that, I'll try my very best. We might even do it the way it's all the
fashion now—the collar will button with silver catches under
appliqué."

It was then that Akakii Akakiievich perceived that there was no
doing without a new overcoat, and his spirits sank utterly. Really, now,
with what means, with what money would he make this overcoat? Of
course he could rely, in part, on the coming holiday bonus, but this
money had been apportioned and budgeted ahead long ago. There was
an imperative need of outfitting himself with new trousers, paying the
shoemaker an old debt for a new pair of vamps to an old pair of
bootlegs, and he had to order from a seamstress three shirts and two
pair of those nethergarments which it is impolite to mention in print;
in short, all the money was bound to be expended entirely, and even
if the director were so gracious as to decide on giving him five and
forty, or even fifty rubles as a bonus, instead of forty, why, even then
only the veriest trifle would be left over, which, in the capital sum

required for the overcoat, would be as a drop in a bucket. Even though
Akakii Akakiievich was, of course, aware of Petrovich's maggot of
popping out with the devil knows how inordinate an asking price, so
that even his wife herself could not restrain herself on occasion from
crying out: "What, are you going out of your mind, fool that you are!
There's times when he won't take on work for anything, but the Foul
One has egged him on to ask a bigger price than all of him is
worth"—even though he knew, of course, that Petrovich would probably undertake the work for eighty rubles, nevertheless and notwithstanding where was he to get those eighty rubles? Half of that sum
might, perhaps, be found; half of it could have been found, maybe even
a little more—but where was he going to get the other half?

But first the reader must be informed where the first half was to
come from. Akakii Akakiievich had a custom of putting away a copper
or so from every ruble he expended, into a little box under lock and
key, with a small opening cut through the lid for dropping money
therein. At the expiration of every half year he made an accounting of
the entire sum accumulated in coppers and changed it into small silver.
He had kept this up a long time, and in this manner, during the course
of several years, the accumulated sum turned out to be more than forty
rubles. And so he had half the sum for the overcoat on hand; but where
was he to get the other half? Where was he to get the other forty rubles?
Akakii Akakiievich mulled the matter over and over and decided that
it would be necessary to curtail his ordinary expenses, for the duration
of a year at the very least; banish the indulgence in tea of evenings;
also, of evenings, to do without lighting candles, but, if there should
be need of doing something, to go to his landlady's room and work
by her candle; when walking along the streets he would set his foot as
lightly and carefully as possible on the cobbles and flagstones, walking
almost on tiptoe, and thus avoid wearing out his soles prematurely;
his linen would have to be given as infrequently as possible to the
laundress and, in order that it might not become too soiled, every time
he came home all of it must be taken off, the wearer having to remain
only in his jean bathrobe, a most ancient garment and spared even by
time itself.

It was, the truth must be told, most difficult for him in the beginning to get habituated to such limitations, but later it did turn into a
matter of habit, somehow, and everything went well; he even became
perfectly trained to going hungry of evenings; on the other hand, however, he had spiritual sustenance, always carrying about in his thoughts
the eternal idea of the new overcoat. From this time forth it seemed as

if his very existence had become somehow fuller, as though he had taken unto himself a wife, as though another person were always present with him, as though he were not alone but as if an amiable feminine helpmate had consented to traverse the path of life side by side with him—and this feminine helpmate was none other than this very same overcoat, with a thick quilting of cotton wool, with a strong lining that would never wear out.

He became more animated, somehow, even firmer of character, like a man who has already defined and set a goal for himself. Doubt, indecision—in a word, all vacillating and indeterminate traits—vanished of themselves from his face and actions. At times a sparkle appeared in his eyes; the boldest and most daring of thoughts actually flashed through his head: Shouldn't he, after all, put marten on the collar? Meditations on this subject almost caused him to make absentminded blunders. And on one occasion, as he was transcribing a paper, he all but made an error, so that he emitted an almost audible "Ugh," and made the sign of the cross.

During the course of each month he would make at least one call on Petrovich, to discuss the overcoat: where would it be best to buy the cloth, and of what color, and at what price—and even though somewhat preoccupied he always came home satisfied, thinking that the time would come, at last, when all the necessary things would be bought and the overcoat made.

The matter went even more quickly than he had expected. Contrary to all his anticipations, the director designated a bonus not of forty or forty-five rubles for Akakii Akakiievich, but all of sixty. Whether he had a premonition that Akakii Akakiievich needed a new overcoat, or whether this had come about of its own self, the fact nevertheless remained: Akakii Akakiievich thus found himself the possessor of an extra twenty rubles. This circumstance hastened the course of things. Some two or three months more of slight starvation—and lo! Akakii Akakiievich had accumulated around eighty rubles. His heart, in general quite calm, began to palpitate. On the very first day possible he set out with Petrovich to the shops. The cloth they bought was very good, and no great wonder, since they had been thinking over its purchase as much as half a year before and hardly a month had gone by without their making a round of the shops to compare prices; but then, Petrovich himself said that there couldn't be better cloth than that. For lining they chose calico, but of such good quality and so closely woven that, to quote Petrovich's words, it was still better than silk and, to look at, even more showy and glossy. Marten they did not buy, for, to be sure, it was expensive, but instead they picked out the best catskin the shop boasted—catskin that could, at a great enough distance, be taken for marten.

Petrovich spent only a fortnight in fussing about with the making of the overcoat, for there was a great deal of stitching to it, and if it hadn't been for that it would have been ready considerably earlier. For his work Petrovich took twelve rubles—he couldn't have taken any less; everything was positively sewn with silk thread, with a small double stitch, and after the stitching Petrovich went over every seam with his own teeth, pressing out various figures with them.

It was on . . . it would be hard to say on precisely what day, but it was, most probably, the most triumphant day in Akakii Akakiievich's life when Petrovich, at last, brought the overcoat. He brought it in the morning, just before Akakii Akakiievich had to set out for his bureau. Never, at any other time, would the overcoat have come in so handy, because rather hard frosts were already setting in and, apparently, were threatening to become still more severe. Petrovich's entrance with the overcoat was one befitting a good tailor. Such a portentous expression appeared on his face as Akakii Akakiievich had never yet beheld. Petrovich felt to the fullest, it seemed, that he had performed no petty labor and that he had suddenly evinced in himself that abyss which lies between those tailors who merely put in linings and alter and fix garments and those who create new ones.

He extracted the overcoat from the bandanna in which he had brought it. (The bandanna was fresh from the laundress; it was only later on that he thrust it in his pocket for practical use.) Having drawn out the overcoat, he looked at it quite proudly and, holding it in both hands, threw it deftly over the shoulders of Akakii Akakiievich, pulled it and smoothed it down the back with his hand, then draped it on Akakii Akakiievich somewhat loosely. Akakiievich, as a man along in his years, wanted to try it on with his arms through the sleeves. Petrovich helped him on with it: it turned out to be fine, even with his arms through the sleeves. In a word, the overcoat proved to be perfect and had come in the very nick of time. Petrovich did not let slip the opportunity of saying that he had done the work so cheaply only because he lived in a place without a sign, on a side street and, besides, had known Akakii Akakiievich for a long time, but on the Nevski Prospect they would have taken seventy-five rubles from him for the labor alone. Akakii Akakiievich did not feel like arguing the matter with Petrovich and, besides, he had a dread of all the fancy sums with which Petrovich liked to throw dust in people's eyes. He paid the tailor off, thanked him, and walked right out in the new overcoat on his way

to the bureau. Petrovich walked out at his heels and, staying behind
on the street, for a long while kept looking after the overcoat from
afar, and then deliberately went out of his way so that, after cutting
across a crooked lane, he might run out again into the street and have
another glance at his overcoat from a different angle—that is, full face.

In the meantime Akakii Akakiievich walked along feeling in the
most festive of moods. He was conscious every second of every minute
that he had a new overcoat on his shoulders, and several times even
smiled slightly because of his inward pleasure. In reality he was a gainer
on two points: for one, the overcoat was warm, for the other, it was
a fine thing. He did not notice the walk at all and suddenly found
himself at the bureau; in the porter's room he took off his overcoat,
looked it all over, and entrusted it to the particular care of the doorman.
No one knows in what manner everybody in the bureau suddenly
learned that Akakii Akakiievich had a new overcoat, and that the
negligee was no longer in existence. They all immediately ran out into
the vestibule to inspect Akakii Akakiievich's new overcoat. They fell
to congratulating him, to saying agreeable things to him, so that at
first he could merely smile, and in a short time became actually embarrassed. And when all of them, having besieged him, began telling
him that the new overcoat ought to be baptized and that he ought, at
the least, to get up an evening party for them, Akakii Akakiievich was
utterly at a loss, not knowing what to do with himself, what answers
to make, or how to get out of inviting them. It was only a few minutes
later that he began assuring them, quite simple-heartedly, that it wasn't
a new overcoat at all, that it was just an ordinary overcoat, that in
fact it was an old overcoat. Finally one of the bureaucrats—some sort
of an assistant to a head of a department, actually—probably in order
to show that he was not at all a proud stick and willing to mingle even
with those beneath him, said: "So be it, then; I'm giving a party this
evening and ask all of you to have tea with me; today, appropriately
enough, happens to be my birthday."

The clerks, naturally, at once thanked the assistant to a head of
a department and accepted the invitation with enthusiasm. Akakii
Akakiievich attempted to excuse himself at first, but all began saying
that it would show disrespect to decline, that it would be simply a
shame and a disgrace, and after that there was absolutely no way for
him to back out. However, when it was all over, he felt a pleasant
glow as he reminded himself that this would give him a chance to take
a walk in his new overcoat even in the evening. This whole day was
for Akakii Akakiievich something in the nature of the greatest and most
triumphant of holidays.

Akakii Akakiievich returned home in the happiest mood, took off the overcoat, and hung it carefully on the wall, once more getting his fill of admiring the cloth and the lining, and then purposely dragged out, for comparison, his former negligee, which by now had practically disintegrated. He glanced at it and he himself had to laugh, so great was the difference! And for a long while thereafter, as he ate dinner, he kept on smiling slightly whenever the present state of the negligee came to his mind. He dined gayly, and after dinner did not write a single stroke; there were no papers of any kind, for that matter; he just simply played the sybarite a little, lounging on his bed, until it became dark. Then, without putting matters off any longer, he dressed, threw the overcoat over his shoulders, and walked out into the street.

We are, to our regret, unable to say just where the official who had extended the invitation lived; our memory is beginning to play us false—very much so—and everything in Petersburg, no matter what, including all its streets and houses, has become so muddled in our mind that it's quite hard to get anything out therefrom in any sort of decent shape. But wherever it may have been, at least this much is certain: that official lived in the best part of town; consequently a very long way from Akakii Akakiievich's quarters. First of all Akakii Akakiievich had to traverse certain deserted streets with but scant illumination; however, in keeping with his progress toward the official's domicile, the streets became more animated; the pedestrians flitted by more and more often; he began meeting even ladies, handsomely dressed; the men he came upon had beaver collars on their overcoats; more and more rarely did he encounter jehus with latticed wooden sleighs, studded over with gilt nails—on the contrary, he kept coming across first-class drivers in caps of raspberry-hued velvet, their sleighs lacquered and with bearskin robes, while the carriages had decorated seats for the drivers and raced down the roadway, their wheels screeching over the snow.

Akakii Akakiievich eyed all this as a novelty—it was several years by now since he had set foot out of his house in the evening. He stopped with curiosity before the illuminated window of a shop to look at a picture, depicting some handsome woman or other, who was taking off her shoe, thus revealing her whole leg (very far from ill-formed), while behind her back some gentleman or other, sporting side whiskers and a handsome goatee, was poking his head out of the door of an adjoining room. Akakii Akakiievich shook his head and smiled, after which he went on his way. Why had he smiled? Was it because he had encountered something utterly unfamiliar, yet about which, neverthe-less, everyone preserves a certain instinct? Or did he think, like so many

other petty clerks: "My, the French they are a funny race! No use
talking! If there's anything they get a notion of, then, sure enough,
there it is!" And yet, perhaps, he did not think even that; after all,
there's no way of insinuating one's self into a man's soul, of finding
out all that he might be thinking about.

At last he reached the house in which the assistant to a head of a
department lived. The assistant to a head of a department lived on a
grand footing; there was a lantern on the staircase; his apartment was
only one flight up. On entering the foyer of the apartment Akakii
Akakiievich beheld row after row of galoshes. In their midst, in the
center of the room, stood a samovar, noisy and emitting clouds of
steam. The walls were covered with hanging overcoats and capes,
among which were even such as had beaver collars or lapels of velvet.
On the other side of the wall he could hear much noise and talk, which
suddenly became distinct and resounding when the door opened and
a flunky came out with a tray full of empty tumblers, a cream pitcher,
and a basket of biscuits. It was evident that the bureaucrats had gathered long since and had already had their first glasses of tea.

Akakii Akakiievich, hanging up his overcoat himself, entered the
room and simultaneously all the candles, bureaucrats, tobacco pipes,
and card tables flickered before him, and the continuous conversation
and the scraping of moving chairs, coming from all sides, struck dully
on his ears. He halted quite awkwardly in the center of the room, at
a loss and trying to think what he ought to do. But he had already
been noticed, was received with much shouting, and everyone immediately went to the foyer and again inspected his overcoat. Akakii
Akakiievich, even though he was somewhat embarrassed, still could
not but rejoice on seeing them all bestow such praises on his overcoat,
since he was a man with an honest heart. Then, of course, they all
dropped him and his overcoat and, as is usual, directed their attention
to the whist tables.

All this—the din, the talk, and the throng of people—all this was
somehow a matter of wonder to Akakii Akakiievich. He simply did
not know what to do, how to dispose of his hands, his feet, and his
whole body; finally he sat down near the cardplayers, watched their
cards, looked now at the face of this man, now of that, and after some
time began to feel bored, to yawn—all the more so since his usual
bedtime had long since passed. He wanted to say good-bye to his host
but they wouldn't let him, saying that they absolutely must toast his
new acquisition in a goblet of champagne. An hour later supper was
served, consisting of mixed salad, cold veal, meat pie, patties from a
pastry cook's, and champagne. They forced Akakii Akakiievich to

empty two goblets, after which he felt that the room had become ever so much more cheerful. However, he absolutely could not forget that it was already twelve o'clock and that it was long since time for him to go home. So that his host might not somehow get the idea of detaining him, he crept out of the room, managed to find his overcoat —which, not without regret, he saw lying on the floor; then, shaking the overcoat and picking every bit of fluff off it, he threw it over his shoulders and made his way down the stairs and out of the house.

It was still dusk out in the street. Here and there small general stores, those around-the-clock clubs for domestics and all other servants, were still open; other shops, which were closed, nevertheless showed, by a long streak of light along the crack either at the outer edge or the bottom, that they were not yet without social life and that, probably, the serving wenches and lads were still winding up their discussions and conversations, thus throwing their masters into utter bewilderment as to their whereabouts. Akakii Akakiievich walked along in gay spirits; for reasons unknown he even made a sudden dash after some lady or other, who had passed by him like a flash of lightning, and every part of whose body was filled with buoyancy. However, he stopped right then and there and resumed his former exceedingly gentle pace, actually wondering himself at the sprightliness that had come upon him from no one knows where.

Soon he again was passing stretch after stretch of those desolate streets which are never too gay even in the daytime, but are even less so in the evening. Now they had become still more deserted and lonely; he came upon glimmering street lamps more and more infrequently— the allotment of oil was now evidently decreasing; there was a succession of wooden houses and fences, with never another soul about; the snow alone glittered on the street, and the squat hovels, with their shutters closed in sleep, showed like depressing dark blotches. He approached a spot where the street was cut in two by an unending square, with the houses on the other side of it barely visible—a square that loomed ahead like an awesome desert.

Far in the distance, God knows where, a little light flickered in a policeman's sentry box that seemed to stand at the end of the world. Akakii Akakiievich's gay mood somehow diminished considerably at this point. He set foot in the square, not without a premonition of something evil. He looked back and on each side of him—it was as though he were in the midst of a sea. "No, it's better even not to look," he reflected and went on with his eyes shut. And when he did open them to see if the end of the square was near, he suddenly saw standing before him, almost at his very nose, two mustachioed strangers—just what sort of men they were was something he couldn't even make out. A mist arose before his eyes and his heart began to pound.

"Why, that there overcoat is mine!" said one of the men in a thunderous voice, grabbing him by the collar. Akakii Akakiievich was just about to yell "Police!" when the other put a fist right up to his mouth, a fist as big as any government clerk's head, adding: "There, you just let one peep out of you!"

All that Akakii Akakiievich felt was that they had taken the overcoat off him, given him a kick in the back with the knee, and that he had fallen flat on his back in the snow, after which he felt nothing more. In a few minutes he came to and got up on his feet, but there was no longer anybody around. He felt that it was cold out in that open space and that he no longer had the overcoat, and began to yell; but his voice, it seemed, had no intention whatsoever of reaching the other end of the square. Desperate, without ceasing to yell, he started off at a run across the square directly toward the sentry box near which the policeman was standing and, leaning on his halberd, was watching the running man, apparently with curiosity, as if he wished to know why the devil anybody should be running toward him from afar and yelling. Akakii Akakiievich, having run up to him, began to shout in a stifling voice that he, the policeman, had been asleep, that he was not watching and couldn't see that a man was being robbed. The policeman answered that he hadn't seen a thing; all he had seen was two men of some sort stop him in the middle of the square, but he had thought they were friends of Akakii Akakiievich's, and that instead of cursing him out for nothing he'd better go on the morrow to the inspector, and the inspector would find out who had taken his overcoat.

Akakii Akakiievich ran home in utter disarray; whatever little hair still lingered at his temples and the nape of his neck was all disheveled; his side and his breast and his trousers were all wet with snow. The old woman, his landlady, hearing the dreadful racket at the door, hurriedly jumped out of bed and, with only one shoe on, ran down to open the door, modestly holding the shift at her breast with one hand; but, on opening the door and seeing Akakii Akakiievich in such a state, she staggered back. When he had told her what the matter was, however, she wrung her hands and said that he ought to go directly to the justice of the peace; the district officer of police would take him in, would make promises to him and then lead him about by the nose; yes, it would be best of all to go straight to the justice. Why, she was even acquainted with him, seeing as how Anna, the Finnish woman who had formerly been her cook, had now gotten a place as a nurse at the justice's; that she, the landlady herself, saw the justice often when he drove past her house, and also that he went to church every Sunday, praying, yet at the same time looking so cheerfully at all the folks, and that consequently, as one could see by all the signs, he was a kindhearted man. Having heard this solution of his troubles through to the end, the saddened Akakii Akakiievich shuffled off to his room, and how he passed the night there may be left to the discernment of him who can in any degree imagine the situation of another.

Early in the morning he set out for the justice's, but was told there that he was sleeping; he came at ten o'clock, and was told again: "He's sleeping." He came at eleven; they told him: "Why, His Honor's not at home." He tried at lunchtime, but the clerks in the reception room would not let him through to the presence under any circumstances and absolutely had to know what business he had come on and what had occurred, so that, at last, Akakii Akakiievich for once in his life wanted to evince firmness of character and said sharply and categorically that he had to see the justice personally, that they dared not keep him out, that he had come from his own bureau on a government matter, and that, now, when he'd lodge a complaint against them, why, they would see, then. The clerks dared not say anything in answer to this and one of them went to call out the justice of the peace.

The justice's reaction to Akakii Akakiievich's story of how he had been robbed of his overcoat was somehow exceedingly odd. Instead of turning his attention to the main point of the matter, he began interrogating Akakii Akakiievich: Just why had he been coming home at so late an hour? Had he, perhaps, looked in at, or hadn't he actually visited, some disorderly house? Akakii Akakiievich became utterly confused and walked out of the office without himself knowing whether the investigation about the overcoat would be instituted or not.

This whole day he stayed away from his bureau (the only time in his life he had done so). On the following day he put in an appearance, all pale and in his old negligee, which had become more woebegone than ever. The recital of the robbery of the overcoat, despite the fact that there proved to be certain ones among his co-workers who did not let pass even this opportunity to make fun of Akakii Akakiievich, nevertheless touched many. They decided on the spot to make up a collection for him, but they collected the utmost trifle, inasmuch as the petty officials had spent a lot even without this, having subscribed for a portrait of the director and for some book or other, at the invitation of the chief of the department, who was a friend of the writer's; and so the sum proved to be most trifling. One of them, moved by compassion, decided to aid Akakii Akakiievich with good advice at least, telling him that he oughtn't to go to the precinct officer of the police, because, even though it might come about that the precinct officer, wishing to merit the approval of his superiors, might locate the overcoat in some way, the overcoat would in the end remain with the police, if Akakii Akakiievich could not present legal proofs that it belonged to him; but that the best thing of all would be to turn to a *certain important person;* that this important person, after conferring and corresponding with the proper people in the proper quarters, could speed things up.

There was no help for it; Akakii Akakiievich summoned up his courage to go to the important person. Precisely what the important person's post was and what the work of that post consisted of, has remained unknown up to now. It is necessary to know that the certain important person had only recently become an Important Person, but, up to then, had been an unimportant person. However, his post was not considered an important one even now in comparison with more important ones. But there will always be found a circle of people who perceive the importance of that which is unimportant in the eyes of others. However, he tried to augment his importance by many other means, to wit: he inaugurated the custom of having the subordinate clerks meet him while he was still on the staircase when he arrived at his office; another, of no one coming directly into his presence, but having everything follow the most rigorous precedence: a collegiate registrar was to report to the provincial secretary, the provincial secretary to a titular one, or whomever else it was necessary to report to, and only thus was any matter to come to him. For it is thus in our Holy Russia that everything is infected with imitativeness; everyone apes his superior and postures like him. They even say that a certain titular councilor, when they put him at the helm of some small individual chancellery, immediately had a separate room for himself partitioned off, dubbing it the reception center, and had placed at the door some doormen or other with red collars and gold braid, who turned the doorknob and opened the door for every visitor, even though there was hardly room in the reception center to hold even an ordinary desk.

The manners and ways of the important person were imposing and majestic, but not at all complex. The chief basis of his system was strictness. "Strictness, strictness, and—strictness," he was wont to say, and when uttering the last word he usually looked very significantly into the face of the person to whom he was speaking, even though, by the way, there was no reason for all this, inasmuch as the half score of clerks constituting the whole administrative mechanism of his chancellery were under the proper state of fear and trembling even as it was: catching sight of him from afar the staff would at once drop whatever they were doing and wait, at attention, until the chief had passed through the room. His ordinary speech with his subordinates reeked of strictness and consisted almost entirely of three phrases: "How dare you? Do you know whom you're talking to? Do you realize in whose presence you are?" However, at soul he was a kindly man, treated his friends well, and was obliging; but the rank of general had knocked him completely off his base. Having received a general's rank he had somehow become muddled, had lost his sense of direction, and did not know how to act. If he happened to be with his equals he was still as human as need be, a most decent man, in many respects—even a man not at all foolish; but whenever he happened to be in a group where there were people even one rank below him, why, there was no holding him; he was taciturn, and his situation aroused pity, all the more since he himself felt that he could have passed the time infinitely more pleasantly. In his eyes one could at times see a strong desire to join in some circle and its interesting conversation, but he was stopped by the thought: Wouldn't this be too much unbending on his part, wouldn't it be a familiar action, and wouldn't he lower his importance thereby? And as a consequence of such considerations he remained forever aloof in that invariably taciturn state, only uttering some monosyllabic sounds at rare intervals, and had thus acquired the reputation of a most boring individual.

It was before such an *important person* that our Akakii Akakiievich appeared, and he appeared at a most inauspicious moment, quite inopportune for himself—although, by the bye, most opportune for the important person. The important person was seated in his private office and had gotten into very, very jolly talk with a certain recently arrived old friend and childhood companion whom he had not seen for several years. It was at this point that they announced to the important person that some Bashmachkin or other had come to see him. He asked abruptly: "Who is he?" and was told: "Some petty clerk or other." "Ah. He can wait; this isn't the right time for him to come," said the important man.

At this point it must be said that the important man had fibbed a little: he had the time; he and his old friend had long since talked over everything and had been long eking out their conversation with protracted silences, merely patting each other lightly on the thigh from time to time and adding, "That's how it is, Ivan Abramovich!" and "That's just how it is, Stepan Varlaamovich!" But despite that he gave orders for the petty clerk to wait a while just the same, in order to show his friend, a man who had been long out of the civil service and rusticating in his village, how long petty clerks had to cool their heels in his anteroom.

Finally, having had his fill of talk, yet having had a still greater fill of silences, and after each had smoked a cigar to the end in a quite restful armchair with an adjustable back, he at last appeared to recall the matter and said to his secretary, who had halted in the doorway with some papers for a report, "Why, I think there's a clerk waiting out there. Tell him he may come in."

On beholding the meek appearance of Akakii Akakiievich and his rather old, skimpy frock coat, he suddenly turned to him and asked, "What is it you wish?"—in a voice abrupt and firm, which he had purposely rehearsed beforehand in his room at home in solitude and before a mirror, actually a week before he had received his present post and his rank of general.

Akakii Akakiievich had already had plenty of time to experience the requisite awe, was somewhat abashed, and, as best he could, insofar as his poor freedom of tongue would allow him, explained, adding even more *now*'s than he would have at another time, that his overcoat had been perfectly new, and that, now, he had been robbed of it in a perfectly inhuman fashion, and that he was turning to him, now, so that he might interest himself through his . . . now . . . might correspond with the head of police or somebody else, and find his overcoat, now. . . . Such conduct, for some unknown reason, appeared familiar to the general.

"What are you up to, my dear sir?" he resumed abruptly. "Don't you know the proper procedure? Where have you come to? Don't you know how matters ought to be conducted? As far as this is concerned, you should have first of all submitted a petition to the chancellery; it would have gone from there to the head of the proper division, then would have been transferred to the secretary, and the secretary would in due time have brought it to my attention—"

"But, Your Excellency," said Akakii Akakiievich, trying to collect whatever little pinch of presence of mind he had, yet feeling at the same time that he was in a dreadful sweat, "I ventured to trouble you, Your Excellency, because secretaries, now . . . aren't any too much to be relied upon—"

"What? What? What?" said the important person. "Where did you get such a tone from? Where did you get such notions? What sort of rebellious feeling has spread among the young people against the administrators and their superiors?" The important person had, it seems, failed to notice that Akakii Akakiievich would never see fifty again, consequently, even if he could have been called a young man it could be applied only relatively, that is, to someone who was already seventy. "Do you know whom you're saying this to? Do you realize in whose presence you are? Do you realize? Do you realize, I'm asking you!" Here he stamped his foot, bringing his voice to such an over-whelming note that even another than an Akakii Akakiievich would have been frightened. Akakii Akakiievich was simply bereft of his senses, swayed, shook all over, and actually could not stand on his feet. If a couple of doormen had not run up right then and there to support him he would have slumped to the floor; they carried him out in a practically cataleptic state. But the important person, satisfied because the effect had surpassed even anything he had expected, and inebriated by the idea that a word from him could actually deprive a man of his senses, looked out of the corner of his eye to learn how his friend was taking this and noticed, not without satisfaction, that his friend was in a most indeterminate state and was even beginning to experience fear on his own account.

How he went down the stairs, how he came out into the street—that was something Akakii Akakiievich was no longer conscious of. He felt neither his hands nor his feet; never in all his life had he been dragged over such hot coals by a general—and a general outside his bureau, at that! With his mouth gaping, stumbling off the sidewalk, he breasted the blizzard that was whistling and howling through the streets; the wind, as is its wont in Petersburg, blew upon him from all the four quarters, from every cross lane. In a second it had blown a quinsy down his throat, and he crawled home without the strength to utter a word; he became all swollen and took to his bed. That's how effective a proper hauling over the coals can be at times!

On the next day he was running a high fever. Thanks to the magnanimous all-around help of the Petersburg climate, the disease progressed more rapidly than could have been expected, and when the doctor appeared he, after having felt the patient's pulse, could not strike on anything to do save prescribing hot compresses, and that solely so that the sick man might not be left without the beneficial help of medical science; but, on the whole, he announced on the spot that in another day and a half it would be curtains for Akakii Akakiievich, after which he turned to the landlady and said: "As for you, Mother, don't you be losing any time for nothing; order a pine coffin for him right now, because a coffin of oak will be beyond his means."

Whether Akakii Akakiievich heard the doctor utter these words, so fateful for him, and, even if he did hear them, whether they had a staggering effect on him, whether he felt regrets over his life of hard sledding—about that nothing is known, inasmuch as he was all the time running a temperature and was in delirium. Visions, each one stranger than the one before, appeared before him ceaselessly: now he saw Petrovich and was ordering him to make an overcoat with some sort of traps to catch thieves, whom he ceaselessly imagined to be under his bed, at every minute calling his landlady to pull out from under his blanket one of them who had actually crawled in there; then he would ask why his old negligee was hanging in front of him, for he had a new overcoat; then once more he had a hallucination that he was standing before the general, getting a proper raking over the coals, and saying: "Forgive me, Your Excellency!"; then, finally, he actually took to swearing foully, uttering such dreadful words that his old landlady could do nothing but cross herself, having never in her life heard anything of the sort from him, all the more so since these words followed immediately after "Your Excellency!"

After that he spoke utter nonsense, so that there was no understanding anything; all one could perceive was that his incoherent words and thoughts all revolved about that overcoat and nothing else.

Finally poor Akakii Akakiievich gave up the ghost. Neither his room nor his things were put under seal; in the first place because he had no heirs, and in the second because there was very little left for anybody to inherit, to wit: a bundle of goose quills, a quire of white governmental paper, three pairs of socks, two or three buttons that had come off his trousers, and the negligee which the reader is already familiar with. Who fell heir to all this treasure trove, God knows; I confess that even the narrator of this tale was not much interested in the matter. They bore Akakii Akakiievich off and buried him. And Petersburg was left without Akakii Akakiievich, as if he had never been therein. There vanished and disappeared a being protected by none, endeared to no one, of no interest to anyone, a being that actually had failed to attract to itself the attention of even a naturalist who wouldn't let a chance slip of sticking an ordinary housefly on a pin and of examining it through a microscope; a being that had submissively endured the jests of the whole chancellery and that had gone to its grave without any extraordinary fuss, but before which, nevertheless, even before the very end of its life, there had flitted a radiant visitor in the guise of an overcoat, which had animated for an instant a poor life, and upon which being calamity had come crashing down just as unbearably as it comes crashing down upon the heads of the mighty ones of this earth!

A few days after his death a doorman was sent to his house from the bureau with an injunction for Akakii Akakiievich to appear immediately; the chief, now, was asking for him; but the doorman had to return empty-handed, reporting back that "he weren't able to come no more," and, to the question: "Why not?" expressed himself in the words, "Why, just so; he up and died; they buried him four days back." Thus did they learn at the bureau about the death of Akakii Akakiievich, and the very next day a new pettifogger, considerably taller than Akakii Akakiievich, was already sitting in his place and putting down the letters no longer in such a straight hand, but considerably more on the slant and downhill.

But whoever could imagine that this wouldn't be all about Akakii Akakiievich, that he was fated to live for several noisy days after his death, as though in reward for a life that had gone by utterly unnoticed? Yet that is how things fell out, and our poor history is taking on a fantastic ending.

Rumors suddenly spread through Petersburg that near the Kalinkin Bridge, and much farther out still, a dead man had started haunting of nights, in the guise of a petty government clerk, seeking for some overcoat or other that had been purloined from him and, because of that stolen overcoat, snatching from all and sundry shoulders, without differentiating among the various ranks and titles, all sorts of overcoats: whether they had collars of catskin or beaver, whether they were quilted with cotton wool, whether they were lined with raccoon, with fox, with bear—in a word, every sort of fur and skin that man has ever thought of for covering his own hide. One of the clerks in the bureau had seen the dead man with his own eyes and had immediately recognized in him Akakii Akakiievich. This had inspired him with such horror, however, that he started running for all his legs were worth and for that reason could not make him out very well but had merely seen the other shake his finger at him from afar. From all sides came an uninterrupted flow of complaints that backs and shoulders—it wouldn't matter so much if they were merely those of titular councilors, but even those of privy councilors were affected—were exposed to the danger of catching thorough colds, because of this oft-repeated snatching off of overcoats.

An order was put through to the police to capture the dead man, at any cost, dead or alive, and to punish him in the severest manner as an example to others—and they all but succeeded in this. To be precise, a policeman at a sentry box on a certain block of the Kirushkin Lane had already gotten a perfect grip on the dead man by his coat collar, at the very scene of his malefaction, while attempting to snatch off the frieze overcoat of some retired musician, who in his time had tootled a flute. Seizing the dead man by the collar, the policeman had summoned two of his colleagues by shouting and had entrusted the ghost to them to hold him, the while he himself took just a moment to reach down in his bootleg for his snuffbox, to relieve temporarily a nose that had been frostbitten six times in his life; but the snuff, probably, was of such a nature as even a dead man could not stand. Hardly had the policeman, after stopping his right nostril with a finger, succeeded in drawing half a handful of powdered tobacco up his left, than the dead man sneezed so heartily that he completely bespattered the eyes of all the three myrmidons. While they were bringing their fists up to rub their eyes, the dead man vanished without leaving as much as a trace, so that they actually did not know whether he had really been in their hands or not.

From then on the policemen developed such a phobia of dead men that they were afraid to lay hands even on living ones and merely shouted from a distance: "Hey, there, get going!" and the dead government clerk began to do his haunting even beyond the Kalinkin Bridge, inspiring not a little fear in all timid folk.

However, we have dropped entirely a certain *important person* who, in reality, had been all but the cause of the fantastic trend taken by what is, by the bye, a perfectly true story. First of all, a sense of justice compels us to say that the *certain important person*, soon after the departure of poor Akakii Akakiievich, done to a turn in the raking over the hot coals, had felt something in the nature of compunction. He was no stranger to compassion; many kind impulses found access to his heart, despite the fact that his rank often stood in the way of their revealing themselves. As soon as the visiting friend had left his private office, he actually fell into a brown study over Akakii Akakiievich. And from that time on, almost every day, there appeared before him the pale Akakii Akakiievich, who had not been able to stand up under an administrative hauling over the coals. The thought concerning him disquieted the certain important person to such a degree that, a week later, he even decided to send a clerk to him to find out what the man had wanted, and how he was, and whether it was really possible to help him in some way. And when he was informed that Akakii Akakiievich had died suddenly in a fever he was left actually stunned, hearkening to the reproaches of conscience, and was out of sorts the whole day.

Wishing to distract himself to some extent and to forget the unpleasant impression this news had made upon him, he set out for an evening party given by one of his friends, where he found a suitable social gathering and, what was best of all, all the men there were of almost the same rank, so that he absolutely could not feel constrained in any way. This had an astonishing effect on the state of his spirits. He relaxed, became amiable and pleasant to converse with—in a word, he passed the time very agreeably. At supper he drank off a goblet or two of champagne—a remedy which, as everybody knows, has not at all an ill effect upon one's gaiety. The champagne predisposed him to certain extracurricular considerations; to be precise, he decided not to go home yet but to drop in on a certain lady of his acquaintance, a Karolina Ivanovna—a lady of German extraction, apparently, toward whom his feelings and relations were friendly. It must be pointed out the important person was no longer a young man, that he was a good spouse, a respected paterfamilias. He had two sons, one of whom was already serving in a chancellery, and a pretty daughter of sixteen, with a somewhat humped yet very charming little nose, who came to kiss his hand every day, adding, "*Bonjour,* Papa," as she did so. His wife, a woman who still had not lost her freshness and was not even in the least hard to look at, would allow him to kiss her hand first, then, turning her own over, kissed the hand that was holding hers.

Yet the important person, who, by the bye, was perfectly contented with domestic tenderness, found it respectable to have a lady friend in another part of the city. This lady friend was not in the least fresher or younger than his wife, but such are the enigmas that exist in this world, and to sit in judgment upon them is none of our affair. And so the important person came down the steps, climbed into his sleigh, and told his driver: "To Karolina Ivanovna's!"—while he himself, after muffling up rather luxuriously in his warm overcoat, remained in that pleasant state than which no better could even be thought of for a Russian—that is, when one isn't even thinking of his own volition, but the thoughts in the meanwhile troop into one's head by themselves, each more pleasant than the other, without giving one even the trouble of pursuing them and seeking them. Filled with agreeable feelings, he lightly recalled all the gay episodes of the evening he had spent, all his mots that had made the select circle go off into peals of laughter; many of them he even repeated in a low voice and found that they were still just as amusing as before, and for that reason it is not to be wondered at that even he chuckled at them heartily.

Occasionally, however, he became annoyed with the gusty wind which, suddenly escaping from God knows where and no one knows for what reason, simply cut the face, tossing tatters of snow thereat, making the collar of his overcoat belly out like a sail, or suddenly, with unnatural force, throwing it over his head and in this manner giving him ceaseless trouble in extricating himself from it.

Suddenly the important person felt that someone had seized him rather hard by his collar. Turning around, he noticed a man of no great height, in an old, much worn frock coat and, not without horror, recognized in him Akakii Akakiievich. The petty clerk's face was wan as snow and looked utterly like the face of a dead man. But the horror of the important person passed all bounds when he saw that the mouth of the man became twisted and, horribly wafting upon him the odor of the grave, uttered the following speech: "Ah, so there you are, now, at last! At last I have collared you, now! Your overcoat is just the one I need! You didn't put yourself out any about mine, and on top of that hauled me over the coals—so now let me have yours!"

The poor important person almost passed away. No matter how firm of character he was in his chancellery and before his inferiors in general, and although after but one look merely at his manly appearance and his figure everyone said: "My, what character he has!"—in this instance, nevertheless, like quite a number of men who have the appearance of doughty knights, he experienced such terror that, not without reason, he even began to fear an attack of some physical disorder. He even hastened to throw his overcoat off his shoulders himself and cried out to the driver in a voice that was not his own, "Go home— fast as you can!"

The driver, on hearing the voice that the important person used only at critical moments and which he often accompanied by something of a far more physical nature, drew his head in between his shoulders just to be on the safe side, swung his whip, and flew off like an arrow. In just a little over six minutes the important person was already at the entrance to his own house. Pale, frightened out of his wits, and minus his overcoat, he had come home instead of to Karolina Ivanovna's, somehow made his way stumblingly to his room, and spent the night in quite considerable distress, so that the next day, during the morning tea, his daughter told him outright: "You're all pale today, Papa." But Papa kept silent and said not a word to anybody of what had befallen him, and where he had been, and where he had intended to go.

This adventure made a strong impression on him. He even badgered his subordinates at rarer intervals with his, "How dare you? Do you realize in whose presence you are?"—and even if he did utter these phrases he did not do so before he had first heard through to the end just what was what. But still more remarkable is the fact that from that time forth the apparition of the dead clerk ceased its visitations utterly; evidently the general's overcoat fitted him to a *t*; at least, no cases of overcoats being snatched off anybody were heard of anymore, anywhere. However, many energetic and solicitous people simply would not calm down and kept on saying from time to time that the dead government clerk was still haunting the remoter parts of the city.

And, sure enough, one policeman at a sentry box in Kolomna had with his own eyes seen the apparition coming out of a house; but, being by nature somewhat puny, so that on one occasion an ordinary full-grown piglet, darting out of a private house, had knocked him off his feet, to the profound amusement of the cab drivers who were standing around, from whom he had exacted a copper each for humiliating him so greatly, to buy snuff with—well, being puny, he had not dared to halt him but simply followed him in the dark until such time as the apparition suddenly looked over its shoulder and, halting, asked him: "What are you after?" and shook a fist at him whose like for size was not to be found among the living. The policeman said: "Nothing," and at once turned back. The apparition, however, was considerably taller by now and was sporting enormous mustachios; setting its steps apparently in the direction of the Obukhov Bridge it disappeared, utterly, in the darkness of night.

EASTER SUNDAY

(Letter number 32 in Gogol's *Selected Passages from a Correspondence with Friends*)

In the Russian there is a special feeling for the feast of Easter Sunday. He feels this kinship more keenly if he happens to be in a foreign country. . . . It seems to him that in Russia people somehow celebrate this day better, and the people themselves are more joyful and better than on other days, and life itself is somehow different, not ordinary everyday. Suddenly it seems to him that this solemn midnight, this ubiquitous ringing of bells, which seems to fuse all the earth into one sound, all the cries, Christ has arisen! which replace on this day all other greetings, that kiss which people give one another only in our country—and he is ready to cry out, Only in Russia is this day celebrated the way it ought to be celebrated. . . .

This day fits our nineteenth century, when thoughts about the happiness of mankind have almost become the favorite thoughts of all people; when embracing all of humanity like our brothers has become the favorite dream of the young people; when many people fantasize only about how to transform all of humanity, how to raise the inner dignity of man; when almost half already have solemnly acknowledged that only Christianity is able to bring that about; when they affirm that Christ's law should be brought more closely into the everyday life of both family and state; when people have even begun to say that everything should be owned in common—houses and land; when heroic feats of charity and helping the unfortunate ones have begun to be subjects of conversation even in fashionable drawing rooms; when, finally, charitable organizations and benevolent shelters and homes have become numerous. The nineteenth century should joyfully celebrate that day which suits the hearts of all the magnanimous and charitable movements! But on that very day, like on a touchstone, you see how pale all the Christian strivings are. They exist only in dreams and thoughts, not in reality. And if, in fact, people on that day had to embrace their brother as their brother—they would not embrace him. People are ready to embrace all of mankind as a brother, but will not embrace their brother.

No, our age cannot celebrate Easter Sunday the way it should be celebrated. There is a terrible obstacle in our way, there is an insurmountable obstacle—*pride*. Pride was known in earlier ages, too, but that was a more childish pride, pride in one's own physical strength, pride in one's wealth, pride in one's birth and rank; but it did not reach that terrible spiritual development in which it has now appeared before us. It stands before us in two forms. The first is pride in one's cleanness. Humanity of our day, rejoicing that it has become better in many ways than our ancestors, has fallen in love with its cleanness and beauty. Nobody is ashamed to boast publicly of his spiritual beauty and to consider himself better than others. We only need to see how everybody speaks as if he were a noble knight. How pitilessly and severely we judge others. We only need to listen to those justifications with which we justify ourselves for not embracing our brother even on Easter Sunday. Without shame or without spiritual tremor, we say: "I cannot embrace that man; he is vile, morally foul, he has besmirched himself with the most dishonorable behavior. I do not let such a person into my front hall; I do not even want to breathe the same air as he; I shall make a detour so that I shall pass without running into him. I cannot live with foul and despicable people. How could I embrace such a person as if he were my brother?" Alas, the poor nineteenth-century person has forgotten that on this day there are no foul or despicable people, that all people are brothers belonging to the same family, every human being has the name of brother, and no other name. . . . All is forgotten.

There is a second kind of pride, the pride of intellect. Never had it grown into such a force as in the nineteenth century. We feel it in everybody's fear of being thought a fool. People of our age can put up with anything: being called a swindler, a scoundrel; give him any name you want, he will put up with it, but he will not put up with the name of fool. He will allow people to laugh at everything, but he will not allow them to laugh at his intelligence. His mind is to him a shrine. At the least sneer at his intelligence, he is immediately ready to place his brother at the proper dueling distance and shoot a bullet in his forehead, without a tremor. He does not believe in anything or anybody; he only believes in his intelligence. What his intelligence does not see, that does not exist for him. . . . Even a shadow of Christian humility cannot touch him because of his pride of intellect. . . .

A man of such an age is to be able to love and to feel Christian love for people? He is to become full of that bright simplicity of mind and angelic childlikeness that unites all people in one family? How could he sense the fragrance of his celestial brotherhood? How could he celebrate this day? Even that externally kindly expression of the former, simple ages, which made it look as if a man were closer to another man, has disappeared. The pride of intelligence of the nineteenth century has annihilated it. The devil has entered the world without a mask now. The spirit of pride ceased to appear in various disguises and to frighten superstitious people. He has appeared in its proper look. Sensing that they acknowledge his domination, he has ceased even to pretend with people. With arrogant shamelessness he now laughs in the face of those who acknowledge him. He issues the stupidest laws to the world, such as had never been issued previously. The world sees it and does not dare to disobey. What does this fashion mean, fashion that is worthless, meaningless, which in the beginning people tolerated as a trifle, as an innocent matter, and which today like a complete master has begun to take charge in our houses, driving out everything that is the main and best thing in man? Nobody is afraid to break several times a day the first and most holy laws of Christ— and meanwhile fears not to fulfill the least little command of fashion, trembling before it like a timid little boy. . . . What do all those innumerable so-called rules of politeness mean which have become stronger than all fundamental principles? What does it mean if seamstresses, tailors, and craftsmen of every kind rule the world, and those anointed by God have remained off to the side? Obscure people, whom nobody knows, who have no ideas or purehearted convictions, rule over the opinions and ideas of intelligent people? The newspaper page, acknowledged by all to be false and to lie, becomes the callous legislator over people who do not respect it. . . .

A strange despondency has taken over the earth. Life has become more and more hard-hearted. Everything is becoming petty and small, only one giant image of boredom has arisen in the sight of all, reaching every day a more and more immeasurable size. Everything is deaf, graves are everywhere. God! How empty and terrible your world is becoming!

Why do only Russians think that this holiday is celebrated as it should be, and is celebrated like that only in our country? Is it a dream? But why is this dream not dreamed by anybody else than the Russians? . . . Not one grain of what is genuinely Russian in our ancestral past and of what Christ himself has illuminated will die out. It will be spread by the resounding strings of poets, promulgated again by fragrant mouths of worshipers, what is going out will flame up again, and the holiday of Easter Sunday will be celebrated as it should be, in our country before it is by other nations! On what basis can we say this, by what qualities contained in our hearts can we support this? Are we better than other nations? Are we nearer to Christ in our lives? We are not better than anybody, and our lives are even less harmonious and more disorderly than all of them. "We are worse than all others"— that is what we should always say about ourselves. But there is something in our nature that does predict this to us. Our disorderliness itself predicts this. We are a metal that is still in a molten state, not yet cast in the form of its national mold. It is still possible for us to reject, to push away from us that which is unsuitable to us, and to take inside us all that other nations which have received their forms and have been set in their molds find it impossible to do. In our basic nature, there is much that we have partly forgotten but that is close to Christ's law. The proof of that is that Christ came here without a sword and the prepared soil of our hearts welcomed his word. The basis for the brotherhood of Christ exists in our Slav nature, and the fraternizing of people was closer to us than that of the house and blood brotherhood. We do not yet have the irreconcilable hatred of one class for another class, and of those angry parties that we see in Europe and that present an insurmountable obstacle to the uniting of people and to brotherly love between them. We have, finally, a courage that nobody else has, and if we find in front of us some kind of task that is decidedly impossible for any other nation, even, for example, such as to reject suddenly and immediately all our faults, and all that makes the noble nature of man feel ashamed—then despite the suffering of our own bodies, not having mercy on ourselves, as in 1812,* not having mercy on our property, we burned our houses and earthly goods, so we shall rush to cast away from us all that shames us and stains us. Not one soul will be left behind another, and at such times all quarrels, hatreds, enmities—all will be forgotten, the brother will cling to the breast of the brother, and all of Russia will be one human being. Basing ourselves on that, we can say that the feast of Easter Sunday will be celebrated in our country before it is in other countries. My soul tells me this with certainty. It is not an idea thought up in the head. Thoughts like this are not thought up. They are born through the suggestion of God, at the same time in the hearts of many people who have never seen one another, who live in different corners of the earth, and such ideas are proclaimed at the same time, as though with one voice. I know with certainty that more than one person in Russia, even though I do not even know him, believes this firmly, and says: "In our country Christ's Easter Sunday† will be celebrated before it is in any other country."

(*1847*)

IN PRAISE OF RUSSIAN PEASANTS

(From *Dead Souls*, vol. 2)

You own peasants so that you may protect them in their peasant way of life. What is that way of life? What is the peasant's occupation? Tilling the soil, is that clear? There are clever people who say, "He must be raised from this state. He leads a life too simple and gross. He must become acquainted with objects of luxury." It is not enough that thanks to this luxury they have themselves become milksops and not human beings, and have picked up the devil knows what diseases, and that there is not an eighteen-year-old boy who has not tried everything, so that he is toothless and bald—now they want to infect the peasants. Thank God one healthy estate is still left that is unacquainted with these fancies. For this we should simply thank God. Yes, for me, the tillers of the soil are the most honorable of all. God grant that all be the tillers of the soil. Experience has shown that the purest morals are

---

* A reference to the burning of Moscow and the driving out of Napoleon's invading armies.
† The Russian word for *Sunday* is the same word as for *Resurrection*. Easter Sunday in Russian is literally "Bright Sunday." In this sentence of the above passage, therefore, "Christ's Easter Sunday" also means, literally, "Christ's Bright Resurrection" (*Svetloe Voskresenie Khristovo*).

those of the man of the agricultural calling. Where tilling the soil is the basis of social life, there is abundance and prosperity. There is neither poverty nor luxury, but there is prosperity. . . . First think of making every one of your peasants rich. Then you yourself will be rich, without factories, without mills, without foolish ventures.

(written between 1840 and 1842)

ON THE CHARACTER OF THE RUSSIANS

(From Gogol's notes for a planned history of Russia)

The character of the Russians is incomparably more subtle and more cunning than that of the inhabitants of all of Europe. Any one of those, even if he has the very sharpest wit, even an Italian, is more simple-minded [than the Russian]. But every Russian, even one who is not intelligent, knows how to pretend so well that he will fool and get the better of anybody.

THE CONTROVERSY OVER GOGOL'S
SELECTED PASSAGES

After writing a negative review of Gogol's *Selected Passages* that was published in the journal *Contemporary*, Vissarion Belinsky received an angry letter of reproach from Gogol himself. In response he wrote the following letter, dated July 15, 1847, which came to represent the views of the radical pro-Western intelligentsia. Although it could not be published in Russia, the text was widely known through manuscript copies, and Herzen had it printed in London in 1855. It was for reading this letter to a meeting of the Petrashevsky Circle in 1849 that Dostoyevsky was sentenced to exile in Siberia:

> You have not noticed that Russia sees her salvation not in mysticism, not in asceticism, not in pietism, but in the progress of civilization, enlightenment, humaneness. Russia does not need sermons (she has heard enough of those!), not prayers (she has said enough of those!), but the awakening in the people of a feeling of human dignity, which has been lost for

so many centuries in dirt and trash, of justice and laws in keeping not with the teaching of the church, but with healthy common sense and justice, and their being applied as strictly as possible. . . . The most acute contemporary national problems in Russia today are: the abolition of serfdom, the ending of physical punishment, the strictest possible carrying out of those laws which do exist. . . . Those are the problems which trouble and preoccupy Russia in her apathetic slumber. But at this very moment, a great writer, who so powerfully helped the self-awareness of Russia with his wonderfully beautiful, deeply true works, who made it possible for Russia as it were to look at herself in a mirror, appears with a book in which in the name of Christ and the church he teaches barbaric landowners how to squeeze more money out of peasants, teaches them how to swear more. No, if you were really filled with the truth of Christ, and not with the teachings of the devil, you would not have written this in your new book. You would tell the landlord that since his peasants are his brothers in Christ, and since a brother cannot be a slave of his brother, he must give them their freedom. At least he must make their work as beneficial as possible for them, realizing in the depth of his conscience that he is in a false position in relation to them. . . . You are a preacher of the knout, an apostle of ignorance, a champion of obscurantism and reaction, a panegyrist of Tartar laws. . . . What is it you are doing? Look down: you stand at the edge of a precipice. You base such teaching on the Orthodox church. I understand that. That church was always a supporter of the knout and a champion of despotism. But why do you bring Christ into this? . . . The meaning of Christ's words has been revealed by the philosophical movement of the last century. That is why a Voltaire, who with the weapon of his mockery extinguished the bonfires of fanaticism and ignorance, is of course much more the son of Christ, the flesh of his flesh, and the bone of his bones than all your priests, archbishops, metropolitans, patriarchs! You say the Russian people are the most religious in the world. That is a lie! . . . The Russian people are not like that. They have too much healthy common sense, clarity, and positive qualities in their minds. . . . I shall not go into your hymn of praise for the loving links between the Russian people and their rulers. I will come right out and say that your hymn of praise did not find agreement in anybody. It even lowered you in the eyes of people whose orientation is in other respects close to yours. . . . The public is right. It sees in Russian writers its only leaders, defenders, saviors from Russian autocracy, orthodoxy, and nationality, and therefore it is always ready to forgive a writer a bad book, but it will never forgive a harmful book.

Here is my final, concluding word: Since you, unfortunately, with proud humility have disavowed your truly great works, then now, with sincere humility, you must disavow your last book and redeem the heavy sin of having published it with new works that will remind us of your earlier ones.

(*1847*)

Gogol was not without his supporters, however, who felt that Belinsky's letter was unfair and one-sided, and that his onslaught on Gogol's vulnerable statements left unnoticed the real value of Gogol's central arguments. Following are the views of three members of what may be called the "minor line" (*minornaya liniya*) of Russian intellectual history.

The first, Gogol's contemporary, Apollon Grigoryev, was a poet and critic. He held the view that Russian national distinctiveness was to be cherished and maintained the original position that the fullest incarnation of Russianness was to be found neither in the nobility (as, for example, in Pushkin) nor in the simple people (as many of the Slavophiles and Tolstoy believed), but rather in the merchants, particularly as portrayed in the plays of Aleksandr Ostrovsky (1823–1886). He expressed this view in a letter to Gogol dated November 17, 1848:

Did you, as a human being, have the right to bare the innermost secrets of your soul before other people? This question reveals again the cynical contempt of contemporary mankind for the highest meaning of their personal lives. . . . Being a great master, you penetrated deeply into the nature of every small creature and into the sad falling away of man from God's image, and you were the first who called the attention of all to the unnoticeable existence of Akakii Akakiievich. . . . In the letter about Easter Sunday, the writer, himself ill with the diseases of our age, unmasks them with sincerity and depth.

The pro-Gogol and anti-Belinsky view surfaced again with the Symbolist poet Aleksandr Blok, who asserted in his essay "The People

and the Intelligentsia" that Gogol's words of love for Russia would
not be understandable to intellectuals; to them they would seem to be
uttered in a delirium. Elsewhere Blok said that Belinsky pointed out a
few sad, weak passages in Gogol, and hence nobody noticed the depth
of thought and the truth in the rest of Gogol's *Selected Passages;* this
was, in his opinion, "Belinsky's great crime." Blok also praised Grigoriev's 1848 letter to Gogol and described Belinsky's role in Russian
history in a remarkable figure of speech:

> One part of *Selected Passages* is small, in a minor key, its
> contents—illness. The rest is huge, truth, man, enthusiasm,
> Russia. . . . [Belinsky] gave a little push so that the Russian
> intelligentsia flew down the stairs, in its Russian Westernizing
> raptures, and hit each stair; and most painfully of all, the last
> stair, the Russian revolution of 1917–1918.

About Grigoryev, Blok wrote:

> In Grigoryev there are preserved the sparks of a vast culture
> which have continued to smolder, down to our own time,
> under the ashes of polemics and indifference.

Grigoryev's collected works were being prepared for publication during
the highly unsettled period between the two Russian Revolutions of
1917, those of February and October. Vladimir Kniazhnin, the historian in charge of the edition, wrote in an introduction dated September
12, 1917:

> Is this book needed, is any book needed at all today? I answer
> with firm conviction: Yes. I believe that the deep decline in
> national feeling is taking place on the eve of its true resur-
> rection and renascence in Russia. And any *Russian* will help
> toward that end. All the more so a book in which anything
> that is national sparkles like a bright, precious stone set in a
> most precious ring. The more terrible the torments, the more
> cruel, the closer we are to the precipice, the more inevitable
> is the hour to create and forge one's national culture.

SERGEY AKSAKOV

AS AN AUTHOR *Sergey Aksakov (1791–1859) was a late bloomer. Born in Ufa, Aksakov spent his childhood in the vast regions of the borderlands of the Russian Empire. He came to know and feel intimately the life of the vast natural surroundings of his early years. Later, as a member of one of the leading Slavophile families in Moscow, he took great interest in the theater. He knew Gogol well and moved in various literary and artistic circles. He served five years as a censor, wrote a book on fishing and another on hunting, and it was only after this that he wrote his masterpieces—*The Family Chronicle *(1856), and its sequel,* The Childhood Years of Bagrov the Grandson *(1858). He also wrote several other works of memoirs and reminiscence.*

For readers living in a world of rapid change and looking for something different, Aksakov's works are an ideal universe in which to immerse oneself. His is a realm that antedates not only the modern and postmodern worlds, but even the nineteenth-century psychosociological realism of George Eliot, Flaubert, Tolstoy, and Turgenev.

"Mikhail Maximovich Kurolesov" is one of the five parts (Aksakov actually called them "fragments" or "excerpts") constituting The Family Chronicle. *This remarkable book, beloved by generations of Russians, chronicles a family called the Bagrovs—thinly disguised portraits of Aksakov's own grandparents. (At the end of the entire volume, the grandfather Bagrov enters on the family tree the birth of his grandson, Sergey Bagrov—in real life Sergey Aksakov.)*

In chronicling events that took place long before his birth, Aksakov of course had to rely on family stories told to him by relatives—mainly his grandmother. (In Aksakov's own lifetime, most of his contemporaries considered The Family Chronicle *an entirely factual, documentary work.) The Kurolesov episode takes us back into the eighteenth century—a world of patriarchal estates as well as unrestrained violence, evil and goodness confronting each other directly and openly.*

Here we find no sophisticated psychological analysis, modern skepticism, problematic perplexity. In the fashion of a historic chronicle, incidents just take place, in sequence, without contrivance by a subtle author. The narrator's Olympian voice is that of someone just telling what really happened, claiming objective reality for the events. He repeatedly tells us that all these events occurred in a different era, long ago, and he endows the men and women of yore, whom he presents as giants and giantesses, with rough-hewn, forceful traits.

We also find ourselves to some extent in the world of the Russian fairy tale or folk tale. We can think of Svetlana (fourteen when married and whisked away) as something of a Cinderella; Kurolesov is like an evil wizard masquerading as a handsome officer. The machinery of a fairy tale comes into play in a folk-tale salvation motif.

The narrator comments on the proceedings the way an elderly family member might, with complete aplomb and unshakable authority. Like so much in vast Russia, the story tends toward excess. The Kurolesov section given here illustrates the propensity of Russians for maximalism—pushing as far as one can go—in this case in debauchery, violence, torture of serfs, and unabashed evil of gigantic dimensions.

Most of The Family Chronicle is idyllic and pastoral, but the Kurolesov section is a tale of growing madness and uninhibited cruelty.

Kathryn B. Feuer, in a brilliant essay, wrote that "the portraits of the good patriarch Bagrov and the evil sadist Kurolesov stand like twin pillars at the entrance of the novel, ushering the reader into its center, the moral and emotional ambiguity of human nature." They represent a moral polarity, opposites within the range of human possibilities. Feuer continues, "The inner drama of The Family Chronicle lies in this struggle between man and his own nature."

It is a curious fact that Aksakov did not return to visit Bashkiria during the nineteen years when he was writing about events that had taken place there. He wrote his books in Moscow and in Abramtsevo, his country estate near Moscow.

MIKHAIL MAXIMOVICH KUROLESOV

I have already promised to relate the full story of Mikhail Maximovich Kurolesov and of his marriage to my grandfather's cousin—Praskovia Ivanovna Bagrova. My chronicles begin in the sixtieth year of the eighteenth century, consequently at an earlier date than the occurrences already related: on the other hand, the end comes very much later. And having explained this much, I hasten to fulfill my promise.

Stepan Mikhailovich was the only son of Mikhail Petrovich Bagrov; Praskovia Ivanovna, the only daughter of his uncle, Ivan Petrovich Bagrov. Hence my grandfather regarded her with a twofold affection, both as the sole female shoot of the Bagrov family, and as his only cousin. The girl lost her mother while still in infancy and was but ten years old when her father died. The mother came of the wealthy stock of the Bakteievs, and the daughter inherited her dowry of nine hundred serfs, a large fortune, and great store of silver and jewels. To these rich possessions were added the three hundred serfs of her late father, and the orphan became a great heiress . . . and a good match! After her father's death, she went, at first, to live with her grandmother, Madame Bakteieva; but as time went on she visited Troitskoie more and more frequently, each time making a longer stay, until in the end Stepan Mikhailovich persuaded her to settle for good and all in his house. Stepan Mikhailovich loved his cousin as well as his own daughters and manifested his tender regard for her in his own fashion; but Praskovia Ivanova was too young, or—to speak more justly—too childish to value her cousin's affection at its true worth; for he never stooped to the flattery and adulation to which the girl had been accustomed in her grandmother's house. Small wonder, then, that she soon grew tired and sick of Troitskoie and began to wish herself back again in the old life with her grandmother Bakteieva. Praskovia Ivanovna was not pretty, but she had regular features, earnest, intelligent gray eyes, and the broad long dark eyebrows that betoken a strong, and even masculine, character. She was tall, and looked fully eighteen when she was but fourteen years old. But in spite of her physical development, she was only a child in heart and mind. Her disposition was very lively and artless, and she would sing and frolic from morning to night. She had a marvelously beautiful voice and loved romantic songs, dancing, and games. When left to herself, she would spend the whole day playing with dolls, while she beguiled her play with every possible variety of folk song, of which she knew an incredible number.

The year before she took up her abode with Stepan Mikhailovich, a young officer of some eight-and-twenty years, one Mikhail Maximovich Kurolesov, one of the native aristocracy, was spending his furlough at his home in the government of Simbirsk. He was fairly good-looking—many indeed considered him handsome—others, however, affirmed that in spite of the beauty of his features his face had something repulsive about it, and, as a child, I recollect hearing my

grandmother and aunts arguing about his looks. Since his fifteenth year
he had served in a regiment that enjoyed a distinguished reputation in
those days, and he was already promoted major. He seldom took any
leave, for with his hundred and fifty serfs and small estate, he was not
able to keep up any sort of establishment. Although he had no real
culture, he was very clever and adroit in conversation, and wrote in a
dashing and correct style. I have several of his letters in my possession,
and they prove him to have been a man of cunning and suave, withal
of a firm and practical mind. I know not indeed how he came to be
related to our immortal Suvorov; but among Kurolesov's papers I find
certain letters from the genial commander in chief, all of which begin
as follows: "Dear Sir, and Cousin Mikhail Maximovich," and conclude
in like manner. "With the expression of deepest respect for yourself,
and my esteemed lady and cousin, Praskovia Ivanovna, I have the honor
to remain . . ." and so forth. Very little was known of Mikhail Maximovich in Simbirsk; nevertheless, "the world is full of rumor," and
during his short furloughs he may have permitted himself sundry ex-
cesses, which were whispered abroad, in spite of the severity he invariably showed toward gossiping servants. Briefly he had earned a certain
reputation, which may be summed up in the following aphorism: "The
major will permit no liberties; you must always be on your guard with
him, and make no slip; he takes an interest in his soldiers and protects
them to the best of his ability; but let one of them commit but the
smallest fault, and he need expect no mercy; Kurolesov's word is final;
as an enemy he is a match for the devil himself—he is a fox, a madcap,
a demon!" All the same he was universally regarded as a sound man
of business. Later rumors, from the same source, had it that the major
was addicted to drink, and his amours were too numerous; the latter
failing however was excused by the old adage: "Such a thing brings
no shame on the man"; the former with similar excuses: "One drink
is no disgrace to a man," or "He who is drunk and keeps his wits is
two steps ahead of anyone else."* And they added that the major always
knew the right place and the right time for his pranks. And so it befell
that Kurolesov was regarded in a charitable and, in some quarters,
even a favorable light. It is only natural to suppose that he was always
careful to be amiable and polite, especially toward old and important
people, so that he was welcomed everywhere. As a near neighbor and
distant relative of the Bakteiev family (through Madame Bakteieva's
son-in-law, Kurmyshev), he soon found means to establish himself in

* With the last two proverbs, a Russian expresses a great deal, very strikingly, and
intelligibly to anybody, despite their apparent indefiniteness. [Aksakov]

her house on the most easy and familiar footing. At first he had no special design, only following his usual custom of ingratiating himself as much as possible with people of wealth and rank; but later, noting the rich and lively young heiress, Praskovia Ivanovna (who already looked almost a woman), he resolved to marry her and secure her fortune for himself. With a view to this end he redoubled his attentions to Praskovia's grandmother and aunt, and had soon assured himself of the support of both ladies; while he courted the girl herself so skillfully that she soon grew very fond of him, merely because he deferred to her in everything, anticipated her wishes, and above all, spoiled her. Mikhail Maximovich disclosed his love to Praskovia's relations, played the role of lover, and everyone believed him when he vowed his passion was wasting him away; that night and day he dreamed only of his Praskovia; and that he was crazy with love for her. He was pitied and lamented—encouraged to hope—in short he was the heartbroken lover. With such sympathetic encouragement from the relations, the rest of the comedy was an easy business. He was able to procure the girl a thousand little pleasures. He took her for drives in his carriage with his beautiful horses, he would spend hours in the swing with her, he sang her favorite folk songs with her; he made her all sorts of little presents, and sent to Moscow for beautiful playthings for her.

The consent of the cousin-guardian being absolutely necessary for the full accomplishment of his design, Mikhail Maximovich next tried his utmost to obtain the goodwill of my grandfather. Under various pretexts, and amply supplied with the highest of high recommendations from Praskovia's relations, he paid several visits to Stepan Mikhailovich at his own house, but he never succeeded in gaining the old gentleman's favor in the least degree. This at first sight may appear somewhat strange, especially as the major possessed so many qualities in common with Stepan Mikhailovich: but over and above his sound judgment the old man possessed such a keen moral instinct for none but upright and honest people that he could instantly detect any crooked or base traits in any man's character; he perceived evil intentions from the start, even when concealed under the most attractive exterior. The smooth speech and courteous bearing of his visitor were of no avail, and did not mislead Stepan Mikhailovich for one moment; for he instantly guessed that some sinister design underlay all this politeness. Withal, my grandfather's principles exacted a blameless course of life; and the reports of the major's profligacy, so easily condoned by others, filled the strict old man with real aversion for Kurolesov: and although he himself in the heat of passion was capable of acts of blind fury, it horrified him to hear of people who could commit barbarities without anger and in cold blood. In consequence of these impressions, he received Mikhail Maximovich on his first visit in the most distant manner, in spite of the latter's interesting conversation on various subjects, especially farming; but the instant the guest turned to Praskovia Ivanovna (who had already made her home with my grandfather) and began treating her quite as an old friend, while the girl listened with obvious delight to his flattering remarks, my grandfather made a wry face, drew his heavy eyebrows together as was his wont when angry, and cast suspicious and unfriendly looks in Kurolesov's direction. The lady of the house and all her daughters, on the contrary, were charmed with the visitor—as he had taken good care from his first entrance into the family that they should be—he flattering them, while they were only too pleased to chat with him in the friendliest way. Unfortunately, however, the very visible signs of the approaching storm depicted upon my grandfather's countenance struck terror into their hearts, and an awkward silence ensued. In vain the guest endeavored to start a cheery general conversation: he only elicited nervous, monosyllabic replies to his polite remarks; and my grandfather became positively rude. Nothing remained possible for the visitor but to take his departure, although it was already late in the evening, and he had been invited, country fashion, to spend the night. "A good-for-nothing fellow, and a scamp: and it's to be hoped he never shows his face here again!" was Stepan Mikhailovich's verdict to his family; who, naturally, did not venture to contradict him; but the stately major was very favorably discussed in the ladies' apartments—and the unsophisticated young heiress talked much, and heard much talk, of his charming manners.

After this unequivocal rebuff Mikhail Maximovich hurried back to Madame Bakteieva and related to her the foregoing events. They knew my grandfather too well to hope that he would ever give his consent to the betrothal, after such a reception. They considered how best to appease him, but could think of nothing feasible. The bold major proposed that the grandmother should invite the girl to stay with her, and then the wedding could take place without Stepan Mikhailovich's consent; but Madame Bakteieva and her daughter, Madame Kurmysheva, guessed rightly that my grandfather would never permit Praskovia to leave his house alone so shortly after the major's visit; and the latter's leave was drawing near its end. Kurolesov next suggested a desperate plan: to persuade Praskovia to elope with him, to carry her off, and to marry her straightway at the nearest parish; the relations, however, would not hear of such a scandal; and so it came about that Mikhail Maximovich had to rejoin his regiment without having attained his object. But mysterious are the ways of providence, nor is it in our power to comprehend how fate willed that such evil business should be carried out successfully. Six months passed, and old Madame Bakteieva heard that Stepan Mikhailovich was preparing for a long journey. I cannot recollect whether it was to Moscow or Astrakhan that he was bound, but his errand must have been one of considerable importance, as his steward accompanied him. Immediately a letter was sent to my grandfather, begging that Praskovia should be allowed to stay with her grandmother during his absence—which request received the prompt and curt reply that Praskovia was perfectly happy at Trotskoie, and anyone who wished to see her must exert themselves to pay her a visit there. After sending this ultimatum, and after solemnly impressing upon his docile Arina Vasilievna that she must guard Praskovia as the very apple of her eye, and on no account permit her to quit Troitskoie, Stepan Mikhailovich departed on his journey.

Madame Bakteieva kept up a brisk correspondence with Praskovia and my grandfather's womenkind. So, as soon as she heard Stepan Mikhailovich was safely out of the way, she wrote and informed Mikhail Maximovich Kurolesov, adding that the old fellow would be a good while absent, and that his best plan would be to come himself and conclude the business that he had in view . . . and that she and her daughter would meet him at Troitskoie. She and Arina Vasilievna had always been on most friendly terms, and when she learned that the latter was very prepossessed by Kurolesov, she described how the charming young major was dying for love of Praskovia, and sang the praises of the suitor with great warmth and energy. She added that her dearest wish was to see her darling, fatherless granddaughter married before she died; and she felt that her beloved child would be happy with this man Kurolesov; that she herself had not long to live, and therefore wished to hurry on the affair. On her side, Arina Vasilievna had nothing to say against the plan, but expressed great doubt whether Stepan Mikhailovich would ever give his consent, as Mikhail Maximovich, in spite of all his perfections, in some extraordinary way had failed to please her husband. The two elder daughters of Arina Vasilievna were called to a family council, presided over by old Madame Bakteieva and her daughter, Madame Kurmysheva—an especially ardent partisan of the major—and it was decided to leave the entire management of the business in the hands of Praskovia's grandmother, as the girl's nearest relative—all this of course on the clear understanding that Stepan Mikhailovich's wife and daughters took no hand in the game, and were supposed to know nothing about the affair. I have

already described Arina Vasilievna as a good-natured and somewhat
weak-minded old lady; and as her daughters were entirely on Madame
Bakteieva's side, it was quite easy to persuade her to a step that was
certain to bring her husband's unbounded wrath upon her. Meanwhile
the gay, heedless Praskovia was quite ignorant of her impending fate.
Many allusions were made in her hearing to Mikhail Maximovich, in
fact no praise was too high for that excellent man—he adored Praskovia, he loved her better than life itself—night and day he thought
but of her, and she might be sure that when he next came on a visit
he would bring all sorts of beautiful presents from Moscow. This sort
of talk was very delightful to Praskovia Ivanovna, and she vowed that
she, too, loved Mikhail Maximovich more than anyone else in the
world. During Madame Bakteieva's stay at Troitskoie, a letter arrived
from Kurolesov, in which he arranged to come over as soon as he could
get leave. Finally the old Bakteieva and her daughter returned to their
own estate, after they had persuaded Arina Vasilievna to say nothing
of their visit in her letters to her husband; and to permit Praskovia to
visit her grandmother at an early date, under the pretext that the latter
was dangerously ill. Praskovia Ivanovna wept and entreated permission
to leave with her grandmother, especially when she heard that the major
was coming soon. But she was not allowed to leave, out of fear of
Stepan Mikhailovich's anger. Kurolesov, meanwhile, had not been able
to get any leave of absence as yet, and it was a good two months before
he arrived on the scene. But soon after his arrival an express messenger
arrived at Troitskoie, with a letter from Madame Kurmysheva, who
wrote that her mother was sick unto death, and desired to see her
grandchild once more before she died; doubtless, the letter continued,
Stepan Mikhailovich would offer no objection to the girl hurrying to
her grandmother's bedside to receive her dying farewell. The letter was
evidently written with the intention of giving Arina Vasilievna every
opportunity of exonerating herself in the eyes of Stepan Mikhailovich.
True to her promise, and quite easy in her mind as to the future, Arina
Vasilievna set off immediately, and conveyed Praskovia to the so-called
deathbed of her grandmother, spent a week with the invalid, and returned home enchanted alike by Mikhail Maximovich's charming manners and the extremely costly presents that he had brought from
Moscow for herself and her daughters. Praskovia Ivanovna was in a
state of rapture; her dearest grandmother was already better when she
arrived; and the dear kind major was there with all sorts of lovely toys
from Moscow. Not a day passed but he came to Madame Bakteieva's
house, always ready to chat and joke with Praskovia—in short, he so
played on the girl's affectionate and grateful heart that, as soon as her

grandmother told her he wished to make her his wife, she, mere child that she was, went wild with joy, and ran about the house telling everyone she met that she was going to marry Mikhail Maximovich— how happy they would be together—what joy to drive with him all day long with his beautiful horses; and to swing, or sing songs, or play with dolls together—even with great big dolls, as big as babies, which could walk and curtsy. This was the sort of life anticipated by the poor little bride. The conspirators hurried on affairs, lest any rumor of what was happening should reach the cousin's ears: friends and neighbors were invited to the betrothal, the young people exchanged rings and kisses, and sat side by side in the place of honor while all present drank to their good health and happiness. At first the bride was extremely bored by all this ceremony, the endless compliments, and the long sitting-in-state; but as she was allowed to have her new Moscow doll to sit beside her, she recovered her good humor, told the guests it was her child, and made the doll bow and curtsy her thanks for their polite congratulations. A week later the pair were married with full obser- vance of all necessary rites, the fifteen-year-old bride being described as seventeen, a statement that her build and height fully justified. Al- though Arina Vasilievna and her daughters must have known that this would be the inevitable end of the plot, they heard of Praskovia's marriage with extreme terror: the scales, as it were, fell from their eyes, and they realized that neither the pretended illness of the grandmother nor the crafty letter of Madame Kurmysheva would save them from Stepan Mikhailovich's fury. Before the actual news of the marriage had reached Troitskoie, Arina Vasilievna had written and told her husband that she had taken Praskovia to visit her dying grandmother, that they had found the old lady somewhat better, but needing her grandchild's company in order to make a full recovery; that she herself had returned home, not wishing to leave the girls too long by themselves—but that it would have taken force to remove Praskovia; nevertheless she was afraid she had incurred his displeasure. Stepan Mikhailovich's reply to this letter was that Arina had behaved very stupidly, and she must set off immediately to Madame Bakteieva's house and bring Praskovia home with her. Arina Vasilievna sighed and wept over his letter, and was at her wits' end how to act in the matter. Shortly after this the young couple paid her a visit. Praskovia appeared to be perfectly happy and cheerful, though less childish and less inclined to give vent to open expressions of her happiness. The husband seemed equally happy, and withal so calm and judicious that he quite comforted poor Arina Vas- ilievna by his sage counsels. He argued in his most convincing and reassuring manner that the whole of Stepan Mikhailovich's wrath would fall on the grandmother's head; that the latter, in consideration of her serious illness, had had a perfect right to anticipate Stepan Mikhailovich's consent, which would certainly have been granted in time; that the wedding would never have taken place had it not been that the grandmother was likely to expire any day, and leave her beloved granddaughter alone in the world—a desolate orphan—whose cousin indeed was a poor exchange for a loving grandparent. A great deal of this sort of soothing conversation took place between him and the Troitskoie ladies, accompanied by the presentation of costly gifts, which they—the ladies—accepted with the greatest pleasure, mingled with a certain amount of guilty fear. Presents were even left for Stepan Mikhailovich himself. The major advised Arina Vasilievna not to mention anything about the marriage in her letters to her husband, but to leave the announcement to be made by the newly married pair themselves; and he promised that he and Praskovia Ivanovna would take the earliest opportunity of sending a long joint letter. But the fact was, he had not the slightest intention of writing to Stepan Mikhailovich: his idea was to postpone the inevitable storm as long as possible, while he made haste to establish himself firmly in his new position. Directly after his marriage he had asked for his discharge from the army, which was promptly granted. His first step was to pay visits, accompanied by his young wife, to all relations, his own as well as hers. In Simbirsk—starting with the governor himself—he paid his respects to every person of any standing whatever. Everyone was delighted with the charming pair; and the major was so successful in currying favor everywhere that very soon all the gentry of the district quite approved of the marriage. And so another few months passed.

Meanwhile Stepan Mikhailovich, who had received no letters for a long time, and whose lawsuit was still undecided, was suddenly seized with such an irresistible longing to see his home that he set off and arrived quite unexpectedly at Troitskoie one fine morning. Arina Vasilievna trembled in every limb when she heard the awful news: the master has arrived! Stepan Mikhailovich rushed joyfully into the house, asked if all were alive and well, clasped his Arina and his children to his heart, and then inquired: "But where is Praskovia?" Encouraged by the loving tones of his voice, Arina Vasilievna replied with a forced laugh: "I really do not exactly know where she is at present: probably with her grandmother. But of course you know, little father, that she is married!" The astonishment and fury of my grandfather at these words were absolutely beyond description. His rage increased when he heard that Praskovia had married Kurolesov. He would have attacked his wife there and then, but she and all her daughters fell at his feet and vowed that everything had been done without their knowledge, and that they had been utterly deceived by Madame Bakteieva. The letter was produced as evidence of their innocence. My grandfather's rage was instantly directed against the old Bakteieva: he ordered fresh horses, and after a few hours' rest set out for her estate. It can well be imagined with what ferocity he attacked Praskovia's old grandmother. After the first outburst the old lady adopted a haughty attitude, and set to work in her turn to abuse my grandfather, growing more and more heated as she proceeded. "How dare you insult me," she screamed, "do you take me for one of your serfs? You seem to forget that I am as good as you are, and my husband was of much higher rank than you! I am much more nearly related to Praskovia than you are: I am her grandmother, and my rights as a guardian are every bit as good as yours! I only had her happiness in view, and I was not going to wait for your consent, because I thought I was dying and had no intention of leaving her at your mercy—I know you only too well, you're a madman and a wild beast! You knock people about in your house. Mikhail Maximovich is a very good match, and Praskovia was in love with him. And I should like to know who objects to him! Only yourself. Ask your daughters and your wife: they can appreciate him." "You lying old harridan," roared my grandfather, "you deceived Arina, you pretended to be ill, and sold Praskovia to that scoundrel Kurolesov, who seems to have bewitched you all!" These remarks sent old Madame Bakteieva nearly beside herself with rage, and she blurted out that Arina Vasilievna, and her daughters too, knew everything there was to know about the marriage, and had accepted plenty of presents from Mikhail Maximovich. These disclosures gave a new direction to my grandfather's anger. Threatening to separate Praskovia from her husband on the ground of her minority, he set off home again, calling on his way at the house of the priest who had married the couple. He called him to account with the utmost vehemence, but the priest calmly produced all the marriage documents, the signatures of the bride, her grandmother, and those of the witnesses, as well as Praskovia's baptismal certificate, which proved she was over seventeen years old. This was a fresh blow for my grandfather, who now lost all hope of ever being able to annul the hateful marriage, and whose fiery wrath kindled more and more against Arina Vasilievna and her daughters. I prefer not to give an exact account of what actually happened when at last he reached home. There was a frightful and horrible scene. Even thirty years later my aunts could not recall that day without a shudder. Enough that the guilty women confessed everything, that all Kurolesov's presents were sent back to Madame Bakteieva with orders to return them to the donor;

that the older daughters were ill for a very long time, that my grandmother lost most of her hair and was compelled to wear a plaster on
her head for a year afterward. The newly married pair were advised
never to show their faces to my grandfather again, and the name of
Kurolesov was forbidden to be mentioned in his house.

Meanwhile time—that healer of soul and body, that queller of
passions—flowed on its peaceful course. At the end of a year not only
was Arina Vasilievna's head mended, but the feeling of resentment in
Stepan Mikhailovich's heart had died away. At first, he would neither
receive the Kurolesovs nor listen to a word about them; he refused
even to read the numerous letters written to him by Praskovia Ivanovna.
But toward the end of a twelvemonth, when from every side news
reached him of the perfect happiness of the young wedded pair and of
the marvelous change in the character of Praskovia, who had suddenly
become quiet and sensible, Stepan Mikhailovich's heart softened, and
he felt a natural longing to see his beloved cousin once again. He
considered rightly that she was the least to blame of anyone connected
with the affair, being but a child, and he granted her permission to
visit Troitskoie, unaccompanied, however, by her husband. Naturally
she hurried over to see her cousin at once. And the vast change in
Praskovia Ivanovna after a year of marriage aroused my grandfather's
veritable astonishment. How could it have been otherwise, indeed! The
past year had awakened a great tenderness and affection for her cousin,
which she had never felt for him in bygone days; and which, considering
the circumstances of her secret marriage, was absolutely incredible.
Could it be that those eyes that overflowed with tears, as he greeted
her on her arrival, revealed to her what deep love was concealed under
the rough exterior and surly obstinacy of this man? Did some vague
foreboding of the dark future warn her that here was the real stay and
support of her life? Did she at last comprehend that among all those
who had flattered and caressed her in childhood, no one had loved her
more truly than the cross old cousin, who had tried to wreck her
happiness and who hated her darling husband? I know not, but all
were astounded at the change in the demeanor of the frivolous girl
toward her cousin. She, who in former days had refused to recognize
his right of guardianship or her duty toward him as his ward (and who
now had real grounds for offense, in consequence of his brutal behavior
toward her own grandmother) met him as an affectionate sister, or
even a devotedly attached daughter, returning to an adored father. Be
that as it may, this sudden sympathy, this deep affection, only ended
with life itself. And how marvelous was the transformation which
Praskovia's whole nature had undergone in this short time! The

thoughtless child had vanished forever, and in her place was a serenely cheerful, but thoughtful woman. She candidly admitted that everyone had done her cousin the greatest wrong; but pleaded in extenuation of their deceit, her own childish ignorance, and the blind love of her grandmother, her husband, and all the other relatives, for herself. She did not press for the immediate pardon of her husband—the greatest offender of all; she only ventured to hope—that in time, and when he saw how happy she was, and with what zeal and ardor her husband looked after all her interests—Cousin Stepan Mikhailovich would forgive Kurolesov, and ask him to come to Troitskoie. Stepan Mikhailovich was so much touched by Praskovia's humility that he could not reply. He did not keep his good little cousin, as he henceforth invariably called her, long, but sent her back home to her husband after a short stay at Troitskoie, saying her place was with the latter. On parting with her, he said: "If, at the end of another year, you and your husband are as happy together as you now are; and if he goes on as well as he has done, then he and I will be reconciled."

And, indeed, at the year's end, during which time he had frequently met his cousin and seen how happy and contented with her lot she was, Stepan Mikhailovich wrote, and said: "Come; and bring your husband to see me!" The old gentleman greeted Kurolesov with the utmost friendliness, told him frankly that he had had serious objections to him at first, and vowed that if he continued to behave well to Praskovia, he should be recognized as a loved and esteemed member of the family. Mikhail Maximovich's behavior was perfect—not so flattering and obsequious as formerly, but most attentive, polite, and respectful. It was plain that he had acquired perfect independence and self-reliance. He talked a great deal about his intention of taking over the full management and control of Praskovia's estates; asked my grandfather for his advice; was very quick to comprehend, and marvelously quick to utilize the latter's valuable information. He even discovered a distant relationship which he explained existed between his family and the Bagrovs before his marriage, and addressed my grandfather as Uncle, while Arina Vasilievna was Aunt, and their children Cousins. Even before the reconciliation he had seized an opportunity of doing Stepan Mikhailovich a service. My grandfather was aware of this, and while thanking him for his kindness, bade him ask a like favor in return. In short, all passed off famously. Appearances were entirely in favor of Mikhail Maximovich, but my grandfather kept his opinion unchanged: "Yes," said he, "the man is clever, and sensible, and prudent; but trust him I never could, and never can."

So another year passed away, in the course of which Stepan Mik-

hailovich emigrated to the province of Ufa. Kurolesov's conduct during
the first three years after his marriage was so orderly and discreet, or
at least so circumspect, that nothing adverse came to light. Besides, he
was very seldom at home, and spent the whole of his time traveling.
At the same time a rumor arose and spread abroad that the young
master was somewhat too severe. During the two following years Kurolesov effected such wonderful improvements in the entire management and direction of his wife's estates that folks were lost in wonder
at his tireless activity, his love of enterprise, and his iron will. Previously
to his taking them in hand, Praskovia's estates had been in a very
neglected state. In many instances they were going to wreck and ruin
owing to the lazy habits of the peasantry. Very little income was paid,
not because there was no market for the country produce, but because
some of the lands were very ill-cultivated, while in other parts the
proportion of arable land was very small; and Praskovia owned the
estates in common with her grandmother Bakteieva and her aunt Kurmysheva. Mikhail Maximovich arranged to transport the serfs to new
properties, and to sell the old property very advantageously. He first
purchased seven thousand desiatins of steppe land in the district of
Stavropol, in the province of Simbirsk (now Samara). This was most
excellent land in the Black Soil Belt, and was two ells deep in rich soil;
it was situated on the banks of the rivulet Berlia, around whose springs
grew but a scanty forest; besides this, the forest preserve, called the
Bears' Glen, was the only wood on the whole estate. To this part he
conveyed three hundred and fifty of the serfs. In this way he established
a highly productive estate, only a hundred versts from Samara; and
distant sixty and forty versts respectively from other Volga ports. It is
a recognized fact that a convenient market for corn and other produce
is the crowning excellence of a good estate. His next act was to journey
to the government of Ufa, where he purchased from the Baskhirs some
twenty thousand desiatins of land, also black earth, but very inferior
to the Simbirsk property as it included a considerable amount of forest
lands. This land lay in several plots on the banks of the river Usen,
and beside the rivulets of the Siuiush, Meleis, Karmalka, and Belebeika;
and at that time belonged, if I recollect aright, to the Menselinsk Circuit:
now it is included in the Belebei Circuit in the government of Orenburg.
Mikhail Maximovich sent four hundred and fifty of his people to the
well-watered neighborhood of the Siuiush; and fifty men were settled
on the banks of the Belebeika. To the larger colony he gave the name
of Parashino, the smaller colony he called Ivanovka, the estate in the
Simbirsk government was called Kurolesovo, and thus the three properties were respectively called by the baptismal, paternal, and married

names of his wife. This piece of sentiment on the part of a man, whom I shall shortly have occasion to portray in such dark colors, has always filled me with astonishment. For his own residence he chose Churasovo, an estate which Praskovia had inherited from her mother, and which was situated only fifty versts distant from the capital of the government. There he built what, in those days, was considered a most magnificent house, surrounded by equally splendid stables and other buildings. The fittings of the house, furniture, indoor and outdoor decorations, chandeliers and candelabra, bronzes, and china and the superb silver plate, were the admiration of all who saw them. This beautiful house was situated on the slope of a gently swelling hill, from which gushed more than twenty most abundant springs. House, wooded slope, and springs were all surrounded by extensive and luxuriant gardens full of the finest fruit trees of every variety. The household arrangements—servants, cuisine, horses and carriages—everything betokened the most refined and fastidious luxury. Visitors, both from the neighborhood—where many landed gentry and nobles resided—and from the city, were never lacking at Churasovo: life there was an endless round of feasting, drinking, singing, card playing, and chatter. Mikhail Maximovich was very particular that his Praskovia should always be richly and elegantly dressed, and, whenever he was at home, seemed solely occupied with her, and the carrying out of her slightest wish. Briefly, at the end of a few years he had attained such a footing in society that good folks admired, while bad folks envied, him. Nor did Mikhail Maximovich neglect his religious duties, and in place of the shabby old wooden church, in two years arose a stately stone-built edifice, decorated in exquisite taste, and even possessing a quite passable choir, chosen from among the servants, and trained under the master's guidance. Four years after her marriage, a little daughter was born to the happy and contented Praskovia, and a year later came a little son. But the children did not live long: the girl died before she was a year old, and the boy when he was scarcely three. Praskovia Ivanovna was most tenderly attached to the little boy, and his loss affected her most deeply. For a whole year she took no interest in anything; her once-blooming health faded and vanished; and she never had another child.

All this time the consequence and dignity of Mikhail Maximovich increased in the country with every day, and every hour. The poor and obscure nobility had certainly a good deal to endure from his arrogant and despotic demeanor; and by this class of neighbors he was more feared than loved: but the upper ranks of nobles were by no means displeased with his methods of reminding the lower ranks of their inferior position. Each year Mikhail Maximovich's absences from home

had grown longer and more frequent, especially since the unhappy year
when Praskovia Ivanovna refused to be comforted for the loss of her
son. It would seem that the tears and lamentations of his wife had been
wearisome to him; and that the deserted house—for Praskovia Ivanovna would receive no company—had bored him. Be that as it may,
there soon came a time when even the glittering company assembled
at Churasovo ceased to charm him.

Strange rumors meanwhile arose, which grew and spread in all
directions: it was whispered that the major was not merely severe, as
had been reported of him in his earlier days, but he had begun to treat
his retainers with cruelty; that he went so frequently to his estates in
Ufa in order that he might give himself up to unrestrained drunkenness
and vice of every possible description; that he had gathered together
an unholy company who practiced abominations under his directions;
that the worst thing about him was the unutterable cruelties that he
inflicted on his serfs when he was intoxicated; and that already two
men had died under torture. It was also said that all the higher officials
in both of the districts where his new estates were situated, were entirely
on his side, he having bribed some and persuaded others to become
his boon companions, while he instilled terror into everyone; the lower
officials and the lesser nobility trembled before him, for he was wont,
if anyone displeased him, to lay hold of him in broad daylight, carry
him off, throw him into a cellar, where he was nearly perished with
cold and hunger, and not infrequently flogged with a frightful whip
called a Cat.*

Not only were these rumors true, but they only gave hints of the
truth, the facts being far worse than the timid peasants dared relate.
The bloodthirsty nature of Kurolesov had developed to such a pitch
under the influence of liquor that humanity shuddered at it. It was a
hideous combination of a tiger's instinct and human intellect.

Finally rumors became certainty, and no one in Praskovia's neighborhood had any more doubts as to the fearful truth. Whenever Mikhail
Maximovich visited Churasovo for a rest between his criminal periods,
his manner of old times was quite unchanged—always friendly and
respectful toward his equals, and polite and affectionate with his wife,
who was now consoled for the loss of her children, and was once more

* The cat was Mikhail Maximovich's favorite instrument of punishment. It was a
whip woven out of seven raw leather straps, each with a knot at the end. In Parashino,
even after Kurolesov's death, these repulsive tools were kept for some time in the
storeroom, of course without being used, and I saw them myself. When the property
came into the possession of Stepan Mikhailovich's son, the cats were burned.
[Aksakov]

surrounded by a cheerful circle of friends. Although Mikhail Maximovich was careful never to lay a finger upon a soul in Churasovo, where all punishment was administered by the steward, yet everyone in the house trembled at the sound of his voice. Likewise, in the manner of any relatives or intimate friends who had any intercourse with him, an unmistakable aversion could be detected. But of all this Praskovia Ivanovna saw nothing, or if she did, she attributed it to some other cause—the universal esteem and the involuntary respect, which her husband's wonderful abilities, self-won wealth, and energetic will, excited in all hearts. Kind folks, who loved Praskovia Ivanovna, rejoiced at her ignorance of the real truth, for she was both gay and serene, and they wished to prolong her happiness as long as possible. It is true that many a female today, and many a woman of small social importance, would have only been too delighted to take an opportunity of revenging herself upon the insolent major—with his high and mighty manners toward his inferiors—by unmasking his real character. But over and above the actual fear inspired by the major himself, another formidable obstacle stood in the way of such exposure. This was the attitude taken by Praskovia Ivanovna herself, who would not tolerate the slightest criticism of her husband. She was too acute not to notice any sly attempt to introduce the subject into the conversation; and without waiting to hear any more, would bring her dark brows close together, remarking in her severest tone that anyone who had a word to say against her husband should never enter her home again. Naturally, after such an outspoken warning, no one dare utter another word. Her own personal attendants—an old and favorite servant of her father and her own faithful nurse—of whom she made great favorites (without, however, making them her confidants, as was customary among ladies of rank in those times) were quite unable to speak frankly to her. Both these old people had only too much reason to wish their mistress to know the real character of her husband, as they had near relations in the master's service, who had plenty to suffer from his unrestrained outbreaks of fury. Finally, however, they decided to tell their mistress everything, and chose a moment when she was alone to speak to her. But scarcely had the name of Mikhail Maximovich been uttered, when the once easygoing Praskovia Ivanovna flew into a rage: she threatened her old nurse with banishment for life to Parashino, if she ever dared to mention the master's name again. By such acts she closed every avenue to the truth and sealed the lips of those who had so much to disclose. Praskovia Ivanovna loved her husband and trusted him implicitly. She knew only too well how ready folks are to interfere with others' concerns; how eager to fish in troubled waters; and once and for all, she made a firm resolution and fixed principle, never to permit her husband's behavior to be discussed in her presence. A most praiseworthy principle, indispensable to the maintenance of family concord! But even to this excellent precept exceptions must sometimes be made, of which the present case is an example. Had Praskovia's strong will—backed up by the circumstance that all the property was hers by right—been brought to bear as a check upon her husband, he might have been persuaded to give up his greed of wealth and power—his unbridled and furious passions would not have had free rein—and like many another, he might have lived a reasonable and happy life.

Another year passed—Mikhail Maximovich gave himself up, unchecked, to his furious instincts, which, increasing and developing, urged him on to commit fouler abominations, which went unpunished. I prefer not to describe the details of the horrible life he led when living on his distant estates, especially at Parashino and the little district town: the story is too loathsome to repeat. I shall therefore confine myself to mentioning only what is necessary to give the reader an idea of this atrocious man. In the year following his marriage he devoted himself in the most energetic and even disinterested way to the numerous duties connected with the administration of his wife's estates. His ability, prudence, and industry were beyond praise. He undertook the arduous, wearisome, and complicated task of conveying great numbers of peasants to distant parts; and his indefatigable and skillful management was exerted solely for the benefit and well-being of the serfs. For this end he spared neither money nor pains, and saw that everyone was duly and fully furnished with everything needful. He thus provided against any risk of want or distress. He himself superintended the departure from the old homestead, accompanied the expedition a great part of the journey, then went on in advance to be ready to receive the emigrants on their arrival at their carefully selected and comfortable new dwelling places. True enough that he was severe, if not cruel, toward offenders. But against this severity might be set his justice to, and fair treatment of, good workers; and he knew when to keep his eyes closed. From time to time, it is true, he would break out, and spend a couple of riotous days in some little town; but he could throw off the effects of his drunkenness as easily as a goose shakes water off her feathers, and after such an interlude would only return with renewed zest to his interrupted labors.

At first this overwhelming mass of duties occupied his mind and hindered him from giving himself up to his ruinous habit of drinking, which aroused all his unnatural instincts. Hard work saved him for a time. But no sooner were the new estates of Parashino and Kurolesovo in working order, and all the houses, huts, and farm buildings ready for occupation, than he had too much time and too little occupation, and gave himself up wholly to drinking with his boon companions. His innate cruelty developed into a mad lust for torture and bloodshed. Encouraged by the terror and submissiveness of all around him, he rapidly lost all sense of humanity, and reveled in unrestrained acts of violence and brigandage. From among his servants and serfs he collected a bodyguard of a couple of dozen infamous rascals, and organized these worthy instruments of his will into a veritable robber band. As these followers observed that their master was permitted to do exactly as he liked and that his maddest tricks went unpunished, they naturally grew to regard him as almighty; and, themselves drunkards and ruffians, were only too ready and willing to carry out his most outrageous commands. Had anyone offended Mikhail Maximovich in word or deed, even in such a small matter as failing to arrive at the appointed hour for a drinking bout, it needed but a sign, and the trusty retainers set off in all haste, seized the delinquent—wherever he might happen to be, either openly or secretly—and dragged him before their master, who ordered him to be chained, knocked about, as often as not soundly flogged, and then locked up in the cellar. Mikhail Maximovich was a great lover of a fine horse; and he also admired fine furniture and pictures. When he took a fancy to anything he saw in a neighbor's or any stranger's house, he invariably offered the owner something of his own in exchange. Should the owner decline the proposal, Mikhail Maximovich, if he happened to be in a good humor, would then offer to buy the coveted possession. If this was also refused, he simply remarked he would have the article for nothing. And he would shortly make his appearance surrounded by his brigand retainers, and take the object by force. Complaints in a court of justice were of no avail, for the police were perfectly aware that any official who dared to take the step of following up a complaint by a visit of inquiry would soon make a close acquaintance with the Cat. The end of all these affairs was that Kurolesov was left in undisturbed possession of his ill-gotten goods, while the unlucky owner as often as not would be nearly beaten to death in his own house, in the presence of his family, who would beseech mercy in vain. Even worse acts of violence were committed, likewise with impunity. After a time Mikhail Maximovich made attempts to conciliate his victims; he either gave them money, or forced them by threats to promise not to bring any further claim against him; and thus the stolen property became legally his. When carousing with his friends, he was fond of boasting that the little portrait in the gold frame, hanging there on the wall, had been taken by him from such-and-such a gentleman; the writing table with gilt-bronze mounts from another; the silver cup out of which he was drinking from a third; and it was not an uncommon thing that the men named were actually sitting at the table, either pretending to hear nothing, or stifling their anger and joining in the general laughter that followed these confessions. Mikhail Maximovich had nerves of iron, and could drink an amazing quantity of brandy without losing his wits. Drunkenness never stupefied him, it excited him and aroused a demoniac activity in his disordered brain and deranged organization. When he was fully primed with drink, his greatest delight was to have horses harnessed to every available vehicle in the place, fill these with his guests and servants, and then, amid the tinkling of the horses' bells and the wild songs and shrieks of the whole company, to dash at full gallop over the neighboring plains and through the villages. A good supply of brandy was always taken on these excursions, and it was one of his jokes to invite anyone he met, irrespective of age or sex, to drink with him. Should the wayfarer refuse the favor, he or she got a thrashing. The offenders were tied to trees, posts, or fences, regardless of rain or cold. I refrain from relating other and more revolting stories. . . . In such a frame of mind as this he galloped one day through a village. As he dashed past a threshing floor, where a peasant and his family were busy threshing, he noticed a woman of singular beauty. "Halt!" shouted Mikhail Maximovich to his servants. "What do you say to this woman, Petrushka?" "The deuce!" cried Petrushka, "she is far too good-looking!" "Will you marry her?" "How can I marry another man's wife?" retorted Petrushka, laughing. "You'll soon see how. Hey, children! Seize her, and pack her into my carriage!" Away they flew to the next parish and in spite of the poor woman's protestations that she already had a husband and two children, she was then and there married to Petrushka. No one dared report this crime to any magistrate, and it was only in later years, when the property came into the hands of the younger Bagrov, that the woman and her husband and children were restored to the real owner; her first husband was long since dead. Bagrov returned a great deal of stolen property to the original owners, but a large portion was never claimed by anyone and moldered away in lumber rooms. I suspect the reader will find it difficult to believe that the commission of such open crimes was possible in Russia, and only eighty years ago; but there is no doubt as to the accuracy of my tale.

But however infamous this unbridled debauchery and boundless tyranny were, something still more horrible developed in Mikhail Maximovich's disposition—an ever-increasing instinct of cruelty and lust of blood. To torture men became an obsession with him. When he had no victim to flog, he grew peevish, restless, even ill; hence his visits to Churasovo became shorter and less frequent. But once back at his beloved Parashino, and he hastened to make up for lost time. Examination and regulation of all domestic affairs furnished him with rich opportunities to inflict punishment; for the slightest irregularity was dealt with in the most barbarous manner; and where is the household where some small fault or act of neglect cannot be found, if it is only sought? In a general way, the whole weight of his tyranny fell almost exclusively on the house servants. It was very rarely, and then only under exceptional circumstance, that he would permit a peasant to be flogged; and in consequence the stewards and overseers had as much to suffer at his hands as the household. He spared no one, and everyone in his personal service had been at least once, and not infrequently several times, beaten nearly to death. It is a fact that Mikhail Maximovich would never order anyone to be flogged when he himself was in a furious passion and screaming with rage, as frequently happened: when he wished to practice his barbarity on anyone, he would address him in a calm, almost gentle, tone, after this manner: "Now, my dear friend, Grigory Kuzmich, I am very sorry indeed to have to do it, but we have a little business to settle between us." With words such as these, he would turn to his head groom, Kovliaga, who, God knows why, was the person most frequently entrusted with the execution of his vile practices. "Let the pussycat scratch him!" he would say, smiling at the other servants, and then would begin a long torture for the unfortunate which Mikhail Maximovich would witness, as he sat comfortably drinking his tea mixed with brandy, smoking his pipe, and cracking jokes about the sufferer, as long as the latter was conscious. Credible witnesses have assured me that the sole means of restoring life to the miserable victims was by wrapping the freshly stripped skins of slaughtered sheep around their bleeding bodies. After gloating his full on the tortured man, Mikhail Maximovich would be sated with the spectacle, and would say: "Enough; carry him off!" and for the rest of the day, and sometimes even for several days, would be especially cheerful and even amiable. But just to finish off the characteristics of this monster, I will add one of his precepts that he was wont to impress upon his boon companions: "I object to sticks and knouts," he often remarked, "you can so easily kill a man with them before anyone has had time to enjoy anything. That's why I prefer my kitten, she makes folks smart and is not dangerous." I have not told the tenth part of what I know of this man's doings, but I think I have told more than enough. I must not forget, however, to observe that a singular freak of human nature was manifested in Mikhail Maximovich, who, throughout all his paroxysms of savagery and tyranny, was busily occupied with the building of his fine stone church at Parashino. At the time reached in my narrative, the outside fabric of the church was already completed, while the whole of his own dwelling house was crowded with carpenters, wood carvers, gilders, painters, etc., etc., who were busy with the beautiful inside decorations.

Praskovia Ivanovna had now been married about fourteen years, and if she noticed anything strange in her husband's manner, who very, very seldom came to see her now, she was still very far from knowing, or even suspecting, his true character. She led her usual quiet and happy life. In the summer she tended her luxuriant gardens and her beautiful gushing springs, which she would never suffer to be enclosed, and which she herself would dredge and clear from all obstructions. In winter she was greatly in request among her hosts of friends, and she had grown passionately fond of card playing. Suddenly a letter arrived from a relative of her husband, an old lady for whom she entertained a great regard. The letter contained a full and detailed account of all Mikhail Maximovich's outrageous doings; and, in conclusion, the writer explained that she considered it nothing short of a crime to leave the mistress of a thousand souls in ignorance of the condition of her retainers—crushed as they were beneath the tyranny of her own husband—when it was a simple matter for her to rescue them by depriving the madman of all authority. The blood of the innocent victims cried to heaven, she wrote, and her own personal servant, Ivan Anufriev, was lying at death's door, in consequence of Kurolesov's ill treatment. As for Praskovia Ivanovna, she need have no fear about acting; she was under the protection of the governor and her own good friends, and Mikhail Maximovich would never dare to come to Churasovo. The letter had the effect of a thunderbolt on Praskovia Ivanovna. She has often told me that, for a few minutes after reading it, she remained as if unconscious. But her extraordinary strength of character and her firm trust in God came to her aid; her agony of soul was conquered, and she resolved on a plan of action over which many a bold man would have hesitated. She ordered the horses to be put in her calash, giving an urgent errand to the government capital as a pretext, and set straightway out for Parashino—accompanied only by one manservant and a maid. The journey was long, more than four hundred versts, and she had plenty of time to reflect on the danger of the step she was taking. But as Praskovia Ivanovna was wont to relate in after days, she made no plans, and came to no decision on the way.

She wished to see, with her own eyes, how her husband really spent his time when on his estates. The frightful letter of the old lady had not entirely convinced her of his guilt, as the writer lived at a great distance, and possibly might have been misled by exaggerated reports. She had not liked to question her old nurse at Churasovo. The idea of personal danger never even entered her mind; her husband had always been so uniformly kind and loving toward her that it appeared to her quite a simple matter to persuade Mikhail Maximovich to return to Churasovo with her. She arrived—as she had intended to arrive—at Parashino late in the evening, left her carriage at the boundary fence, and went very softly, accompanied only by her two servants, through all the outbuildings to the back door of the wing of the house, where she saw lights and from whence issued a confused medley of songs, shouts, and laughter. Her hand never trembled as she opened the door. The scene that presented itself to her gaze lacked nothing to prove the manner of life led by her husband. Even tipsier than usual, he sat drinking with his already drunken guests. Clad in a red silk shirt, his face a mask of coarse sensuality, he grasped a glass of punch in one hand, while his left arm encircled the waist of a beautiful woman who was seated in his lap. Before him sang and danced the whole household of half-intoxicated servants. Praskovia Ivanovna took everything in with a glance—almost fainting she tottered back, shut the door behind her, and left the house. Outside, on the steps, she met one of her husband's servants, an elderly—and fortunately sober—man. He recognized his mistress and exclaimed: "Little mother, Praskovia Ivanovna, is it you?" Here Praskovia Ivanovna made signs to him to keep silence, until they reached the middle of the courtyard, when she spoke to him in very severe tones: "So this is the way you all spend your time here! Your merry life shall soon come to an end!" The man threw himself at her feet and, weeping, exclaimed: "Little mother, do you really believe we have merry lives here? God Himself has sent you!" Praskovia Ivanovna again ordered him to be quiet, and to show her where Ivan Anufriev, who she heard was still alive, was lying ill. She was conducted to the covered cattle sheds, and there, in a hut near the cows' stalls, she found the dying Anufriev. He was so exhausted that he was unable to speak a word. But his brother Aleksey, a poor youth who had been unmercifully flogged on the preceding day, crawled slowly and painfully from his pallet of straw, knelt down, and told the dreadful stories of his brother, himself, and many others. Praskovia's heart was like to break with pity and horror: her conscience reproached her bitterly, and she resolved to make a speedy end to Mikhail Maximovich's cruel reign—a simple matter, as she then thought. She gave strict orders that the master should not be informed of her arrival; and, as she heard that in the unfinished part of the great house there was a quite habitable room, where Mikhail Maximovich was accustomed to dispatch business and regulate his accounts, she resolved to spend the rest of the night there, intending to talk to her husband in the morning, when he should be sober. But the report of her arrival had already gotten abroad. One of the most sinister of Mikhail Maximovich's companions whispered a word in his master's ear. In an instant Kurolesov's intoxication vanished: he recognized his danger. Although he knew but little of his wife's brave and steadfast character, having so far done nothing to bring it into play, still he had a suspicion of her real strength of mind. He dismissed his drunken crew, two pails of cold water were dashed over his head, and, refreshed in mind and body, he dressed himself decently and tried to ascertain whether his wife was asleep or not. Already he had resolved on his plan of action. He was quite convinced, and rightly, too, that someone had informed Praskovia Ivanovna of his conduct; and not being quite satisfied as to the truth of the tale, she had come to see the state of things for herself. He knew that she had been a witness of the midnight revels; but what he did *not* know was that she had seen Ivan Anufriev and spoken to Aleksey. In spite of the nocturnal saturnalia, he still hoped to make his peace with her. He prepared to play the part of the repentant sinner with great pathos, to appeal to his wife's affection, and to get her out of Parashino as quickly as possible.

Meanwhile the morning dawned and the sun rose. Mikhail Maximovich went softly to Praskovia Ivanovna's room, opened the door cautiously, and saw from the condition of the bed, hastily prepared for her overnight, that it had never been occupied. He gazed into the interior of the chamber. Praskovia Ivanovna knelt weeping and praying to the cross on the spire of the newly built church, which could be seen glittering against the sky from the open window, as there was no icon suspended in the room. After a pause, Kurolesov addressed his wife quite gaily, and said: "My dearest, you have prayed quite long enough! Now, what put it into your head to pay me this delightful visit?" Praskovia Ivanovna rose to her feet, and without losing any of her composure refused her husband's embrace, while in cold and severe tones she told him that she knew everything and had seen Ivan Anufriev. Relentlessly she expressed her utter abhorrence of the bloodthirsty wretch, and told him that henceforth he was no husband of hers. She informed him that he must instantly deliver up the power of attorney for the administration of all her estates, and leave Parashino; should he ever venture to show himself in her presence again, or even be seen upon any of her land, she would inform the government of his misdeeds and have him sent to penal servitude in Siberia. Mikhail Maximovich was not prepared for this sort of talk. He fairly foamed with rage. "How dare you speak to me like this!" he bellowed. "Very good, my little pigeon! Then I can speak to you in a different tone. You shall never leave Parashino until you have given me a deed of purchase of the whole of your estates. If you do not agree to this, you may go and starve in the cellar." And without more ado, he seized a stick that stood in a corner, threw his Praskovia violently on the floor, and beat her until she lost consciousness. Then, calling some of his trusty servants, he bade them carry the mistress down to the vault, fastened the door with a massive padlock, and put the key in his pocket. All the household were summoned to his presence, and in the most stern and threatening tones he inquired who had conducted Praskovia Ivanovna to the cattle sheds. But that guilty person had long since absconded, and Praskovia's coachman and manservant had fled with him; only the servant maid could not make up her mind to abandon her mistress. Mikhail Maximovich did not hurt the girl, but, giving her some instructions as to how to persuade her lady to listen to reason, he himself locked her up in the cellar with Praskovia. And what did the monster then? He recommenced his orgies with the most unbounded zest. But in vain he swallowed his brandy, in vain his besotted crew of servants danced and sang around him. . . . Mikhail Maximovich grew gloomy and uneasy. Still this gloom in no way discouraged him from pursuing his purpose in the most indefatigable way. He had a legal deed of purchase of the estates of Parashino and Kurolesovo drawn up in the name of one of his worthy friends, and duly executed in the neighboring district town. As an act of grace, Churasovo was left in Praskovia's possession. Twice a day he visited his wife in the cellar and tried to persuade her to sign the deed. He entreated her to pardon him for his violence, which was the act of a moment of rage; promised never to come near her if she would only consent; and assured her that in the event of his death all should be left to her. But Praskovia Ivanovna, aching from his blows, exhausted by hunger, and ravaged by fever, would not give up her rights. So passed five days. Heaven alone knows how it all might have ended.

All this time Stepan Mikhailovich was living tranquilly in his New Bagrovo, about a hundred and twenty versts distant from Parashino. I have already said that he had long since been perfectly reconciled to Mikhail Maximovich and, although he had no special liking for the man, still on the whole he was quite satisfied with his behavior. On his side, Kurolesov always treated my grandfather and his whole family with the greatest respect and politeness. Since the establishment of Parashino, and his own residence on that estate, he had paid a yearly visit to Bagrovo, on which occasions he was exceedingly pleasant and amiable; consulted Stepan Mikhailovich, as one experienced in all matters concerned with settlements and emigration; took notes of all he heard, for which he expressed extreme gratitude; and knew, too, how to profit by the information. Twice he had invited Stepan Mikhailovich to visit him at Parashino, in order to see for himself how his advice had been followed. My grandfather was quite enchanted by the perfection of the new estate, and, on his last visit, after examining all the fields and buildings, had exclaimed: "Well, friend Mikhail, you are young, but already a master farmer: you have nothing more to learn from me!" And, in truth, Kurolesov's management of the estate left nothing to be desired. As may well be imagined, he parted from his old guest with every conceivable expression of regard and respect. After a few years, however, unfavorable reports of Kurolesov began to be whispered in Bagrovo. At first these rumors were never mentioned in my grandfather's hearing, as he would never tolerate any slander or scandal: all the same, the rumors grew and increased. Stepan Mikhailovich's family got to hear about Kurolesov's behavior, and one fine day Arina Vasilievna resolved to enlighten her husband as to the sort of debauched life led by Mikhail Maximovich. The old man refused to believe the report, and said that if anyone chose to pay heed to gossip he might expect to hear the vilest tales about his neighbors. "I am only too well aware," he added, "of the sort of folks the Bakteievian peasants are—a pack of lazy ne'er-do-wells and sluggards; even my brother's own serfs were ruined by those women. Small wonder that they find regular work burdensome! Perhaps Mikhail has changed everything a little too suddenly, but the fellows ought to be accustomed to the new management by now. And if he does take a drop too much now and then, after slaving himself nearly to death, it's no very great crime for a man, especially if it doesn't lead him to neglect his work. What you have told me would be disgusting enough, if it were true, but it is nothing but a pack of lies; and I cannot understand how you and your daughters can listen to such servants' tittle-tattle!" After this withering reply no one ventured to refer to the subject again. Eventually, however, certain peasants who had formerly belonged to the Bagrov family, who from time to time came to visit their relations at New Bagrovo, brought the most frightful tales of their master's cruelty. Arina Vasilievna thereupon tackled her husband a second time, and entreated him to interview the parish magistrate of Parashino, a former Bagrov peasant himself, and a man whose integrity and veracity were beyond all question. This man was on a visit to New Bagrovo, and my grand-father consented to see him. After hearing the magistrate's tale of hor-ror, which fairly made his hair stand on end, my grandfather was completely at a loss as to how to act. It was very rarely indeed that he heard from Praskovia Ivanovna, and when he had news she seemed to be perfectly happy and peaceful. Evidently she suspected nothing of her husband's conduct. He himself, in earlier days, had advised her never to permit anyone to criticize her husband's behavior in her pres-ence; and he now perceived that his counsel had been only too well observed. Moreover he reflected that if she were informed of the actual state of affairs, she could do nothing to help, and the knowledge would only cause her useless pain. Under the circumstances he preferred to let her remain in ignorance. He always had the utmost objection to interfering in anyone's business, and in the case of Kurolesov he con-sidered it quite unnecessary. "May he break his neck, or be called up for a criminal inquiry—and serve him right, too. Only God Himself can cure the fellow. He treats his peasants decently, and if he knocks the house servants about, they are a lot of idle vagabonds who deserve what they get. I am not going to be mixed up with any disgusting tales." With this resolve my grandfather let the matter rest. He contented himself by not replying to Kurolesov's letters and by ceasing to hold any communication with him. The latter understood perfectly what was meant by this and left the old gentleman alone. The correspondence between Stepan Mikhailovich and Praskovia Ivanovna, however, grew more frequent and more affectionate than ever.

Such was the state of affairs when suddenly the three fugitives from Parashino made their appearance at New Bagrovo. The day fol-lowing their escape had been spent in the impenetrable marshy forests that lay around the great threshing ground of Parashino. During the night they had received secret visits from peasants on the estate, who had told them all that had happened to their mistress; and they had hurried directly to Stepan Mikhailovich, as Praskovia Ivanovna's nat-ural protector. One may well imagine the state of Stepan Mikhailovich's mind when he heard of the happenings at Parashino. He loved his cousin as dearly, if not indeed more dearly, than his own daughters. Praskovia cruelly used by her ruthless husband, Praskovia starving in a damp dungeon—perhaps already dead—the awful picture stood so clearly before his eyes that the old man sprang to his feet almost beside himself with agony, and, rushing through the courtyard and into the village, summoned his serfs and servants together. All crowded round him; the laborers quitted the fields; all—sharing the sorrow and anxiety of their beloved master—cried with one voice that they would accompany him and rescue Praskovia Ivanovna. In less than two hours three great wagons, to which my grandfather's own fiery stallions were harnessed, were dashing on their way to Parashino. They carried twelve of the sturdiest young men among the peasantry and servants, as well as the refugees from Parashino, who were armed with muskets, swords, pikes, and pitchforks. Toward evening two similar wagons set out, drawn by the pick of the peasants' horses, and each containing ten men similarly equipped, ready to help Stepan Mikhailovich in case of need. On the evening of the following day the first expedition halted only seven versts distant from Parashino; the weary horses were baited, and, in the first twilight of the summer dawn, the carts clattered into the wide courtyard of the mansion and drew up before the door of the vault, close to the neighboring building occupied by Kurolesov. Stepan Mikhailovich sprang to the door and knocked loudly. From within a feeble voice said: "Who is there?" My grandfather recognized the voice of his cousin, and weeping for joy at finding her still living, crossed himself and shouted: "God be praised! It is I—your cousin—Stepan Mikhailovich. You have nothing to fear now!" He instantly gave the servants orders to find Praskovia's calash and harness the horses, and six armed men were ordered to guard the approach to the cellar, while he himself, with the assistance of the rest, broke in the door with axes and crowbars. This was but the work of a moment. Stepan Mikhailovich took Praskovia Ivanovna in his arms, laid her in the cart between himself and her faithful maid, and went tranquilly away with his armed retinue. The sun had just risen, and its glittering rays illuminated the golden cross on the church spire. It was but six days ago that Praskovia Ivanovna had prayed to that cross: now she prayed to it once more, and with tears of gratitude for her wonderful deliverance. Five versts beyond Parashino they were overtaken by the calash, and Stepan Mikhailovich and his cousin continued their journey in it to Bagrovo.

And how could all this come about? you will ask. Had no one witnessed their arrival? Where were Mikhail Maximovich and his trusty band? Had he seen and heard nothing, or was he absent? No! Many there heard the uproar and witnessed the rescue of Praskovia. Mikhail Maximovich was at home, knew perfectly well what was happening, and had not dared to cross the threshold of his own house.

The facts were as follows. The servants had spent the greater part of the night drinking with their master, and it was impossible to awaken a great number of them. Kurolesov's favorite servant, who never drank spirits, and who, consequently, was perfectly sober, had great difficulty in rousing his drunken master. Trembling with fear, he informed him of the arrival of Stepan Mikhailovich, and of the row of guns leveled at the house. "Where are our men?" inquired Mikhail Maximovich. "Some of them are asleep, and the rest have hidden themselves," replied the servant, but he lied, for at that moment a drunken crew gathered at the door of the room. Mikhail Maximovich regained his senses somewhat, and shrieked: "May the Devil fly away with you! Shut all the doors, and observe what happens through the window!" In a minute or two the servant exclaimed: "They have battered the door down. . . . Now they are carrying off the mistress. . . . They are going!" "Be off to bed!" retorted Mikhail Maximovich, and he covered himself up with the quilt and went to sleep, or pretended to do so.

Ah yes, there is a moral power in good that overcomes the might of evil. Mikhail Maximovich recognized the steady and intrepid courage of Stepan Mikhailovich: he felt that he had only wrong on his side, and, in spite of his desperate and bold character, he dared not attempt to snatch his victim from her deliverer.

With what loving and anxious care was the poor suffering little cousin brought home by Stepan Mikhailovich! His love and pity for Praskovia were redoubled. He refrained from asking her any questions on the journey home, and, when Bagrovo was reached, he forbade his family to weary her by any sort of conversation. Her marvelous constitution, however, and equally marvelous strength of character together sufficed to restore her to her wonted good health by the end of a fortnight. This being the case, Stepan Mikhailovich determined to ask for a full account of what had happened to her, it being absolutely necessary that he should know the truth about the whole affair, as he was not one to attach importance to any but authentic histories. Praskovia Ivanovna told him all, reserving nothing; but at the same time entreated him not to let her relatives know anything about the affair, and also expressed a wish that the subject should be allowed to drop. Knowing the irascible nature of her cousin as she did, she begged him not to take any revenge on Mikhail Maximovich, telling him candidly that she had reconsidered her former decision, and had resolved not to expose her husband and thereby bring dishonor upon a name that was her own as long as life lasted. She added that she regretted the words spoken to her husband on their first meeting, and was determined not to lay any charge against him: all the same she recognized it as her bounden duty to release her retainers as soon as possible from his merciless tyranny, and therefore intended to withdraw all authority from Kurolesov and appoint her cousin as sole administrator of her estates. She begged Stepan Mikhailovich to write a letter at once to Mikhail Maximovich, reclaiming the power of attorney given to the latter: in the event of the request being refused, she would then give orders to have it legally annulled. She expressed the wish that the letter should spare her husband's pride as much as possible; but in order to give it full weight and significance, she desired to put her own signature to it. And here I must add that she could only write very bad Russian. Stepan Mikhailovich was so devoted to her that he restrained his just anger, and carried out all her wishes faithfully. Only in one matter did he refuse to oblige her, the control of her property. "I dislike meddling in other folks' business," said he, "and I don't wish your relatives to be able to say that I make a good thing out of your thousand serfs. Your affairs are bound to be mismanaged now, but you are rich enough not to make a trouble of it. On my own account, though, I will write and tell your rascal of a husband that I am taking over the management of the estates, just to give him the fright he deserves. As for anything else that you ask, I am only too pleased to do it for you." As the result of this conference he strictly forbade any of his family to ask Praskovia any questions. The letter to Mikhail Maximovich was duly written by my grandfather; Praskovia Ivanovna added a few words, and a messenger took it to Parashino. But while all these consultations and decisions and letter writing were in process of happening, the Parashino matter had been closed, once and for all. At the end of four days, the messenger returned with the news that God had willed that Mikhail Maximovich should die a sudden death, and that he was already in his grave. On hearing these tidings Stepan Mikhailovich involuntarily crossed himself, and exclaimed: "Thank God!" His wife and daughters, who in spite of their previous partiality for Mikhail Maximovich now as cordially detested him, also praised heaven for this deliverance. Not so Praskovia. Judging of her feelings in the matter by their own, everyone hastened to tell her the news, which they expected her to receive with great joy. But their astonishment was great, for the news was like a thunderbolt: she fell into a state of the deepest despondency, and became ill again. Once more her strong constitution got the better of her malady, but she continued melancholy and depressed. For many weeks she wept incessantly, and she wasted away to such an extent that her cousin was filled with anxious forebodings. No one could comprehend such grief and such bitter tears shed for a man who was of the veriest dregs of humanity, and who had forfeited all claim to her affection by his inhuman treatment of her. This may help to explain the mystery.

Some ten years after the foregoing events, my mother—who was a great favorite of Praskovia Ivanovna, and who had been listening with the deepest interest to an account of the tragedy, of which Praskovia Ivanovna spoke but seldom and then only to her most intimate friends—said: "Tell me, dearèst Aunt, why did you grieve so over the death of Mikhail Maximovich? In your place I should have commended his soul to the mercy of God, and have been rejoiced to be rid of him." "Stupid child!" replied Praskovia Ivanovna, "I had loved him for four-teen long years: such a love is not destroyed in a month. And what concerns me most is the welfare of his soul: he died with no time for repentance."

Six weeks after the death of Kurolesov, Praskovia Ivanovna re-gained somewhat of her ordinary composure. She went, accompanied by her cousin and the whole family, to Parashino to repeat the cus-tomary prayers for the dead. It astonished everyone that, on reaching Parashino, and even during the sorrowful ceremony, Praskovia Iva-novna never shed a tear—an effort that taxed her shattered mind and enfeebled frame to the utmost degree. In deference to her wishes the party only remained a few hours at Parashino, and she herself never entered the wing of the house occupied by her late husband, in which he died.

It is not difficult to guess how Kurolesov's sudden death was brought about. After Praskovia's rescue, every soul on the estate was firmly convinced that the master's reign would soon come to an end. All were extremely anxious that the old master of Bagrovo, their mis-tress's second father, would turn her good-for-nothing husband out of the estate. No one had the slightest doubt that the ill-used and insulted young mistress would hesitate a moment in setting the law in motion against the criminal. Each day they momentarily expected Stepan Mik-hailovich and the officers of justice to make their appearance; but one week followed another, and no one came. Mikhail Maximovich drank and raved as usual, flogged everyone who approached him—even his quiet sober-living servant, who had awakened him and warned him of Praskovia's deliverance—because he had been thus left in the lurch. He boasted that his wife had settled all her property legally upon him. The cup of human endurance was overflowing: the future promised no hope, and so it came about that two scoundrels of his bodyguard—and, be it noted, among those persons who had the least to dread from his cruelty—carried out a frightful plan: they poisoned him with ar-senic, which they mixed with the kvass that he was accustomed to drink during the night. They put such a quantity of poison into the decanter that Kurolesov only lived two hours after drinking from it. The criminals had no accomplices, and the awful event filled everyone with indescribable terror. Each one suspected the other, but for a long time the real culprits remained undiscovered. Six months later, one of these fell ill, and, when near death, confessed his crime. His fellow murderer, although the dying man had not disclosed his name, fled and disappeared, leaving no trace.

There is not the slightest doubt that this sudden death of Kurolesov would have been followed by a strict judicial inquiry had it not happened that a short time previously he had removed a young secretary, bearing the same name as his own, from Churasovo, and established him in the counting house at Parashino. This young man acted with remarkable promptitude and prudence, and succeeded in hushing up the affair. As one result of his good offices he was eventually appointed administrator of the whole of Praskovia Ivanovna's estates, and—as Mikhailushka—he became known and respected far and near in the governments of Orenburg and Simbirsk. This worthy and indefatigable steward amassed a considerable fortune, and for a long time led a most temperate life; he received his freedom after Praskovia Ivanovna's death; but the loss of his beloved wife drove him to drink—he wasted all his savings and died in poverty. One of his sons, however, had a brilliant career in government service, and, if I recollect aright, was raised to the rank of a noble.

I cannot deny that even forty years afterward, when Stepan Mikhailovich's grandson succeeded to the estate of Parashino, he found the memory of Mikhail Maximovich still held in affection by the peasantry. His barbarity, which, after all, had been principally practiced upon the household staff, was quite forgotten. On the other hand, the unerring sagacity with which he could pick out the guilty from the innocent—the good from the bad laborers—his disinterested efforts to improve the condition of the serfs, and his readiness to help anyone in genuine need were recollected and extolled. The old men would smile as they told the following story of him: It seems Kurolesov was accustomed to say: "Rob and betray me as much as you like, so long as I know nothing about it: but if I catch you—don't complain!"

After her return to Bagrovo, Praskovia Ivanovna gradually recovered her health, consoled by the fervent affection of her cousin and the kindly care of the whole family, who expected to see a great change in her. This, however, was not the case; her former good health was restored, her broken heart was healed, and at the end of a year she decided to return to Churasovo. Stepan Mikhailovich was grieved to part with his cousin. He felt himself especially responsible for her wellbeing, and he had grown accustomed to her constant companionship: never once in his life had he really been angry with her. Notwithstanding this, he in no way sought to persuade her to remain, but rather urged her to take her departure. "What sort of a life is this for you, my dear cousin?" he was wont to ask. "Life here is very dull; we don't mind it, because we have never been used to any other. But you are still young;" (she was thirty years old) "you are rich, and accustomed to a very different style of living. Go back to Churasovo, and to your fine house and gardens and fountains. There are plenty of rich friends there who are fond of you and will help you to be happy. Who knows but you may make a happy marriage yet. At any rate you must not lose your chances here."

Praskovia Ivanovna postponed her departure from day to day, finding it difficult to part from the cousin who had rescued her from a terrible fate, and who had been her kind friend from her earliest childhood. But at last the day was fixed. The preceding day she had risen very early and gone to Stepan Mikhailovich, who was sitting on the balcony, sunk in melancholy meditation. She embraced him, weeping, and said: "Cousin, I know how much you love me, and I love and honor you as my own father. God, who reads all hearts, knows my gratitude. But I wish everyone to know it, and so I beg of you to let me settle the estates that my mother left me on you. My father's estates, in any case, will go to your boy Aleksey. All my relations on my mother's side are rich; and you know there is no just reason why I should leave my property to them. I shall never marry again. I want the Bagrov family to be rich. Now, consent, dear cousin, if you wish me to be happy, and easy in my mind!" And with these words she sank down at his feet, covering his hands with kisses. "Listen to me, cousin," replied Stepan Mikhailovich in a stern tone, "you know little of me, or you would never propose that I should accept another's property, or deprive your legitimate heirs of their own. No one shall ever tell that tale of Stepan Bagrov. Take heed that you never mention the subject to me again, or I shall be angry with you, for the first time in my life!"

On the following day Praskovia Ivanovna set out on her journey to Churasovo, where she began a new and independent life.

(1856)

FYODOR TYUTCHEV

ACCORDING TO THE TWENTIETH-CENTURY *philosopher Nikolay Ber-dyayev, modern Russian literature followed not the directions set by Pushkin, but those of Tyutchev (1803–1873), "who wrote not in the spirit of the Renaissance but in torment and anxiety."*

Born in Ovstug near Bryansk, Tyutchev was brought up on his family's country estate in a conservative, patriotic, and patriarchal spirit. He was educated at home by an outstanding scholarly tutor, and from 1819 to 1821 studied at the University of Moscow. He then left for St. Petersburg, entered the foreign service, and spent the next twenty-two years abroad, mainly in Germany. In 1839 he was dismissed from his diplomatic position for having left his post in Turin without permission. He stayed in Germany for five more years after that without a job, and then returned to Russia, to become fully reintegrated in St. Petersburg life.

Already married twice before (he remarried in 1839, after his first wife died), in 1850 Tyutchev fell in love with twenty-four-year-old Elena Deniseva, who had been the governess to his daughter. Over the course of their fourteen-year affair she bore him three children. He devoted a cycle of passionate poems to her, outlived her by almost ten years, and died after suffering several strokes.

Though he used mainly French in everyday life, Tyutchev reserved Russian, as the English literary scholar Henry Gifford has said, for his deepest intimacies, for supreme perceptions. His lyrical and reflective poetry falls into two periods. First, when he was a young man and a contemporary of Pushkin's, he became known through a group of sixteen poems that Pushkin published in a magazine in 1836. The second period came in the nineteenth century's Russian "Age of Prose," after 1840, when he wrote philosophical and nature poems, as well as a body of extraordinary poems inspired by his love for Elena Deniseva. These lyrics belong to the best love poems in the Russian language.

Tyutchev spoke often of the ultimate inexpressibility of human thoughts and feelings. The poem "Silentium" contains lines that are among the most frequently quoted by Russians of every walk of life ("A thought once uttered is untrue"). The later symbolist poets took the poem to be an intimation of the ineffability of that mysterious experience they saw as the single source of all the creation of art. It is usually taken to be a Russian expression of the belief in the intuitive, the mysterious, and the enigmatic, as opposed to the rational and intellectually definable. Thus it speaks for those elements in Russian culture that assert the superiority of feeling and oppose what they view as the Western predilection for the formal and verbal.

Tyutchev was fascinated by ceaseless change in nature, its unrest, the wildness of the elements alternating with a trancelike peace. He achieved his effects by means unfamiliar to the English-speaking reader—not by verbal daring and allusions, but by the strength of internal organization of the poem: he confined himself to simple phrases and the language of normal perception. Tyutchev was a poet of destructive love, of havoc, of agitation. He often struck a rhetorical tone reminiscent of the eighteenth century—grand, declamatory, archaic. He wrote of shivers, storms, the abyss. He lived for the moment of divination.

He is important in the history of Russian thought as a creator of images of Russianness, of qualities the Russians came to perceive as distinctively Russian. His articles, quirky at times, are of high political interest. They present the conservative, Slavophile point of view of Russian affairs. He was a patriot who defended Czar Nicholas's foreign policy. His articles and letters were not republished during the Soviet era and are being rediscovered by Russians only since the fall of the Communist regime in Russia.

TEARS

O lacrimarum fons. *
—THOMAS GRAY

Friends, with my eyes I love caressing
the purple of a flashing wine,
nor do I scorn the fragrant ruby
of clustered fruit that leaves entwine.

I love to look around when Nature
seems as it were immersed in May;
when bathed in redolence she slumbers
and smiles throughout her dreamy day.

I love to see the face of Beauty
flushed with the air of Spring that seeks
softly to toy with silky ringlets
or deepen dimples on her cheeks.

But all voluptuous enchantments,
lush grapes, rich roses—what are you
compared to tears, that sacred fountain,
that paradisal morning dew!

Therein divinest beams are mirrored,
and in those burning drops they break,
and breaking—what resplendent rainbows
upon Life's thunderclouds they make!

As soon as mortal eyes thou touchest,
with wings, Angel of Tears, the world
dissolves in mist, and lo! a skyful
of Seraph faces is unfurled.

(1823)

---

* *O lacrimarum fons,* a quotation of the first words of Thomas Gray's four-line
Latin poem "Alcaic Fragment," means "Oh fountain of tears." Thomas Gray (1716–
1771) was an English poet and scholar, for Tyutchev, a model of Romantic poetic
melancholy.

SUMMER NIGHTFALL

Down from her head the earth has rolled
the low sun like a red-hot ball.
Down went the evening's peaceful blaze
and sea waves have absorbed it all.

Heavy and near the sky had seemed.
But now the stars are rising high,
they glow and with their humid heads
push up the ceiling of the sky.

The river of the air between
heaven and earth now fuller flows.
The breast is ridded of the heat
and breathes in freedom and repose.

And now there goes through Nature's veins
a liquid shiver, swift and sweet,
as though the waters of a spring
had come to touch her burning feet.

(1829)

APPEASEMENT

The storm withdrew, but Thor had found his oak,
and there it lay magnificently slain,
and from its limbs a remnant of blue smoke
spread to bright trees repainted by the rain—

—while thrush and oriole made haste to mend
their broken melodies throughout the grove,
upon the crests of which was propped the end
of a virescent rainbow edged with mauve.

(1830)

SILENTIUM!

Speak not, lie hidden, and conceal
the way you dream, the things you feel.
Deep in your spirit let them rise
akin to stars in crystal skies
that set before the night is blurred:
delight in them and speak no word.

How can a heart expression find?
How should another know your mind?
Will he discern what quickens you?
A thought once uttered is untrue.
Dimmed is the fountainhead when stirred:
drink at the source and speak no word.

Live in your inner self alone
within your soul a world has grown,
the magic of veiled thoughts that might
be blinded by the outer light,
drowned in the noise of day, unheard . . .
take in their song and speak no word.

                                        (*1830*)

THE ABYSS

When sacred Night sweeps heavenward, she takes
the glad, the winsome day, and folding it,
rolls up its golden carpet that had been
spread over an abysmal pit.
Gone visionlike is the external world,
and man, a homeless orphan, has to face
in utter helplessness, naked, alone,
the blackness of immeasurable space.

Upon himself he has to lean; with mind
abolished, thought unfathered, in the dim
depths of his soul he sinks, for nothing comes
from outside to support or limit him.

All life and brightness seem an ancient dream—
while in the very substance of the night,
unraveled, alien, he now perceives
a fateful something that is his by right.

(1848–1850)

HUMAN TEARS

Human tears, O the tears! you that flow
when life is begun—or half-gone,
tears unseen, tears unknown, you that none
can number or drain, you that run
like the streamlets of rain from the low
clouds of Autumn, long before dawn. . . .

(1849?)

LAST LOVE

Love at the closing of our days
is apprehensive and very tender.
Glow brighter, brighter, farewell rays
of one last love in its evening splendor.

Blue shade takes half the world away:
through western clouds alone some light is slanted.
O tarry, O tarry, declining day,
enchantment, let me stay enchanted.

The blood runs thinner, yet the heart
remains as ever deep and tender.
O last belated love, thou art
a blend of joy and of hopeless surrender.

(1852–1854)

IS RUSSIA DISTINCT FROM THE WEST?

What is Russia, what is the meaning of her existence, what is the law of her history? Whence has she appeared? Whither is she going? What does she express? . . . For centuries Western Europe believed, with great simplicity of mind, that there was not and could not be a Europe other than herself. . . . That another Europe should exist, an Eastern Europe, a lawful sister of the Christian West, that a whole world should exist over there, united in its principle, with solidarity among its parts, living its own organic, distinctive life—that was impossible to admit . . . but in the end, fate accomplished its goal. The hand of the giant tore away the curtain. The Europe of Charlemagne found itself face-to-face with the Europe of Peter the Great. [From Tyutchev's article "Russia and Germany," 1853]

For two generations we have locked away Russia's national self-awareness inside an enchanted circle. We really need God to give us a healthy kick to make us break up this circle and return to our own road. [From a letter dated November 24, 1853]

KAROLINA PAVLOVA

KAROLINA PAVLOVA (1807–1893) was one of the few female Russian authors of the nineteenth century. The opening of universities to women and the changed position of the sexes—social as well as ideological— toward the end of the century was followed very quickly by a veritable explosion of female literary talent. Anna Akhmatova, Marina Tsvetayeva, and many others were at the forefront of the poetic scene around the time of World War I, and women writers have been prominent in all the literary genres since then.

The daughter of Karl Jaenisch, a physician of German origin who became professor of physics and chemistry at the Moscow Medical Academy, Karolina Pavlova met many literary figures in her youth. She knew many of the shining lights of Russian literature, including Pushkin, and fell in love with the exiled Polish poet Adam Mickiewicz in the late 1820s. In 1837, however, she married Nikolay Pavlov, a writer who never rose above mediocrity.

For many years she presided over a glittering literary salon in Moscow. After Karolina Pavlova inherited a fortune, her husband began squandering it and mortgaged some of her property. The marriage finally broke up when he set up a household with a young cousin of Karolina Pavlova's. She sued him and managed to have him sentenced and sent into exile.

Pavlova's literary career began with translations of Russian poetry into German. She knew many languages and wrote poems in Russian, French, and German. Her own Russian poetry was highly praised by the critic Vissarion Belinsky and others, but many comments on it (and its author) were negative. The main objections seemed to be that she emphasized verbal qualities, sound, and individual words and phrases rather than content. These same attributes of her works, however, were

*the reason why the symbolists half a century later revived and praised
her by then forgotten poetry.*

*Pavlova is best known for one short novel, A Double Life (1848),
in which the prose narrative is interspersed with poems. The novel
belongs to the genre of the "society tale" popular in the 1830s and
1840s in Russia as well as in France. It presents a rich, well-placed
young society woman around whom her elders spin intrigues, mainly
concerning her marriage and her fortune. She is poetic and ambitious,
but her social surroundings are shallow and worthless. At the end
Pavlova's sensitive heroine feels lonely and alienated. The selections
included here consist of Chapter 6 of A Double Life, and a poem
Pavlova included in the introduction to her novel.*

*Pavlova left Russia in 1853 and spent most of the rest of her life
abroad. Also in 1853, she met a student twenty-five years younger than
herself, who became the deepest love of her life. The poem "Strange,
the Way We Met" describes their first meeting. She continued to publish
translations of Russian poetry and to write her own poetry, in Russian,
French, and German. She lived mostly in Dresden and died there, far
from Moscow, lonely and forgotten. A hundred years after her death,
her works (and her life, with its many reversals) were to become the
object of renewed interest.*

*Professor Barbara Heldt, who translated Pavlova's A Double Life
into English, summed up her role as a woman writer in the Russia of
her age:*

> *In the nineteenth century, when its literature equaled that
> written at any place at any time in history, Russia had no
> great woman writer—no Sappho, no Ono or Komachi or
> Murasaki Shikibu, no Madame de Staël or George Sand, no
> Jane Austen or George Eliot—or so we might say when sur-
> veying the best-known works of the age. And it would be
> almost true, but not quite.*

Karolina Pavlova was the exception.

FROM *A DOUBLE LIFE* (CHAPTER VI)

The day was drawing near that Vera Vladimirovna always
celebrated—Cecily's birthday. This time, too, she had made various
preparations to spend it as gaily as possible: a dinner, a concert, a *bal*

champêtre, a supper—every possible thing that could be done was done, with great effort and at great expense. The gaiety of people of the highest circles is incredibly expensive. When Cecily woke up that day, she found her mother's gifts lying on her sofa: two charming dresses, one a dinner dress, the other an evening dress, and the most marvelous lace scarf, ordered from Paris. In the course of the morning she received approximately two dozen bouquets and three dozen notes from friends—all saying precisely · the same thing, to which it was necessary to respond with precisely the same variations. Society women have attained the wondrous art of contriving thirty variations on a phrase that means nothing even the first time. Then Madame Valitsky arrived with her daughter (on that morning no other people were received). Cecily went into the garden with Olga to rest from her correspondence a bit. They settled into a corner where there was some shade and began to chatter away; they talked of twenty different subjects, and then Olga's voice grew lower and more secretive.

"Listen," she said, "you're killing Ivachinsky. He was so upset by your coolness yesterday that out of desperation he lost all night at cards at Ilichev's and almost went out of his mind."

"Who told you that?" Cecily asked.

"A cousin told it to Mama. He was there and saw Dmitri. You're really driving him to goodness knows what. He's becoming a gambler."

It was not Olga herself who was saying these things: it was her mother's prompting. Only Madame Valitsky knew the great power and naïveté of female egotism; only Madame Valitsky knew how much more interesting to a woman a man becomes, and how much dearer, the moment she sees the possibility of changing him in her own fashion, reforming him from vice, saving him from destruction. The greater the danger, the deeper the abyss ready to swallow him, the more glorious is the triumph, the more tempting the success, the greater the pleasure in stretching out to the one who is perishing a saving hand, fragile and yet all-powerful. Madame Valitsky had decided that Cecily must become Dmitri's wife so that she would not somehow become the wife of Prince Victor, and Madame Valitsky proceeded toward her goal. And Olga, for her part, was also of a mind to keep the precious prince for herself and did not trust Cecily too much in this respect. Although Olga was too young to know what levers to pull, she was clever enough to use them according to her mother's directions. In society's lexicon, this sort of move is called "adroit" or "clever."

Instead of answering, Cecily bowed her head and fell to thinking. But there wasn't much time to think that day; it was time to dress for dinner. Madame Valitsky and her daughter left, so that they too could dress and return in a couple of hours, and Cecily went to her room, called the maid, and sat down at her dressing table, loosening her black braids. She was so full of thoughts and daydreams that she paid no attention to the hairdo Annushka was laboring over. Looking into her mirror, she thought only of what Olga had said. So she was capable of bringing Dmitri to desperation. A possibility always flattering and satisfying to a woman, and as a result of which she began to await him with great impatience.

But however much these thoughts possessed her she could not help but be distracted, if only briefly, while putting on the splendid new dress. And indeed, when she was all ready and standing before her mirror, it presented such a picture of grace that, looking at it, she understood perfectly poor Dmitri's torments of the heart.

The dinner was, like all dinners of this sort, long and boring. Aside from Vera Vladimirovna's husband and two or three guests like him, who ate with great appetite, everyone was waiting for it to end—Cecily and Olga more than anyone, because Prince Victor and Dmitri were not expected until evening. Once dinner was over with, they could still have a few pleasant hours to themselves.

The time for the concert finally arrived. The guests, whose number had increased, pressed into the room and began listening very patiently to variations and fantasias, arias and duets, accompanied by the constant movement of chairs set down for new arrivals. An Italian duet sung by Olga and Cecily ended the concert. It was, of course, delightful, since it had been taken from the latest opera and, of course, it gave the listeners enormous delight. The entire three rows of toques and mobcaps in front of the pianos rippled. All the men, mercilessly squeezed into the corners and along the walls, clapped their hands in a storm of delight. Dmitri Ivachinsky, who had just come in the door, was so unsparing of himself that he tore his gloves to shreds. Prince Victor himself applauded more than when he had heard Grisi in Paris. The duet, in a word, produced a huge effect, after which they all dispersed into the garden with frank delight.

Cecily took Olga by the arm and ran with her toward her own room in order to escape the general thanks, comb her hair, and change for the ball. In the doorway stood Dmitri Ivachinsky. He bowed to her and whispered five or six words. Cecily nodded her head and passed swiftly by.

"Olga," she said, after running upstairs to her room and gazing at the dark waves of her hair in the mirror, "are you promised for the mazurka?"

"Since yesterday morning," Olga answered in a voice so content that one could have no doubt as to whom she was promised. "And you?"

"Since just a minute ago," Cecily said, even more content, throwing her marvelous scarf on the sofa.

She felt extraordinarily happy, somehow wildly and boldly happy. She gave herself over to new, engrossing feelings. She was dimly aware of certain unknown possibilities. The daughter of Eve was tasting the forbidden fruit. The young captive was breathing in free, fragrant, unfamiliar air and growing drunk on it. Vera Vladimirovna had never wished to admit such an eventuality. Those prudent, vigilant, cautious women never do. They rely totally on their maternal efforts. They are extremely consistent with their daughters. In place of the spirit they give them the letter, in place of live feeling a dead rule, in place of holy truth a preposterous lie. And they often manage through these clever, precautionary machinations to steer their daughters safely to what is called "a good match." Then their goal is attained. Then they leave her, confused, powerless, ignorant, and uncomprehending, to God's will; and afterward they sit down tranquilly to dinner and lie down to sleep. And this is the very same daughter whom at the age of six they could not bring themselves to leave alone in her room, lest she fall off a chair. But that was a matter of bodily injuries (blood is quite visible, physical pain is frightening), not of an obscure, mute pain of the spirit.

One could be consoled if it were only bad mothers that acted like this. There are not many bad mothers. But it is the very best mothers who do it and will go on doing it forever. And all these bringers-up were young once, were brought up in the same way! Were they really so satisfied with their own lives and with themselves that they are happy to renew the experience with their children? Is all this absurdity as long-lived as those reptiles that continue to exist after they are cut into pieces? Didn't these poor women weep? Didn't they blame themselves and other people? Didn't they look for help in vain? Didn't they feel the meaninglessness of the support given them? Didn't they recognize the bitter fruit of this lie?

But many of them, perhaps, did not! There are incredible cases and strange exceptions. There are examples of people falling from the third floor onto the pavement and remaining unharmed; then why not give one's daughter, too, a shove?

And it must be said, too, that so much is forgotten in life, the years change and reshape us so strangely! So many young, inspired dreamers in time become tax farmers and distillers. So many carefree

young idlers become owners of Siberian gold mines. So many flighty
scoundrels become merciless punishers of every kind of passion. Time
is a strange force!

When the friends came downstairs together in their ball gowns and
appeared among the guests, they were truly beautiful. Olga, in a white
dress of exceedingly expensive simplicity, with cornflowers in her long
blond curls, was astonishingly lovely; but Cecily, who was also all in
white, with a crown of white roses set over her proud black braids,
was even lovelier. Olga was still searching for something; Cecily had
already found it. Olga glowed with hope; Cecily shone with victory.
In her face, her smile, her whole glance, in every movement there was
something too beautiful for good form, something splendidly ravishing,
a sort of victory of Poltava. And this was only the shadow of love! But
love is so inexpressibly exciting that even its shadow is full of charm
and better than anything else in the world.

The weather was most propitious. The starry night wafted a marvelous life-giving warmth. The ball, or rustic ball, as it was called, was
set up on the model of a certain Parisian party given not long before
and quite in the new fashion. The carefully rolled courtyard in front
of the house entrance served as a ballroom. It was tightly encircled by
a double row of laurels and orange trees and tall rare flowers. Among
the branches gas lamps were burning, pouring their bright light onto
the whole scene. The adjacent garden was also illuminated, but more
dimly, with small flames in translucent porcelain globes and alabaster
vases. It had been transformed into a drawing room, study tables and
a buffet. Opulent furniture was artfully arranged throughout. Tea tables
were standing under fragrant shrubs. Pyramids of fruit rose in the
middle of multicolored dahlias and beautiful camellias composed into
luxuriant bunches. Mysterious lights glowed fantastically through the
dark green. All this was indeed surprisingly pleasant.

From behind a thick mass of acacias an invisible orchestra started
to play; the ball had begun. Thanks to that unusual setting and the
attractive novelty of it all, the decorous, indolent aristocratic company
came unexpectedly to life. Dances followed swiftly one after the other.
At times light feminine laughter was heard in the night air. Everything
was movement, noise, and gaiety. The tranquil stars looked down from
their heights, a few old trees stood in sullen silence, gloomy and motionless among the crowd.

Time passed. The dances continued. Cecily, always quickly tired,
felt no fatigue that evening. A new, inexplicable existence was growing
in her. One of those rich hours of life had struck when the heart is so

full of itself that no happiness is capable of taking it by surprise. At that moment a miracle would have seemed natural and ordinary to her: she would not even have noticed it. If one of those shining stars had fallen to earth before her, she would have simply pushed it away with her foot.

Providence sometimes bestows such moments on earthly existence! It was close to midnight. The party, as always happens around this time, reached its most brilliant moment. Din and motion were everywhere. Everywhere through the greenery glimmered dresses of different colors, floating scarves, glittering bracelets on white arms. Everywhere voices were heard; the jokes, mockery, compliments, slander, vulgarity of some, the wit of others, the coquetry of still others— all mixed and blended into one general sound of voices. From its fathomless darkness, the night sky shone strangely above this turmoil. Those drawing room speeches, those empty words sounded somehow insolent in the dark infinity; the worldly, false, overcivilized mode of life made a sinful, sacrilegious noise in God's free expanse.

After many quadrilles Olga, Cecily, and another young girl sat down to rest, the three of them on a small divan in a cozy half-hidden corner of the garden. Dmitri Ivachinsky came up to them and began to talk with the third girl; she laughed and answered him animatedly. Suddenly the mazurka started up. Olga took her neighbor who had been talking with Dmitri by the hand and ran off with her. Cecily also stood up, took a couple of steps, looked around, and stopped. For a minute she was alone with Ivachinsky.

"Dmitri Andreyevich," she said suddenly, with a charming blush, "I have to ask you something; don't play cards as you did yesterday at Ilichev's. You will promise, won't you? You won't gamble anymore?"

"I won't," he answered, "if you'll give me that flower you tore off your bouquet and are holding in your hand."

The mazurka thundered louder. Cecily flitted through the garden, but the flower fell from her hands onto the path.

She stopped for a second, at the turning of the path: did she really have to look, to know whether it had been found? It was lying in Dmitri's hand, and he was following behind her. She stretched out her own hand a little with the insincere intention of taking it back, but her look was more honest than her hand. There was no one in the garden. Dmitri grasped her outstretched fingers and kissed them swiftly.

Two minutes later she began dancing the mazurka with him and slipped into the bright circle, surrounded by chairs, among the crowd of onlookers. But who among them could see how tenderly that trembling little hand, which had been kissed for the first time, was grasped?

It was the same simple story once again, old and forever new! It was true that Dmitri was captivated with Cecily. The magnetism of others' opinions always had an astonishing effect on him. Seeing her that evening so dazzling and so surrounded, he could not fail to be satisfied with her, and far more satisfied with himself. He was one of those weak creatures who grow drunk on success. At that moment he was no longer merely calculating: he saw himself placed higher than all the rest by Cecily, higher even than Prince Victor, the arrogant object of his secret envy; and his head began to turn. Inside him there started up youth's wildness and its irresistible burst of passion, as at the height of battle, when the warrior rushes blindly forward to tear the standard from the enemy ranks at any cost. This actually resembled love. It was, perhaps, mixed with some attraction of the heart as well, but this was only that ruthless masculine feeling which, if the woman inspiring him had committed some awkwardness, had worn some ugly hairdo or unfashionable hat, could at any moment change into fierce malice.

But one could lay odds that Cecily was incapable of committing the slightest awkwardness and would always be perfectly dressed and coiffed.

The mazurka ended at last. Supper was waiting on various tables, large and small, placed about the garden. Cecily and Dmitri sat as far as they could from one another. They now intentionally kept their distance; they were already two conspirators hiding their association.

The party was coming to a close. Coaches and carriages were brought around. As Madame Valitsky had requested, Dmitri found her carriage and accompanied her to it. While they were walking he bent toward her a little and whispered in a conspiratorial voice:

"Let me visit you tomorrow morning, Natalia Afanasevna. I'm going to ask you to do me an important service."

"I'll be waiting with great pleasure," she answered. "Come about one."

The lackey opened the doors of the carriage. Madame Valitsky sat down feeling almost as lively and happy as her daughter.

The short summer night was already turning pale by the time the guests had all left. It may be said that everyone, or nearly everyone at least, was satisfied. They had rushed about, danced, made noise, and amused themselves to exhaustion. For her part, Vera Vladimirovna lay down to sleep quite satisfied. Her party had been a complete success, and Prince Victor had looked at Cecily often and had stated at two different times that she was extremely lovely. Madame Valitsky also lay down to sleep very satisfied: just one more little push was needed to get that dangerous Cecily out of the way. Olga lay down to sleep even more satisfied: the prince had talked a lot of nonsense to her during the mazurka and had remarked that her dress was exceptionally becoming. Dmitri could not be dissatisfied: his egotism was still in full carouse and, as he fell asleep, he felt inwardly victorious. Prince Victor always went to sleep completely satisfied with himself and with others. Finally, even poor Nadezhda Ivanovna, who never succeeded in anything, who never arranged anything or expected anything, whom no one danced with or spoke to—even she fell asleep satisfied, for no reason at all.

But Cecily lay down to sleep with that abounding happiness which sometimes fills an eighteen-year-old heart for a moment, and which is so alive that in quiet and solitude one becomes almost ill with it. She could not think, but there was a turmoil in her chest, and fantasies began. Her closed eyes still saw the ball, the bright-colored crowd, and the illuminated garden. And her drowsing consciousness grew inexplicably somber with some unaccountable feeling. Happy, she sighed sorrowfully, not knowing why. And comfortingly, a languorous drowsiness descended on her. It seemed as if echoes of the orchestra were carrying through the hush—distant, half-sorrowful harmonies, now stopping, now starting up again, and melting into strange talk, mysterious conversations, marvelous, wished-for sounds, *his* call, into *his* greeting:

> *"The far-off star*
> *Has long been flaming;*
> *Long have I waited,*
> *The hour goes by.*
> *Languishing in an evil dream*
> *In this strange land,*
> *Awake, beloved,*
> *In your own country;*
> *Among the victorious*
> *Sacred things of night,*
> *Leave the deception*
> *Of material worry."*

> *Sad is the smile on his lips,*
> *His words flow more gently:*
> *"O, eternal error of the heart,*
> *How early you have grown close to her!*

How soon the voice of bold convictions
Has been awakened in her!
How many painful revelations,
How many sorrows lie ahead!
How life will try in vain to disenchant
Her soul to the very end!
Alas! There in the world all is unclear,
There all is blind and false raving!
With dark, mute thought, you
Will search there for me alone:
It is in me your soul believes,
Me that you love, not him.
But in the midst of changing vanity
In your routine of every day,
I will remain an unclear sadness,
A dream of the heart unrealized.
And sensing light in the depths of gloom,
Trusting in an unearthly secret,
You will travel from ghost to ghost,
From one sorrow to another.
In all that will be dear to your heart,
In all you will see the same lie;
You have loved the infinite,
You wait for the immeasurable.
It is not life, O fateful thirsting,
That will assuage your pain!
You will have another future,
Other streams of life.
Thus let your fate turn out a bitter one,
The bright paradise of hopes vanish!
Get used to a difficult path
And learn the strength of the weak.
Understand that the Lord's commandments
Have doomed you, defenseless ones,
To unconditional patience
To a task higher than that on earth.
Learn, as a wife, the suffering of a wife,
Know that, submissive, she
Must not seek the path
To her own dreams, her own desires;
That her heart protests in vain,
That her duty is implacable,

> *That all her soul is in his power,*
> *That even her thoughts are fettered.*
> *Prepare all the strength of youth*
> *For mute tears, for an obscure struggle,*
> *And may the heavenly father give you*
> *An unconquerable love!"*
>
> (1848)

STRANGE, THE WAY WE MET

Strange, the way we met. In a drawing-room circle
    With its empty conversation,

Almost furtively, not knowing one another,
    We guessed at our kinship.

And we realized our souls' likeness
    Not by passionate words tumbling at
                            random from our lips,
But by mind answering mind,
    And the gleam of hidden thoughts.

Diligently absorbed by modish nonsense,
    Uttering witty remarks,
We suddenly looked at each other
    With a curious, attentive glance,

And each of us, successfully fooling them all
    With our chatter and joking,
Heard in the other the arrogant, terrible
    Laughter of the Spartan boy.

And, meeting, we did not try to find
    In the other's soul an echo of our own.
All evening the two of us spoke stiffly
    Locking up our sadness.

Not knowing whether we would meet again,
    Meeting unexpectedly that evening,

With strange truthfulness, cruelly, sternly,
    We waged war until morning.

Abusing every habitual notion,
    Like foe with merciless foe,
Silently and firmly, like brothers,
    Later we shook hands.

(1854)

IVAN GONCHAROV

IVAN GONCHAROV (1812–1891) was born in the town of Simbirsk on the Volga River, into a family that brought him up as a small child in the values and customs of traditional Russian merchant culture. Orphaned, he was then transferred to relatives who belonged to the aristocracy. Thus, when he later came to write of the ways of country landowners, such as the Oblomovs, he was able to view them with the double perspective of the ethos of the gentry as well as of the very different merchant class.

Goncharov studied at the University of Moscow and then spent most of his life in the government service, during the last twelve years of which he worked as a censor. He also showed signs of being unbalanced, suffering from a paranoia that led him to accuse Turgenev of having plagiarized various themes from Goncharov's own works.

Oblomov (1859), his most famous novel, gives a marvelous sense of the tension between being attracted by some of the feckless gentry's finer, poetic traits, and repelled by others. Goncharov wrote two other important novels, A Common Story (1847) and The Precipice (1869), and a travel account of his sea journey around Africa and as far as Japan, The Frigate Pallas (1858). Oblomov's Dream was written by Goncharov in 1849 as a separate work, and then incorporated by him as a chapter in the novel Oblomov, which he wrote through the 1850s and completed in August 1857.

In the village of Oblomovka, and in Goncharov's images of the Russian countryside, life is isolated, mild, gentle, not heroic, not sublime. The inhabitants are set in their ways, which they regard as the only ways. There is excess in food, kissing, sheltering the youngster, resting, laziness.

Goncharov gives us an image of ancient Russia as idyllic but also flawed—pristine, rich in fairy tales, resting its faith in miracles, pampered. Like Aksakov's premodern Russia, this is a world of the ancient epics, where all is slowed down, presenting a picture of mixed charm and repulsiveness.

The novel is supposed to take place in Goncharov's own days, but the retrospective chapter, Oblomov's Dream, the vision of his childhood, is inserted out of chronological order, as a flashback of etiological explanation.

Oblomov's Dream conveys to us the feel of a premodern society —isolated, fearful of the stranger, self-satisfied, smug—with a cyclical sense of time, based on the return of the seasons. The voice of the chronicler is a slightly ironic one. There is full acceptance of whatever happens: "The rain will wet me, the sun will dry me," one peasant says. There is no dynamism, no desire for change, for any conquest of new territories—material or spiritual—no self-assertion.

Prosaic, down-to-earth attitudes are held by all in common. They live in their little unchanging community outside of history isolated from the surrounding world, convinced that "everything was as it should be." There is a narrow definition of who is and who is not a fellow human being. "Not one of ours" rules out the Other. The gentry does little work. They eat and eat. They sleep after the midday meal. Fairy tales nurture the imagination of little Oblomov. Nothing strengthens his willpower.

The inhabitants of Oblomovka are only little connected to the cash economy. They are largely autarkic, self-sufficient. There is little attempt to arouse the reader against such idle, privileged drones, with only touches of covert condemnation of their idleness. It is understandable that in the Russian context, with its proclivity to turn literary characters into models, Oblomov became a psychological-social-pathological type, a label. Oblomovism (or Oblomovshchina in Russian) immediately became a tag, a buzzword for indolence. Even in our days the Russians still proclaim this to be one of their distinctive traits. (The question of whether Oblomovism is a matter of pathology—an individual disease—or a product of society—caused by the ills and inertias of Russian feudal society—continues to be debated.)

Oblomov presents the life story of its hero or antihero, Ilya Oblomov, from childhood to death (and even a little beyond his death, to the tiny obituaries pronounced on him by three of his best friends and his servant). Oblomov is the ultimate of nonaction. His refusal to become interested in any activity, his preference for contemplation, for indolence, for allowing himself to be loved—his passivity and his min-

gling of passivity with receptivity—are traced slowly, over and over, with infinite patience and delightful, amusing completeness.

Goncharov's narrative is old-fashioned, slow, meticulous, exhaustive. He does everything fully and at complete leisure. Otherwise we would not receive its full impact. The narrator generalizes and draws conclusions freely. His imagery parallels the traditional content. Oblomov is devoid of high metaphysics and other political and philosophical concerns that are abundant in the works of Dostoyevsky and others.

There is neither the modern realism of Turgenev or Chekhov, nor the soul-searching and intensity of Tolstoy and Dostoyevsky, nor the absurdity of Gogol. We find instead in Goncharov's text the narrative method of painstaking accumulation of detail, of working out every theme and scene fully, in an aesthetic of accumulation. And through these means Goncharov has created his Oblomov, with an extreme ideal of inactivity, a man convinced he sees through the vanity of all action and holds on to his own values.

OBLOMOV'S DREAM

Where are we? In what blessed little corner of the earth has Oblomov's dream transferred us? What a lovely spot!

It is true there is no sea there, no high mountains, cliffs, or precipices, no virgin forests—nothing grand, gloomy, and wild. But what is the good of the grand and the wild? The sea, for instance? Let it stay where it is! It merely makes you melancholy: looking at it, you feel like crying. The heart quails at the sight of the boundless expanse of water, and the eyes grow tired of the endless monotony of the scene. The roaring and the wild pounding of the waves do not caress your feeble ears; they go on repeating their old, old, song, gloomy and mysterious, the same since the world began; and the same old moaning is heard in it, the same complaints as though of a monster condemned to torture, and piercing, sinister voices. No birds twitter around; only silent sea gulls, like doomed creatures, mournfully fly to and fro near the coast and circle over the water.

The roar of a beast is powerless beside these lamentations of nature, the human voice, too, is insignificant, and man himself is so little and weak, so lost among the small details of the vast picture! Perhaps it is because of this that he feels so depressed when he looks at the sea.

Yes, the sea can stay where it is! Its very calm and stillness bring no
comfort to a man's heart; in the barely perceptible swell of the mass
of waters man still sees the same boundless, though slumbering, force
that can so cruelly mock his proud will and bury so deeply his brave
schemes, and all his labor and toil.

Mountains and precipices, too, have not been created for man's
enjoyment. They are as terrifying and menacing as the teeth and claws
of a wild beast rushing upon him; they remind us too vividly of our
frailty and keep us continually in fear of our lives. And the sky over
the peaks and the precipices seems so far and unattainable, as though
it had recoiled from men.

The peaceful spot where our hero suddenly found himself was not
like that. The sky there seems to hug the earth, not in order to fling
its thunderbolts at it, but to embrace it more tightly and lovingly; it
hangs as low overhead as the trustworthy roof of the parental house,
to preserve, it would seem, the chosen spot from all calamities. The
sun there shines brightly and warmly for about six months of the year
and withdraws gradually, as though reluctantly, as though turning back
to take another look at the place it loves and to give it a warm, clear
day in the autumn, amid the rain and slush.

The mountains there seem to be only small-scale models of the
terrifying mountains far away that frighten the imagination. They form
a chain of gently sloping hillocks, down which it is pleasant to slide
on one's back in play, or to sit on watching the sunset dreamily.

The river runs gaily, sporting and playing; sometimes it spreads
into a wide pond, and sometimes it rushes along in a swift stream, or
grows quiet, as though lost in meditation, and creeps slowly along the
pebbles, breaking up into lively streams on all sides, whose rippling
lulls you pleasantly to sleep.

The whole place, for ten or fifteen miles around, consists of a series
of picturesque, smiling, gay landscapes. The sandy, sloping banks of
the clear stream, the small bushes that steal down to the water from
the hills, the twisting ravine with a brook running at the bottom, and
the birch copse—all seem to have been carefully chosen and composed
with the hand of a master.

A heart worn out by tribulations or wholly unacquainted with
them cries out to hide itself in that secluded spot and live there happily
and undisturbed. Everything there promises a calm, long life, till the
hair turns white with age and death comes unawares, like sleep.

The year follows a regular and imperturbable course there. Spring
arrives in March, according to the calendar, muddy streams run down
the hills, the ground thaws, and a warm mist rises from it; the peasant

throws off his sheepskin, comes out into the open only in his shirt and, shielding his eyes with a hand, stands there enjoying the sunshine and shakes his shoulders with pleasure; then he pulls the overturned cart first by one shaft, then by the other, or examines and kicks with his foot at the plow that lies idle in the shed, getting ready for his usual labors. No sudden blizzards return in the spring, covering the fields or breaking down the trees with snow. Like a cold and unapproachable beauty, winter remains true to its character till the lawfully appointed time for warmth; it does not tease with sudden thaws or bend one double with unheard-of frosts; everything goes on in the usual way prescribed by nature. In November snow and frost begin, and by Twelfth-day it grows so cold that a peasant leaving his cottage for a minute returns with hoarfrost on his beard; and in February a sensitive nose already feels the soft breath of approaching spring in the air. But the summer—the summer is especially enchanting in that part of the country. The air there is fresh and dry; it is not filled with the fragrance of lemons and laurels, but only with the scent of wormwood, pine, and wild cherry; the days are bright with slightly burning but not scorching sunshine, and for almost three months there is not a cloud in the sky. As soon as clear days come, they go on for three or four weeks; the evenings are warm and the nights are close. The stars twinkle in such a kindly and friendly way from the sky. If rain comes, it is such a beneficent summer rain! It falls briskly, abundantly, splashing along merrily like the big, warm tears of a man overcome with sudden joy; and as soon as it stops the sun once more looks down with a bright smile of love on the hills and fields and dries them; and the whole countryside responds to the sun with a happy smile. The peasant welcomes the rain joyfully. "The rain will wet me and the sun will dry me," he says, holding up delightedly his face, shoulders, and back to the warm shower. Thunderstorms are not a menace but a blessing there; they always occur at the appointed times, hardly ever missing St. Elijah's day on the second of August, as though to confirm the well-known legend among the people. The strength and number of thunderclaps also seem to be the same each year, as though a definite amount of electricity had been allotted annually for the whole place. Terrible storms, bringing devastation in their wake, are unheard-of in those parts, and no report of them has ever appeared in the newspapers. And nothing would ever have been published about that thrice-blessed spot had not a twenty-eight-year-old peasant widow, Marina Kulkov, given birth to quadruplets, an event the press could not possibly have ignored.

The Lord has never visited those parts either by Egyptian or ordinary plagues. No one of the inhabitants has ever seen or remembered any terrible heavenly signs, fiery balls, or sudden darkness; there are no poisonous snakes there; locusts do not come; there are no roaring lions, nor growling tigers, nor even bears nor wolves, because there are no forests. Only ruminating cows, bleating sheep, and cackling hens walk about the villages and fields in vast numbers.

It is hard to say whether a poet or a dreamer would have been pleased with nature in this peaceful spot. These gentlemen, as everyone knows, love to gaze at the moon and listen to the song of the nightingale. They love the coquette moon when she dresses up in amber clouds and peeps mysteriously through the branches or flings sheaves of silvery beams into the eyes of her admirers. But in that country no one has even heard of the moon being anything but an ordinary moon. It stares very good-naturedly at the villages and the fields, looking very like a polished brass basin. The poet would have looked at her in vain with eyes of rapture; she gazes as good-naturedly at a poet as does a round-faced village beauty in response to the eloquent and passionate glances of a city philanderer.

There are no nightingales in those parts, either—perhaps because there are no shady nooks and roses there. But what an abundance of quail! At harvest time in the summer boys catch them with their hands. Do not imagine, however, that quail are regarded there as a gastronomic luxury—no, the morals of the inhabitants had not been corrupted to that extent: a quail is a bird that is not mentioned in the dietary rules. In that part of the country it delights the ear with its singing; that is why almost every house has a quail in a string cage under the roof.

The poet and dreamer would have remained dissatisfied by the general appearance of that modest and unpretentious district. They would never have succeeded in seeing an evening in the Swiss or Scottish style, when the whole of nature—the woods, the river, the cottage walls, and the sandy hills—is suffused by the red glow of the sunset, against which is set off a cavalcade of gentlemen, riding on a twisting, sandy road after having escorted a lady on a trip to some gloomy ruin and now returning at a smart pace to a strong castle, where an ancient native would tell them a story about the Wars of the Roses and where, after a supper of wild goat's meat, a young girl would sing them a ballad to the accompaniment of a lute—scenes with which the pen of Walter Scott has so richly filled our imagination. No, there is nothing like that in our part of the country.

How quiet and sleepy everything is in the three or four villages that compose this little plot of land! They lie close to one another and look as though they had been flung down accidentally by a giant's hand and scattered about in different directions, where they had remained to this day. One cottage, dropped on the edge of a ravine, has remained hanging there since time immemorial, half of it suspended in the air and propped up by three poles. People have lived quietly and happily there for three or four generations. One would think that a hen would be afraid to go into it, and yet Onisim Suslov, a steady man, who is too big to stand up in his own cottage, lives there with his wife. Not everyone would be able to enter Onisim's cottage, unless, indeed, the visitor persuaded it to stand *with its back to the forest and its front to him*. For its front steps hang over the ravine, and in order to enter it one has to hold on to the grass with one hand and its roof with the other, and then lift one's foot and place it firmly on the steps.

Another cottage clings precariously to the hillside like a swallow's nest; three other cottages have been thrown together accidentally not far away, and two more stand at the very bottom of the ravine.

Everything in the village is quiet and sleepy: the doors of the silent cottages are wide open; not a soul is to be seen; only the flies swarm in clouds and buzz in the stuffy air. On entering a cottage, you will call in vain in a loud voice: dead silence will be your answer; very seldom will some old woman, who is spending her remaining years on the stove, reply with a painful sigh or a sepulchral cough; or a three-year-old child, long-haired, barefoot, and with only a torn shirt on, will appear from behind a partition, stare at you in silence, and hide himself again.

In the fields, too, peace and a profound silence reign; only here and there a plowman can be seen stirring like an ant on the black earth—and, scorched by the heat and bathed in perspiration, pitching his plow forward. The same imperturbable peace and quiet prevail among the people of that locality. No robberies, murders, or fatal accidents ever happened there; no strong passions or daring enterprises ever agitated them. And, indeed, what passions or daring enterprises could have agitated them? Everyone there knew what he was capable of. The inhabitants of those villages lived far from other people. The nearest villages and the district town were twenty and twenty-five miles away. At a certain time the peasants carted their corn to the nearest landing stage of the Volga, which was their Colchis or Pillars of Hercules, and some of them went to the market once a year, and that was all the intercourse they had with the outside world. Their interests centered upon themselves and they never came into contact with or ran foul of anyone else's. They knew that the administrative city of the province was sixty miles away, but very few of them ever went there; they also knew that farther away in the same direction was Saratov or Nizhny-Novgorod; they had heard of Petersburg and Moscow, and

that French and Germans lived beyond Petersburg, and the world farther away was for them as mysterious as it was for the ancients—
unknown countries, inhabited by monsters, people with two heads,
giants; farther away still there was darkness, and at the end of it all
was the fish that held the world on its back. And as their part of the
country was hardly ever visited by travelers, they had no opportunity
of learning the latest news of what was going on in the world: the
peasants who supplied them with their wooden vessels lived within
fifteen miles of their villages and were as ignorant as they. There was
nothing even with which they could compare their way of living and
find out in this way whether they lived well or no, whether they were
rich or poor, or whether there was anything others had that they, too,
would like.

These lucky people imagined that everything was as it should be
and were convinced that everyone else lived like them and to live
otherwise was a sin. They would not believe it if someone told them
that there were people who had other ways of plowing, sowing, har-
vesting, and selling. What passions and excitements could they possibly
have? Like everyone else, they had their worries and weaknesses, rent
and taxes, idleness and sleep; but all this did not amount to a great
deal and did not stir their blood. For the last five years not one of the
several hundred peasants of that locality had died a natural, let alone
a violent, death. And when someone had gone to his eternal sleep either
from old age or from some chronic illness, the people there had gone
on marveling at such an extraordinary event for months. And yet it
did not surprise them at all that, for instance, Taras the blacksmith
had nearly steamed himself to death in his mud hut so that he had to
be revived with cold water. The only crime that was greatly prevalent
was the theft of peas, carrots, and turnips from the kitchen gardens,
and on one occasion two suckling pigs and a chicken had suddenly
disappeared—an event that outraged the whole neighborhood and was
unanimously attributed to the fact that carts with wooden wares had
passed through the village on their way to the fair. But, generally
speaking, accidents of any kind were extremely rare.

Once, however, a man had been found lying in a ditch by the
bridge outside a village, evidently a member of a cooperative group of
workmen who had passed by on their way to the town. The boys were
the first to discover him, and they ran back terrified to the village with
the news that some terrible serpent or werewolf was lying in a ditch,
adding that he had chased them and nearly eaten Kuzka. The braver
souls among the peasants armed themselves with pitchforks and axes
and went in a crowd to the ditch.

"Where are you off to?" The old men tried to stop them. "Think yourselves stout fellows, do you? What do you want there? Leave it alone, no one's driving you."

But the peasants went, and about a hundred yards from the spot began calling to the monster in different voices, and as there was no reply, they stopped, then moved on again. A peasant lay in the ditch, leaning his head against its side; a bundle and a stick with two pairs of bast shoes tied on it, lay beside him. They did not venture near him or touch him.

"Hey you, there!" they shouted in turn, scratching their heads or their backs. "What's your name? Hey, you! What do you want here?"

The stranger tried to raise his head but could not; evidently he was either ill or very tired. One peasant nearly brought himself to touch him with his pitchfork.

"Don't touch him! Don't touch him!" many of the others cried. "How do we know what sort of a man he is? He hasn't said a word. He may be one of them—don't touch him, lads!"

"Let's go," some said. "Come on now: he isn't one of ours, is he? He'll only bring us trouble!"

And they all went back to the village, telling the old men that a stranger was lying there who would not speak and goodness only knows what he was up to.

"Don't have anything to do with him if he is a stranger," the old men said, sitting on the mound of earth beside their cottages, with their elbows on their knees. "Let him do as he likes! You shouldn't have gone at all!"

Such was the spot where Oblomov suddenly found himself in his dream. Of the three or four villages scattered there, one was Sosnovka and another Vavilovka, about a mile from each other. Sosnovka and Vavilovka were the hereditary property of the Oblomov family and were therefore known under the general name of Oblomovka. The Oblomov country seat was in Sosnovka. About three and a half miles from Sosnovka lay the little village of Verkhlyovo, which had once belonged to the Oblomov family but which had long since passed into other hands, and a few more scattered cottages that went with it. This village belonged to a rich landowner who was never to be seen on his estate, which was managed by a German steward.

Such was the whole geography of the place.

Oblomov woke up in the morning in his small bed. He was only seven. He felt lighthearted and gay. What a pretty, red-cheeked, and plump boy he was! He had such sweet, round cheeks that were the envy of many a little rogue who would blow up his own on purpose, but could never get cheeks like that. His nurse was waiting for him to wake up. She began putting on his stockings, but he did not let her; he played about, dangling his legs. His nurse caught him, and they both laughed. At last she succeeded in making him get up. She washed his face, combed his hair, and took him to his mother. Seeing his mother, who had been dead for years, Oblomov even in his sleep thrilled with joy and his ardent love for her; two warm tears slowly appeared from under his eyelashes and remained motionless. His mother covered him with passionate kisses, then looked at him anxiously to see if his eyes were clear, if anything hurt him, asked the nurse if he had slept well, if he had waked in the night, if he had tossed in his sleep, if he had a temperature. Then she took him by the hand and led him to the icon. Kneeling down and putting her arm around him, she made him repeat the words of a prayer. The boy repeated them after her absentmindedly, gazing at the window, through which the cool of the morning and the scent of lilac poured into the room.

"Are we going for a walk today, Mummy?" he suddenly asked in the middle of the prayer.

"Yes, darling," she replied hurriedly, without taking her eyes off the icon and hastening to finish the holy words.

The boy repeated them listlessly, but his mother put her whole soul into them. Then they went to see his father, and then they had breakfast.

At the breakfast table Oblomov saw their aunt, an old lady of eighty; she was constantly grumbling at her maid, who stood behind her chair waiting on her and whose head shook with age. Three elderly spinsters, his father's distant relations, were also there, as well as his father's slightly mad brother, and a poor landowner by the name of Chekmenev, the owner of seven serfs, who was staying with them, and several old ladies and old gentlemen. All these members of the Oblomov retinue and establishment picked up the little boy and began showering caresses and praises on him; he had hardly time to wipe away the traces of the unbidden kisses. After that they began stuffing him with rolls, biscuits, and cream. Then his mother hugged and kissed him again and sent him for a walk in the garden, the yard, and the meadow, with strict instructions to his nurse not to leave the child alone, not to let him go near the horses, the dogs, and the goat or wander too far from the house, and, above all, not to let him go to the ravine, which had a bad name as the most terrible place in the neighborhood. Once they found a dog there that was reputed to be mad only because it ran away and disappeared behind the hills when attacked with pitchforks and axes; carcasses were thrown into the ravine, and wolves and robbers and other creatures that did not exist in those parts or anywhere else in the world were supposed to live there.

The child did not wait for his mother to finish her warnings: he was already out in the yard. He examined his father's house and ran around it with joyful surprise, as though he had never seen it before: the gates that leaned to one side; the wooden roof that had settled in the middle and was overgrown with tender green moss; the rickety front steps; the various outbuildings and additions built onto it; and the neglected garden. He was dying to climb on to the projecting gallery that went all around the house and to have a look at the stream from there; but the gallery was very old and unsafe, and only the servants were allowed to go there—nobody else used it. He didn't heed his mother's prohibition and was already running to the inviting steps when his nurse appeared and succeeded in catching him. He rushed away from her to the hayloft, intending to climb up the steep ladder leading to it, and she had no sooner reached the hayloft than she had to stop him climbing up the dovecote, getting into the cattle yard, and—Lord forbid—the ravine.

"Dear me, what an awful child—what a fidget, to be sure!" his nurse said. "Can't you sit still for a minute, sir? Fie, for shame!"

The nurse's days—and nights—were one continuous scurrying and dashing about: one moment in agony, another full of joy, afraid that he might fall and hurt himself, deeply moved by his unfeigned childish affection, or vaguely apprehensive about his distant future—this was all she lived for, these agitations warmed the old woman's blood and sustained her sluggish existence which might otherwise have come to an end long before.

The child, however, was not always so playful; sometimes he suddenly grew quiet and gazed intently at everything as he sat beside his nurse. His childish mind was observing closely all that was going on around him; these impressions sank deeply into his soul, and grew and matured with him.

It was a glorious morning; the air was cool; the sun was still low. Long shadows fell from the house, the trees, the dovecote, and the gallery. The garden and the yard were full of cool places, inviting sleep and daydreaming. Only the rye fields in the distance blazed and shimmered, and the stream sparkled and glittered in the sun so that it hurt one's eyes to look at it.

"Why, Nanny, is it so dark here and so light there, and why will it be light here soon as well?"

"Because the sun is going to meet the moon, my dear, and frowns when it can't find it, but as soon as it sees it in the distance it grows brighter."

The little boy grew thoughtful and went on looking all about him: he saw Antip going to get water and another Antip, ten times bigger than the real one, walking beside him along the ground, and the water barrel looked as big as a house, and the horse's shadow covered the whole of the meadow, and after taking only two steps across the meadow, it suddenly moved across the hill, and Antip had had no time to leave the yard. The child, too, took two steps—another step and he would be on the other side of the hill. He would like to have gone there to see where the horse had disappeared to. He ran to the gate, but his mother's voice could be heard from the window:

"Nurse, don't you see that the child has run out in the sun! Take him where it's cool. If his head gets hot, he'll be sick and lose his appetite. If you're not careful, he'll run to the ravine."

"Oh, you naughty boy!" the nurse grumbled softly as she took him back to the house.

The boy watched with his keen and sensitive eyes what the grown-ups were doing and how they were spending the morning. Not a single detail, however trifling, escaped the child's inquisitive attention; the picture of his home life was indelibly engraved on his memory; his malleable mind absorbed the living examples before him and unconsciously drew up the program of his life in accordance with the life around him.

The morning could not be said to be wasted in the Oblomov house. The clatter of knives chopping meat and vegetables in the kitchen could be heard as far as the village. From the servants' hall came the hum of the spindle and the soft, thin voice of a woman: it was difficult to say whether she was crying or improvising a melancholy song without words. As soon as Antip returned to the yard with the barrel of water, the women and the coachmen came trudging toward it from every direction with pails, troughs, and jugs. Then an old woman carried a basinful of flour and a large number of eggs from the storehouse to the kitchen; the cook suddenly threw some water out through the window and splashed Arapka, which sat all morning with its eyes fixed on the window, wagging its tail and licking its chops.

Oblomov's father was not idle, either. He sat at the window all morning, keeping a wary eye on all that was going on in the yard.

"Hey, Ignashka, what are you carrying there, you fool?" he would ask a servant walking across the yard.

"I'm taking the knives to be sharpened, sir," the man would answer, without looking at his master.

"Very well, and mind you sharpen them properly."

Then he would stop a peasant woman.

"Hey, my good woman, where have you been?"

"To the cellar, sir," she would stop and reply, shielding her eyes and gazing at the window. "Been to fetch some milk for dinner."

"All right, go, go," her master would reply. "And mind you don't spill the milk. And you, Zakharka, where are you off to again, you rogue?" he shouted later. "I'll show you how to run! It's the third time I've seen you. Back to the hall with you!"

And Zakharka went back to the hall to doze.

If the cows came back from the fields, Oblomov's father would be the first to see that they were watered; if he saw from the window that the dog was chasing a hen, he would at once take stern measures to restore order.

His wife, too, was very busy: she spent three hours explaining to Averka, the tailor, how to make a tunic for Oblomov out of her husband's jacket, drawing the pattern in chalk and watching that Averka did not steal any cloth; then she went to the maids' room to tell each girl what her daily task of lace making was; then she called Nastasya Ivanovna, or Stepanida Agapovna, or someone else from her retinue for a walk in the garden with the practical purpose of seeing how ripe the apples were, if the one that was ripe the day before had fallen off the tree, to do some grafting or pruning, and so on. Her chief concern, however, was the kitchen and the dinner. The whole household was consulted about the dinner: the aged aunt, too, was invited to the council. Everyone suggested a dish: giblet soup, noodles, brawn, tripe, red or white sauce. Every advice was taken into consideration, thoroughly discussed, and then accepted or rejected in accordance with the final decision of the mistress of the house. Nastasya Petrovna or Stepanida Ivanovna* was constantly being sent to the kitchen to remind the cook of something or other, to add one dish or cancel another, to take sugar, honey, wine for the cooking, and see whether the cook had used all that he had been given.

Food was the first and foremost concern at Oblomovka. What calves were fattened there every year for the festival days! What birds were reared there! What deep understanding, what hard work, what care were needed in looking after them! Turkeys and chickens for name

* Goncharov cavalierly mixes the maids' names throughout.

days and other solemn occasions were fattened on nuts. Geese were deprived of exercise and hung up motionless in a sack a few days before a festival so that they should get covered with fat. What stores of jams, pickles, and biscuits! What meads, what kvasses, were brewed, what pies baked at Oblomovka!

And so up to midday everyone was busy, everyone was living a full, conspicuous, antlike life. These industrious ants were not idle on Sundays and holidays, either: on those days the clatter of knives in the kitchen was louder than ever; the kitchen maid journeyed a few times from the barn to the kitchen with a double quantity of flour and eggs; in the poultry yard there was a greater uproar and more bloodshed than ever. An enormous pie was baked, which was served cold for dinner on the following day; on the third and fourth day its remnants were sent to the maids' room, where it lasted till Friday, when one stale end of it without stuffing descended by special favor to Antip, who, crossing himself, proudly and fearlessly demolished this interesting fossil, enjoying the consciousness that it was his master's pie more than the pie itself, like an archaeologist who will enjoy drinking some wretched wine out of what remains of some vessel a thousand years old.

The child kept observing and watching it all with his childish mind, which did not miss anything. He saw how often a usefully and busily spent morning was followed by midday and dinner.

At midday it was hot; not a cloud in the sky. The sun stood motionless overhead scorching the grass. There was not the faintest breeze in the motionless air. Neither tree nor water stirred; an imperturbable stillness fell over the village and the fields, as though everything were dead. The human voice sounded loud and clear in the empty air. The flight and the buzzing of a beetle could be heard a hundred yards away, and from the thick grass there came the sound of snoring, as if someone were fast asleep there. In the house, too, dead silence reigned. It was the hour of after-dinner sleep. The child saw that everyone— father, mother, the old aunt, and their retinue—had retired to their rooms; and those who had no rooms of their own went to the hayloft, the garden, or sought coolness in the hall, while some, covering their faces from the flies with a handkerchief, dropped off to sleep where the heat and the heavy dinner had overcome them. The gardener stretched himself out under a bush in the garden beside his mattock, and the coachman was asleep in the stables. Oblomov looked into the servants' quarters: there everyone was lying stretched out side by side on the floor, on the benches, and in the passage, and the children, left to their own devices, were crawling about and playing in the sand. The dogs, too, stole into their kennels, there being no one to bark at. One could walk through the house from one end to the other without meeting a soul; it would have been easy to steal everything and take it away in carts, if there were any thieves in those parts, for no one would have interfered with them. It was a sort of all-absorbing and invincible sleep, a true semblance of death. Everything was dead, except for the snoring that came in all sorts of tones and variations from every corner of the house. Occasionally someone would raise his head, look around senselessly, in surprise, and turn over, or spit without opening his eyes, and munching his lips or muttering something under his breath, fall asleep again. Another would suddenly, without any preliminary preparations, jump up from his couch, as though afraid of losing a precious moment, seize a mug of kvass, and blowing away the flies that floated in it, which made the hitherto motionless flies begin to move about in the hope of improving their position, have a drink, and then fall back on the bed as though shot dead.

The child went on watching and watching. He ran out into the open with his nurse again after dinner. But in spite of the strict injunctions of her mistress and her own determination, the nurse could not resist the fascination of sleep. She, too, was infected by the epidemic that raged in Oblomovka. At first she looked sedulously after the child, did not let him go far from her, scolded him for being naughty; then, feeling the symptoms of the infection, she begged him not to go out of the gate, not to tease the goat, and not to climb on the dovecote or the gallery. She herself sat down in some shady nook—on the front steps, at the entrance to the cellar, or simply on the grass, with the apparent intention of knitting a sock and looking after the child. But soon her admonitions grew more sluggish and she began nodding. "Oh, dear," she thought, falling asleep, "that fidget is sure to climb on the gallery or—run off to—the ravine. . . ." At this point the old woman's head dropped forward and the sock fell out of her hands; she lost sight of the child and, opening her mouth slightly, began to snore softly.

The child had been waiting impatiently for that moment, with which his independent life began. He seemed to be alone in the whole world; he tiptoed past his nurse and ran off to see where everybody was asleep; he stopped and watched intently if someone woke for a minute, spat and mumbled in his sleep, then, with a sinking heart, ran up on the gallery, raced around it on the creaking boards, climbed the dovecote, penetrated into the remotest corners of the garden, where he listened to the buzzing of a beetle and watched its flight in the air for a long time; he listened to the chirring in the grass and tried to catch the disturbers of peace; caught a dragonfly, tore off its wings to see what it would do, or stuck a straw through it and watched it fly with that appendage; observed with delight, holding his breath, a spider sucking a fly and the poor victim struggling and buzzing in its clutches. In the end the child killed both the victim and its torturer. Then he went to a ditch, dug up some roots, peeled them, and enjoyed eating them more than the jams and apples his mother gave him. He ran out of the gate, too: he would like to go to the birch wood, which seemed to him so near that he was sure he would get there in five minutes, not by the road, but straight across the ditch, the wattle fences, and the pits; but he was afraid, for he had been told that there were wood demons and robbers and terrible beasts there. He wanted to go to the ravine, too, for it was only about a hundred yards from the garden; he ran to the very edge of it, to peer into it as into the crater of a volcano, when suddenly all the stories and legends about the ravine rose before his mind's eye; he was thrown into a panic, and rushed more dead than alive back to his nurse trembling with fear, and woke the old woman. She awoke with a start, straightened the kerchief on her head, pushed back the wisps of gray hair under it with a finger, and, pretending not to have been asleep at all, glanced suspiciously at Oblomov and at the windows of her master's house and, with trembling fingers, began clicking with the knitting needles of the sock that lay on her lap.

Meanwhile the heat had begun to abate a little; everything in nature was getting more animated; the sun had moved toward the woods. In the house, too, the silence was little by little broken; a door creaked somewhere; someone could be heard walking in the yard; someone else sneezed in the hayloft. Soon a servant hurriedly brought an enormous samovar from the kitchen, bending under its weight. The company began to assemble for tea; one had a crumpled face and swollen eyelids; another had a red spot on the cheek and on the temple; a third was still too sleepy to speak in his natural voice. They wheezed, groaned, yawned, scratched their heads, stretched themselves, still barely awake. The dinner and the sleep had made them terribly thirsty. Their throats were parched; they drank about twelve cups of tea each, but this did not help; they moaned and groaned; they tried cranberry water, pear water, kvass, and some medicinal drinks to quench their thirst. All sought deliverance from it as though it were some punishment inflicted on them by God; all rushed about, panting for a drink, like a caravan of travelers in the Arabian desert looking in vain for a spring of water.

The little boy was there beside his mother, watching the strange faces around him and listening to their languid and sleepy conversation.

He enjoyed looking at them, and thought every stupid remark they made interesting. After tea they all found something to do: one went down to the river and walked slowly along the bank, kicking the pebbles into the water; another sat by the window watching everything that went on outside; if a cat ran across the yard or a magpie flew by, he followed it with his eyes and the tip of his nose, turning his head to right and left. So dogs sometimes like to sit for a whole day on the windowsill, basking in the sun and carefully examining every passerby. Oblomov's mother would put his head on her lap and slowly comb his hair, admiring its softness and making Nastasya Ivanovna and Stepanida Tikhonovna admire it too. She talked to them of his future, conjuring up a vision of him as the hero of some brilliant exploit, while they predicted great riches for him.

But presently it was getting dark, again a fire crackled in the kitchen and again there was a loud clatter of knives; supper was being prepared. The servants had gathered at the gates; sounds of the balalaika and of laughter were heard there. They were playing catch.

The sun was setting behind the woods; its last few warm rays cut straight across the woods like shafts of fire, brightly gilding the tops of the pines. Then the rays were extinguished one by one, the last one lingering for a long time and piercing the thicket of branches like a thin quill; but it, too, was extinguished. Objects lost their shapes: at first everything was merged into a gray, and then into a black, mass. The birds gradually stopped singing; soon they fell silent altogether, except one, which, as though in defiance of the rest, went on chirping monotonously amid the general silence and at intervals that were getting longer and longer till, finally, it gave one last low whistle, slightly rustled the leaves around it, and fell asleep. All was silent. Only the grasshoppers chirped louder than ever. White mists rose from the ground and spread over the meadows and the river. The river, too, grew quieter; a few more moments and something splashed in it for the last time, and it grew motionless. There was a smell of damp in the air. It grew darker and darker. The trees began to look like groups of monsters; the woods were full of nameless terrors; someone suddenly moved about there with a creaking noise, as though one of the monsters shifted from one place to another, a dead twig cracking under its foot. The first star, like a living eye, gleamed brightly in the sky, and lights appeared in the windows of the house.

It was the time of solemn and universal stillness in nature, a time when the creative mind is most active, when poetic thoughts are fanned into flames, when passion burns more brightly or anguish is felt more acutely in the heart, when the seed of a criminal design ripens more imperturbably and more strongly in the cruel heart, and when everybody in Oblomovka is once more peacefully and soundly asleep.

"Let's go for a walk, Mummy," said Oblomov.

"Good heavens, child," she replied, "go for a walk at this hour! It's damp, you'll get your feet wet, and it's so frightening: the wood-demon is walking about in the woods now, carrying off little children."

"Where to? What is he like? Where does he live?" the little boy asked.

And his mother gave full rein to her unbridled fancy. The boy listened to her, opening and closing his eyes, till at last he was overcome by sleep. The nurse came and, taking him from his mother's lap, carried him off to bed asleep, his head hanging over her shoulder.

"Well, thank goodness, another day gone," the Oblomovka inhabitants said, getting into bed, groaning, and crossing themselves. "We've lived through it safely, God grant it may be the same tomorrow! Praise be unto thee, O Lord!"

Then Oblomov dreamed of another occasion: one endless winter evening he was timidly pressing closely to his nurse, who was whispering a fairy story to him about some wonderful country where there was no night and no cold, where all sorts of miracles happened, where the rivers flowed with milk and honey, where no one did a stroke of work all the year round, and fine fellows, like Oblomov, and maidens more beautiful than words can tell did nothing but enjoy themselves all day long. A fairy godmother lived there, who sometimes took the shape of a pike and who chose for her favorite some quiet and harmless man—in other words, some loafer, ill-treated by everyone, and for no reason in the world, bestowed all sorts of treasures on him, while he did nothing but eat and drink and dressed in costly clothes, and then married some indescribable beauty, Militrisa Kirbityevna. The little boy listened breathlessly to the story, pricking up his ears, and his eyes glued to his nurse's face. The nurse or the traditional tale so artfully avoided every reference to reality that the child's imagination and intellect, having absorbed the fiction, remained enslaved by it all his life. The nurse told him good-humoredly the story of Yemelya-the-Fool, that wickedly insidious satire on our forefathers and, perhaps, on ourselves, too. Though when he grew up Oblomov discovered that there were no rivers flowing with milk and honey, nor fairy godmothers, and though he smiled at his nurse's tales, his smile was not sincere, and it was accompanied by a secret sigh: the fairy tale had become mixed up with real life in his mind, and sometimes he was sorry that fairy tale was not life and life was not fairy tale. He could not help dreaming of Militrisa Kirbityevna; he was always drawn to the land where people do nothing but have a good time and where there are no worries or sorrows; he preserved for the rest of his life a predisposition for doing no work, walking about in clothes that had been provided for him, and eating at the fairy godmother's expense.

Oblomov's father and grandfather, too, had heard as children the same fairy stories, handed down for centuries and generations in their stereotyped form by their nurses.

In the meantime the nurse was drawing another picture for the little boy's imagination. She was telling him about the heroic exploits of our Achilles and Ulysses, about the great bravery of Ilya Muromets, Dobryna Nikitich, Alyosha Popovich, Polkan the Giant, Kolechishche the Traveler, about how they had journeyed all over Russia, defeating numberless hosts of infidels, how they vied with each other in drinking big goblets of wine at one gulp without uttering a sound; she then told him of wicked robbers, sleeping princesses, towns and people turned to stone; finally, she passed on to our demonology, dead men, monsters, and werewolves.

With Homer's simplicity and good humor and his eye for vivid detail and concrete imagery, she filled the boy's memory and imagination with the Iliad of Russian life, created by our Homers in the far-off days when man was not yet able to stand up to the dangers and mysteries of life and nature, when he trembled at the thought of werewolves and wood-demons and sought Alyosha Popovich's help against the adversities threatening him on all sides, and when the air, water, forests, and plains were full of marvels. Man's life in those days was insecure and terrible; it was dangerous for him to go beyond his own threshold; a wild beast might fall upon him any moment, or a robber might kill him, or a wicked Tartar rob him of all his possessions, or he might disappear without a trace. Or else signs from heaven might appear, pillars or balls of fire; or a light might glimmer above a new grave; or some creature might walk about in the forest as though swinging a lantern, laughing terribly and flashing its eyes in the dark. And so many mysterious things happened to people, too: a man might live for years happily without mishap, and all of a sudden he would begin to talk strangely or scream in a wild voice, or walk in his sleep; another would for no reason at all begin to writhe on the ground in convulsions. And before it happened, a hen had crowed like a cock or a raven had croaked over the roof. Man, weak creature that he is, felt bewildered, and tried to find in his imagination the key to his own being and to the mysteries that encompassed him. And perhaps it was the everlasting quiet of a sleepy and stagnant life and the absence of movement and of any real terrors, adventures, and dangers that made

man create amid the real life another fantastic one where he might find
amusement and true scope for his idle imagination or an explanation
of ordinary events and the causes of the events outside the events
themselves. Our poor ancestors groped their way through life, they
neither controlled their will nor let it be inspired, and then marveled
naively or were horrified at the discomforts and evils of life, and sought
for an explanation of them in the mute and obscure hieroglyphics of
nature. A death, they thought, was caused by the fact that, shortly
before, a corpse had been carried out of the house head and not feet
foremost, and a fire because a dog had howled for three nights under
the window; and they took great care that a corpse should be carried
out feet foremost, but went on eating the same food and sleeping on
the bare grass as before; a barking dog was beaten or driven away,
but still they shook the sparks from a burning splinter down the cracks
of the rotten floor. And to this day the Russian people, amid the stark
and commonplace realities of life, prefer to believe in seductive legends
of the old days, and it may be a long, long time before they give up
this belief.

Listening to his nurse's stories of our Golden Fleece—the Fire
Bird—of the obstacles and secret passages in the enchanted castle, the
little boy plucked up courage, imagining himself the hero of some great
exploit—and a shiver ran down his back, or he grieved over the misfortunes of the brave hero of the tale. One story followed another. The
nurse told her stories picturesquely, with fervor and enthusiasm, sometimes with inspiration, because she half believed them herself. Her eyes
sparkled, her head shook with excitement, her voice rose to unaccustomed notes. Overcome by a mysterious terror, the boy clung to her
with tears in his eyes. Whether she spoke of dead men rising from their
graves at midnight, or of the victims of some monster, pining away in
captivity, or of the bear with the wooden leg walking through large
and small villages in search of the leg that had been cut off—the boy's
hair stood on end with horror; his childish imagination was paralyzed
and then worked feverishly; he was going through an agonizing, sweet,
and painful experience; his nerves were taut like chords. When his
nurse repeated the bear's words grimly: "Creak, creak, limewood leg;
I've walked through large villages, I've walked through a small village,
all the women are fast asleep, but one woman does not sleep, she is
sitting on my skin, she is cooking my flesh, she is spinning my own
fur," and so on, when the bear entered the cottage and was about to
seize the woman who had robbed him of his leg, the little boy could
stand it no longer: he flung himself shrieking into his nurse's arms,
trembling all over; he cried with fright and laughed with joy because

he was not in the wild beast's claws, but on the stove beside his nurse. The little boy's imagination was peopled with strange phantoms; fear and anguish struck root in his soul for years, perhaps forever. He looked sadly about him, and seeing only evil and misfortune everywhere in life, dreamed constantly of that magic country where there were no evils, troubles, or sorrows, where Militrisa Kirbityevna lived, where such excellent food and such fine clothes could be had for nothing. . . .

Fairy tales held sway not only over the children in Oblomovka, but also over the grown-ups to the end of their lives. Everyone in the house and the village, from the master and mistress down to the burly blacksmith Taras, was afraid of something on a dark night: every tree was transformed into a giant and every bush into a den of brigands. The rattling of a shutter and the howling of the wind in the chimney made men, women, and children turn pale. At Epiphany no one went out of the gate by himself at ten o'clock at night; on Easter night no one ventured into the stables, afraid of meeting the house-demon there. They believed in everything at Oblomovka: in ghosts and werewolves. If they were told that a stack of hay walked about the field, they believed it implicitly; if someone spread a rumor that a certain ram was not really a ram but something else, or that a certain Marfa or Stepanida was a witch, they were afraid of both the ram and Marfa; it never occurred to them to ask why the ram was not a ram or why Marfa had become a witch, and, indeed, they would attack anyone who dared to doubt it—so strong was their belief in the miraculous at Oblomovka!

Oblomov realized afterward that the world was a very simple affair, that dead men did not rise from their graves, that as soon as there were any giants about, they were put in a sideshow, and robbers were clapped into jail; but if his belief in phantoms disappeared, there remained a sort of sediment of fear and a vague feeling of anguish. Oblomov discovered that no misfortunes were caused by monsters, and he scarcely knew what misfortunes there were, and yet he expected something dreadful to happen any moment and he could not help being afraid. Even now, if he were left in a dark room or if he saw a corpse, he would still be frightened because of the sinister feeling of anguish sown in his mind as a child; laughing at his fears in the morning, he could not help turning pale again in the evening.

Then Oblomov saw himself as a boy of thirteen or fourteen. He was going to school at Verkhlyovo, about three miles from Oblomovka. The steward of the estate, a German by the name of Stolz, had started a small boarding school for the children of the local gentry. He had a son, Andrey, who was almost of the same age as Oblomov, and there was another boy, who hardly ever worked at all. He was scrofulous and spent all his childhood with his eyes or ears in bandages, and was always weeping surreptitiously because he lived with wicked strangers and not with his grandmother and had no one to fondle him and make him his favorite pasty. So far there were no other children at the school.

There was nothing for it: Oblomov's father and mother decided to send their darling child to school. The boy protested violently at first, shrieking, crying, and being as unreasonable about it as he possibly could, but in the end he was sent off to Verkhlyovo. The German was a strict and businesslike man like most Germans. Oblomov might have learned something from him had Oblomovka been three hundred miles from Verkhlyovo. But under the circumstances, how could he have learned anything? The fascination of the Oblomovka atmosphere, way of life, and habits extended to Verkhlyovo, which had also once belonged to the Oblomovs; except for Stolz's house, everything there was imbued with the same primitive laziness, simplicity of customs, peace, and inertia. The child's heart and mind had been filled with the scenes, pictures, and habits of that life long before he set eyes on his first book. And who can tell when the development of a child's intellect begins? How can one trace the birth of the first ideas and impressions in a child's mind? Perhaps when a child begins to talk, or even before he can talk or walk, but only gazes at everything with that dumb, intent look that seems blank to grown-ups, he already catches and perceives the meaning and the connections of the events of his life, but is not able to tell it to himself or to others. Perhaps Oblomov had observed and understood long ago what was being said and done in his presence: that his father, dressed in velveteen trousers and a brown quilted cotton coat, did nothing but walk up and down the room all day with his hands behind his back, take snuff, and blow his nose, while his mother passed on from coffee to tea, from tea to dinner; that it never entered his father's head to check how many stacks of hay or corn had been mown or reaped, and call to account those who were guilty of neglecting their duties, but if his handkerchief was not handed to him soon enough, he would make a scene and turn the whole house upside down. Perhaps his childish mind had decided long ago that the only way to live was how the grown-ups around him lived. What other decision could he possibly have reached? And how did the grown-ups live at Oblomovka? Did they ever ask themselves why life had been given them? Goodness only knows. And how did they answer it? Most probably they did not answer it at all: everything seemed so clear and simple to them. They had never heard of the so-called hard life, of people who were constantly worried, who rushed about from place to place, or who devoted their lives to everlasting, never-ending work. They did not really believe in mental worries, either; they did not think that life existed so that man should constantly strive for some barely apprehended aims; they were terribly afraid of strong passions, and just as with other people bodies might be consumed by the volcanic action of inner, spiritual fire, so their souls wallowed peacefully and undisturbed in their soft bodies. Life did not mark them, as it did other people, with premature wrinkles, devastating moral blows, and diseases. The good people conceived life merely as an ideal of peace and inactivity, disturbed from time to time by all sorts of unpleasant accidents, such as illness, loss of money, quarrels, and, incidentally, work. They suffered work as a punishment imposed upon our forefathers, but they could not love it and avoided it wherever and whenever they could, believing it both right and necessary to do so. They never troubled themselves about any vague moral and intellectual problems, and that was why they were always so well and happy and lived so long. Men of forty looked like boys; old men did not struggle with a hard, painful death, but, having lived to an unbelievably old age, died as if by stealth, quietly growing cold and imperceptibly breathing their last. This is why it is said that in the old days people were stronger. Yes, indeed they were: in those days they were in no hurry to explain to a boy the meaning of life and prepare him for it as though it were some complicated and serious business; they did not worry him with books that arouse all sorts of questions, that corrode your heart and mind and shorten life. Their way of life was ready-made and was taught to them by their parents, who in turn received it ready-made from their grandparents, and their grandparents from their great-grandparents, being enjoined to keep it whole and undefiled like Vesta's fire. Whatever was done in the time of Oblomov's father, had been done in the times of his grandfather and great-grandfather and, perhaps, is still being done at Oblomovka.

What, then, had they to worry or get excited about, or to learn? What aims had they to pursue? They wanted nothing: life, like a quiet river, flowed past them, and all that remained for them was to sit on the bank of that river and watch the inevitable events that presented themselves uncalled for to every one of them in turn. And so, too, like living pictures, there unrolled themselves in turn before the imagination of Oblomov in his sleep the three main events of life, as they happened in his family and among his relations and friends: births, marriages, and funerals. Then there followed a motley procession of their gay and mournful subdivisions: christenings, name days, family celebrations, fast and feast days, noisy dinner parties, assemblies of relatives, greetings, congratulations, conventional tears and smiles. Everything was done with the utmost precision, gravity, and solemnity. He even saw the familiar faces and their expression on these different occasions, their preoccupied looks and the fuss they made. Present them with any ticklish problem of matchmaking, any solemn wedding or name day you like, and they would arrange it according to all the accepted rules and without the least omission. No one in Oblomovka made the slightest mistake about the right place for a guest at the table, what dishes were to be served, who were to drive together on a ceremonial occasion, what observances were to be kept. Did they not know how to rear a child? Why, you had only to look at the rosy and well-fed darlings that their mothers carried or led by the hand! It was their ambition that their children should be plump, white-skinned, and healthy. They would do without spring altogether rather than to fail to bake a cake in the shape of a lark at its beginning. They did not belong to those who did not know how important that was and did not do it. All their life and learning, all their joys and sorrows were in these things, and that was the main reason why they banished all other griefs and worries and knew no other joys. Their life was full of these fundamental and inevitable events that provided endless food for their hearts and minds. They waited with beating hearts for some ceremony, rite, or feast, and then, having christened, married, or buried a man, they forgot him completely and sank into their usual apathy, from which some similar event—a name day, a wedding, etc.—roused them once again. As soon as a baby was born, the first concern of his parents was to carry out as precisely as possible and without any omissions all the customary rites that decorum demanded, that is to say, to have a feast after the christening; then the careful rearing of the baby began. Its mother set herself and the nurse the task of rearing a healthy child, guarding it from colds, the evil eye, and other hostile influences. They took great care that the child should always be happy and eat a lot. As soon as the boy was firmly on his feet—that is to say, when he no longer needed a nurse—the mother was already secretly cherishing the desire to find him a mate—also as rosy and as healthy as possible. Again the time came for rites, feasts, and, at last, weddings: that was all they lived for. Then came the repetitions: the birth of children, rites, and feasts, until a funeral brought about a change of scenery, but not for long: one set of people made way for another, the children grew up into young men and in due course married and had children of their own —and so life, according to this program, went on in an uninterrupted and monotonous sequence of events, breaking off imperceptibly at the very edge of the grave.

Sometimes, it is true, other cares were thrust upon them, but the inhabitants of Oblomovka met them for the most part with stoic impassivity, and after circling over their heads, the troubles flew past them like birds that, coming to a smooth wall and finding no shelter there, flutter their wings in vain near the hard stones and fly away. Thus, for instance, a part of the gallery around the house suddenly collapsed one day, burying under its ruins a hen with its chicks; Aksinya, Antip's wife, who had sat down under the gallery with her spinning, would have been badly injured had she not gone to fetch some more flax. There was a great commotion in the house: everyone, big and small, rushed to the spot and expressed dismay at the thought that instead of the hen and chicks the mistress herself might have been walking under the gallery with Oblomov. They all gasped with horror and began reproaching one another that it had never occurred to them before to remind each other to order someone to repair the gallery. They were all astonished that it should have collapsed, although only the day before they were surprised at its having stood so long! They began discussing how to repair the damage; they expressed regret about the hen and her chicks and then slowly dispersed to where they had come from, having first been strictly forbidden to take Oblomov anywhere near the gallery. Three weeks later, orders were given to Andrushka, Petrushka, and Vaska to take the fallen planks and banisters out of the way and put them near the barn, where they remained till the spring. Every time Oblomov's father caught sight of them out of the window, he would think of having the gallery repaired: he would call for the carpenter and consult him as to whether it would be better to build a new gallery or break down what remained of the old, then he would let him go home, saying, "You can go now and I'll think it over." That went on till Vaska or Motka told his master that, having climbed onto what remained of the gallery that morning, he noticed that the corners had broken away from the walls and might collapse any moment. Then the carpenter was called for a final consultation, as a result of which it was decided to prop up the part of the gallery that was still standing with the fragments of the old, which was actually done at the end of the month.

"Why," said Oblomov's father to his wife, "the gallery is as good as new. Look how beautifully Fyodor has fixed the planks, just like the pillars of the marshal's house! It's perfectly all right now: it will last for years!"

Someone reminded him that it would be a good opportunity for repairing the gate and the front steps, for the holes between them were so big that pigs, let alone cats, got through them into the cellar.

"Yes, yes, to be sure," Oblomov's father replied, looking worried, and went at once to inspect the front steps.

"Yes, indeed, look how rickety they are," he said, rocking the steps with his foot like a cradle.

"But it rocked like that when it was made," someone observed.

"Well, what about it?" Oblomov's father replied. "They haven't fallen down, though they have stood there for sixteen years without any repairs. Luka made a good job of it. He was a real carpenter, Luka was! He's dead, may his soul rest in peace. They've gotten spoiled now—no carpenter could do such a job now!"

He turned his eyes away and, they say, the steps still rock but have not fallen to pieces yet. Luka, it would seem, was indeed an excellent carpenter!

One must do the Oblomovs justice, though: sometimes when things went wrong, they would take a great deal of trouble and even flew into a temper and grew angry. How could one thing or another have been neglected for so long? Something must be done about it at once! And they went on talking interminably about repairing the little bridge across the ditch or fencing off part of the garden to prevent the cattle from spoiling the trees because the wattle fence had collapsed in one place.

One day, while taking a walk in the garden, Oblomov's father had even gone so far as to lift, groaning and moaning, the fence off the ground with his own hands and told the gardener to prop it up at once with two poles; thanks to his promptness, the fence remained standing like that all through the summer, and it was only in winter that the snow brought it down again. At last even the bridge had three new planks laid across it after Antip had fallen through it with his horse and water barrel. He had not had time to recover from his injuries before the bridge was as good as new. Nor did the cows and goats profit much from the fresh fall of the wattle fence in the garden: they had only had time to eat the currant bushes and to start stripping the bark off the tenth lime tree, and never reached the apple trees, when an order was given to put the fence right and even to dig a ditch around it. The two cows and a goat that were caught in the act had received a good beating!

Oblomov also dreamed of the big, dark drawing room in his parents' house, with its ancient ashwood armchairs, which were always covered, a huge, clumsy, and hard sofa, upholstered in faded and stained blue oriental cloth, and one large leather armchair. A long winter evening; his mother sat on the sofa with her feet tucked under her, lazily knitting a child's stocking, yawning, and occasionally

scratching her head with a knitting needle. Nastasya Ivanovna and
Pelageya Ignatyevna sat beside her and, bending low over their work,
were diligently sewing something for Oblomov for the holidays or for
his father or for themselves. His father paced the room with his hands
behind his back, looking very pleased with himself, or sat down in the
armchair, and after a time once more walked up and down the room,
listening attentively to the sound of his own footsteps. Then he took
a pinch of snuff, blew his nose, and took another pinch. One tallow
candle burned dimly in the room, and even this was permitted only on
autumn and winter evenings. In the summer months everyone tried to
get up and go to bed by daylight. This was done partly out of habit
and partly out of economy. Oblomov's parents were extremely sparing
with any article that was not produced at home but had to be bought.
They gladly killed an excellent turkey or a dozen chickens to entertain
a guest, but they never put an extra raisin in a dish, and turned pale
when their guest ventured to pour himself out another glass of wine.
Such depravity, however, was a rare occurrence at Oblomovka: that
sort of thing would be done only by some desperate character, a social
outcast, who would never be invited to the house again. No, they had
quite a different code of behavior there: a visitor would never dream
of touching anything before he had been asked at least three times. He
knew very well that if he was asked only once to savor some dish or
drink some wine, he was really expected to refuse it. It was not for
every visitor, either, that two candles were lit: candles were bought in
town for money and, like all purchased articles, were kept under lock
and key by the mistress herself. Candle ends were carefully counted
and safely put away. Generally speaking, they did not like spending
money at Oblomovka, and however necessary a purchase might be,
money for it was issued with the greatest regret and that, too, only if
the sum was insignificant. Any considerable expense was accompanied
by moans, shrieks, and abuse. At Oblomovka they preferred to put up
with all sorts of inconveniences, and even stopped regarding them as
such, rather than spend money. That was why the sofa in the drawing
room had for years been covered in stains; that was why the leather
armchair of Oblomov's father was leather only in name, being all rope,
a piece of leather remaining only on the back, the rest having all peeled
off five years before; and that was perhaps why the gate was lopsided
and the front steps rickety. To pay two hundred, three hundred, or
five hundred rubles all at once for something, however necessary it
might be, seemed almost suicidal to them. Hearing that a young local
landowner had been to Moscow and bought a dozen shirts for three
hundred rubles, a pair of boots for twenty-five rubles, and a waistcoat

for his wedding for forty rubles, Oblomov's father crossed himself and said, with a look of horror on his face, that "such a scamp must be locked up." They were, generally speaking, impervious to economic truths about the desirability of a quick turnover of capital, increased production, and exchange of goods. In the simplicity of their souls they understood and put into practice only one way of using capital—keeping it under lock and key—in a chest.

The other inhabitants of the house and the usual visitors sat in the armchairs in the drawing room in different positions, breathing hard. As a rule, deep silence reigned among them: they saw each other every day, and had long ago explored and exhausted all their intellectual treasures, and there was little news from the outside world. All was quiet; only the sound of the heavy, homemade boots of Oblomov's father, the muffled ticking of a clock in its case on the wall, and the snapping of a thread by the teeth or the hands of Pelageya Ignatyevna or Nastasya Ivanovna broke the dead silence from time to time. Half an hour sometimes passed like that, unless of course someone yawned aloud and muttered, as he made the sign of the cross over his mouth, "Lord, have mercy upon us!" His neighbor yawned after him, then the next person, as though at a word of command, opened his mouth slowly, and so the infectious play of the air and lungs spread among them all, moving some of them to tears.

Oblomov's father would go up to the window, look out, and say with mild surprise:

"Good Lord, it's only five o'clock, and how dark it is outside!"

"Yes," someone would reply, "It is always dark at this time of the year: the evenings are drawing in."

And in the spring they would be surprised and happy that the days were drawing out. But if asked what they wanted the long days for, they did not know what to say.

And again they were silent. Then someone snuffed the candle and suddenly extinguished it, and they all gave a start.

"An unexpected guest!" someone was sure to say. Sometimes this would serve as topic for conversation.

"Who would that be?" the mistress would ask. "Not Nastasya Faddeyevna? I wish it was! But no, she won't come before the holiday. That would have been nice! How we should embrace each other and have a good cry! And we should have gone to morning and afternoon Mass together. . . . But I'm afraid I couldn't keep up with her! I may be the younger one, but I can't stand as long as she can!"

"When was it she left here?" Oblomov's father asked. "After St. Elijah's Day, I believe."

"You always get the dates mixed up," his wife corrected him. "She left before Whitsun."

"I think she was here on the eve of St. Peter's Fast," retorted Oblomov's father.

"You're always like that," his wife said reprovingly. "You will argue and make yourself ridiculous."

"Of course she was here. Don't you remember we had mushroom pies because she liked them?"

"That's Maria Onisimovna: she likes mushroom pies—I do remember that! And Maria Onisimovna did not stop till St. Elijah's Day, but only till St. Prokhov's and Nikanor's."

They reckoned the time by holy days, by the seasons of the years, by different family and domestic occurrences, and never referred to dates or months. That was perhaps partly because, except for Oblomov's father, they all got mixed up with the dates and the months. Defeated, Oblomov's father made no answer, and again the whole company sank into drowsiness. Oblomov, snuggled up behind his mother's back, was also drowsing and occasionally dropped off to sleep.

"Aye," some visitor would then say with a deep sigh, "Maria Onisimovna's husband, the late Vasily Fomich, seemed a healthy chap, if ever there was one, and yet he died! Before he was fifty, too! He should have lived to be a hundred!"

"We shall all die at the appointed time—it's God's will," Pelageya Ignatyevna replied with a sigh. "Some people die, but the Khlopovs have one christening after another—I am told Anna Andreyevna has just had another baby—her sixth!"

"It isn't only Anna Andreyevna," said the lady of the house. "Wait till her brother gets married—there'll be one child after another—there's going to be plenty of trouble in that family! The young boys are growing up and will soon be old enough to marry; then the daughters will have to get married, and where is one to find husbands for them? Today everyone is asking for a dowry, and in cash, too."

"What are you saying?" asked Oblomov's father, going up to them.

"Well, we're saying that . . ."

And they told him what they were talking about.

"Yes," Oblomov's father said sententiously, "that's life for you! One dies, another one is born, a third one marries, and we just go on getting older. There are no two days that are alike, let alone two years. Why should it be so? Wouldn't it have been nice if one day were just like the day before, and yesterday were just like tomorrow? It's sad, when you come to think of it."

"The old are aging and the young are growing up," someone muttered sleepily in a corner of the room.

"One has to pray more and try not to think of anything," the lady of the house said sternly.

"True, true," Oblomov's father, who had meant to indulge in a bit of philosophy, remarked apprehensively and began pacing the room again.

There was another long silence; only the faint sound made by the wool as it was pulled through the material by the needles could be heard. Sometimes the lady of the house broke the silence.

"Yes," she said, "it is dark outside. At Christmastime, when our people come to stay, it will be merrier and we shan't notice the evenings pass. If Malanya Petrovna comes, there will be no end of fun! The things she does! Telling fortunes by melting down tin or wax, or running out of the gate; my maids don't know where they are when she's here. She'd organized all sorts of games—she is a rare one!"

"Yes," someone observed, "a society lady! Two years ago she took it into her head to go tobogganing—that was when Luka Savich injured his forehead."

They all suddenly came to life and burst out laughing as they looked at Luka Savich.

"How did you manage to do that, Luka Savich?" said Oblomov's father, dying with laughter. "Come on, tell us!"

And they all went on laughing, and Oblomov woke up, and he, too, laughed.

"Well, what is there to tell?" Luka Savich said, looking put out. "Aleksey Naumich has invented it all: there was nothing of the kind at all."

"Oh!" they shouted in chorus. "What do you mean—nothing happened at all? We're not dead, are we? And what about that scar on your forehead? You can still see it."

And they shook with laughter.

"What are you laughing at?" Luka Savich tried to put in a word between the outbursts of laughter. "I—I'd have been all right if that rascal Vaska had not given me that old toboggan—it came to pieces under me—I—"

His voice was drowned in the general laughter. In vain did he try to finish the story of his fall: the laughter spread to the hall and the maids' room, till the whole house was full of it; they all recalled the amusing incident, they all laughed and laughed in unison, *ineffably*, like the Olympian gods. When the laughter began to die down, someone would start it anew and—off they went again.

At last they managed somehow to compose themselves.

"Will you go tobogganing this Christmas?" Luka Savich asked Oblomov's father after a pause.

Another general outburst of laughter which lasted for about ten minutes.

"Shall I ask Antip to get the hill ready before the holidays?" Oblomov's father said suddenly. "Luka Savich is dying to have another go—he can't bear to wait—"

The laughter of the whole company interrupted him.

"But is that toboggan still in working order?" one of them asked, choking with laughter.

There was more laughter.

They all went on laughing for a long time, then gradually began quieting down: one was wiping his tears, another blowing his nose, a third coughing violently and clearing his throat, saying with difficulty: "Oh dear, oh dear, this will be the death of me! Dear me, the way he rolled over on his back with the skirts of his coat flying—"

This was followed by another outburst of laughter, the last and the longest of all, and then all was quiet. One man sighed, another yawned aloud, muttering something under his breath, and everyone fell silent.

As before, the only sounds that could be heard were the ticking of the clock, Oblomov's father's footfalls, and the sharp snapping of a thread broken off by one of the ladies. Suddenly Oblomov's father stopped in the middle of the room, looking dismayed and touching the tip of his nose.

"Good heavens," he said, "what can this mean? Someone's going to die: the tip of my nose keeps itching."

"Goodness," his wife cried, throwing up her hands, "no one's going to die if it's the tip of the nose that's itching. Someone's going to die when the bridge of the nose is itching. Really, my dear, you never can remember anything! You'll say something like this when strangers or visitors are in the house, and you will disgrace yourself!"

"But what does it mean when the tip of your nose is itching?" Oblomov's father asked, looking embarrassed.

"Looking into a wineglass! How could you say a thing like that! Someone's going to die, indeed!"

"I'm always mixing things up!" said Oblomov's father. "How is one to remember—the nose itching at the side, or at the tip, or the eyebrows—"

"At the side means news," Pelageya Ivanovna chimed in. "If the eyebrows are itching, it means tears; the forehead, bowing, if it's on

the right—to a man, and if it's on the left side—to a woman; if the
ears are itching, it means that it's going to rain; lips—kissing;
mustache—eating sweets; elbow—sleeping in a new place; soles of the
feet—a journey—"

"Well done, Pelageya Ivanovna!" said Oblomov's father. "And I
suppose when butter is going to be cheap, your neck will be itching—"

The ladies began to laugh and whisper to one another; some of
the men smiled; it seemed as though they would burst out laughing
again, but at that moment there came a sound like a dog growling and
a cat hissing when they are about to throw themselves upon each other.
That was the clock striking.

"Good Lord, it's nine o'clock already!" Oblomov's father cried
with joyful surprise. "Dear me, I never noticed how the time was
passing. Hey, there! Vaska! Vanka! Motka!"

Three sleepy faces appeared at the door.

"Why don't you lay the table?" Oblomov's father asked with
surprise and vexation. "You never think of your masters! Well, what
are you standing there for? Come on, vodka!"

"That's why the tip of your nose was itching," Pelageya Ivanovna
said quickly. "When you drink vodka, you'll be looking into your
glass."

After supper, having kissed and made the sign of the cross over
each other, they all went to bed, and sleep descended over their un-
troubled heads. In his dream Oblomov saw not one or two such evenings, but weeks, months, and years of days and evenings spent in this
way. Nothing interfered with the monotony of their life, and the inhabitants of Oblomovka were not tired of it because they could not
imagine any other kind of existence; and if they could, they would
have recoiled from it in horror. They did not want any other life, and
they would have hated it. They would have been sorry if circumstances
had brought any change in their mode of living, whatever its nature.
They would have been miserable if tomorrow were not like yesterday
and if the day after tomorrow were not like tomorrow. What did they
want with variety, change, or unforeseen contingencies, which other
people were so keen on? Let others make the best of them if they could;
at Oblomovka they did not want to have anything to do with it. Let
others live as they liked. For unforeseen contingencies, though they
might turn out well in the end, were disturbing: they involved constant
worry and trouble, running about, restlessness, buying and selling or
writing—in a word, doing something in a hurry, and that was no joking
matter: they went on for years snuffling and yawning, or laughing good-
humoredly at country jokes or, gathering in a circle, telling each other

their dreams. If a dream happened to be frightening, they all looked depressed and were afraid in good earnest; if it was prophetic, they were all unfeignedly glad or sad, according to whether the dream was comforting or ominous. If the dream required the observance of some rite, they took the necessary steps at once. Or they played cards— ordinary games on weekdays, and Boston with their visitors on holy days—or they played patience, told fortunes for a king of hearts or a queen of clubs, foretelling a marriage. Sometimes some woman named Natalya Faddeyevna came to stay for a week or a fortnight. To begin with, the two elderly ladies would tell each other all the latest news in the neighborhood, what everyone did or how everyone lived; they discussed not only all the details of their family life and what was going on behind the scenes, but also everyone's most secret thoughts and intentions, prying into their very souls, criticizing and condemning the unworthy, especially the unfaithful husbands, and then they would go over all the important events: name days, christenings, births, who invited or did not invite whom and how those who had been invited were entertained. Tired of this, they began showing each other their new clothes, dresses, coats, even skirts and stockings. The lady of the house boasted of her linen, yarn, and lace of home manufacture. But that topic, too, would be exhausted. Then they would content themselves with coffee, tea, jam. Only after that would they fall silent. They sat for some time looking at each other and from time to time sighing deeply. Occasionally one of them would burst out crying.

"What's the matter, my dear?" the other one asked anxiously.

"Oh, I feel so sad, my dear," the visitor replied with a heavy sigh. "We've angered the good Lord, sinners that we are. No good will come of it."

"Oh, don't frighten me, dear, don't scare me," the lady of the house interrupted.

"Oh, yes, yes," Natalya Faddeyevna went on, "the day of judgment is coming: nation will rise against nation and kingdom against kingdom—the end of the world is near!" she exclaimed at last, and the two ladies burst out crying bitterly.

Natalya Faddeyevna had no grounds at all for her final conclusion, no one having risen against anyone and there not having been even a comet that year, but old ladies sometimes have dark forebodings.

Only very seldom was this way of passing the time interrupted by some unexpected event, such as, for instance, the whole household being overcome by the fumes from the stoves. Other sicknesses were practically unknown in the house and the village, except when a man would accidentally stumble in the dark against the sharp end of a stake, or fall off the hayloft, or be hit on the head by a plank dropping from the roof. But this happened only seldom, and against such accidents there was a score of well-tried domestic remedies: the bruise would be rubbed with a freshwater sponge or with daphne, the injured man was given holy water to drink or had some spell whispered over him—and he would be well again. But poisoning by charcoal fumes was a fairly frequent occurrence. If that happened, they all took to their beds, moaning and groaning were heard all over the house, some tied pickled cucumbers around their heads, some stuffed cranberries into their ears and sniffed horseradish, some went out into the frost with nothing but their shirts on, and some simply lay unconscious on the floor. This happened periodically once or twice a month, because they did not like to waste the heat in the chimney and shut the flues while flames like those in *Robert the Devil* still flickered in the stoves. It was impossible to touch a single stove without blistering one's hand.

Only once was the monotony of their existence broken by a really unexpected event. Having rested after a heavy dinner, they had all gathered around the tea table, when an Oblomov peasant, who had just returned from town, came suddenly into the room and after a great deal of trouble pulled out from the inside of his coat a crumpled letter addressed to Oblomov's father. They all looked dumbfounded; Mrs. Oblomov even turned slightly pale; they all craned their necks toward the letter and fixed their eyes upon it.

"How extraordinary! Who could it be from?" Mrs. Oblomov said at last, having recovered from her surprise.

Mr. Oblomov took the letter and turned it about in bewilderment, not knowing what to do with it.

"Where did you get it?" he asked the peasant. "Who gave it to you?"

"Why, sir, at the inn where I stopped in town," replied the peasant. "A soldier came twice from the post office, sir, to ask if there was any peasant there from Oblomovka. He'd gotten a letter for the master, it seems."

"Well?"

"Well, sir, at first I hid myself, so the soldier, sir, he went away with this here letter. But the sexton from Verkhlyovo had seen me and he told them. So he comes a second time, the soldier, sir. And as he comes the second time, he starts swearing at me and gives me the letter. Charged me five kopecks for it, he did. I asks him what I was to do with the letter, and he told me to give it to you, sir."

"You shouldn't have taken it," Mrs. Oblomov observed vexedly.

"I didn't take it, ma'am. I said to him, I said, 'What do we want your letter for—we don't want no letters,' I said. 'I wasn't told to take letters and I durstn't,' I said. 'Take your letter and go away,' I said. But he started cursing me something awful, he did, threatening to go to the police, so I took it."

"Fool!" said Mrs. Oblomov.

"Who could it be from?" Mr. Oblomov said wonderingly, examining the address. "The writing seems familiar!"

He passed the letter around and they all began discussing who it could be from and what it was about. They were all completely at a loss. Mr. Oblomov asked for his glasses and they spent an hour and a half looking for them. He put them on and was already about to open the letter when his wife stopped him.

"Don't open it," she said apprehensively. "Who knows, it might be something dreadful—some awful trouble. You know what people are nowadays. There's plenty of time: you can open it tomorrow or the day after: it won't run away."

The letter was locked up in a drawer with the glasses. They all sat down to tea, and the letter might have lain in the drawer for years had they not all been so greatly excited by the extraordinary event. At tea and all next day they talked of nothing but the letter. At last they could not stand it any longer, and on the fourth day, having all gathered in a crowd, they opened it nervously, Mr. Oblomov glanced at the signature.

"Radishchev," he read. "Why, that's Filip Matveich."

"Oh, so that's who it is from!" they cried from all sides. "Is he still alive? Good Lord, fancy he's not dead! Well, thank God! What does he say?"

Mr. Oblomov began reading the letter aloud. It seemed that Radishchev was asking for a recipe of beer that was brewed particularly well at Oblomovka.

"Send it to him! Send it to him!" they all shouted. "You must write him a letter!"

A fortnight passed.

"Yes, I must write to him," Mr. Oblomov kept saying to his wife. "Where's the recipe?"

"Where is it?" his wife replied. "I must try and find it. But why all this hurry? Wait till the holy days; the fast will be over, and then you can write to him. There's plenty of time. . . ."

"Yes, indeed. I'd better write during the holy days," said Mr. Oblomov.

The question of the letter was raised again during the holy days. Mr. Oblomov made up his mind to write the letter. He withdrew to

his study, put on his glasses, and sat down at the table. Dead silence
reigned in the house; the servants were told not to stamp their feet or
make a noise. "The master's writing," everyone said, speaking in a
timid and respectful voice as though someone were lying dead in the
house. He had just time to write, "Dear Sir," in a trembling hand,
slowly, crookedly, and as carefully as though performing some dangerous operation, when his wife came into the room.

"I'm very sorry," she said, "but I can't find the recipe. I must have
a look in the bedroom cupboard. It may be there. But how are you
going to send the letter?"

"By post, I suppose," replied Mr. Oblomov.

"And what will the postage be?"

Mr. Oblomov produced an old calendar.

"Forty kopecks," he said.

"Waste forty kopecks on such nonsense!" she observed. "Let's
rather wait till we can send it by someone. Tell the peasants to find
out."

"Yes," said Mr. Oblomov, "it would certainly be better to send
it by hand." And tapping the pen on the table a few times, he put it
back in the inkstand and took off his glasses.

"Yes, indeed," he concluded. "It won't run away; there's plenty
of time."

It is doubtful whether Filip Matveich ever received the recipe.

Sometimes Oblomov's father picked up a book. It made no difference to him what book it was. He did not feel any need for reading,
but regarded it as a luxury, as something that one could easily do
without, just as one could do without a picture on the wall or without
taking a walk. That was why he did not mind what book he picked
up: he looked upon it as something that was meant as an entertainment,
something that would help to distract him when he was bored or had
nothing better to do.

"I haven't read a book for ages," he would say, or sometimes he
would change the phrase to, "Now, then, let's read a book." Or he
would simply happen to see the small pile of books that was left him
by his brother and pick one up at random. Whether it happened to be
Golikov, or the latest *Dream Book*, or Kheraskov's *Rossiade*, or Su-
marokov's tragedies, or the *Moscow News* of two years ago, he read
it all with equal pleasure, remarking at times: "Whatever will he think
of next! What a rascal! Damn the fellow!" These exclamations referred
to the authors, for whose calling he had no respect whatever; he had
even adopted the attitude of semi-indulgent contempt for a writer that
is so characteristic of old-fashioned people. He, like many other people

of his day, thought that an author must be a jovial fellow, a rake, a drunkard, and a mountebank, something like a clown. Sometimes he read the two-year-old papers aloud for the edification of everybody or just told them a piece of news from them. "They write from The Hague," he would say, "that His Majesty the King has safely returned to his palace after a short journey," and as he spoke he glanced at his listeners over his glasses. Or: "The ambassador of such and such a country has presented his credentials in Vienna. And here they write," he went on, "that the works of Madame Genlis have been translated into Russian."

"I suppose," remarked one of his listeners, a small landowner, "they do all these translations to extract some money from us gentry."

Meanwhile poor Oblomov had still to go for his lessons to Stolz. As soon as he woke up on Monday morning, he felt terribly depressed. He heard Vaska's raucous voice shouting from the front steps:

"Antip, harness the piebald one to take the young master to the German!"

His heart sank. Sadly he went to his mother. She knew what was the matter with him and began gilding the pill, secretly sighing herself at the thought of parting with him for a whole week.

Nothing was good enough for him to eat that morning. They baked rolls of different shapes for him, loaded him with pickles, biscuits, jams, all sorts of sweetmeats, cooked and uncooked dainties, and even provisions. He was given it all on the supposition that he did not get enough to eat at the German's house.

"You won't get anything decent to eat there," they said at Oblomovka. "For dinner they'll give you nothing but soup, roast meat, and potatoes, and bread and butter for tea. As for supper—not a crumb, old man!"

Oblomov, however, dreamed mostly of Mondays on which he did not hear Vaska's voice shouting for the piebald to be harnessed, but his mother greeting him at breakfast with a smile and pleasant news.

"You're not going today, dear; Thursday is a great holy day, and it isn't worth traveling there and back for three days."

Or sometimes she would announce to him suddenly:

"Today is commemoration week—it's no time for lessons: we shall be baking pancakes."

Or his mother would look at him intently on a Monday morning and say:

"Your eyes look tired this morning, darling. Are you well?" and shake her head.

The sly little boy was perfectly well, but he said nothing.

"You'd better stay at home this week," she said, "and we shall see how you feel."

And they were all convinced in the house that lessons and Commemoration Saturday must never be allowed to interfere with each other and that a holy day on a Thursday was an insurmountable obstacle to lessons during the whole of the week. Only from time to time would a servant or a maid, who had been punished because of the young master, grumble:

"Oh, you spoiled little brat! When will you clear out to your German?"

At other times Antip would suddenly turn up at the German's on the familiar piebald in the middle or at the beginning of the week to fetch Oblomov.

"Maria Savishna or Natalya Faddeyevna or the Kuzovkovs with all their children have come on a visit and you're wanted back home!"

And Oblomov stayed at home for three weeks, and then Holy Week was not far off, followed by Easter; or someone in the house decided that for some reason or other one did not study in the week after Easter; there would be only a fortnight left till summer, and it was not worth going back to school, for the German himself had a rest in summer, so that it was best to put the lessons off till the autumn. Oblomov spent a most enjoyable six months. How tall he grew during that time! And how fat he grew! How soundly he slept! They could not admire him enough at home, nor could they help observing that when the dear child returned home from the German on Saturdays, he looked pale and thin.

"He can easily come to harm," his mother would remark. "He'll have plenty of time to study, but you cannot buy health for money: health is the most precious thing in life. The poor boy comes back from school as from a hospital: all his fat is gone, he looks so thin—and such a naughty boy, too: always running about!"

"Yes," his father observed, "learning is no joke: it will take it out of anyone!"

And the fond parents went on finding excuses for keeping their son at home. There was no difficulty in finding excuses besides holy days. In winter they thought it was too cold, in summer it was too hot to drive to the next village, and sometimes it rained; in the autumn the roads were too muddy. Sometimes Antip aroused their doubts: he did not seem to be drunk, but he had a sort of wild look in his eyes—there might be trouble, he might get stuck in the mud or fall into a ditch. The Oblomovs, however, tried to make their excuses as legitimate as possible in their own eyes, and particularly in the eyes of Stolz, who did not spare *Donnerwetters* to their faces and behind their backs for pampering the child.

The days of the heroes of Fonvizin's comedy *The Minor*—the Prostakovs and Skotinins—had gone long before. The proverb "Knowledge is light and ignorance is darkness" was already penetrating into the big and small villages together with the books sold by book peddlers. Oblomov's parents understood the advantages of education, but only its material advantages. They saw that it was only education that made it possible for people to make a career, that is, to acquire rank, decorations, and money; that old-fashioned lawyers, case-hardened and corrupt officials, who had grown old in their pettifogging ways and chicaneries, were having a bad time. Ominous rumors were abroad that not only reading and writing but all sorts of hitherto unheard-of subjects were required. A gulf opened up between the higher and the lower grades of civil servants that could be bridged only by something called a diploma. Officials of the old school, children of habit and nurslings of bribes, began to disappear. Many of those who had survived were dismissed as unreliable, and others were put on trial; the luckiest were those who, giving up the new order of things as a bad job, retired to their well-feathered nests while the going was good. Oblomov's parents grasped all this and understood the advantages of education, but only these obvious advantages. They had only the vaguest and remotest idea of the intrinsic need for education, and that was why they wanted to obtain for their son some of its brilliant advantages. They dreamed of a gold-embroidered uniform for him; they imagined him as a councilor at court, and his mother even imagined him as a governor of a province. But they wanted to obtain all this as cheaply as possible, by all sorts of tricks, by secretly dodging the rocks and obstacles scattered on the path of learning and honors, without bothering to jump over them—that is, for instance, by working a little, not by physical exhaustion or the loss of the blessed plumpness acquired in childhood. All they wanted was that their son should merely comply with the prescribed rules and regulations and obtain in some way or other a certificate that said that their darling Ilya *had mastered all the arts and sciences*. The whole of this Oblomov system of education met with strong opposition in Stolz's system. Each fought stubbornly for his own ideas. Stolz struck at his opponents directly, openly, and persistently, and they parried his blows by all sorts of cunning devices, including those already described. Neither side won; German pertinacity might have overcome the stubbornness and obduracy of the

Oblomovs, had not the German met opposition in his own camp. The fact was that Stolz's own son spoiled Oblomov, prompting him at lessons and doing his translations for him.

Oblomov clearly saw his life at home and at Stolz's. As soon as he woke up at home, he saw Zakhar, later his famous valet, Zakhar Trofimych, standing by his bed. Zakhar, like his old nurse, pulled on his stockings and put on his shoes, while Oblomov, a boy of fourteen, merely stretched out to him first one leg, then the other, as he lay on the bed; and if something seemed to him amiss, he hit Zakhar on the nose with a foot. If Zakhar resented it and had the impudence to complain, he would get a hiding from the grown-ups as well. Then Zakhar combed his hair, helped him on with his coat, forcing his arms carefully through the sleeves so as not to disturb him unduly, and reminded him of the things he had to do, washing as soon as he got up, and so on. If Oblomov wanted something, he had only to wink and three or four servants rushed to carry out his wish; if he dropped something, or if he had to get something, someone else would pick it up or get it for him; if he wanted to fetch something or run out of the house for something and, being a lively boy, would like to run out and do it all himself, his father, mother, and three aunts shouted all at once: "What for? Where are you off to? And what are Vaska, Vanka, and Zakharka for? Hey, Vaska! Vanka! Zakharka! What are you gaping at, you idiots! I'll show you!"

And try as he might, Oblomov could never do anything for himself. Later he found that it was much less trouble and learned to shout himself:

"Hey, Vaska! Vanka! Bring me this! Bring me that! I don't want this, I want that! Run and fetch it!"

At times he got tired of the tender solicitude of his parents. If he ran down the stairs or across the yard, a dozen desperate voices shouted after him: "Oh, hold him by the hand! Stop him! He'll fall down and hurt himself! Stop!" If he tried to run out into the hall in winter, or to open a window, there were again shouts: "Where are you off to? You can't do that! Don't run, don't go, don't open it: you'll hurt yourself, you'll catch a cold . . . !" And sadly Oblomov remained indoors, cherished like an exotic flower in a hothouse, and like it he grew slowly and languidly. His energies, finding no outlet, turned inward and withered, drooping. Sometimes he woke up feeling so bright and cheerful, so fresh and gay; he felt as though something inside him were full of life and movement, just as if some imp had taken up its quarters there, daring him to climb on the roof, or mount the gray mare and gallop to the meadows where they were haymaking, or sit astride on the fence, or tease the village dogs; or he suddenly wanted to run like mad through the village, then across the field and the gullies into the birch wood, and down to the bottom of the ravine in three jumps, or get the village boys to play a game of snowball with him and try out his strength. The little imp egged him on; he resisted as long as he could, and at last jumped down the front steps into the yard in winter, without his cap, ran through the gate, seized a ball of snow in each hand, and flew toward a group of boys. The fresh wind cut into his face, the frost pinched his ears, the cold air entered his mouth and throat, his chest expanded with joy—he ran along faster and faster, laughing and screaming. There were the boys; he flung a snowball at them but missed; he was not used to it. He was about to pick up another when his face was smothered by a huge lump of snow: he fell; his face hurt from the new sensation; he was enjoying it all, he was laughing, and there were tears in his eyes.

Meanwhile there was an uproar at home: darling Ilya had vanished! A noise, shouts. Zakhar rushed into the yard, followed by Vaska, Mitka, Vanka—all running about in confusion. Two dogs ran madly after them, catching them by the heels, for, as everyone knows, dogs cannot bear to see a running man. Shouting and yelling, the servants raced through the village, followed by the barking dogs. At last they came across the boys and began meting out justice: pulled them by the hair and ears, hit them across the back, and told off their fathers. Then they got hold of the young master, wrapped him in the sheepskin they had brought, then in his father's fur coat and two blankets, and carried him home in triumph. At home they had despaired of seeing him again, giving him up for lost; but the joy of his parents at seeing him alive and unhurt was indescribable. They offered up thanks to the Lord, then gave him mint and elderberry tea to drink, followed by raspberry tea in the evening, and kept him three days in bed—yet only one thing could have done him good—playing snowball again. . . .

(1849; 1859 as part of the novel Oblomov)

IVAN TURGENEV

Ivan Turgenev (1818–1883) was the first Russian writer to become widely known in the West. This was due in part to his prolonged stay in France and Germany, during which he made the acquaintance of leading French and English writers—the Goncourt brothers, Flaubert, Henry James—and became accepted in Parisian literary life, and in part to the qualities of the novels and stories he wrote. They seemed to be very "European"—similar to what French and English writers were writing—and therefore found a ready-made audience in the West. His works are "meticulously crafted," in the words of Milton Ehre, a scholar of Russian novels, in contrast to the open-ended, expansive form of the central stream of nineteenth-century Russian fiction.

Turgenev was brought up on his mother's family's country estate in the Orel Province. His mother was brutal, dominating, and extremely rich. His father came from a distinguished but impoverished aristocratic family; their marriage was one of convenience. Turgenev reacted to the bullying of his mother (who ruled the serfs with an iron hand) with intense revulsion. This sensitive, gentle writer (whom friends in France later called "the tender barbarian") was deeply wounded by his mother's brutalities.

He studied successively at the universities of Moscow and St. Petersburg, and in 1838 left for a European journey. He became acquainted with the intellectual elite of Europe as well as of his own country.

Turgenev had a lifelong liaison, some of the time a ménage à trois, with a celebrated singer (half gypsy, half Spanish), Madame Pauline Garcia Viardot, who was married to a wealthy French count. Turgenev spent most of his life abroad, living in Baden and in Paris. His long residence in Europe and some aspects of his novels aroused the dis-

pleasure both of Dostoyevsky, who felt Turgenev had abandoned Russia, was too pro-Western, and did not keep in close enough touch with life inside Russia, and of Tolstoy, who objected to Turgenev's aristocratic attitudes.

In Russia, Turgenev's reception had mixed literary and sociopolitical causes. He won his first literary acclaim with a series of sketches, with minimal plot, in which a sensitive, upper-class narrator, usually a hunter, described with warm sympathy his meetings with peasants and other members of the lower classes—and also gave beautiful nature descriptions. These brief, lyrical stories were first published individually and later collected in one volume under the title Notes of a Hunter (1852). Like Harriet Beecher Stowe's Uncle Tom's Cabin in the United States, Turgenev's sketches had a great political and social impact in stirring Russian opinion against the system of serfdom and aroused sympathy for the life of poor, simple people. The stories were a factor in eventually bringing about the freeing of the serfs in the Emancipation Decrees of 1861.

His Diary of a Superfluous Man (1850) popularized the label "superfluous man" for a category of the Russian character, which Griboedov, Pushkin, Lermontov, and others had already made a familiar Russian literary as well as social type. In 1852 he was arrested and briefly imprisoned for having published a eulogistic obituary of Gogol, of whom the government disapproved at that time. This arrest gave Turgenev highly esteemed credentials as a dissident.

Turgenev's best known work, Fathers and Sons (1861), is one of the two high points of Russian realism in nineteenth-century fiction— the other being Tolstoy's Anna Karenina. The novel presents three major love relationships between three major couples, and conflicts between and within two generations. The novel caused much controversy about the views advanced by the characters and about where Turgenev's own sympathies lay in the conflicts between the "nihilism" of Bazarov, a member of the younger generation, and the traditional attitudes of the older generation.

Turgenev's novels are all quite short. Several of them mingle personal concerns—mainly love—with social inquiry. Turgenev's later socially focused novels are exemplified by Virgin Soil (1871). Those dealing primarily with love are exemplified by Spring Torrents (1872). Turgenev also wrote several plays. A Month in the Country (written in 1850, published in 1855), a delicate psychological drama, has been performed frequently all over the world.

The glory of Turgenev's writing is in the creation of poetic moods, atmosphere, and nuances of subtle feelings. His genius lies also in *rendering the poetry of natural settings. His characters are subtle, delicate, fine. One wonders at such contrasting images of Russians of the nineteenth century as those of Gogol and those of Turgenev.*

Turgenev was a gentle person. His fiction is full of reticences, of the suggestion half spoken, of beautiful female characters. There is no such unrestrained feverishness as that in Dostoyevsky; rather, there are the closely worked out, orderly architectonics of the story as a whole. He does not deal with supercelestial questions. "When I am not dealing with concrete characters," Turgenev wrote, "I am completely lost, and I do not know where to turn. It always seems to me that the exact opposite of what I am saying could be asserted with equal justice. But if I am speaking of a red nose and blond hair, then the hair is blond and the nose red; no amount of reflection will change that."

Among the wide range of emotional situations Turgenev excelled at rendering, love is preeminent. "First Love" (1860) is a story that shows repeated discoveries—of what love can be, as well as of domination and self-control. All this is crowned by the vision of overpowering passion and self-sacrifice for love. "First Love" is not a social or ideological novel; the frame story is conventional, even stereotypical. The structure is that of ever higher gradations, of seeing with ever deeper and closer insight loves of increasingly greater intensity. The theme can be seen as an unusual initiation. The rich tissue of social detail, class distinctions, and literary references is melted down in the caldron of passion and self-destruction.

In politics Turgenev was a democrat and a liberal, deeply convinced of the values of social justice and enlightenment. His portrait of Belinsky conveys as much about Turgenev's own sensibility and ideals as about Belinsky. It is the best that could be said about the entire peculiar grouping known as the Russian intelligentsia.

FIRST LOVE

The guests had gone long ago. The clock struck half past twelve. Besides the host there was no one left in the room but Sergey Nikolaich and Vladimir Petrovich. The host rang for the servant to take away the remains of the supper.

"So we are agreed," he said, settling himself comfortably in his armchair and lighting a cigar. "Each of us is to tell the story of his first love. You begin, Sergey Nikolaich."

Sergey Nikolaich, a chubby little man with puffy features and a fair complexion, looked at the host and raised his eyes to the ceiling. "I never had a first love," he said at last. "I started straight away with my second."

"How was that?"

"Quite simple. I was eighteen when I first began paying court to a certain charming young lady, but I behaved as if this were nothing new for me, exactly as I afterward made love to others. As a matter of fact I fell in love for the first and last time at the age of six, with my nurse; but that was a very long time ago, and the details of our relations have escaped my memory, and even if I could remember them, whom could they interest?"

"So what shall we do?" began the host. "There was nothing very entertaining about my first love, either; I was never in love before I met Anna Ivanovna, my present wife, and the course of our love ran smooth from the very first: our parents made the match, we soon became fond of one another, and got married without delay. My story can be told in very few words. I admit, gentlemen, that when I raised the question of first love I was counting on you, who are—well, if not exactly old—still not young bachelors; perhaps *you* can tell us something interesting, Vladimir Petrovich?"

Vladimir Petrovich, a man of about forty with grizzled black hair, said hesitatingly: "The story of my first love really is somewhat unusual."

"Ha!" exclaimed the host and Sergey Nikolaich both at once. "All the better. . . . Let us hear it."

"Very well . . . but no, I will not tell you the story, I am a poor storyteller, I'm sure to make it either dry and brief, or lengthy and false. If you don't mind, I'd rather put down all I can remember in a notebook, and then read it to you."

His companions protested at first, but Vladimir Petrovich had his own way in the end. They met again a fortnight later, and Vladimir Petrovich proved as good as his word.

This is what he read to his listeners out of his notebook:

I

I was sixteen years old at the time. What I am going to relate took place during the summer of 1833.

I was living in Moscow with my parents. They had rented a house outside the town, at Kaluga Gate, just opposite Neskuchny Gardens. I was studying at the university, but by no means overexerting myself.

I enjoyed perfect liberty and did just as I pleased, especially after parting with my last tutor, a Frenchman, who was unable to forget that he had descended upon Russia *comme une bombe*, and who lolled on his bed all day with a defiant air. My father treated me with indulgent indifference; my mother hardly took any notice of me, though she had no other children; other cares engrossed all her attention. My father, still a young man and very good-looking, had married her for her money; she was ten years his senior. My mother led a melancholy life: always anxious, jealous, low-spirited, though never in my father's presence; she stood in great awe of him, and he bore himself coldly aloof, with an air of severity. I have never met anyone so exquisitely refined, so confident, so imperious as my father.

I shall never forget my first weeks in that house. The weather was perfect; we moved on the ninth of May, the feast of St. Nicholas. I strolled about the grounds and Neskuchny Gardens, sometimes wandering beyond the confines of the city; I usually took a book with me, Kaidanov's *History* or something of that sort, but seldom so much as opened it; I chiefly occupied myself in reciting poetry, for which I had a very good memory; my blood tingled, and my heart ached with a strange, exquisite pain; I was in constant expectation and fear of something, marveling at everything, ready for anything; my imagination played and hovered around the same set of ideas all the time, like swifts hovering over a belfry at dawn. I fell into reveries, grew melancholy, sometimes even shed tears; but, through all these tears and sudden fits of sadness, whether occasioned by some melodious line or by the beauty of the evening, the joyous sensation of youthful life, turbulent and seething, made itself felt, like the grass sending up its blades through the earth in the spring.

I had a pony for my own use. I would saddle it myself and ride far away, setting it at a gallop and imagining myself a knight at a tournament (how cheerfully the wind whistled past my ears!), or, raising my face to the sky, I would absorb its radiant light and blueness with my receptive soul.

As I remember it, the image of woman, the faintest apparition of a woman's love, seldom, if at all, took definite shape in my mind; but in all that I thought or felt there lurked the half-conscious, shy presentiment of something new, ineffably sweet—in a word, something feminine.

This presentiment, this constant expectation, permeated my whole being; I breathed it, I felt it coursing through my veins, in every drop of my blood . . . and very soon it was destined to come true.

The main building in our country abode was a wooden house with columns and two low-roofed wings; a tiny factory turning out cheap wallpaper was housed in the one on the left side. I often went there to watch a dozen lean, unkempt, sallow-faced urchins in dirty overalls leap on the wooden levers, which bore down on the rectangular frame of the press, to stamp out the gaudy patterns with the weight of their puny bodies. The annex on the right was unoccupied and to let. One day, three weeks or so after the ninth of May, its shutters were flung open and female faces showed at the windows; some family had taken the annex. I remember my mother asking our butler that day at dinner who our new neighbors were, and on hearing the name of Princess Zasekina, saying first, not without a certain respect: "Oh, Princess . . ." and then: "Probably hard up."

"They had three *izvozchiks* for their move," the butler remarked, placing a dish on the table respectfully. "They have no carriage of their own, and the furniture is very cheap looking."

"Yes," said my mother. "But still I'm glad. . . ."

My father cast an icy glance at her and she said no more.

And truly, Princess Zasekina could not have been a rich woman: the annex she had rented was so rickety, small, and low-ceilinged that no family of the slightest affluence would have consented to live there. But I did not take much heed of the conversation at the time. The rank of princess did not impress me much: I had just read Schiller's *Robbers*.

II

I was in the habit of sauntering about the grounds with a gun every evening, in the hope of shooting crows. I had long felt hatred for those furtive, cunning, predatory birds. On the day of which I am speaking, I went out on my usual quest, and, after having followed every path in vain (the crows caught sight of me and were uttering short caws somewhere in the distance), I found myself close to the low fence between our part of the grounds and the narrow slip of garden behind the right-hand annex and pertaining to it. I walked by with my eyes lowered. Suddenly I heard voices; I glanced over the fence and stood as if petrified—a strange spectacle presented itself to my eyes.

A few paces away, in a clearing among green raspberry bushes, stood a tall, slender girl in a dress of pink, striped material, a white kerchief on her head; four young men crowded around her, and she was striking each of them by turns on the forehead with those small gray-blue flowers so familiar to children, though I do not know their name. Their petals form tiny sacks that burst open with a pop when struck against a firm surface. The young men offered their foreheads so eagerly, and in all the girl's movements (she had her profile turned to me) there was so much that was imperious, affectionate, mocking, and attractive that I almost cried out in my wonder and delight, and felt I would have given anything to have my own forehead slapped by those dainty fingers. My gun slipped to the grass, I forgot everything, devouring with my eyes the slender waist, the graceful neck, the beautiful arms, the slightly disheveled fair hair showing beneath the white kerchief, the intelligent eyes, half hidden by the lashes, the delicate cheek below the lashes. . . .

"Young man—hi! young man!" cried a voice close to my ear. "Is that the way to behave, staring at strange young ladies?"

I started, dumbfounded. Quite near, on the other side of the fence, stood a man with short black hair, regarding me ironically. At that very moment the girl turned toward me. I saw two large gray eyes set in a lively and animated face, and suddenly the face broke out into laughter, white teeth gleamed, the brows were raised in a comical manner. . . . I flushed, snatched up my gun, and, pursued by peals of ringing but by no means unfriendly laughter, rushed into my room, flung myself on the bed, and covered my face with my hands. My heart was plunging wildly; I felt at the same time ashamed and happy; never before had I been so agitated.

After resting for a short time, I combed my hair, brushed my coat, and went down to tea. The image of the young girl was before me all the time, and though my heart no longer plunged wildly, I was conscious of an exquisite pang now and then.

"What's the matter?" my father asked me suddenly. "Have you killed a crow?"

I wanted to tell him all, but refrained, merely indulging in a secret smile. Before going to bed I twirled two or three times on my heel for some reason, put pomade on my hair, and lying down, slept like a top all night. Toward morning I woke for a moment, raised my head from the pillow, cast a delighted look all around, and went to sleep again.

III

"How can I get to know them?" was my first thought on waking. I went into the garden before breakfast, but I did not venture too close to the fence and I saw no one. After breakfast I strolled up and down the street in front of their house, looking into the windows from a distance. . . . Once I thought I saw *her* face behind the curtain and retreated in alarm. "But I must get to know her," I thought as I paced about the stretch of sandy ground in front of Neskuchny Gardens. "But how? That is the question." I recalled the minutest details of yesterday's encounter; somehow the picture of her laughing at me remained clearest of all in my memory. Destiny, however, had been busying itself on my account while I was fretting and laying plans.

While I was away, my mother received from her new neighbor a letter written on gray paper and sealed with the dark sealing wax generally used on postal orders and bottles of cheap wine. In this letter, which was written in an unrefined hand, and full of bad grammar, the princess begged my mother to use her influence on her behalf: my mother, she wrote, was on good terms with certain influential folk on whom the fate of the princess depended, and that of her children, for she had some very important lawsuits on. "I appeal to you," she wrote, "as one well-bread lady to another, and at the same time I take pleasure in this oppertunity." She wound up her letter with a request to be received by my mother. I found my mother in a very bad humor: my father was away and she had no one to advise her. Not to answer "a well-bread lady," and a princess at that, was out of the question, but how to answer, my mother did not quite know. To write a note in French she felt would be not quite the thing, but my mother was not very strong in the spelling of Russian herself, and she knew it and was loath to expose herself. So she was glad when I came and immediately sent me to the princess, bidding me to tell her by word of mouth that my mother would be glad to oblige Her Ladyship in any way she could, and was prepared to receive her between twelve and one o'clock. This unexpectedly rapid fulfillment of my secret wishes, while it made me very happy, at the same time alarmed me; but I did not show the embarrassment I felt, and went up to my room—to put on a new tie and frock coat. I had to go about in a jacket and turn-down collar at home, much to my displeasure.

IV

In the shabby, cramped passage of the wing, which I entered trembling all over, I was met by an ancient, gray-haired manservant, with a dark, coppery complexion, morose, piglike eyes, and such deep wrinkles on his brow and temples as I had never before seen. In his hand was a plate with the remains of a salted herring on it, and he asked me gruffly, closing the door of the room with his foot:

"What do you want?"

"Is Princess Zasekina at home?" I asked.

"Vonifaty!" came in a shaky female voice from behind the door.

Without a word, the servant turned on his heel, revealing the well-worn back of his livery, adorned by a solitary rusty button stamped with a coat of arms, and walked away, putting the plate on the floor.

"Have you been to the police station?" the same shaky voice asked. The servant mumbled something in answer. "What did you say?" went on the voice. "Somebody to see me? The young gentleman from next door? Well, ask him in."

"Go into the drawing room, please," said the servant, reappearing and lifting the plate from the floor. I straightened my tie and went into the "drawing room."

I found myself in a small, not very tidy room, with shabby furniture, which looked as if it had been dumped down in a hurry. By the window, in an armchair with a broken arm, sat a woman of fifty or so, with a plain face; she had no cap on and wore an old green dress with a gaudy worsted scarf at the neck. Her small black eyes were fixed on my person.

I walked up to her and made my bow.

"Have I the honor of addressing Princess Zasekina?"

"I am Princess Zasekina; are you the son of Mr. V.?"

"Yes, madam. I have come with a message from my mother."

"Won't you sit down? Vonifaty! Where are my keys, have you seen them anywhere?"

I informed Princess Zasekina of my mother's reply to her letter. She listened to me, drumming on the windowsill with thick red fingers, and when I was finished, again fixed her gaze on me.

"Very good; I will be sure to come," she at last brought out. "You look very young! How old may you be?"

"Sixteen," I faltered.

The princess pulled some greasy papers, scribbled all over, out of her pocket and, holding them close to her eyes, began looking through them.

"A very nice age," she said suddenly, turning and fidgeting in her chair. "You mustn't stand on ceremony with us. We are all very simple here."

"Much too simple," I thought to myself, casting a look of instinctive repulsion over her ungainly person.

At that moment the other door into the drawing room was flung open, and the girl I had seen the day before appeared in the doorway. She raised her hand, and a smile flitted over her lips.

"My daughter," said the princess, pointing with her elbow in the direction of the door. "Zina, this is the son of our neighbor, Mr. V. What is your name, pray?"

"Vladimir," I answered, rising and almost stammering with excitement.

"And your patronymic?"

"Petrovich."

"Fancy! I used to know a chief of police called Vladimir Petrovich. You needn't look for my keys, Vonifaty, they're in my pocket."

The young girl went on looking at me with her mocking smile, her eyes slightly narrowed, her head a little on one side.

"I have seen Monsieur Voldemar before," she began. (The silvery tones of her voice sent a thrill through me.) "You don't mind me calling you by your Christian name?"

"Why, of course not!" I stammered out.

"Where was that?" asked the princess. The young princess did not answer her mother.

"Have you anything to do just now?" she asked, not taking her eyes off me.

"No, indeed!"

"Would you like to help me wind up some wool? Come with me."

With a nod of her head she left the drawing room. I followed her.

The furniture was less shabby and arranged with more taste in the room that we now entered. Not that I was in a condition to notice anything at the moment: I moved about as one in a dream; a sensation of bliss carried almost to the point of imbecility seemed to affect all my limbs.

The younger princess sat down, got out a skein of red wool, and, pointing to a chair opposite her, carefully unwound it on to my out-stretched hands. She did all this in silence, with a comical air of leisure, a serene, arch smile on her parted lips. She began winding the wool around a card bent in two, and suddenly shot such a swift radiant glance at me that I involuntarily lowered my eyes. When her eyes, which were usually narrowed, opened wide for a moment, her face was completely changed—her features seemed to be suddenly irradiated.

"I wonder what you thought of me yesterday, Monsieur Volde-mar?" she said, breaking the silence. "I suppose you thoroughly dis-approved of me."

"I . . . Princess . . . I did not think anything. . . . How could I? . . ." I answered in confusion.

"Look here!" she said. "You don't know me yet; I'm a strange creature; I always want everyone to tell me the truth. I heard you say you were sixteen. I am twenty-one; you see how much older I am, and therefore you must always speak the truth to me . . . and obey me," she added. "Look at me, why don't you look me in the face?"

My embarrassment became still greater; I raised my eyes to hers, however. She smiled, but not as before; this time it was a smile of approval.

"Go on, look at me!" she said, lowering her voice indulgently. "I don't mind. I like your face; I have a feeling we are going to be friends. Do you like me?" she added archly.

"Princess . . ." I began.

"In the first place, you are to call me Zinaida Alexandrovna, and in the second, I can't bear the way children . . . young men," she corrected herself, "have of not saying what they think straight out. Leave that to grown-ups. You do like me, don't you?"

Although her frankness delighted me, I could not help being somewhat offended. Anxious to show her she was not dealing with a little boy, I said, trying to assume an air of ponderous familiarity:

"I like you very much, Zinaida Alexandrovna, of course I do, I have not the slightest desire to conceal the fact. . . ."

She slowly shook her head at me.

"Have you got a tutor?" she suddenly asked.

"No, I haven't had a tutor for a long time." This was a lie; hardly a month had elapsed since I had parted with my French tutor.

"Oh, I see you are quite grown up."

She tapped lightly on my fingers. "Hold your arms straight!" And she began unwinding the wool with great diligence.

Taking advantage of the fact that she was looking down at her work, I proceeded to study her, first surreptitiously, then more and more boldly. Her face seemed still more charming to me than it had the day before, the features were so delicate, so intelligent, so sweet. She sat with her back to the window, on which hung a white curtain; a sunbeam, penetrating through the curtain, streamed softly over her fluffy golden hair, her innocent neck, sloping shoulders, her tender, calm bosom. I looked at her, and how close and familiar she seemed to have become! I felt as if I had known her for ages, and that I had known nothing, had never really lived before I met her. . . . She was wearing a dark, rather worn dress with an apron over it. I felt as if I would like to stroke every pleat of this dress and this apron. The toes of her shoes peeped out from beneath her dress. I would have loved to prostrate myself in adoration at those shoes. . . . "And here I am," I mused, "sitting before her. . . . I have made her acquaintance. . . . Good heavens—what bliss!" I all but leaped from my seat in my ecstasy, but checked myself in time and only shuffled my feet like a child who has been given something nice to eat.

I was as content as a fish in its native element, and I wished I could stay in that room, on that chair, forever.

The lowered eyelids were gently raised, and again her luminous eyes shed their kindly radiance on me, and again she smiled.

"How you look at me!" she said slowly, shaking her finger at me.

I flushed crimson. "She understands everything, she sees everything," flashed through my mind. "And how could she help seeing and understanding everything?"

There was a sudden sound in the next room—the clatter of a sword.

"Zina!" cried the princess from the drawing room. "Belovzorov has brought you a kitten."

"A kitten!" exclaimed Zinaida, and leaping from her chair, she flung the ball of wool on my lap and ran out of the room.

I, too, rose and, placing the wool on the windowsill, walked into the drawing room and stood still in amazement: in the middle of the room, its four paws spread out on the floor, lay a tabby kitten; Zinaida was kneeling over it, gently holding up its head. Beside the old princess, taking up almost the whole space between the windows, stood a fine young man, a Hussar, fair, curly-haired, with a ruddy face and prominent eyes.

"What a funny little thing!" cooed Zinaida. "Its eyes aren't gray, they're green, and look what great big ears! Thank you, Victor Yegorych! You're a dear!"

The Hussar, in whom I recognized one of the young men I had seen the day before, smiled and bowed, his spurs clicking, and the metal rings of his scabbard tinkling.

"You were pleased to say yesterday you wished to have a tabby kitten with big ears . . . so I got one. Your word is law." The young man made another bow.

The kitten mewed faintly and began sniffing at the floor.

"It's hungry!" exclaimed Zinaida. "Vonifaty! Sonya! Bring some milk!"

A maid in a shabby yellow dress, with a faded kerchief around her neck, came in, carrying a saucer of milk, which she placed before the kitten. The kitten started, screwed up its eyes, and began lapping.

"How rosy its tongue is!" remarked Zinaida, bending her head almost to the floor and trying to peer sideways right under the kitten's chin.

The kitten drank its fill and began purring, lifting its front paws up and down primly. Zinaida got up and turned to the maid. "Take it away," she said indifferently.

"Your hand—for the kitten," said the Hussar, smirking, his massive frame wriggling in the tight new uniform.

"Both!" replied Zinaida, and held her hands out to him. While he was kissing them, she looked at me over her shoulder.

I stood motionless, unable to make up my mind whether to laugh, make some remark, or remain silent. Suddenly, through the open door into the passage, I saw our footman Fyodor making signs at me. I walked over to him mechanically.

"What is it?" I asked.

"Your mama sent me for you," he whispered. "She is angry with you for not coming back with the answer."

"Why, how long have I been here?"

"Over an hour."

"Over an hour!" I repeated involuntarily and, going back to the drawing room, began to take my leave, bowing and scraping my feet.

"Where are you going?" the younger princess asked me, shooting me a glance over the Hussar's shoulder.

"I've got to go home. So I may tell my mother," I added, turning toward the old lady, "to expect you sometime after one, I presume."

"Yes, tell her that, sir!"

The old princess hastily pulled out her snuffbox and inhaled a pinch so loudly that I actually started. "Tell her that," she repeated, blinking tearfully and wheezing.

I made another bow, turned on my heel, and walked out of the room, with that sensation of discomfort in my back so familiar to any very young man who knows he is being watched.

"Mind you come and see us again, Monsieur Voldemar," cried Zinaida with another of her laughs.

"Why does she laugh so much?" I thought as I walked home, accompanied by Fyodor, who, though he said nothing, followed me in obvious disapproval. My mother scolded me and wondered what I could have been doing all that time at the princess's. I did not answer, but went up to my room. All of a sudden I felt profoundly melancholy. It was all I could do not to burst into tears. . . . I was jealous of the Hussar!

V

The princess, true to her promise, called on my mother, and—failed to make herself liked. I was not present at the meeting, but I heard my mother tell my father at the table that that Princess Zasekina seemed *une femme très vulgaire*, that she had tired her out with requests to speak to Prince Sergey about her, that she was full of lawsuits and disputes—*des vilaines affaires d'argent*—and that she must be a regular *intrigante*. My mother added, however, that she had invited her and her daughter to dinner for the next day (when I heard the words "and her daughter," I bent low over my plate), for, after all, they were neighbors, and the name was a good one. In answer to all this, my father told my mother he remembered now who this lady was; that in his youth he had known the late Prince Zasekin, a very well bred, but vain and foolish man; that he was known to society as *le Parisien*, owing to his prolonged sojourn in Paris; that he had once been very rich but had gambled away his fortune, and had then, for some reason, or other, probably for money—though he could have made a better choice—here my father gave one of his icy smiles—married the daughter of some petty official, and afterward gone in for speculation, and finally ruined himself.

"I hope she does not mean to try and borrow money," remarked my mother.

"I wouldn't be surprised if she did," my father said calmly. "Does she speak French?"

"Very badly."

"Hm. But what does that matter? I think you said you had invited her daughter, too; someone told me she was a nice girl, and well educated."

"If so, she does not take after her mother."

"Nor her father," retorted my father. "For though an educated man, he was very stupid."

My mother sighed and fell into a reverie. My father said no more. I felt exceedingly uncomfortable during this entire conversation.

After dinner I went into the garden but did not take my gun. I had vowed to myself that I would not go near the "Zasekin garden," but some irresistible force seemed to draw me toward it, and not in vain. Hardly had I approached the fence when I saw Zinaida. This time she was alone. She held a book in her hands and was walking slowly along the path. She did not notice me.

I almost let her pass, but caught myself in time and gave a little cough.

She turned around without stopping, merely putting aside the broad blue ribbon of her round straw hat and looking at me with a faint smile before turning her eyes to the page again. I took off my cap, loitered about for a while, and left the spot with a heavy heart. *"Que suis-je pour elle?"* I said to myself in French (God knows why).

Familiar steps sounded behind me; I looked back and saw my father walking toward me with his usual brisk, light gait.

"Was that the princess's daughter?" he asked.

"Yes."

"So you know her?"

"I saw her this morning at her mother's."

My father stopped, turned sharply on his heel, and walked back. When he reached Zinaida's side, he bowed courteously. She returned the bow, though not without a certain expression of surprise on her face, and lowered her book. I saw her eyes follow him as he walked away. My father was always elegantly dressed, quite simply but with a taste that was all his own; but never had his figure seemed more graceful, or his gray hat set more becomingly on his ever so slightly thinning wavy hair.

I took a few steps toward Zinaida, but she did not so much as look at me, and raising her book once more, walked away.

VI

I spent the whole of the evening and the following morning in a kind of numb misery. I remember trying to work and taking up Kaidanov, but in vain did the rounded periods in the famous textbook flash before my eyes. I read at least ten times the words: "Julius Caesar was renowned for his valor in battle," and, finding I could make no sense of them, finally put the book down. Just before dinner I pomaded my hair again and again dressed myself up in my frock coat and tie.

"What's that for?" asked my mother. "You're not a student yet, and who knows whether you'll pass the examinations. Besides, your jacket is quite new; is it to be thrown aside?"

"But we have visitors to dinner," I whispered, almost desperate.

"Nonsense! Those visitors don't matter!"

There was nothing for it but to submit. I changed into my jacket but did not take off my tie. The princess and her daughter arrived half an hour before dinnertime; the old woman had thrown a yellow shawl over the green dress that was already familiar to me, and wore an old-fashioned bonnet with flame-colored ribbons. She embarked immediately upon the subject of her promissory notes, sighed, complained of her poverty, whined, but deported herself without a trace of bashfulness, taking snuff as noisily and fidgeting in her chair as unconstrainedly as if she were at home. The idea that she was a princess did not seem to enter her mind. Zinaida, on the other hand, was prim, almost supercilious, every inch a princess. A cold rigidity and gravity showed in her face, and I hardly recognized her; her smile and glance were different, too; but in this new guise she was no less beautiful in my eyes. She wore a barege dress patterned with irregular pale-blue scrolls; her hair fell in long ringlets on either side of her face, in the English manner—a style well suited to the cold expression of her face. My father sat next to her during dinner and kept his neighbor entertained with his refined and quiet courtesy. Every now and then he would look into her face, and every now and then she would look at him; and there was something strange, almost hostile, in those glances! They conversed in French; I remember being struck with the purity of Zinaida's pronunciation. The older princess behaved at the table with the freedom she had already displayed, and seemed perfectly at her ease, eating a great deal and praising the food. My mother obviously found her tiresome, and answered her with a kind of melancholy disdain; my father occasionally winced almost imperceptibly. My mother did not care for Zinaida, either. "Proud girl!" she said on the next day. "I'd like to know what she finds to be so proud of, *avec sa mine de grisette!*"

"You have evidently never seen a *grisette* in your life," remarked my father.

"And thank God for that!"

"Thank God, indeed . . . but that being the case, you are not entitled to judge of them."

Zinaida took not the slightest notice of me. Soon after dinner, her mother took her leave.

"So I may count on your protection, Maria Nikolayevna and Pyotr Vasilyevich?" she said in a singsong voice, addressing both my parents. "There it is! I have known better times, and now they're gone. Here I am—Her Ladyship, if you please!" she added with an unpleasant laugh. "Honor's not much good when there isn't any food."

My father made her a deferential bow and saw her out of the room. I stood there, in my short jacket, gazing at the floor like one condemned to death. Zinaida's treatment had completely annihilated me. Judge of my surprise, therefore, when, on passing me, she said in a rapid whisper, the former kindly look in her eyes: "Come and see us at eight this evening, mind you do, now. . . ." I could only fling out my arms in astonishment—but she had gone, throwing a white scarf over her head.

VII

Punctually at eight, dressed in my frock coat, my hair brushed into a tuft on the top of my head, I entered the passage of the wing occupied by the princess. The old manservant, casting a morose glance at me, rose reluctantly from the bench on which he was sitting. The sound of merry voices came from the drawing room. I opened the door and stepped back in amazement. In the middle of the room, on a chair, stood the young princess, holding a man's hat in her hands; five men crowded around the chair. They were all trying to get their hands into the inside of the hat, while she held it out of their reach, shaking it. On catching sight of me, she shouted: "Wait, wait! Here's a fresh visitor, he must have a ticket, too," and, jumping lightly off the chair, she took me by my coat sleeve. "Come on," she said, "don't stand there! Messieurs, allow me to introduce you to one another: this is Monsieur Voldemar, our neighbor's son. And these"—here she turned to me, pointing to the guests one after another—"are Count Malevsky, Dr. Lushin, the poet Maidanov, retired Captain Nirmatsky, and Belovzorov of the Hussars—you've already met him. I hope you'll all be friends."

I was too embarrassed even to make a bow; in the person of Dr. Lushin I recognized the dark-haired gentleman who had ridiculed me so cruelly in the garden; the rest were all strangers to me.

"Count!" Zinaida went on. "Write out a ticket for Monsieur Voldemar."

"That's not fair," objected the count, speaking with a slight Polish accent. He was a handsome, dandified, dark individual with expressive brown eyes, a thin pale nose and a neat little mustache above the smallest of mouths. "*He* didn't play forfeits with us."

"Not fair, not fair!" echoed Belovzorov and the gentleman who had been introduced to me as a retired captain, a man of about forty years of age, his face atrociously pitted with smallpox, his hair as curly as a Negro's, round-shouldered, bandy-legged, and wearing an unbuttoned military coat without epaulets.

"Make him out a ticket, I tell you," repeated the princess. "I won't have sedition! It is Monsieur Voldemar's first day with us, and the law may be relaxed in his favor. Stop grumbling, now, and do as I tell you!"

The count shrugged his shoulders, but inclining his head submissively, he took up a pen in his white ringed fingers, tore a strip of paper, and began writing.

"Will you at least allow us to explain the rules to Monsieur Voldemar?" asked Lushin in a sneering voice. "He seems to be entirely at a loss. You see, young man, we're playing forfeits; the princess has been fined, and whoever gets the lucky ticket will be entitled to kiss her hand. Have I made myself clear?"

I only stared at him and stood there as if stunned, while the princess once more leaped onto the chair and began shaking the hat. Everybody reached out for it, I among them.

"Maidanov," said the princess, addressing a tall young man with a lean face, small myopic eyes, and long black hair, "being a poet, you must show magnanimity and let Monsieur Voldemar have your ticket as well as his own, so that he has two chances instead of one."

But Maidanov only shook his head, tossing back his long hair. I put my hand into the hat last, pulled out my ticket . . . and unfolded it. Judge of my feelings when I saw the word *kiss* on it!

"Kiss!" I cried out involuntarily.

"Bravo! He's won!" cried the princess instantly. "I'm so glad!" Descending from the chair, she looked into my eyes with a smile so sweet and calm that my heart seemed to turn within me. "Are *you* glad?"

"Me?" was all I could bring out.

"Sell me your ticket," blurted out Belovzorov close to my ear. "I'll give you a hundred rubles."

I shot the Hussar a withering glance that caused Zinaida to clap her hands and Lushin to exclaim: "Bravo!"

"But," continued Lushin, "as master of ceremonies I must insist on strict adherence to the rules. Monsieur Voldemar, go down on one knee! That is our custom."

Zinaida stood before me, her head a little on one side—as if to get a better view of me—and extended her hand to me with the utmost gravity. My vision went dim; I meant to go down on one knee, but fell on both, and touched Zinaida's fingers with my lips so awkwardly that I got a scratch on the tip of my nose from one of her nails.

"That'll do," said Lushin, helping me to get up.

The game of forfeits went on. Zinaida made me sit beside her. What penalties she invented! One of them fell to her own lot; she was called upon to represent "a monument." Choosing the ungainly Nirmatsky for her pedestal, she made him lie flat on his face and draw his head into his shoulders. Laughter never ceased for a moment. Brought

up as I had been in the sober seclusion of a respectable upper-class
home, was it to be wondered that all this noise and clatter, the unconstrained, almost riotous merry-making, the incredible intimacy with
strangers, fairly went to my head? I was intoxicated as with wine. I
began laughing and talking louder than anyone else in the room, so
that even the old princess, who was in the next room with some official
she had summoned for a consultation, came in to see what was the
matter. But I felt so happy that, as the saying goes, I did not turn a
hair, nor did I give a straw for the derisive remarks of some or the
black looks of others. Zinaida continued to single me out and never
let me leave her side. One of the penalties I received was to sit close
to her, the same silk kerchief covering both our heads, and tell her *my
secret*. I remember my sensations when our two heads were suddenly
enveloped by a fragrant, stifling, diaphanous haze, when through this
haze her eyes shone so soft and so near, and her breath came so warm,
and her teeth gleamed, and the ends of her hair tickled and stung me.
I was silent; she smiled mysteriously and archly, and at last whispered:
"Well?" while I only blushed, and laughed, and turned my head away,
almost breathless. We soon got tired of forfeits and turned to a game
with a piece of string. Heavens, what delight I felt when, during a fit
of abstraction, I received a sharp rap on the knuckles from her! How
I pretended to be woolgathering again, and how she purposely avoided
touching my hands, just to tease me!

The pranks and tricks we played that evening! We played the
piano, we sang and we danced, we pretended to be Gypsies camping,
dressing up Nirmatsky as a bear and making him drink salty water.
Count Malevsky showed us all manner of card tricks, finishing up by
shuffling the cards for whist and dealing them out so that he got all
the trumps, for which Lushin "heartily congratulated" him. Maidanov
recited a few passages from his poem "The Assassin" (the romantic
movement was then at its height), which he intended to have published
in a black binding with blood-red capital letters. We stole the cap from
the knees of the official and made him dance the *Kazachok* before we
would return it. A woman's cap was put on old Vonifaty's head, and
Zinaida donned a man's hat. . . . But it would be impossible to relate
all we did. Belovzorov alone kept aloof in a corner for the most part,
knitting his brows and sulking. . . . Every now and then his eyes became
bloodshot, an angry flush suffused his features, and it seemed as if he
were just about to rush upon us all and scatter us like so many chips;
but the young princess would look at him, shaking an admonishing
finger, and he would go back to his corner again.

At last we were exhausted. Though the old princess was still perfectly game, as she herself put it, and did not mind the noise, even she felt tired and wished for a rest. Soon after eleven supper was served; it consisted of a piece of old dry cheese and cold pies with minced ham, all of which I found more delicious than any pâté; there was only one bottle of wine, and there was something queer about it—it was very dark, with a bulgy neck, and the wine itself tasted of red paint; nobody drank it, anyhow. Faint and worn out with happiness, I left the annex; Zinaida pressed my hand firmly as she bade me good-bye, smiling her mysterious smile again.

I felt the heavy, moist breath of the night on my heated face; there was thunder in the air; black clouds were gradually increased in size as they crept across the sky, their vague contours continually changing. A breeze shuddered restlessly among the dark treetops, and somewhere far away, on the other side of the sky, the thunder seemed to be grumbling to itself, with angry hollow sounds.

I went to my room by the back door. My servant slept on the floor and I had to step over him. He woke up, saw me, and reported that my mother was displeased with me again and had wanted to send for me, but my father would not let her. (Never before had I gone to bed without bidding good night to my mother and asking for her blessing.) Well—it could not be helped!

Telling the man I would take my clothes off myself and go to bed, I snuffed out the candle. . . . But I neither undressed nor lay down.

I sat down on a chair, remaining on it long, like one under a spell. . . . What I felt was so new, so sweet! I sat motionless, looking around me, taking deep breaths, every now and then giving vent to soundless laughter at some recollection, or going all cold inside, as I thought: now I am in love, so this is what it is like, love. Zinaida's face floated gently before my eyes, never quite out of sight, her lips smiled mysteriously, she looked at me from the corners of her eyes, interrogative, musing, affectionate . . . as she had when she bade me good-bye. At last I got up, went on tiptoe toward my bed, carefully, without taking my clothes off, laid my head on the pillow, as if afraid an abrupt movement would disturb that with which I was filled to the brim. . . .

I lay down but did not even close my eyes. Soon I noticed that faint reflections were stealing into the room. I sat up and looked toward the window. Its frame stood out distinctly against the mysterious whiteness of the panes. A storm, I said to myself, and that is exactly what it was; but it was somewhere far away, so far that the sound of thunder did not reach my ears; only faint, long forks of lightning flashed incessantly across the sky; or rather they did not so much flash as quiver and twitch, like the wing of a dying bird. I got out of bed, went over to the window, and stood there till daylight. . . .

The lightning did not stop for a single instant; it was what the Russian country folk call a "sparrow's night." I gazed at the mute stretch of sand, at the massed shadows in Neskuchny Gardens, at the pale-yellow facades of distant buildings, which seemed to quiver with each faint flash of lightning. . . . I gazed and could not tear myself away from the sight; those mute lightnings, that restrained brilliance, seemed like a response to the mute, mysterious impulses flashing within me. The day was beginning; the dawn showed in crimson patches. With the approach of the sun the flashes of lightning grew paler and shorter; they quivered at longer and longer intervals, until they finally disappeared in the sober, prosaic light of the coming day. . . .

The lightning within me disappeared, too. I felt a great fatigue and stillness . . . but the image of Zinaida continued to hover triumphantly over my soul. This image, however, seemed calm now; like the swan rising from the reeds, it detached itself from its unbeautiful surroundings, and as I fell asleep, I once more prostrated myself before it in trusting adoration. . . .

Oh, submissive emotions, low sounds, gentleness and serenity of a soul deeply moved, the melting radiance of first love—where are you now, where?

VIII

The next morning, when I came down to tea, my mother scolded me, though less than I had expected, and made me tell her how I had spent the evening. I told her briefly, omitting most of the details and endeavoring to make it all sound as innocent as possible.

"But still they're not quite *comme il faut*," remarked my mother, "and you have no call to hang around them; you have your examinations to prepare for."

Being well aware that my mother's anxiety about my studies would not go further than these few words, I did not take the trouble to argue with her; but after morning tea, my father, taking my arm, led me into the garden and made me tell him all I had seen at the Zasekins'.

My father had a strange influence over me, and our relations were altogether strange. He took scarcely any interest in my education, but at the same time never said anything to wound me; he respected my liberty, he was even, if the expression is permissible, polite to me . . .

but he never admitted me to the slightest intimacy. I loved him, I admired him, I considered him the embodiment of masculine excellence, and oh, how I could have worshiped him but for my constant awareness of being kept deliberately at arm's length! When he wished to, he could instantaneously, with a single word, a single gesture, instill in me boundless confidence. At such moments my soul would expand, and I would chatter away, as I would with an intelligent friend or indulgent mentor. . . . And then, with the same abruptness, he would abandon me, and once again I would feel myself repulsed—very kindly and gently, but nevertheless repulsed.

A mood of gaiety would sometimes come over him and then he could romp and gambol with me like a boy (he was fond of every form of violent physical exercise); and once—only once!—he fondled me so lovingly that I nearly wept. . . . But both his gaiety and his moods of tenderness vanished without leaving any trace, and I could never found any hopes for the future on what passed between us—it all seemed to have been nothing but a dream. Sometimes I would gaze at his clever, handsome, serene face, till my heart throbbed and my whole being strained toward him . . . and he, as if guessing what was going on within me, would stroke my cheek casually, and either go out of the room and busy himself over something, or suddenly freeze, as only he could freeze, when I would immediately shrink and freeze, too. His rare fits of indulgence toward myself were never caused by my mute though perfectly obvious prayers; they always came unexpectedly.

Thinking over my father's character in later life, I came to the conclusion that he had other things beside me—and our domestic life—to think of; his heart was in something quite different, something that he enjoyed to the full. "Take what you can," he once said to me, "but never surrender your own self. To belong entirely to oneself— that is what constitutes the thing we call life." Another time, in my capacity of youthful democrat, I began to hold forth on freedom in his presence (he was in one of his "kind" moods that day, when one could say what one liked to him). "Freedom," he repeated. "And do you know the only thing that can give man freedom?"

"What's that?"

"Will, his own will, and it will give him power, too, which is better than any freedom. Learn to know what you want, and you will be free and able to command others."

My father's first and foremost aim was to live, and live he did; perhaps he had a foreboding that he had not much time to enjoy "the thing we call life": he died at the age of forty-two.

I gave my father a full description of my visit to the Zasekins'. He

listened to me with a kind of absentminded attention, sitting on a bench
and drawing in the sand with the end of his riding crop. He laughed
once or twice, cast a bright, amused glance at me, egging me on with
brief questions and remarks. At first I hardly ventured so much as to
utter Zinaida's name, but soon could restrain myself no longer and
began singing her praises. My father kept chuckling to himself. Then,
becoming thoughtful, he stretched and rose from the bench.

I remembered that, while leaving the house, he had ordered his
horse to be saddled. He was an excellent horseman and could break
in the most savage horses long before Mr. Reri displayed his skill.

"Shall I go with you, Father?" I asked.

"No," he said, and his face assumed its usual expression of affectionate indifference. "You can go alone if you want to; and tell the
groom I shan't be riding."

Turning his back on me, he walked briskly away. I followed him
with my eyes till he passed through the gate and disappeared. I saw
his hat moving along the top of the fence; then I saw him walk into
the Zasekins' house.

He was there less than an hour, and on leaving went straight to
town, returning home only toward the evening.

After dinner I went to the Zasekins' myself. I found the old princess
alone in the drawing room. When she saw me, she scratched her head
under her cap with the end of a knitting needle and asked me abruptly
if I could copy out an application for her.

"With pleasure," I replied, sitting down on the edge of a chair.

"Mind you make the letters big enough," said the princess, handing
me a page scribbled all over. "And do you think you could have it
ready today, young sir?"

"Yes, I'll do it today."

The door of the next room opened a crack, and Zinaida's face,
pale, thoughtful, with the hair combed carelessly back, appeared in the
opening; she glanced at me with her big cold eyes and quietly closed
the door.

"Zina! I say, Zina!" cried her mother. But Zina made no answer.
I took the old woman's application home with me and spent the rest
of the evening over it.

IX

My "passion" dated from that day. I think my feelings must have been
something like those of a man starting upon a career of service. I was

no longer just a young boy; I was a lover. I have said that my passion dated from that day, but I ought to add that my sufferings, too, began on that day. I pined when I was away from Zinaida; I could not concentrate, I could do nothing but think of her all day long. . . . I pined when I was away from her . . . but her presence brought me no relief, either. I was jealous, conscious of my own insignificance, sulked foolishly, and prostrated myself before her no less foolishly; but an irresistible force drew me to her, and every time I could not cross the threshold of her room without a joyous pang. Zinaida very soon divined that I was in love with her, indeed I had no thought of concealment; she made merry over my infatuation, fooled, petted, and tormented me in turns. It is sweet to be the sole source, the absolute and unchallengeable cause of the greatest happiness or the profoundest grief of another—and Zinaida found me as wax in her hands. But I was not the only one in love with her: all the men who visited the house raved about her, and she kept them all on a tether—at her feet. It amused her to excite in them hopes and misgivings by turns, to twist them around her little finger (she called it knocking people against one another), and they had no thought of resistance and submitted gladly to her will. Her vivacious and lovely being was imbued with an entrancing blend of cunning and recklessness, of artificiality and simplicity, of tranquility and animal spirits; over everything she said or did, over all her movements, there seemed to hover a light, subtle grace; a peculiar power was in play everywhere. And her face, which changed constantly, also seemed to be in play; it expressed almost instantaneously derision, thought, and fervor. The most conflicting emotions, light and swift as the shadows of clouds on a sunny windy day, seemed to be ever chasing one another over her eyes and lips.

Each of her admirers was necessary to her. Belovzorov, whom she called "My Beast," or sometimes simply "Mine," would have rushed into the flames for her; not relying upon his mental powers or other qualities, he kept offering her his hand, hinting that the others were not serious. Maidanov answered to the poetic strain in her; though, like most authors, cold by nature, he assured her earnestly, and himself, too, perhaps, that he adored her, eulogizing her in endless poetic effusions, which he recited to her with a kind of ecstasy that was at once affected and sincere. And she, while feeling a certain sympathy for him, treated him with a shade of mockery; she had not much faith in him, and after listening to his effusions, made him recite Pushkin, to clear the atmosphere, as she said. Lushin, the droll doctor, whose words sounded so cynical, understood her better and loved her more than all the rest, though he abused her, both to her face and behind her back.

She respected him, but showed him no mercy and found a malicious delight in letting him see that he, too, was in her power. "I am a flirt, I have no heart, I am an actress by nature," she once said to him in my presence. "Very well, then! Give me your hand, now, and I will stick a pin into it; you will feel humiliated before the young man here, you will feel pain, and yet you will be so good as to laugh, Monsieur Truthful." Lushin flushed up, averted his face, bit his lip, but ended by stretching his hand out to her. She pricked it, and he actually laughed . . . and she laughed, too, thrusting the pin deep into his flesh and looking into his eyes, which he vainly tried to keep away from her face.
. . . Least of all could I understand her relations with Count Malevsky. He was good-looking, alert, and intelligent, but there was something dubious, something false about him that even I, a lad of sixteen, could feel, and I could not help marveling that Zinaida failed to notice it. But who knows—perhaps she noticed the falseness and did not mind it! The defects of her education, her strange acquaintances and habits, the constant presence of her mother, the poverty and disorder in the house, everything, from the freedom that this young girl enjoyed to the consciousness of her superiority over those surrounding her, had developed a kind of half-contemptuous negligence and moral callousness in her. Whatever happened in their household, whether Vonifaty came to announce there was no sugar, or some shabby piece of gossip came to light, or her guests quarreled among themselves, she only tossed her curls and said: "Nonsense!" refusing to be moved.

As for me, my blood boiled whenever Malevsky stole up to her, sly as a fox, lolled elegantly over the back of her chair, and began whispering in her ear with a complacent and unctuous simper, while she, her arms folded, looked at him gravely, smiling and shaking her head from side to side.

"What makes you receive Count Malevsky?" I once asked her.

"He has such a darling little mustache, you see," she answered. "But of course you wouldn't understand that."

"You don't mean to say you think I'm in love with him?" she volunteered another time. "No, I could never love a man like that, a man I can't help looking down on. I need someone capable of breaking my will. But I shall never come across such a person, thank God! I'm not going to fall into anyone's talons, not I!"

"Does that mean you will never love anyone?"

"What about you? Don't I love you?" she retorted, flicking my nose with her glove.

Oh yes, Zinaida got a lot of entertainment at my expense. For three weeks I saw her every day, and the life she led me during that time! She did not often come to our house, and I was not sorry for it, for whenever she did, she acted the young lady, the princess, and I turned shy. I was afraid of giving myself away before my mother, who thoroughly disapproved of Zinaida and watched us with hostile eyes.

I did not mind my father nearly as much; he ignored me, and scarcely spoke to her, but when he did, it was always to say something clever and pointed. I gave up study and reading, I even gave up my country rambles and my riding. Like a beetle fastened by the leg I spun around the beloved wing of the house; I would have stayed there forever, if that had been possible . . . but my mother grumbled and Zinaida herself sometimes drove me away. When she did this, I locked myself up in my room or went to the farthest end of the garden, where I clambered up onto the crumbling wall of the high, brick-built conservatory and sat there for hours, my legs dangling over the wall on the side facing the road, gazing in front of me with unseeing eyes. White butterflies fluttered languidly over the dusty nettles; a perky little sparrow alighted on a broken brick nearby, chirruping exasperatingly, turning around and around, and spreading its tail; the crows, who still regarded me with suspicion, cawed now and then from the bare top of a birch, and the sun and wind played among its thin branches; sometimes the calm, austere boom of the bells from the Donskoi Monastery reached my ears, and I would sit there looking and listening, my heart overflowing with a sensation I could not define; it embraced everything—sadness and joy, anxious forebodings, desire for life, and fear of life. But I understood nothing of all this at the time, and would not have been able to put a name to what was fermenting within me, or, if I had tried, would have found one name for it all—Zinaida.

And all the while Zinaida played with me as a cat plays with a mouse. She flirted with me, and I immediately melted and became agitated, or she suddenly repulsed me, and I did not dare to approach her or even look at her.

I remember she was very distant with me for several days running; I lost heart, and sneaking timidly into the annex, tried to keep near the old princess, although she was in the worst of tempers at the time; her financial affairs were very bad, and she had twice been obliged to explain her situation at the local police station.

Once, passing the familiar garden fence, I caught sight of Zinaida; she was sitting motionless on the grass, leaning back on her hands. I made as if to go quietly away, but she suddenly lifted her head, motioning to me imperiously. I stood rooted to the ground; I was not quite sure what her gesture meant. She repeated it. I promptly leaped over the palings and ran joyously toward her; but she stopped me with her eyes, pointing toward the path two paces from where she was sitting. Perplexed and abashed, I knelt at the side of the path. She was so pale, every feature of her face breathed such bitter grief, such profound weariness that it wrung my heart, and I could not help asking:

"What's the matter?"

Zinaida stretched out her hand, plucked a blade of grass, chewed it, and flung it away from her.

"You love me very much, don't you?" she asked at last. "You do, don't you?"

I did not answer; there was no need to do so.

"Yes," she said, still looking at me, "I know you do. The same eyes," she added, turning thoughtful and covering her face with her hands. "I'm sick of it all," she whispered. "I'd like to go to the end of the world, I can't stand it any longer, I can't bear it. . . . And what's in store for me? . . . Oh, I'm so unhappy, so unhappy!"

"But why?" I asked timidly.

For an answer, Zinaida shrugged her shoulders. I remained kneeling, gazing at her in profound misery. Every word she said pierced my heart. I would have given my life at that moment to relieve her sorrow. I looked at her, still unable to think what could have made her so unhappy, and vividly imagined how, in a fit of uncontrollable sadness, she had gone out into the garden and dropped to the ground as if she had been mowed down. All around was so green, so radiant; a breeze ruffled the leaves, every now and then shaking the raspberry canes above Zinaida's head.

Doves cooed in the distance, and the bees murmured, flying low over the sparse grass. The blue sky shed its kindly radiance from above, but I felt so melancholy. . . .

"Do you feel like reciting some poetry?" asked Zinaida gently, supporting herself on one elbow. "I like to hear you recite. You chant, rather, it's true, but I don't mind it, it's so very young. Recite 'The Hills of Georgia.' Only do sit down, first."

I sat down and recited "The Hills of Georgia."

" 'For not to love is quite beyond its powers.' " Zinaida repeated the last line. "That is what we love poetry for: it treats of unreal things and makes them sound not only better but even more real than real things. . . . 'For not to love is quite beyond its powers'—that's it, the heart would like not to love, but it can't help loving." She fell silent again, then with a sudden start got on to her feet. "Come on! Maidanov is sitting with my mother; he brought me his poem, and I went away. He's upset, too. . . . But it can't be helped! One day you'll know all . . . don't be angry with me, now!"

Giving a quick pressure to my hand, Zinaida ran ahead. We went back to the annex together. Maidanov began reading us his "Assassin," which had just come out, but I did not listen to him. He declaimed his four-foot iambics in a singsong voice, the rhymes alternating and jingling like sleigh bells, loud and empty, while I studied Zinaida's face, trying to probe the meaning of what she had been saying to me.

> *Or is it that a secret rival*
> *Has overwhelmed you all at once?*

Maidanov suddenly declaimed in nasal accents, and my eyes met Zinaida's. She lowered hers, reddening slightly. I saw her flush and went numb with fear. I had been jealous before, but never before had the idea that she might have fallen in love crossed my mind. "Lord! She is in love!"

X

My real tortures only began then. I racked my brains thinking, turning things over, and kept a constant watch, as secretly as I could, over Zinaida. Some change had come over her—that was quite evident. She now went for long, solitary walks. Sometimes she did not come out to her visitors, locking herself up in her room by the hour. That was not like her. All of a sudden I became, or at least so I imagined, extraordinarily perspicacious. "Was this the one? Or that?" I kept asking myself, shifting my suspicions anxiously from one admirer to another. Count Malevsky (though the admission made me blush for Zinaida) seemed to me the most dangerous of all.

I was doubtless not very acute, and my secretiveness could have hardly deceived anyone; Dr. Lushin, for one, very soon saw through me. But he, too, had changed considerably of late; he had grown thinner, and though he laughed as much as ever, his laughter was now hollow, bitter, and brief, and his former light irony and forced cynicism had given place to a nervous irritability he seemed unable to repress.

"What makes you come here so often, young man?" he once said to me when we were alone in the Zasekin drawing room. (The young princess had not returned from her walk, but we could hear the shrill voice of her mother from the mezzanine, scolding her maid.) "You ought to be studying, working, while you are still young—and what d'you think you're doing?"

"How do you know I don't work when I'm at home?" I answered, trying to sound supercilious and only succeeding in betraying my confusion.

"Oh, don't I? No, no, it's not work you're thinking about. I won't argue with you . . . at your age it's only natural. But your choice is so very unfortunate. Don't you see what sort of household this is?"

"I'm afraid I don't understand you," I said.

"You don't? So much the worse for you! I consider it my duty to warn you. Old bachelors like myself may visit here with impunity. We are a hardened lot, nothing can hurt us, but your skin is still tender. The air here is bad for you, believe me; you may catch the infection."

"What do you mean?"

"I'll tell you what I mean. Do you consider your present state as healthy? Is it normal? Do you really think all you're going through just now is good for you? Do you?"

"Why, what am I going through?" I asked, although in the depths of my heart I knew the doctor was right.

"Young man, young man!" continued the doctor, stressing the words as if they contained something extremely humiliating for me. "Diplomacy isn't your line. Your face is still the mirror of your soul, and thank God for that! But what's the use of talking! I wouldn't be hanging about here if I weren't . . ." the doctor ground his teeth, "if I weren't the same sort of fool myself. One thing I can't help wondering at: that an intelligent person like yourself can remain ignorant of what is going on here."

"What *is* going on?" I reiterated, on the alert at once.

The doctor cast a glance of quizzical compassion at me.

"I'm a fine fellow, too," he said as if to himself. "Why should I tell him? In a word," he added, raising his voice, "I repeat: this atmosphere is bad for you. You may enjoy it, but what of that! A hothouse smells nice, too, but you can't live in a hothouse. Listen to me, my friend, take up your Kaidanov again."

At this moment the old princess came in to complain to the doctor of toothache. Then Zinaida appeared.

"There," said her mother, "give her a good scolding, Doctor. She drinks iced water all day long. Is it good for her with her weak chest?"

"Why do you do that?" asked the doctor.

"And what harm can it do me?"

"Harm? You might catch cold and die."

"Do you mean it? Really? Well, I wouldn't mind that much."

"So that's how it is," the doctor muttered. Her mother left the room.

"Yes, that's how it is," said Zinaida. "Is life such a fine thing, after all? Look around you. . . . Are things so good? Do you think I can't understand, can't feel? Drinking iced water gives me pleasure, and you come and gravely assure me that I ought not to risk my life, such as it is, for a moment of pleasure—I say nothing of happiness."

"I see," remarked Lushin, "whims and independence, these words sum you up—your whole nature is in them."

Zinaida laughed nervously.

"You're behind the times, my dear Doctor. You're a poor observer, you're out of date. Put on your glasses and you'll see that I am in no mood for whims now. It's intensely entertaining to fool you all, and myself into the bargain, but as for independence. . . . Monsieur Voldemar," she said suddenly, stamping her small foot, "stop pulling a long face! I can't stand being pitied!" She walked rapidly away.

"The atmosphere is bad for you, young man, very bad," repeated Dr. Lushin.

XI

That evening the usual guests assembled at the Zasekins'; I was among them.

The conversation turned on Maidanov's poem; Zinaida praised it sincerely. "But I'll tell you what!" she said. "If I were a poet, I would choose quite different subjects. Perhaps it's all nonsense, but strange thoughts come into my head, especially when I can't sleep, just before daybreak, when the sky turns all pink and gray. For example, I would . . . But I'm afraid you'll laugh at me!"

"No, we won't!" we cried, all speaking at once.

"I would describe," she went on, folding her arms and looking away, "a company of young girls in a great boat at night on a calm stream. The moon is shining, they are all in white, with wreaths of white flowers, and they sing a kind of hymn or something."

"I see, I see, go on," drawled Maidanov with dreamy significance.

"Suddenly—noise, laughter, torches and the sound of a tambourine on the shore. . . . A crowd of bacchantes comes running, singing, shouting. It is for you, Mr. Poet, to paint the picture . . . only I would like the torches to be very red and smoke terribly, and the bacchantes' eyes to shine beneath their wreaths, and the wreaths themselves must be dark. Don't forget tiger skins, goblets, and gold, lots of gold."

"Where would you put the gold?" asked Maidanov, tossing back his straight hair, his nostrils dilating.

"Where? On their shoulders, arms, legs, everywhere! They say women used to wear anklets of gold in the olden times. The bacchantes call to the maidens in the boat. The maidens have stopped singing—they cannot go on—but they sit motionless; they drift toward the shore. And all of a sudden, one of them gets up gently. . . . This needs a masterful description: the way she gets quietly up, in the moonlight, the panic among her companions. . . . She steps over the side of the boat, the bacchantes cluster around her and carry her away, into the night, into the dark. . . . I can see smoke, clouds of smoke, confusion. . . . And through it all the shrieks of the bacchantes, and her white wreath lying on the shore."

Zinaida stopped speaking. "She is in love!" I said to myself again.

"Is that all?" asked Maidanov.

"That's all," she answered.

"It isn't a subject for a long poem," he remarked pompously, "but I might use your idea for a lyrical work."

"In the romantic vein?" asked Malevsky.

"In the romantic vein, of course, Byronic."

"I prefer Victor Hugo to Byron," the young count dropped out carelessly, "he's more interesting."

"Victor Hugo is a first-rate writer," said Maidanov, "and my friend Tonkosheyev, in his Spanish novel *El Trovador*—"

"Do you mean the book with the question marks upside down?" interrupted Zinaida.

"Yes, it is a custom with the Spanish. I was going to say that Tonkosheyev—"

"Oh, now you're going to begin arguing about classicism and romanticism again!" said Zinaida, interrupting him once more. "We'd better play at something. . . ."

"Forfeits?" asked Lushin.

"No, I'm sick of forfeits; let's play similes." (This was a game of Zinaida's invention: an object was selected and everyone had to find a simile for it, the one whose simile was the happiest receiving a prize.) She walked up to the window. The sun had just set; long crimson clouds stretched high up in the sky.

"What are those clouds like?" asked Zinaida, and without waiting for anyone to answer, said: "To me they are like the crimson sails on Cleopatra's golden barge, when she sailed to meet Antony. You told me about it not long ago, Maidanov, do you remember?"

And we all, like Polonius, decided then and there that the clouds exactly resembled those sails, and that no one could find a better simile.

"How old was Antony then?" asked Zinaida.

"Quite a young man, probably," replied Malevsky.

"Yes, he was young," said Maidanov positively.

"Excuse me," said Lushin, "he was over forty."

"Over forty!" echoed Zinaida, darting a swift glance at Lushin.

Soon after that I went home. "She is in love," I whispered involuntarily, "but with whom is she in love?"

XII

The days passed, and Zinaida became ever stranger and more incomprehensible. I went into her room once and found her sitting on a wicker chair, her head pressed against the hard edge of the table. She sat up, and I saw that her cheeks were wet with tears.

"Oh, it's you," she said, smiling spitefully. "Come here!"

I went up to her; she put her hand on my head and, catching hold of a lock of my hair, began twisting it.

"You're hurting me," I said at last.

"Oh, it hurts, does it? And do you think I don't suffer?" she said.

"Oh!" she cried suddenly as she saw she had pulled out a tuft of hair by the roots. "Look what I've done! Poor Monsieur Voldemar!"

Carefully smoothing out the tuft, she wound it around her finger, making a ring of it.

"I will put your hair in my locket and wear it," she said, her eyes glistening with tears. "Perhaps that will give you some comfort. . . . Now, go!"

There was trouble at home when I returned. My father and mother were having some kind of an explanation; she was reproaching him for something, while he, as usual, coldly and politely held his peace, and soon left. I could not hear what it was my mother said; besides, I had other things to think of; all I remember is that after this explanation she summoned me into her room and expressed her displeasure at my frequent visits to the princess, who, according to her, was *une femme capable de tout*. I kissed her hand (I always resorted to this when I wished to put a stop to the conversation) and went to my room. Zinaida's tears had completely baffled me; I did not know what to think of them and was ready to cry myself: notwithstanding my sixteen years, I was still only a child. I no longer thought of Malevsky, though Belovzorov was growing more savage every day, staring at the sleek count as a wolf stares at a lamb; in fact, I thought of nothing and no one. I lost myself in surmises and sought secluded spots. I acquired a special fondness for the broken-down conservatory. I would clamber up its high wall and sit there, a sad, lonely youth, feeling exceedingly sorry for myself—and how I enjoyed these melancholy sensations, how I wallowed in them!

One day I sat on the wall, looking into the distance and listening to the tolling of the church bell. . . . Suddenly I was aware of a creepy sensation in my skin—it was not a passing breeze and it was not a shudder, it was a feeling that someone was near me. . . . I looked down. Zinaida was hurrying along the road beneath me in a light-gray dress, with a pink sunshade resting on one shoulder. She saw me, too, and stopped, turning up the brim of her straw hat and raising her velvety eyes to me.

"What are you doing up there?" she asked, smiling strangely. "There!" she said. "You are always assuring me of your love—well, if you really love me, jump down onto the road."

The words were scarcely out of her mouth when I flew down, as if pushed from behind. The wall was about fourteen feet high. I fell on my feet, but the shock was so violent that I could not remain standing, and fell, losing consciousness for a moment. When I came to, without opening my eyes, I felt Zinaida's presence near me. "Oh, my darling!" she was saying, bending over me, and her voice sounded anxious and affectionate. "How could you do such a thing, why did you listen to me? You know I love you! Do get up!"

I could feel her bosom heaving so near me, her hands touching my head, and then—oh, then!—her soft, fresh lips showered kisses on my face, they even touched my own lips. . . . But Zinaida must have seen, by the expression of my face, that I was no longer unconscious, for she rose abruptly, saying:

"Well, get up, you naughty boy, you mad creature! Don't lie there in the dust!" I got to my feet. "Give me my sunshade," said Zinaida, "see where I dropped it! And stop looking at me like that . . . it's silly! Did you hurt yourself? I suppose you got stung by the nettles! Don't you look at me like that, I tell you! But there, he doesn't hear me, he can't even answer," she added, as if to herself. "Go home, now, Monsieur Voldemar, brush your clothes, and mind you don't follow me, or I'll be angry and never again . . ."

Without finishing the sentence she walked away at a brisk pace, while I sat down by the roadside, for my knees were shaking. My hands had been stung by the nettles, my back ached, and my head was reeling, but never since have I experienced such bliss as I did then. I could feel it like a sweet pain in all limbs, and finally it vented itself in ecstatic leaps and cries. In very truth I was still but a child.

XIII

I was so proud and happy all that day, the sensation of Zinaida's kisses
on my face was still so vivid, I recalled every word she had said to me
with such quivering ecstasy, cherished my sudden good fortune so
lovingly, that I was almost frightened and did not even want to see
her—the source of all these new sensations. I felt as if I had nothing
more to ask of fate, as if it were time for me to "draw one last breath
and die." The next day, however, as I set off for the annex, I felt
exceedingly self-conscious and tried in vain to conceal this beneath a
cloak of modest familiarity, which I considered suitable to one desirous
of showing that he can keep a secret. Zinaida received me just as usual,
without the slightest sign of emotion, only shaking her finger at me
and asking me if I had any bruises. My air of modest familiarity and
mystery deserted me instantly, and with it my self-consciousness. I had
not expected any particular demonstration, of course, and yet Zinaida's
calm reception acted upon me like a cold douche: I realized that I was
nothing but a child in her eyes—and how sad this made me! Zinaida
paced up and down the floor, bestowing a fleeting smile upon me every
time her eyes rested on me, but her thoughts were far away, I could
see that. "Should I mention yesterday's affair myself?" I mused. "Ask
her where she had been going in such a hurry, just to put an end to
my doubts? . . ." But I discarded the idea and seated myself quietly in
an obscure corner of the room.

Belovzorov came in and I was actually glad to see him.

"I couldn't find a saddle horse quiet enough to carry you," he said
austerely. "Freytag vouches for one, but I am not sure of its temper,
I'm afraid."

"And what are you afraid of?" asked Zinaida. "Be so good as to
explain."

"Why? You see, you can't really ride. Supposing anything happened to you, which God forbid! And what makes you want to ride
all of a sudden?"

"That is no concern of yours, my dear Mr. Beast. But of course I
could ask Pyotr Vasilyevich. . . ." (My father's name was Pyotr Vasilyevich. I was amazed at the easy, careless way she used it, as if confident
of his readiness to oblige her.)

"I see," said Belovzorov, "so it's *him* you want to go riding with!"

"Whether I ride with him or with anyone else, makes no difference
to you. It won't be with you, anyhow."

"Not with me," echoed Belovzorov. "Just as you like. All right,
I'll get a horse for you."

"And mind it *is* a horse, and not a cow. I warn you I mean to gallop."

"Gallop away, then! Is it Malevsky you want to gallop with?"

"And why not with Malevsky, my brave soldier? Now, now, calm yourself, don't glare like that! I'll take you, too. You know what Malevsky is to me now—ugh!" She tossed her head.

"You only say that to console me," grumbled Belovzorov.

Zinaida looked at him with narrowed eyes.

"And does it console you? Oh, you . . . soldier!" she said, bringing out the last word as if unable to find any other epithet. "And you, Monsieur Voldemar, will you come with us?"

"I . . . I don't like being with a lot of people . . ." I muttered, not daring to lift my eyes.

"Oh, you would prefer a tête-à-tête, would you? Very well, each to his own." She sighed. "Go on, then, Belovzorov, see what you can do! I shall want the horse tomorrow."

"And where is the money to come from?" interpolated the old princess.

Zinaida frowned.

"I shan't ask you for it. Belovzorov will trust me."

"Trust . . . trust," muttered the princess, and suddenly shouted at the top of her voice: "Dunyashka!"

"*Maman*—what did I give you a bell for?" expostulated her daughter.

"Dunyashka!" called the old woman again.

Belovzorov took his leave; I went out with him. . . . Zinaida made no attempt to keep me.

XIV

I got up early next morning, cut myself a stick, and sauntered out of the city gates. I would go out, I told myself, and try and shake off my grief. It was a fine day, bright and not too warm; there was a fresh, sportive ground breeze, rustling with gentle playfulness, stirring everything, disturbing nothing. I roamed long over hills and through woods; I did not feel happy, for I had gone out determined to give myself up to grief; but youth, the beautiful weather, the fresh air, the pleasure of rapid walking, the luxury of reposing in solitude on the dense grass, had their effect; the thought of those unforgettable words, of those kisses, once more filled my soul. I dwelt with satisfaction on the thought that Zinaida would not be able to deny that I had both resolution and courage. . . . "She prefers others to me—well and good! But others only talk of what they would do, while *I* acted! And that was nothing in comparison with what I am capable of doing for her sake. . . ."

I gave free rein to my fancy, imagining myself saving her from the hands of enemies, seeing myself covered with blood from head to foot, rescuing her from some dungeon, dying at her feet. I remembered the picture of Malec-Adel bearing Matilde away on his horse, which hung on the drawing-room wall, and then my attention was attracted to a large speckled woodpecker, fussily climbing the trunk of a slender birch tree, anxiously peering out, first on one side, then on the other, like a double-bass player seated behind his instrument.

Then I sang "'Twas not the white snow," which led me to a ballad popular at the time: "I await thee, whilst the playful breeze"; then I began shouting out Yermak's address to the stars, from Khomyakov's tragedy; I tried to invent something myself in a sentimental vein, even going so far as to compose the line with which the poem was to conclude—"Oh, Zinaida, Zinaida!" but nothing came of the attempt. And now the dinner hour was approaching. I descended to the valley, along which a narrow sandy path wound its way to the town. While I was still on this path I heard the hollow sound of horses' hoofs behind me. Looking back, I involuntarily halted and took off my cap, for the riders were Zinaida and my father. They were riding side by side. My father was saying something to her, leaning over in the saddle, his hand resting on the neck of his horse; he was smiling; Zinaida listened to him in silence, her eyes austerely lowered, her lips compressed. At first I only saw the two of them, but a few seconds later I caught sight of Belovzorov, who had been hidden by a turn of the path, riding a fiery coal-black horse and clad in his Hussar's uniform and fur-trimmed cloak. His good steed tossed its head, snorting and prancing, its rider reining it in and urging it forward with his spurs at the same time. I stepped to the side of the path. My father gathered up the reins and moved away from Zinaida, who directed a slow glance at him—and they galloped past me. Belovzorov dashed after them, his sword clattering. . . . "He's as red as a lobster," I thought, "and she—why is she so pale? Riding all morning, and pale?"

I redoubled my steps and got home just in time for dinner. My father had already changed, and was seated, washed and refreshed, beside my mother's armchair, reading an article from the *Journal des Débats* to her in his mellow, even voice. My mother was listening absently, and asked me as soon as I appeared what I had been doing all this time, adding that she hated people hanging about goodness knows where and goodness knows in what company. It was on the tip of my tongue to say I had been out for a walk all by myself, but a glance at my father made me decide to hold my tongue.

XV

During the next five or six days I hardly saw Zinaida: she pleaded illness, but this did not prevent the usual frequenters of the annex from "going on duty," as they called it—all of them, that is to say, with the exception of Maidanov, who always lost heart and fell into dejection as soon as there was no cause about which he could be enthusiastic. Belovzorov sulked in his corner, red-faced and buttoned up to the neck. A sneering smile flickered continually over the subtle features of Count Malevsky; he really had fallen into disgrace with Zinaida, and was more obliging than ever to the old princess; he actually drove her to the governor general in a hired carriage; but the visit turned out a failure and even led to unpleasantness for Malevsky himself, who was reminded of an incident involving certain artillery officers and could only plead his inexperience at the time in his defense. Lushin called once or twice a day, but never stayed long; I was rather afraid of him since our last talk and at the same time was genuinely attracted to him. Once he went for a walk with me in Neskuchny Gardens, and was very amiable and good-natured, telling me the names and peculiarities of the various plants and flowers, suddenly interrupting himself to smite his brow and exclaim, with complete irrelevance: "Fool that I was, I thought her a mere flirt! There are evidently people who enjoy sacrificing themselves."

"What do you mean by that?" I asked.

"Nothing—for your ears, anyhow!" Lushin answered sharply.

Zinaida avoided me. I could not fail to notice that the sight of me was disagreeable to her. She seemed to avert her face from me instinctively; and it was this that was so painful, so hard to bear. But there was no help for it, and I strove to keep out of her sight, only watching her from afar, but in this I did not always succeed. There was still something inexplicable going on within her: her face was different, her whole bearing was changed. The change in her came home to me with special force one warm, still evening. I was sitting on a low bench beneath a spreading elder bush; it was a favorite spot of mine: I could see Zinaida's window from there. As I sat there, a small bird flitted about among the darkening leaves over my head; a gray cat, elongating its back, crept stealthily into the garden, and some early insects were filling the air—still limpid, though there was no longer any light—with their ponderous hum. I sat looking at the window, hoping it would open; and soon it really was flung open, and Zinaida appeared in it. She was wearing a white dress, and was herself—her face, her shoulders, her arms—almost as white as the dress. For a long time she stood motionless, gazing steadily from under knitted brows in front of her. I had never seen her gaze like this. Then she clasped her hands tight, raising them to her lips and then to her forehead, and suddenly, spreading her fingers wide, tossed her hair behind her ears, shook her head, gave a single resolute nod, and closed the window with a bang.

Three days later she came across me in the garden. I was going to turn away, but she stopped me.

"Come, give me your hand," she said in her old affectionate manner. "You and I haven't had a nice chat for ages."

I looked at her: her eyes shone with a gentle light; she seemed to be smiling through a mist.

"Are you still unwell?" I asked.

"No, no, that's all over," she said, plucking a small red rose. "I'm a little tired still, but that will pass, too."

"And will you be like you used to be before?" I asked.

Zinaida raised the flower to her face, and it seemed to me that the vivid petals cast their reflections on her cheeks.

"Why, have I changed?"

"You have," I said quietly.

"I've been horrid to you—I know that," said Zinaida, "but you shouldn't have taken any notice. . . . I couldn't help it. . . . But what's the good of talking about it?"

"You don't want me to love you, that's what it is!" I exclaimed moodily, giving way to a sudden impulse.

"Oh, yes, I do, but not the way you loved me before."

"How, then?"

"Let's be friends, that's how." Zinaida held out the rose for me to smell. "I'm so much older than you, I could be your aunt, you know; or your elder sister, if you like. And you . . ."

"And I am only a child for you. . . ."

"Of course you are, but a sweet, good, intelligent child whom I love dearly. I'll tell you what! I appoint you my page from this day; and don't forget that a page must never leave his queen. Here's your badge," she added, putting the rose in my buttonhole. "A token of our goodwill toward you."

"You showed me other tokens of goodwill before," I muttered.

"Oh," said Zinaida, "what a memory he has! Well, I don't mind giving you one now. . . ."

And leaning over me, she imprinted a pure, calm kiss on my brow.

I could only look at her, and she turned, saying: "Follow me, my page," and walked toward the annex. I followed her in a state of amazement. "Can it be," I thought, "that this gentle, sensible girl is the same Zinaida I used to know?" Her very gait seemed calmer to me now, her figure more dignified, more graceful. . . .

But God, how my love for her blazed up!

XVI

After dinner the usual guests assembled in the annex, and the young princess came out of her room to receive them. They were all there, in full strength, as on that first, unforgettable evening. Even Nirmatsky dragged himself there; Maidanov was the first to come this time, bringing a new poem with him. We played forfeits again, but without the former wild capers, without the fooling and noise—the Gypsy element was gone from our revels. Zinaida set a new tone to the party. I sat next to her in my capacity of her page. Among other penalties she suggested that the one who drew the lot with a mark on it should tell us what he had dreamed. But nothing came of this. The dreams turned out to be either dull (Belovzorov had dreamed that he fed his horse on carp, and that its head was of wood), or unnatural and obvious fabrications. . . . Maidanov entertained us with a regular novel, bristling with funeral vaults, angels with lyres, and talking flowers . . . not to mention distant strains. . . . Zinaida would not let him go on. "Well, if it comes to inventing," she said, "let everyone relate something that never happened at all." Again it fell to Belovzorov's lot to begin.

The young Hussar was completely at a loss. "I can't think of anything," he exclaimed.

"Nonsense!" cried Zinaida. "Imagine you are married, or something like that, and tell us how you would treat your wife. Would you lock her up?"

"Yes, I would."

"And would you sit with her yourself?"

"Certainly I would."

"Very well. And supposing she got tired of it and deceived you?"

"I would kill her."

"And if she ran away?"

"I would run after her and kill her."

"All right. And now supposing *I* were your wife, what would you do?"

Belovzorov was silent for a moment.

"I would kill myself."

Zinaida laughed.

"I see your story is not very long," she said.

The next lot was drawn by Zinaida. She looked up at the ceiling, thinking.

"Now listen," she said at last. "This is what I have made up. Imagine a beautiful palace, a summer night, and a wonderful ball. The young queen is receiving her guests. Everywhere are gold, marble, crystal, silk, lights, diamonds, flowers, incense, every luxury the heart could desire."

"You love luxury, don't you?" interrupted Lushin.

"Luxury is elegant," she retorted, "and I love elegance."

"More than beauty?" he asked.

"You're too clever for me, I don't know what you mean. Now, don't interrupt. And so, the ball is a splendid one. There are hosts of guests, all young, good-looking, brave, and all head over ears in love with the queen."

"Are there no women among the guests?" asked Malevsky.

"No . . . let me see . . . yes, there are."

"And all very plain?"

"All charming, but the men are all in love with the queen. She is tall and slender. . . . She wears a small gold diadem on her dark hair."

I looked at Zinaida, and at that moment she seemed to be taller than any of us, her white forehead, her straight eyebrows were stamped with such bright intelligence and power that I thought: "You yourself are that queen."

"Everyone is crowding around her," Zinaida went on, "with the most flattering speeches."

"So she likes flattery?" asked Lushin.

"Oh, you're impossible, interrupting all the time. . . . Who isn't fond of flattery?"

"One last question," put in Malevsky, "has the queen a husband?"

"I haven't thought of that. No, what does she want a husband for?"

"Of course," put in Malevsky, "what does she want a husband for?"

"*Silence!*" cried Maidanov, who spoke atrocious French.

"*Merci!*" said Zinaida. "So the queen sits listening to the flattering speeches and the music, but she does not look at any of her guests. Six tall windows are open from ceiling to floor, and beyond them are the dark sky studded with enormous stars and a dark park with enormous trees in it. The queen looks out at the park. There, among the trees, is a fountain looming white in the dark, and very tall—as tall as a ghost. The queen hears through the din of voices and music the quiet splashing of the water; as she looks out of the window she thinks to herself: 'Yes, gentlemen, you are all noble, wise, rich, you cluster around me, you cherish every word I let fall, each of you is ready to die at my feet, you are all in my power . . . but there, by the fountain, by the splashing water, the one I love, the one who has power over me, stands waiting for me. He has neither rich garments nor jewels, and no one knows him, but he stands waiting for me, and he knows I will go out to him. And I will, there is no force strong enough to prevent me if I wish to go out to him, to stay with him, to lose myself with him there, in the darkness of the park, where the trees are rustling and the fountain splashes its waters. . . .' "

Zinaida broke off.

"Is that . . . pure invention?" asked Malevsky insinuatingly.

Zinaida did not deign even to look at him.

"I wonder what we would have done, gentlemen," said Lushin suddenly, "if we had been among the guests and had known of the fortunate man standing by the fountain?"

"Wait, wait!" interrupted Zinaida, "I'll tell you myself how each of you would have behaved. You, Belovzorov, would have called him out; you, Maidanov, would have written an epigram on him . . . no, no, you wouldn't, you can't write epigrams; you would have composed lengthy iambics, in the manner of Barbier, and published them in the *Telegraph*. You, Nirmatsky, would have borrowed from him, no, you would have lent him money at high interest; as for you, Doctor—" she paused, "I don't know what you would have done."

"In my capacity of court physician," replied Lushin, "I would probably have advised the queen not to give a ball when she did not feel in the mood for entertaining."

"Perhaps you would have been right. What about you, Count?"

"Me?" said the count with his malevolent smile.

"You would have offered him a poisoned chocolate."

Malevsky winced and looked very sly, but the next moment burst out laughing.

"As for you, Voldemar . . ." Zinaida went on, "but I think we've had enough of this sort of thing; let's play at something else."

"Monsieur Voldemar, as a faithful page, would have held his queen's train as she ran off into the park," said Malevsky venomously.

I flushed crimson, but Zinaida, laying her hand on my shoulder and getting up, said in a rather shaky voice: "I never gave you the right to be insolent, Count, and I would therefore request you to leave my house." She pointed to the door.

"Really, Princess," muttered Malevsky, turning pale.

"The princess is quite right!" exclaimed Belovzorov, also getting up.

"I swear I never expected," continued Malevsky, "I did not think there was anything in my words to . . . I did not for a moment intend to give offense . . . I beg your pardon."

Zinaida cast an icy glance at him and laughed coldly.

"Stay if you like," she said with a negligent gesture. "Monsieur Voldemar and I were wrong to lose our tempers. You're fond of stinging—sting away, then!"

"I beg your pardon," repeated Malevsky, and I, recalling Zinaida's gesture, told myself that a real queen could not have shown an offender the door with greater majesty.

The game of forfeits did not go on for long after this incident. Everyone felt rather awkward, not so much on account of the little scene just enacted, as from some indefinable but oppressive emotion. No one mentioned it, but everyone was conscious of this emotion and knew that his neighbor shared it. Maidanov recited his poem, and Malevsky praised it with exaggerated enthusiasm.

"How anxious he is to show his good nature now!" Lushin whispered in my ear.

Soon we all went home. Zinaida had turned suddenly thoughtful, and her mother had sent word that she had a headache. Nirmatsky complained of rheumatism.

I could not sleep for a long time—Zinaida's story had made a great impression on me. "Was a hint intended?" I asked myself. "And if so, what and whom was she hinting at? And if there was any truth in it, surely she would not have dared . . . no, no, it's impossible," I whispered, turning continually, with burning cheeks, on my pillow. . . . But I remembered the expression on Zinaida's face as she told her story. . . . I remembered Lushin's involuntary exclamation on our walk in Neskuchny Gardens, the sudden changes in her treatment of me . . . and I exhausted myself in surmises.

"Who is *he*?" The words stood constantly before my eyes, as if engraved on the darkness in letters of fire; a low, ominous cloud seemed to be hanging over me, and I kept expecting it to burst any moment. I had become accustomed to a great deal of late, I had seen many strange things at the Zasekins'; the disorder, the tallow candle ends, the broken knives and forks, the gloomy Vonifaty, the shabby maids, the strange manners of the old princess, nothing in this eccentric household could astonish me anymore. . . . But I could not get used to what I was beginning vaguely to guess at in Zinaida. . . . Adventuress, my mother had once called her. She, my idol, my divinity—an adventuress! The word stung me, I tried to escape from it by burying my face in the pillow, I chafed at it . . . and yet, and yet, what would I not have given to be that happy he of the fountain!

My blood surged madly in my veins. "The park . . . the fountain . . ." thought I. "Suppose I go out into the park?" I was dressed in a moment and slipped out. It was a dark night. The trees were whispering almost inaudibly. A still coolness came from above, and the smell of fennel was wafted from the vegetable garden. I visited all the paths; the sound of my own light footsteps at the same time alarmed and cheered me; I stopped to listen to the beating of my heart—full, rapid beats. At last I came up to the fence and leaned against the thin palings. Suddenly—or was it my imagination?—a female form slipped past me. . . . I strained my eyes into the darkness, holding my breath. . . . What was that? Was it the sound of steps, or only the beating of my heart again? "Who's there?" I lisped indistinctly. Again! Was it a stifled laugh . . . or the rustling of branches . . . or had someone sighed, close to my ear? I was seized with panic. "Who's there?" I repeated still more softly.

A light breeze rose for a moment; something flashed across the sky: a shooting star. "Is it Zinaida?" I wanted to ask, but the words died on my lips. And all of a sudden, as it often happens in the middle of the night, a profound stillness prevailed. . . . Even the grasshoppers stopped chirping in the bushes, and from somewhere came the sound of a window being closed. I stood there for a short time, then returned to my room, to my cold bed. I felt a strange excitement, as if I had kept a tryst but found myself alone, brushing past another's happiness.

XVII

Next day I was only able to catch a glimpse of Zinaida as she and her mother drove by. I did see Lushin, who, however, merely bestowed upon me the briefest of greetings, and I saw Malevsky. The young count smirked at me and spoke to me in a friendly fashion. Of all the people visiting at the annex he alone had managed to insinuate himself into our house and get into my mother's good graces. My father did not take to him and treated him with an almost insulting politeness.

"*Ah, monsieur le page!*" said Malevsky. "Glad to see you! What is your beauteous queen doing?"

His handsome, healthy face was at that moment so detestable to me, and the look he turned on me was so insultingly facetious, that I made no reply.

"What, still angry with me?" he went on. "You shouldn't be. It wasn't I who called you a page, you know, and it's usually queens who have pages. But allow me to observe that you are somewhat negligent of your duties."

"My duties?"

"Yes. A page should never leave his mistress's side; a page should know what she is doing all the time—should watch all her movements," he added, lowering his voice. "By day—and by night."

"What d'you mean by that?"

"Mean? I should have thought my meaning was clear enough. By day—and by night. The day doesn't matter so much. It is light in the day, and there are always plenty of people about. But in the night— that's when you must be on the alert. I would advise you not to sleep at night, but watch, watch, for all you are worth. Remember the park, the night, the fountain—that is where you should watch. You will thank me for this one day."

Malevsky laughed and turned his back on me. In all probability he did not attach much importance to his words; he enjoyed the reputation of a first-rate hoaxer and was famous for his ability to take people in at masked balls, in which he was greatly aided by the falseness that had become second nature to him. . . . He had only been teasing me, but every word was like a drop of poison in my veins. The blood rushed to my head. "Ha, so that's it, is it!" I said to myself. "Very well! So it was not for nothing that I was drawn toward the park! But I won't have it!" I cried aloud, smiting my chest, though I would not have been able to say exactly what it was I would not have. "Whether I find Malevsky himself in the park," I told myself (perhaps it was his own secret he blurted out, he is brazen enough for that), "or anyone else" (the fence around our garden was low, and there would be no difficulty in climbing over it), "whoever it is, had better look out for himself, it is me he will have to do with! . . . I will prove to the world and to the false one" (yes, that is what I called her!) "that I know how to revenge myself!"

I went back to my room, took out of a drawer in my desk an English penknife that I had purchased a few days ago, felt its sharp blades, and, with knitted brows and an air of cold, steadfast resolution, as if I were thoroughly accustomed to this sort of thing, slipped it into my pocket. My heart throbbed angrily, and then seemed to turn to stone. I went about all day with knitted brows and tightly compressed lips, pacing up and down the floor of my room, gripping the knife, which had gotten quite warm in my pocket, and preparing myself for some terrible event. These sensations were so new, so unprecedented that they quite entertained me, and I was so elated by them that I hardly gave a thought to Zinaida herself. I kept picturing to myself Aleko and the young Gypsy—"Whither, young fellow? Lie there! . . ." and then: "You are covered with blood! Oh, what have you done? . . ." "Nothing!" With what a cruel smile I repeated that word: "Nothing!" My father was not at home, but my mother, who was now in a perpetual state of repressed irritation, noted my air of fatality and asked me at suppertime:

"You look like a cat watching a mouse—what's the matter?"

For a reply I gave a condescending smile, thinking to myself: "If they only knew!" Eleven o'clock struck; I went up to my room but did not undress. I was waiting for midnight to strike; and at last it struck. "Now!" I whispered through clenched teeth, and made for the garden, having first taken the precaution to button up my jacket and, for some reason, turn up my sleeves.

I had selected in advance the spot where I intended to keep my watch: at the very end of the garden, where the fence dividing our grounds from those of the Zasekins ended in the wall that surrounded both, there stood a solitary fir tree; by taking up my post beneath its dense low-growing branches I could see all around me, as far as the darkness of the night allowed: there was a little path here that had always seemed mysterious to me; it wound its way snakelike beneath the fence and was trampled at this particular spot by the feet of those who clambered over the palings; farther it led to a circular arbor, formed by the branches of acacias. Reaching this fir tree, I leaned against its trunk and began my watch.

It was a still night like the one before, but the sky was not so cloudy, and the outlines of the bushes and of the taller flowers showed more distinctly. The first minutes of waiting were wearisome, almost eerie. I was ready to do anything! But I had not quite made up my mind as to the manner in which I ought to proceed. Should I thunder out: "Whither away? Halt! Confess, or die!" or simply stab in the dark? Every sound, every rustle, every flutter seemed to me unusual, significant. . . . I got ready to spring, bending forward. . . . But half an hour passed, then an hour; I grew calmer and cooler; the realization that what I was doing was futile, that I had made a fool of myself, that Malevsky had only been making fun of me, gradually came over me. I abandoned my ambush and made a round of the garden. As if to spite me, there was not a sound to be heard; all was still; even our dog was asleep, curled up in a ball at the garden gate. I climbed up to the top of the ruined conservatory, gazed at the distant field beneath, remembered my encounter with Zinaida, and fell into a reverie.

Suddenly I started. . . . I thought I could hear the creaking of a door being opened, followed by the light snapping of twigs. . . . In two bounds I was on the ground again and froze to the spot. Light steps, rapid and stealthy, could be distinctly heard in the garden. . . . They were approaching me. "Here he is at last!" flashed across my mind. I pulled the knife convulsively out of my pocket, opened it no less convulsively—red sparks whirled in front of my eyes, my hair stood on end with fear and rage. . . . The steps were approaching the very spot where I was standing—I crouched, straining toward them. . . . The figure of a man appeared—good heavens! It was my father!

I recognized him at once, though he was muffled in a dark cloak and his hat was pulled down over his brows. He passed me on tiptoe. There was nothing to conceal me, but he did not notice me, for I had crouched so low and was so huddled up as to seem almost one with the earth itself. In a single moment the jealous, bloodthirsty Othello was transformed into a schoolboy. . . . The unexpected apparition of my father had so terrified me that at first I did not even notice where he was coming from, or the direction in which he disappeared. It was only when all was quiet again that I allowed my limbs to relax and asked myself what my father could be doing in the garden at night. In my fright I had dropped the knife into the grass but was too much ashamed to look for it. I had sobered down instantaneously. On my way home, however, I went to my bench beneath the elder bush and looked up at Zinaida's window. The small, slightly convex panes of the window were a dim blue in the feeble light shed by the nocturnal sky. Suddenly their color changed . . . and behind them—I saw it distinctly—a curtain of some light color was cautiously and gently lowered till it touched the windowsill, where it hung motionless.

"What does it all mean?" I said aloud, almost involuntarily, when I was back in my own room. "A dream, a chance occurrence, or . . .?" The suspicions that now entered my mind were so new and strange that I scarcely dared to admit them.

XVIII

I got up with an aching head the next morning. The excitement of the day before had vanished. In its place were nothing but painful bewil-

derment and a melancholy such as I had never before known, as if something within me were dying.

"You look like a rabbit with half its brains removed," said Lushin when we chanced to meet that day.

I shot stealthy glances at my mother and father at the breakfast table. He was calm as usual, she, as usual, full of suppressed irritation. I half expected my father to say a kind word to me, as he sometimes did. . . . But this time he did not even bestow on me his daily cool caress. "Should I tell Zinaida all? . . ." I wondered. "For nothing matters now, all is over between us." I went to her, but not only was unable to tell her anything, I did not even get a chance to speak to her properly. The old princess's son, a twelve-year-old cadet, had arrived from Petersburg for the holidays. Zinaida at once turned her brother over to me. "Here's a friend for you, dearest Volodya." (She had never called me that before.) "His name is Volodya, too. I hope you'll like him; he's rather shy, but he has a good heart. Show him Neskuchny Gardens, go for walks with him, in a word, take him under your wing. You will, won't you? You're a kindhearted boy yourself!" She placed her hands affectionately on my shoulders, and I lost my heart to her all over again. The arrival of this boy turned me back into a boy myself. I looked at the cadet in silence, and he stared back as silently. Zinaida burst out laughing and pushed us toward one another. "Come on, children, embrace!" We obeyed.

"Would you like to see the park?" I asked the cadet.

"Yes, please, sir," he answered in a husky voice, like a real cadet. Zinaida laughed again. . . . I noted that her complexion had never been so lovely as it was that day. The cadet and I set off. There was an old swing in our garden; I helped him onto the narrow seat and began swinging him. He sat motionless in his new uniform of thick cloth adorned with broad strips of gold braid holding on to the ropes with all his might.

"Why don't you unfasten your collar?" I asked.

"Oh, we're used to it," he said, clearing his throat. He was very like his sister; his eyes, in particular, reminded me of hers. I enjoyed looking after him, but the old grief still gnawed at my heart. "Today I'm just a child," I told myself, "while only yesterday . . ." I remembered the spot where I had dropped my knife and went to look for it. I found it and the cadet begged me for it, broke off a thick stem of hemlock, made himself a whistle, and began blowing it. Othello whistled a bit, too.

But in the evening poor Othello wept bitterly in the arms of Zinaïda, when, discovering him in a secluded nook in the garden, she asked him what made him look so sad. My tears gushed out so violently that she was quite alarmed. "What's the matter, Voldemar? What is it?" she kept asking, and getting no answer and seeing that I did not stop crying, she tried to kiss my wet cheek. But I turned from her, whispering through my sobs: "I know all. Why did you play with me? What did you need my love for?"

"Yes, I am much to blame, Volodya," said Zinaida, "I know I am," and she clasped her hands. "There is so much that is bad, dark, sinful in me. . . . But I am not playing with your affections now, I really am fond of you, you can have no idea why. . . . But . . . what do you know?"

What was there for me to say? She stood before me, looking at me, and I was hers, all hers, from head to foot, whenever she looked at me. . . . A quarter of an hour later, I was running races with the cadet and Zinaida. I was laughing now, not weeping, but the laughter made the tears spill from swollen eyelids; I wore a ribbon of Zinaida's around my neck instead of a tie, and shouted with joy when I managed to catch her around her waist. She could do what she liked with me.

XIX

If I were asked to give a detailed account of my feelings during the week following my unsuccessful nocturnal expedition, I should not know how to set about it. It was a strange, feverish period, a kind of chaos in which feelings, thoughts, suspicions, hopes, joys, and sufferings of the most conflicting nature were caught up in a mad vortex; I was afraid of looking into my heart, if a boy of sixteen may be considered capable of looking into his own heart, afraid of thinking seriously about anything; I simply scrambled through the day as best I could; but I slept well . . . here my childish levity came to my relief. I did not want to know whether I was loved, and I did not want to admit to myself that I was not loved; I avoided my father, but Zinaida I could not avoid. . . . Her presence consumed me like a flame . . . and what did I care what was the fire that burned and melted me, so long as it was sweet to burn and melt? Yielding to every impression as it came, I played hide-and-seek with myself, shunned memories, and closed my eyes to what I felt was in store for me. . . . This feverish state could not have lasted long. A thunderbolt put a sudden end to it and quite changed the stream of my existence.

Returning to dinner one day, after rather a long walk, I learned to my surprise that I was to dine alone; that my father had gone out, and my mother did not feel well, did not want any dinner, and had locked herself in her bedroom. I could see by the faces of the servants that something unusual had happened. . . . I did not dare to question them, but I had one friend among them, Philip, the young footman, a passionate lover of poetry and a skilled performer on the guitar, and I turned to him. I learned that there had been a terrible scene between my father and my mother (every word of it could be heard in the maids' room; the conversation had been carried on chiefly in French, but Masha, one of the maids, had worked five years in the house of a seamstress from Paris, and understood it all); that my mother had accused my father of having been unfaithful to her, of carrying on an affair with the next-door young lady; that my father had at first denied the charge, but had afterward flared up himself and said something nasty about "a woman of her age," which had made my mother cry; that my mother had also mentioned a promissory note which my father was supposed to have given the old princess, adding harsh words about the latter, as well as about the young lady, and it was then that my father had spoken so unkindly.

"And it all started," concluded Philip, "with an anonymous letter; nobody knows who wrote it; that's how it all came out, it never would have come out but for the letter."

"Why—do you mean there was anything?" I forced myself to ask, my feet and hands going cold and a quiver starting somewhere inside me. Philip gave a significant wink.

"There was. You can't conceal that sort of thing; your father was ever so careful this time, but there's always a carriage to be hired, or something . . . you can't do without servants."

I dismissed Philip and threw myself on my bed. I did not burst into tears or give myself up to despair; I did not ask myself how and when had it all happened; I did not ask myself how it was that I had not discovered it long ago—I did not even murmur against my father. . . . What I had just learned was too much for me: the sudden revelation had crushed me. . . . All was over. All my flowers had been torn up by the roots and lay around me, scattered and trampled.

XX

The next day my mother announced her intention of going back to town. My father went into her bedroom in the morning and had a long talk with her. No one heard what he said, but my mother stopped crying; she calmed down and called for her breakfast, without however leaving her room or changing her decision. I remember strolling about all day, but I did not go into the garden, and never so much as glanced in the direction of the annex. And that evening I was the witness of an extraordinary scene: taking Count Malevsky's arm, my father led him out of the drawing room into the hall and said coldly, in the presence of one of the footmen: "A few days ago Your Honor was shown the door in a certain house; and now, without going into any explanations, it is my privilege to inform you that if you ever try to come here again, I will throw you out of the window. I don't like your handwriting." The count cringed, ground his teeth, shrugged his shoulders, and slunk away.

Preparations began for the move to town, to our house in Arbat Street. My father himself probably had no desire to stay any longer in the country; but he had evidently succeeded in dissuading my mother from making any scandal; everything was done quietly, without haste, my mother even sending her compliments to the princess and expressing her regret that a slight indisposition prevented her from taking leave of her. I wandered about as if possessed, desiring one thing only—for all this to come to an end as soon as possible. There was one thought I could not shake off—how could she, a young girl, and after all a princess, have brought herself to act as she had knowing that my father was not a free man, and well aware that she could easily have married—Belovzorov, for instance! What had she expected to come of it? Did she not fear to ruin her whole future? "There," thought I, "that's what love is, that's passion, that's devotion!" And Lushin's words came to my mind: "There are evidently people who enjoy sacrificing themselves." Once during this period I caught sight of something pale at one of the windows of the wing. . . . "Could it be Zinaida's face?" I wondered . . . and that was just what it was. I could no longer restrain myself. I could not bear to part with her without a word of farewell. I watched for an opportunity and made my way to the wing of the house.

The old princess received me in the drawing room in her usual careless and dingy manner.

"How is it your people are taking wing so early, sir?" she asked, cramming snuff into both her nostrils. I looked at her, and a load fell from my shoulders. The term promissory note, which Philip had let drop, had been torturing me. She suspected nothing, or so at least it seemed to me at the time. Zinaida appeared from the other room, in a black dress, pale, her hair out of curl; she took my hand in hers silently and led me away.

"I heard your voice," she said, "and came out immediately. And was it so easy for you to desert us, cruel boy?"

"I have come to bid you farewell, Princess," I said in answer, "and probably forever. You have heard that we are moving back to town?"

Zinaida looked searchingly at me.

"Yes, I have. Thank you for coming. I began to think I should never see you again. Think kindly of me, if you can. I tormented you sometimes, I know, but I am not what you think me."

She turned away, leaning against the window frame.

"Really I'm not. I know you have a bad opinion of me."

"*I* have?"

"Yes, you . . . you."

"I?" I repeated sorrowfully, and my heart was shaken as before under the spell of her irresistible, indescribable charm. "I? Believe me, Zinaida Alexandrovna, whatever you have done, however you have tortured me, I shall love and adore you to the end of my days."

She turned swiftly, her arms spread wide, and then flung them around my neck, kissing me passionately and firmly. God knows whom that long farewell kiss was intended for, but I drank up its sweetness eagerly, I knew it would never be repeated. "Good-bye, good-bye," I said again and again.

She tore herself from me and went out of the room. I, too, went away. I am incapable of describing the feelings with which I went away. I should not like to have to go through all this again, and yet I should count myself an unhappy man if I had missed it.

We moved back to town. It was long before I was able to shake off the past and begin working again. My wound healed slowly; but I bore no grudge against my father. On the contrary, he had grown in my eyes; let psychologists explain the paradox as they may. I was walking along a boulevard one day when to my great joy whom should I run into but Lushin! I liked him for his frank, sincere ways, and he was dear to me for the memories he aroused in me. I rushed up to him.

"Ha!" he said, knitting his brows. "It's you, young man, is it? Let's have a look at you! Still a bit sallow, but the moping expression has gone from your eyes. You look like a human being, not a lapdog. That's good. Well, how are you? Working?"

I heaved a sigh. I did not want to lie, and was ashamed of owning the truth.

"Never mind," continued Lushin, "don't lose heart! The chief thing is to lead a normal life and not let yourself be carried away by your feelings. For what's the good of that? Wherever the wave carries you, it is bad; but as long as a man has so much as a stone beneath him—at least he stands on his two feet. I do nothing but cough—and Belovzorov—have you heard about him?"

"Why, what about him?"

"Completely disappeared; they say he went to the Caucasus. Let it be a lesson to you, young man! And all because people don't know when it's time to part, to tear the net. You seem to have come out of it unscathed. Mind you don't get caught another time! Good-bye!"

"I'll never be caught again," thought I. "I'll never see her again." But I was destined to see Zinaida once more.

XXI

My father was in the habit of taking a ride every day; he had a fine English russet stallion with a long thin neck and long legs; it was a savage, indomitable animal; its name was Electric. Nobody but my father could manage it. One day he came into my room in a good-natured mood, a rare thing with him of late; he was going out riding and had his spurs on. I begged him to take me with him.

"We'd better play leapfrog, instead," my father answered, "you won't be able to keep up with me on your little German nag."

"Oh yes, I will; I'll put on spurs."

"Come on, then!"

We set out. I had a shaggy black pony, surefooted and spirited; true, it had to go at a gallop to keep up with Electric's trot, but I did not fall behind. I have never seen a horseman like my father; his seat was so carelessly easy, so elegant, and the horse seemed to feel it and to be proud of its rider. We rode through the boulevards, spent some time on the Devichye Polye, jumped several fences (at first I had been afraid of jumping, but my father despised timid people—and so I had stopped being afraid), crossed the Moscow River twice, and I was beginning to think we were going back, especially as my father remarked that my horse seemed tired, when he suddenly turned sharply from me and made for the Krymsky ford, sending his horse at a gallop along the bank. I galloped after him. When we reached a towering pile of old logs, he jumped lightly off Electric, bade me dismount, threw the reins of his horse into my hands, and told me to wait there, by the logs; then he turned into a narrow side street and disappeared from my sight. I began pacing backward and forward along the bank, leading the horses and scolding Electric, who kept tossing his head, shaking all over, snorting and neighing; whenever I stood still, he pawed the ground, squealed, and bit my nag on the neck, in a word, behaved like the spoiled thoroughbred he was. Still my father did not come back. An unpleasant dampness rose from the river; a drizzling rain fell soundlessly, mottling with tiny dark patches those tiresome gray logs, around which I kept wandering till heartily sick of them. I felt bored and dejected, and still my father did not come. A policeman, evidently a Finn, as gray as the logs, with an enormous potlike hat on his head, and carrying a halberd (and what on earth was a policeman doing on the bank of the Moscow River?) approached me, and turning a face like that of a wrinkled beldame toward me, asked:

"What are you doing here with those horses, master? Let me hold them for you."

I did not answer him; he begged for some tobacco. To get rid of him (and also because my impatience was becoming intolerable) I took a few paces in the direction in which my father had gone; then I went down the side street, turned the corner—and stopped short. About forty paces away, at the open window of a small wooden house, stood my father, his back to me; he was leaning against the windowsill, and inside, half concealed by the curtain, sat a woman in a dark dress, talking to my father; the woman was Zinaida.

I was dumbfounded. I had certainly not expected this. My first impulse was to turn tail. "If my father looks back, I am lost," I thought. But a strange feeling, which was stronger than curiosity, stronger even than jealousy, stronger than fear, kept me rooted to the spot. I stood gazing and straining my ears to catch their words. My father seemed to be insisting on something to which Zinaida would not consent. I can still see her face—sorrowful, grave, beautiful, stamped with an indescribable blend of devotion, sadness, and love, and with a kind of despair—I can find no other word for it. She spoke in monosyllables, never raising her eyes, merely smiling humbly and stubbornly. The smile alone would have told me it was Zinaida. My father shrugged his shoulders and straightened his hat—a sure sign of impatience with him. . . . Then I made out the words: "*Vous devez vous séparer de cette.* . . ." Zinaida drew herself up and stretched out her arm. . . . An extraordinary scene was enacted before my eyes: my father lifted his riding crop, with which he had been flicking the dust from the skirts of his coat, and brought it down with a smart crack on that bared forearm. It was all I could do not to cry out, but Zinaida only started, looked at my father in silence, lifted her arm slowly up to her lips, kissing the weal crimsoning on it. Flinging away the riding crop, my father rushed up the steps of the porch and burst into the house. . . . Zinaida turned away from the window, her arms outstretched and her head thrown back. . . .

I retreated, faint with fear, my heart filled with an anguish of amazement; I ran to the end of the side street, almost letting Electric break loose from the halter, and returned to the riverbank. My thoughts were in utter confusion. I had known before that my father, usually so cool and reserved, was given to sudden fits of fury, and yet I found it impossible to realize what it was I had just witnessed. . . . But I knew I should never be able to forget, as long as I lived, Zinaida's gesture, look, smile; I knew that her image, so suddenly revealed to me in this new aspect, would be engraved forever on my memory. I gazed vacantly at the river, unconscious of the tears trickling down my cheeks. "He beat her," I kept repeating, "beat her, beat her. . . ."

"Come on, give me the reins, won't you?" It was my father's voice behind me.

I handed him the reins mechanically. He leaped onto Electric's back. . . . The horse, chilled from the long wait, reared, and then sprang forward ten feet or so. But my father soon got the better of it, plunging his spurs into the animal's sides and striking it on the neck with his fist. . . . "Ah—I haven't got my whip!" he muttered.

I thought of the crack with which the riding crop had come down, and shuddered.

"What have you done with it?" I asked my father after a short pause.

He galloped ahead without answering. I overtook him. I felt I simply must see his face.

"Did you get tired waiting?" my father asked through his teeth.

"Rather. But where did you drop your whip?" I insisted.

My father darted a swift glance at me.

"I didn't drop it," he said, "I threw it away."

He turned thoughtful and bent his head . . . and it was then, for the first and probably last time, that I saw what kindness and compassion his severe features were capable of expressing.

Again he set his horse at a gallop, and this time I was not able to overtake him. I arrived home a quarter of an hour after he did.

"That's what love is!" I told myself once more that night, seated at my desk, on which books and notebooks were gradually accumulating. "That's passion! You would think *anyone* would be roused to anger, *no one* would submit to a blow, however dear the hand that dealt it! But apparently even this can be endured by one who loves. . . . And I . . . and I thought . . ."

This last month had matured me considerably, and my own love, with its agitation and sufferings, now seemed to me petty, childish, insignificant, in comparison with that other unknown thing as to which

I could only form vague surmises, that thing which was as terrifying
to me as an unfamiliar countenance, beautiful but stern, which one
seeks in vain to make out through the gloom. . . .

I had a strange and terrible dream that night. I dreamed I went
into a dark, low-ceilinged room. . . . My father stood there, whip in
hand, stamping his foot; Zinaida crouched in the corner, and there was
a red gash, not on her arm, but across her brow. Behind them both
rose the figure of Belovzorov, covered with blood. He opened his pale
lips and uttered angry threats at my father. . . .

Two months later I entered the university, and six months after
that my father died (of a stroke) in Petersburg, where we had just
moved. A few days before his death he received a letter from Moscow
that caused him great agitation. He went to my mother and asked her
for something, they say he actually wept—my father wept! On the
morning of the day when he had his stroke, he began a letter to me in
French: "My son," he wrote, "beware of the love of woman, beware
of that joy, that poison. . . ." After his death, my mother sent a considerable sum of money to Moscow.

XXII

Three or four years passed. I had just graduated from the university
but had not yet made up my mind what to take up, what door to
knock at; in the meantime I merely idled. One evening I met Maidanov
at the theater. He was married and was employed in a government
office, but I did not find any changes in him. He still indulged in futile
enthusiasm and sudden fits of depression.

"Do you know," he said casually, "that Madame Dolskaya is
here?"

"Who is Madame Dolskaya?"

"Have you forgotten? She's the former Princess Zasekina, with
whom we were all, including yourself, in love. In the country, near
Neskuchny Gardens—remember?"

"Is she married to Dolsky?"

"Yes."

"And is she here, at the theater?"

"No, but she arrived in Petersburg a few days ago; she's going
abroad."

"And what sort of man is her husband?"

"Oh, he's an excellent fellow, rich, too. We used to work together,
in Moscow. You understand, after that affair—but you know all about

that, of course"—Maidanov gave a significant smile—"it was not so easy for her to find a husband; there were consequences. . . . But a woman of her ability can manage anything. Go and call on her, she'll be very glad to see you. She's lovelier than ever."

Maidanov gave me Zinaida's address. She was staying at the Demuth Hotel. Old memories stirred within me. . . . I promised myself I would visit my old flame the very next day. But all sorts of things turned up; I let a week go by, and another, and when at last I set out for the Demuth Hotel and asked for Madame Dolskaya, I was told she died four days ago, rather unexpectedly, in childbirth.

I felt as if someone had struck me right over the heart. The thought that I might have seen her, and had not, and would never see her again, this bitter thought ate into my soul with all the power of stark reproach. "Dead!" I echoed, staring blankly at the porter, and then went quietly out into the street and walked off, without any idea where I was going. The entire past surged up before me. So this is how that young, brilliant, eager life was fated to end, this is the destiny to which it had aspired with such haste and perturbation! Thus musing, I recalled those dear features, those eyes, those tresses, all shut up in a narrow wooden box, reposing in the damp dark earth somewhere not far from me—who was still living—perhaps only a few yards away from my father. . . . Turning over all these things in my mind, I tried to concentrate on them, but the words:

Indifferent lips pronounced the fatal tidings
To my indifferent ears . . .

echoed in my soul. Oh, youth, youth! You care for nothing, you seem to possess all the treasures of the universe, grief itself is a source of entertainment for you, even sorrow is becoming to you! Confident and arrogant, you declare: behold, I alone live, while your days flee, vanishing unreckoned and leaving not a trace behind them, and everything within you vanishes, like wax melting in sunlight, like snow. . . . And it may be that the whole secret of your charm lies, not in your ability to achieve whatsoever you will, but in your ability to believe there is nothing you could not achieve, in the fact that you expend so recklessly forces for which you can find no other uses, that each one of us is firmly convinced of his right to say: what would not I have done, if I had not wasted my time so vainly!

Take myself, for example: on what were my expectations based, what did I hope for, what brilliant future did I anticipate, that I scarcely

gave a sigh, scarcely felt a moment's grief, as I bade farewell to the
specter of my first love?

And what, of all I hoped for, has come true? And now, as the
evening shadows begin to fall across my path, is there anything more
radiant, more precious to me than the memories of that short-lived
early morning storm in spring?

But why do I seek to calumniate myself? Even then, in those reckless youthful days, I was not deaf to the sorrowful voice calling to me,
to the solemn sound reaching me from the grave. I remember a few
days after that on which I heard of Zinaida's death, I attended, of my
own accord, obeying an irresistible impulse, the deathbed of a poor
old woman who lived in the same building as I did. She lay there in
her agony, struggling for her life, beneath a covering of rags, her mat-
tress a couple of hard planks, her pillow a sack. Her life had been one
grinding struggle with incessant poverty. She had never known any
joys, never tasted the sweets of happiness—she might have been expected to welcome death, to see in it her peace and freedom. And yet,
while her decrepit body held out, while her bosom still rose and fell
painfully beneath the icy hand that had her in its grip, while there was
still a vestige of strength left in her, the old woman crossed herself
continually, whispering: "O Lord, forgive my sins . . ." and the horror,
the fear of death that could be seen in her eyes only disappeared as
the last spark of consciousness left her. . . . I remember that there, at
the deathbed of this poor old woman, I thought with anguish of Zinaida, and a desire rose in me to pray for her, for my father, for myself.

(*1860*)

ON BELINSKY

Some of my readers will perhaps be surprised at the word *idealist* with
which I thought it necessary to characterize Belinsky. . . . Such a description suited him admirably. Belinsky was as much an idealist as a
negationist. He negated in the name of his ideal. That ideal had quite
a definite and homogeneous quality, though it was called and still is
called by different names: science, progress, humanity, civilization—
the West, in short. Well-meaning but ill-disposed people even use the
word *revolution*. What matters is not the name, but the substance,
which is so clear and indubitable that it is not worthwhile dwelling
upon it. There can be no misunderstandings here. Belinsky devoted
himself wholly to the service of this ideal. He belonged to the camp of

the "Westernizers," as their opponents called them, with all his sympathies and with the whole of his activity. He was a Westerner not only because he acknowledged the superiority of Western science, Western art, and the Western social order, but also because he was deeply convinced of the need for Russia to absorb everything the West had produced for the development of her own powers and her own importance. He believed there was no salvation for us other than to follow the path Peter the Great pointed out to us and upon which the Slavophiles hurled their choicest execrations at that time. To accept the results of Western life, to adapt them to ours, taking into account the peculiarities of our history and climate and, treating them, too, of course, freely and critically—it was in this way that he thought we could at last achieve originality, a quality he prized much more than is generally believed. . . . Yes, Belinsky loved Russia; but he loved freedom and enlightenment as ardently. To combine what to him were the highest interests—therein lay the whole meaning of his work, that was what he aspired to.

(1869)

ON THE RUSSIAN LANGUAGE

In these days of doubt, in these days of painful brooding over the fate of my country, you alone are my rod and my staff, O great, mighty, true, and free Russian language! If it were not for you, how could one keep from despairing at the sight of what is going on at home? It is inconceivable that such a language should not belong to a great people.

ALEKSANDR HERZEN

*ALEKSANDR HERZEN (1812–1870) was the son of a prominent and very
wealthy Russian nobleman, Ivan Yakovlev, and Yakovlev's German
mistress. He was given the name Herzen to suggest he was a child of
the heart—Herz in German means "heart." From 1847 till his death
he lived as an émigré outside of Russia. When Herzen's father died in
Russia, the czarist government permitted the father's fortune to be
transferred to Herzen abroad—thanks to pressure from the Rothschild
international banking family, which advanced loans to the government.
Hence Herzen's exile was materially well cushioned.*

Herzen published a magazine, The Bell, *which had great influence outside and inside Russia, and was the author of several stories,
philosophical studies, the novel* Who Is to Blame, *and many articles.
Between 1852 and 1868 he produced his outstanding work, the voluminous and engrossing* My Past and Thoughts (Byloe i dumy), *from
which the passages here have been taken.*

My Past and Thoughts *combines historical analyses, philosophical
observations, autobiographical anecdotes, reminiscences, descriptions
of travels, vignettes of individuals, and frank and emotional accounts
of events in Herzen's own family life (deaths, wrenching marital sufferings). According to Isaiah Berlin, the book represents "perhaps the
most extraordinary self-revelation on the part of a sensitive and fastidious man ever written down for the benefit of the general public."*

*Herzen was a liberal in the truest sense: wishing for the free and
full development of every human being. His instincts were for moderation, gentleness, kindness, understanding. He represents the very
best of nineteenth-century Russian culture.*

*Herzen had a mind exceptionally attuned to the effects on indi-
vidual human beings of belonging to groups. Although he assigned the*

highest value to individuals, he saw human beings as deeply grounded
in the historical era to which they belonged. He is one of the most
historically oriented Russians who ever lived.

He considered the bourgeoisie of Western Europe to be vulgar
and petty. He found it ironic and pathetic that the middle class, with
its paucity of spiritual aspiration, had become the leading force in the
nineteenth century. In this view he agreed with other leading Russian
thinkers of his as well as later times, such as Dostoyevsky. However,
he differed from the predominant current of Russian opinion in rejecting its and others' utopian strivings.

Herzen focused on the lives of individual human beings, not on
abstractions and blueprints for perfecting society as a whole. He believed that no theory or doctrine (such as romantic idealism or socialism) could supply, as Isaiah Berlin termed it, "any simple or final answer
to any genuine human problem." He deplored the terrible power over
human lives exercised by ideological abstractions. The goal of life to
him was life itself. Herzen wrote: "We think the purpose of the child
is to grow up because it does grow up. But its purpose is to play, to
enjoy itself, to be a child. If we merely look to the end of the process,
the purpose of all life is death." Herzen was terrified of the oppressors,
but he was also terrified of the liberators. He cared mainly for the
preservation of individual liberty. His writings embodied a strong libertarian humanism, which became eclipsed in Russia in October 1917.

RECOLLECTIONS OF RUSSIAN
INTELLECTUALS—1830s AND 1860s

(From My Past and Thoughts)

Thirty years ago,* the Russia of the *future* existed exclusively among
a few boys, hardly more than children, so small and inconspicuous that
there was room for them under the heels of the jackboots of the
autocracy—yet in them lay the heritage of December 14,† the heritage
of a purely national Russia, as well as of the learning of all humanity.
This new life struggled on like the grass sprouting at the mouth of the
still smoldering crater.

In the very maw of the monster these children, so unlike other

---

* Herzen wrote this portion of his memoirs in the 1850s.
† December 14, 1825: the date of the Decembrist uprising, after the death of Alexander I. The uprising failed; the reign of Nicholas I (1825–55) followed.

children, grew, developed, and began to live a different life. Weak, insignificant, unsupported, and persecuted by everybody, they might have easily perished, leaving no trace, but they *survived*, or, if they died on their way, all did not die with them. They were the rudimentary cells, the embryos of history, barely perceptible and barely existing—like all embryos.

Little by little, groups of them were formed. Those elements that had traits in common gathered round their centers: then the groups repelled one another. This splitting up gave them breadth of vision and many-sidedness in their development; after developing to the end, that is, to the extreme, the branches united again by whatever names they may be called—Stankevich's circle, the Slavophiles, or our own circle.

The leading characteristic of them all was a profound feeling of aversion for official Russia, for their environment, and at the same time the urge to escape out of it—and, in some of them, a vehement desire to change the contemporary state of affairs.

The objection that these circles, unnoticed both from above and from below, formed an exceptional, a casual, a disconnected phenomenon, that the education of the young people was for the most part exotic, alien, and that they would rather express the translation of French and German ideas into Russian than anything of their own, seems to us quite groundless.

Possibly about the turn of the last century there was in the aristocracy a sprinkling of Russian foreigners who had sundered all ties with the national life; but they had neither practical interests, nor environment sharing their convictions, nor a literature of their own. They died out barren. Victims of the divorce from the people brought about by Czar Peter, they remained eccentric and whimsical, not merely superfluous but undeserving of pity. The War of 1812 put an end to them—the old generation lived on, but none of the younger developed in that direction. To bracket with them men of the stamp of Chaadayev* would be the greatest mistake.

Protest, denunciation, hatred for one's country, has a completely different significance from indifferent aloofness. Byron, lashing at English life, fleeing from England as from the plague, remained a typical

---

* Pyotr Chaadayev (1794–1856) aroused a storm with his *Philosophical Letters*, written in French in 1829 and only privately circulated. The czarist regime officially declared him insane because of his harsh critique of Russia. In the words of George L. Kline, a historian of Russian philosophy, Chaadayev found "unity, universality, and 'conciliarity' in Western Europe, with its tradition of Roman Catholic Christianity, but exclusiveness, divisiveness, and self-centeredness in Russia, with its tradition of Russian Orthodox Christianity."

Englishman. Heine,* trying, out of exasperation at the loathsome political state of Germany, to become French, remained a genuine German. The highest protest against Judaism—Christianity—is permeated
with the spirit of Judaism. The separation of the states of North America
from England could lead to war and hatred, but it could not make the
Americans un-English.

As a rule, it is with great difficulty that people can get rid of their
physiological memories and the mold in which they are cast by heredity.
To achieve that one must either be peculiarly trite and apathetic or else
be absorbed in abstract pursuits. The impersonality of mathematics or
the nonhuman objectivity of nature does not call forth this faculty of
the mind, does not awaken it; but as soon as we touch upon questions
of life, of art, of morals, in which a man is not only an observer and
investigator, but also a participant, then we find a physiological limit
—which the inherited blood and brains make it very hard to overstep
unless one could erase from them all traces of the cradle songs of the
home fields and hills, of the customs and the whole setting of the past.

The poet or the artist is always national in his truest work. Whatever he does, whatever aim and thought may be contained in his work,
he expresses, whether he wishes it or not, some elemental forces at
work in the national character, and expresses them more deeply and
more clearly than the very history of the people. Even when renouncing
everything national, the artist does not lose the chief traits that reveal
his origin. Both in the Greek *Iphigenia* and in the Oriental *Divan* Goethe
was a German. Poets really are, as the Romans called them, prophets;
only they do not foretell what is not and will be by chance, but give
expression to *what exists, though still unknown*, in the dim consciousness of the masses, what is still slumbering in them.

Everything that has existed from time immemorial in the soul of
the Anglo-Saxon peoples is linked together as in a chain by one
personality—and every fiber, every hint, every urge, fermenting from
generation to generation and *unconscious* of itself, has received at his
hands form and language.

No one is likely to suppose that the England of the Elizabethan
times—the majority of the people, anyway—had a clear understanding
of Shakespeare; nor have they such now—but for that matter they
have no distinct understanding of themselves, either. Yet I do not doubt
that when an Englishman goes to the theater he does understand
Shakespeare—instinctively, through sympathy. At the moment when

* Heinrich Heine (1797–1856) was a German lyrical and satirical poet and prose
writer who settled in Paris in 1831.

he is listening to the play, something becomes clearer and more familiar to him. One would think that a people so quick-witted as the French might understand Shakespeare, too. The character of Hamlet, for instance, is so universally human, especially in the stage of doubts and hesitation, of the realization of some black deeds being perpetrated, some betrayal of what is great for the sake of what is mean and trivial, that it is hard to imagine that anybody could fail to understand him, but in spite of every trial and effort, Hamlet remains alien to the Frenchman.

If the aristocrats of the past century, who consistently ignored everything Russian, remained in reality incredibly more Russian than the house serfs remained peasants, it is even more impossible that the younger generation could have lost their Russian character because they studied science and philosophy in French and German books. A section of our Moscow Slavs reached the point of ultra-Slavism with Hegel in their hands.

The very circles of which I am speaking sprang into existence in natural response to a deep inner need of the Russian life of that period.

We have spoken many times of the stagnation that followed the crisis of 1825. The moral level of society sank, development was interrupted, everything progressive and energetic was effaced. Those who remained—frightened, weak, distracted—were petty and shallow; the worthless generation of Alexander occupied the foremost place. As time went on they changed into cringing officials, lost the savage poetry of revelry and aristocratic ways together with every shadow of independent dignity; they served assiduously, they made the grade, but they never became high dignitaries in the full sense of the word. Their day was over.

Under this great world of society, the great world of the people maintained an indifferent silence; nothing was changed for them—their plight was bad, indeed, but not worse than before—the new blows were not intended for their scourged backs. *Their time had not yet come*. It was between this roof and this foundation that our children were the first to raise their heads—perhaps because they did not suspect how dangerous it was; anyway, by means of these children, Russia, stunned and stupefied, began to come to life again.

What impressed them was the complete contradiction of the *words* they were taught with the *realities* of life around them. Their teachers, their books, their university spoke one language that was intelligible to heart and mind. Their father and mother, their relations, and all their surroundings spoke other things with which neither mind nor

heart was in agreement, but with which the powers that be and pe-
cuniary interests were in accord. Nowhere did this contradiction between education and real life reach such proportions as among the
nobility of Russia. The uncouth German student with his round cap
covering a seventh part of his head, with his world-shaking sallies, is
far nearer to the German *Spiessbürger* than is supposed, while the
French *collégien*, thin with vanity and emulation, is already *en herbe
l'homme raisonnable, qui exploite sa position.*

The number of educated people among us has always been extremely small; but those who were educated have always received an
education, not perhaps very thorough, but fairly general and humane:
it humanized them all. But a *human* being was just what the bureaucratic hierarchy or the successful maintenance of the landowning regime
did not require. The young man had either to dehumanize himself—
and the greater number did so—or to stop short and ask himself: "But
is it absolutely essential to go into the service? Is it really a good thing
to be a landowner?" After that for some, the weaker and more impatient, there followed the idle existence of a cornet on the retired list,
the sloth of the country, the dressing gown, eccentricities, cards, wine,
etc.; for others a time of ordeal and inner travail. They could not live
in complete moral disharmony, nor could they be satisfied with a negative attitude of withdrawal; awakened thought demanded an outlet.
The various solutions of these questions, all equally harassing for the
young generation, determined their distribution into various circles.

Thus, for instance, our little circle was formed in the university
and found Sungurov's circle already in existence. His, like ours, was
concerned rather with politics than with learning. Stankevich's circle,
which came into existence at the same time, was equally near and
equally remote from both. It followed another path, and its interests
were purely theoretical.

Between 1830 and 1840 our convictions were too youthful, too
ardent and passionate, not to be exclusive. We could feel a cold respect
for Stankevich's circle, but we could not come into closer contact with
it. They traced philosophical systems, were absorbed in self-analysis,
and found peace in a luxurious pantheism from which Christianity was
not excluded. The stuff of our dreams was woven out of ways of
organizing a new league in Russia on the pattern of the Decembrists
and we looked upon knowledge as merely a means. The government
did its best to strengthen us in our revolutionary tendencies.

In 1834 the whole of Sungurov's circle was sent into exile and—
vanished.

In 1835 we were exiled. Five years later we came back, hardened
by our experience. The dreams of youth had become the irrevocable
determination of maturity. That was the heydey of Stankevich's circle.
Stankevich himself I did not find in Moscow—he was in Germany; but
it was just at that moment that Belinsky's articles were beginning to
attract universal attention.

On our return we measured our strength with them. The battle
was an unequal one for both sides; origins, weapons, and language—
all were different. After fruitless skirmishes we saw that it was our turn
now to undertake serious study and we too set to work upon Hegel
and the German philosophy. When we had made a sufficient study of
it, it became evident that there was no ground for dispute between us
and Stankevich's circle.

The latter was inevitably bound to break up. It had done its bit
—and had done it most brilliantly; its influence on the whole of literature and academic teaching was immense—one need but recall the
names of Belinsky and Granovsky; Koltsov was formed in it; Botkin,
Katkov, and others belonged to it.* But it could not remain an exclusive
circle without lapsing into German doctrinairism—men who were alive
and Russian had no leanings that way.

In addition to Stankevich's circle, there was another one, formed
during our exile, and, like us, it was at swords' points with Stankevich's
circle; its members were afterward called Slavophiles. The Slavophiles
approached the vital questions that occupied us from the opposite side,
and were far more absorbed in practical work and real conflict than
Stankevich's circle.

It was natural that Stankevich's society should split up between
them and us. The Aksakovs and Samarin joined the Slavophiles, that
is, Khomyakov and the Kireyevskys. Belinsky and Bakunin went over
to us. Stankevich's closest friend, one most kindred to his spirit, Granovsky, was one of us from the day he came back from Germany.

If Stankevich had lived, his circle would nonetheless have broken
up. He would himself have gone over to Khomyakov or to us.

By 1842 the sifting in accordance with natural affinity had long

* Timofey N. Granovsky (1813–1855) was a liberal, pro-Western professor of European history at Moscow University. He was the prototype for Stepan Trofimovich
Verkhovensky, a character satirized in Dostoyevsky's novel *The Devils (The Possessed)*. Aleksey V. Koltsov (1809–1842) was one of the very few peasant poets of
the nineteenth century in Russia. Vasily P. Botkin (1811–1869) was a music and
art critic and friend of Belinsky; Mikhail N. Katkov (1818–1887) was editor of an
important conservative magazine, *Russky Vestnik* ("Russian Messenger"), which
published a great number of the best Russian novels of the nineteenth century in
installments.

been over, and our camp stood in battle array face-to-face with the Slavophiles. Of that conflict we will speak elsewhere.

What inspiration touched these men? What was it that recreated them? They had no thought, no care for their social position, or for their personal gain or for their security; their whole life, all their efforts were devoted to the public weal regardless of all personal interests; some forgot their wealth, others their poverty, and went forth, without looking back, to the solution of theoretical questions. The interests of truth, the interests of learning, the interests of art, *humanitas*, absorbed everything else.

And the renunciation of this world was not confined to the time at the university and two or three years of youth. The best men of Stankevich's circle are dead; the others have remained what they were to this day. Belinsky, worn out by work and suffering, fell a fighter and a beggar. Granovsky, delivering his message of learning and humanity, died as he mounted his platform. Botkin did not, in fact, become a merchant; indeed, none of them *distinguished* themselves in the government service.

It was just the same in the two other circles, the Slavophiles and ours. Where, in what corner of the Western world today, do you find such groups of devotees of thought, such zealots of learning, such fanatics of conviction—whose hair turns gray but whose enthusiasm is forever young?

Where? Point them out. I boldly challenge you—I only except for the moment one country, Italy—and demarcate the field for the contest, i.e., I stipulate that my opponent should not escape from the domain of statistics into that of history.

We know how great were the interest in theory and the passion for truth and religion in the days of such martyrs for science and reason as Bruno, Galileo, and the rest; we know, too, what the France of the Encyclopedists was in the second half of the eighteenth century; but later? Later *sta, viator*!

In the Europe of today there is no youth and there are no young men. The most brilliant representative of the France of the last years of the Restoration and of the July dynasty, Victor Hugo, has taken exception to my saying this. Properly speaking he refers to the young France of the twenties, and I am ready to admit that I have been too sweeping—but beyond that I will not yield one iota to him. I have their own admissions. Take *Confession d'un enfant du siècle*, and the poems of Alfred de Musset, recall the France depicted in George Sand's

letters, in the contemporary drama and novels, and in the cases in the
law courts.

But what does all that prove? A great deal; and in the first place
that the Chinese shoes of German make in which Russia has hobbled
for a hundred and fifty years, though they have caused many painful
corns, have evidently not crippled her bones, since whenever she has
had a chance of stretching her limbs, the result has been the exuberance
of fresh young energies. That does not guarantee the future, but it does
make it extremely *possible*.

                                                    (*written 1850s, published 1861*)

RUSSIAN FOLK PROVERBS

RUSSIAN POPULAR SAYINGS are a treasure trove of deeply embedded attitudes toward a tremendous variety of subjects. They are the crystallized feelings of Russians about themselves and their lives— picturesque, colorful formulations, even if sometimes obscure and ambiguous—that have stood the test of time. Repeated, committed to memory, and passed on by successive generations, they are pithy, often epigrammatic, funny fragments of traditional Russian national perceptions. For non-Russians, they provide little windows into the Russians' self-imagery.

Russian written literature was created by literate people, of course—for the most part members of the educated classes. But there was another sphere in which culture expressed itself—oral folk literature, folk art, folk culture.

The two cultures, literate and oral, educated and folk, did meet at certain points, overlapping and interacting. Proverbial expressions are one such channel between the literate and oral Russias. Culture not only trickled down from the top, but also rose in various capillary tubes from the bottom up. The folk, the people—mostly peasants, also some urban craftsmen and artisans—lived in a traditional culture based largely on their ancient preliterate or subliterate folk roots. These people passed on their values through their accumulated sayings, saws, proverbs, riddles. Their tradition made incursions into written literature—as may be seen in Goncharov's Oblomov's Dream *and Aksakov's* Family Chronicle—*through the influence of proverbs, songs, fairy tales.*

Russians of all classes came in contact with these sayings—learned them, added new ones, stored them in their memories, and cited them—and they do so to this day, in everyday life as well as in learned

disquisitions or political oratory—when appropriate to a given situa-
tion. Acquaintance with these ready-made formulations—contradic-
tory though they may often be—gives insight into the true collective
memory of the Russian people. They are the helm that helps steer the
Russians' reactions—in commerce, family life, political life, and factory
life. They are the formulations of attitudes that spring to the fore the
most quickly, the most automatically.

Unlike most Westerners, who have become converted to the idea
of the primacy and superiority of generalized, abstract discourse, the
Russians to this day are fond of the concreteness of their proverbs.
Traditional images and the folksy aura of ancient sayings have main-
tained their appeal.

The group of proverbs selected here deal with the theme of the
familiar versus the alien, "we" versus "they," the motherland Russia
in opposition to the "other," the "Pole and the German." Such cate-
gories are separated by a particularly sharp dividing line in Russian
culture, as is evident in anthropologists' research as well as literature.
The selections here are culled from the collection of proverbs by the
famous Russian folklorist Vladimir Dal (1801–1872), a collection
which contains about 28,000 proverbs arranged in 180 thematic cat-
egories. The proverbs praise loyalty to Russia, advise staying put and
not straying away from one's home, support conformity, and deprecate
foreign countries. They particularly emphasize the need to remain at-
tached to the home. The qualities admired are hospitality, military
prowess, and a "slow" or "rear" intelligence, while rationality, intel-
lectuality, and systematic inventiveness (all three often attributed to the
Germans) are ridiculed.

Praise the place that is beyond the sea, but sit at home.

Water doesn't flow under a stone that's lying down.

A stone grows moss.

Whatever nation you live with, hold on to its customs.

Among whatever people you find yourself, put on their cap.

That country is dear where your belly button got cut.

It is a poor bird that soils its own nest.

Without a roof even wormwood doesn't grow.

People praise the drums on the other side of the mountains, but when we see them over here, they turn out to be just plain baskets.

Springtime is beautiful, but in foreign parts even spring is not beautiful.

Woe to him who is in a foreign country and doesn't know the language.

Foreign countries are like a stepmother. They don't stroke the fur the right direction.

One's own country rubs one the right way.

At home you don't feel a burden.

At home smoke doesn't burn one's eyes.

At home even straw is good to eat.

At home even the walls help.

Even beyond the mountains there are human beings.

Even across the river there live people.

It doesn't matter where you live, just so you are not hungry.

A dog will gnaw off its leg and run away.

A pine tree waves to its own forest.

Russia and summer have nothing in common.

Russia has gotten stiff under the snow.

Russian bones like warmth.

Steam doesn't break any bones.

The crane says, "Good-bye, Mother Russia, I'll go where it's warm."

The goose goes south, the peasant goes to his stove.

In Russia nobody ever starved to death.

The joy of Russia is to drink.

One Russian finished off one hundred Moslem pagans.

The Russian peasant has a rear intelligence.

The words *perhaps if you're lucky* and *somehow* are typical of the Russian.

What is health to the Russian is death to the German.

The German is cunning.

The Germans have instruments for everything.

The Germans are clever; they invented the monkey.

The German gets there with his brain, the Russian with his eyes.

Here it is not like in Poland; here we have bigger people.

Holy Russia is large and everywhere the sun shines.

Holy Russian land is large, but there is no room for justice in it.

KOZMA PRUTKOV

IF ONE WERE TO JUDGE *from the stereotype (such as Woody Allen's film* Love and Death*), then Russian literature is one long high-flown debate about the human soul, the nature of good and evil, and the depths of human psychology, and in general is a valley of tears populated by anguished philosophers, fools in Christ, and saintly prostitutes.*

The comic nonsense of Kozma Prutkov shows that to picture Russian culture as uniformly lugubrious is a sad error, which is due not to Woody Allen but to solemn literary historians. Playfulness and fun did exist in nineteenth-century Russia; so did irreverence. Russian literature was never all gloom and doom. Western critics and scholars (and the Russian ones, whom Western critics have tended to parrot) did us a disservice in either omitting any mention of Kozma Prutkov altogether or giving him very short shrift.

Not only does Kozma Prutkov embody the spirit of laughter but also of the grotesque and the absurd (which flowered profusely a century later in Central Europe, in the works of Franz Kafka, Ionesco, and others).

Kozma Prutkov never actually existed as one person. In 1850 two cousins, Aleksey Tolstoy (1817–1875) and Aleksey Zhemchuzhnikov (1821–1908) happened to share an apartment in St. Petersburg. Tolstoy was a well-known author of historical dramas and novels. The two cousins began the practice of writing a silly, satirical poem every day. Then they wrote a little playlet, Fantasia, *which they published on January 8, 1851, under the pseudonym Kozma Prutkov. (They lifted this name from a valet of theirs who they thought was the acme of obtuseness.) The comic skit presents a rich lady who loves her pug-*

dog *Fantasia* above all else, and who promises to marry off her young ward to whichever one of her six suitors will find the lost animal.

Kozma Prutkov caught on. It did not harm his reputation that at the performance of *Fantasia* Czar Nicholas I walked out and the audience jeered. The Kozma Prutkov team produced aphorisms, little satirical poems, and a book of fake memoirs by a grandfather supposed to have lived in the eighteenth century. The qualities they display for our amusement are self-importance, stuffiness, pseudo-profound platitudes, and a passion for resounding, fatuous truisms.

The productions of Kozma Prutkov have one foot in the world of nonsense (akin to the creations of Lewis Carroll and Edward Lear) and the other foot in the realm of satire.

Many of Prutkov's saws have become proverbial with Russians, who sometimes quote him without realizing it. His aphorisms have merged with the fund of anonymous Russian proverbial lore.

Kozma Prutkov's oeuvre includes a four-page article proposing to establish "unithink"—unanimity—in the Russian empire. The czar is besought to impose views to be published in "one official organ," views which would then be copied and reprinted in all other newspapers throughout the country. Officials were to report on all employees under them, listing what newspapers and magazines they subscribed to and read. Those who did not subscribe to the official organs or who expressed views different from the official ones were to be penalized. Thus unofficial, reprehensible ideas would be eliminated. Little did Kozma Prutkov's creators expect that a Soviet regime would one day actually put into practice this centrally planned unanimity.

The comic aphorisms that follow have been drawn from the hundreds written by Kozma Prutkov. We find truly asinine comic maxims and witticisms alongside utterly banal pompous pronouncements. To some extent they parody traditional Russian proverbs, but they are also close to Flaubert's Dictionary of Accepted Ideas. It is part of their charm that often the mind boggles at how to interpret them.

THE FRUITS OF REFLECTION:
THOUGHTS AND APHORISMS

The engagement ring is the first link in the chains of married life.

Our life can be compared to a capricious river, on the surface of which a boat sails, sometimes rocked by a gentle wave, not infrequently held up in its course by shoals and broken rocks under the surface of the water. Is it necessary to remind ourselves that this delicate boat on the marketplace of quickly passing time is none other than we ourselves?

One cannot embrace the unembraceable.

Nothing is so big that a still bigger thing will not surpass it in size. Nothing is so small that a still smaller thing cannot be placed inside it.

Look to the root!

Better say little but say it well.

Scholarship sharpens the mind; studying sharpens the memory.

What will others say about you if you yourself cannot say anything about yourself?

Self-sacrifice is what every shooter's bullet aims at.

One's memory is a sheet of white paper; sometimes one writes on it well and other times badly.

A failing memory is like a lamp that is going out.

A failing memory can also be compared to a forget-me-not that is withering.

Failing eyesight I shall always compare to an old, tarnished mirror, even to a cracked one.

The imagination of a poet oppressed by misery is like a foot enclosed in a new shoe.

A person who is passionately in love with somebody endures someone else only out of calculation.

If you want to be handsome, join the Hussars.

Human beings were not clothed by beneficent nature, they have received from above the gift of sartorial art.

If there were no tailors, pray tell: how could you tell the civil service departments apart?

If you conceal the truth from your friends, to whom will you reveal yourself?

What is better? When you compare the past, compare it with the present.

To walk to the end of the road of life is worth more than walking through the entire universe.

If you have a fountain, turn it off; let even a fountain have a rest.

A married rake is like a sparrow.

An eager doctor is like a pelican.

An egoist is like someone sitting in a well.

The man dies but his decorations remain on the face of the earth.

Why does a foreigner strive less to live in our country than we do to live in his country? Because he is already abroad.

Even turpentine is good for something.

Punch a horse in the nose—it will wave its tail.

Three things are hard to stop doing: (a) eating a good dish, (b) talking with a friend who has come back from an expedition, (c) scratching where you are scratching.

If they ask you what is more useful, the sun or the moon, answer: the moon. The sun shines in the daytime, when it is light anyway; the moon shines at night.

On the other hand, the sun is better inasmuch as it shines and warms; the moon only shines, and even that only on moonlit nights.

If shadows of objects did not depend on the size of those objects, but grew at their own will, soon there might be no lighted place in the whole world.

The infant's first step is its first step toward death.

Death has been placed at the end of life so that it would be more convenient to prepare for it.

Do not carry anything to the extreme. A man who wants to dine too late risks that he will dine in the morning of the following day.

The beginning of a clear day I shall boldly compare to the birth of an innocent baby. The former will perhaps not end without rain, the life of the latter without tears.

(1854; 1860; 1884)

A MEMORY OF BYGONE DAYS

(After Heine)

I remember you in childhood,
Almost forty years ago;
With your rumpled pinafore on,
With your corset laced in so.

In it you were feeling awkward,
And you told me secretly:
"Let my corset out in back now;
In it I cannot run free."

All suffused with agitation,
I your corset then unwound. . . .
You ran off with happy laughter,
I stood still in thought profound.

(1860)

FYODOR DOSTOYEVSKY

OUTSIDE OF RUSSIA, Dostoyevsky (1821–1881) is generally considered the greatest, most influential Russian author of all time. The Russian philosopher Nikolay Berdyayev even went so far as to say that having produced Dostoyevsky was a sufficient justification for the existence of the Russian people in this world.

Dostoyevsky was the son of an army medical doctor. He studied in an officers' academy for military engineers. After graduation, he worked briefly for the army in St. Petersburg, but by then he was already associating with journalistic and literary circles and soon resigned his commission. He had a sensational success with his first published work, a novel in letters, Poor Folk (1846), and went on to write a series of short stories. However, he was at the same time involved in an underground political group that circulated forbidden publications and discussed dissident ideas and plans. In 1849 he was arrested and sentenced to death, went through a mock execution that was halted at the last moment, and then was informed of his real punishment, ten years of penal and military service in Siberia. His harsh years in a Siberian prison camp were a turning point in his life: he became acquainted with common criminals, various fellow inmates who were peasants and nonintellectuals, and he underwent a drastic change of views. He described his Siberian experiences in the thinly fictionalized Notes from the House of the Dead (1860–1862).

After his release in 1859, he resumed his literary career, spent several years in Europe—mainly Germany—and was also very active as a journalist, editor, and publisher of magazines. His intellectual development took him from his youthful subversive radicalism to Russian nationalism and Russian Orthodox religious faith. In his work as editor and journalist, his nationalistic views are sometimes hard to *swallow; in his fiction, they are transmuted into art of the highest order.*

Dostoyevsky suffered from recurring attacks of epilepsy. Attacks of the illness were preceded by moments of ecstasy and intensity of feeling; they were followed by depression and temporary loss of memory. He was intimately acquainted, through self-observation, with extreme emotional states. His writings (personal letters as well as fiction) describe these and other intense psychological experiences, which Dostoyevsky studied and re-created in his literary art.

Dostoyevsky was also a passionate, pathological gambler. It was with the greatest difficulty that he finally succeeded in curing himself of this addiction. He was often in financial difficulties. His many journalistic ventures (some undertaken together with his brother) were motivated to a considerable extent by his personal financial needs. His novels were slow to receive recognition abroad; their psychology and construction were too far ahead of the times. In Germany, France, and England, it was only after World War I that the psychology of his characters as well as the philosophical and political implications of his ideas were understood and appreciated. Three European writers—Hermann Hesse, André Gide, and Virginia Woolf—stand out among the many pioneers in the process of making Dostoyevsky the most influential Russian writer in the twentieth century.

*Dostoyevsky's four great novels—*Crime and Punishment *(1866),* The Idiot *(1868–1869),* The Possessed, *also translated as* The Devils *(1871–1872), and* The Brothers Karamazov *(1879–1880)—together with Tolstoy's* War and Peace *and* Anna Karenina, *are the works of Russian literature that are the most widely known throughout the world. Dostoyevsky's works, once recognized, had a cataclysmic effect on psychology and on literary art in the West. Virginia Woolf described her encounter with the Russian novel as being similar to the experience of seeing naked men crawl from a train wreck; her figure of speech expresses aptly the impact of Dostoyevsky's novels on many other English, German, French, and American writers. The absence in Dostoyevsky of various reticences conventional in nineteenth-century Western fiction and the intensity of his dramatizations of new psychological and intellectual insights seemed to many readers to amount to a complete baring of the depths of the human heart and mind.*

The architectonics of The Brothers Karamazov *is that of the four-ring circus; the aesthetic is that of fantastic realism. "The Grand Inquisitor," a section from* The Brothers Karamazov, *is a political prophecy of twentieth-century totalitarian movements. It contains startling insight into what Erich Fromm has called the "flight from freedom,"* the drive toward uniformity of worship and conviction, the tendency to seek regimentation, banning dissent and independent thinking, such as seen in Communist Russia and Nazi Germany.

The Brothers Karamazov *sums up and crowns Dostoyevsky's life's work. Its themes are suffering, human freedom, and the limitations of reason (recalling one of Gogol's themes). It is also (again similarly to Gogol) an attack on Western European rationalism and the smugness of the contemporary Western-educated Russians who thought of themselves as progressives and rationalists. When Dostoyevsky pilloried and satirized these intellectuals, he meant to indict all of the nineteenth-century scientific, secularist, and irreligious attitudes.*

The Brothers Karamazov *is a book about various seekers. It is also a theodicy—an attempt at justifying God's goodness—an attempt that had been made by many philosophers and theologians long before Dostoyevsky. To some extent Dostoyevsky's book grapples with Voltaire's philosophical novelette* Candide (1759), *which ridiculed the optimistic views that "this is the best of all possible worlds" and that if we only understood the ultimate design, we would come to agree that the seeming cruelties and injustices are in reality justified and necessary.*

It is a novel based on the question "If there is no immortality, then is everything permitted?" and on the psychology of the nearness to each other of joy and pain, of pride and humility. It presents many versions of love and hate and greed, all set in a provincial Russian town, like that of Staraya Russa, in which Dostoyevsky resided from time to time.

In the novel, the epic—or "poema," as Ivan Karamazov calls it —of "The Grand Inquisitor" is preceded by the intellectual and rebellious Ivan Karamazov's account—delivered to his religious, kindly brother Alyosha—of his reasons for rejecting God's world: his revulsion at the ubiquitous cruelties inflicted on little children and innocent creatures, who cannot in any way be held to be deserving of such suffering. Hence, Ivan explains, he puts his earthly, "Euclidian" sense of what is evil above philosophical or theological arguments that God's justice is incomprehensible since it exists in a higher realm of more than rational dimensions. The reply to Ivan's poem of "The Grand Inquisitor" is contained in the entire novel, with all its episodes and dialogues, not merely in Alyosha's enigmatic kiss which he gives Ivan at the conclusion of this section.

Mikhail Bakhtin, the influential Russian philosopher who popularized the concept of polyphony as a central feature of the modern novel, considered that "a plurality of independent and unmerged voices

*and consciousnesses, a genuine polyphony of fully valid voices, is in
fact the chief characteristic of Dostoyevsky's novels. . . . The author,
however, is the orchestrator and the conductor of his voices. The author
is active—interrupting although not drowning out the voice of the
Other."*

*While this may be true of Dostoyevsky's novels, in his articles and
speeches the great novelistic dialogist becomes a vehement and partisan
monologist. His was a powerful voice of the Slavophile movement, of
the "native soil" party, very much concerned with creating an image
of Russian national identity that was inclusive and universal. Dostoyevsky's speech at the Pushkin Festival in 1881—of which an extract
is given here—is an eloquent, even if somewhat muddy and verbose,
expression of his views, which have left a tremendous mark on Russians' conceptions of their own self-image.*

THE GRAND INQUISITOR

(From *The Brothers Karamazov*)

"Brother," Alyosha said suddenly, his eyes beginning to flash, "you
asked just now if there is in the whole world a being who could and
would have the right to forgive. But there is such a being, and he can
forgive everything, forgive all *and for all*, because he himself gave his
innocent blood for all and for everything. You've forgotten about him,
but it is on him that the structure is being built, and it is to him that
they will cry out: 'Just art thou, O Lord, for thy ways have been
revealed!' "

"Ah, yes, the 'only sinless One' and his blood! No, I have not
forgotten about him; on the contrary, I've been wondering all the while
why you hadn't brought him up for so long, because in discussions
your people usually trot him out first thing. You know, Alyosha—
don't laugh!—I composed a poem once, about a year ago. If you can
waste ten more minutes on me, I'll tell it to you."

"You wrote a poem?"

"Oh, no, I didn't write it," Ivan laughed. "I've never composed
two lines of verse in my whole life. But I made up this poem and
memorized it. I made it up in great fervor. You'll be my first reader—
I mean, listener. Why, indeed, should an author lose even one listener?"
Ivan grinned. "Shall I tell it or not?"

"I'm listening carefully," said Alyosha.

"My poem is called 'The Grand Inquisitor'—an absurd thing, but I want you to hear it."

THE GRAND INQUISITOR

"But here, too, it's impossible to do without a preface, a literary preface, that is—pah!" Ivan laughed, "and what sort of writer am I! You see, my action takes place in the sixteenth century, and back then—by the way, you must have learned this in school—back then it was customary in poetic works to bring higher powers down to earth. I don't need to mention Dante. In France, court clerks, as well as monks in the monasteries, gave whole performances in which they brought the Madonna, angels, saints, Christ, and God himself onstage. At the time it was all done quite artlessly. In Victor Hugo's *Notre Dame de Paris*, in the Paris of Louis XI, to honor the birth of the French dauphin, an edifying performance is given free of charge for the people in the city hall, entitled *Le bon jugement de la très sainte et gracieuse Vierge Marie*, in which she herself appears in person and pronounces her *bon jugement*. With us in Moscow, in pre-Petrine antiquity, much the same kind of dramatic performances, especially from the Old Testament, were given from time to time; but, besides dramatic performances, there were many stories and 'verses' floating around the world in which saints, angels, and all the powers of heaven took part as needed. In our monasteries such poems were translated, recopied, even composed—and when?—under the Tartars. There is, for example, one little monastery poem (from the Greek, of course): *The Mother of God Visits the Torments*, with scenes of a boldness not inferior to Dante's. The Mother of God visits hell and the Archangel Michael guides her through 'the torments.' She sees sinners and their sufferings. Among them, by the way, there is a most amusing class of sinners in a burning lake: some of them sink so far down into the lake that they can no longer come up again, and 'these God forgets'—an expression of extraordinary depth and force. And so the Mother of God, shocked and weeping, falls before the throne of God and asks pardon for everyone in hell, everyone she has seen there, without distinction. Her conversation with God is immensely interesting. She pleads, she won't go away, and when God points out to her the nail-pierced hands and feet of her Son and asks: 'How can I forgive his tormentors?' she bids all the saints, all the martyrs, all the angels and archangels to fall down together with her and plead for the pardon of all without discrimination. In the end she extorts from God a cessation of torments every year, from Holy Friday to Pentecost, and the sinners in hell at once thank the Lord and cry out to him: 'Just art thou, O Lord, who has judged so.' Well, my little poem would have been of the same kind if it had appeared back then. He comes onstage in it; actually, he says nothing in the poem, he just appears and passes on. Fifteen centuries have gone by since he gave the promise to come in his Kingdom, fifteen centuries since his prophet wrote: 'Behold, I come quickly.' 'Of that day and that hour knoweth not even the Son, but only my heavenly Father,' as he himself declared while still on earth. But mankind awaits him with the same faith and the same tender emotion. Oh, even with greater faith, for fifteen centuries have gone by since men ceased to receive pledges from heaven:

> *Believe what the heart tells you,*
> *For heaven offers no pledge.*

Only faith in what the heart tells you! True, there were also many miracles then. There were saints who performed miraculous healings; to some righteous men, according to their biographies, the Queen of Heaven herself came down. But the devil never rests, and there had already arisen in mankind some doubt as to the authenticity of these miracles. Just then, in the north, in Germany, a horrible new heresy appeared. A great star, 'like a lamp' (that is, the Church), 'fell upon the fountains of waters, and they were made bitter.' These heretics began blasphemously denying miracles. But those who still believed became all the more ardent in their belief. The tears of mankind rose up to him as before, they waited for him, loved him, hoped in him, yearned to suffer and die for him as before. . . . And for so many centuries mankind had been pleading with faith and fire: 'God our Lord, reveal thyself to us,' for so many centuries they had been calling out to him, that he in his immeasurable compassion desired to descend to those who were pleading. He had descended even before then, he had visited some righteous men, martyrs, and holy hermits while they were still on earth, as is written in their 'lives.' Our own Tyutchev, who deeply believed in the truth of his words, proclaimed that:

> *Bent under the burden of the Cross,*
> *The King of Heaven in the form of a slave*
> *Walked the length and breadth of you,*
> *Blessing you, my native land.*

It must needs have been so, let me tell you. And so he desired to appear to people if only for a moment—to his tormented, suffering people, rank with sin but loving him like children. My action is set in Spain, in Seville, in the most horrible time of the Inquisition, when fires blazed every day to the glory of God, and

> *In the splendid auto-da-fé*
> *Evil heretics were burnt.*

Oh, of course, this was not that coming in which he will appear, according to his promise, at the end of time, in all his heavenly glory, and which will be as sudden 'as the lightning that shineth out of the east unto the west.' No, he desired to visit his children if only for a moment, and precisely where the fires of the heretics had begun to crackle. In his infinite mercy he walked once again among men, in the same human image in which he had walked for three years among men fifteen centuries earlier. He came down to the 'scorched squares' of a southern town where just the day before, in a 'splendid auto-da-fé,' in the presence of the king, the court, knights, cardinals, and the loveliest court ladies, before the teeming populace of all Seville, the Cardinal Grand Inquisitor had burned almost a hundred heretics at once *ad majorem gloriam Dei*. He appeared quietly, inconspicuously, but, strange to say, everyone recognized him. This could be one of the best passages in the poem, I mean, why it is exactly that they recognize him. People are drawn to him by an invincible force, they flock to him, surround him, follow him. He passes silently among them with a quiet smile of infinite compassion. The sun of love shines in his heart, rays of Light, Enlightenment, and Power stream from his eyes and, pouring over the people, shake their hearts with responding love. He stretches forth his hands to them, blesses them, and from the touch of him, even only of his garments, comes a healing power. Here an old man, blind from childhood, calls out from the crowd: 'Lord, heal me so that I, too, can see you,' and it is as if the scales fell from his eyes, and the blind man sees him. People weep and kiss the earth he walks upon. Children throw down flowers before him, sing and cry 'Hosanna!' to him. 'It's he, it's really he,' everyone repeats, 'it must be he, it can be no one but he.' He stops at the porch of the Seville cathedral at the very moment when a child's little open white coffin is being brought in with weeping: in it lies a seven-year-old girl, the only daughter of a noble citizen. The dead child is covered with flowers. 'He will raise your child,' people in the crowd shout to the weeping mother. The cathedral padre, who has come out to meet the coffin, looks perplexed and frowns. Suddenly a wail comes from the dead child's mother. She throws herself down at his feet: 'If it is you, then raise my child!' she exclaims, stretching her hands out to him. The procession halts, the little coffin is lowered down onto the porch at his feet. He looks with compassion and his lips once again softly utter: '*Talitha cumi*'—'and the damsel arose.' The girl rises in her coffin, sits up and, smiling, looks around her in wide-eyed astonishment. She is still holding the bunch of white roses with which she had been lying in the coffin. There is a commotion among the people, cries, weeping, and at this very moment the Cardinal Grand Inquisitor himself crosses the square in front of the cathedral. He is an old man, almost ninety, tall and straight, with a gaunt face and sunken eyes, from which a glitter still shines like a fiery spark. Oh, he is not wearing his magnificent cardinal's robes in which he had displayed himself to the people the day before, when the enemies of the Roman faith were burned—no, at this moment he is wearing only his old, coarse monastic cassock. He is followed at a certain distance by his grim assistants and slaves, and by the 'holy' guard. At the sight of the crowd he stops and watches from afar. He has seen everything, seen the coffin set down at his feet, seen the girl rise, and his face darkens. He scowls with his thick, gray eyebrows, and his eyes shine with a sinister fire. He stretches forth his finger and orders the guard to take him. And such is his power, so tamed, submissive, and tremblingly obedient to his will are the people, that the crowd immediately parts before the guard, and they, amid the deathly silence that has suddenly fallen, lay their hands on him and lead him away. As one man the crowd immediately bows to the ground before the aged Inquisitor, who silently blesses the people and moves on. The guards lead their prisoner to the small, gloomy, vaulted prison in the old building of the holy court, and lock him there. The day is over, the Seville night comes, dark, hot, and 'breathless.' The air is 'fragrant with laurel and lemon.' In the deep darkness, the iron door of the prison suddenly opens, and the old Grand Inquisitor himself slowly enters carrying a lamp. He is alone, the door is immediately locked behind him. He stands in the entrance and for a long time, for a minute or two, gazes into his face. At last he quietly approaches, sets the lamp on the table, and says to him: 'Is it you? You?' But receiving no answer, he quickly adds: 'Do not answer, be silent. After all, what could you say? I know too well what you would say. And you have no right to add anything to what you already said once. Why, then, have you come to interfere with us? For you have come to interfere with us and you know it yourself. But do you know what will happen tomorrow? I do not know who you are, and I do not want to know: whether it is you, or only his likeness; but tomorrow I shall condemn you and burn you at the stake as the most evil of heretics, and the very people who today kissed your feet, tomorrow, at a nod from me, will rush to heap the coals up around your stake, do you know that? Yes, perhaps you do know it,' he added, pondering deeply, never for a moment taking his eyes from his prisoner."

"I don't quite understand what this is, Ivan," Alyosha, who all the while had been listening silently, smiled. "Is it boundless fantasy, or some mistake on the old man's part, some impossible *qui pro quo*?"

"Assume it's the latter, if you like," Ivan laughed, "if you're so spoiled by modern realism and can't stand anything fantastic—if you want it to be *qui pro quo*, let it be. Of course," he laughed again, "the man is ninety years old, and might have lost his mind long ago over his idea. He might have been struck by the prisoner's appearance. It might, finally, have been simple delirium, the vision of a ninety-year-old man nearing death, and who is excited, besides, by the auto-da-fé of a hundred burned heretics the day before. But isn't it all the same to you and me whether it's *qui pro quo* or boundless fantasy? The only thing is that the old man needs to speak out, that finally after all his ninety years, he speaks out, and says aloud all that he has been silent about for ninety years."

"And the prisoner is silent, too? Just looks at him without saying a word?"

"But that must be so in any case," Ivan laughed again. "The old man himself points out to him that he has no right to add anything to what has already been said once. That, if you like, is the most basic feature of Roman Catholicism, in my opinion at least: 'Everything,' they say, 'has been handed over by you to the pope, therefore everything now belongs to the pope, and you may as well not come at all now, or at least don't interfere with us for the time being.' They not only speak this way, they also write this way, at least the Jesuits do. I've read it in their theologians myself. 'Have you the right to proclaim to us even one of the mysteries of that world from which you have come?' my old man asks him, and answers the question himself: 'No, you have not, so as not to add to what has already been said once, and so as not to deprive people of freedom, for which you stood so firmly when you were on earth. Anything you proclaim anew will encroach upon the freedom of men's faith, for it will come as a miracle, and the freedom of their faith was the dearest of all things to you, even then, one and a half thousand years ago. Was it not you who so often said then: "I want to make you free"? But now you have seen these "free" men,' the old man suddenly adds with a pensive smile. 'Yes, this work has cost us dearly,' he goes on, looking sternly at him, 'but we have finally finished this work in your name. For fifteen hundred years we have been at pains over this freedom, but now it is finished, and well finished. You do not believe that it is well finished? You look at me meekly and do not deign even to be indignant with me. Know, then, that now, precisely now, these people are more certain than ever before that they are completely free, and at the same time they themselves have brought us their freedom and obediently laid it at our feet. It is our doing, but is it what you wanted? This sort of freedom?' "

"Again I don't understand," Alyosha interrupted. "Is he being ironic? Is he laughing?"

"Not in the least. He precisely lays it .o his and his colleagues' credit that they have finally overcome free~om, and have done so in order to make people happy. 'For only now'—he is referring, of course, to the Inquisition—'has it become possible to think for the first time about human happiness. Man was made a rebel; can rebels be happy? You were warned,' he says to him, 'you had no lack of warnings and indications, but you did not heed the warnings, you rejected the only way of arranging for human happiness, but fortunately, on your departure, you handed the work over to us. You promised, you established with your word, you gave us the right to bind and loose, and surely you cannot even think of taking this right away from us now. Why, then, have you come to interfere with us?' "

"What does it mean, that he had no lack of warnings and indications?" Alyosha asked.

"You see, that is the main thing that the old man needs to speak about.

" 'The dread and intelligent spirit, the spirit of self-destruction and nonbeing,' the old man goes on, 'the great spirit spoke with you in the wilderness, and it has been passed on to us in books that he supposedly "tempted" you. Did he really? And was it possible to say anything more true than what he proclaimed to you in his three questions, which you rejected, and which the books refer to as "temptations"? And at the same time, if ever a real, thundering miracle was performed on earth, it was on that day, the day of those three temptations. The miracle lay precisely in the appearance of those three questions. If it were possible to imagine, just as a trial and an example, that those three questions of the dread spirit had been lost from the books without a trace, and it was necessary that they be restored, thought up and invented anew, to be put back into the books, and to that end all the wise men on earth—rulers, high priests, scholars, philosophers, poets —were brought together and given this task: to think up, to invent three questions such as would not only correspond to the scale of the event, but, moreover, would express in three words, in three human phrases only, the entire future history of the world and mankind—do you think that all the combined wisdom of the earth could think up anything faintly resembling in force and depth those three questions that were actually presented to you then by the powerful and intelligent spirit in the wilderness? By the questions alone, simply by the miracle of their appearance, one can see that one is dealing with a mind not human and transient but eternal and absolute. For in these three questions all of subsequent human history is as if brought together into a single whole and foretold; three images are revealed that will take in all the insoluble historical contradictions of human nature over all the earth. This could not have been seen so well at the time, for the future was unknown, but now that fifteen centuries have gone by, we can see that in these three questions everything was so precisely divined and foretold, and has proved so completely true, that to add to them or subtract anything from them is impossible.

" 'Decide yourself who was right: you or the one who questioned you then? Recall the first question; its meaning, though not literally, was this: "You want to go into the world, and you are going empty-handed, with some promise of freedom, which they in their simplicity and innate lawlessness cannot even comprehend, which they dread and fear—for nothing has ever been more insufferable for man and for human society than freedom! But do you see these stones in this bare, scorching desert? Turn them into bread and mankind will run after you like sheep, grateful and obedient, though eternally trembling lest you withdraw your hand and your loaves cease for them." But you did not want to deprive man of freedom and rejected the offer, for what sort of freedom is it, you reasoned, if obedience is bought with loaves of bread? You objected that man does not live by bread alone, but do you know that in the name of this very earthly bread, the spirit of the earth will rise against you and fight with you and defeat you, and everyone will follow him exclaiming: "Who can compare to this beast, for he has given us fire from heaven!" Do you know that centuries will pass and mankind will proclaim with the mouth of its wisdom and science that there is no crime, and therefore no sin, but only hungry men? "Feed them first, then ask virtue of them!"—that is what they will write on the banner they raise against you, and by which your temple will be destroyed. In place of your temple a new edifice will be raised, the terrible Tower of Babel will be raised again, and though, like the former one, this one will not be completed either, still you could have avoided this new tower and shortened people's suffering by a thousand years—for it is to us they will come after suffering for a thousand years with their tower! They will seek us out again, underground, in catacombs, hiding (for again we shall be persecuted and tortured), they will find us and cry out: "Feed us, for those who promised us fire from heaven did not give it." And then we shall finish building their tower, for only he who feeds them will finish it, and only we shall feed them, in your name, for we shall lie that it is in your name. Oh, never, never will they feed themselves without us! No science will give them bread as long as they remain free, but in the end they will lay their freedom at our feet and say to us: "Better that you enslave us, but feed us." They will finally understand that freedom and earthly bread in plenty for everyone are inconceivable together, for never, never will they be able to share among themselves. They will also be convinced that they are forever incapable of being free, because they are feeble, depraved, nonentities and rebels. You promised them heavenly bread, but, I repeat again, can it compare with earthly bread in the eyes of the weak, eternally depraved, and eternally ignoble human race? And if in the name of heavenly bread thousands and tens of thousands will follow you, what will become of the millions and tens of thousands of millions of creatures who will not be strong enough to forgo earthly bread for the sake of the heavenly? Is it that only the tens of thousands of the great and strong are dear to you, and the remaining millions, numerous as the sands of the sea, weak but loving you, should serve only as material for the great and the strong? No, the weak, too, are dear to us. They are depraved and rebels, but in the end it is they who will become obedient. They will marvel at us, and look upon us as gods, because we, standing at their head, have agreed to suffer freedom and to rule over them—so terrible will it become for them in the end to be free! But we shall say that we are obedient to you and rule in your name. We shall deceive them again, for this time we shall not allow you to come to us. This deceit will constitute our suffering, for we shall have to lie. This is what that first question in the wilderness meant, and this is what you rejected in the name of freedom, which you placed above everything. And yet this question contains the great mystery of this world. Had you accepted the "loaves," you would have answered the universal and everlasting anguish of man as an individual being, and of the whole of mankind together, namely: "before whom shall I bow down?" There is no more ceaseless or tormenting care for man, as long as he remains free, than to find someone to bow down to as soon as possible. But man seeks to bow down before that which is indisputable, so indisputable that all men at once would agree to the universal worship of it. For the care of these pitiful creatures is not just to find something before which I or some other man can bow down, but to find something that everyone else will also believe in and bow down to, for it must needs be *all together*. And this need for *communality* of worship is the chief torment of each man individually, and of mankind as a whole, from the beginning of the ages. In the cause of universal worship, they have destroyed each other with the sword. They have made gods and called upon each other: "Abandon your gods and come and worship ours, otherwise death to you and your gods!" And so it will be until the end of the world, even when all gods have disappeared from the earth: they will still fall down before idols. You knew, you could not but know, this essential mystery of human nature, but you rejected the only absolute banner, which was offered to you to make all men bow down to you indisputably—the banner of earthly bread; and you rejected it in the name of freedom and heavenly bread. Now see what you did next. And all again in the name of freedom! I tell you that man has no more tormenting care than to find someone to whom he can hand over as quickly as possible that gift of freedom with which the miserable creature is born. But he alone can take over the freedom of men who appeases their conscience. With bread you were given an indisputable banner: give man bread and he will bow down to you, for there is nothing more indisputable than bread. But if at the same time someone else takes over his conscience—oh, then he will even throw down your bread and follow him who has seduced his conscience. In this you were right. For the mystery of man's being is not only in living, but in what one lives for. Without a firm idea of what he lives for, man will not consent to live and will sooner destroy himself than remain on earth, even if there is bread all around him. That is so, but what came of it? Instead of taking over men's freedom, you increased it still more for them! Did you forget that peace and even death are dearer to man than free choice in the knowledge of good and evil? There is nothing more seductive for man than the freedom of his conscience, but there is nothing more tormenting, either. And so, instead of a firm foundation for appeasing human conscience once and for all, you chose everything that was unusual, enigmatic, and indefinite, you chose everything that was beyond men's strength, and thereby acted as if you did not love them at all—and who did this? He who came to give his life for them! Instead of taking over men's freedom, you increased it and forever burdened the kingdom of the human soul with its torments. You desired the free love of man, that he should follow you freely, seduced and captivated by you. Instead of the firm ancient law, man had henceforth to decide for himself, with a free heart, what is good and what is evil, having only your image before him as a guide—but did it not occur to you that he would eventually reject and dispute even your image and your truth if he was oppressed by so terrible a burden as freedom of choice? They will finally cry out that the truth is not in you, for it was impossible to leave them in greater confusion and torment than you did, abandoning them to so many cares and insoluble problems. Thus you yourself laid the foundation for the destruction of your own kingdom, and do not blame anyone else for it. Yet is this what was offered you? There are three powers, only three powers on earth, capable of conquering and holding captive forever the conscience of these feeble rebels, for their own happiness—these powers are miracle, mystery, and authority. You rejected the first, the second, and the third, and gave yourself as an example of that. When the dread and wise spirit set you on a pinnacle of the Temple and said to you: "If you would know whether or not you are the Son of God, cast yourself down; for it is written of him, that the angels will bear him up, and he will not fall or be hurt, and then you will know whether you are the Son of God, and will prove what faith you have in your Father." But you heard and rejected the offer and did not yield and did not throw yourself down. Oh, of course, in this you acted proudly and magnificently, like God, but mankind, that weak, rebellious tribe—are they gods? Oh, you knew then that if you made just one step, just one movement toward throwing yourself down, you would immediately have tempted the Lord and would have lost all faith in him and been dashed against the earth you came to save, and the intelligent spirit who was tempting you would rejoice. But, I repeat, are there many like you? And, indeed, could you possibly have assumed, even for a moment, that mankind, too, would be strong enough for such a temptation? Is that how human nature was created—to reject the miracle, and in those terrible moments of life, the moments of the most terrible, essential, and tormenting questions of the soul, to remain only with the free decision of the heart? Oh, you knew that your deed would be preserved in books, would reach the depths of the ages and the utmost limits of the earth, and you hoped that, following you, man, too, would remain with God, having no need of miracles. But you did not know that as soon as man rejects miracles, he will at once reject God as well, for man seeks not so much God as miracles. And since man cannot bear to be left without miracles, he will go and create new miracles for himself, his own miracles this time, and will bow down to the miracles of quacks, or women's magic, though he be rebellious, heretical, and godless a hundred times over. You did not come down from the cross when they shouted to you, mocking and reviling you: "Come down from the cross and we will believe that it is you." You did not come down because, again, you did not want to enslave man by a miracle and thirsted for faith that is free, not miraculous. You thirsted for love that is free, and not for the servile raptures of a slave before a power that has left him permanently terrified. But here, too, you overestimated mankind, for, of course, they are slaves, though they were created rebels. Behold and judge, now that fifteen centuries have passed, take a look at them: whom have you raised up to yourself? I swear, man is created weaker and baser than you thought him! How, how can he ever accomplish the same things as you? Respecting him so much, you behaved as if you had ceased to be compassionate, because you demanded too much of him—and who did this? He who loved him more than himself! Respecting him less, you would have demanded less of him, and that would be closer to love, for his burden would be lighter. He is weak and mean. What matter that he now rebels everywhere against our power, and takes pride in this rebellion? The pride of a child and a schoolboy! They are little children, who rebel in class and drive out the teacher. But there will also come an end to the children's delight, and it will cost them dearly. They will tear down the temples and drench the earth with blood. But finally the foolish children will understand that although they are rebels, they are feeble rebels, who cannot endure their own rebellion. Pouring out their foolish tears, they will finally acknowledge that he who created them rebels no doubt intended to laugh at them. They will say it in despair, and what they say will be a blasphemy that will make them even more unhappy, for human nature cannot bear blasphemy and in the end always takes revenge for it. And so, turmoil, confusion, and unhappiness—these are the present lot of mankind, after you suffered so much for their freedom! Your great prophet tells in a vision and an allegory that he saw all those who took part in the first resurrection and that they were twelve thousand from each tribe. But even if there were so many, they, too, were not like men, as it were, but gods. They endured your cross, they endured scores of years of hungry and naked wilderness, eating locusts and roots, and of course you can point with pride to these children of freedom, of free love, of free and magnificent sacrifice in your name. But remember that there were only several thousand of them, and they were gods. What of the rest? Is it the fault of the rest of feeble mankind that they could not endure what the mighty endured? Is it the fault of the weak soul that it is unable to contain such terrible gifts? Can it be that you indeed came only to the chosen ones and·for the chosen ones? But if so, there is a mystery here, and we cannot understand it. And if it is a mystery, then we, too, had the right to preach mystery and to teach them that it is not the free choice of the heart that matters, and not love, but the mystery, which they must blindly obey, even setting aside their own conscience. And so we did. We corrected your deed and based it on *miracle, mystery*, and *authority*. And mankind rejoiced that they were once more led like sheep, and that at last such a terrible gift, which had brought them so much suffering, had been taken from their hearts. Tell me, were we right in teaching and doing so? Have we not, indeed, loved mankind, in so humbly recognizing their impotence, in so lovingly alleviating their burden and allowing their feeble nature even to sin, with our permission? Why have you come to interfere with us now? And why are you looking at me so silently and understandingly with your meek eyes? Be angry! I do not want your love, for I do not love you. And what can I hide from you? Do I not know with whom I am speaking? What I have to tell you is all known to you already, I can read it in your eyes. And is it for me to hide our secret from you? Perhaps you precisely want to hear it from my lips. Listen, then: we are not with you, but with *him*, that is our secret! For a long time now—eight centuries already—we have not been with you, but with *him*. Exactly eight centuries ago we took from him what you so indignantly rejected, that last gift he offered you when he showed you all the kingdoms of the earth: we took Rome and the sword of Caesar from him, and proclaimed ourselves sole rulers of the earth, the only rulers, though we have not yet succeeded in bringing our cause to its full conclusion. But whose fault is that? Oh, this work is still in its very beginnings, but it has begun. There is still long to wait before its completion, and the earth still has much to suffer, but we shall accomplish it and we shall be caesars, and then we shall think about the universal happiness of mankind. And yet you could have taken the sword of Caesar even then. Why did you reject that last gift? Had you accepted that third counsel of the mighty spirit, you would have furnished all that man seeks on earth, that is: someone to bow down to, someone to take over his conscience, and a means for uniting everyone at last into a common, concordant, and incontestable anthill—for the need for universal union is the third and last torment of men. Mankind in its entirety has always yearned to arrange things so that they must be universal. There have been many great nations with great histories, but the higher these nations stood, the unhappier they were, for they were more strongly aware than others of the need for a universal union of mankind. Great conquerors, Tamerlanes and Genghis Khans, swept over the earth like a whirlwind, yearning to conquer the cosmos, but they, too, expressed, albeit unconsciously, the same great need of mankind for universal and general union. Had you accepted the world and

Caesar's purple, you would have founded a universal kingdom and granted universal peace. For who shall possess mankind if not those who possess their conscience and give them their bread? And so we took Caesar's sword, and in taking it, of course, we rejected you and followed *him*. Oh, there will be centuries more of the lawlessness of free reason, of their science and anthropophagy—for, having begun to build their Tower of Babel without us, they will end in anthropophagy. And it is then that the beast will come crawling to us and lick our feet and spatter them with tears of blood from its eyes. And we shall sit upon the beast and raise the cup, and on it will be written: "Mystery!" But then, and then only, will the kingdom of peace and happiness come for mankind. You are proud of your chosen ones, but you have only your chosen ones, while we will pacify all. And there is still more: how many among those chosen ones, the strong ones who might have become chosen ones, have finally grown tired of waiting for you, and have brought and will yet bring the powers of their spirit and the ardor of their hearts to another field, and will end by raising their *free* banner against you! But you raised that banner yourself. With us everyone will be happy, and they will no longer rebel or destroy each other, as in your freedom, everywhere. Oh, we shall convince them that they will only become free when they resign their freedom to us, and submit to us. Will we be right, do you think, or will we be lying? They themselves will be convinced that we are right, for they will remember to what horrors of slavery and confusion your freedom led them. Freedom, free reason, and science will lead them into such a maze, and confront them with such miracles and insoluble mysteries, that some of them, unruly and ferocious, will exterminate themselves; others, unruly but feeble, will exterminate each other; and the remaining third, feeble and wretched, will crawl to our feet and cry out to us: "Yes, you were right, you alone possess his mystery, and we are coming back to you —save us from ourselves." Receiving bread from us, they will see clearly, of course, that we take from them the bread they have procured with their own hands, in order to distribute it among them, without any miracle; they will see that we have not turned stones into bread; but, indeed, more than over the bread itself, they will rejoice over taking it from our hands! For they will remember only too well that before, without us, the very bread they procured for themselves turned to stones in their hands, and when they came back to us, the very stones in their hands turned to bread. Too well, far too well, will they appreciate what it means to submit once and for all! And until men understand this, they will be unhappy. Who contributed most of all to this lack of understanding, tell me? Who broke up the flock and scattered it upon paths unknown? But the flock will gather again, and again submit, and this time once and for all. Then we shall give them quiet, humble happiness, the happiness of feeble creatures, such as they were created. Oh, we shall finally convince them not to be proud, for you raised them up and thereby taught them pride; we shall prove to them that they are feeble, that they are only pitiful children, but that a child's happiness is sweeter than any other. They will become timid and look to us and cling to us in fear, like chicks to a hen. They will marvel and stand in awe of us and be proud that we are so powerful and so intelligent as to have been able to subdue such a tempestuous flock of thousands of millions. They will tremble limply before our wrath, their minds will grow timid, their eyes will become as tearful as children's or women's, but just as readily at a gesture from us they will pass over to gaiety and laughter, to bright joy and happy children's song. Yes, we will make them work, but in the hours free from labor we will arrange their lives like a children's game, with children's songs, choruses, and innocent dancing. Oh, we will allow them to sin, too; they are weak and powerless, and they will love us like children for allowing them to sin. We will tell them that every sin will be redeemed if it is committed with our permission; and that we allow them to sin because we love them, and as for the punishment for these sins, very well, we take it upon ourselves. And we will take it upon ourselves, and they will adore us as benefactors, who have borne their sins before God. And they will have no secrets from us. We will allow or forbid them to live with their wives and mistresses, to have or not to have children—all depending on their obedience—and they will submit to us gladly and joyfully. The most tormenting secrets of their conscience—all, all they will bring to us, and we will decide all things, and they will joyfully believe our decision, because it will deliver them from their great care and their present terrible torments of personal and free decision. And everyone will be happy, all the millions of creatures, except for the hundred thousand of those who govern them. For only we, we who keep the mystery, only we shall be unhappy. There will be thousands of millions of happy babes, and a hundred thousand sufferers who have taken upon themselves the curse of the knowledge of good and evil. Peacefully they will die, peacefully they will expire in your name, and beyond the grave they will find only death. But we will keep the secret, and for their own happiness we will entice them with a heavenly and eternal reward. For even if there were anything in the next world, it would not, of course, be for such as they. It is said and prophesied that you will come and once more be victorious, you will come with your chosen ones, with your proud and mighty ones, but we will say that they saved only themselves, while we have saved everyone. It is said that the harlot who sits upon the beast and holds *mystery* in her hands will be disgraced, that the feeble will rebel again, that they will tear her purple and strip bare her "loathsome" body. But then I will stand up and point out to you the thousands of millions of happy babes who do not know sin. And we, who took their sins upon ourselves for their happiness, we will stand before you and say: "Judge us if you can and dare." Know that I am not afraid of you. Know that I, too, was in the wilderness, and I, too, ate locusts and roots; that I, too, blessed freedom, with which you have blessed mankind, and I, too, was preparing to enter the number of your chosen ones, the number of the strong and mighty, with a thirst "that the number be complete." But I awoke and did not want to serve madness. I returned and joined the host of those who have *corrected your deed*. I left the proud and returned to the humble, for the happiness of the humble. What I am telling you will come true, and our kingdom will be established. Tomorrow, I repeat, you will see this obedient flock, which at my first gesture will rush to heap hot coals around your stake, at which I shall burn you for having come to interfere with us. For if anyone has ever deserved our stake, it is you. Tomorrow I shall burn you. *Dixi.*' "

Ivan stopped. He was flushed from speaking, and from speaking with such enthusiasm; but when he finished, he suddenly smiled.

Alyosha, who all the while had listened to him silently, though toward the end, in great agitation, he had started many times to interrupt his brother's speech but obviously restrained himself, suddenly spoke as if tearing himself loose.

"But . . . that's absurd!" he cried, blushing. "Your poem praises Jesus, it doesn't revile him . . . as you meant it to. And who will believe you about freedom? Is that, is that any way to understand it? It's a far cry from the Orthodox idea. . . . It's Rome, and not even the whole of Rome, that isn't true—they're the worst of Catholicism, the Inquisitors, the Jesuits . . . ! But there could not even possibly be such a fantastic person as your Inquisitor. What sins do they take on themselves? Who are these bearers of the mystery who took some sort of curse upon themselves for men's happiness? Has anyone ever seen them? We know the Jesuits, bad things are said about them, but are they what you have there? They're not that, not that at all. . . . They're simply a Roman army, for a future universal earthly kingdom, with the emperor—the pontiff of Rome—at their head . . . that's their ideal, but without any mysteries or lofty sadness. . . . Simply the lust for power, for filthy earthly lucre, enslavement . . . a sort of future serfdom with them as the landowners . . . that's all they have. Maybe they don't even believe in God. Your suffering Inquisitor is only a fantasy. . . ."

"But wait, wait," Ivan was laughing, "don't get so excited. A fantasy, you say? Let it be. Of course it's a fantasy. But still, let me ask: do you really think that this whole Catholic movement of the past few centuries is really nothing but the lust for power only for the sake of filthy lucre? Did Father Paissy teach you that?"

"No, no, on the contrary, Father Paissy once even said something like what you . . . but not like that, of course, not at all like that," Alyosha suddenly recollected himself.

"A precious bit of information, however, despite your 'not at all like that.' I ask you specifically: why should your Jesuits and Inquisitors have joined together only for material wicked lucre? Why can't there happen to be among them at least one sufferer who is tormented by great sadness and loves mankind? Look, suppose that one among all those who desire only material and filthy lucre, that one of them, at least, is like my old Inquisitor, who himself ate roots in the desert and raved, overcoming his flesh, in order to make himself free and perfect, but who still loved mankind all his life, and suddenly opened his eyes and saw that there is no great moral blessedness in achieving perfection of the will only to become convinced, at the same time, that millions of the rest of God's creatures have been set up only for mockery, that they will never be strong enough to manage their freedom, that from such pitiful rebels will never come giants to complete the tower, that it was not for such geese that the great idealist had his dream of harmony. Having understood all that, he returned and joined . . . the intelligent people. Couldn't this have happened?"

"Whom did he join? What intelligent people?" Alyosha exclaimed, almost passionately. "They are not so very intelligent, nor do they have any great mysteries and secrets. . . . Except maybe for godlessness, that's their whole secret. Your Inquisitor doesn't believe in God, that's his whole secret!"

"What of it! At last you've understood. Yes, indeed, that alone is the whole secret, but is it not suffering, if only for such a man as he, who has wasted his whole life on a great deed in the wilderness and still has not been cured of his love for mankind? In his declining years he comes to the clear conviction that only the counsels of the great and dread spirit could at least somehow organize the feeble rebels, 'the unfinished, trial creatures created in mockery,' in a tolerable way. And so, convinced of that, he sees that one must follow the directives of the intelligent spirit, the dread spirit of death and destruction, and to that end accept lies and deceit, and lead people, consciously now, to death and destruction, deceiving them, moreover, all along the way, so that they somehow do not notice where they are being led, so that at least on the way these pitiful, blind men consider themselves happy. And deceive them, notice, in the name of him in whose ideal the old man believed so passionately all his life! Is that not a misfortune? And if even one such man, at least, finds himself at the head of that whole army 'lusting for power only for the sake of filthy lucre,' is one such man, at least, not enough to make a tragedy? Moreover, one such man standing at its head would be enough to bring out finally the real ruling idea of the whole Roman cause, with all its armies and Jesuits—the highest idea of this cause. I tell you outright that I firmly believe that this one man has never been lacking among those standing at the head of the movement. Who knows, perhaps such 'ones' have even been found among the Roman pontiffs. Who knows, maybe this accursed old man, who loves mankind so stubbornly in his own way, exists even now, in the form of a great host of such old men, and by no means accidentally, but in concert, as a secret union, organized long ago for the purpose of keeping the mystery, of keeping it from unhappy and feeble mankind with the aim of making them happy. It surely exists, and it should be so. I imagine that even the Masons have something like this mystery as their basis, and that Catholics hate the Masons so much because they see them as competitors, breaking up the unity of the idea, whereas there should be one flock and one shepherd. . . . However, the way I'm defending my thought makes me seem like an author who did not stand up to your criticism. Enough of that."

"Maybe you're a Mason yourself!" suddenly escaped from Alyosha. "You don't believe in God," he added, this time with great sorrow. Besides, it seemed to him that his brother was looking at him mockingly. "And how does your poem end," he asked suddenly, staring at the ground, "or was that the end?"

"I was going to end it like this: when the Inquisitor fell silent, he waited some time for his prisoner to reply. His silence weighed on him. He had seen how the captive listened to him all the while intently and calmly, looking him straight in the eye, and apparently not wishing to contradict anything. The old man would have liked him to say something, even something bitter, terrible. But suddenly he approaches the old man in silence and gently kisses him on his bloodless, ninety-year-old lips. That is the whole answer. The old man shudders. Something stirs at the corners of his mouth; he walks to the door, opens it, and says to him: 'Go and do not come again . . . do not come at all . . . never, never!' And he lets him out into the 'dark squares of the city.' The prisoner goes away."

"And the old man?"

"The kiss burns in his heart, but the old man holds to his former idea."

"And you with him!" Alyosha exclaimed ruefully. Ivan laughed.

"But it's nonsense, Alyosha, it's just the muddled poem of a muddled student who never wrote two lines of verse. Why are you taking it so seriously? You don't think I'll go straight to the Jesuits now, to join the host of those who are correcting his deed! Good lord, what do I care? As I told you: I just want to drag on until I'm thirty, and then—smash the cup on the floor!"

"And the sticky little leaves, and the precious graves, and the blue sky, and the woman you love! How will you live, what will you love them with?" Alyosha exclaimed ruefully. "Is it possible, with such hell in your heart and in your head? No, you're precisely going in order to join them . . . and if not, you'll kill yourself, you won't endure it!"

"There is a force that will endure everything," said Ivan, this time with a cold smirk.

"What force?"

"The Karamazov force . . . the force of the Karamazov baseness."

"To drown in depravity, to stifle your soul with corruption, is that it?"

"That, too, perhaps . . . only until my thirtieth year maybe I'll escape it, and then . . ."

"How will you escape it? By means of what? With your thoughts, it's impossible."

"Again, in Karamazov fashion."

"You mean 'everything is permitted'? Everything is permitted, is that right, is it?"

Ivan frowned, and suddenly turned somehow strangely pale.

"Ah, you caught that little remark yesterday, which offended Miusov so much . . . and that brother Dmitri so naively popped up and rephrased?" He grinned crookedly. "Yes, perhaps 'everything is permitted,' since the word has already been spoken. I do not renounce it. And Mitenka's version is not so bad."

Alyosha was looking at him silently.

"I thought, brother, that when I left here I'd have you, at least, in all the world," Ivan suddenly spoke with unexpected feeling, "but now I see that in your heart, too, there is no room for me, my dear hermit. The formula, 'everything is permitted,' I will not renounce, and what then? Will you renounce me for that? Will you?"

Alyosha stood up, went over to him in silence, and gently kissed him on the lips.

"Literary theft!" Ivan cried, suddenly going into some kind of rapture. "You stole that from my poem! Thank you, however. Get up, Alyosha, let's go, it's time we both did."

They went out, but stopped on the porch of the tavern.

"So, Alyosha," Ivan spoke in a firm voice, "if, indeed, I hold out for the sticky little leaves, I shall love them only remembering you. It's enough for me that you are here somewhere, and I shall not stop wanting to live. Is that enough for you? If you wish, you can take it as a declaration of love. And now you go right, I'll go left—and enough, you hear, enough. I mean, even if I don't go away tomorrow (but it seems I certainly shall), and we somehow meet again, not another word to me on any of these subjects. An urgent request. And with regard to brother Dmitri, too, I ask you particularly, do not ever even mention him to me again," he suddenly added irritably. "It's all exhausted, it's all talked out, isn't it? And in return for that, I will also make you a promise: when I'm thirty and want 'to smash the cup on the floor,' then, wherever you may be, I will still come to talk things over with you once more . . . even from America, I assure you. I will make a point of it. It will also be very interesting to have a look at you by then, to see what's become of you. Rather a solemn promise, you see. And indeed, perhaps we're saying good-bye for some seven or ten years. Well, go now to your Pater Seraphicus; he's dying, and if he dies without you, you may be angry with me for having kept you. Good-bye, kiss me once more—so—and now go. . . .'"

Ivan turned suddenly and went his way without looking back. It was similar to the way his brother Dmitri had left Alyosha the day before, though the day before it was something quite different. This strange little observation flashed like an arrow through the sad mind of Alyosha, sad and sorrowful at that moment. He waited a little, looking after his brother. For some reason he suddenly noticed that his brother Ivan somehow swayed as he walked, and that his right shoulder, seen from behind, appeared lower than his left. He had never noticed it before. But suddenly he, too, turned and almost ran to the monastery. It was already getting quite dark, and he felt almost frightened; something new was growing in him, which he would have been unable to explain. The wind rose again as it had yesterday, and the centuries-old pine trees rustled gloomily around him as he entered the hermitage woods. He was almost running. "Pater Seraphicus—he got that name from somewhere—but where?" flashed through Alyosha's mind. "Ivan, poor Ivan, when shall I see you again . . . ? Lord, here's the hermitage! Yes, yes, that's him, Pater Seraphicus, he will save me . . . from him, and forever!"

Several times, later in his life, in great perplexity, he wondered how he could suddenly, after parting with his brother Ivan, so completely forget about his brother Dmitri, when he had resolved that morning, only a few hours earlier, that he must find him, and would not leave until he did, even if it meant not returning to the monastery that night.

ON THE MISSION OF RUSSIA

Slavophilism is the spiritual union of all those who believe that our great Russia will speak its new word, a healthy word, not previously heard by the world—to all the world. This word will be spoken for the good of all humanity and in favor of its associating in one new, fraternal, worldwide union. I also belong to those who are convinced of this and believe in this. . . . In many respects I hold pure Slavophile views.

ON RUSSIAN DISTINCTIVENESS AND
UNIVERSALITY

(From a speech on Pushkin published in the August 1880 issue of *Writer's Diary*, a journal that Dostoyevsky single-handedly wrote and edited.)

I shall state it emphatically: there has never been a poet with such a universal responsiveness as Pushkin. The point is not just in his responsiveness, but in its amazing depth, and in the reincarnation of his spirit in the spirit of foreign nations, in an almost perfect, and therefore also miraculous, reincarnation, because no such phenomenon has taken place anywhere else in any other poet. This can be found only in Pushkin, and in this sense, I repeat, he is an unheard-of phenomenon and, in our opinion, even a prophetic one, for it was precisely here that his national Russian force expressed itself the most: precisely in the national quality of his poetry, the national quality in furthest development, that of our future, which exists at present in concealment, and it expressed itself prophetically. For what is the strength of the spirit of Russian nationality if not Russia's striving toward its ultimate goals of worldwide and international universality? When Pushkin became a national poet, as he came in close contact with the people's strength, he acquired a presentiment of the great future mission of that force. Here he is prescient, here he is a prophet.

(*1880*)

In fact what has Peter's reform meant to us, not only for the future, but also for what has already taken place, what has happened, what has appeared before our eyes? What did that reform signify to us? For us it was not merely the adoption of European costumes, customs, inventions, and European science. Let us penetrate into the essence of what took place, let us look closely. Yes, it is very possible that Peter originally began to carry it out only in the narrowest utilitarian sense, but subsequently, when he developed his idea to its furthest limit, he doubtlessly yielded to some secret intuition, which pulled him, in this matter, toward future goals that were indubitably far greater than narrow utilitarianism.

In exactly the same way the Russian people also did not accept the reform merely out of utilitarianism, but rather they already sensed with their foresight, almost immediately, some kind of very remote, incomparably higher goal than mere narrow utilitarianism.

The Russian people, I repeat, of course felt this goal unconsciously, but immediately and fully. We strove toward a vital, universal, humanistic union. We admitted the genius of other nations into our soul, not in a hostile fashion (as it might appear it would have to be), but in a friendly manner. We took in all nations, not making discriminatory distinctions between nations, being able from the first to abolish contradictions and to excuse and reconcile differences. We thereby demonstrated our readiness and inclination (which appeared to us ourselves only then) to a universal international uniting with all the nations of the great Aryan family. Yes, the mission of the Russian people is certainly all-European and worldwide. To become truly Russian, to become fully Russian can in the last analysis only mean (I emphasize this) becoming a brother to all human beings, a universal human being, if you wish. Oh, all that Slavophilism and Westernism of ours is only a big misunderstanding, although historically it was inevitable. To a true Russian, Europe and the fate of the great Aryan clan are as precious as Russia herself, as the fate of our native land, because worldwide universality is our fate, not through conquest by the sword, but by the strength of brotherhood and our brotherly striving toward a uniting of people. If you try to understand our history after Peter's reform, you will find traces and signs of this idea, of my dream, if you wish, in the character of our relations with European nations, even in our governmental policy. What has Russia been doing these two entire centuries in its policy, if not serve Europe much more than herself? I do not think this happened only because of the incompetence of our politicians. The nations of Europe do not have any idea how precious they are to us! And in the future, I believe this, we, that is, of course not we, but the Russian people of the future, will come to understand down to the last one that to become real Russians will mean precisely this: to strive to reconcile European conflicts, finally and definitely, and to show to the Europeans how to put an end to their European anguish inside our Russian soul, which unites all humanity, to enclose in it with brotherly love all our brothers, and in the end maybe even to speak the final word of the great, general harmony, of the ultimate brotherly assent of all peoples to the law of Christ's gospels.

I know all too well that my words may seem enthusiastic, exaggerated, fanatical. Let it be so; I do not regret that I spoke them. They had to be spoken, and they are essential particularly now, especially now, when we are celebrating and honoring our great genius, who embodied this very idea in his artistic work. This idea had been expressed previously more than once; I am not saying anything at all new. This may seem smug: "That is the fate decreed for us, for our beggarly, rough land? We are fated to speak a new word to humanity?" Am I talking about economic power, about glory of the sword or science? I am speaking only about the brotherhood of human beings and about how the Russian heart may be predestined more than all other nations for universal, brotherly fellowship. I see signs of this in our history, in our talented people, in the artistic genius of Pushkin.

Let our land be impoverished. "Christ walked up and down in the serf's guise and blessed it." [from a poem by Tyutchev] Why should we not accept his last word? Was He Himself not born in a manger? I repeat: at least we can point to Pushkin, to the universality of his genius. He was able to embrace foreign geniuses in his heart as if they were close relatives. At least in his artistic creation, he revealed irrefutably this universality of the Russian spirit, and there is an important lesson in this. If this idea is a fantasy, at least in Pushkin there is something on which to base it. If he had lived longer, maybe he would have shown immortal and great images of the Russian soul that would be understandable to our European brothers. He would have drawn them to us much more closely than they are now. Maybe he would have succeeded in explaining to them all the truth of our strivings, and they would have understood us better than they do now. They might have sensed what we are, they would have stopped looking at us distrustingly and condescendingly, as they look on us still. If Pushkin had lived longer, perhaps there would be less misunderstanding and quarreling even among ourselves. But God decided otherwise. Pushkin died in the full spread of his powers, and doubtless carried away with him some great secret into the grave. And now, we, without him, are trying to divine what that secret is.

(1880)

LEO TOLSTOY

LEO TOLSTOY (1828–1910) is generally considered one of the two or three greatest Russian novelists. Many critics and readers consider him the best.

He was born into an aristocratic landowning family in the Tula Province. Both his parents died before he was ten years old, but he was brought up by a succession of kindly, loving female relatives, and his childhood could hardly have been more serene and calm. Later Tolstoy studied law and then Near Eastern languages at the University of Kazan, and alternated years of a landowner's life at his Yasnaya Polyana estate with periods of observing military life in the Caucasus and participating, as an officer, in the war on the Danube and in the Crimea. After serving in the Crimean War he wrote the autobiographical Sevastapol Stories, which established his reputation. Returning to civilian life, he again lived on his estate and became engrossed in organizing a school for peasant children and in preparing pedagogical texts for them. When he moved to St. Petersburg, he soon found the circles of professional writers insufferable. In 1862 he married Sofya Andreyevna Behrs, the daughter of a neighboring landowner, and settled for a decade of the happy life of a married landowner and family man, which he combined with the strenuous effort of writing War and Peace, which he completed in 1869.

Tolstoy had always been both a moralist and a lover of ordinary, sensuous life. His serious, brooding side led him into increasingly somber philosophical reflections. His feeling that he encountered the actual presence of death one night in a country inn in the small town of Arzamas, while on a trip to arrange the purchase of some forests, precipitated a crisis that brought his life to a standstill. He undertook the study of various religions and philosophies in an attempt to resolve *his inability to cope with the fact of death. After rejecting all the systems and all traditional answers that he considered, he found his own—in the unspoiled Russian peasant's simple acceptance of death. Tolstoy also decided these same untutored peasants were the bearers of authentic Christianity. His* Confession *(1879–1892) sets forth the history of his inner struggles and of the conversion.*

In his later years Tolstoy went on to become a moral teacher to followers all over the globe. He preached his own personal form of Christian anarchism, pacifism, and nonviolent resistance to evil. Tolstoy opposed both the Orthodox church and the czarist regime of Russia, and became an influential leader of a worldwide movement. Gandhi in India, many Americans and Englishmen of Tolstoy's own time, and Martin Luther King, Jr., were among those influenced by Tolstoy's views.

His various pedagogic and humanitarian activities were also interspersed with the writing of marvelous literary works, in many genres—including the novels Anna Karenina *and* Resurrection, *various tales such as the late* Hadji Murad, *and the play* Power of Darkness.

It would be wrong to draw a sharp line between Tolstoy as the passionate lover of life in all its manifestations when he was a young man, and Tolstoy as the stern, puritanical teacher when he was old. Both sides of his character coexisted in him from the beginning. He enjoyed keenly the physical and animal side of the world, and he also sought spiritual perfection through abnegation. He was both a sensualist and a moralist. It is the tension between the two strivings in him that is in part responsible for the power of his works. Tolstoy can be a stern judge who starts with a full awareness of the power and attraction of temptation; he is not one of those who preach abstinence while feeling little appetite to indulge. Throughout his life, Tolstoy's passionate attachment to all aspects of this world led him to see it clearly and deeply. At the same time his moral fervor has few equals in the Western world.

His adopting peasant clothes, his resolve not to profit from royalties for his literary works—and not least his becoming the destination for pilgrimages of not only serious idealists from all over the world but also cranks and eccentrics, if not lunatics—understandably put a heavy burden on his marriage. They led to friction with his wife, who had not expected such developments in the man she had married. Her jealousy and her demands often led to bitter marital strife. In the end, in 1910, at the age of eighty-two, Tolstoy fled from his home intending to take refuge in a monastery. He fell ill on the train and died at a small railroad station along the way.

During his long life, besides novels, stories, and plays, he wrote religious, educational, and political treatises and pamphlets and numerous letters, and kept diaries; his collected works fill ninety large volumes, and an even larger edition is being planned in Russia.

Tolstoy has been called a netoshchik, *a man inclined to say "no" (nye-to), to deny in many situations—to rail against the way society was organized, against dominant conventions, against manners, against cruelty, against reprehensible individual motives and actions. He was a champion of exposing, of unmasking—as well as of analyzing and dissecting. He was also a man and artist most susceptible to physical stimuli, whether those of music, hunting, sex, or mowing grass. He had tremendous vital energy.*

The analysis of human behavior in Tolstoy's works is deceptively plain. We might mistakenly conclude that nothing could be easier than giving such utterly transparent renderings of who did and thought what, and how. Yet nothing is more difficult to achieve than Tolstoyan simplicity. He arrived at it through countless rewritings, painstaking elimination of clichés, and by seeking and selecting the right detail and the exact, most direct phrase. His sentences are lapidary, brutally direct. Reading Tolstoy changes us forever; we notice aspects of human behavior of which we had been previously unaware; we see life around us and our own subjectivity differently than before having read him.

His focusing on the extreme situation—the fatal illness and the impending death of Ivan Ilych, for example—is akin to the central point of the existentialists of the twentieth century. He was drawn to human beings involved in extreme situations—such as death—as well as the most ordinary, even banal routines, and he juxtaposed and contrasted these two types of human circumstances.

The thrust of his attacks was anti-establishment. He believed the Christian Russian peasants had the best understanding of the true values of life, even though he saw very clearly their dark sides. He opposed the organized Orthodox Church, but admired the peasants' simple faith. (His play The Power of Darkness *presents horrible murders perpetrated by peasants—but also their capacity to repent and be redeemed.) The peasant servant Gerasim in "The Death of Ivan Ilych" is a minor character, but he is not just an extra in Tolstoy's cast—he has unflinching honesty and feels human brotherhood.*

"The Death of Ivan Ilych" is a merciless portrait of the social establishment and of the vanity of a successful life within society. Tolstoy's seemingly impersonal, detached, aloof narrator speaks with a voice that is nevertheless magisterial, self-assured, authoritative.

Tolstoy's eye for the telling detail is displayed on every page: from the motto respice finem *("be mindful of your end"—that is, death) on the watch chain of the very unmindful Ivan Ilych, to the ironic circumstance that the fatal illness Ivan Ilych contracts was probably caused by his bumping his side while he was trying to take care of the furnishing of his new house.*

Like his great Danish contemporary Kierkegaard, Tolstoy believed that facing a crisis was necessary, even desirable, if a person was to arrive at a genuine understanding of what he or she wanted to achieve in life. Both stressed the need to confront extreme situations in order to discover what is truly important and what is not, as in the story of Ivan Ilych. Ilych, a high official, successful in his rise upward through society, supremely well adjusted socially, esteemed by society, in every way a man who had made it, found only when he was facing death that everything had been a falsehood and a chimera. Direct, warm human contact had come very seldom, perhaps only through the peasant Gerasim, who does not think it is taboo to refer to illness and death, and through Ilych's pitiful son. Death is the big presence, which in the end eclipses concern with promotions, money, social approval, clean linen, the furniture of life. There is something very stark about this direct, devastating story.

"Master and Man" puts still greater emphasis on death, in this case the simplicity and acceptance of death by a peasant. Tolstoy's strong feeling for lowly Russians—who in his view were deeply, truly Christian human beings—placed in an extreme, existential confrontation with death is a hallmark of his compassionate realism and also a feature of his writing that has drawn to him his perennial worldwide readership.

THE DEATH OF IVAN ILYCH

I

During an interval in the Melvinsky trial in the large building of the law courts, the members and public prosecutor met in Ivan Egorovich Shebek's private room, where the conversation turned on the celebrated Krasovsky case. Fyodor Vasilyevich warmly maintained that it was not subject to their jurisdiction, Ivan Egorovich maintained the contrary, while Pyotr Ivanovich, not having entered into the discussion at the start, took no part in it but looked through the *Gazette* that had just been handed in.

"Gentlemen," he said, "Ivan Ilych has died!"

"You don't say so!"

"Here, read it yourself," replied Pyotr Ivanovich, handing Fyodor Vasilyevich the paper still damp from the press. Surrounded by a black border were the words: "Praskovya Fyodorovna Golovina, with profound sorrow, informs relatives and friends of the demise of her beloved husband Ivan Ilych Golovin, Member of the Court of Justice, which occurred on February the 4th of this year 1882. The funeral will take place on Friday at one o'clock in the afternoon."

Ivan Ilych had been a colleague of the gentlemen present and was liked by them all. He had been ill for some weeks with an illness said to be incurable. His post had been kept open for him, but there had been conjectures that in case of his death Alekseyev might receive his appointment, and that either Vinnikov or Shtabel would succeed Alekseyev. So on receiving the news of Ivan Ilych's death the first thought of each of the gentlemen in that private room was of the changes and promotions it might occasion among themselves or their acquaintances.

"I shall be sure to get Shtabel's place or Vinnikov's," thought Fyodor Vasilyevich. "I was promised that long ago, and the promotion means an extra eight hundred rubles a year for me besides the allowance."

"Now I must apply for my brother-in-law's transfer from Kaluga," thought Pyotr Ivanovich. "My wife will be very glad, and then she won't be able to say that I never do anything for her relations."

"I thought he would never leave his bed again," said Pyotr Ivanovich aloud. "It's very sad."

"But what really was the matter with him?"

"The doctors couldn't say—at least they could, but each of them said something different. When last I saw him I thought he was getting better."

"And I haven't been to see him since the holidays. I always meant to go."

"Had he any property?"

"I think his wife had a little—but something quite trifling."

"We shall have to go to see her, but they live so terribly far away."

"Far away from you, you mean. Everything's far away from your place."

"You see, he never can forgive my living on the other side of the river," said Pyotr Ivanovich, smiling at Shebek. Then, still talking of the distances between different parts of the city, they returned to the court.

Besides considerations as to the possible transfers and promotions likely to result from Ivan Ilych's death, the mere fact of the death of a near acquaintance aroused, as usual, in all who heard of it the complacent feeling that "it is he who is dead and not I."

Each one thought or felt, "Well, he's dead but I'm alive!" But the more intimate of Ivan Ilych's acquaintances, his so-called friends, could not help thinking also that they would now have to fulfill the very tiresome demands of propriety by attending the funeral service and paying a visit of condolence to the widow.

Fyodor Vasilyevich and Pyotr Ivanovich had been his nearest acquaintances. Pyotr Ivanovich had studied law with Ivan Ilych and had considered himself to be under obligations to him.

Having told his wife at dinnertime of Ivan Ilych's death and of his conjecture that it might be possible to get her brother transferred to their circuit, Pyotr Ivanovich sacrificed his usual nap, put on his evening clothes, and drove to Ivan Ilych's house.

At the entrance stood a carriage and two cabs. Leaning against the wall in the hall downstairs near the cloak stand was a coffin lid covered with cloth of gold, ornamented with gold cord and tassels, that had been polished up with metal powder. Two ladies in black were taking off their fur cloaks. Pyotr Ivanovich recognized one of them as Ivan Ilych's sister, but the other was a stranger to him. His colleague Schwartz was just coming downstairs, but on seeing Pyotr Ivanovich enter he stopped and winked at him, as if to say: "Ivan Ilych has made a mess of things—not like you and me."

Schwartz's face with his Piccadilly whiskers and his slim figure in evening dress, had as usual an air of elegant solemnity that contrasted with the playfulness of his character and had a special piquancy here, or so it seemed to Pyotr Ivanovich.

Pyotr Ivanovich allowed the ladies to precede him and slowly followed them upstairs. Schwartz did not come down but remained where he was, and Pyotr Ivanovich understood that he wanted to arrange where they should play bridge that evening. The ladies went upstairs to the widow's room, and Schwartz with seriously compressed lips but a playful look in his eyes, indicated by a twist of his eyebrows the room to the right where the body lay.

Pyotr Ivanovich, like everyone else on such occasions, entered feeling uncertain of what he would have to do. All he knew was that at such times it is always safe to cross oneself. But he was not quite sure whether one should make obeisances while doing so. He therefore adopted a middle course. On entering the room he began crossing himself and made a slight movement resembling a bow. At the same time, as far as the motion of his head and arm allowed, he surveyed the room. Two young men—apparently nephews, one of whom was a high-school pupil—were leaving the room, crossing themselves as they did so. An old woman was standing motionless, and a lady with strangely arched eyebrows was saying something to her in a whisper. A vigorous, resolute church reader, in a frock coat, was reading something in a loud voice with an expression that precluded any contradiction. The butler's assistant, Gerasim, stepping lightly in front of Pyotr Ivanovich, was strewing something on the floor. Noticing this, Pyotr Ivanovich was immediately aware of a faint odor of a decomposing body.

The last time he had called on Ivan Ilych, Pyotr Ivanovich had seen Gerasim in the study. Ivan Ilych had been particularly fond of him and he was performing the duty of a sick nurse.

Pyotr Ivanovich continued to make the sign of the cross, slightly inclining his head in an intermediate direction between the coffin, the reader, and the icons on the table in a corner of the room. Afterward, when it seemed to him that this movement of his arm in crossing himself had gone on too long, he stopped and began to look at the corpse.

The dead man lay, as dead men always lie, in a specially heavy way, his rigid limbs sunk in the soft cushions of the coffin, with the head forever bowed on the pillow. His yellow waxen brow with bald patches over his sunken temples was thrust up in the way peculiar to the dead, the protruding nose seeming to press on the upper lip. He was much changed and had grown even thinner since Pyotr Ivanovich had last seen him, but, as is always the case with the dead, his face was handsomer and above all more dignified than when he was alive. The expression on the face said that what was necessary had been accomplished, and accomplished rightly. Besides this there was in that expression a reproach and a warning to the living. This warning seemed to Pyotr Ivanovich out of place, or at least not applicable to him. He felt a certain discomfort and so he hurriedly crossed himself once more and turned and went out of the door—too hurriedly and too regardless of propriety, as he himself was aware.

Schwartz was waiting for him in the adjoining room with legs spread wide apart and both hands toying with his top hat behind his back. The mere sight of that playful, well-groomed, and elegant figure refreshed Pyotr Ivanovich. He felt that Schwartz was above all these happenings and would not surrender to any depressing influences. His very look said that this incident of a church service for Ivan Ilych could not be a sufficient reason for infringing the order of the session—in other words, that it would certainly not prevent his unwrapping a new pack of cards and shuffling them that evening while a footman placed four fresh candles on the table: in fact, that there was no reason for supposing that this incident would hinder their spending the evening agreeably. Indeed he said this in a whisper as Pyotr Ivanovich passed him, proposing that they should meet for a game at Fyodor Vasilyevich's. But apparently Pyotr Ivanovich was not destined to play bridge that evening. Praskovya Fyodorovna (a short, fat woman who despite all efforts to the contrary had continued to broaden steadily from her shoulders downward and who had the same extraordinarily arched eyebrows as the lady who had been standing by the coffin), dressed all in black, her head covered with lace, came out of her own room with some other ladies, conducted them to the room where the dead body lay, and said: "The service will begin immediately. Please go in."

Schwartz, making an indefinite bow, stood still, evidently neither accepting nor declining this invitation. Praskovya Fyodorovna, recognizing Pyotr Ivanovich, sighed, went close up to him, took his hand, and said: "I know you were a true friend to Ivan Ilych . . ." and looked at him, awaiting some suitable response. And Pyotr Ivanovich knew that, just as it had been the right thing to cross himself in that room, so what he had to do here was to press her hand, sigh, and say, "Believe me. . . ." So he did all this and as he did it felt that the desired result had been achieved: that both he and she were touched.

"Come with me. I want to speak to you before it begins," said the widow. "Give me your arm."

Pyotr Ivanovich gave her his arm and they went to the inner rooms, passing Schwartz, who winked at Pyotr Ivanovich compassionately.

"That does for our bridge! Don't object if we find another player. Perhaps you can cut in when you do escape," said his playful look.

Pyotr Ivanovich sighed still more deeply and despondently, and Praskovya Fyodorovna pressed his arm gratefully. When they reached the drawing room, upholstered in pink cretonne and lighted by a dim lamp, they sat down at the table—she on a sofa and Pyotr Ivanovich on a low pouf, the springs of which yielded spasmodically under his weight. Praskovya Fyodorovna had been on the point of warning him to take another seat, but felt that such a warning was out of keeping with her present condition and so changed her mind. As he sat down on the pouf Pyotr Ivanovich recalled how Ivan Ilych had arranged this room and had consulted him regarding this pink cretonne with green leaves. The whole room was full of furniture and knickknacks, and on her way to the sofa the lace of the widow's black shawl caught on the carved edge of the table. Pyotr Ivanovich rose to detach it, and the springs of the pouf, relieved of his weight, rose also and gave him a push. The widow began detaching her shawl herself, and Pyotr Ivanovich again sat down, suppressing the rebellious springs of the pouf under him. But the widow had not quite freed herself and Pyotr Ivanovich got up again, and again the pouf rebelled and even creaked. When this was all over she took out a clean cambric handkerchief and began to weep. The episode with the shawl and the struggle with the pouf had cooled Pyotr Ivanovich's emotions and he sat there with a sullen look on his face. This awkward situation was interrupted by Sokolov, Ivan Ilych's butler, who came to report that the plot in the cemetery that Praskovya Fyodorovna had chosen would cost two hundred rubles. She stopped weeping and, looking at Pyotr Ivanovich with the air of a victim, remarked in French that it was very hard for her. Pyotr Ivanovich made a silent gesture signifying his full conviction that it must indeed be so.

"Please smoke," she said in a magnanimous yet crushed voice, and turned to discuss with Sokolov the price of the plot for the grave.

Pyotr Ivanovich while lighting his cigarette heard her inquiring very circumstantially into the prices of different plots in the cemetery and finally decide which she would take. When that was done she gave instructions about engaging the choir. Sokolov then left the room.

"I look after everything myself," she told Pyotr Ivanovich, shifting the albums that lay on the table; and noticing that the table was endangered by his cigarette ash, she immediately passed him an ashtray, saying as she did so: "I consider it an affectation to say that my grief prevents my attending to practical affairs. On the contrary, if anything can—I won't say console me, but—distract me, it is seeing to everything concerning him." She again took out her handkerchief as if preparing to cry, but suddenly, as if mastering her feeling, she shook herself and began to speak calmly. "But there is something I want to talk to you about."

Pyotr Ivanovich bowed, keeping control of the springs of the pouf, which immediately began quivering under him.

"He suffered terribly the last few days."

"Did he?" said Pyotr Ivanovich.

"Oh, terribly! He screamed unceasingly, not for minutes but for hours. For the last three days he screamed incessantly. It was unendurable. I cannot understand how I bore it; you could hear him three rooms off. Oh, what I have suffered!"

"Is it possible that he was conscious all that time?" asked Pyotr Ivanovich.

"Yes," she whispered. "To the last moment. He took leave of us a quarter of an hour before he died, and asked us to take Volodya away."

The thought of the sufferings of this man he had known so intimately, first as a merry little boy, then as a schoolmate, and later as a grown-up colleague, suddenly struck Pyotr Ivanovich with horror, despite an unpleasant consciousness of his own and this woman's dissimulation. He again saw that brow, and that nose pressing down on the lip, and felt afraid for himself.

"Three days of frightful suffering and then death! Why, that might suddenly, at any time, happen to me," he thought, and for a moment felt terrified. But—he did not himself know how—the customary reflection at once occurred to him that this had happened to Ivan Ilych and not to him, and that it should not and could not happen to him, and that to think that it could would be yielding to depression which he ought not to do, as Schwartz's expression plainly showed. After which reflection Pyotr Ivanovich felt reassured, and began to ask with interest about the details of Ivan Ilych's death, as though death were an accident natural to Ivan Ilych but certainly not to himself.

After many details of the really dreadful physical sufferings Ivan Ilych had endured (which details he learned only from the effect those sufferings had produced on Praskovya Fyodorovna's nerves) the widow apparently found it necessary to get to business.

"Oh, Pyotr Ivanovich, how hard it is! How terribly, terribly hard!" and she again began to weep.

Pyotr Ivanovich sighed and waited for her to finish blowing her nose. When she had done so he said, "Believe me . . ." and she again began talking and brought out what was evidently her chief concern with him—namely, to question him as to how she could obtain a grant of money from the government on the occasion of her husband's death. She made it appear that she was asking Pyotr Ivanovich's advice about her pension, but he soon saw that she already knew about that to the minutest detail, more even than he did himself. She knew how much could be gotten out of the government in consequence of her husband's death, but wanted to find out whether she could not possibly extract something more. Pyotr Ivanovich tried to think of some means of doing so, but after reflecting for a while and, out of propriety, condemning the government for its niggardliness, he said he thought that nothing more could be gotten. Then she sighed and evidently began to devise means of getting rid of her visitor. Noticing this, he put out his cigarette, rose, pressed her hand, and went out into the anteroom.

In the dining room where the clock stood that Ivan Ilych had liked so much and had bought at an antique shop, Pyotr Ivanovich met a priest and a few acquaintances who had come to attend the service, and he recognized Ivan Ilych's daughter, a handsome young woman. She was in black and her slim figure appeared slimmer than ever. She had a gloomy, determined, almost angry expression, and bowed to Pyotr Ivanovich as though he were in some way to blame. Behind her, with the same offended look, stood a wealthy young man, an examining magistrate, whom Pyotr Ivanovich also knew and who was her fiancé, as he had heard. He bowed mournfully to them and was about to pass into the death chamber, when from under the stairs appeared the figure of Ivan Ilych's schoolboy son, who was extremely like his father. He seemed a little Ivan Ilych, such as Pyotr Ivanovich remembered from when they studied law together. His tear-stained eyes had in them the look that is seen in the eyes of boys of thirteen or fourteen who are not pure-minded. When he saw Pyotr Ivanovich he scowled morosely and shamefacedly. Pyotr Ivanovich nodded to him and entered the death chamber. The service began: candles, groans, incense, tears, and sobs. Pyotr Ivanovich stood looking gloomily down at his feet. He did not look once at the dead man, did not yield to any depressing influence, and was one of the first to leave the room. There was no one in the anteroom, but Gerasim darted out of the dead man's room, rummaged with his strong hands among the fur coats to find Pyotr Ivanovich's, and helped him on with it.

"Well, friend Gerasim," said Pyotr Ivanovich, so as to say something. "It's a sad affair, isn't it?"

"It's God's will. We shall all come to it someday," said Gerasim, displaying his teeth—the even, white teeth of a healthy peasant—and, like a man in the thick of urgent work, he briskly opened the front door, called the coachman, helped Pyotr Ivanovich into the sleigh, and sprang back to the porch as if in readiness for what he had to do next.

Pyotr Ivanovich found the fresh air particularly pleasant after the smell of incense, the dead body, and carbolic acid.

"Where to, sir?" asked the coachman.

"It's not too late even now. . . . I'll call around on Fyodor Vasilyevich."

He accordingly drove there and found them just finishing the first rubber, so that it was quite convenient for him to cut in.

II

Ivan Ilych's life had been most simple and most ordinary and therefore most terrible.

He had been a member of the court of justice, and died at the age of forty-five. His father had been an official who after serving in various ministries and departments in Petersburg had made the sort of career that brings men to positions from which by reason of their long service they cannot be dismissed, though they are obviously unfit to hold any responsible position, and for whom therefore posts are specially created, which though fictitious carry salaries of from six to ten thousand rubles that are not fictitious, and in receipt of which they live on to a great age.

Such was the privy councillor and superfluous member of various superfluous institutions, Ilya Epimovich Golovin.

He had three sons, of whom Ivan Ilych was the second. The eldest son was following in his father's footsteps, only in another department, and was already approaching that stage in the service at which a similar sinecure would be reached. The third son was a failure. He had ruined his prospects in a number of positions and was now serving in the railway department. His father and brothers, and still more their wives, not merely disliked meeting him, but avoided remembering his existence unless compelled to do so. His sister had married Baron Greff, a Petersburg official of her father's type. Ivan Ilych was *le phénix de la famille* as people said. He was neither as cold and formal as his elder brother nor as wild as the younger, but was a happy mean between them—an intelligent, polished, lively, and agreeable man. He had studied with his younger brother at the School of Law, but the latter had failed to complete the course and was expelled when he was in the fifth class. Ivan Ilych finished the course well. Even when he was at the School of Law he was just what he remained for the rest of his life: a capable, cheerful, good-natured, and sociable man, though strict in the fulfillment of what he considered to be his duty: and he considered his duty to be what was so considered by those in authority. Neither as a boy nor as a man was he a toady, but from early youth was by nature attracted to people of high station as a fly is drawn to the light, assimilating their ways and views of life and establishing friendly relations with them. All the enthusiasms of childhood and youth passed without leaving much trace on him; he succumbed to sensuality, to vanity, and latterly among the highest classes to liberalism, but always within limits that his instinct unfailingly indicated to him as correct.

At school he had done things that had formerly seemed to him very horrid and made him feel disgusted with himself when he did them; but when later on he saw that such actions were done by people of good position and that they did not regard them as wrong, he was able not exactly to regard them as right, but to forget about them entirely or not be at all troubled at remembering them.

Having graduated from the School of Law and qualified for the tenth rank of the civil service, and having received money from his father for his equipment, Ivan Ilych ordered himself clothes at Scharmer's, the fashionable tailor, hung a medallion inscribed *respice finem* on his watch chain, took leave of his professor and the prince who was patron of the school, had a farewell dinner with his comrades at Donon's first-class restaurant, and with his new and fashionable portmanteau, linen, clothes, shaving and other toilet appliances, and a traveling rug, all purchased at the best shops, he set off for one of the provinces where, through his father's influence, he had been attached to the governor as an official for special service.

In the province Ivan Ilych soon arranged as easy and agreeable a position for himself as he had had at the School of Law. He performed his official tasks, made his career, and at the same time amused himself pleasantly and decorously. Occasionally he paid official visits to country districts, where he behaved with dignity both to his superiors and inferiors, and performed the duties entrusted to him, which related chiefly to the sectarians, with an exactness and incorruptible honesty of which he could not but feel proud.

In official matters, despite his youth and taste for frivolous gaiety, he was exceedingly reserved, punctilious, and even severe; but in society he was often amusing and witty, and always good-natured, correct in his manner, and *bon enfant*, as the governor and his wife—with whom he was like one of the family—used to say of him.

In the province he had an affair with a lady who made advances to the elegant young lawyer, and there was also a milliner; and there were carousals with aides-de-camp who visited the district, and after-supper visits to a certain outlying street of doubtful reputation; and there was too some obsequiousness to his chief and even to his chief's wife, but all this was done with such a tone of good breeding that no hard names could be applied to it. It all came under the heading of the French saying: *"Il faut que jeunesse se passe."** It was all done with clean hands, in clean linen, with French phrases, and above all among people of the best society and consequently with the approval of people of rank.

* Youth must have its fling.

So Ivan Ilych served for five years and then came a change in his official life. The new and reformed judicial institutions were introduced, and new men were needed. Ivan Ilych became such a new man. He was offered the post of examining magistrate, and he accepted it though the post was in another province and obliged him to give up the connections he had formed and to make new ones. His friends met to give him a send-off; they had a group photograph taken and presented him with a silver cigarette case, and he set off to his new post.

As examining magistrate Ivan Ilych was just as *comme il faut* and decorous a man, inspiring general respect and capable of separating his official duties from his private life, as he had been when acting as an official on special service. His duties now as examining magistrate were far more interesting and attractive than before. In his former position it had been pleasant to wear an undress uniform made by Scharmer, and to pass through the crowd of petitioners and officials who were timorously awaiting an audience with the governor, and who envied him as with free and easy gait he went straight into his chief's private room to have a cup of tea and a cigarette with him. But not many people had then been directly dependent on him—only police officials and the sectarians when he went on special missions—and he liked to treat them politely, almost as comrades, as if he were letting them feel that he who had the power to crush them was treating them in this simple, friendly way. There were then but few such people. But now, as an examining magistrate, Ivan Ilych felt that everyone without exception, even the most important and self-satisfied, was in his power, and that he need only write a few words on a sheet of paper with a certain heading, and this or that important, self-satisfied person would be brought before him in the role of an accused person or a witness, and if he did not choose to allow him to sit down, would have to stand before him and answer his questions. Ivan Ilych never abused his power; he tried on the contrary to soften its expression, but the consciousness of it and of the possibility of softening its effect supplied the chief interest and attraction of his office. In his work itself, especially in his examinations, he very soon acquired a method of eliminating all considerations irrelevant to the legal aspect of the case, and reducing even the most complicated case to a form in which it would be presented on paper only in its externals, completely excluding his personal opinion of the matter, while above all observing every prescribed formality. The work was new and Ivan Ilych was one of the first men to apply the new Code of 1864.

On taking up the post of examining magistrate in a new town, he made new acquaintances and connections, placed himself on a new footing, and assumed a somewhat different tone. He took up an attitude of rather dignified aloofness toward the provincial authorities, but picked out the best circle of legal gentlemen and wealthy gentry living in the town and assumed a tone of slight dissatisfaction with the government, of moderate liberalism, and of enlightened citizenship. At the same time, without at all altering the elegance of his toilet, he ceased shaving his chin and allowed his beard to grow as it pleased.

Ivan Ilych settled down very pleasantly in this new town. The society there, which inclined toward opposition to the governor, was friendly, his salary was larger, and he began to play *vint* [a form of bridge], which he found added not a little to the pleasure of life, for he had a capacity for cards, played good-humoredly, and calculated rapidly and astutely, so that he usually won.

After living there for two years he met his future wife, Praskovya Fyodorovna Mikhel, who was the most attractive, clever, and brilliant girl of the set in which he moved, and among other amusements and relaxations from his labors as examining magistrate, Ivan Ilych established light and playful relations with her.

While he had been an official on special service he had been accustomed to dance, but now as an examining magistrate it was exceptional for him to do so. If he danced now, he did it as if to show that though he served under the reformed order of things, and had reached the fifth official rank, yet when it came to dancing he could do it better than most people. So at the end of an evening he sometimes danced with Praskovya Fyodorovna, and it was chiefly during these dances that he captivated her. She fell in love with him. Ivan Ilych had at first no definite intention of marrying, but when the girl fell in love with him he said to himself: "Really, why shouldn't I marry?"

Praskovya Fyodorovna came of a good family, was not bad looking, and had some little property. Ivan Ilych might have aspired to a more brilliant match, but even this was good. He had his salary, and she, he hoped, would have an equal income. She was well connected, and was a sweet, pretty, and thoroughly correct young woman. To say that Ivan Ilych married because he fell in love with Praskovya Fyodorovna and found that she sympathized with his views of life would be as incorrect as to say that he married because his social circle approved of the match. He was swayed by both these considerations: the marriage gave him personal satisfaction, and at the same time it was considered the right thing by the most highly placed of his associates.

So Ivan Ilych got married.

The preparations for marriage and the beginning of married life, with its conjugal caresses, the new furniture, new crockery, and new linen, were very pleasant until his wife became pregnant—so that Ivan Ilych had begun to think that marriage would not impair the easy, agreeable, gay, and always decorous character of his life, approved of by society and regarded by himself as natural, but would even improve it. But from the first months of his wife's pregnancy, something new, unpleasant, depressing, and unseemly, and from which there was no way of escape, unexpectedly showed itself.

His wife, without any reason—*de gaieté de cœur* as Ivan Ilych expressed it to himself—began to disturb the pleasure and propriety of their life. She began to be jealous without any cause, expected him to devote his whole attention to her, found fault with everything, and made coarse and ill-mannered scenes.

At first Ivan Ilych hoped to escape from the unpleasantness of this state of affairs by the same easy and decorous relation to life that had served him heretofore: he tried to ignore his wife's disagreeable moods, continued to live in his usual easy and pleasant way, invited friends to his house for a game of cards, and also tried going out to his club or spending his evenings with friends. But one day his wife began upbraiding him so vigorously, using such coarse words, and continued to abuse him every time he did not fulfill her demands, so resolutely and with such evident determination not to give way till he submitted—that is, till he stayed at home and was bored just as she was—that he became alarmed. He now realized that matrimony—at any rate with Praskovya Fyodorovna—was not always conducive to the pleasures and amenities of life, but on the contrary often infringed on both comfort and propriety, and that he must therefore entrench himself against such infringement. And Ivan Ilych began to seek for means of doing so. His official duties were the one thing that imposed upon Praskovya Fyodorovna, and by means of his official work and the duties attached to it he began struggling with his wife to secure his own independence.

With the birth of their child, the attempts to feed it, and the various failures in doing so, and with the real and imaginary illnesses of mother and child, in which Ivan Ilych's sympathy was demanded but about which he understood nothing, the need of securing for himself an existence outside his family life became still more imperative.

As his wife grew more irritable and exacting and Ivan Ilych transferred the center of gravity of his life more and more to his official work, so did he grow to like his work better and became more ambitious than before.

Very soon, within a year of his wedding, Ivan Ilych had realized that marriage, though it may add some comforts to life, is in fact a very intricate and difficult affair toward which in order to perform one's duty, that is, to lead a decorous life approved of by society, one must adopt a definite attitude just as toward one's official duties.

And Ivan Ilych evolved such an attitude toward married life. He only required of it those conveniences—dinner at home, housewife, and bed—which it could give him, and above all that propriety of external forms required by public opinion. For the rest he looked for lighthearted pleasure and propriety, and was very thankful when he found them, but if he met with antagonism and querulousness he at once retired into his separate fenced-off world of official duties, where he found satisfaction.

Ivan Ilych was esteemed a good official, and after three years was made assistant public prosecutor. His new duties, their importance, the possibility of indicting and imprisoning anyone he chose, the publicity his speeches received, and the success he had in all these things, made his work still more attractive.

More children came. His wife became more and more querulous and ill-tempered, but the attitude Ivan Ilych had adopted toward his home life rendered him almost impervious to her grumbling.

After seven years' service in that town he was transferred to another province as public prosecutor. They moved, but were short of money and his wife did not like the place they moved to. Though the salary was higher the cost of living was greater, besides which two of their children died and family life became still more unpleasant for him.

Praskovya Fyodorovna blamed her husband for every inconvenience they encountered in their new home. Most of the conversations between husband and wife, especially as to the children's education, led to topics that recalled former disputes, and those disputes were apt to flare up again at any moment. There remained only those rare periods of amorousness that still came to them at times but did not last long. These were islets at which they anchored for a while and then again set out upon that ocean of veiled hostility that showed itself in their aloofness from one another. This aloofness might have grieved Ivan Ilych had he considered that it ought not to exist, but he now regarded the position as normal, and even made it the goal at which he aimed in family life. His aim was to free himself more and more from those unpleasantnesses and to give them a semblance of harmlessness and propriety. He attained this by spending less and less time with his family, and when obliged to be at home he tried to safeguard his position by the presence of outsiders. The chief thing, however, was that he had his official duties. The whole interest of his life now centered in the official world and that interest absorbed him. The consciousness of his power, being able to ruin anybody he wished to ruin, the importance, even the external dignity, of his entry into court, or meetings with his subordinates, his success with superiors and inferiors, and above all his masterly handling of cases, of which he was conscious— all this gave him pleasure and filled his life, together with chats with his colleagues, dinners, and bridge. So that on the whole Ivan Ilych's life continued to flow as he considered it should—pleasantly and properly.

So things continued for another seven years. His eldest daughter was already sixteen, another child had died, and only one son was left, a schoolboy and a subject of dissension. Ivan Ilych wanted to put him in the School of Law, but to spite him Praskovya Fyodorovna entered him at the high school. The daughter had been educated at home and had turned out well: the boy did not learn badly, either.

III

So Ivan Ilych lived for seventeen years after his marriage. He was already a public prosecutor of long standing, and had declined several proposed transfers while awaiting a more desirable post, when an unanticipated and unpleasant occurrence quite upset the peaceful course of his life. He was expecting to be offered the post of presiding judge in a university town, but Happe somehow came to the front and obtained the appointment instead. Ivan Ilych became irritable, reproached Happe, and quarreled both with him and with his immediate superiors—who became colder to him and again passed him over when other appointments were made.

This was in 1880, the hardest year of Ivan Ilych's life. It was then that it became evident on the one hand that his salary was insufficient for them to live on, and on the other that he had been forgotten, and not only this, but that what was for him the greatest and most cruel injustice appeared to others a quite ordinary occurrence. Even his father did not consider it his duty to help him. Ivan Ilych felt himself abandoned by everyone, and that they regarded his position with a salary of 3,500 rubles as quite normal and even fortunate. He alone knew that with the consciousness of the injustices done him, with his wife's incessant nagging, and with the debts he had contracted by living beyond his means, his position was far from normal.

In order to save money that summer he obtained leave of absence and went with his wife to live in the country at her brother's place.

In the country, without his work, he experienced ennui for the first time in his life, and not only ennui but intolerable depression, and he decided that it was impossible to go on living like that, and that it was necessary to take energetic measures.

Having passed a sleepless night pacing up and down the veranda, he decided to go to Petersburg and bestir himself, in order to punish those who had failed to appreciate him and to get transferred to another ministry.

Next day, despite many protests from his wife and her brother, he started for Petersburg with the sole object of obtaining a post with a salary of five thousand rubles a year. He was no longer bent on any particular department, or tendency, or kind of activity. All he now wanted was an appointment to another post with a salary of five thousand rubles, either in the administration, in the banks, with the railways, in one of the Empress Marya's Institutions, or even in the customs— but it had to carry with it a salary of five thousand rubles and be in a ministry other than that in which they had failed to appreciate him.

And this quest of Ivan Ilych's was crowned with remarkable and unexpected success. At Kursk an acquaintance of his, F. I. Ilyin, got into the first-class carriage, sat down beside Ivan Ilych, and told him of a telegram just received by the governor of Kursk announcing that a change was about to take place in the ministry: Pyotr Ivanovich was to be superseded by Ivan Semenovich.

The proposed change, apart from its significance for Russia, had a special significance for Ivan Ilych, because by bringing forward a new man, Pyotr Petrovich, and consequently his friend Zachar Ivanovich, it was highly favorable for Ivan Ilych, since Zachar Ivanovich was a friend and colleague of his.

In Moscow this news was confirmed, and on reaching Petersburg Ivan Ilych found Zachar Ivanovich and received a definite promise of an appointment in his former department of justice.

A week later he telegraphed to his wife: "Zachar in Miller's place. I shall receive appointment on presentation of report."

Thanks to this change of personnel, Ivan Ilych had unexpectedly obtained an appointment in his former ministry that placed him two stages above his former colleagues besides giving him five thousand rubles salary and three thousand five hundred rubles for expenses connected with his removal. All his ill humor toward his former enemies and the whole department vanished, and Ivan Ilych was completely happy.

He returned to the country more cheerful and contented than he had been for a long time. Praskovya Fyodorovna also cheered up and a truce was arranged between them. Ivan Ilych told of how he had been feted by everybody in Petersburg, how all those who had been his enemies were put to shame and now fawned on him, how envious they were of his appointment, and how much everybody in Petersburg had liked him.

Praskovya Fyodorovna listened to all this and appeared to believe it. She did not contradict anything, but only made plans for their life in the town to which they were going. Ivan Ilych saw with delight that these plans were his plans, that he and his wife agreed, and that, after a stumble, his life was regaining its due and natural character of pleasant lightheartedness and decorum.

Ivan Ilych had come back for a short time only, for he had to take up his new duties on the tenth of September. Moreover, he needed time to settle into the new place, to move all his belongings from the province, and to buy and order many additional things: in a word, to make such arrangements as he had resolved on, which were almost exactly what Praskovya Fyodorovna, too, had decided on.

Now that everything had happened so fortunately, and that he and his wife were at one in their aims and moreover saw so little of one another, they got along together better than they had since the first years of marriage. Ivan Ilych had thought of taking his family away with him at once, but the insistence of his wife's brother and her sister-in-law, who had suddenly become particularly amiable and friendly to him and his family, induced him to depart alone.

So he departed, and the cheerful state of mind induced by his success and by the harmony between his wife and himself, the one intensifying the other, did not leave him. He found a delightful house, just the thing both he and his wife had dreamed of. Spacious, lofty reception rooms in the old style, a convenient and dignified study, rooms for his wife and daughter, a study for his son—it might have been specially built for them. Ivan Ilych himself superintended the arrangements, chose the wallpapers, supplemented the furniture (preferably with antiques which he considered particularly *comme il faut*), and supervised the upholstering. Everything progressed and progressed and approached the ideal he had set himself: even when things were only half completed they exceeded his expectations. He saw what a refined and elegant character, free from vulgarity, it would all have when it was ready. On falling asleep he pictured to himself how the reception room would look. Looking at the yet unfinished drawing room he could see the fireplace, the screen, the whatnot, the little chairs dotted here and there, the dishes and plates on the walls, and the bronzes, as they would be when everything was in place. He was pleased by the thought of how his wife and daughter, who shared his taste in this matter, would be impressed by it. They were certainly not expecting as much. He had been particularly successful in finding, and buying cheaply, antiques that gave a particularly aristocratic character to the whole place. But in his letters he intentionally understated everything in order to be able to surprise them. All this so absorbed him that his new duties—though he liked his official work—interested him less than he had expected. Sometimes he even had moments of absentmindedness during the court sessions, and would consider whether he should have straight or curved cornices for his curtains. He was so interested in it all that he often did things himself, rearranging the furniture, or re-hanging the curtains. Once when mounting a stepladder to show the upholsterer, who did not understand, how he wanted the hangings draped, he made a false step and slipped, but being a strong and agile man he clung on and only knocked his side against the knob of the window frame. The bruised place was painful but the pain soon passed, and he felt particularly bright and well just then. He wrote: "I feel fifteen years younger." He thought he would have everything ready by September, but it dragged on till mid-October. But the result was charming not only in his eyes but to everyone who saw it.

In reality it was just what is usually seen in the houses of people of moderate means who want to appear rich, and therefore succeed only in resembling others like themselves: there were damasks, dark wood, plants, rugs, and dull and polished bronzes—all the things people of a certain class have in order to resemble other people of that class. His house was so like the others that it would never have been noticed, but to him it all seemed to be quite exceptional. He was very happy when he met his family at the station and brought them to the newly furnished house all lit up, where a footman in a white tie opened the door into the hall decorated with plants, and when they went on into the drawing room, and the study, uttering exclamations of delight. He conducted them everywhere, drank in their praises eagerly, and beamed with pleasure. At tea that evening, when Praskovya Fyodorovna among other things asked him about his fall, he laughed and showed them how he had gone flying and had frightened the upholsterer.

"It's a good thing I'm a bit of an athlete. Another man might have been killed, but I merely knocked myself, just here; it hurts when it's touched, but it's passing off already—it's only a bruise."

So they began living in their new home—in which, as always happens, when they got thoroughly settled in they found they were just one room short—and with the increased income, which as always was just a little (some five hundred rubles) too little, but it was all very nice.

Things went particularly well at first, before everything was finally arranged and while something had still to be done: this thing bought, that thing ordered, another thing moved, and something else adjusted. Though there were some disputes between husband and wife, they were both so well satisfied and had so much to do that it all passed off without any serious quarrels. When nothing was left to arrange it became rather dull and something seemed to be lacking, but they were then making acquaintances, forming habits, and life was growing fuller.

Ivan Ilych spent his mornings at the law court and came home to dinner, and at first he was generally in a good humor, though he occasionally became irritable just on account of his house. (Every spot on the tablecloth or the upholstery, and every broken window-blind string, irritated him. He had devoted so much trouble to arranging it all that every disturbance of it distressed him.) But on the whole his life ran its course as he believed life should do: easily, pleasantly, and decorously.

He got up at nine, drank his coffee, read the paper, and then put on his undress uniform and went to the law courts. There the harness in which he worked had already been stretched to fit him and he donned it without a hitch: petitioners, inquiries at the chancery, the chancery itself, and the sittings public and administrative. In all this the thing was to exclude everything fresh and vital, which always disturbs the regular course of official business, and to admit only official relations with people, and then only on official grounds. A man would come, for instance, wanting some information. Ivan Ilych, as one in whose sphere the matter did not lie, would have nothing to do with him: but if the man had some business with him in his official capacity, something that could be expressed on officially stamped paper, he would do everything, positively everything he could within the limits of such relations, and in doing so would maintain the semblance of friendly human relations, that is, would observe the courtesies of life. As soon as the official relations ended, so did everything else. Ivan Ilych possessed this capacity to separate his real life from the official side of affairs and not mix the two, in the highest degree, and by long practice and natural aptitude had brought it to such a pitch that sometimes, in the manner of a virtuoso, he would even allow himself to let the human and official relations mingle. He let himself do this just because he felt that he could at any time he chose resume the strictly official attitude again and drop the human relation. And he did it all easily, pleasantly, correctly, and even artistically. In the intervals between the sessions he smoked, drank tea, chatted a little about politics, a little about general topics, a little about cards, but most of all about official appointments. Tired, but with the feelings of a virtuoso—one of the first violins who has played his part in an orchestra with precision—he would return home to find that his wife and daughter had been out paying calls, or had a visitor, and that his son had been to school, had done his homework with his tutor, and was duly learning what is taught at high schools. Everything was as it should be. After dinner, if they had no visitors, Ivan Ilych sometimes read a book that was being much discussed at the time, and in the evening settled down to work, that is, read official papers, compared the depositions of witnesses, and noted paragraphs of the code applying to them. This was neither dull nor amusing. It was dull when he might have been playing bridge, but if no bridge was available it was at any rate better than doing nothing or sitting with his wife. Ivan Ilych's chief pleasure was giving little dinners to which he invited men and women of good social position, and just as his drawing room resembled all other drawing rooms so did his enjoyable little parties resemble all other such parties.

Once they even gave a dance. Ivan Ilych enjoyed it and everything went off well, except that it led to a violent quarrel with his wife about the cakes and sweets. Praskovya Fyodorovna had made her own plans, but Ivan Ilych insisted on getting everything from an expensive confectioner and ordered too many cakes, and the quarrel occurred because some of those cakes were left over and the confectioner's bill came to forty-five rubles. It was a great and disagreeable quarrel. Praskovya Fyodorovna called him "a fool and an imbecile," and he clutched at his head and made angry allusions to divorce.

But the dance itself had been enjoyable. The best people were there, and Ivan Ilych had danced with Princess Trufonova, a sister of the distinguished founder of the Society "Bear My Burden."

The pleasures connected with his work were pleasures of ambition; his social pleasures were those of vanity; but Ivan Ilych's greatest pleasure was playing bridge. He acknowledged that whatever disagreeable incident happened in his life, the pleasure that beamed like a ray of light above everything else was to sit down to bridge with good players, not noisy partners, and of course to four-handed bridge (with five players it was annoying to have to stand out, though one pretended not to mind), to play a clever and serious game (when the cards allowed it), and then to have supper and drink a glass of wine. After a game of bridge, especially if he had won a little (to win a large sum was unpleasant), Ivan Ilych went to bed in specially good humor.

So they lived. They formed a circle of acquaintances among the best people and were visited by people of importance and by young folk. In their views as to their acquaintances, husband, wife, and daughter were entirely agreed, and tacitly and unanimously kept at arm's length and shook off the various shabby friends and relations who, with much show of affection, gushed into the drawing room with its Japanese plates on the walls. Soon these shabby friends ceased to obtrude themselves and only the best people remained in the Golovins' set.

Young men made up to Lisa, and Petrishchev, an examining magistrate and Dmitri Ivanovich Petrishchev's son and sole heir, began to be so attentive to her that Ivan Ilych had already spoken to Praskovya Fyodorovna about it, and considered whether they should not arrange a party for them, or get up some private theatricals.

So they lived, and all went well, without change, and life flowed pleasantly.

IV

They were all in good health. It could not be called ill health if Ivan Ilych sometimes said that he had a queer taste in his mouth and felt some discomfort in his left side.

But this discomfort increased and, though not exactly painful, grew into a sense of pressure in his side accompanied by ill humor. And his irritability became worse and worse and began to mar the agreeable, easy, and correct life that had established itself in the Golovin family. Quarrels between husband and wife became more and more frequent, and soon the ease and amenity disappeared and even the decorum was barely maintained. Scenes again became frequent, and very few of those islets remained on which husband and wife could meet without an explosion. Praskovya Fyodorovna now had good reason to say that her husband's temper was trying. With characteristic exaggeration she said he had always had a dreadful temper, and that it had needed all her good nature to put up with it for twenty years. It was true that now the quarrels were started by him. His bursts of temper always came just before dinner, often just as he began to eat his soup. Sometimes he noticed that a plate or dish was chipped, or the food was not right, or his son put his elbow on the table, or his daughter's hair was not done as he liked it, and for all this he blamed Praskovya Fyodorovna. At first she retorted and said disagreeable things to him, but once or twice he fell into such a rage at the beginning of dinner that she realized it was due to some physical derangement brought on by taking food, and so she restrained herself and did not answer, but only hurried to get the dinner over. She regarded this self-restraint as highly praiseworthy. Having come to the conclusion that her husband had a dreadful temper and made her life miserable, she began to feel sorry for herself, and the more she pitied herself the more she hated her husband. She began to wish he would die; yet she did not want him to die because then his salary would cease. And this irritated her against him still more. She considered herself dreadfully unhappy just because not even his death could save her, and though she concealed her exasperation, that hidden exasperation of hers increased his irritation also.

After one scene in which Ivan Ilych had been particularly unfair and after which he had said in explanation that he certainly was irritable but that it was due to his not being well, she said that if he was ill it should be attended to, and insisted on his going to see a celebrated doctor.

He went. Everything took place as he had expected and as it always does. There was the usual waiting and the important air assumed by the doctor, with which he was so familiar (resembling that which he himself assumed in court), and the sounding and listening, and the questions that called for answers that were foregone conclusions and were evidently unnecessary, and the look of importance that implied that "if only you put yourself in our hands we will arrange everything—we know indubitably how it has to be done, always in the same way for everybody alike." It was all just as it was in the law courts. The doctor put on just the same air toward him as he himself put on toward an accused person.

The doctor said that so-and-so indicated that there was so-and-so inside the patient, but if the investigation of so-and-so did not confirm this, then he must assume that and that. If he assumed that and that, then . . . and so on. To Ivan Ilych only one question was important: was his case serious or not? But the doctor ignored that inappropriate question. From his point of view it was not the one under consideration, the real question was to decide between a floating kidney, chronic catarrh, or appendicitis. It was not a question of Ivan Ilych's life or death, but one between a floating kidney and appendicitis. And that question the doctor solved brilliantly, as it seemed to Ivan Ilych, in favor of the appendix, with the reservation that should an examination of the urine give fresh indications the matter would be reconsidered. All this was just what Ivan Ilych had himself brilliantly accomplished a thousand times in dealing with men on trial. The doctor summed up just as brilliantly, looking over his spectacles triumphantly and even

gaily at the accused. From the doctor's summing up Ivan Ilych concluded that things were bad, but that for the doctor, and perhaps for
everybody else, it was a matter of indifference, though for him it was
bad. And this conclusion struck him painfully, arousing in him a great
feeling of pity for himself and of bitterness toward the doctor's indifference to a matter of such importance.

He said nothing of this, but rose, placed the doctor's fee on the
table, and remarked with a sigh: "We sick people probably often put
inappropriate questions. But tell me, in general, is this complaint dangerous, or not? . . ."

The doctor looked at him sternly over his spectacles with one eye,
as if to say: "Prisoner, if you will not keep to the questions put to you,
I shall be obliged to have you removed from the court."

"I have already told you what I consider necessary and proper.
The analysis may show something more." And the doctor bowed.

Ivan Ilych went out slowly, seated himself disconsolately in his
sleigh, and drove home. All the way home he was going over what the
doctor had said, trying to translate those complicated, obscure, scientific phrases into plain language and find in them an answer to the
question: "Is my condition bad? Is it very bad? Or is there as yet nothing
much wrong?" And it seemed to him that the meaning of what the
doctor had said was that it was very bad. Everything in the streets
seemed depressing. The cabmen, the houses, the passersby, and the
shops, were dismal. His ache, this dull gnawing ache that never ceased
for a moment, seemed to have acquired a new and more serious significance from the doctor's dubious remarks. Ivan Ilych now watched
it with a new and oppressive feeling.

He reached home and began to tell his wife about it. She listened,
but in the middle of his account his daughter came in with her hat on,
ready to go out with her mother. She sat down reluctantly to listen to
this tedious story, but could not stand it long, and her mother, too,
did not hear him to the end.

"Well, I am very glad," she said. "Mind, now, to take your medicine regularly. Give me the prescription and I'll send Gerasim to the
chemist's." And she went to get ready to go out.

While she was in the room Ivan Ilych had hardly taken time to
breathe, but he sighed deeply when she left it.

"Well," he thought, "perhaps it isn't so bad after all."

He began taking his medicine and following the doctor's directions,
which had been altered after the examination of the urine. But then it
happened that there was a contradiction between the indications drawn
from the examination of the urine and the symptoms that showed

themselves. It turned out that what was happening differed from what the doctor had told him, and that he had either forgotten, or blundered, or hidden something from him. He could not, however, be blamed for that, and Ivan Ilych still obeyed his orders implicitly and at first derived some comfort from doing so.

From the time of his visit to the doctor, Ivan Ilych's chief occupation was the exact fulfillment of the doctor's instructions regarding hygiene and the taking of medicine, and the observation of his pain and his excretions. His chief interests came to be people's ailments and people's health. When sickness, deaths, or recoveries were mentioned in his presence, especially when the illness resembled his own, he listened with agitation that he tried to hide, asked questions, and applied what he heard to his own case.

The pain did not grow less, but Ivan Ilych made efforts to force himself to think that he was better. And he could do this so long as nothing agitated him. But as soon as he had any unpleasantness with his wife, any lack of success in his official work, or held bad cards at bridge, he was at once acutely sensible of his disease. He had formerly borne such mischances, hoping soon to adjust what was wrong, to master it and attain success, or make a grand slam. But now every mischance upset him and plunged him into despair. He would say to himself: "There, now, just as I was beginning to get better and the medicine had begun to take effect, comes this accursed misfortune, or unpleasantness. . . ." And he was furious with the mishap, or with the people who were causing the unpleasantness and killing him, for he felt that this fury was killing him but could not restrain it. One would have thought that it should have been clear to him that this exasperation with circumstances and people aggravated his illness, and that he ought therefore to ignore unpleasant occurrences. But he drew the very opposite conclusion: he said that he needed peace, and he watched for everything that might disturb it and became irritable at the slightest infringement of it. His condition was rendered worse by the fact that he read medical books and consulted doctors. The progress of his disease was so gradual that he could deceive himself when comparing one day with another—the difference was so slight. But when he consulted the doctors it seemed to him that he was getting worse, and even very rapidly. Yet despite this he was continually consulting them.

That month he went to see another celebrity, who told him almost the same as the first had but put his questions rather differently, and the interview with this celebrity only increased Ivan Ilych's doubts and fears. A friend of a friend of his, a very good doctor, diagnosed his illness again quite differently from the others, and though he predicted recovery, his questions and suppositions bewildered Ivan Ilych still more and increased his doubts. A homoeopathist diagnosed the disease in yet another way, and prescribed medicine that Ivan Ilych took secretly for a week. But after a week, not feeling any improvement and having lost confidence both in the former doctor's treatment and in this one's, he became still more despondent. One day a lady acquaintance mentioned a cure effected by a wonder-working icon. Ivan Ilych caught himself listening attentively and beginning to believe that it had occurred. This incident alarmed him. "Has my mind really weakened to such an extent?" he asked himself. "Nonsense! It's all rubbish. I mustn't give way to nervous fears but having chosen a doctor must keep strictly to his treatment. That is what I will do. Now it's all settled. I won't think about it, but will follow the treatment seriously till summer, and then we shall see. From now there must be no more of this wavering!" This was easy to say but impossible to carry out. The pain in his side oppressed him and seemed to grow worse and more incessant, while the taste in his mouth grew stranger and stranger. It seemed to him that his breath had a disgusting smell, and he was conscious of a loss of appetite and strength. There was no deceiving himself: something terrible, new, and more important than anything before in his life, was taking place within him of which he alone was aware. Those about him did not understand or would not understand it, but thought everything in the world was going on as usual. That tormented Ivan Ilych more than anything. He saw that his household, especially his wife and daughter, who were in a perfect whirl of visiting, did not understand anything of it and were annoyed that he was so depressed and so exacting, as if he were to blame for it. Though they tried to disguise it he saw that he was an obstacle in their path, and that his wife had adopted a definite line in regard to his illness and kept to it regardless of anything he said or did. Her attitude was this: "You know," she would say to her friends, "Ivan Ilych can't do as other people do, and keep to the treatment prescribed for him. One day he'll take his drops and keep strictly to his diet and go to bed in good time, but the next day unless I watch him he'll suddenly forget his medicine, eat sturgeon—which is forbidden—and sit up playing cards till one o'clock in the morning."

"Oh, come, when was that?" Ivan Ilych would ask in vexation. "Only once at Pyotr Ivanovich's."

"And yesterday with Shebek."

"Well, even if I hadn't stayed up, this pain would have kept me awake."

"Be that as it may you'll never get well like that, but will always make us wretched."

Praskovya Fyodorovna's attitude to Ivan Ilych's illness, as she expressed it both to others and to him, was that it was his own fault and was another of the annoyances he caused her. Ivan Ilych felt that this opinion escaped her involuntarily—but that did not make it easier for him.

At the law courts, too, Ivan Ilych noticed, or thought he noticed, a strange attitude toward himself. It sometimes seemed to him that people were watching him inquisitively as a man whose place might soon be vacant. Then again, his friends would suddenly begin to chaff him in a friendly way about his low spirits, as if the awful, horrible, and unheard-of thing that was going on within him, incessantly gnawing at him and irresistibly drawing him away, was a very agreeable subject for jests. Schwartz in particular irritated him by his jocularity, vivacity, and savoir faire, which reminded him of what he himself had been ten years ago.

Friends came to make up a set and they sat down to cards. They dealt, bending the new cards to soften them, and he sorted the diamonds in his hand and found he had seven. His partner said "No trumps" and supported him with two diamonds. What more could be wished for? It ought to be jolly and lively. They would make a grand slam. But suddenly Ivan Ilych was conscious of that gnawing pain, that taste in his mouth, and it seemed ridiculous that in such circumstances he should be pleased to make a grand slam.

He looked at his partner Mikhail Mikhailovich, who rapped the table with his strong hand and instead of snatching up the tricks pushed the cards courteously and indulgently toward Ivan Ilych that he might have the pleasure of gathering them up without the trouble of stretching out his hand for them. "Does he think I am too weak to stretch out my arm?" thought Ivan Ilych, and forgetting what he was doing he overtrumped his partner, missing the grand slam by three tricks. And what was most awful of all was that he saw how upset Mikhail Mikhailovich was about it but did not himself care. And it was dreadful to realize why he did not care.

They all saw that he was suffering, and said: "We can stop if you are tired. Take a rest." Lie down? No, he was not at all tired, and he finished the rubber. All were gloomy and silent. Ivan Ilych felt that he had diffused this gloom over them and could not dispel it. They had supper and went away, and Ivan Ilych was left alone with the consciousness that his life was poisoned and was poisoning the lives of others, and that this poison did not weaken but penetrated more and more deeply into his whole being.

With this consciousness, and with physical pain besides the terror, he must go to bed, often to lie awake the greater part of the night. Next morning he had to get up again, dress, go to the law courts, speak, and write; or if he did not go out, spend at home those twenty-four hours a day each of which was a torture. And he had to live thus all alone on the brink of an abyss, with no one who understood or pitied him.

V

So one month passed and then another. Just before the New Year his brother-in-law came to town and stayed at their house. Ivan Ilych was at the law courts and Praskovya Fyodorovna had gone shopping. When Ivan Ilych came home and entered his study he found his brother-in-law there—a healthy, florid man—unpacking his portmanteau himself. He raised his head on hearing Ivan Ilych's footsteps and looked up at him for a moment without a word. That stare told Ivan Ilych everything. His brother-in-law opened his mouth to utter an exclamation of surprise but checked himself, and that action confirmed it all.

"I have changed, eh?"

"Yes, there is a change."

And after that, try as he would to get his brother-in-law to return to the subject of his looks, the latter would say nothing about it. Praskovya Fyodorovna came home and her brother went out to her. Ivan Ilych locked the door and began to examine himself in the glass, first full face, then in profile. He took up a portrait of himself taken with his wife, and compared it with what he saw in the glass. The change in him was immense. Then he bared his arms to the elbow, looked at them, drew the sleeves down again, sat down on an ottoman, and grew blacker than night.

"No, no, this won't do!" he said to himself, and jumped up, went to the table, took up some law papers, and began to read them, but could not continue. He unlocked the door and went into the reception room. The door leading to the drawing room was shut. He approached it on tiptoe and listened.

"No, you are exaggerating!" Praskovya Fyodorovna was saying.

"Exaggerating! Don't you see it? Why, he's a dead man! Look at his eyes—there's no light in them. But what is it that is wrong with him?"

"No one knows. Nikolayevich (that was another doctor) said something, but I don't know what. And Leshchetitsky (this was the celebrated specialist) said quite the contrary . . ."

Ivan Ilych walked away, went to his own room, lay down, and began musing: "The kidney, a floating kidney." He recalled all the doctors had told him of how it detached itself and swayed about. And by an effort of imagination he tried to catch that kidney and arrest it and support it. So little was needed for this, it seemed to him. "No, I'll go to see Pyotr Ivanovich again." (That was the friend whose friend was a doctor.) He rang, ordered the carriage, and got ready to go.

"Where are you going, Jean?" asked his wife, with a specially sad and exceptionally kind look.

This exceptionally kind look irritated him. He looked morosely at her.

"I must go to see Pyotr Ivanovich."

He went to see Pyotr Ivanovich, and together they went to see his friend, the doctor. He was in, and Ivan Ilych had a long talk with him.

Reviewing the anatomical and physiological details of what in the doctor's opinion was going on inside him, he understood it all.

There was something, a small thing, in the vermiform appendix. It might all come right. Only stimulate the energy of one organ and check the activity of another, then absorption would take place and everything would come right. He got home rather late for dinner, ate his dinner, and conversed cheerfully, but could not for a long time bring himself to go back to work in his room. At last, however, he went to his study and did what was necessary, but the consciousness that he had put something aside—an important, intimate matter that he would revert to when his work was done—never left him. When he had finished his work he remembered that this intimate matter was the thought of his vermiform appendix. But he did not give himself up to it, and went to the drawing room for tea. There were callers there, including the examining magistrate who was a desirable match for his daughter, and they were conversing, playing the piano, and singing. Ivan Ilych, as Praskovya Fyodorovna remarked, spent that evening more cheerfully than usual, but he never for a moment forgot that he had postponed the important matter of the appendix. At eleven o'clock he said good night and went to his bedroom. Since his illness he had slept alone in a small room next to his study. He undressed and took up a novel by Zola, but instead of reading it he fell into thought, and in his imagination that desired improvement in the vermiform appendix occurred. There was the absorption and evacuation and the reestablishment of normal activity. "Yes, that's it!" he said to himself. "One need only assist nature, that's all." He remembered his medicine, rose, took it, and lay down on his back watching for the beneficent action of the medicine and for it to lessen the pain. "I need only take it regularly and avoid all injurious influences. I am already feeling better, much better." He began touching his side: it was not painful to the touch. "There, I really don't feel it. It's much better already." He put out the light and turned on his side. . . . "The appendix is getting better, absorption is occurring." Suddenly he felt the old, familiar, dull, gnawing pain, stubborn and serious. There was the same familiar loathsome taste in his mouth. His heart sank and he felt dazed. "My God! My God!" he muttered. "Again, again! and it will never cease." And suddenly the matter presented itself in a quite different aspect. "Vermiform appendix! Kidney!" he said to himself. "It's not a question of appendix or kidney, but of life and . . . death. Yes, life was there and now it is going, going and I cannot stop it. Yes. Why deceive myself? Isn't it obvious to everyone but me that I'm dying, and that it's only a question of weeks, days . . . it may happen this moment. There was light and now there is darkness. I was here and now I'm going there! Where?" A chill came over him, his breathing ceased, and he felt only the throbbing of his heart.

"When I am not, what will there be? There will be nothing. Then where shall I be when I am no more? Can this be dying? No, I don't want to!" He jumped up and tried to light the candle, felt for it with trembling hands, dropped candle and candlestick on the floor, and fell back on his pillow.

"What's the use? It makes no difference," he said to himself, staring with wide-open eyes into the darkness. "Death. Yes, death. And none of them know or wish to know it, and they have no pity for me. Now they are playing." (He heard through the door the distant sound of a song and its accompaniment.) "It's all the same to them, but they will die too! Fools! I first, and they later, but it will be the same for them. And now they are merry . . . the beasts!"

Anger choked him and he was agonizingly, unbearably miserable. "It is impossible that all men have been doomed to suffer this awful horror!" He raised himself.

"Something must be wrong. I must calm myself—must think it all over from the beginning." And he again began thinking. "Yes, the beginning of my illness: I knocked my side, but I was still quite well that day and the next. It hurt a little, then rather more. I saw the doctors, then followed despondency and anguish, more doctors, and I drew nearer to the abyss. My strength grew less and I kept coming nearer and nearer, and now I have wasted away and there is no light in my eyes. I think of the appendix—but this is death! I think of mending the appendix, and all the while here is death! Can it really be death?" Again terror seized him and he gasped for breath. He leaned down and began feeling for the matches, pressing with his elbow on the stand beside the bed. It was in his way and hurt him, he grew furious with it, pressed on it still harder, and upset it. Breathless and in despair he fell on his back, expecting death to come immediately.

Meanwhile the visitors were leaving. Praskovya Fyodorovna was seeing them off. She heard something fall and came in.

"What has happened?"

"Nothing. I knocked it over accidentally."

She went out and returned with a candle. He lay there panting heavily, like a man who has run a thousand yards, and stared upward at her with a fixed look.

"What is it, Jean?"

"No . . . o . . . thing. I upset it." ("Why speak of it? She won't understand," he thought.)

And in truth she did not understand. She picked up the stand, lit his candle, and hurried away to see another visitor off. When she came back he still lay on his back, looking upward.

"What is it? Do you feel worse?"

"Yes."

She shook her head and sat down.

"Do you know, Jean, I think we must ask Leshchetitsky to come and see you here."

This meant calling in the famous specialist, regardless of expense. He smiled malignantly and said, "No." She remained a little longer and then went up to him and kissed his forehead.

While she was kissing him he hated her from the bottom of his soul and with difficulty refrained from pushing her away.

"Good night. Please God you'll sleep."

"Yes."

VI

Ivan Ilych saw that he was dying, and he was in continual despair.

In the depth of his heart he knew he was dying, but not only was he not accustomed to the thought, he simply did not and could not grasp it.

The syllogism he had learned from Kiezewetter's logic—"Caius is a man, men are mortal, therefore Caius is mortal"—had always seemed to him correct as applied to Caius, but certainly not as applied to himself. That Caius—man in the abstract—was mortal, was perfectly correct, but he was not Caius, not an abstract man, but a creature quite, quite separate from all others. He had been little Vanya, with a mama and a papa, with Mitya and Volodya, with the toys, a coachman, and a nurse, afterward with Katenka and with all the joys, griefs, and delights of childhood, boyhood, and youth. What did Caius know of the smell of that striped leather ball Vanya had been so fond of? Had Caius kissed his mother's hand like that, and did the silk of her dress rustle so for Caius? Had he rioted like that at school when the pastry was bad? Had Caius been in love like that? Could Caius preside at a session as he did? "Caius really was mortal, and it was right for him to die; but for me, little Vanya, Ivan Ilych, with all my thoughts and emotions, it's altogether a different matter. It cannot be that I ought to die. That would be too terrible."

Such was his feeling.

"If I had to die like Caius I should have known it was so. An inner voice would have told me so, but there was nothing of the sort in me and I and all my friends felt that our case was quite different from that of Caius. And now here it is!" he said to himself. "It can't be. It's impossible! But here it is. How is this? How is one to understand it?"

He could not understand it, and tried to drive this false, incorrect, morbid thought away and to replace it by other proper and healthy thoughts. But that thought, and not the thought only but the reality itself, seemed to come and confront him.

And to replace that thought he called up a succession of others, hoping to find in them some support. He tried to get back into the former current of thoughts that had once screened the thought of death from him. But strange to say, all that had formerly shut off, hidden, and destroyed, his consciousness of death, no longer had that effect. Ivan Ilych now spent most of his time in attempting to reestablish that old current. He would say to himself: "I will take up my duties again—after all I used to live by them." And banishing all doubts he would go to the law courts, enter into conversation with his colleagues, and sit carelessly as was his wont, scanning the crowd with a thoughtful look and leaning both his emaciated arms on the arms of his oak chair; bending over as usual to a colleague and drawing his papers nearer he would interchange whispers with him, and then suddenly raising his eyes and sitting erect would pronounce certain words and open the proceedings. But suddenly in the midst of those proceedings the pain in his side, regardless of the stage the proceedings had reached, would begin its own gnawing work. Ivan Ilych would turn his attention to it and try to drive the thought of it away, but without success. *It* would come and stand before him and look at him, and he would be petrified and the light would die out of his eyes, and he would again begin asking himself whether *It* alone was true. And his colleagues and subordinates would see with surprise and distress that he, the brilliant and subtle judge, was becoming confused and making mistakes. He would shake himself, try to pull himself together, manage somehow to bring the sitting to a close, and return home with the sorrowful consciousness that his judicial labors could not as formerly hide from him what he wanted them to hide, and could not deliver him from *It*. And what was worst of all was that *It* drew his attention to itself not in order to make him take some action but only that he should look at *It*, look it straight in the face: look at it and without doing anything, suffer inexpressibly.

And to save himself from this condition Ivan Ilych looked for consolations—new screens—and new screens were found and for a while seemed to save him, but then they immediately fell to pieces or rather became transparent, as if *It* penetrated them and nothing could veil *It*.

In these latter days he would go into the drawing room he had arranged—that drawing room where he had fallen and for the sake of which (how bitterly ridiculous it seemed) he had sacrificed his life— for he knew that his illness originated with that knock. He would enter and see that something had scratched the polished table. He would look for the cause of this and find that it was the bronze ornamentation of an album, that had gotten bent. He would take up the expensive album which he had lovingly arranged, and feel vexed with his daughter and her friends for their untidiness—for the album was torn here and there and some of the photographs turned upside down. He would put it carefully in order and bend the ornamentation back into position. Then it would occur to him to place all those things in another corner of the room, near the plants. He could call the footman, but his daughter or wife would come to help him. They would not agree, and his wife would contradict him, and he would dispute and grow angry. But that was all right, for then he did not think about *It*. *It* was invisible.

But then, when he was moving something himself, his wife would say: "Let the servants do it. You will hurt yourself again." And suddenly *It* would flash through the screen and he would see it. It was just a flash, and he hoped it would disappear, but he would involuntarily pay attention to his side. "It sits there as before, gnawing just the same!" And he could no longer forget *It*, but could distinctly see it looking at him from behind the flowers. "What is it all for?"

"It really is so! I lost my life over that curtain as I might have done when storming a fort. Is that possible? How terrible and how stupid. It can't be true! It can't, but it is."

He would go to his study, lie down, and again be alone with *It:* face-to-face with *It*. And nothing could be done with *It* except to look at it and shudder.

VII

How it happened it is impossible to say because it came about step by step, unnoticed, but in the third month of Ivan Ilych's illness, his wife, his daughter, his son, his acquaintances, the doctors, the servants, and above all he himself, were aware that the whole interest he had for other people was whether he would soon vacate his place, and at last release the living from the discomfort caused by his presence and be himself released from his sufferings.

He slept less and less. He was given opium and hypodermic injections of morphine, but this did not relieve him. The dull depression he experienced in a somnolent condition at first gave him a little relief, but only as something new; afterward it became as distressing as the pain itself or even more so.

Special foods were prepared for him by the doctors' orders, but all those foods became increasingly distasteful and disgusting to him.

For his excretions also special arrangements had to be made, and this was a torment to him every time—a torment from the uncleanliness, the unseemliness, and the smell, and from knowing that another person had to take part in it.

But just through this most unpleasant matter, Ivan Ilych obtained comfort. Gerasim, the butler's young assistant, always came in to carry the things out. Gerasim was a clean, fresh peasant lad, grown stout on town food and always cheerful and bright. At first the sight of him, in his clean Russian peasant costume, engaged on that disgusting task embarrassed Ivan Ilych.

Once when he got up from the commode too weak to draw up his trousers, he dropped into a soft armchair and looked with horror at his bare, enfeebled thighs with the muscles so sharply marked on them.

Gerasim with a firm light tread, his heavy boots emitting a pleasant smell of tar and fresh winter air, came in wearing a clean Hessian apron, the sleeves of his print shirt tucked up over his strong bare young arms; and refraining from looking at his sick master out of consideration for his feelings, and restraining the joy of life that beamed from his face, he went up to the commode.

"Gerasim!" said Ivan Ilych in a weak voice.

Gerasim started, evidently afraid he might have committed some blunder, and with a rapid movement turned his fresh, kind, simple young face which just showed the first downy signs of a beard.

"Yes, sir?"

"That must be very unpleasant for you. You must forgive me. I am helpless."

"Oh, why, sir"—and Gerasim's eyes beamed and he showed his glistening white teeth—"what's a little trouble? It's a case of illness with you, sir."

And his deft strong hands did their accustomed task, and he went out of the room stepping lightly. Five minutes later he as lightly returned.

Ivan Ilych was still sitting in the same position in the armchair.

"Gerasim," he said when the latter had replaced the freshly washed utensil. "Please come here and help me." Gerasim went up to him. "Lift me up. It is hard for me to get up, and I have sent Dmitri away."

Gerasim went up to him, grasped his master with his strong arms deftly but gently, in the same way that he stepped—lifted him, supported him with one hand, and with the other drew up his trousers and would have set him down again, but Ivan Ilych asked to be led to the sofa. Gerasim, without an effort and without apparent pressure, led him, almost lifting him, to the sofa and placed him on it.

"Thank you. How easily and well you do it all!"

Gerasim smiled again and turned to leave the room. But Ivan Ilych felt his presence such a comfort that he did not want to let him go.

"One thing more, please move up that chair. No, the other one —under my feet. It is easier for me when my feet are raised."

Gerasim brought the chair, set it down gently in place, and raised Ivan Ilych's legs on to it. It seemed to Ivan Ilych that he felt better while Gerasim was holding up his legs.

"It's better when my legs are higher," he said. "Place that cushion under them."

Gerasim did so. He again lifted the legs and placed them, and again Ivan Ilych felt better while Gerasim held his legs. When he set them down Ivan Ilych fancied he felt worse.

"Gerasim," he said. "Are you busy now?"

"Not at all, sir," said Gerasim, who had learned from the towns-folk how to speak to gentlefolk.

"What have you still to do?"

"What have I to do? I've done everything except chopping the logs for tomorrow."

"Then hold my legs up a bit higher, can you?"

"Of course I can. Why not?" And Gerasim raised his master's legs higher and Ivan Ilych thought that in that position he did not feel any pain at all.

"And how about the logs?"

"Don't trouble about that, sir. There's plenty of time."

Ivan Ilych told Gerasim to sit down and hold his legs, and began to talk to him. And strange to say it seemed to him that he felt better while Gerasim held his legs up.

After that Ivan Ilych would sometimes call Gerasim and get him to hold his legs on his shoulders, and he liked talking to him. Gerasim did it all easily, willingly, simply, and with a good nature that touched Ivan Ilych. Health, strength, and vitality in other people were offensive to him, but Gerasim's strength and vitality did not mortify but soothed him.

What tormented Ivan Ilych most was the deception, the lie, which for some reason they all accepted, that he was not dying but was simply ill, and that he only need keep quiet and undergo a treatment and then something very good would result. He, however, knew that do what they would nothing would come of it, only still more agonizing suffering and death. This deception tortured him—their not wishing to admit what they all knew and what he knew, but wanting to lie to him concerning his terrible condition, and wishing and forcing him to participate in that lie. Those lies—lies enacted over him on the eve of his death and destined to degrade this awful, solemn act to the level of their visitings, their curtains, their sturgeon for dinner—were a terrible agony for Ivan Ilych. And strangely enough, many times when they were going through their antics over him he had been within a hairbreadth of calling out to them: "Stop lying! You know and I know that I am dying. Then at least stop lying about it!" But he had never had the spirit to do it. The awful, terrible act of his dying was, he could see, reduced by those about him to the level of a casual, unpleasant, and almost indecorous incident (as if someone entered a drawing room diffusing an unpleasant odor) and this was done by that very decorum which he had served all his life long. He saw that no one felt for him, because no one even wished to grasp his position. Only Gerasim recognized it and pitied him. And so Ivan Ilych felt at ease only with him. He felt comforted when Gerasim supported his legs (sometimes all night long) and refused to go to bed, saying: "Don't you worry, Ivan Ilych. I'll get sleep enough later on," or when he suddenly became familiar and exclaimed: "If you weren't sick it would be another matter, but as it is, why should I grudge a little trouble?" Gerasim alone did not lie; everything showed that he alone understood the facts of the case and did not consider it necessary to disguise them, but simply felt sorry for his emaciated and enfeebled master. Once when Ivan Ilych was sending him away he even said straight out: "We shall all of us die, so why should I grudge a little trouble?"—expressing the fact that he did not think his work burdensome, because he was doing it for a dying man and hoped someone would do the same for him when his time came.

Apart from this lying, or because of it, what most tormented Ivan Ilych was that no one pitied him as he wished to be pitied. At certain moments after prolonged suffering he wished most of all (though he would have been ashamed to confess it) for someone to pity him as a sick child is pitied. He longed to be petted and comforted. He knew he was an important functionary, that he had a beard turning gray, and that therefore what he longed for was impossible, but still he longed for it. And in Gerasim's attitude toward him there was something akin to what he wished for, and so that attitude comforted him. Ivan Ilych wanted to weep, wanted to be petted and cried over, and then his colleague Shebek would come, and instead of weeping and being petted, Ivan Ilych would assume a serious, severe, and profound air, and by force of habit would express his opinion on a decision of the court of cassation and would stubbornly insist on that view. This falsity around him and within him did more than anything else to poison his last days.

VIII

It was morning. He knew it was morning because Gerasim had gone, and Pyotr the footman had come and put out the candles, drawn back one of the curtains, and begun quietly to tidy up. Whether it was morning or evening, Friday or Sunday, made no difference, it was all just the same: the gnawing, unmitigated, agonizing pain, never ceasing for an instant, the consciousness of life inexorably waning but not yet extinguished, the approach of that ever dreaded and hateful Death which was the only reality, and always the same falsity. What were days, weeks, hours, in such a case?

"Will you have some tea, sir?"

"He wants things to be regular, and wishes the gentlefolk to drink tea in the morning," thought Ivan Ilych, and only said "No."

"Wouldn't you like to move onto the sofa, sir?"

"He wants to tidy up the room, and I'm in the way. I am uncleanliness and disorder," he thought, and said only:

"No, leave me alone."

The man went on bustling about. Ivan Ilych stretched out his hand. Pyotr came up, ready to help.

"What is it, sir?"

"My watch."

Pyotr took the watch which was close at hand and gave it to his master.

"Half-past eight. Are they up?"

"No, sir, except Vladimir Ivanich" (the son) "who has gone to school. Praskovya Fyodorovna ordered me to wake her if you asked for her. Shall I do so?"

"No, there's no need to." "Perhaps I'd better have some tea," he thought, and added aloud: "Yes, bring me some tea."

Pyotr went to the door, but Ivan Ilych dreaded being left alone. "How can I keep him here? Oh yes, my medicine." "Pyotr, give me my medicine." "Why not? Perhaps it may still do me some good." He took a spoonful and swallowed it. "No, it won't help. It's all tomfoolery, all deception," he decided as soon as he became aware of the familiar, sickly, hopeless taste. "No, I can't believe in it any longer. But the pain, why this pain? If it would only cease just for a moment!" And he moaned. Pyotr turned toward him. "It's all right. Go and fetch me some tea."

Pyotr went out. Left alone Ivan Ilych groaned not so much with pain, terrible though that was, as from mental anguish. Always and forever the same, always these endless days and nights. If only it would come quicker! If only *what* would come quicker? Death, darkness? . . . No, no! Anything rather than death!

When Pyotr returned with the tea on a tray, Ivan Ilych stared at him for a time in perplexity, not realizing who and what he was. Pyotr was disconcerted by that look and his embarrassment brought Ivan Ilych to himself.

"Oh, tea! All right, put it down. Only help me to wash and put on a clean shirt."

And Ivan Ilych began to wash. With pauses for rest, he washed his hands and then his face, cleaned his teeth, brushed his hair, and looked in the glass. He was terrified by what he saw, especially by the limp way in which his hair clung to his pallid forehead.

While his shirt was being changed he knew that he would be still more frightened at the sight of his body, so he avoided looking at it.

Finally he was ready. He drew on a dressing gown, wrapped himself in a plaid, and sat down in the armchair to take his tea. For a moment he felt refreshed, but as soon as he began to drink the tea he was again aware of the same taste, and the pain also returned. He finished it with an effort, and then lay down stretching out his legs, and dismissed Pyotr.

Always the same. Now a spark of hope flashes up, then a sea of despair rages, and always pain; always pain, always despair, and always the same. When alone he had a dreadful and distressing desire to call someone, but he knew beforehand that with others present it would be still worse. "Another dose of morphine—to lose consciousness. I will tell him, the doctor, that he must think of something else. It's impossible, impossible, to go on like this."

An hour and another pass like that. But now there is a ring at the doorbell. Perhaps it's the doctor? It is. He comes in fresh, hearty, plump, and cheerful, with that look on his face that seems to say: "There, now, you're in a panic about something, but we'll arrange it all for you directly!" The doctor knows this expression is out of place here, but he has put it on once for all and can't take it off—like a man who has put on a frock coat in the morning to pay a round of calls.

The doctor rubs his hands vigorously and reassuringly.

"Brr! How cold it is! There's such a sharp frost; just let me warm myself!" he says, as if it were only a matter of waiting till he was warm, and then he would put everything right.

"Well, now, how are you?"

Ivan Ilych feels that the doctor would like to say: "Well, how are our affairs?" but that even he feels that this would not do, and says instead: "What sort of a night have you had?"

Ivan Ilych looks at him as much as to say: "Are you really never ashamed of lying?" But the doctor does not wish to understand this question, and Ivan Ilych says: "Just as terrible as ever. The pain never leaves me and never subsides. If only something . . ."

"Yes, you sick people are always like that. . . . There, now I think I am warm enough. Even Praskovya Fyodorovna, who is so particular, could find no fault with my temperature. Well, now I can say good morning," and the doctor presses his patient's hand.

Then, dropping his former playfulness, he begins with a most serious face to examine the patient, feeling his pulse and taking his temperature, and then begins the sounding and auscultation.

Ivan Ilych knows quite well and definitely that all this is nonsense and pure deception, but when the doctor, getting down on his knee, leans over him, putting his ear first higher then lower, and performs various gymnastic movements over him with a significant expression on his face, Ivan Ilych submits to it all as he used to submit to the speeches of the lawyers, though he knew very well that they were all lying and why they were lying.

The doctor, kneeling on the sofa, is still sounding him when Praskovya Fyodorovna's silk dress rustles at the door and she is heard scolding Pyotr for not having let her know of the doctor's arrival.

She comes in, kisses her husband, and at once proceeds to prove that she has been up a long time already, and only owing to a misunderstanding failed to be there when the doctor arrived.

Ivan Ilych looks at her, scans her all over, holds against her the whiteness and plumpness and cleanness of her hands and neck, the gloss of her hair, and the sparkle of her vivacious eyes. He hates her with his whole soul. And the thrill of hatred he feels for her makes him suffer from her touch.

Her attitude toward him and his disease is still the same. Just as the doctor had adopted a certain relation to his patient that he could not abandon, so had she formed one toward him—that he was not doing something he ought to do and was himself to blame, and that she reproached him lovingly for this—and she could not now change that attitude.

"You see he doesn't listen to me and doesn't take his medicine at the proper time. And above all he lies in a position that is no doubt bad for him—with his legs up."

She described how he made Gerasim hold his legs up.

The doctor smiled with a contemptuous affability that said: "What's to be done? These sick people do have foolish fancies of that kind, but we must forgive them."

When the examination was over the doctor looked at his watch, and then Praskovya Fyodorovna announced to Ivan Ilych that it was of course as he pleased, but she had sent today for a celebrated specialist who would examine him and have a consultation with Mikhail Danilovich (their regular doctor).

"Please don't raise any objections. I am doing this for my own sake," she said ironically, letting it be felt that she was doing it all for his sake and only said this to leave him no right to refuse. He remained silent, knitting his brows. He felt that he was so surrounded and involved in a mesh of falsity that it was hard to unravel anything.

Everything she did for him was entirely for her own sake, and she told him she was doing for herself what she actually was doing for herself, as if that was so incredible that he must understand the opposite.

At half-past eleven the celebrated specialist arrived. Again the sounding began and the significant conversations in his presence and in another room, about the kidneys and the appendix, and the questions and answers, with such an air of importance that again, instead of the real question of life and death that now alone confronted him, the question arose of the kidney and appendix that were not behaving as they ought to and would now be attacked by Mikhail Danilovich and the specialist and forced to amend their ways.

The celebrated specialist took leave of him with a serious though not hopeless look, and in reply to the timid question Ivan Ilych, with eyes glistening with fear and hope, put to him as to whether there was a chance of recovery, said that he could not vouch for it but there was a possibility. The look of hope with which Ivan Ilych watched the doctor out was so pathetic that Praskovya Fyodorovna, seeing it, even wept as she left the room to hand the doctor his fee.

The gleam of hope kindled by the doctor's encouragement did not last long. The same room, the same pictures, curtains, wallpaper, medicine bottles, were all there, and the same aching suffering body, and Ivan Ilych began to moan. They gave him a subcutaneous injection and he sank into oblivion.

It was twilight when he came to. They brought him his dinner and he swallowed some beef tea with difficulty, and then everything was the same again and night was coming on.

After dinner, at seven o'clock, Praskovya Fyodorovna came into the room in evening dress, her full bosom pushed up by her corset, and with traces of powder on her face. She had reminded him in the morning that they were going to the theater. Sarah Bernhardt was visiting the town and they had a box, which he had insisted on their taking. Now he had forgotten about it and her toilet offended him, but he concealed his vexation when he remembered that he had himself insisted on their securing a box and going because it would be an instructive and aesthetic pleasure for the children.

Praskovya Fyodorovna came in, self-satisfied but yet with a rather guilty air. She sat down and asked how he was, but, as he saw, only for the sake of asking and not in order to learn about it, knowing that there was nothing to learn—and then went on to what she really wanted to say: that she would not on any account have gone but that the box had been taken and Helen and their daughter were going, as well as Petrishchev (the examining magistrate, their daughter's fiancé) and that it was out of the question to let them go alone; but that she would have much preferred to sit with him for a while; and he must be sure to follow the doctor's orders while she was away.

"Oh, and Fyodor Petrovich" (the fiancé) "would like to come in. May he? And Lisa?"

"All right."

Their daughter came in in full evening dress, her fresh young flesh exposed (making a show of that very flesh that in his own case caused so much suffering), strong, healthy, evidently in love and impatient with illness, suffering, and death, because they interfered with her happiness.

Fyodor Petrovich came in, too, in evening dress, his hair curled à la Capoul, a tight stiff collar around his long sinewy neck, an enormous white shirtfront and narrow black trousers tightly stretched over his strong thighs. He had one white glove tightly drawn on, and was holding his opera hat in his hand.

Following him the schoolboy crept in unnoticed, in a new uniform, poor little fellow, and wearing gloves. Terribly dark shadows showed under his eyes, the meaning of which Ivan Ilych knew well.

His son had always seemed pathetic to him, and now it was dreadful to see the boy's frightened look of pity. It seemed to Ivan Ilych that Vasya was the only one besides Gerasim who understood and pitied him.

They all sat down and again asked how he was. A silence followed. Lisa asked her mother about the opera glasses, and there was an altercation between mother and daughter as to who had taken them and where they had been put. This occasioned some unpleasantness.

Fyodor Petrovich inquired of Ivan Ilych whether he had ever seen Sarah Bernhardt. Ivan Ilych did not at first catch the question, but then replied: "No, have you seen her before?"

"Yes, in Adrienne Lecouvreur."

Praskovya Fyodorovna mentioned some roles in which Sarah Bernhardt was particularly good. Her daughter disagreed. Conversation sprang up as to the elegance and realism of her acting—the sort of conversation that is always repeated and is always the same.

In the midst of the conversation Fyodor Petrovich glanced at Ivan Ilych and became silent. The others also looked at him and grew silent. Ivan Ilych was staring with glittering eyes straight before him, evidently indignant with them. This had to be rectified, but it was impossible to do so. The silence had to be broken, but for a time no one dared to break it and they all became afraid that the conventional deception would suddenly become obvious and the truth become plain to all. Lisa was the first to pluck up courage and break that silence, but by trying to hide what everybody was feeling, she betrayed it.

"Well, if we are going it's time to start," she said, looking at her watch, a present from her father, and with a faint and significant smile at Fyodor Petrovich relating to something known only to them. She got up with a rustle of her dress.

They all rose, said good night, and went away.

When they had gone it seemed to Ivan Ilych that he felt better; the falsity had gone with them. But the pain remained—that same pain and that same fear that made everything monotonously alike, nothing harder and nothing easier. Everything was worse.

Again minute followed minute and hour followed hour. Everything remained the same and there was no cessation. And the inevitable end of it all became more and more terrible.

"Yes, send Gerasim here," he replied to a question Pyotr asked.

IX

His wife returned late at night. She came in on tiptoe, but he heard her, opened his eyes, and made haste to close them again. She wished to send Gerasim away and to sit with him herself, but he opened his eyes and said: "No, go away."

"Are you in great pain?"

"Always the same."

"Take some opium."

He agreed and took some. She went away.

Till about three in the morning he was in a state of stupefied misery. It seemed to him that he and his pain were being thrust into a narrow, deep black sack, but though they were pushed farther and farther in they could not be pushed to the bottom. And this, terrible enough in itself, was accompanied by suffering. He was frightened yet wanted to fall through the sack, he struggled but yet cooperated. And suddenly he broke through, fell, and regained consciousness. Gerasim was sitting at the foot of the bed dozing quietly and patiently, while he himself lay with his emaciated stockinged legs resting on Gerasim's shoulders; the same shaded candle was there and the same unceasing pain.

"Go away, Gerasim," he whispered.

"It's all right, sir. I'll stay awhile."

"No. Go away."

He removed his legs from Gerasim's shoulders, turned sideways onto his arm, and felt sorry for himself. He only waited till Gerasim had gone into the next room and then restrained himself no longer but wept like a child. He wept on account of his helplessness, his terrible loneliness, the cruelty of man, the cruelty of God, and the absence of God.

"Why hast Thou done all this? Why hast Thou brought me here? Why, why dost Thou torment me so terribly?"

He did not expect an answer and yet wept because there was no answer and could be none. The pain again grew more acute, but he did not stir and did not call. He said to himself: "Go on! Strike me! But what is it for? What have I done to Thee? What is it for?"

Then he grew quiet and not only ceased weeping but even held his breath and became all attention. It was as though he were listening not to an audible voice but to the voice of his soul, to the current of thoughts arising within him.

"What is it you want?" was the first clear conception capable of expression in words, that he heard.

"What do you want? What do you want?" he repeated to himself. "What do I want? To live and not to suffer," he answered.

And again he listened with such concentrated attention that even his pain did not distract him.

"To live? How?" asked his inner voice.

"Why, to live as I used to—well and pleasantly."

"As you lived before, well and pleasantly?" the voice repeated.

And in imagination he began to recall the best moments of his pleasant life. But strange to say none of those best moments of his pleasant life now seemed at all what they had then seemed—none of them except the first recollections of childhood. There, in childhood, there had been something really pleasant with which it would be possible to live if it could return. But the child who had experienced that happiness existed no longer, it was like a reminiscence of somebody else.

As soon as the period began that had produced the present Ivan Ilych, all that had then seemed joys now melted before his sight and turned into something trivial and often nasty.

And the further he departed from childhood and the nearer he came to the present the more worthless and doubtful were the joys. This began with the School of Law. A little that was really good was still found there—there was lightheartedness, friendship, and hope. But in the upper classes there had already been fewer of such good moments. Then during the first years of his official career, when he was in the service of the governor, some pleasant moments again occurred: they were the memories of love for a woman. Then all became confused and there was still less of what was good; later on again there was still less that was good, and the further he went the less there was. His marriage, a mere accident, then the disenchantment that followed it, his wife's bad breath and the sensuality and hypocrisy: then that deadly official life and those preoccupations about money, a year of it, and two, and ten, and twenty, and always the same thing. And the longer it lasted the more deadly it became. "It is as if I had been going downhill while I imagined I was going up. And that is really what it was. I was going up in public opinion, but to the same extent life was ebbing away from me. And now it is all done and there is only death."

"Then what does it mean? Why? It can't be that life is so senseless and horrible. But if it really has been so horrible and senseless, why must I die and die in agony? There is something wrong!"

"Maybe I did not live as I ought to have," it suddenly occurred to him. "But how could that be, when I did everything properly?" he replied, and immediately dismissed from his mind this, the sole solution of all the riddles of life and death, as something quite impossible.

"Then what do you want now? To live? Live how? Live as you lived in the law courts when the usher proclaimed 'The judge is coming!' The judge is coming, the judge!" he repeated to himself. "Here he is, the judge. But I am not guilty!" he exclaimed angrily. "What is it for?" And he ceased crying, but turning his face to the wall continued to ponder on the same question: Why, and for what purpose, is there all this horror? But however much he pondered he found no answer. And whenever the thought occurred to him, as it often did, that it all resulted from his not having lived as he ought to have, he at once recalled the correctness of his whole life and dismissed so strange an idea.

X

Another fortnight passed. Ivan Ilych now no longer left his sofa. He would not lie in bed but lay on the sofa, facing the wall nearly all the time. He suffered ever the same unceasing agonies and in his loneliness pondered always on the same insoluble question: "What is this? Can it be that it is Death?" And the inner voice answered: "Yes, it is Death."

"Why these sufferings?" And the voice answered, "For no reason—they just are so." Beyond and besides this there was nothing.

From the very beginning of his illness, ever since he had first been to see the doctor, Ivan Ilych's life had been divided between two contrary and alternating moods: now it was despair and the expectation of this uncomprehended and terrible death, and now hope and an intently interested observation of the functioning of his organs. Now before his eyes there was only a kidney or an intestine that temporarily evaded its duty, and now only that incomprehensible and dreadful death from which it was impossible to escape.

These two states of mind had alternated from the very beginning of his illness, but the further it progressed the more doubtful and fantastic became the conception of the kidney, and the more real the sense of impending death.

He had but to call to mind what he had been three months before and what he was now, to call to mind with what regularity he had been going downhill, for every possibility of hope to be shattered.

Latterly during that loneliness in which he found himself as he lay facing the back of the sofa, a loneliness in the midst of a populous town and surrounded by numerous acquaintances and relations but that yet could not have been more complete anywhere—either at the bottom of the sea or under the earth—during that terrible loneliness Ivan Ilych had lived only in memories of the past. Pictures of his past rose before him one after another. They always began with what was nearest in time and then went back to what was most remote—to his childhood—and rested there. If he thought of the stewed prunes that had been offered him that day, his mind went back to the raw shriveled French plums of his childhood, their peculiar flavor and the flow of saliva when he sucked their stones, and along with the memory of that taste came a whole series of memories of those days: his nurse, his brother, and their toys. "No, I mustn't think of that. . . . It is too painful," Ivan Ilych said to himself, and brought himself back to the present—to the button on the back of the sofa and the creases in its morocco. "Morocco is expensive, but it does not wear well: there had been a quarrel about it. It was a different kind of quarrel and a different kind of morocco that time when we tore Father's portfolio and were punished, and Mama brought us some tarts. . . ." And again his thoughts dwelt on his childhood, and again it was painful and he tried to banish them and fix his mind on something else.

Then again together with that chain of memories another series passed through his mind—of how his illness had progressed and grown worse. There also the further back he looked the more life there had been. There had been more of what was good in life and more of life itself. The two merged together. "Just as the pain went on getting worse and worse, so my life grew worse and worse," he thought. "There is one bright spot there at the back, at the beginning of life, and afterward all becomes blacker and blacker and proceeds more and more rapidly—in inverse ratio to the square of the distance from death," thought Ivan Ilych. And the example of a stone falling downward with increasing velocity entered his mind. Life, a series of increasing suffer-

ings, flies farther and farther toward its end—the most terrible suffering. "I am flying. . . ." He shuddered, shifted himself, and tried to
resist, but was already aware that resistance was impossible, and again
with eyes weary of gazing but unable to cease seeing what was before
them, he stared at the back of the sofa and waited—awaiting that
dreadful fall and shock and destruction.

"Resistance is impossible!" he said to himself. "If I could only
understand what it is all for! But that, too, is impossible. An explanation
would be possible if it could be said that I have not lived as I ought
to. But it is impossible to say that," and he remembered all the legality,
correctitude, and propriety of his life. "That at any rate can certainly
not be admitted," he thought, and his lips smiled ironically as if someone could see that smile and be taken in by it. "There is no explanation!
Agony, death. . . . What for?"

XI

Another two weeks went by in this way and during that fortnight an
event occurred that Ivan Ilych and his wife had desired. Petrishchev
formally proposed. It happened in the evening. The next day Praskovya
Fyodorovna came into her husband's room considering how best to
inform him of it, but that very night there had been a fresh change for
the worse in his condition. She found him still lying on the sofa but in
a different position. He lay on his back, groaning and staring fixedly
straight in front of him.

She began to remind him of his medicines, but he turned his eyes
toward her with such a look that she did not finish what she was
saying; so great an animosity, to her in particular, did that look express.

"For Christ's sake let me die in peace!" he said.

She would have gone away, but just then their daughter came in
and went up to say good morning. He looked at her as he had at his
wife, and in reply to her inquiry about his health said dryly that he
would soon free them all of himself. They were both silent and after
sitting with him for a while went away.

"Is it our fault?" Lisa said to her mother. "It's as if we were to
blame! I am sorry for Papa, but why should we be tortured?"

The doctor came at his usual time. Ivan Ilych answered "Yes" and
"No," never taking his angry eyes from him, and at last said: "You
know you can do nothing for me, so leave me alone."

"We can ease your sufferings."

"You can't even do that. Let me be."

The doctor went into the drawing room and told Praskovya Fyodorovna that the case was very serious and that the only resource left was opium to allay her husband's sufferings, which must be terrible.

It was true, as the doctor said, that Ivan Ilych's physical sufferings were terrible, but worse than the physical sufferings were his mental sufferings, which were his chief torture.

His mental sufferings were due to the fact that that night, as he looked at Gerasim's sleepy, good-natured face with its prominent cheekbones, the question suddenly occurred to him: "What if my whole life has really been wrong?"

It occurred to him that what had appeared perfectly impossible before, namely that he had not spent his life as he should have, might after all be true. It occurred to him that his scarcely perceptible attempts to struggle against what was considered good by the most highly placed people, those scarcely noticeable impulses that he had immediately suppressed, might have been the real thing, and all the rest false. And his professional duties and the whole arrangement of his life and of his family, and all his social and official interests, might all have been false. He tried to defend all those things to himself and suddenly felt the weakness of what he was defending. There was nothing to defend.

"But if that is so," he said to himself, "and I am leaving this life with the consciousness that I have lost all that was given me and it is impossible to rectify it—what then?"

He lay on his back and began to pass his life in review in quite a new way. In the morning when he saw first his footman, then his wife, then his daughter, and then the doctor, their every word and movement confirmed to him the awful truth that had been revealed to him during the night. In them he saw himself—all that for which he had lived—and saw clearly that it was not real at all, but a terrible and huge deception that had hidden both life and death. This consciousness intensified his physical suffering tenfold. He groaned and tossed about, and pulled at his clothing which choked and stifled him. And he hated them on that account.

He was given a large dose of opium and became unconscious, but at noon his sufferings began again. He drove everybody away and tossed from side to side.

His wife came to him and said:

"Jean, my dear, do this for me. It can't do any harm and often helps. Healthy people often do it."

He opened his eyes wide.

"What? Take communion? Why? It's unnecessary! However . . ."

She began to cry.

"Yes, do, my dear. I'll send for our priest. He is such a nice man."

"All right. Very well," he muttered.

When the priest came and heard his confession, Ivan Ilych was softened and seemed to feel a relief from his doubts and consequently from his sufferings, and for a moment there came a ray of hope. He again began to think of the vermiform appendix and the possibility of correcting it. He received the sacrament with tears in his eyes.

When they laid him down again afterward he felt a moment's ease, and the hope that he might live awoke in him again. He began to think of the operation that had been suggested to him. "To live! I want to live!" he said to himself.

His wife came in to congratulate him after his communion, and when uttering the usual conventional words she added:

"You feel better, don't you?"

Without looking at her he said, "Yes."

Her dress, her figure, the expression of her face, the tone of her voice, all revealed the same thing. "This is wrong, it is not as it should be. All you have lived for and still live for is falsehood and deception, hiding life and death from you." And as soon as he admitted that thought, his hatred and his agonizing physical suffering again sprang up, and with that suffering a consciousness of the unavoidable, approaching end. And to this was added a new sensation of grinding shooting pain and a feeling of suffocation.

The expression of his face when he uttered that "yes" was dreadful. Having uttered it, he looked her straight in the eyes, turned on his face with a rapidity extraordinary in his weak state, and shouted:

"Go away! Go away and leave me alone!"

XII

From that moment the screaming began that continued for three days, and was so terrible that one could not hear it through two closed doors without horror. At the moment he answered his wife he realized that he was lost, that there was no return, that the end had come, the very end, and his doubts were still unsolved and remained doubts.

"Oh! Oh! Oh!" he cried in various intonations. He had begun by screaming "I won't!" and continued screaming on the letter O.

For three whole days, during which time did not exist for him, he struggled in that black sack into which he was being thrust by an invisible, resistless force. He struggled as a man condemned to death struggles in the hands of the executioner, knowing that he cannot save himself. And every moment he felt that despite all his efforts he was drawing nearer and nearer to what terrified him. He felt that his agony was due to his being thrust into that black hole and still more to his not being able to get right into it. He was hindered from getting into it by his conviction that his life had been a good one. That very justification of his life held him fast and prevented his moving forward, and it caused him most torment of all.

Suddenly some force struck him in the chest and side, making it still harder to breathe, and he fell through the hole and there at the bottom was a light. What had happened to him was like the sensation one sometimes experiences in a railway carriage when one thinks one is going backward while one is really going forward and suddenly becomes aware of the real direction.

"Yes, it was all not the right thing," he said to himself, "but that's no matter. It can be done. But what *is* the right thing?" he asked himself, and suddenly grew quiet.

This occurred at the end of the third day, two hours before his death. Just then his schoolboy son had crept softly in and gone up to the bedside. The dying man was still screaming desperately and waving his arms. His hand fell on the boy's head, and the boy caught it, pressed it to his lips, and began to cry.

At that very moment Ivan Ilych fell through and caught sight of the light, and it was revealed to him that though his life had not been what it should have been, this could still be rectified. He asked himself, "What *is* the right thing?" and grew still, listening. Then he felt that someone was kissing his hand. He opened his eyes, looked at his son, and felt sorry for him. His wife came up to him and he glanced at her. She was gazing at him open-mouthed, with undried tears on her nose and cheek and a despairing look on her face. He felt sorry for her, too.

"Yes, I am making them wretched," he thought. "They are sorry, but it will be better for them when I die." He wished to say this but had not the strength to utter it. "Besides, why speak? I must act," he thought. With a look at his wife he indicated his son and said: "Take him away . . . sorry for him . . . sorry for you, too. . . ." He tried to add, "forgive me," but said "forgo" and waved his hand, knowing that He whose understanding mattered would understand.

And suddenly it grew clear to him that what had been oppressing him and would not leave him was all dropping away at once from two sides, from ten sides, and from all sides. He was sorry for them, he must act so as not to hurt them: release them and free himself from these sufferings. "How good and how simple!" he thought. "And the

pain?" he asked himself. "What has become of it? Where are you,
pain?"

He turned his attention to it.

"Yes, here it is. Well, what of it? Let the pain be."

"And death . . . where is it?"

He sought his former accustomed fear of death and did not find
it. "Where is it? What death?" There was no fear because there was
no death.

In place of death there was light.

"So that's what it is!" he suddenly exclaimed aloud. "What joy!"

To him all this happened in a single instant, and the meaning of
that instant did not change. For those present his agony continued for
another two hours. Something rattled in his throat, his emaciated body
twitched, then the gasping and rattle became less and less frequent.

"It is finished!" said someone near him.

He heard these words and repeated them in his soul.

"Death is finished," he said to himself. "It is no more!"

He drew in a breath, stopped in the midst of a sigh, stretched out,
and died.

(1886)

MASTER AND MAN

I

It happened in the seventies, in winter, on the day after St. Nicholas's
day. There was a holiday in the parish, and the village innkeeper and
second-guild merchant, Vasily Andreyevich Brekhunov, could not go
away, as he had to attend church (he was a church warden), and go
receive and entertain friends and acquaintances at home. But at last all
the guests were gone, and Vasily Andreyevich began preparations for
a drive over to a neighboring landowner to buy from him the forest
for which they had been bargaining this long while. He was very anxious to go, so as to forestall the town merchants, who might snatch
away this profitable purchase. The youthful landowner only asked ten
thousand rubles for the forest, while Vasily Andreyevich offered seven
thousand. In reality, seven thousand was but a third of the real worth
of the property. Vasily Andreyevich might, perhaps, be able to drive

the better bargain, because the forest stood in his district, and by an old-standing agreement between him and the other village-merchants, no one of them competed in another's territory. But Vasily Andreyevich had learned that the timber merchants from the capital town of the province intended to bid for the Goryachkin forest, and he decided to go at once and conclude the bargain. Accordingly, as soon as the feast was over, he took seven hundred rubles of his own from the strongbox, added to them twenty-three hundred belonging to the church, and after carefully counting the whole, he put the money in his pocketbook and made haste to be gone. Nikita, the laborer, the only one of Vasily Andreyevich's men who was not drunk that day, ran to harness the horse. He was not drunk on this occasion because he was a drunkard; since the last day before the fast, when he spent his coat and boots in drink, he had forsworn his debauchery and kept sober for a month. He was not drinking even now, in spite of the temptation arising from the universal absorption of alcohol during the first two days of the holiday.

Nikita was a fifty-year-old muzhik from the neighboring village; an "unreliable" man, as folk called him, "one who lived most of his life with other people" and not at his own home. He was esteemed everywhere for his industry, quickness, and strength, and still more for his kindliness and pleasantness. But he could never live long in one place because about twice a year, or even more often he gave way to drink; and at such times, besides spending all he had, he became turbulent and quarrelsome. Vasily Andreyevich had dismissed him several times, and afterward engaged him again, valuing his honesty and kindness to animals, but chiefly his cheapness. The merchant did not pay Nikita eighty rubles, the worth of such a man, but forty; and even that he paid without regular account, in small installments, and mostly not in cash, but in high-priced goods from his own shop.

Nikita's wife, Martha, a vigorous and once-beautiful woman, carried on the home, with a boy and two girls. She never pressed Nikita to live at home; first, because she had lived for about twenty years with a cooper, a muzhik from another village, who lodged with them; and second, because, although she treated her husband as she pleased when he was sober, she feared him like fire when he was drinking. Once, when drunk at home, Nikita, perhaps to counterbalance his sober humility, broke open his wife's box, took her best clothes, and seizing an ax, cut to shreds all her gala dress and garments. The whole wages that Nikita earned went to his wife, without objection from him. It was in pursuance of this arrangement that Martha, two days before the holiday, came to Vasily Andreyevich, and got from him wheat flour, tea, sugar, with a pint of vodka—about three rubles worth in all—and five rubles in cash; for which she gave thanks as for a great and special favor, when in fact, and at the lowest figure, the merchant owed twenty rubles.

"What agreement did I make with you?" said Vasily Andreyevich to Nikita. "If you want anything, take it; you will work it out. I am not like other folks, with their putting off, and accounts, and fines. We are dealing straightforwardly. You work for me, and I stand by you. What you need, I give it to you."

Talking in this way, the merchant was honestly convinced of his beneficence to Nikita; and he spoke with such assertion that everyone, beginning with Nikita, confirmed him in this conviction.

"I understand, Vasily Andreyevich, I do my best, I try to do as I would for my own father. I understand all right," answered Nikita, understanding very well that he is cheated, but at the same time feeling that it is useless to try to get the accounts cleared up. While there is nowhere else to go, he must stay where he is, and take what he can get.

When Nikita was told by his master to put the horse in, willingly and cheerfully as always, and with a firm and easy stride, he stepped to the cart shed, took down from the nail the heavy, tasseled leather bridle, and jingling the rings of the bit, went to the stable where stood the horse that Vasily Andreyevich had bidden to be harnessed.

"Well, silly, are you tired, tired?" said Nikita, in answer to the soft whinny that greeted him from the stallion, a fairly good dark bay of medium height, with sloping quarters, who stood solitary in his stall. "Quiet, quiet, there's plenty of time! Let me give you a drink first," he went on to the horse, as though speaking to a creature with reason. With the skirt of his coat he swept down the horse's broad, double-ridged back, roughed and dusty as it was; then he put the bridle on the handsome young head, arranged his ears and mane, and led him away to drink. Picking his way out of the dung-strewn stable, the dark bay began to plunge, making play with his hind foot, as though to kick Nikita, who was hurrying him to the well.

"Now, then, now, then, you rogue," said Nikita, knowing Moukhorta was careful that the hind foot went no farther than his fur coat, doing no hurt, and knowing how the horse liked this play.

After the cold water, the horse stood awhile, breathing, and moving his wet, strong lips, from which transparent drops fell into the trough; then he sniffed.

"If you want no more, you needn't take it. Well, let it be at that; but don't ask again for more," said Nikita, quite seriously emphasizing to Moukhorta the consequences of his behavior. Then he briskly led him back to the shed, pulling the rein on the young horse, who lashed out all the way along the yard.

No other men were about, except a stranger to the place, the husband of the cook, who had come for a holiday.

"Go and ask, there's a good fellow, which sleigh is wanted, the wide one or the little one," said Nikita to him.

The cook's husband went away, and soon returned with the answer, that the small one was ordered. By this time, Nikita had harnessed the horse, fixed the brass-studded saddle, and carrying in one hand the light-painted yoke, with the other hand he led the horse toward the two sleighs that stood under the shed.

"All right, let us have the small one," said he, backing the intelligent horse (which all the time pretended to bite at him) into the shafts; and with the help of the cook's husband, he began to harness.

When all was nearly ready, and only the reins needed fixing, Nikita sent the cook's husband to the shed for straw, and to the storehouse for the rug.

"That's nice. Don't, don't, don't bristle up!" said Nikita, squeezing into the sleigh the freshly thrashed oat straw that the cook's husband had brought. "Now give me the sacking, while we spread it out, and put the rug over it. That's all right, just the thing, comfortable to sit on," said he, doing that which he was talking about, and making the rug tight over the straw all around.

"Thanks, my dear fellow," said Nikita to the cook's husband. "When two work, it's done quicker." Then, disentangling the leather reins, the ends of which were brought together and tied on a ring, he took the driver's seat on the sleigh and shook up the good horse, who stirred himself, eager to make across the frozen refuse that littered the yard, toward the gate.

"Uncle Mikit, eh, Uncle!" came a shout behind him from a seven-year-old boy in black fur cloak, new white felt boots, and warm cap, who slammed the door as he hurried from the entrance hall toward the yard. "Put me in!" he asked, in a shrill voice, buttoning his cloak as he ran.

"All right, come, my dove," said Nikita; and stopping the sleigh, he put in the master's son, full of joy, and drove out into the road.

It was three o'clock, and cold (about ten degrees of frost), gloomy, and windy. In the yard it seemed quiet, but in the street a strong breeze blew. The snow showered down from the roof of the barn close by and, at the corner by the baths, flew whirling around. Nikita had scarcely driven out and turned around by the front door when Vasily Andreyevich, too, with a cigarette in his mouth, wearing a sheepskin overcoat tightly fastened by a girdle placed low, came out from the entrance hall. He strode down the trampled snow of the steps, which creaked under his boots, and stopped to turn in the corners of his overcoat collar on both sides of his ruddy face (clean-shaven, except for a mustache), so as to keep the fur clear from the moisture of his breath.

"See there! What a manager! Here he is!" said he, smiling and showing his white teeth, on catching sight of his little son on the sleigh. Vasily Andreyevich was excited by the wine he had taken with his guests, and was therefore more than usually pleased with everything that belonged to him, or that was of his doing. His wife, a pale and meager woman, about to become a mother, stood behind him in the entrance hall, with a woolen plaid so wrapped about her head and shoulders that only her eyes could be seen.

"Would it not be better to take Nikita with you?" she asked, timidly, stepping out from the door. Vasily Andreyevich answered nothing, but spat. "You have money with you," the wife continued, in the same plaintive voice. "What if the weather gets worse. Be careful, for God's sake."

"Do you think I don't know the road, that I need a guide?" retorted Vasily Andreyevich, with that affected compression of the lips that he used when speaking among dealers in the market, as though he valued his own speech.

"Really, do take him, I ask you, for God's sake!" repeated his wife, folding her plaid closer.

"Just listen! She sticks to it like a leaf in the bath! Why, where must I take him to?"

"Well, Vasily Andreyevich, I'm ready," said Nikita cheerfully. "If I'm away, there are only the horses to be fed," he added, turning to his mistress.

"I'll look after that, Nikitushka; I'll tell Simon," answered the mistress.

"Shall I come, Vasily Andreyevich?" asked Nikita, waiting.

"It seems we must consider the old women. But if you come, go and put on something warmer," said Vasily Andreyevich, smiling once more, and winking at Nikita's fur coat, which was very old, torn under the arms and down the back, and soiled and crease-worn around the skirts.

"Hey, friend, come and hold the horse awhile!" shouted Nikita to the cook's husband in the yard.

"I'll hold him myself," said the little boy, taking his cold red hands out of his pockets and seizing the cold leather reins.

"Only don't be too long putting your best coat on! Be quick!" shouted Vasily Andreyevich jestingly to Nikita.

"In a breath, good master Vasily Andreyevich!" said Nikita, and he ran down the yard to the laborers' quarters.

"Now, Arinushka, give me my overcoat off the oven, I have to go with the master!" said Nikita, hastening into the room and taking his girdle down from the nail.

The cook, who had just finished her after-dinner nap, and was about to get ready the samovar for her husband, turned to Nikita merrily, and catching his haste, moved about quickly, took the worn-out woolen overcoat off the oven where it was drying, and shook and rubbed it.

"How comfortable you must be, with your husband here," said Nikita to the cook, always, as part of his good-natured politeness, ready to say something to anyone whom he came across. Then putting around himself the narrow and worn girdle, he drew in his breath and tightened it about his spare body.

"There," he said, afterward, addressing himself not to the cook but to the girdle, while tucking the ends under his belt. "This way you won't jump out." Then working his shoulders up and down to get his arms loose, he put on the overcoat, again stretching his back to free his arms; and that done, he took his mittens from the shelf. "Now we're all right."

"You ought to change your boots," said the cook, "those boots are very bad."

Nikita stopped, as if remembering something.

"Yes, I ought. . . . But it will be all right; it's not far." And he ran out into the yard.

"Won't you be cold, Nikitushka?" said his mistress, as he came up to the sleigh.

"Why should I be cold? It is quite warm," answered Nikita, arranging the straw in the forepart of the sleigh, so as to bring it over the feet, and stowing under it the whip that a good horse would not need.

Vasily Andreyevich was already in the sleigh, almost filling up the whole of the curved back with the bulk of his body wrapped in two great fur coats; and taking up the reins, he started at once. Nikita jumped in, seating himself in front to the left and hanging one leg over the side.

II

The good stallion sped the sleigh along at a brisk pace over the trodden and frozen road, the runners creaking faintly as they went.

"Look at him there, hanging on! Give me the whip, Nikita," shouted Vasily Andreyevich, evidently enjoying the sight of his boy holding to the sleigh runners behind. I'll give it to you! Run to your mother, you young dog!"

The boy jumped off. The dark bay began to amble, and then, getting his breath, broke into a trot.

Kresty, the village where the home of Vasily Andreyevich stood, consisted of six houses. Scarcely had they passed the blacksmith's house when they suddenly felt the wind to be stronger than they had thought. The road was no longer visible. The tracks of the sleigh as they were left behind were instantly covered with snow, and the road was only to be distinguished by its rise above the land on either side. The snow swept over the plain like thick smoke, and the horizon disappeared. The Telyatin forest, always particularly visible, loomed dimly through the driving snow dust. The wind came from the left hand, persistently blowing aside the mane on Moukhorta's lofty neck, turning away even his knotted tail, and pressing the deep collar of Nikita's overcoat (he sat on the windward side) against his face and nose.

"There is no chance of his showing speed with this snow," said Vasily Andreyevich, proud of his horse. "I once went to Pashutino with him, and we got there in half an hour."

"What?"

"Pashutino, I said, and he did it in half an hour."

"A good horse that, no question," said Nikita.

They became silent. But Vasily Andreyevich wanted to talk.

"Now I think of it, did you tell your good woman not to give any drink to the cooper?" asked the merchant, who was wholly of opinion that Nikita must feel flattered, talking with such an important and sensible man as himself. He was so pleased with this, his own jest, that it never entered his head that the subject might be unpleasant to Nikita.

Again the man failed to catch his master's words, the voice being carried away by the wind.

Vasily Andreyevich, in his clear and loud voice, repeated the jest about the cooper.

"God help them, master, I don't think about the matter. I only watch that she does no harm to the boy; if she does—then God help her!"

"That is right," said Vasily Andreyevich. "Well, are you going to buy a horse in the spring?" Thus he began a new topic of conversation.

"I must buy one," answered Nikita, turning aside the collar of his coat and leaning toward his master. The conversation had become interesting to him, and he did not wish to lose a word.

"My lad is grown up, and it is time he plowed for himself and gave up hiring out," said he.

"Well, then, take that horse with the thin loins; the price will not be high," shouted Vasily Andreyevich, eagerly entering into his favorite business of horse dealing, to which he gave all his powers.

"You had better give me fifteen rubles, and I'll buy in the market," said Nikita, who knew that at the highest price, the horse with the thin loins that his master wanted to sell to him was not worth more than seven rubles, but would cost him, at his master's hands, twenty-five; and that meant half a year's wages gone.

"The horse is a good one. I treat you as I would myself. Honestly. Brekhunov injures no man. Let me stand the loss, and me only. Honestly," he shouted in the voice that he used in cheating his customers, "a genuine horse."

"As you think," said Nikita, sighing, sure that it was useless to listen further; and he again drew the collar over his ear and face.

They drove in silence for about half an hour. The wind cut sharply into Nikita's side and arm, where his coat was torn. He huddled himself up and breathed in his coat collar, which covered his mouth, and breathing this way seemed to make him warmer.

"What do you think, shall we go through Karamyshevo, or keep the straight road?" said Vasily Andreyevich.

The road through Karamyshevo was more frequented, and staked on both sides, but it was longer. The straight road was nearer, but it was little used, and the stakes, now snow-covered, marked it out but badly.

Nikita thought awhile.

"Through Karamyshevo is farther, but it is better going," he said.

"But straight on, we have only to be careful in passing the little valley, and then the way is fairly good," said Vasily Andreyevich, who favored the direct road.

"As you say," replied Nikita.

So the merchant went his own way. After driving about half a verst, passing a waymark, a long branch of oak, which shook in the wind and on which a dry leaf hung here and there, he turned to the left.

Upon turning, the wind blew almost directly against them, and the snow showered from on high. Vasily Andreyevich stirred up the horse and inflated his cheeks, blowing his breath upon his mustache. Nikita dozed.

They drove thus silently for about ten minutes. Then the merchant began to say something.

"What?" asked Nikita, opening his eyes.

Vasily Andreyevich did not answer, but bent himself about, looking behind them, and then ahead of the horse. The sweat had curled the animal's coat on the groin and neck, and he was going at a walk.

"I say, what's the matter?" repeated Nikita.

"What is the matter?" mocked Vasily Andreyevich, irritated. "I see no waymarks. We must be off the road."

"Well, pull up, then, and I will find the road," said Nikita, and lightly jumping down, he drew out the whip from the straw and struck out to the left from his own side of the sleigh.

The snow was not deep that season, but in places it was up to one's knee, and Nikita got it into his boots. He walked about, feeling with his feet and the whip, but could nowhere find the road.

"Well?" said the merchant when Nikita returned to the sleigh.

"There is no road on this side. I must try the other."

"What is that dark thing in front? Go and see," said Vasily Andreyevich.

Nikita walked ahead, got near the dark patch, and found it was black earth that the wind had strewn over the snow from some fields of winter wheat. After searching to the right also, he returned to the sleigh, shook the snow off himself, cleared his boots, and took his seat.

"We must go to the right," he said decidedly. "The wind was on our left before, now it is straight ahead. To the right," he repeated, with the same decision.

Vasily Andreyevich turned accordingly. But yet no road was found. He drove on for some time. The wind kept up, and the snow still fell.

"We seem to be astray altogether, Vasily Andreyevich," said Nikita suddenly, and as pleasantly as possible. "What is that?" he said, pointing to some black potato leaves that thrust themselves through the snow.

Vasily Andreyevich stopped the horse, which by this time was in heavy perspiration and stood with its deep sides heaving. "What can it mean?" asked he.

"It means that we are on the Zakharian lands. Why, we are ever so far astray!"

"Bosh!" remarked Vasily Andreyevich, who now spoke quite otherwise than when at home, in an unconstrained and vulgar tone.

"I am telling you no lie; it is true," said Nikita. "You can feel that the sleigh is moving over a potato field, and there are the heaps of old leaves. It is the Zakharian factory land."

"What a long way we are off!" said the other. "What are we to do?"

"Go straight ahead, that's all. We shall reach someplace," said Nikita. "If we do not get to Zakharovka, we shall come out at the owner's farm."

Vasily Andreyevich assented and let the horse go as Nikita had said. They drove in this way for a long while. At times they passed winter wheat fields, where the wind had turned up and blown loose soil over the snow-covered dikes and the snowdrifts. Sometimes they passed a stubble field, sometimes a cornfield, where they could see the upstanding wormwood and straw beaten by the wind; sometimes they saw on all sides deep white snow, with nothing above it. The snow whirled down from on high, and up from below. Now they seemed to be going downhill, and now uphill; then they seemed as though standing still, while the snowfield ran past them. Both were silent. The horse was evidently tiring; his coat grew crisp and white with frost, and he no better than walked. Suddenly he stumbled in some ditch or watercourse and went down. Vasily Andreyevich wanted to halt, but Nikita opposed him.

"Why should we stop? We have gone astray, and we must find our road. Hey, old fellow, hey," he shouted in an encouraging voice to the horse; and he jumped from the sleigh, sinking into the ditch. The horse dashed forward and quickly landed upon a frozen heap. Obviously it was a made ditch.

"Where are we, then?" said Vasily Andreyevich.

"We shall see," answered Nikita. "Go ahead, we shall get to somewhere."

"Is not that the Goryachkin forest?" asked the merchant, pointing out a dark mass that showed across the snow in front of them.

"When we get nearer, we shall see what forest it is," said Nikita.

He noticed that from the side of the dark mass long dry willow leaves were fluttering toward them; and he knew thereby that it was no forest, but houses; yet he chose not to say so. And in fact they had scarcely gone twenty-five yards when they distinctly made out the trees and heard a new and melancholy sound. Nikita was right; they had come upon not a forest but a row of tall willow trees, whereon a few scattered leaves still shivered. The willows were evidently ranged along the ditch and around a barn. Coming up to the trees, through which the wind moaned and sighed, the horse suddenly planted his forefeet above the height of the sleigh, then drew up his hind legs after him, and they were out of the snow and on the road.

"Here we are," said Nikita, "but we don't know where."

The horse went right away along the snow-covered road, and they had not gone many yards when they saw a fence around a barn, from which the snow was flying in the wind. Passing the barn the road turned in the direction of the wind and brought them upon a snowdrift. But ahead of them was a passage between two houses; the drift was merely blown across the road, and must be crossed. Indeed, after passing the drift, they found a village street. In front of the end house of the village, the wind was shaking desperately the frozen linen that hung there: shirts, one red, one white, some leg cloths, and a skirt. The white shirt especially shook frantically, tugging at the sleeves.

"Look there, either a lazy woman, or a dead one, left her linen out over the holiday," said Nikita, seeing the fluttering shirts.

III

At the beginning of the street the wind was still felt and the road was snow-covered. But well within the village there was shelter, more warmth, and life. At one house a dog barked; at another, a woman, with her husband's coat over her head, came running from within and stopped at the door to see who was driving past. In the middle of the village could be heard the sound of girls singing. Here the wind, the snow, the frost, seemed subdued.

"Why, this is Grishkino," said Vasily Andreyevich.

"It is," said Nikita.

Grishkino it was. It turned out they had strayed eight versts to the left, out of their proper direction; still, they had gotten somewhat nearer to their destination. From Grishkino to Goryachkino was about five versts more.

In the middle of the village they almost ran into a tall man walking in the center of the road.

"Who is driving?" said this man, and he held the horse. Then, recognizing Vasily Andreyevich, he took hold of the shaft and leaped up to the sleigh, where he sat himself on the driver's seat.

It was the muzhik Isai, well-known to the merchant, and known through the district as a first-rate horsethief.

"Ah, Vasily Andreyevich, where is God sending you?" said Isai, from whom Nikita caught the smell of vodka.

"We are going to Goryachkino."

"You've come a long way around! You had better have gone through Malakhovo."

"Yes, but we got astray," said Vasily Andreyevich, pulling up.

"A good horse," said Isai, examining him and dexterously tightening the loosened knot in his tail. "Are you going to stay the night here?"

"No, friend, we must go on."

"Your business must be pressing. And who is that? Ah, Nikita Stepanovich!"

"Who else?" answered Nikita. "Look here, good friend, can you tell us how not to miss the road again?"

"How can you possibly miss it? Just turn back straight along the street, and then, outside the houses, keep straight ahead. Don't go to the left until you reach the high road, then turn to the left."

"And which turning do we take out of the high road? The summer or the winter road?" asked Nikita.

"The winter road. As soon as you get clear of the village there are some bushes, and opposite them is a waymark, an oaken one, all branches. There is the road."

Vasily Andreyevich turned the horse back and drove through the village.

"You had better stay the night," Isai shouted after them. But the merchant did not answer; five versts of smooth road, two versts of it through the forest, was easy enough to drive over, especially as the wind seemed quieter and the snow seemed to have ceased.

After passing along the street, darkened and trodden with fresh horse tracks, and after passing the house where the linen was hung out (a sleeve of the white shirt was by this time torn off, and the garment hung by one frozen sleeve), they came to the weirdly moaning and sighing willows, and then were again in the open country. Not only was the snowstorm still raging, but it seemed to have gained strength. The whole road was under snow, and only the stakes, the waymarks, proved that they were keeping right. But even these signs of the road were difficult to make out, for the wind blew right in their faces.

Vasily Andreyevich screwed up his eyes and bent his head, examining the marks; but for the most part he left the horse alone, trusting to his sagacity. And, in fact, the creature went correctly, turning now to the left, now to the right, along the windings of the road which he sensed under his feet. So that in spite of the thickening snow and strengthening wind, the waymarks were still to be seen, now on the left, now on the right.

They had driven thus for ten minutes when suddenly, straight in front of their horse, a black object sprang up, moving through the snow. Moukhorta had caught up to a sleigh containing other travelers, and he struck his forefeet against it.

"Drive around! Go ahead!" cried these others.

Vasily Andreyevich shaped to go around them. In the sleigh were four peasants, three men and a woman, evidently returning from a feast. One of the men whipped the quarters of their poor horse with a switch, while two of them, waving their arms from the fore part of the sleigh, shouted out something. The woman, muffled up and covered with snow, sat quiet and rigid at the back.

"Who are you?" asked Vasily Andreyevich.

"A-a-a!" was all that could be heard.

"I say, who are you?"

"A-a-a!" shouted one of the peasants with all his strength; but nevertheless it was impossible to make out the name.

"Go on! Don't give up!"

"You have been enjoying yourselves."

"Get on! Get on! Up, Semka! Step out! Up, up!"

The sleighs struck together, almost locked their sides, then fell apart, and the peasants' sleigh began to drop behind. The shaggy, snow-covered, big-bellied pony, obviously distressed, was making his last efforts with his short legs to struggle along through the deep snow, which he trod down with labor. For a moment, with distended nostrils and ears set back in distress, he kept his muzzle, which was that of a young horse, near Nikita's shoulder; then he began to fall still farther behind.

"See what drink does," said Nikita. "They have tired that horse to death. What heathens!"

For a few minutes the pantings of the tired-out horse could be heard, with the drunken shouts of the peasants. Then the pantings become inaudible, and the shouts, also. Again all was silent, except for the whistling wind and the occasional scrape of the sleigh runners upon a bare spot of road.

This encounter livened up and encouraged Vasily Andreyevich, who drove more boldly, not examining the waymarks, and again trusting to his horse.

Nikita had nothing to occupy him, and dozed. Suddenly the horse stopped, and Nikita was jerked forward, knocking his nose against the front.

"It seems we are going wrong again," said Vasily Andreyevich.

"What is the matter?"

"The waymarks are not to be seen. We must be out of the road."

"Well, if so, let us look for the road," said Nikita laconically, and he got out again to explore the snow. He walked for a long time, now out of sight, now reappearing, then disappearing; at last he returned.

"There is no road here; it may be farther on," said he, sitting down in the sleigh.

It began to grow dark. The storm neither increased nor diminished.

"I should like to meet those peasants again," said Vasily Andreyevich.

"Yes, but they won't pass near us; we must be a good distance off the road. Maybe they are astray, too," said Nikita.

"Where shall we make for, then?"

"Leave the horse to himself. He will find his way. Give me the reins."

The merchant handed over the reins, the more willingly that his hands, in spite of his warm gloves, felt the frost.

Nikita took the reins and held them lightly, trying to give no pressure; he was glad to prove the good sense of his favorite. The intelligent horse, turning one ear and then the other, first in this, then in that direction, presently began to wheel around.

"He only stops short of speaking," said Nikita. "Look how he manages it! Go on, go on, that's good."

The wind was now at their backs; they were warmer.

"Is he not wise?" continued Nikita, delighted with his horse. "A Kirghiz beast is strong, but stupid. But this one—look what he is after with his ears. There is no need of a telegraph wire; he can feel through a mile."

Hardly half an hour had gone when a forest, or a village, or something loomed up in front; and to their right, the waymarks again showed. Evidently they were upon the road again.

"We are back at Grishkino, are we not?" exclaimed Nikita suddenly.

Indeed, on the left hand rose the same barn, with the snow flying from it; and farther on was the same line with the frozen shirts and drawers, so fiercely shaken by the wind.

Again they drove through the street, again felt the quiet and shelter, again saw the road with the horse tracks, heard voices, songs, the barking of a dog. It was now so dark that a few windows were lighted.

Halfway down the street, Vasily Andreyevich turned around the horse toward a large house and stopped at the yard gate.

"Call out Taras," he ordered Nikita.

Nikita went up to the snow-dimmed window, in the light from

which glittered the flitting flakes, and knocked with the handle of the whip.

"Who is there?" a voice answered to his knock.

"The Brekhunovs, from Kresty, my good man," answered Nikita. "Come out for a minute."

Someone moved from the window, and in about two minutes the door in the entrance hall was heard to open, the latch of the front door clicked, and holding the door against the wind, there peeped out an old, white-bearded man, who wore a high cap and a fur coat over a white holiday shirt. Behind him was a young fellow in a red shirt and leather boots.

"Glad to see you," said the old man.

"We have lost our road, friend," said Vasily Andreyevich. "We set out for Goryachkino and found ourselves here. Then we went on, but lost the road again."

"I see; what a wandering!" answered the old man. "Petrushka, come, open the gates," he said to the young man in the red shirt.

"Of course I will," said the young fellow cheerfully as he ran off through the entrance hall.

"We are not stopping for the night, friend," said Vasily Andreyevich.

"Where can you go in darkness? You had better stop."

"Should be very glad to, but I must go on."

"Well, then, at least warm yourself a little; the samovar is just ready," said the old man.

"Warm ourselves? We can do that," said Vasily Andreyevich. "It cannot get darker, and when the moon is up, it will be still lighter. Come, Nikita, let us go in and warm up a bit."

"I don't object; yes, let us warm ourselves," said Nikita, who was very cold, and whose one desire was to warm his benumbed limbs over the oven.

Vasily Andreyevich went with the old man into the house. Nikita drove through the gate that Petrushka opened, and by the latter's advice, stood the horse under a shed, the floor of which was strewn with stable litter. The high bow over the horse caught the roof beam, and the hens and a cock perched up there began to cackle and scratch on the wood. Some startled sheep, pattering their feet on the frozen floor, huddled themselves out of the way. A dog, evidently a young one, yelped desperately in fright and barked fiercely at the stranger.

Nikita held conversation with them all. He begged pardon from the fowls, and calmed them with assurances that he would give them no more trouble; he reproved the sheep for being needlessly frightened; and while fastening up the horse, he kept on exhorting the little dog.

"That will do," said he, shaking the snow from himself. "Hear how he is barking!" added he, for the dog's benefit. "That's quite enough for you, quite enough, stupid! That will do! Why do you bother yourself? There are no thieves or strangers about."

"It is like the tale of the Three Domestic Counselors," said the young man, thrusting the sleigh under the shed with his strong arm.

"What counselors?"

"The tale is in P'uls'n. A thief sneaks up to a house; the dog barks—that means 'Don't idle, take care'; the cock crows—that means 'Get up'; the cat washes itself—that means 'A welcome guest is coming, be ready for him,' " said the young man, with a broad smile.

Petrushka could read and write, and knew almost by heart the only book he possessed, which was Paulsen's primer; and he liked, especially when, as now, he had a little too much to drink, to quote from the book some saying that seemed appropriate to the occasion.

"Quite true," said Nikita.

"I suppose you are cold, uncle," said Petrushka.

"Yes, something that way," said Nikita. They both crossed the yard and entered the house.

IV

The house at which Vasily Andreyevich had drawn up was one of the richest in the village. The family had five fields, and besides these, hired others outside. Their belongings included six horses, three cows, two heifers, and a score of sheep. In the house lived twenty-two souls; four married sons, six grandchildren (of whom one, Petrushka, was married), two great-grandchildren, three orphans, and four daughters-in-law with their children. It was one of the few families that maintain their unity; yet even here was beginning that indefinable interior discord—as usual, among the women—that must soon bring about separation. Two sons were water carriers in Moscow; one was in the army. At present, those at home were the old man, his wife, one son who was head of the house, another son who came from Moscow on a holiday, and all the women and children. Besides the family there was a guest, a neighbor, who was the elder of the village.

In the house there hung over the table a shaded lamp, which threw a bright light down upon the tea service, a bottle of vodka, and some eatables, and upon the brick wall of the corner where hung the holy images with pictures on each side of them. At the head of the table sat Vasily Andreyevich in his black fur coat, sucking his frozen mustache and scrutinizing the people and the room with his eyes of a hawk. Beside him at the table sat the white-bearded bald old father of the house, in a white homespun shirt; by him, wearing a thin cotton shirt, sat a son with sturdy back and shoulders, the one who was holiday-making from Moscow; then the other son, the strapping eldest brother who acted as head of the house; then the village elder, a lean and red-haired muzhik.

The muzhiks, having drunk and eaten, prepared to take tea; the samovar already boiled, standing on the floor near the oven. The children were in evidence about the oven and the sleeping shelves. On the bench along the wall sat a woman with a cradle beside her. The aged mother of the house, whose face was wrinkled all over, even to the lips, waited on Vasily Andreyevich. As Nikita entered the room, she filled up a coarse glass with vodka and handed it to Vasily Andreyevich.

"No harm done, Vasily Andreyevich, but you must drink our good health," said the old man.

The sight and smell of vodka, especially in his cold and tired condition, greatly disturbed Nikita's mind. He became gloomy, and after shaking the snow from his coat and hat, stood before the holy images; without noticing the others, he made the sign of the cross thrice, and bowed to the images; then, turning to the old man, he bowed to him first, afterward to all who sat at the table, and again to the women beside the oven, saying, "Good fortune to your feast." Without looking at the table, he began to take off his overcoat.

"Why, you are all over frost, uncle," said the eldest brother, looking at the rime on Nikita's face, eyes, and beard.

Nikita got his coat off, shook it, hung it near the oven, and came to the table. They offered him vodka also. There was a moment's bitter struggle; he wavered on the point of taking the glass and pouring the fragrant, transparent liquid into his mouth. But he looked at Vasily Andreyevich, remembered his vow, remembered the lost boots, the cooper, his son for whom he had promised to buy a horse when the spring came; he sighed, and refused.

"I don't drink, thank you humbly," he said gloomily, and sat down on the bench near the second window.

"Why not?" asked the eldest brother.

"I don't drink, that's all," said Nikita, not daring to raise his eyes, and looking at the thawing icicles in his beard and mustache.

"It is not good for him," said Vasily Andreyevich, munching a biscuit after emptying his glass.

"Then have some tea," said the kindly old woman. "I daresay you are quite benumbed, good soul. What a while you women are with the samovar."

"It is ready," answered the youngest, and wiping around the samovar with an apron, she bore it heavily to the table and set it down with a thud.

Meanwhile, Vasily Andreyevich told how they had gone astray and worked their way back twice to the same village, what mistakes they had made, and how they had met the drunken peasants. Their hosts expressed surprise, showed why and where they had missed the road, told them the names of the revelers they had met, and made plain how they ought to go.

"From here to Molchanovka, a child might go; the only thing is to make sure where to turn out of the high road, just beside the bushes. But yet you did not get there," said the village elder.

"You ought to stop here. The women will make up a bed," said the old woman persuasively.

"You would make a better start in the morning; much pleasanter, that," said the old man, affirming what his wife had said.

"Impossible, friend! Business!" said Vasily Andreyevich. "If you let an hour go, you may not be able to make it up in a year," added he, remembering the forest and the dealers who were likely to compete with him. "By all means, let us stretch out," he said, turning to Nikita.

"We may lose ourselves again," said Nikita moodily. He was gloomy because of the intense longing he felt for the vodka; and the tea, the only thing that could quench that longing, had not yet been offered to him.

"We have only to reach the turning, and there is no more danger of losing the road, as it goes straight through the forest," said Vasily Andreyevich.

"Just as you say, Vasily Andreyevich; if you want to go, let us go," said Nikita, taking the glass of tea offered to him.

"Well, let us drink up our tea, and then march!"

Nikita said nothing, but shook his head, and carefully pouring the tea into the saucer, began to warm his hands over the steam. Then, taking a small bite of sugar in his mouth, he turned to their hosts, said "Your health," and drank down the warming liquid.

"Could anyone come with us to the turning?" asked Vasily Andreyevich.

"Why not? Certainly," said the eldest son. "Petrushka will put in the horse and go with you as far as the turning."

"Then put in your horse, and I shall be in your debt."

"My dear man," said the kindly old woman, "we are right glad to do it."

"Petrushka, go and put in the mare," said the eldest son.

"All right," said Petrushka, with his broad smile; and taking his cap from the nail, he hurried away to harness the horse.

While the harnessing was in progress, the talk turned back to the point where it stood when Vasily Andreyevich arrived. The old man had complained to the village elder about the conduct of his third son, who had sent him no present this holiday time, though he had sent a French shawl to his wife.

"These young folk are getting worse and worse," said the old man.

"Very much worse!" said the village elder. "They are unmanageable. They know too much. There's Demochkin, now, who broke his father's arm. It all comes from too much learning."

Nikita listened, watched the faces, seeming as though he, too, would like to have a share in the conversation, were he not so busy with his tea; as it was, he only nodded his head approvingly. He emptied glass after glass, growing warmer and more and more comfortable. The talk kept on in the one strain, all about the harm that comes from family division; clearly, no theoretical discussion, but concerned with a rupture in this very house, arising through the second son, who sat there in his place, morosely silent. The question was a painful one, and absorbed the whole family; but in politeness they refrained from discussing their private affairs before strangers. At last, however, the old man could endure no longer. In a tearful voice, he began to say that there should be no breakup of the family while he lived, that the house had much to thank God for, but if they fell apart—they must become beggars.

"Just like the Matvayeffs," said the village elder. "There was plenty among them all, but when they broke up the family, there was nothing for any of them."

"That's just what you want to do," said the old man to his son.

The son answered nothing, and there was a painful pause. Petrushka broke the silence, having by this time harnessed the horse and returned to the room, where he had been standing for a few minutes, smiling all the time.

"There is a tale in P'uls'n, just like this," said he. "A father gave his sons a besom to break. They could not break it while it was bound together, but they broke it easily by taking every switch by itself. That's the way here," he said, with his broad smile. "All's ready!" he added.

"Well, if we're ready, let us start," said Vasily Andreyevich. "As to this quarrel, don't you give in, grandfather. You got everything together, and you are the master. Apply to the magistrate; he will show you how to keep your authority."

"And he gives himself such airs, such airs," the old man continued to complain, appealingly. "There is no ordering him! It is as though Satan lived in him."

Meanwhile, Nikita, having drunk his fifth glass of tea, did not stand it upside down, in sign that he had finished, but laid it by his side, hoping they might fill it a sixth time. But as the samovar had run dry, the hostess did not fill up for him again; and then Vasily Andreyevich began to put on his things. There was no help; Nikita, too, rose, put back his nibbled little cake of sugar into the sugar basin, wiped the moisture from his face with the skirt of his coat, and moved to put on his overcoat.

After getting into the garment, he sighed heavily; then, having thanked their hosts and said good-bye, he went out from the warm, bright room and through the dark, cold entrance hall, where the wind creaked the doors and drove the snow in at the chinks, into the dark yard. Petrushka, in his fur coat, stood in the center of the yard with the horse, and smiling as ever, recited a verse from "P'uls'n":

> *The storm covers the heaven with darkness,*
> *Whirling the driven snow,*
> *Now, howling like a wild beast,*
> *Now, crying like a child.*

Nikita nodded appreciatively, and arranged the reins.

The old man, coming out with Vasily Andreyevich, brought a lantern, wishing to show the way; but the wind put it out at once. Even in the enclosed yard, one could see that the storm had risen greatly.

"What weather!" thought Vasily Andreyevich. "I'm afraid we shall not get there. But it must be! Business! And then, I have put our friend to the trouble of harnessing his horse, God helping, we'll get there."

Their aged host also thought it better not to go; but he had offered his arguments already, and they had not been listened to. "Maybe it is old age makes me overcautious; they will get there all right," thought he. "And we can all go to bed at the proper time. It will be less bother."

Petrushka likewise saw danger in going, and felt uneasy; but he would not let anyone see it, and put on a bold front, as though he had not a fear; the lines about "whirling the driven snow" encouraged him, because they were a quite true description of what was going on out in the street. As to Nikita, he had no wish to go at all; but he was long used to following other people's wishes, and to give up his own. Therefore nobody withheld the travelers.

V

Vasily Andreyevich went over to the sleighs, found them with some groping through the darkness, got in, and took the reins.

"Go ahead!" he shouted. Petrushka, kneeling in his sleigh, started the horse. The dark bay, who had before been whinnying, aware of the mare's nearness, now dashed after her, and they drove out into the street. They rode once more through the village, down the same road, past the space where the frozen linen had hung, but hung no longer; past the same barn, now snowed-up almost as high as the roof, from which the snow flew incessantly; past the moaning, whistling, and bending willows. And again they came to where the sea of snow raged from above and below. The wind had such power that, taking the travelers sideways when they were crossing its direction, it heeled the sleigh over so that the horse was pushed aside. Petrushka drove his good mare in front, at an easy trot, giving her an occasional lively shout of encouragement. The dark bay pressed after her.

After driving thus for about ten minutes, Petrushka turned around and called out something. But neither Vasily Andreyevich nor Nikita could hear for the wind, but they guessed that they had reached the turning. In fact, Petrushka had turned to the right; the wind came in their front, and to the right, through the snow, loomed something black. It was the bush beside the turning.

"Well, good-bye to you!"

"Thanks, Petrushka!"

" 'The storm covers the heaven with darkness!' " shouted Petrushka, and disappeared.

"Quite a poet," said Vasily Andreyevich, and shook the reins.

"Yes, a fine young man, a genuine fellow," said Nikita.

They drove on. Nikita sank and pressed his head between his shoulders, so that his short beard covered up his throat. He sat silent, trying to keep the warmth that the tea had given him. Before him he saw the straight lines of the shafts, which to his eyes looked like the ruts of the road; he saw the shifting quarters of the horse, with the knotted tail swayed in the wind; beyond, he saw the high bow between the shafts, and the horse's rocking head and neck, with the floating mane. From time to time he noticed waymarks, and knew that, thus far, they had kept right, and he need not concern himself.

Vasily Andreyevich drove on, trusting to the horse to keep to the road. But Moukhorta, although he had picked himself up a little in the village, went unwillingly, and seemed to shirk from the road, so that Vasily Andreyevich had to press him at times.

"Here is a waymark on the right, here's another, and there's a third," reckoned Vasily Andreyevich, "and here, in front, is the forest," he thought, examining a dark patch ahead. But that which he took for a forest was only a bush. They passed the bush, drove about fifty yards farther, and there was neither the fourth waymark nor the forest.

"We must reach the forest soon," thought Vasily Andreyevich; and buoyed up by the vodka and the tea, he shook the reins. The good, obedient animal responded, and now at an amble, now at an easy trot, made in the direction he was sent, although he knew it was not the way in which he should have been going. Ten minutes went by, but no forest.

"I'm afraid we are lost again!" said Vasily Andreyevich, pulling up.

Nikita silently got out from the sleigh, and holding with his hand the flaps of his coat, which pressed against him or flew from him as he stood and turned in the wind, began to tread the snow, first to one side, then to the other. About three times he went out of sight altogether. At last he returned and took the reins from the hands of Vasily Andreyevich.

"We must go to the right," he said sternly and peremptorily; and he turned the horse.

"Well, if it must be to the right, let us go to the right," said Vasily Andreyevich, passing over the reins and thrusting his hands into his sleeves. "I should be glad to be back at Grishkino, anyway," he said.

Nikita did not answer.

"Now, then, old fellow, stir yourself," he called to the horse; but the latter, in spite of the shake of the reins, went on only slowly. In places the snow was knee-deep, and the sleigh jerked at every movement of the horse.

Nikita took the whip, which hung in front of the sleigh, and struck once. The good creature, unused to the lash, sprang forward at a trot, but soon fell again to a slow amble. Thus they went for five minutes. All was so dark, and so blurred with snow from above and below, that sometimes they could not make out the bow between the shafts. At times it seemed as though the sleigh was standing, and the ground running back. Suddenly the horse stopped, feeling something wrong in front of him. Nikita once more lightly jumped out, throwing down the reins, and went in front to find out what was the matter. But hardly had he taken a pace clear ahead, when his feet slipped and he fell down some steep place.

"Whoa, whoa!" he said to himself, trying to stop his fall, and falling. There was nothing to seize hold of, and he only brought up when his feet plunged into a thick bed of snow that lay in the ravine. The fringe of snow that hung on the edge of the ravine, disturbed by Nikita's fall, showered upon him, and got into his coat collar.

"That's bad treatment!" said Nikita, reproaching the snow and the ravine, as he cleared out his coat collar.

"Mikit, ha, Mikit," shouted Vasily Andreyevich, from above. But Nikita did not answer. He was too much occupied in shaking away the snow, then in looking for the whip, which he lost in rolling down the bank. Having found the whip, he started to climb up the bank, but failed, rolling back every time, so that he was compelled to go along the foot of the bank to find a way up. About ten yards from the place where he fell, he managed to struggle up again, and turn back along the bank toward where the horse should have been. He could not see horse nor sleigh; but by going over in the direction to which the wind was blowing, he heard the voice of Vasily Andreyevich and the whinny of Moukhorta calling him, before he saw them.

"I'm coming. Don't make a noise for nothing," he said.

Only when quite near the sleigh could he make out the horse and Vasily Andreyevich, who stood close by, and looked gigantic.

"Where the devil have you gotten lost? We've got to drive back. We must get back to Grishkino anyway," the master began to rebuke him angrily.

"I should be glad to get there, Vasily Andreyevich, but how are we to do it? Here is a ravine where if we once get in, we shall never come out. I pitched in there in such a way that I could hardly get out."

"Well, surely we can't stay here; we must go somewhere," said Vasily Andreyevich.

Nikita made no answer. He sat down on the sleigh with his back to the wind, took off his boots and emptied them of snow, then, with a little straw that he took from the sleigh, he stopped from the inside a gap in the left boot.

Vasily Andreyevich was silent, as though leaving everything to Nikita alone. Having put on his boots, Nikita drew his feet into the sleigh, took the reins, and turned the horse along the ravine. But they had not driven a hundred paces when the horse stopped again. Another ditch confronted him.

Nikita got out again and began to explore the snow. He was afoot a long while. At last he reappeared on the side opposite to that from which he started.

"Vasily Andreyevich, are you alive?" he called.

"Here! What is the matter?"

"I can't make anything out, it is too dark; except some ditches. We must drive to windward again."

They set off once more; Nikita explored again, stumbling in the snow, or resting on the sleigh; at last, falling down, he was out of breath, and stopped beside the sleigh.

"How now?" asked Vasily Andreyevich.

"Well, I'm quite tired out. And the horse is done up."

"What are we to do?"

"Wait a minute." Nikita moved off again, and soon returned.

"Follow me," he said, going in front of the horse.

Vasily Andreyevich gave orders no more, but implicitly did what Nikita told him.

"Here, this way," shouted Nikita, stepping quickly to the right. Seizing Moukhorta's head, he turned him toward a snowdrift. At first the horse resisted, then dashed forward, hoping to leap the drift, but failed and sank in snow up to the hams.

"Get out!" called Nikita to Vasily Andreyevich, who still sat in the sleigh; and taking hold of a shaft, he began to push the sleigh after the horse.

"It's a hard job, friend," he said to Moukhorta, "but it can't be helped. Stir yourself! Once more! Ah-oo-oo! Just a little!" he called out. The horse leaped forward, once, twice, but failed to clear himself, and sank again. He pricked his ears and sniffed at the snow, putting his head down to it as if thinking out something.

"Well, friend, this is no good," urged Nikita to Moukhorta. "A-ah, just a little more!" Nikita pulled on the shaft again; Vasily Andreyevich did the same on the opposite side. The horse lifted his head and made a sudden dash.

"A-ah, A-ah, don't be afraid, you won't sink," shouted Nikita. One plunge, a second, a third, and at last the horse was out from the snowdrift and stood still, breathing heavily and shaking himself clear. Nikita wanted to lead him on farther; but Vasily Andreyevich, in his two fur coats, had so lost his breath that he could walk no more, and dropped into the sleigh.

"Let me get my breath a little," he said, unbinding the handkerchief that tied the collar of his coat.

"We are all right here, you might as well lie down," said Nikita.

"I'll lead him along"; and with Vasily Andreyevich in the sleigh, he led the horse by the head, about ten paces farther, then up a slight rise, and stopped.

The place where Nikita drew up was not in a hollow, where the snow might gather, but was sheltered from the wind by rising ground. At moments the wind, outside this protection, seemed to become quieter; but these intervals did not last long, and after them the storm, as if to compensate itself, rushed on with tenfold vigor, and tore and whirled the more. Such a gust of wind swept past as Vasily Andreyevich, with recovered breath, got out of the sleigh and went up to Nikita to talk over the situation. They both instinctively bowed themselves, and waited until the stress should be over. Moukhorta laid back his ears and shook himself discontentedly. When the blast had abated a little, Nikita took off his mittens, stuck them in his girdle, and having breathed a little on his hands, began to undo the strap from the bow over the shafts.

"Why are you doing that?" asked Vasily Andreyevich.

"I'm taking out the horse. What else can we do? I'm worn out," said Nikita, as though apologizing.

"But we could drive out to somewhere."

"No, we could not. We should only do harm to the horse. The poor beast is worn out," said Nikita, pointing to the creature, who stood there, awaiting the next move with heavily heaving sides. "We must put up for the night," he repeated, as though they were at their inn. He began to undo the collar straps, and detached the collar.

"But we shall be frozen?" queried Vasily Andreyevich.

"Well, if we are, we cannot help it," said Nikita.

VI

In his two fur coats, Vasily Andreyevich was quite warm, especially after the exertion in the snowdrift. But a cold shiver ran down his back when he learned that they must stay where they were the night long. To calm himself, he sat down in the sleigh and got out his cigarettes and matches.

Meanwhile, Nikita continued to take out the horse. He undid the belly band, took away the reins and collar strap, and laid the bow aside from the shafts, continuing to encourage Moukhorta by speaking to him.

"Now, come out, come out," he said, leading the horse clear of the shafts. "We must tie you here. I'll put a bit of straw for you, and take off your bridle," he went on, doing as he said. "After a bite, you'll feel ever so much better."

But Moukhorta was not calmed by Nikita's words; uneasily he shifted his feet, pressed against the sleigh, turned his back to the wind, and rubbed his head on Nikita's sleeve.

As if not wholly to reject the treat of straw that Nikita put under his nose, Moukhorta just once seized a wisp out of the sleigh, but quickly deciding that there was more important business than to eat straw, he threw it down again, and the wind instantly tore it away and hid it in the snow.

"Now we must make a signal," said Nikita, turning the front of the sleigh against the wind; and having tied the shafts together with a strap, he set them on end in the front of the sleigh. "If the snow covers us, the good folk will see the shafts and dig us up," said Nikita. "That's what old hands advise."

Vasily Andreyevich had meanwhile opened his fur coat, and making a shelter with its folds, he rubbed match after match on the box. But his hands trembled, and the kindled matches were blown out by the wind, one after another, some when just struck, others when he thrust them to the cigarette. At last one match burned fully and lighted up for a moment the fur of his coat, his hand with the gold ring on the bent forefinger, and the snow-sprinkled straw that stuck out from under the sacking. The cigarette took light. Twice he eagerly whiffed the smoke, drew it in, blew it through his mustache, and would have gone on, but the wind tore away the burning tobacco. Even these few whiffs of tobacco smoke cheered up Vasily Andreyevich.

"Well, we will stop here," he said authoritatively.

Looking at the raised shafts, he thought to make a still better signal, and to give Nikita a lesson.

"Wait a minute, and I'll make a flag," he said picking up the handkerchief that he had taken from around his collar and put down in the sleigh. Drawing off his gloves and reaching up, he tied the handkerchief tightly to the strap that held the shafts together. The handkerchief at once began to beat about wildly, now clinging around a shaft, now streaming out, and cracking like a whip.

"That's fine," said Vasily Andreyevich, pleased with his work, and getting into the sleigh. "We should be warmer together, but there's not room for two," he said.

"I can find room," said Nikita, "but the horse must be covered; he's sweating, the good fellow. Excuse me," he added, going to the sleigh and drawing the sacking from under Vasily Andreyevich. This

he folded, and after taking off the saddle and breeching, covered the dark bay with it.

"Anyway, it will be a bit warmer, silly," he said, putting the saddle and heavy breeching over the sacking.

"Can you spare the rug? and give me a little straw?" said Nikita, after finishing with the horse.

Taking these from under Vasily Andreyevich, he went behind the sleigh, dug there a hole in the snow, put in the straw, and pulling his hat over his eyes and covering himself with the rug, sat down on the straw, with his back against the bark matting of the back of the sleigh, which kept off the wind and snow.

Vasily Andreyevich, seeing what Nikita was doing, shook his head disapprovingly, in the way he usually did over the signs of peasant folks' ignorance and denseness; and he began to make arrangements for the night.

He smoothed the remaining straw, heaped it more thickly under his side, thrust his hands into his sleeves, and adjusted his head in the corner of the sleigh in front, where he was sheltered from the wind. He did not wish to sleep. He lay down and thought; about one thing only, which was the aim, reason, pleasure, and pride of his life; about the money he had made, and might make, the amount his neighbors had, and the means whereby they gained it and were gaining it; and how he, like them, could gain a great deal more.

"The oak can be sold for sleigh runners. And certainly, the trees for building. And there are a hundred feet of firewood to the acre"— so he estimated the forest, which he had seen in the autumn, and which he was going to buy. "But for all that, I won't pay ten thousand; say eight thousand; and besides, in allowing for the bare spaces, I'll oil the surveyor—a hundred rubles will do it—a hundred and fifty, if necessary, and get him to take about thirteen acres out of the forest. He is sure to sell for eight; three thousand down. Yes, sure; he will weaken at that," he thought, pressing his forearm on the pocketbook beneath. "And how we've gotten astray, God knows! The forest and the keeper's hut should be just by. I should like to hear the dogs, but they never bark when they're wanted, the cursed brutes." He opened his collar a little to look and listen; there was only the dark head of the horse, and his back, on which the sackcloth fluttered; there was only the same whistle of the wind, the flapping and cracking of the handkerchief on the shafts, and the lashing of the snow on the bark matting of the sleigh. He covered himself again. "If one had only known this beforehand, we had better have stayed where we were. But no matter; tomorrow will be time enough. It is only a day later. In this weather, the other fellows won't dare to go." Then he remembered that on the ninth he had to receive the price of some cattle from the butcher. He wanted to do the business himself, for his wife had no experience, and was not competent in such matters. "She never knows what to do," he continued to reflect, remembering how she had failed in her behavior toward the commissary of police when he visited them yesterday at the feast. "Just a woman, of course. What has she ever seen? In my father's and mother's time, what sort of a house had we? Nothing out of the way; a well-to-do countryman's; a barn, and an inn, and that was the whole property. And now what a change I've made, these fifteen years! A general store, two taverns, a flour mill, a stock of grain, two farms rented, a house and warehouse all iron-roofed," he remembered proudly. "Not like in the old people's time! Who is known over the whole place? Brekhunov.

"And why is all this? Because I stick to business, I look after things; not like others, who idle, or waste their time in foolishness. I give up sleep at night. Storm or no storm, I go. And of course, the thing is done. They think money is made easily, by just playing. Not at all; it's work and trouble. They think luck makes men. Look at the Mironovs, who have their millions, now. Why? They worked. Then God gives. If God only grants us health!" And the idea that he, also, might become a millionaire like Mironov, who began with nothing, so excited Vasily Andreyevich that he suddenly felt a need to talk to someone. But there was nobody. If he could only have reached Goryachkino, he might have talked with the landowner, and got around him.

"What a gale! It will snow us in so that we can't get out in the morning," he thought, listening to the sound of the wind, which blew against the front of the sleigh and lashed the snow against the bark matting.

"And I did as Nikita said, all for nothing," he thought. "We ought to have driven on, and gotten to somewhere. We might have gone back to Grishkino and stayed at Taras's. Now we must sit here all night. Well, what was I thinking about? Yes, that God gives to the industrious, and not to the lazy, loafers, and fools. It's time for a smoke, too." He sat up, got his cigarette case, and stretched himself flat on his stomach, to protect the light from the wind with the flaps of his coat; but the wind got in and put out match after match. At last he managed to get a cigarette lit. It began to burn, and the achievement of his object greatly delighted him. Although the wind had more of his cigarette than he himself, nevertheless he got about three puffs, and felt better. He again threw himself back in the sleigh, wrapped himself up, and

returned to his recollections and dreams; he fell asleep. But suddenly
something pushed and awoke him. Was it the dark bay pulling the
straw from under him, or some fancy of his own? At all events he
awoke, and his heart began to beat so quickly and strongly that the
sleigh seemed to be shaking under him. He opened his eyes. Everything
around was the same as before; but it seemed a shade brighter. "The
morning," he thought, "it can't be far from morning." But he suddenly
remembered that the light was only due to the rising of the moon. He
lifted himself, and looked first at the horse. Moukhorta stood with his
back to the wind and shivered all over. The sacking, snow-covered and
turned up at one corner; the breeching, which had slipped aside; the
snowy head and fluttering mane; all was now more clearly visible.
Vasily Andreyevich bent over the back of the sleigh and looked behind.
Nikita sat in his old position. The rug and his feet were covered with
snow. "I'm afraid he will be frozen, his clothes are so bad. I might be
held responsible. He is tired out, and has not much resisting power,"
reflected Vasily Andreyevich; and he thought of taking the sacking
from the horse, to put over Nikita; but it was cold to disturb himself,
and besides, he did not want the horse frozen. "What was the use of
bringing him? It is all her stupidity!" thought Vasily Andreyevich,
remembering the unloved wife; and he turned again to his former place
in the front of the sleigh. "My uncle once sat in snow all night like
this," he reflected, "and no harm came of it. And Sebastian also was
dug out," he went on, remembering another case, "but he was dead,
stiff like a frozen carcass.

"It would have been all right if we had stopped at Grishkino."
Carefully covering himself, not to waste the warmth of the fur, and so
as to protect his neck, knees, and the soles of his feet, he shut his eyes,
trying to sleep. But however much he tried, no sleep came; on the
contrary, he felt alert and excited. He began again to count his gains
and the debts due to him; again he began to boast to himself, and to
feel proud of himself and his position; but he was all the while disturbed
by a lurking fear, and by the unpleasant reflection that he had not
stopped at Grishkino. He changed his attitude several times; he lay
down and tried to find a better position, more sheltered from wind and
snow, but failed; he rose again and changed his position, crossed his
feet, shut his eyes, and lay silent; but either his crossed feet, in their
high felt boots, began to ache, or the wind blew in somewhere. Thus
lying for a short time, he again began the disagreeable reflection, how
comfortably he would have lain in the warm house at Grishkino. Again
he rose, changed his position, wrapped himself up, and again lay down.
Once Vasily Andreyevich fancied he heard a distant cock crow.

He brightened up and began to listen with all his might; but however he strained his ear, he heard nothing but the sound of the wind whistling against the shafts, and the snow lashing the bark matting of the sleigh. Nikita had been motionless all the time, not even answering Vasily Andreyevich, who spoke to him twice.

"He doesn't worry; he seems to be asleep," Vasily Andreyevich thought angrily, looking behind the sleigh at the snow-covered Nikita.

Twenty times Vasily Andreyevich thus rose and lay down. It seemed to him this night would never end. "It must be near morning now," he thought once, rising and looking around him. "Let me see my watch. It is cold to unbutton oneself; but if I only knew it was near morning, it would be better. Then we might begin to harness the horse." At the bottom of his mind, Vasily Andreyevich knew that the dawn could be nowhere near; but he began to feel more and more afraid, and he chose both to deceive himself and to find himself out. He began cautiously to undo the hooks of the inside fur coat, then putting his hand in at the bosom, he felt about until he got at the vest. With great trouble, he drew out his silver, flower-enameled watch, and began to examine it. Without a light, he could make out nothing. Again he lay down flat, as when he lit the cigarette, got the matches, and began to strike. This time he was particularly careful, and selecting a match with most phosphorus on, at one attempt lit it. Lighting up the face of the watch, he could not believe his eyes. It was not later than ten minutes past twelve. The whole night was yet before him.

"Oh, what a weary night!" thought Vasily Andreyevich, a cold shiver running down his back; and buttoning up again, he hugged himself close in the corner of the sleigh. Suddenly, through the monotonous wail of the wind, he distinctly heard a new and a living sound. It grew gradually louder and became quite clear, then began to die away. There could be no doubt; it was a wolf. And this wolf's howl was so near that down the wind one could hear how he changed his cry by the movement of his jaws. Vasily Andreyevich turned back his collar and listened attentively. Moukhorta listened likewise, pricking up his ears, and when the wolf had ceased howling, he shifted his feet and sniffed warningly. After this Vasily Andreyevich not only was unable to sleep, but even to keep calm. The more he tried to think of his accounts, of his business, reputation, importance, and property, more and more fear grew upon him; and above all his thoughts, one thought stood out predominantly and penetratingly: the thought of his rashness in not stopping at Grishkino.

"The forest—what do I care about the forest? There is plenty of business without that, thank God! Ah, why did I not stay the night?"

said he to himself. "They say people who drink are soon frozen," he thought, "and I have had some drink." Then testing his own sensations, he felt that he began to shiver, not knowing whether from cold or fear. He tried to wrap himself up and to lie down as before; but he could not. He was unable to rest, wanted to rise, to do something to suppress his gathering fears, against which he felt helpless. Again he got his cigarettes and matches; but only three of the latter remained, and these were bad ones. All three rubbed away without lighting.

"To the devil, curse it, to—!" he broke out, himself not knowing why, and he threw away the cigarette, broken. He was about to throw away the matchbox, but stayed his hand, and thrust it in his pocket instead. He was so agitated that he could no longer remain in one place. He got out of the sleigh, and standing with his back to the wind, set his girdle again, tightly and low down.

"What is the use of lying down; it is only waiting for death; much better mount the horse and get away!" The thought suddenly flashed into his mind. "The horse will not stand still with someone on his back. He"—thinking of Nikita—"must die anyway. What sort of a life has he? He does not care much even about his life, but as for me—thank God, I have something to live for!"

Untying the horse from the sleigh, he threw the reins over his neck and tried to mount, but failed. Then he clambered on the sleigh, and tried to mount from that; but the sleigh tilted under his weight, and he failed again. At last, on a third attempt, he backed the horse to the sleigh, and cautiously balancing on the edge, got his body across the horse. Lying thus for a moment, he pushed himself once, twice, and finally threw one leg over and seated himself, supporting his feet on the breeching in place of stirrups. The shaking of the sleigh roused Nikita, and he got up; Vasily Andreyevich thought he was speaking.

"Listen to you, fool? What, must I die in this way, for nothing?" exclaimed Vasily Andreyevich. Tucking under his knees the loose skirts of his fur coat, he turned the horse around and rode away from the sleigh in the direction where he expected to find the forest and the keeper's hut.

VII

Nikita had not stirred since, covered by the rug, he took his seat behind the sleigh. Like all people who live with nature, and endure much, he was patient and could wait for hours, even days, without growing restless or irritated. When his master called to him, he heard, but made no answer, because he did not wish to stir. The thought that he might, and very likely must, die that night came to him at the moment he was taking his seat behind the sleigh. Although he still felt the warmth from the tea he had taken, and from the exercise of struggling through the snowdrift, he knew the warmth would not last long, and that he could not warm himself again by moving about, for he was exhausted and felt as a horse may when it stops and must have food before it can work again. Besides, his foot, the one in the torn boot, was numbed, and already he could not feel the great toe. And the cold began to creep all over his body.

The thought that he would die that night came upon him, seeming not very unpleasant, nor very awful. Not unpleasant, because his life had been no unbroken feast, but rather an incessant round of toil of which he began to weary. And not awful, because, beyond the masters whom he served here, like Vasily Andreyevich, he felt himself dependent upon the Great Master; upon Him who had sent him into this life. And he knew that even after death he must remain in the power of that Master, who would not treat him badly. "Is it a pity to leave what you are practiced in and used to? Well, what's to be done? You must get used to fresh things as well.

"Sins?" he thought, and recollected his drunkenness, the money wasted in drink, his ill treatment of his wife, neglect of church and of the fasts, and all things for which the priest reprimanded him at the confessional. "Of course, these are sins. But then, did I bring them on me myself? Whatever I am, I suppose God made me so. Well, and about these sins? How can one help it?"

So he thought, concerning what might happen to him that night, and having reached his conclusion, he gave himself up to the thoughts and recollections that ran through his mind of themselves. He remembered the visit of his wife, Martha; the drunkenness among the peasants, and his own abstinence from drink; the beginning of their journey; Tarass's house, and the talk about the breakup of the family; his own lad; Moukhorta, with the sacking over him for warmth; and his master, rolling around in the sleigh and making it creak. "He is uneasy," thought Nikita, "most likely because a life like his makes one want not to die; different from people of my kind." And all these recollections and thoughts interwove and jumbled themselves in his brain, until he fell asleep.

When Vasily Andreyevich mounted the horse, he twisted aside the sleigh, and the back of it slid away from behind Nikita, who was struck by one of the runner ends. Nikita awoke, thus compelled to move. Straightening his legs with difficulty, and throwing off the snow that covered them, he got up. Instantly an agony of cold penetrated his whole frame. On making out what was happening, he wanted Vasily Andreyevich to leave him the sacking that lay over the horse, which was no longer needed there, so that he might put it around himself. But Vasily Andreyevich did not wait, and disappeared in the midst of snow. Thus left alone, Nikita considered what he had better do. He felt unable to move off in search of some house; and it was already impossible for him to sit down in the place he had occupied, for it was already covered with snow; and he knew he could not get warm in the sleigh, having nothing to cover him. He felt as cold as though he stood in his shirt; there seemed no warmth at all from his coat and overcoat. For a moment he pondered, then sighed, and keeping the rug over his head, he threw himself into the sleigh, in the place where his master had lain. He huddled himself up into the smallest space, but still got no warmth. Thus he lay for about five minutes, shivering through his whole body; then the shivering ceased, and he began to lose consciousness, little by little. Whether he was dying or falling asleep, he knew not; but he was as ready for the one as for the other. If God should bid him get up again, still alive in the world, to go on with his laborer's life, to care for other men's horses, to carry other men's grain to the mill, to again start drinking and renouncing drink, to continue the money supply to his wife and that same cooper, to watch his lad growing up—well, so be His holy will. Should God bid him arise in another world, where all would be as fresh and bright as this world was in his young childhood, with the caresses of his mother, the games among the children, the fields, forests, skating in winter—arise to a life quite out of the common—then, so be His holy will. And Nikita wholly lost consciousness.

VIII

During this while, Vasily Andreyevich, guiding with his feet and the gathered reins, rode the horse in the direction where he, for some cause, expected to find the forest and the forester's hut. The snow blinded him, and the wind, it seemed, was bent on staying him; but with head bent forward, and continually pulling up his fur coat between him and the cold, nail-studded pad on which he could not settle himself, he urged on the horse. The dark bay, though with difficulty, obediently ambled on in the direction to which he was turned.

For some minutes he rode on—as it seemed to him, in a straight line—seeing nothing but the horse's head and the white waste, and hearing only the whistling of the wind about the horse's ears and his own coat collar.

Suddenly a dark patch showed in front of him. His heart began to beat with joy, and he rode on toward the object, already seeing in it the house walls of a village. But the dark patch was not stationary, it moved. It was not a village, but a ridge, covered with tall mugwort, which rose up through the snow, and bent to one side under the force of the wind. The sight of the high grass, tormented by the pitiless wind, somehow made Vasily Andreyevich tremble, and he started to ride away hastily, not perceiving that in approaching the place, he had quite turned out of his first direction, and that now he was heading the opposite way. He was still confident that he rode toward where the forester's hut should be. But the horse seemed always to make toward the right, and Vasily Andreyevich had to guide it toward the left.

Again a dark patch appeared before him; again he rejoiced, believing that now surely he saw a village. But once more it was the ridge, covered with high grass, shaking ominously, and as before, frightening Vasily Andreyevich. But it was not the same ridge of grass, for near it was a horse track, now disappearing in the snow. Vasily Andreyevich stopped, bent down, and looked carefully: a horse track, not yet snow-covered; it could only be the hoofprints of his own horse. He was evidently moving in a small circle. "And I am perishing in this way," he thought. To repress his terror, he urged on the horse still more, peering into the mist of snow, in which he saw nothing but flitting and fitful points of light. Once he thought he heard either the barking of dogs or the howling of wolves, but the sounds were so faint and indistinct that he could not be sure whether he had heard them or imagined them; and he stopped to strain his ears and listen.

Suddenly a terrible, deafening cry beat upon his ears, and everything began to tremble and quake about him. Vasily Andreyevich seized the horse's neck, but that also shook, and the terrible cry rose still more frightfully. For some moments Vasily Andreyevich was beside himself and could not understand what had happened. It was only this: Moukhorta, whether to encourage himself or to call for help, had neighed, loudly and resonantly.

"The devil! How that cursed horse frightened me!" said Vasily Andreyevich to himself. But even when he understood the cause of his terror, he could not shake it off.

"I must bethink myself, steady myself," he went on, even while, unable to regain his self-control, he urged forward the horse without noting that he was now going with the wind instead of against it. His body, especially where his fur coat did not protect it against the pad, was freezing, shivering and aching all over. He forgot all about the forester's hut and desired one thing only—to get back to the sleigh, that he might not perish alone, like that mugwort in the midst of the terrible waste of snow.

Without warning, the horse suddenly stumbled under him, caught in a snowdrift, began to plunge, and fell on his side. Vasily Andreyevich jumped off, dragged down the breeching with his foot, and turned the pad around by holding to it as he jumped. As soon as he was clear, the horse righted itself, plunged forward one leap and then another, and neighing again, with the sacking and breeching trailed after him, disappeared, leaving Vasily Andreyevich alone in the snowdrift. The latter pressed on after the horse, but the snow was so deep, and his fur coat so heavy, that, sinking over the knee at each step, he was out of breath after not more than twenty paces, and stopped. "The forest, the sheep, the farms, the shop, the taverns," thought he, "how can I leave them? What is really the matter? This is impossible!" surged through his head. And he had a strange recollection of the wind-shaken mugwort that he had ridden past twice, and such a terror seized him that he lost all sense of the reality of what was happening. He thought, "Is not this all a dream?"—and tried to wake himself. But there was no awakening. The snow was real, lashing his face and covering him; and it was a real desert in which he was now alone, like that mugwort, waiting for inevitable, speedy, and incomprehensible death.

"Queen in heaven, Nicholas the miracle doer, sustainer of the faithful!"—He recalled yesterday's Te Deums; the shrine with the black image in a golden chasuble; the tapers that he sold for the shrine, and that, as they were at once returned to him, he used to put back in the store chest hardly touched by the flame. And he began to implore that same Nicholas—the miracle doer—to save him, vowing to the saint a Te Deum and tapers. But in some way, here, he clearly and without a doubt realized that the image, chasuble, tapers, priests, thanksgivings, and so forth, while very important and necessary in their place, in the church, were of no service to him now; and that between those tapers and Te Deums, and his own disastrous plight, there could be no possible relation.

"I must not give up; I must follow the horse's tracks, or they, too, will be snowed over." The thought struck him, and he made on. But despite his resolution to walk quietly, he found himself running, falling down every minute, rising and falling again. The hoofprints were already almost indistinguishable where the snow was shallow. "I am lost!" thought Vasily Andreyevich, "I shall lose this track as well!" But at that instant, casting a glance in front, he saw something dark. It was the horse, and not him alone, but the sleigh, the shafts. Moukhorta, with the pad twisted around and the trailed breeching and sacking, was standing, not in his former place, but nearer to the shafts, and was shaking his head, drawn down by the reins beneath his feet. It appeared that Vasily Andreyevich had stuck in the same ravine into which they had, with Nikita, previously plunged, that the horse had led him back to the sleigh, and that he had dismounted at not more than fifty paces from the place where the sleigh lay.

IX

When Vasily Andreyevich, with great difficulty, regained the sleigh, he seized upon it and stood motionless for a long time, trying to calm himself and to take breath. Nikita was not in his old place, but something was lying in the sleigh, something already covered with snow; and Vasily Andreyevich guessed it to be Nikita. His terror had now quite left him; if he felt any fear, it was lest that terror should return upon him in the way he had experienced it when on the horse, and especially when he was alone in the snowdrift. By any and every means, he must keep away that terror; to do that, he must forget himself, think about something else; something must be done. Accordingly, the first thing he did was to turn his back to the wind and throw open his fur cloak. As soon as he felt a little refreshed, he shook out the snow from his boots and gloves, bound up his girdle again, tight and low down, as though making ready for work, as he did when going out to buy grain from the peasants' carts. The first step to take, it appeared to him, was to free the horse's legs. And he did this; then clearing the rein, he tied Moukhorta to the iron cramp in front of the sleigh, as before, and walking around the horse's quarters, he adjusted the pad, breeching, and sacking. But as he did this, he perceived a movement in the sleigh; and Nikita's head rose out of the snow that was about it. With obvious great difficulty, the peasant rose and sat up; and in a strange fashion, as though he were driving away flies, waved his hand before his face, saying something which Vasily Andreyevich interpreted as a call to himself.

Vasily Andreyevich left the sack unadjusted and went to the sleigh. "What is the matter with you?" he asked. "What are you saying?"

"I am dy-y-ing, that's what's the matter," said Nikita brokenly, struggling for speech. "Give what I have earned to the lad. Or to the wife; it's all the same."

"What, are you really frozen?" asked Vasily Andreyevich.

"I can feel I've got my death. Forgiveness . . . for Christ's sake . . ." said Nikita in a sobbing voice, continuing to wave his hand before his face, as if driving away flies.

Vasily Andreyevich stood for half a minute quiet and still; then suddenly, with the same resolution with which he used to strike hands over a good bargain, he took a step back, turned up the sleeves of his fur coat, and using both hands, began to rake the snow from off Nikita and the sleigh. That done, Vasily Andreyevich quickly took off his belt, made ready the fur coat, and moving Nikita with a push, he lay down on him, covering him not only with the fur coat, but with the full length of his own body, which glowed with warmth.

Adjusting with his hands the skirts of his coat, so as to come between Nikita and the bark matting of the sleigh, and tucking the tail of the coat between his knees, Vasily Andreyevich lay flat, with his head against the bark matting in the sleigh front. He no longer could hear, either the stirring of the horse or the wind's whistling; he had ears only for the breathing of Nikita. At first, and for a long time, Nikita lay without a sign; then he sighed deeply, and moved, evidently with returning warmth.

"Ah, there you are! And yet you say 'die.' Lie still, get warm, and we shall . . ." began Vasily Andreyevich. But to his own surprise, he could not speak: because his eyes were filled with tears, and his lower jaw began to quiver strongly. He said no more; only swallowed down the risings in his throat.

"I have been frightened, that is clear, and have lost my nerve," he thought of himself. But this weakness came not as an unpleasant sensation; rather as a notable, and hitherto unknown, delight.

"That's what we are!" he said to himself, with a strange, tender, and tranquil sense of victory. He lay quiet for some time, wiping his eyes with the fur of his coat, and returning the right skirt under his knees as the wind continually turned it up.

He felt a passionate desire to let someone else know of his happy condition.

"Nikita!" he said.

"It's comfortable," came an answer from below.

"So it is, friend! I was nearly lost. And you would have been frozen, and I should . . ."

But here again his face began to quiver, and his eyes once more filled with tears; he could say no more.

"Well, never mind," he thought, "I know well enough myself what I know," and he kept quiet.

Several times he looked at the horse, and saw that his back was uncovered and the sacking and breeching were hanging down nearly to the snow. He ought to get up and cover the horse; but he could not bring himself to leave Nikita for even a moment and so disturb that happy situation in which he felt himself; for he had no fear now.

Nikita warmed him from below, and the fur coat warmed him from above; but his hands, with which he held the coat skirts down on both sides of Nikita, and his feet, from which the wind continually lifted the coat, began to freeze. But he did not think of them. He thought only of how to restore the man who lay beneath him.

"No fear, he will not escape," he said to himself as Nikita grew warmer; and he said this boastingly, in the way he used to speak of his buying and selling.

Then he lay for a long while. At first his thoughts were filled with impressions of the snowstorm, the shafts of the sleigh, the horse under the sleigh bow, all jostling before his eyes; he recollected Nikita, lying under him; then upon these impressions rose others, of the feast, his wife, the commissary of police, the taper box; then again of Nikita, this time lying under the taper box. Then came apparitions of peasants at their trafficking, and white walls, and iron-roofed houses, with Nikita stretched out beneath; then all was confused, one thing running into another, like the colors in the rainbow, which blend into one whiteness, all the different impressions fused into one nothing; and he fell asleep. For a long time he slept dreamlessly; but before daybreak dreams visited him again. He was once more standing beside the taper box, and Tikhon's wife asked him for a five-kopeck taper, for the feast; he wanted to take the taper and give it to her, but he could not move his hands, which hung down, thrust tightly into his pockets. He wanted to walk around the box; but his feet would not move; his goloshes, new and shiny, had grown to the stone floor, and he could neither move them nor take out his feet. All at once the box ceased to be a taper box, and turned into a bed; and Vasily Andreyevich saw himself lying, face downward, on the taper box, which was his own bed at home. Thus lying, he was unable to get up; and yet he must get up, because Ivan Matveich, the commissary of police, would soon call upon him, and with Ivan Matveich he must either bargain for the forest or set the breeching right on Moukhorta. He asked his wife, "Well, has he not come?" "No," she said, "he has not." He heard someone drive up to the front door. It must be he. No, whoever it was, he has gone past. "Mikolayevna, Mikolayevna! What, has he not come yet?" No. And he lay on the bed, still unable to rise, and still waiting, a waiting that was painful, and yet pleasant. All at once, his joy was fulfilled; the expected one came; not Ivan Matveich, the commissary of police, but another; and yet the one for whom he had waited. He came, and called to him; and he that called was he who had bidden him lie down upon Nikita. Vasily Andreyevich was glad because that one had visited him. "I am coming," he cried joyfully. And the cry awoke him.

He wakes, but wakes in quite another state than when he fell asleep. He wants to rise, and cannot; to move his arm, and cannot—his leg, and he cannot do that. He wants to turn his head, and cannot do even so much. He is surprised, but not at all disturbed by this. He divines that this is death, and is not at all disturbed even by that. And he remembers that Nikita is lying under him, and that he has gotten warm and is alive; and it seems to him that he is Nikita, and Nikita is he, that his life is not in himself, but in Nikita. He makes an effort to listen, and hears the breathing, even the slight snoring, of Nikita. "Nikita is alive, and therefore I also am alive!" he says to himself triumphantly. And something quite new, such as he had never known in all his life, is stealing down upon him.

He remembers his money, the shop, the house, the buying and selling, the Mironovs' millions; and he really cannot understand why that man, called Vasily Brekhunov, had troubled with all those things with which he had troubled himself. "Well, he did not know what it was all about," he thinks, concerning this Vasily Brekhunov. "He did not know, but now I know. No mistake this time; *now I know.*" And again he hears the summons of that one who had before called him. "I am coming, I am coming," all his being speaks joyfully and tenderly. And he feels himself free; with nothing to encumber him more. And nothing more, in this world, saw, heard, or felt Vasily.

Around about, all was as before. The same whirling snow, driving upon the fur coat of the dead Vasily Andreyevich, upon Moukhorta, whose whole body shivered, and upon the sleigh now hardly to be seen, with Nikita lying in the bottom of it, kept warm beneath his now dead master.

X

Toward daybreak, Nikita awoke. The cold roused him, again creeping along his back. He had dreamed that he was driving from the mill with a cartload of his master's flour, and that near Liapin's, in turning at the bridge end, he got the cart stuck. And he saw that he went beneath the cart, and lifted it with his back, adjusting his strength to it. But, wonderful!—the cart did not stir, it stuck to his back, so that he could neither lift nor get from under. It crushed his back. And how cold it was! He must get away somehow.

"That's enough," he cried to whoever, or whatever, it was that pressed his back with the cart. "Take the sacks out!" But the cart still pressed him, always colder and colder; and suddenly a peculiar knocking awoke him completely, and he remembered all. The cold cart— that was his dead and frozen master, lying upon him. The knocking was from Moukhorta, who struck twice on the sleigh with his hooves.

"Andreyevich, eh, Andreyevich!" says Nikita inquiringly, straightening his back and already guessing the truth. But Andreyevich does not answer, and his body and legs are hard, and cold, and heavy, like iron weights.

"He must have died. May his be the kingdom of heaven!" thinks Nikita. He turns his head, digs with his hand through the snow about him, and opens his eyes. It is daylight. The wind still whistles through the shafts, and the snow is still falling, but with a difference, not lashing upon the bark matting as before, but silently covering the sleigh and horse, ever deeper and deeper; and the horse's breathing and stirring are no more to be heard. "He must be frozen too," thinks Nikita. And in fact, those hoof strokes upon the sleigh were the last struggles of Moukhorta, by that time quite benumbed, to feel his legs.

"God, Father, it seems thou callest me as well," says Nikita to himself. "Let Thy holy will be done. But it is. . . . Still, one cannot die twice, and must die once. If it would only come quicker! . . ." And he draws in his arm again, shutting his eyes; and he loses consciousness, with the conviction that this time he is really going to die altogether.

About dinnertime on the next day, the peasants with their shovels dug out Vasily Andreyevich and Nikita, only seventy yards from the road, and half a mile from the village. The wind had hidden the sleigh in snow, but the shafts and the handkerchief were still visible. Moukhorta, over his belly in snow, with the breeching and sacking trailing from his back, stood all whitened, his dead head pressed in upon the apple of his throat; his nostrils were fringed with icicles, his eyes filled with rime and frozen around as with tears. In that one night he had become so thin that he was nothing but skin and bone. Vasily Andreyevich was stiffened like a frozen carcass, and he lay with his legs spread apart, just as he was when they rolled him off Nikita. His prominent hawk eyes were shriveled up, and his open mouth under his clipped mustache was filled with snow. But Nikita, though chilled through, was alive. When he was roused, he imagined he was already dead and that the happenings about him were by this time not in this world, but in another. When he heard the shouts of the peasants, who were digging him out and rolling the frozen Vasily Andreyevich from him, he was surprised at first to think that in the other world, also, peasants should be making noise. But when he understood that he was still here, in this world, he was rather sorry than glad, especially when he realized that the toes of both his feet were frozen.

Nikita lay in the hospital for two months. They cut off three toes from him, and the others recovered, so that he was able to work. For twenty years more, he went on living, first as a farm laborer, lately as a watchman. He died at home, just as he wished, only this year; laid under the holy images, with a lighted taper in his hands. Before his death, he asked forgiveness from his old wife, and forgave her for the cooper; he took leave of his son and the grandchildren and went away, truly pleased that, in dying, he released his son and daughter-in-law from the added burden of his keep, and that he himself was, this time really, going out of a life grown wearisome to him, into that other one which with every passing year had grown clearer and more desirable to him. Is he better off, or worse off, there in the place where he awoke after that real death? Is he disappointed? Or has he found things there to be such as he expected? That we shall all of us soon learn.

(1895)

HOW LITERATURE TEACHES US
ABOUT MORAL AND PSYCHOLOGICAL LIFE

(From Tolstoy's essay "Why Do Men Stupefy Themselves?" written in 1890, when he was sixty-one, as an introduction to a book on drunkenness by P. A. Alekseyev. The essay, little known in the West, illustrates Tolstoy's approach to literature as a repository of moral lessons.)

The mainspring that activates all human life lies not in human beings' moving their arms, legs, and backs, but in their consciousness. In order for a human being to do something with his legs or arms, it is first necessary for a certain change to take place in his consciousness. This change, which defines all subsequent actions of that person, is always minute, almost imperceptible.

The painter Bryullov once made a correction on a student's sketch. The pupil, looking at the transformed sketch, said: "You hardly at all touched my study, yet it has become entirely different." Bryullov answered: "Hardly-at-all is where art begins."

That saying is strikingly true, not only in relation to art, but also in relation to all life. One can say that true life begins where hardly-at-all begins, at the point where changes occur that seem to us infinitely small, barely perceptible. True life does not take place where large external changes occur, where people move, collide, fight, kill one another. It takes place where hardly-at-all differentiating changes are made.

Raskolnikov's real life did not take place when he was killing the old woman or her sister.* When he was killing the first old woman and still more her sister, he was not living his real life; rather, he was acting like a machine, he was doing something that he was not capable of doing: he was firing a charge that had been loaded inside him a long time before. One old woman had been killed, the other stood there in front of him, the ax was in his hand.

Raskolnikov's real life took place not when he was facing the old woman's sister, but before he had killed either old woman, when he had not yet stood in a strange apartment in order to murder, when he had not yet held an ax in his hand, and did not have a loop in the overcoat on which he hung the ax—it took place before he had even thought of the old woman, when he was lying at home on his sofa, not thinking at all about the old woman or even about whether one could, on the basis of an individual's decision, wipe another human being, a superfluous and harmful being, off the face of the earth. His real life took place when he was thinking about whether or not he ought to live in Petersburg, whether or not he should accept money from his mother, about questions which had nothing to do with the old woman. The decision whether or not he would kill the old woman was made then, in that animal sphere of life completely independent of reality. Those decisions were not made when he stood in front of the other woman with an ax in his hand, but rather when he was not yet acting but only thinking, when only his consciousness was active, when barely perceptible changes were taking place in that consciousness. It is then that the greatest possible lucidity of thought is particularly important for the correct solution of the question that arises, and it is then that one glass of beer, one smoked cigarette can impair the solution to the problem, hinder its solution, deafen the voice of the conscience, and cause the question to be decided in favor of one's lower animal nature, as it was with Raskolnikov.

The changes are just barely perceptible, but their consequences are colossal, terrible. The instant when a human being makes a decision

* In Dostoyevsky's *Crime and Punishment*.

and begins to act can change many material things. Houses, fortunes, peoples' bodies can perish, but nothing that is brought about is more important than that which is deposited in the human being's consciousness. Consciousness limits what can take place. From barely perceptible changes that take place in the area of consciousness, the most unimaginably important, limitless consequences can follow.

(1890)

ANTON CHEKHOV

ANTON CHEKHOV (1860–1904) was one of those few authors in the history of world literature who not only wrote in two different genres, but excelled in both—in Chekhov's case, drama and the short story.

The grandson of a serf and son of a grocer, Chekhov grew up in Taganrog, a small town near the Black Sea, and at the age of nineteen moved to Moscow. He studied medicine, and some of his procedures as a creator of fiction have been compared to the methods of an observant physician. While still a medical student, Chekhov began to write, at first specializing in comic sketches and short farces. He gradually drifted away from medicine and became a professional writer. His stories grew more serious and more lyrical. After having numerous stories published in newspapers and books, he wrote his four great plays, The Seagull (1896), Uncle Vanya (1899), The Three Sisters (1901), and The Cherry Orchard (1903).

In 1890 Chekhov traveled across Siberia (in the days before the Trans-Siberian Railroad) to the Pacific island of Sakhalin, and studied the conditions of the Russian convicts and the native Ainu and Gilyak; he observed the mistreatment of the native population and the horrible conditions in general. He wrote travel sketches for newspapers as he went, and later a short book, Sakhalin Island (1893–1895), about his experiences.

For the last three years of his life, when he was already very seriously ill with tuberculosis, he was happily married to the actress Olga Knipper. Chekhov died of his disease in 1904.

Chekhov's fame grew steadily after his death, in Russia and abroad. His plays became classics of the stage; his short stories have served as models to Western European and American twentieth-century authors. They have influenced the development of the genre of short fiction all over the world.

Chekhov did not share the frequent Russian practice of using literature for open preaching. Some contemporaries regarded Chekhov as indifferent and condemned him for it. Tolstoy considered a hands-off attitude on the writer's part immoral—an abdication of moral obligations. Chekhov was attracted by the ironies of human existence and presented them in detail, as though matter-of-factly, and thereby all the more poignantly.

The Lady with the Dog *is based on the ironic twist inherent in the situation in which a man accustomed to light seductions, who has frequently been unfaithful to his wife, discovers that for the first time in his life, after plunging into what at first seems another superficial affair, he is totally—and hopelessly—in love. What begins as something utterly conventional turns into a unique situation. The sadness of the story, the sense of a long stretch of days in which nothing essential will change, as though looking ahead into an infinitely long corridor, are characteristic of Chekhov. Yet neither the compassion nor the irony would have been effective if Chekhov had not presented the characters and events with high finesse. Every detail is placed gently, nothing is overstated, all is subtly prepared for. There is a plainness about the story that, in contrast to Tolstoy's vigor of presentation, seems soft— yet direct and powerful.*

The Lady with the Dog *renders masterfully specific, never-repeated incidents (the meetings of the two lovers, the circumstances accompanying the events) as well as the general course of their lives—that is, it gives both the microscopic and macroscopic views. Much of the story depends on significant concrete details: the fence around Anna Sergeyevna's house, the two high-school students smoking on the landing when the lovers meet again at the opera, the man's conversation with his daughter on his way to meeting his mistress in a hotel, his glimpse of himself in the mirror. Chekhov's sympathy with the characters—with all human beings' desire to live—pervades the story. An utterly private, routine tale has a flabbergasting emotional impact.*

Chekhov sees the characters he describes, feels with them, and pities them. In his stories, he expresses the attitudes that Maksim Gorky, in his remarkable reminiscences of his meetings with Chekhov, says were visible in Chekhov's facial expression—a "sad and gentle smile . . . a lovable modesty and delicate sensitiveness." In his stories, says critic Pyotr Bitsilli, "we are seized by a sense of anxiety, an agonizing and yet enrapturing experience of life's inexpressible mystery,

concealed in all its countless manifestations . . . so familiar to one
another and yet unique, in their ephemerality and apparent uselessness.
We sense that what happened to them could have happened to us; and
it begins to seem that indeed it has."

Uncle Vanya (1899) belongs to the four plays that established
Chekhov's standing as one of the world's great dramatists. It is a study
in different levels of communication—failed, half successful, or (more
rarely and momentarily) fully achieved. The boredom of Russian provincial life is exacerbated by the emotional sensitivity of some of the
characters. It is a play of inner action and of waiting. The professor
reveals his complete selfishness and ingratitude, while other characters
confess their love for one another. As the drama critic Eric Bentley
wrote in What Is Theatre, "Chekhov's major plays are punctuated with
superb jokes, they are informed with a profound comic sense, but they
are also suffused with emotion." Bentley called the exquisite, touching
final scene of Uncle Vanya one of the "beauties of modern literature."

Typically for Chekhov's major plays, in Uncle Vanya dramatic
interest is spread among several characters, not concentrated on one
or two of them. Failure of human communication through the slippage
of attention away from the focus of the other characters' conversation
is a pervasive feature. The long, grand view taken by Astrov, with his
one-thousand-year-long vision and the mixture of idealism and love of
nature—wishing to foster, not destroy, human and natural resources
—is admirable as well as pathetic.

Chekhov's plays changed the course of world drama and continue
to be studied by young playwrights all over the world.

THE LADY WITH THE DOG

I

The appearance on the front of a new arrival—a lady with a lapdog
—became the topic of general conversation. Dmitri Dmitrich Gurov,
who had been a fortnight in Yalta and gotten used to its ways, was
also interested in new arrivals. One day, sitting on the terrace of Ver-
net's restaurant, he saw a young woman walking along the promenade;
she was fair, not very tall, and wore a toque; behind her trotted a white
Pomeranian.

Later he came across her in the park and in the square several times a day. She was always alone, always wearing the same toque, followed by the white Pomeranian. No one knew who she was, and she became known simply as the lady with the dog.

"If she's here without her husband and without any friends," thought Gurov, "it wouldn't be a bad idea to strike up an acquaintance with her."

He was not yet forty, but he had a twelve-year-old daughter and two schoolboy sons. He had been married off when he was still in his second year at the university, and his wife seemed to him now to be almost twice his age. She was a tall, black-browed woman, erect, dignified, austere, and, as she liked to describe herself, a "thinking person." She was a great reader, preferred the new "advanced" spelling, called her husband by the more formal "Dimitri" and not the familiar "Dmitri"; and though he secretly considered her not particularly intelligent, narrow-minded, and inelegant, he was afraid of her and disliked being at home. He had been unfaithful to her for a long time, he was often unfaithful to her, and that was why, perhaps, he almost always spoke ill of women, and when men discussed women in his presence, he described them as *the lower breed.*

He could not help feeling that he had had enough bitter experience to have the right to call them as he pleased, but all the same without *the lower breed* he could not have existed a couple of days. He was bored and ill at ease among men, with whom he was reticent and cold, but when he was among women he felt at ease, he knew what to talk about with them and how to behave; even when he was silent in their company he experienced no feeling of constraint. There was something attractive, something elusive in his appearance, in his character and his whole person, that women found interesting and irresistible; he was aware of it, and was himself drawn to them by some irresistible force.

Long and indeed bitter experience had taught him that every new affair, which at first relieved the monotony of life so pleasantly and appeared to be such a charming and light adventure, among decent people and especially among Muscovites, who are so irresolute and so' hard to rouse, inevitably developed into an extremely complicated problem and finally the whole situation became rather cumbersome. But at every new meeting with an attractive woman he forgot all about this experience, he wanted to enjoy life so badly and it all seemed so simple and amusing.

And so one afternoon, while he was having dinner at a restaurant in the park, the woman in the toque walked in unhurriedly and took a seat at the table next to him. The way she looked, walked, and dressed, wore her hair, told him that she was of good social standing, that she was married, that she was in Yalta for the first time, that she was alone and bored. . . . There was a great deal of exaggeration in the stories about the laxity of morals among the Yalta visitors, and he dismissed them with contempt, for he knew that such stories were mostly made up by people who would gladly have sinned themselves if they had had any idea how to go about it; but when the woman sat down at the table three yards away from him he remembered these stories of easy conquests and excursions to the mountains, and the tempting thought of a quick and fleeting affair, an affair with a strange woman whose very name he did not know, suddenly took possession of him.

He tried to attract the attention of the dog by calling softly to it, and when the Pomeranian came up to him he shook a finger at it. The Pomeranian growled. Gurov again shook a finger at it.

The woman looked up at him and immediately lowered her eyes.

"He doesn't bite," she said, and blushed.

"May I give him a bone?" he asked, and when she nodded, he said amiably: "Have you been long in Yalta?"

"About five days."

"And I am just finishing my second week here."

They said nothing for the next few minutes.

"Time flies," she said without looking at him, "and yet it's so boring here."

"That's what one usually hears people saying here. A man may be living in Belev and Zhizdra or some other godforsaken hole and he isn't bored, but the moment he comes here all you hear from him is 'Oh, it's so boring! Oh, the dust!' You'd think he'd come from Granada!"

She laughed. Then both went on eating in silence, like complete strangers; but after dinner they strolled off together, and they embarked on the light playful conversation of free and contented people who do not care where they go or what they talk about. They walked, and talked about the strange light that fell on the sea; the water was of such a soft and warm lilac, and the moon threw a shaft of gold across it. They talked about how close it was after a hot day. Gurov told her that he lived in Moscow, that he was a graduate in philology but worked in a bank, that he had at one time thought of singing in a private opera company but had given up the idea, that he owned two houses in Moscow. . . . From her he learned that she had grown up in Petersburg, but had gotten married in the town of S—, where she had been living for the past two years, that she would stay another month in Yalta, and that her husband, who also needed a rest, might join her. She was quite unable to tell him what her husband's job was, whether he served in the offices of the provincial governor or the rural council, and she found this rather amusing herself. Gurov also found out that her name and patronymic were Anna Sergeyevna.

Later, in his hotel room, he thought about her and felt sure that he would meet her again the next day. It had to be. As he went to bed he remembered that she had only recently left her boarding school, that she had been a schoolgirl like his own daughter; he recalled how much diffidence and angularity there was in her laughter and her conversation with a stranger—it was probably the first time in her life she had found herself alone, in a situation when men followed her, looked at her, and spoke to her with only one secret intention, an intention she could hardly fail to guess. He remembered her slender, weak neck, her beautiful gray eyes.

"There's something pathetic about her, all the same," he thought as he fell asleep.

II

A week had passed since their first meeting. It was a holiday. It was close indoors, while in the streets a strong wind raised clouds of dust and tore off people's hats. All day long one felt thirsty, and Gurov kept going to the terrace of the restaurant, offering Anna Sergeyevna fruit drinks and ices. There was nowhere to go.

In the evening, when the wind had dropped a little, they went to the pier to watch the arrival of the steamer. There were a great many people taking a walk on the landing pier; some were meeting friends, they had bunches of flowers in their hands. It was there that two peculiarities of the Yalta smart set at once arrested attention: the middle-aged women dressed as if they were still young girls and there was a great number of generals.

Because of the rough sea the steamer arrived late, after the sun had set, and she had to swing backward and forward several times before getting alongside the pier. Anna Sergeyevna looked at the steamer and the passengers through her lorgnette, as though trying to make out some friends, and when she turned to Gurov her eyes were sparkling. She talked a lot, asked many abrupt questions, and immediately forgot what it was she had wanted to know; then she lost her lorgnette in the crowd of people.

The smartly dressed crowd dispersed; soon they were all gone, the wind had dropped completely, but Gurov and Anna were still standing there as though waiting to see if someone else would come off the boat.

Anna Sergeyevna was no longer talking. She was smelling her flowers without looking at Gurov.

"It's a nice evening," he said. "Where shall we go now? Shall we go for a drive?"

She made no answer.

Then he looked keenly at her and suddenly put his arms around her and kissed her on the mouth. He felt the fragrance and dampness of the flowers and immediately looked around him fearfully: had anyone seen them?

"Let's go to your room," he said softly.

And both walked off quickly.

It was very close in her hotel room, which was full of the smell of the scents she had bought in a Japanese shop. Looking at her now, Gurov thought: "Life is full of strange encounters!" From his past he preserved the memory of carefree, good-natured women, whom love had made gay and who were grateful to him for the happiness he gave them, however short-lived; and of women like his wife, who made love without sincerity, with unnecessary talk, affectedly, hysterically, with such an expression, as though it were not love or passion, but something much more significant; and of two or three very beautiful, frigid women, whose faces suddenly lit up with a predatory expression, an obstinate desire to take, to snatch from life more than it could give; these were women no longer in their first youth, capricious, unreasoning, despotic, unintelligent women, and when Gurov lost interest in them, their beauty merely aroused hatred in him and the lace trimmings on their negligees looked to him then like the scales of a snake.

But here there was still the same diffidence and angularity of inexperienced youth—an awkward feeling; and there was also the impression of embarrassment, as if someone had just knocked at the door. Anna Sergeyevna, this lady with the dog, apparently regarded what had happened in a peculiar sort of way, very seriously, as though she had become a fallen woman—so it seemed to him, and he found it odd and disconcerting. Her features lengthened and drooped, and her long hair hung mournfully on either side of her face; she sank into thought in a despondent pose, like a woman taken in adultery in an old painting.

"It's wrong," she said. "You'll be the first not to respect me now."

There was a watermelon on the table. Gurov cut himself a slice and began to eat it slowly. At least half an hour passed in silence.

Anna Sergeyevna was very touching; there was an air of a pure, decent, naive woman about her, a woman who had very little experience of life; the solitary candle burning on the table scarcely lighted up her face, but it was obvious that she was unhappy.

"But, darling, why should I stop respecting you?" Gurov asked. "You don't know yourself what you're saying."

"May God forgive me," she said, and her eyes filled with tears. "It's terrible."

"You seem to wish to justify yourself."

"How can I justify myself? I am a bad, despicable creature. I despise myself and have no thought of justifying myself. I haven't deceived my husband, I've deceived myself. And not only now. I've been deceiving myself for a long time. My husband is, I'm sure, a good and honest man, but, you see, he is a flunky. I don't know what he does at his office, all I know is that he is a flunky. I was only twenty when I married him, I was eaten up by curiosity, I wanted something better. There surely must be a different kind of life, I said to myself. I wanted to live. To live, to live! I was burning with curiosity. I don't think you know what I am talking about, but I swear I could no longer control myself, something was happening to me, I could not be held back, I told my husband I was ill, and I came here. . . . Here, too, I was going about as though in a daze, as though I was mad, and now I've become a vulgar worthless woman whom everyone has a right to despise."

Gurov could not help feeling bored as he listened to her; he was irritated by her naive tone of voice and her repentance, which was so unexpected and so out of place; but for the tears in her eyes, he might have thought that she was joking or playacting.

"I don't understand," he said gently, "what it is you want."

She buried her face on his chest and clung close to him.

"Please, please believe me," she said. "I love a pure, honest life. I hate immorality. I don't know myself what I am doing. The common people say 'the devil led her astray.' I, too, can now say about myself that the devil has led me astray."

"There, there . . ." he murmured.

He gazed into her staring, frightened eyes, kissed her, spoke gently and affectionately to her, and gradually she calmed down and her cheerfulness returned; both of them were soon laughing.

Later, when they went out, there was not a soul on the promenade, the town with its cypresses looked quite dead, but the sea was still roaring and dashing itself against the shore; a single launch tossed on the waves, its lamp flickering sleepily.

They hailed a cab and drove to Oreanda.

"I've just found out your surname, downstairs in the lobby," said Gurov. "Von Diederitz. Is your husband a German?"

"No. I believe his grandfather was German. He is of the Orthodox faith himself."

In Oreanda they sat on a bench not far from the church, looked down on the sea, and were silent. Yalta could scarcely be seen through the morning mist. White clouds lay motionless on the mountaintops. Not a leaf stirred on the trees, the cicadas chirped, and the monotonous, hollow roar of the sea, coming up from below, spoke of rest, of eternal sleep awaiting us all. The sea had roared like that down below when there was no Yalta or Oreanda, it was roaring now, and it would go on roaring as indifferently and hollowly when we were here no more. And in this constancy, in this complete indifference to the life and death of each one of us, there is perhaps hidden the guarantee of our eternal salvation, the never-ceasing movement of life on earth, the never-ceasing movement toward perfection. Sitting beside a young woman who looked so beautiful at the break of day, soothed and enchanted by the sight of all that fairyland scenery—the sea, the mountains, the clouds, the wide sky—Gurov reflected that, when you came to think of it, everything in the world was really beautiful, everything but our own thoughts and actions when we lose sight of the higher aims of existence and our dignity as human beings.

Someone walked up to them, a watchman probably, looked at them, and went away. And there seemed to be something mysterious and also beautiful in this fact, too. They could see the Theodosia boat coming toward the pier, lit up by the sunrise, and with no lights.

"There's dew on the grass," said Anna Sergeyevna, breaking the silence.

"Yes. Time to go home."

They went back to the town.

After that they met on the front every day at twelve o'clock, had lunch and dinner together, went for walks, admired the sea. She complained of sleeping badly and of her heart beating uneasily, asked the same questions, alternately worried by feelings of jealousy and by fear that he did not respect her sufficiently. And again and again in the park or in the square, when there was no one in sight, he would draw her to him and kiss her passionately. The complete idleness, these kisses in broad daylight, always having to look around for fear of someone watching them, the heat, the smell of the sea, and the constant looming into sight of idle, well-dressed, and well-fed people seemed to have made a new man of him; he told Anna Sergeyevna that she was beautiful, that she was desirable, made passionate love to her, never left her side, while she was often lost in thought and kept asking him to admit that he did not really respect her, that he was not in the least in love with her and only saw in her a vulgar woman. Almost every night they drove out of town, to Oreanda or to the waterfall; the excursion was always a success, and every time their impressions were invariably grand and beautiful.

They kept expecting her husband to arrive. But a letter came from him in which he wrote that he was having trouble with his eyes and implored his wife to return home as soon as possible. Anna Sergeyevna lost no time in getting ready for her journey home.

"It's a good thing I'm going," she said to Gurov. "It's fate."

She took a carriage to the railway station, and he saw her off. The drive took a whole day. When she got into the express train, after the second bell, she said:

"Let me have another look at you. . . . One last look. So."

She did not cry, but looked sad, just as if she were ill, and her face quivered.

"I'll be thinking of you, remembering you," she said. "Good-bye. You're staying, aren't you? Don't think badly of me. We are parting forever. Yes, it must be so, for we should never have met. Well, good-bye. . . ."

The train moved rapidly out of the station; its lights soon disappeared, and a minute later it could not even be heard, just as though everything had conspired to put a quick end to this sweet trance, this madness. And standing alone on the platform gazing into the dark distance, Gurov listened to the chirring of the grasshoppers and the humming of the telegraph wires with a feeling as though he had just woken up. He told himself that this had been just one more affair in his life, just one more adventure, and that it, too, was over, leaving nothing but a memory. He was moved and sad, and felt a little penitent that the young woman, whom he would never see again, had not been happy with him; he had been amiable and affectionate with her, but all the same in his behavior to her, in the tone of his voice and in his caresses, there was a suspicion of light irony, the somewhat coarse arrogance of the successful male, who was, moreover, almost twice her age. All the time she called him good, wonderful, high-minded; evidently she must have taken him to be quite different from what he really was, which meant that he had involuntarily deceived her.

At the railway station there was already a whiff of autumn in the air; the evening was chilly.

"Time I went north, too," thought Gurov as he walked off the platform. "High time!"

Anton Chekhov

III

At home in Moscow everything was already like winter: the stoves were heated, and it was still dark in the morning when the children were getting ready to go to school and having breakfast, so that the nurse had to light the lamp for a short time. The frosts had set in. When the first snow falls and the first day one goes out for a ride in a sleigh, one is glad to see the white ground, the white roofs, the air is so soft and wonderful to breathe, and one remembers the days of one's youth. The old lime trees and birches, white with rime, have such a benign look, they are nearer to one's heart than cypresses and palms, and beside them one no longer wants to think of mountains and the sea.

Gurov had been born and bred in Moscow, and he returned to Moscow on a fine frosty day; and when he put on his fur coat and warm gloves and took a walk down Petrovka Street, and when on Saturday evening he heard the church bells ringing, his recent holiday trip and the places he had visited lost their charm for him. Gradually he became immersed in Moscow life, eagerly reading three newspapers a day and declaring that he never read Moscow papers on principle. Once more he could not resist the attraction of restaurants, clubs, banquets, and anniversary celebrations, and once more he felt flattered that well-known lawyers and actors came to see him and that in the Medical Club he played cards with a professor as his partner. Once again he was capable of eating a whole portion of the Moscow speciality of sour cabbage and meat served in a frying pan. . . .

Another month and, he thought, nothing but a memory would remain of Anna Sergeyevna; he would remember her as through a haze and only occasionally dream of her with a wistful smile, as he did of the others before her. But over a month passed, winter was at its height, and he remembered her as clearly as though he had only parted from her the day before. His memories haunted him more and more persistently. Every time the voices of his children doing their homework reached him in his study in the stillness of the evening, every time he heard a popular song or some music in a restaurant, every time the wind howled in the chimney—it all came back to him: their walks on the pier, early morning with the mist on the mountains, the Theodosia boat, and the kisses. He kept pacing the room for hours remembering it all and smiling, and then his memories turned into daydreams and the past mingled in his imagination with what was going to happen. He did not dream of Anna Sergeyevna, she accompanied him everywhere like his shadow and followed him wherever he went. Closing his eyes, he saw her as clearly as if she were before him, and she seemed to him lovelier, younger, and tenderer than she had been; and he thought that he, too, was much better than he had been in Yalta. In the evenings she gazed at him from the bookcase, from the fireplace, from the corner—he heard her breathing, the sweet rustle of her dress. In the street he followed women with his eyes, looking for anyone who resembled her. . . .

He was beginning to be overcome by an overwhelming desire to share his memories with someone. But at home it was impossible to talk of his love, and outside his home there was no one he could talk to. Not the tenants who lived in his house, and certainly not his colleagues in the bank. And what was he to tell them? Had he been in love then? Had there been anything beautiful, poetic, edifying, or even anything interesting about his relations with Anna Sergeyevna? So he had to talk in general terms about love and women, and no one guessed what he was driving at, and his wife merely raised her black eyebrows and said:

"Really, Dimitri, the role of a coxcomb doesn't suit you at all!"

One evening, as he left the Medical Club with his partner, a civil servant, he could not restrain himself, and said:

"If you knew what a fascinating woman I met in Yalta!"

The civil servant got into his sleigh and was about to be driven off, but suddenly he turned around and called out:

"I say!"

"Yes?"

"You were quite right: the sturgeon *was* a bit off."

These words, so ordinary in themselves, for some reason hurt Gurov's feelings: they seemed to him humiliating and indecent. What savage manners! What faces! What stupid nights! What uninteresting, wasted days! Crazy gambling at cards, gluttony, drunkenness, endless talk about one and the same thing. Business that was of no use to anyone and talk about one and the same thing absorbed the greater part of one's time and energy, and what was left in the end was a sort of dock-tailed, barren life, a sort of nonsensical existence, and it was impossible to escape from it, just as though you were in a lunatic asylum or a convict chaingang!

Gurov lay awake all night, fretting and fuming, and had a splitting headache the whole of the next day. The following nights, too, he slept badly, sitting up in bed thinking, or walking up and down his room. He was tired of his children, tired of the bank, he did not feel like going out anywhere or talking about anything.

In December, during the Christmas holidays, he packed his things,

told his wife that he was going to Petersburg to get a job for a young
man he knew, and set off for the town of S—. Why? He had no very
clear idea himself. He wanted to see Anna Sergeyevna, to talk to her,
to arrange a meeting, if possible.

He arrived in S— in the morning and took the best room in a
hotel, with a fitted carpet of military gray cloth and an inkstand gray
with dust on the table, surmounted by a horseman with raised hand
and no head. The hall porter supplied him with all the necessary information: Von Diederitz lived in a house of his own in Old Potter's
Street, not far from the hotel. He lived well, was rich, kept his own
carriage horses, the whole town knew him. The hall porter pronounced
the name: Dridiritz.

Gurov took a leisurely walk down Old Potter's Street and found
the house. In front of it was a long gray fence studded with upturned
nails.

"A fence like that would make anyone wish to run away," thought
Gurov, scanning the windows and the fence.

As it was a holiday, he thought, her husband was probably at
home. It did not matter either way, though, for he could not very well
embarrass her by calling at the house. If he were to send in a note it
might fall into the hands of the husband and ruin everything. The best
thing was to rely on chance. And he kept walking up and down the
street and along the fence, waiting for his chance. He watched a beggar
enter the gate and the dogs attack him; then, an hour later, he heard
the faint indistinct sounds of a piano. That must have been Anna
Sergeyevna playing. Suddenly the front door opened and an old woman
came out, followed by the familiar white Pomeranian. Gurov was about
to call to the dog, but his heart began to beat violently and in his
excitement he could not remember its name.

He went on walking up and down the street, hating the gray fence
more and more, and he was already saying to himself that Anna Sergeyevna had forgotten him and had perhaps been having a good time
with someone else, which was indeed quite natural for a young woman
who had to look at that damned fence from morning till night. He
went back to his hotel room and sat on the sofa for a long time, not
knowing what to do, then he had dinner and after dinner a long sleep.

"How stupid and disturbing it all is," he thought, waking up and
staring at the dark windows: it was already evening. "Well, I've had
a good sleep, so what now? What am I going to do tonight?"

He sat on a bed covered by a cheap gray blanket looking exactly
like a hospital blanket, and taunted himself in vexation:

"A *lady* with a dog! Some adventure, I must say! Serves you right!"

At the railway station that morning he had noticed a poster announcing in huge letters the first performance of *The Geisha Girl* at the local theater. He recalled it now, and decided to go to the theater.

"Quite possibly she goes to first nights," he thought.

The theater was full. As in all provincial theaters, there was a mist over the chandeliers and the people in the gallery kept up a noisy and excited conversation; in the first row of the stalls stood the local dandies with their hands crossed behind their backs; here, too, in the front seat of the governor's box, sat the governor's daughter, wearing a feather boa, while the governor himself hid modestly behind the portiere so that only his hands were visible; the curtain stirred, the orchestra took a long time tuning up. Gurov scanned the audience eagerly as they filed in and occupied their seats.

Anna Sergeyevna came in, too. She took her seat in the third row, and when Gurov glanced at her his heart missed a beat and he realized clearly that there was no one in the world nearer and dearer or more important to him than that little woman with the stupid lorgnette in her hand, who was in no way remarkable. That woman lost in a provincial crowd now filled his whole life, was his misfortune, his joy, and the only happiness that he wished for himself. Listening to the bad orchestra and the wretched violins played by second-rate musicians, he thought how beautiful she was. He thought and dreamed.

A very tall, round-shouldered young man with small whiskers had come in with Anna Sergeyevna and sat down beside her; he nodded at every step he took and seemed to be continually bowing to someone. This was probably her husband, whom in a fit of bitterness at Yalta she had called a flunky. And indeed there was something of a lackey's obsequiousness in his lank figure, his whiskers, and the little bald spot on the top of his head. He smiled sweetly, and the gleaming insignia of some scientific society which he wore in his buttonhole looked like the number on a waiter's coat.

In the first interval the husband went out to smoke and she was left in her seat. Gurov, who also had a seat in the stalls, went up to her and said in a trembling voice and with a forced smile:

"Good evening!"

She looked up at him and turned pale, then looked at him again in panic, unable to believe her eyes, clenching her fan and lorgnette in her hand and apparently trying hard not to fall into a dead faint. Both were silent. She sat and he stood, frightened by her embarrassment and not daring to sit down beside her. The violinists and the flutist began tuning their instruments, and they suddenly felt terrified, as though they were being watched from all the boxes. But a moment later she got up and walked rapidly toward one of the exits; he followed her, and both of them walked aimlessly along corridors and up and down stairs. Figures in all sorts of uniforms—lawyers, teachers, civil servants, all wearing badges—flashed by them; ladies, fur coats hanging on pegs, the cold draft bringing with it the odor of cigarette ends. Gurov, whose heart was beating violently, thought:

"Oh, Lord, what are all these people, that orchestra, doing here?"

At that moment he suddenly remembered how after seeing Anna Sergeyevna off he had told himself that evening at the station that all was over and that they would never meet again. But how far they still were from the end!

She stopped on a dark, narrow staircase with a notice over it: "To the Upper Circle."

"How you frightened me!" she said, breathing heavily, still looking pale and stunned. "Oh, dear, how you frightened me! I'm scarcely alive. Why did you come? Why?"

"But, please, try to understand, Anna," he murmured hurriedly. "I beg you, please, try to understand. . . ."

She looked at him with fear, entreaty, love, looked at him intently, so as to fix his features firmly in her mind.

"I've suffered so much," she went on, without listening to him. "I've been thinking of you all the time. The thought of you kept me alive. And yet I tried so hard to forget you—why, oh, why did you come?'

On the landing above two schoolboys were smoking and looking down, but Gurov did not care. He drew Anna Sergeyevna toward him and began kissing her face, her lips, her hands.

"What are you doing? What are you doing?" she said in horror, pushing him away. "We've both gone mad. You must go back tonight, this minute. I implore you, by all that's sacred. . . . Somebody's coming!"

Somebody was coming up the stairs.

"You must go back," continued Anna Sergeyevna in a whisper. "Do you hear? I'll come to you in Moscow. I've never been happy, I'm unhappy now, and I shall never be happy, never! So please don't make me suffer still more. I swear I'll come to you in Moscow. But now we must part. Oh, my sweet, my darling, we must part!"

She pressed his hand and went quickly down the stairs, looking back at him all the time, and he could see from the expression in her eyes that she really was unhappy. Gurov stood listening for a short time, and when all was quiet he went to look for his coat and left the theater.

IV

Anna Sergeyevna began going to Moscow to see him. Every two or three months she left the town of S—, telling her husband that she was going to consult a Moscow gynecologist, and her husband believed and did not believe her. In Moscow she stayed at the Slav Bazaar and immediately sent a porter in a red cap to inform Gurov of her arrival. Gurov went to her hotel, and no one in Moscow knew about it.

One winter morning he went to her hotel as usual (the porter had called with his message at his house the evening before, but he had not been in). He had his daughter with him, and he was glad of the opportunity of taking her to school, which was on the way to the hotel. Snow was falling in thick wet flakes.

"It's three degrees above zero," Gurov was saying to his daughter, "and yet it's snowing. But then, you see, it's only warm on the earth's surface, in the upper layers of the atmosphere the temperature's quite different."

"Why isn't there any thunder in winter, Daddy?"

He explained that, too. As he was speaking, he kept thinking that he was going to meet his mistress and not a living soul knew about it. He led a double life: one for all who were interested to see, full of conventional truth and conventional deception, exactly like the lives of his friends and acquaintances; and another that went on in secret. And by a kind of strange concatenation of circumstances, possibly quite by accident, everything that was important, interesting, essential, everything about which he was sincere and did not deceive himself, everything that made up the quintessence of his life, went on in secret, while everything that was a lie, everything that was merely the husk in which he hid himself to conceal the truth, like his work at the bank, for instance, his discussions at the club, his ideas of the lower breed, his going to anniversary functions with his wife—all that happened in the sight of all. He judged others by himself, did not believe what he saw, and was always of the opinion that every man's real and most interesting life went on in secret, under cover of night. The personal, private life of an individual was kept a secret, and perhaps that was partly the reason why civilized man was so anxious that his personal secrets should be respected.

Having seen his daughter off to her school, Gurov went to the Slav Bazaar. He took off his fur coat in the cloakroom, went upstairs, and knocked softly on the door. Anna Sergeyevna, wearing the gray dress he liked most, tired out by her journey and by the suspense of waiting for him, had been expecting him since the evening before; she was pale, looked at him without smiling, but was in his arms the moment he went into the room. Their kiss was long and lingering, as if they had not seen each other for two years.

"Well," he asked, "how are you getting on there? Anything new?"

"Wait, I'll tell you in a moment. . . . I can't . . ."

She could not speak because she was crying. She turned away from him and pressed her handkerchief to her eyes.

"Well, let her have her cry," he thought, sitting down in an armchair. "I'll wait."

Then he rang the bell and ordered tea; while he was having his tea, she was still standing there with her face to the window. She wept because she could not control her emotions, because she was bitterly conscious of the fact that their life was so sad: they could only meet in secret, they had to hide from people, like thieves! Was not their life ruined?

"Please, stop crying!" he said.

It was quite clear to him that their love would not come to an end for a long time, if ever. Anna Sergeyevna was getting attached to him more and more strongly, she worshiped him, and it would have been absurd to tell her that all this would have to come to an end one day. She would not have believed it, anyway.

He went up to her and took her by the shoulders, wishing to be nice to her, to make her smile; and at that moment he caught sight of himself in the looking glass.

His hair was already beginning to turn gray. It struck him as strange that he should have aged so much, that he should have lost his good looks in the last few years. The shoulders on which his hands lay were warm and quivering. He felt so sorry for this life, still so warm and beautiful, but probably soon to fade and wilt like his own. Why did she love him so? To women he always seemed different from what he was, and they loved in him not himself, but the man their imagination conjured up and whom they had eagerly been looking for all their lives; and when they discovered their mistake they still loved him. And not one of them had ever been happy with him. Time had passed, he had met women, made love to them, parted from them, but not once had he been in love; there had been everything between them, but no love.

It was only now, when his hair was beginning to turn gray, that he had fallen in love properly, in good earnest—for the first time in his life.

He and Anna Sergeyevna loved each other as people do who are very dear and near, as man and wife or close friends love each other; they could not help feeling that fate itself had intended them for one another, and they were unable to understand why he should have a wife and she a husband; they were like two migrating birds, male and female, who had been caught and forced to live in separate cages. They had forgiven each other what they had been ashamed of in the past, and forgave each other everything in their present, and felt that this love of theirs had changed them both.

Before, when he felt depressed, he had comforted himself by all sorts of arguments that happened to occur to him on the spur of the moment, but now he had more serious things to think of, he felt profound compassion, he longed to be sincere, tender. . . .

"Don't cry, my sweet," he said. "That'll do, you've had your cry. . . . Let's talk now, let's think of something."

Then they had a long talk. They tried to think how they could get rid of the necessity of hiding, telling lies, living in different towns, not seeing one another for so long. How were they to free themselves from their intolerable chains?

"How? How?" he asked himself, clutching at his head. "How?"

And it seemed to them that in only a few more minutes a solution would be found and a new, beautiful life would begin; but both of them knew very well that the end was still a long, long way away and that the most complicated and difficult part was only just beginning.

(1899)

UNCLE VANYA

Country Scenes in Four Acts

CHARACTERS

ALEKSANDR VLADIMIROVICH SEREBRYAKOV, *a retired university professor*

YELENA ANDREYEVNA SEREBRYAKOV, *his wife, aged twenty-seven*

SONYA ALEXANDROVNA, *his daughter by his first marriage*

MARIA VASILYEVNA VOYNITSKY, *the mother of the professor's first wife*

IVAN PETROVICH VOYNITSKY, *her son*

MIKHAIL LVOVICH ASTROV, *a country doctor*

ILYA ILYCH TELEGIN, *an impoverished landowner*

MARINA, *an old nurse*

A LABORER

A WATCHMAN

The action takes place on SEREBRYAKOV'S *estate.*

ACT ONE

A garden. Part of the house can be seen, with the veranda. Under an old poplar, by the avenue of trees, a table set for tea. Benches, chairs; a guitar on one of the benches. Not far from the table, a swing. About three o'clock in the afternoon. An overcast sky.

MARINA, *a heavily built old woman, who moves with difficulty, sits by the samovar, knitting a sock;* ASTROV *is walking up and down near her.*

MARINA (*Pours out a glass of tea*)
Have some tea, dear.

ASTROV (*Accepts the glass reluctantly*)
Thank you. I don't feel like it, somehow.

MARINA
You wouldn't like a drop of vodka, would you?

ASTROV
No, thank you. I don't drink vodka every day, you know. Besides, it's so close. (*Pause*) How long have we known each other, Nanny?

MARINA (*Thinking it over*)
How long? Dear me, let me think. . . . You first came here—into these parts—when? . . . Sonya's mother was still living then. You visited us regularly for two winters before she died. Well, that makes eleven years to my way of reckoning. (*After a moment's thought*) Perhaps even longer.

ASTROV
Have I changed much since then?

MARINA
Yes, I'm afraid you have, dear. You were young and handsome then, but now you look much older. And you aren't as handsome as you used to be. If you don't mind me mentioning it, you drink a lot, too.

ASTROV

Yes. . . . In ten years I've grown a different man. And the reason? Overwork, Nanny. Overwork. On my feet from morning till night. Don't know the meaning of rest. And at night I lie awake under the bedclothes in constant fear of being dragged out to a patient. Haven't had a single free day ever since I've known you. I couldn't help growing old, could I? And, besides, life here is dull, stupid, sordid. . . . This sort of life wears you down. You're surrounded by cranks—cranks, all of them. Spend two or three years with them and gradually, without noticing it, you become a crank yourself. It's inevitable—sure as fate. *(Twisting his long mustache)* Just look at this enormous mustache I've grown. An idiotic mustache. I've become a crank, Nanny. . . . Haven't grown stupid yet, thank God; there's nothing wrong with my brains, but my feelings have, I'm afraid, grown numb. I want nothing, I need nothing, there's no one I'm fond of—except, perhaps, you, Nanny. *(Kisses her on the head)* I had a nurse like you when I was a little boy.

MARINA

You wouldn't like something to eat, would you?

ASTROV

No, thank you. In the third week of Lent I went to Malitskoye. There was an epidemic there. Spotted fever. In the cottages people were lying side by side on the floor. . . . Filth, stench, smoke . . . Calves, too, lying about on the floor, among the sick. And pigs. Spent a whole day there looking after the patients without sitting down and without a bite of food, and when I got back home, they wouldn't let me rest. Brought a signalman from the railway. I got him on the table and was about to operate on him when damned if he didn't go and die on me under the chloroform. It was then, when I didn't want them, that my feelings awakened and my conscience pricked me, as though I had killed him on purpose. . . . I sat down, closed my eyes like this, and thought to myself: Will those who will be living a hundred or two hundred years after us spare a thought for us who are now blazing a trail for them? Will they have a good word to say for us? No, Nanny, they won't, they won't!

MARINA

Men won't, but God will.

ASTROV

Thank you, Nanny. You spoke well.

(VOYNITSKY enters from the house; he has had a nap after lunch

and looks rumpled. He sits down on a bench and straightens his fash-
ionable tie)

VOYNITSKY
Yes. *(Pause)* Yes. . . .

ASTROV
Had a good sleep?

VOYNITSKY
Yes. Very. *(Yawns)* Ever since the professor and his wife have come to
live with us, our life has been turned upside down. . . . I go to sleep
at the wrong time, at lunch and dinner I eat all sorts of fancy concoc-
tions, drink wine—all this can't be good for me. Before I hadn't a free
minute to myself. Sonya and I worked like Trojans, but now only Sonya
works, while I sleep, eat, and drink—it's too bad!

MARINA *(Shaking her head)*
Shameful's what I call it! The professor gets up at twelve o'clock, and
the samovar's kept on the boil all morning waiting for him. Before they
came, we used to have dinner at one o'clock, like everybody else, but
now we're having it at about seven. The professor spends the night
reading and writing and all of a sudden at two in the morning he rings
his bell. Why, what is it? Tea, if you please! Wake the servants for
him. Put on the samovar. Shameful—that's what it is!

ASTROV
And are they going to stay here long?

VOYNITSKY *(Whistles)*
A hundred years. The professor has decided to stay here for good.

MARINA
Same thing now. The samovar has been on the table for the last two
hours, and they've gone for a walk.

VOYNITSKY
They're coming, they're coming. Keep calm, Nanny.
   (Voices are heard; from the far end of the garden, returning from
their walk, enter SEREBRYAKOV, YELENA, SONYA, *and* TELEGIN)

SEREBRYAKOV
Excellent, excellent. . . . Wonderful scenery.

TELEGIN
Remarkable, sir.

SONYA

We'll go to the plantation tomorrow, Father. Would you like to?

VOYNITSKY

Let's have tea, ladies and gentlemen.

SEREBRYAKOV

My friends, be so kind as to send my tea up to my study. I've still some work to do today.

SONYA

I'm sure you'll like the plantation, Father.

(YELENA, SEREBRYAKOV, and SONYA go into the house; TELEGIN goes up to the table and sits down beside MARINA)

VOYNITSKY

It's hot, close, and our eminent scholar walks about in an overcoat and galoshes, wearing gloves, and carrying an umbrella.

ASTROV

Which shows that he takes good care of himself.

VOYNITSKY

But how lovely she is, how lovely! I've never seen a more beautiful woman in my life.

TELEGIN *(To* MARINA*)*

Whether I drive through the fields or take a walk in the shade of the trees in the garden or look on this table, I experience a feeling of indescribable bliss! The weather is enchanting, the birds are singing, we all live in peace and harmony—what more do we want? *(Accepting a glass from* MARINA*)* I'm infinitely obliged to you!

VOYNITSKY *(Dreamily)*

Her eyes . . . A wonderful woman!

ASTROV

Tell us something.

VOYNITSKY *(Phlegmatically)*

What do you want me to tell you?

ASTROV

Is there nothing new at all?

VOYNITSKY

Nothing. Everything's old. I'm the same as I was. Grown worse, I daresay, for I've grown lazy, do nothing, just grumble like an old fogy.

My mother, the old crow, still goes about croaking about women's emancipation. She's got one foot in the grave, but she's still looking in her clever books for the dawn of a new life.

ASTROV

And the professor?

VOYNITSKY

The professor, as always, spends all his time from morning till late at night in his study—writing. "Racking his wits, with furrowed brow, odes, odes, odes we write, without one word of praise for them or us, our labor to requite." Pity the poor paper! He'd much better write his autobiography. What a wonderful subject! A retired professor, you understand, an old dry-as-dust, a learned minnow. . . . Gout, rheumatism, migraine. Got himself an enlarged liver from jealousy and envy. . . . This minnow lives on the estate of his first wife. Lives there against his will, for he can't afford to live in the town. Always complaining of his hard luck, though as a matter of fact he's damned lucky. *(Nervously)* Just think how lucky he is! The son of an ordinary sacristan, a divinity student, he obtained all sorts of degrees and was given a chair at a university. Now he is the son-in-law of a senator, and so on, and so on. All that is not important, though. What is important is this: the man has been lecturing and writing about art for exactly twenty-five years, and yet he doesn't know a thing about art. For twenty-five years he's been chewing over other men's ideas about realism, naturalism, and all sorts of other nonsense. For twenty-five years he has been lecturing and writing on things intelligent people have known about for ages and stupid people aren't interested in, anyway. Which means that for twenty-five years he's been wasting his time. And yet the self-conceit of the man! What pretensions! He has retired, and not a living soul knows or cares about him. He's totally unknown, which means that for twenty-five years he's been doing somebody else out of a job. But look at him: struts about like a demigod!

ASTROV

You're jealous!

VOYNITSKY

Yes, I'm jealous! And the success he has with women! No Don Juan has ever known such amazing success! His first wife, my sister, a sweet, gentle creature, pure as this blue sky, noble, generous, a woman who had had more admirers than he has had students, loved him as only pure angels can love beings as pure and beautiful as themselves. My mother, his mother-in-law, dotes on him to this day, and he still inspires a feeling of reverential awe in her. His second wife, a beautiful, clever woman—you've just seen her—married him when he was already an old man. She sacrificed her youth, her beauty, her freedom, her brilliance to him. Whatever for? Why?

ASTROV

Is she faithful to the professor?

VOYNITSKY

Unfortunately, yes.

ASTROV

Why unfortunately?

VOYNITSKY

Because that loyalty of hers is false from beginning to end. There's a lot of fine sentiment in it, but no logic. To be unfaithful to an old husband whose company is insufferable—that is immoral. But to try to stifle your unhappy youth and your natural feelings—that's not immoral.

TELEGIN *(In a tearful voice)*

Vanya, I don't like to hear you talk like that. Really, you know, anyone who betrays a wife or husband is a person you cannot trust, a person who might betray his country, too.

VOYNITSKY *(With vexation)*

Dry up, Waffles!

TELEGIN

No, listen, Vanya. My wife ran away from me with her lover the day after our wedding because of my unprepossessing appearance. I never swerved from my duty after that. I still love her and I'm still faithful to her. I do all I can to help her. I gave her all I had for the education of her children by the man she loved. My happiness may have been ruined, but I've still got my pride. And what about her? She's no longer young: under the influence of the laws of nature her beauty has faded; the man she loved is dead. . . . What has she got left?

(Enter SONYA *and* YELENA; *a little later enter* MARIA VOYNITSKY *with a book. She sits down and reads, is given tea, and drinks it without raising her head)*

SONYA *(Hurriedly to nurse)*

Some peasants have come, Nanny. Please go and talk to them. I'll see to the tea myself. *(Pours out the tea)*

(MARINA *goes out.* YELENA *takes her cup of tea and drinks, sitting on the swing*)

ASTROV (*To* YELENA)

I've really come to see your husband. You wrote to me that he was very ill—rheumatism and something else—but it seems there's nothing the matter with him at all.

YELENA

He felt very depressed last night. Complained of pains in his legs. But today he's quite all right.

ASTROV

And I've galloped like mad for twenty miles! Oh, well, never mind. It's not the first time. I can stay with you now till tomorrow and at least have a good night's sleep.

SONYA

Yes, do. It's not often you stay the night with us. I don't expect you've had dinner, have you?

ASTROV

No, as a matter of fact I haven't.

SONYA

Well, in that case you will have some dinner, too. We dine at about seven now. (*Drinks*) The tea's cold!

TELEGIN

I'm afraid the temperature has dropped considerably in the samovar.

YELENA

Never mind, Ivan Ivanych, we'll drink it cold.

TELEGIN

Beg your pardon, ma'am, but I'm not Ivan Ivanych. I'm Ilya Ilych—er—Ilya Ilych Telegin, ma'am, or just Waffles, as some people call me because of my pockmarked face. I stood godfather to Sonya, and your husband knows me very well. I live here now, ma'am, on your estate. I expect—er—the fact that I dine with you every day has not escaped your notice.

SONYA

Mr. Telegin is our assistant, our right-hand man. (*Tenderly*) Won't you have another cup, dear Godfather?

MARIA

Good heavens.

SONYA

What's the matter, Granny?

MARIA

I forgot to tell Aleksandr—I'm afraid it must have slipped my memory—I had a letter from Kharkov today—from Pavel Aleksandrovich. He's sent me his new pamphlet.

ASTROV

Interesting?

MARIA

Yes, but rather peculiar. He flatly contradicts everything he defended seven years ago. This is terrible!

VOYNITSKY

There's nothing terrible about it. Drink your tea, Mother.

MARIA

But I want to talk!

VOYNITSKY

You've been talking for fifty years, talking and reading pamphlets. Time you put a stop to it.

MARIA

I don't know why you always seem to find my conversation disagreeable. I'm sorry, Jean, but you've changed so much during the last year that I simply cannot recognize you. You used to be a man of definite convictions, a man of enlightened views.

VOYNITSKY

Oh, yes, to be sure! I was a man of enlightened views that did not enlighten anyone. *(Pause)* A man of enlightened views! What a cruel joke! I'm forty-seven now. Till a year ago I did my best to hoodwink myself with that pedantic stuff of yours so as not to see what real life was like. And I thought I was doing the right thing! And now, if you only knew! I can't sleep at night, so vexed, so furious, am I with myself for having so stupidly frittered away my time when I could have had everything that my age now denies me.

SONYA

Uncle Vanya, this is boring!

MARIA *(To her son)*

You seem to be putting all the blame for something on your former convictions. But it is not they that are at fault but yourself. You seem to forget that convictions are nothing by themselves, a dead letter. You should have been doing some real work.

VOYNITSKY

Some real work? Not everyone has the ability to be some sort of scribbling *perpetuum mobile* like that Herr Professor of yours.

MARIA

What are you suggesting by that, pray?

SONYA *(Imploringly)*

Granny, Uncle Vanya, please!

VOYNITSKY

All right, all right. I shut up and apologize.
    (Pause)

YELENA

It's such a lovely day today. . . . Not too hot.

VOYNITSKY

A lovely day to hang oneself.
    (TELEGIN tunes his guitar. MARINA walks near the house, calling a hen)

MARINA

Chuck-chuck-chuck . . .

SONYA

What did the peasants come for, Nanny?

MARINA

Oh, always the same thing. About the wasteland again. Chuck-chuck-chuck . . .

SONYA

Which one are you calling?

MARINA

Old Speckly has gone off with her chicks. The crows might get them.
. . . *(Goes out)*
    (TELEGIN plays a polka; they all listen in silence; enter a LABORER)

LABORER

Is the doctor here? *(To ASTROV)* If you please, sir, they've sent for you.

ASTROV

Where from?

LABORER

From the factory.

ASTROV *(With vexation)*

Thank you very much. Well, I suppose I'd better go. *(Looks around for his cap)* A pity, though, damn it.

SONYA

What a shame you have to go. Do come back to dinner from the factory.

ASTROV

Afraid it'll be too late. Yes, afraid so ... afraid so ... *(To the* LABORER*)* Look here, be a good chap and fetch me a glass of vodka. *(The* LABORER *goes out)* Where on earth ... ? Where ... ? *(Finds his cap)* There's a character in one of Ostrovsky's plays who has a big mustache but little wit. . . . Well, that's me. Oh, well, good-bye, ladies and gentlemen. *(To* YELENA*)* If you care to look me up sometimes with Sonya, I'd be delighted to see you. I have a little estate of about eighty acres, but if you're interested, there's a model orchard and nursery such as you wouldn't find within a thousand miles. Next to my estate is the government plantation. The forester there is old and always ill, so it's I who have really to look after things there.

YELENA

I've been told already that you make a hobby of forestry. I suppose it could be of the greatest use, but don't you think it interferes with your real work? After all, you're a doctor.

ASTROV

God alone knows what our real work is.

YELENA

Do you find it interesting?

ASTROV

Yes, it's interesting work.

VOYNITSKY *(Ironically)*

Very!

YELENA *(To* ASTROV*)*

You're still a young man. You don't look more than, well, thirty-six or thirty-seven, and I don't supppose it's really as interesting as you

say. Nothing but trees and trees. Must be awfully monotonous, I should
think.

SONYA

Oh, no, it's extremely interesting. Dr. Astrov is planting new forests
every year, and already he's been awarded a bronze medal and a diploma. He does his best to prevent the destruction of the old forests.
If you listen to him, you'll agree with him entirely. He says forests
adorn the earth, teach man to understand the beautiful, and instill in
him a lofty attitude of mind. Forests temper the severity of the climate.
In countries with a mild climate less energy is spent in the struggle with
nature, and that is why men there are beautiful, supple, more sensitive,
their speech refined, and their movements graceful. Art and learning
flourish there. Their outlook on life is not so gloomy, and their attitude
to women is full of exquisite refinement.

VOYNITSKY *(Laughing)*

Bravo, bravo! All this is charming but hardly convincing, so that *(To*
ASTROV*)*, allow me, my friend, to go on stoking my stoves with logs
and building my barns of wood.

ASTROV

You can stoke your stoves with peat and build your barns of brick.
Well, all right, cut down the woods if you have to, but why destroy
them? The Russian forests echo with the sound of the ax, millions of
trees are perishing, the homes of wild animals and birds are being laid
waste, the rivers are growing shallow and running dry, exquisite scenery
is disappearing forever, and all because men are too lazy and too stupid
to bend down and pick up their fuel from the ground. *(To* YELENA*)*
Isn't that so, madam? One has to be a barbarian to burn this beauty
in one's stove, to destroy what we cannot create. Man has been endowed with reason and creative powers to increase what has been given
him, but so far he has not created but destroyed. There are fewer and
fewer forests, the rivers are drying up, the game birds are becoming
extinct, the climate is ruined, and every day the earth is becoming
poorer and more hideous. *(To* VOYNITSKY*)* Here you're looking at me
ironically, and you don't think that what I am telling you is serious—
and perhaps I really am a crank, but when I walk past the peasants'
woods I saved from the ax, or when I hear a young wood planted with
my own hands rustling over my head, I realize that the climate is to
some extent in my power and that if in a thousand years men are happy
and contented, I shall have done my bit toward it. When I plant a birch
tree and then see its green branches swaying in the wind, I cannot help

feeling proud and thrilled with the thought that I—*(Seeing the LA-BORER, who has brought a glass of vodka on a tray)* However *(Drinks)* it's time I was going. All that is, I suppose, just the talk of a crank when all is said and done. Good-bye! *(Goes toward the house)*

SONYA *(Takes his arm and goes with him)*
When are you coming again?

ASTROV
Don't know.

SONYA
Not for another month again?
(ASTROV and SONYA go into the house; MARIA and TELEGIN remain sitting at the table; YELENA and VOYNITSKY go toward the veranda)

YELENA
And you, Vanya, have again been behaving disgracefully. What did you want to irritate your mother for with your talk about the *perpetuum mobile*? And at lunch today you quarreled with Aleksandr again. All this is so petty!

VOYNITSKY
But if I hate him!

YELENA
There's no reason why you should hate Aleksandr. He's just like everybody else. No worse than you.

VOYNITSKY
Oh, if you could only see your face, your movements! You're too lazy to be alive! Too lazy!

YELENA
Oh, dear, lazy and bored! Everyone's abusing my husband; everyone looks at me with compassion: Poor woman, she has an old husband! This tender concern for me—oh, how well I understand it! As Astrov said just now: You're all recklessly destroying the forests, and soon there will be nothing left on the earth. And in the same way you're recklessly destroying human beings, and thanks to you, there will be no more loyalty, no more purity, nor any capacity for self-sacrifice. Why can't you ever look with indifference at a woman if she doesn't happen to belong to you? Why? Because—again the doctor is right—there's a devil of destruction in all of you. You don't care what happens to the forests, nor to the birds, nor to women, nor to one another.

VOYNITSKY
I don't like this sort of talk!
  (Pause)

YELENA
That doctor has a tired, sensitive face. An interesting face. Sonya quite obviously finds him attractive. She's in love with him, and I quite understand her. This is the third time he's been here since we arrived, but I feel shy with him, and I have never really been nice to him or spoken to him as I should have liked. He must think I'm a detestable creature. I expect the reason why we are such good friends is that we are both such tiresome, such dull people! Tiresome! Don't look at me like that! I don't like it!

VOYNITSKY
How else can I look at you if I love you? You're my happiness, my life, my youth! I know the chances that you should return my feeling are nil, but I'm not asking for anything. All I want is to be allowed to look at you, to listen to your voice—

YELENA
Shhh . . . They might hear you! *(Goes toward the house)*

VOYNITSKY *(Following her)*
Let me talk to you of my love. Don't drive me away. That alone will make me the happiest man on earth—

YELENA
This has gone far enough!
  (YELENA and VOYNITSKY go into the house; TELEGIN strikes a chord on the guitar and plays a polka; MARIA writes something on the margin of the pamphlet)

ACT TWO

(A dining room in SEREBRYAKOV's house. Night. The watchman can be heard knocking in the garden.*

SEREBRYAKOV is sitting in an armchair before an open window, dozing. YELENA is sitting beside him, also dozing)

---

* Watchmen had to knock together pieces of wood as they patrolled the grounds, to show they were on the job.

SEREBRYAKOV *(Waking)*

Who's there? You, Sonya?

YELENA

It's me.

SEREBRYAKOV

You, darling . . . Oh, what excruciating pain!

YELENA

Your rug has fallen on the floor. *(Wraps the rug around his legs)* I think I'd better close the window, Aleksandr.

SEREBRYAKOV

No, don't. I can't breathe. I dropped off just now, and I dreamed that my left leg did not belong to me. I was awakened by the frightful pain. No, it's not gout. More likely rheumatism. What's the time?

YELENA

Twenty past twelve.
(Pause)

SEREBRYAKOV

Please find Batyushkov for me in the library in the morning. I believe we've got his works.

YELENA

I'm sorry, what did you say?

SEREBRYAKOV

See if you can find Batyushkov for me in the morning. I seem to remember we had his works. But why can't I breathe?

YELENA

You're tired. You haven't slept for two nights.

SEREBRYAKOV

I've been told Turgenev got angina pectoris from gout. I'm afraid I may get it, too. This damnable, disgusting old age! The devil take it. Ever since I've become ill, I've become disgusting to myself. And I shouldn't be in the least surprised if you all find me repugnant.

YELENA

You talk of your old age as though it were our fault that you are old.

SEREBRYAKOV

You most of all, I expect, must find me odious.
(YELENA gets up and sits down farther away)

SEREBRYAKOV

And you're quite right, of course. I'm not a fool and I understand. You're a young, healthy, beautiful woman. You want to live. And I'm an old man, practically a corpse. Isn't that so? Don't I realize it? And, of course, it's stupid of me to go on living. But wait, I shall soon set you all free. I shan't last much longer.

YELENA

I can't stand it anymore. For God's sake, be quiet.

SEREBRYAKOV

What it comes to is that, thanks to me, everyone is worn out, bored, wasting their youth, and only I am satisfied and enjoying life. Why, of course!

YELENA

Do be quiet! You've exhausted me!

SEREBRYAKOV

I've exhausted everyone. Of course.

YELENA *(Through tears)*

It's unbearable! Tell me, what do you want of me?

SEREBRYAKOV

Nothing.

YELENA

Well, in that case be quiet. I beg you.

SEREBRYAKOV

It's a funny thing, but every time Ivan or that old idiot Maria starts talking, no one objects, everyone listens. But I've only to open my mouth, and everyone begins to feel miserable. Even my voice disgusts them. Well, suppose I am disgusting, suppose I am an egoist, a despot, but haven't I got some right to be an egoist even in my old age? Haven't I earned it? Haven't I the right, I ask, to enjoy a quiet old age, to be treated with consideration by the people around me?

YELENA

No one's disputing your rights. *(The window bangs in the wind)* The wind is rising. I'd better close the window. *(Closes window)* It's going to rain soon. No one disputes your rights.
    (A pause; the watchman in the garden knocks and sings)

SEREBRYAKOV

All my life I've worked in the interests of learning; I got used to my study, my lecture room, my colleagues, and now I find myself buried alive in this tomb, and every day I'm obliged to see stupid people and listen to their absurd talk. I want to live! I like success, I like fame, I like people to talk about me, and here—why, it's like living in exile! Every minute to be grieving for the past, watching others making a name for themselves, being afraid of death . . . I can't put up with it! I haven't the strength. And here they won't even forgive me for being old!

(*Enter* SONYA)

SONYA

You told me to send for Dr. Astrov yourself, Father, and now that he's here, you won't see him. It's not nice. We seem to have troubled him for nothing.

SEREBRYAKOV

What good is your Astrov to me? He knows as much about medicine as I do about astronomy.

SONYA

You don't want us to send for the whole medical faculty for your gout, do you?

SEREBRYAKOV

I refuse even to talk to that crazy fellow.

SONYA

Just as you like. (*Sits down*) I don't care.

SEREBRYAKOV

What's the time?

YELENA

Nearly one o'clock.

SEREBRYAKOV

I can't breathe. . . . Sonya, fetch me the drops from the table!

SONYA

Here you are. (*Gives him the drops*)

SEREBRYAKOV (*Irritably*)

Good Lord, not those! You can't ask anyone for anything!

SONYA

Kindly keep your temper. Some people may put up with it, but I won't.
So spare me, for goodness' sake. I haven't the time, either. I have to
get up early in the morning. We are haymaking.

(*Enter* VOYNITSKY *in dressing gown with a candle*)

VOYNITSKY

There's going to be a storm. (*Lightning*) Dear me, what a flash! Helen,
Sonya, go to bed. I've come to take your place.

SEREBRYAKOV (*Frightened*)

No, no! Don't leave him with me. He'll talk me to death!

VOYNITSKY

But you must let them have some rest! It's the second night they've
had no sleep.

SEREBRYAKOV

Let them go to bed, but you go, too. Thank you. I implore you. In the
name of our past friendship don't raise any objections. We'll talk another time.

VOYNITSKY (*With a grin*)

Our past friendship . . . Past—

SONYA

Do be quiet, Uncle Vanya.

SEREBRYAKOV (*To his wife*)

Darling, don't leave me alone with him! He'll talk me to death.

VOYNITSKY

This is really becoming absurd.

(*Enter* MARINA *with a candle*)

SONYA

Why don't you go to bed, Nanny? It's late.

MARINA

I can't very well go to bed while the samovar's still on the table,
can I?

SEREBRYAKOV

No one's asleep, everyone's exhausted. I'm the only one to have a hell
of a good time.

MARINA (*Goes up to* SEREBRYAKOV, *tenderly*)

What's the matter, sir? Does it hurt very badly? I've a gnawing pain
in my legs, too: it keeps on gnawing something terrible. (*Puts his rug*

right) You've had this trouble for a long time, sir. I remember Sonya's mother sitting up night after night with you. She took it so much to heart, poor dear. Aye, she was very fond of you, she was. *(Pause)* The old are just like children. They want someone to be sorry for them. But no one ever cares for the old. *(Kisses* SEREBRYAKOV *on the shoulder)* Come along, sir, come along to bed. . . . Come along, love. I'll give you some lime tea and warm your poor legs. . . . Say a prayer for you, I will. . . .

SEREBRYAKOV *(Deeply touched)*
Let's go, Marina.

MARINA
I've a gnawing pain in my legs, too, sir. Keeps on gnawing something terrible. *(Leads him away together with* SONYA*)* Sonya's mother used to worry over you so much, poor dear. Cried her heart out, she did. You were only a silly little girl then, Sonya. . . . Come along, sir, come along. . . .

(SEREBRYAKOV, SONYA, *and* MARINA *go out)*

YELENA
I'm absolutely worn out with him. I can hardly stand on my feet.

VOYNITSKY
You with him and I with myself. This is the third night I've had no sleep.

YELENA
There's something the matter with this house. Your mother hates everything except her pamphlets and the professor. The professor is in a state of exasperation: he doesn't trust me and he's afraid of you. Sonya is angry with her father, angry with me, and hasn't spoken to me for a fortnight. You hate my husband and don't conceal your contempt for your mother. I am exasperated and was about to burst into tears a dozen times today. . . . There's something the matter with this house.

VOYNITSKY
Let's drop this silly talk!

YELENA
You, Vanya, are an educated and intelligent person, and I should have thought you ought to understand that the world is not being destroyed by bandits and by fires, but by hatred, enmity, and all these petty squabblings. You ought to stop grumbling and try to reconcile everyone.

VOYNITSKY

Reconcile me to myself first! Oh, my dear—
(Presses his lips to her hand)

YELENA

Don't do that! *(Takes her hand away)* Go away!

VOYNITSKY

The rain will be over in a moment, and everything in nature will be refreshed and breathe freely. I alone will not be refreshed by the storm. Day and night the thought that my life has been hopelessly wasted weighs upon me like a nightmare. I have no past. It has been stupidly wasted on trifles. And the present frightens me by its senselessness. That's what my life and my love are like. What on earth am I to do with them? My whole inner life is being wasted to no purpose, like a ray of sunshine in a pit, and I'm running to waste, too.

YELENA

When you talk to me about your love, it somehow makes me go all dead inside and I don't know what to say. I'm sorry, but I've nothing to say to you. *(Is about to go out)* Good night.

VOYNITSKY *(Barring her way)*

Oh, if you knew how miserable I am at the thought that by my side in this very house another life is being wasted—yours! What is it you're waiting for? What damned reason prevents you from doing something? Understand, do understand. . . .

YELENA *(Looks at him intently)*

Vanya, you're drunk!

VOYNITSKY

Possibly, possibly . . .

YELENA

Where's the doctor?

VOYNITSKY

He's in there. He's staying the night with me. Possibly, possibly—everything is possible!

YELENA

Have you been drinking today again? Why do you do it?

VOYNITSKY

At least it's something like life. Don't stop me, Helen.

YELENA

You never used to drink before, and you never used to talk so much before. Go to bed. You bore me.

VOYNITSKY *(Presses his lips to her hand)*

My darling—my wonderful one!

YELENA *(With vexation)*

Leave me alone, please. This really is the end! *(Goes out)*

VOYNITSKY *(Alone)*

She's gone. *(Pause)* Ten years ago I used to meet her at my sister's. She was seventeen then and I—thirty-seven. Why didn't I fall in love with her then and propose to her? I could have married her easily. And now she would have been my wife. . . . Yes. . . . Now we should have both been awakened by the storm. She'd have been frightened by the thunder, and I'd have held her in my arms and whispered: "Don't be afraid, darling, I'm here." Oh, what wonderful thoughts! I can't help laughing, so happy do they make me feel. Oh, dear, I'm getting all confused. Why am I old? Why doesn't she understand me? Her fine phrases, her lazy morals, her absurd, her lazy ideas about the destruction of the world—oh, I hate it all so much! *(Pause)* Oh, how I've been cheated! I adored that professor, that miserable, gouty nonentity; I worked for him like a horse. Sonya and I squeezed the last penny out of the estate. Like greedy peasants we haggled over linseed oil, peas, curds, half starving ourselves to save up every farthing and send him thousands of rubles. I was proud of him and his learning. He was everything in the world to me. Everything he wrote, every word he uttered, seemed the highest achievement of genius to me. . . . Good God, and now? Now he has retired and now one can see what his life's work amounts to. He won't leave behind a single worthwhile page; he is a mere cipher—a soap bubble! And I have been cheated. I can see it now. Stupidly cheated. . . .

(Enter ASTROV, *without waistcoat and tie; he is tipsy; he is followed by* TELEGIN *with the guitar)*

ASTROV

Play!

TELEGIN

But everyone's asleep.

ASTROV

Play, damn you! *(*TELEGIN *begins to play softly. To* VOYNITSKY*)* All alone? No ladies? *(Arms akimbo, sings softly)* "Dance cottage, dance stove, dance bed, I've nowhere to lay my head. . . ." You see, the storm woke me. Lovely drop of rain. What's the time?

VOYNITSKY

Hanged if I know.

ASTROV

I thought I heard Helen's voice.

VOYNITSKY

She was here a minute ago.

ASTROV

A gorgeous woman. *(Examines bottles on table)* Medicines. Good Lord, look at these prescriptions! From Kharkov, from Moscow, from Tula . . . Every town must be sick and tired of his gout. Is he ill or is he shamming?

VOYNITSKY

He's ill.
    (Pause)

ASTROV

Why are you so down in the mouth today? Not sorry for the professor, are you?

VOYNITSKY

Leave me alone.

ASTROV

Or can it be that you're in love with the professor's wife?

VOYNITSKY

She's my friend.

ASTROV

Already?

VOYNITSKY

What do you mean—already?

ASTROV

A woman can be a man's friend in the following sequence: first a good companion, then a mistress, and only then a friend.

VOYNITSKY

What a vulgar idea!

ASTROV

Oh? Well, yes, I admit I'm growing vulgar. Bèsides, as you see, I'm drunk, too. As a rule, I get drunk like this once a month. When in this condition, I become as brazen and insolent as you please. I don't care a damn for anything then. I don't hesitate to do the most difficult operations, and I do them beautifully. I make the most ambitious plans for the future. At such a time I do not think of myself as a crank, and I believe that I'm being of enormous service to humanity—enormous! At such a time, too, I have my own special philosophic system, and all of you, my friends, seem to me such teeny-weeny insects—such microbes. *(To* TELEGIN*)* Play, Waffles!

TELEGIN

My dear chap, I'd be only too glad to play for you, but please understand—everyone's asleep!

ASTROV

Play, damn you! (TELEGIN *plays softly)* We really must have a drink. Come along, we've still got some brandy left. And as soon as it's daylight, we'll go to my place. All right? *(Seeing* SONYA *entering)* Excuse my dishabille.

(He goes out quickly; TELEGIN *follows after him)*

SONYA

And you have again got drunk with the doctor, Uncle Vanya. Birds of a feather. Thick as thieves. Oh, well, he's always like that, but what made you do it? At your age it certainly doesn't suit you.

VOYNITSKY

Age has nothing to do with it. When there's no real life, one has to live on illusions. It's better than nothing, anyway.

SONYA

The hay is all cut, it rains every day, it's all rotting, and you're amusing yourself with illusions. You don't care about the estate at all anymore. I'm the only one who does any work here, and I'm all done up. *(Alarmed)* Uncle, you have tears in your eyes.

VOYNITSKY

Tears? Not at all—nonsense. You looked at me just now as your mother used to do. My dear! *(Kisses her hands and face)* My sister, my dear, dear sister. . . . Where is she now? Oh, if she knew! If only she knew!

SONYA

What? Knew what, Uncle?

VOYNITSKY

Oh, I feel so miserable—so unhappy. . . . Never mind. . . . Later . . .
I'm going. . . . *(Goes out)*

SONYA *(Knocks on the door)*

Doctor, you're not asleep, are you? Please come out for a minute.

ASTROV *(Behind the door)*

One moment! *(A minute later comes out with waistcoat and tie on)*
What can I do for you?

SONYA

You can drink yourself if you don't think it's disgusting, but please
don't let my uncle drink. It's bad for him.

ASTROV

All right. We won't drink anymore. *(Pause)* Not a drop. I'm going
home now. By the time the horses are harnessed, it will be daylight.

SONYA

It's raining. Wait till morning.

ASTROV

The storm is passing over; we shall get only the tail end of it. I'm going.
And please don't send for me to see your father again. I tell him it's
gout, and he tells me it's rheumatism. I ask him to stay in bed, and he
will sit in a chair. And today he refused to talk to me at all.

SONYA

He's spoiled. *(Looks in the sideboard)* Won't you have something to
eat?

ASTROV

Thank you, I think I will.

SONYA

I like to have a bite of something at night. I think we shall find something
here. They say Father has been a great favorite with the ladies and
they've spoiled him. Here, have some cheese.
    (Both of them stand at the sideboard and eat)

ASTROV

I've had nothing to eat today. I've only been drinking. Your father is
a very difficult man. *(Takes a bottle from the sideboard)* May I? There's
no one here, so I can speak frankly. You know, I don't think I'd survive
a month in your house. The atmosphere would stifle me. Your father
can think of nothing but his gout and his books, Uncle Vanya with his

depressions, your grandmother, and last but not least, your step-mother. . . .

SONYA

What's wrong with my stepmother?

ASTROV

In a human being everything ought to be beautiful: face, dress, soul, thoughts. She is very beautiful, there's no denying it, but all she does is eat, sleep, go for walks, fascinate us all by her beauty and—nothing more. She has no duties. Other people work for her. Isn't that so? And an idle life cannot be pure. *(Pause)* However, I may be too hard on her. Like your Uncle Vanya, I'm dissatisfied with life, and both of us have become a pair of old grumblers.

SONYA

Are *you* dissatisfied with life?

ASTROV

I love life in general, but I simply can't stand our Russian provincial, philistine life. I have the utmost contempt for it. And as for my own personal life, I wish to goodness I could say there was something good in it. But there's absolutely nothing. You know, if there's only one glimmer of light in the distance as you walk through the woods on a dark night, you don't notice your weariness, nor the darkness, nor the thorns and twigs that strike your face as you pass. . . . I work harder than anyone in our district, fate is forever hitting out at me and some-times I suffer unbearably, but there's no light gleaming in the distance for me. I don't expect anything for myself anymore. I dislike people and it's years since I cared for anyone.

SONYA

Not for anyone?

ASTROV

No, not for anyone. I feel a certain affection only for your old nurse —for old times' sake. There doesn't seem to be much to distinguish one peasant from another. They're all uncivilized, and they all live in squalor; and I find it difficult to get on with our educated people. They make me tired. Our dear old friends all have petty minds and petty feelings, and they don't see farther than their noses. In fact, they are simply stupid. And those who are bigger and more intelligent are hys-terical, given to self-analysis and morbid introspection. They whine, hate, and slander each other, sidle up to a man, look at him askance, and decide: "He has a bee in his bonnet!" or "He's a windbag!" And when they don't know what label to stick on me, they say: "He's a queer fellow, a queer one!" I like forests, that's queer; I don't eat meat, that's queer, too. They no longer have a spontaneous, pure, and objective attitude to nature or to men. None whatever! (*Is about to drink*)

SONYA (*Prevents him*)
Don't, please. I beg you. Don't drink any more.

ASTROV
Why not?

SONYA
Because you're not that kind of man. You have such natural good manners, such a nice, gentle voice, and—and more than that. You're unlike anyone I know: You are—the salt of the earth! Why do you want to be like ordinary people, who drink and play cards? Oh, please, don't do it, I beseech you! You keep on saying that people do not create but only destroy what heaven has given them. Then why do you destroy yourself? You mustn't, you mustn't—I beseech you, I beg you!

ASTROV (*Holds out his hand to her*)
I won't drink any more.

SONYA
Give me your word.

ASTROV
My word of honor.

SONYA (*Presses his hand warmly*)
Thank you!

ASTROV
No more! I've come to my senses. You see I'm quite sober now, and I shall remain sober to the end of my days. (*Looks at his watch*) And so, let's continue. I say: My time is over, it's too late for me. . . . I've grown old, I've worked too hard, I've become vulgar, all my feelings have become blunted, and I don't think I could form an attachment to anyone any more. I don't love anyone and I don't think I shall ever love anyone. The only thing that still continues to exercise the strongest possible appeal on me is beauty. I can't remain indifferent to it. I can't help feeling that if, for example, Helen wanted to, she could turn my head in one day. . . . But then that's not love. That's not affection. (*Covers his eyes with his hands and shudders*)

SONYA

What's the matter?

ASTROV

Oh, nothing. . . . In Lent one of my patients died under chloroform.

SONYA

It's time you forgot about it. *(Pause)* Tell me, if—if I had a friend or a younger sister, and if you were to discover that—well, that she had fallen in love with you, what would your reaction be to that?

ASTROV *(Shrugging)*

Don't know. I'd give her to understand that I couldn't care for her and—er—that I had other things on my mind. Well, if I am to go, I must go now. Good-bye, my dear child, or we shall not finish till morning. *(Presses her hand)* I'll go through the drawing room, if I may. I'm afraid your uncle will detain me. *(Goes out)*

SONYA *(Alone)*

He has said nothing to me. . . . His heart and his mind are still hidden from me, but why do I feel so happy? *(Laughs happily)* I told him: You're fine, you're noble, you have such a gentle voice. . . . Shouldn't I have said that? His voice trembles, it is so caressing. I—I can still almost feel it in the air. But when I spoke to him about a younger sister, he didn't understand. . . . *(Wringing her hands)* Oh, how awful it is not to be beautiful! How awful! And I know that I'm not beautiful. I know. I know. Last Sunday when people were coming out of church, I heard them talking about me, and one woman said: "She's such a good and generous girl, but what a pity she is so plain." So plain . . .

(Enter YELENA*)*

YELENA *(Opens the window)*

The storm is over. What sweet air! *(Pause)* Where's the doctor?

SONYA

Gone.
(Pause)

YELENA

Sonya!

SONYA

Yes?

YELENA

How long are you going to be cross with me? We've done one another
no harm. Why should we be enemies? Don't you think it's time we
made it up?

SONYA

Oh, I've been wishing it myself. *(Embraces her)* Don't let's be cross
ever again.

YELENA

That's different.
    (Both are agitated)

SONYA

Has Father gone to bed?

YELENA

No, he's sitting in the drawing room. . . . You and I haven't been
speaking to one another for weeks, and goodness only knows why.
. . . *(Seeing that the sideboard is open)* What's this?

SONYA

The doctor has had something to eat.

YELENA

And there's wine, too. Come, let's drink to our friendship.

SONYA

Yes, let's.

YELENA

Out of one glass . . . *(Fills it)* That's better. Well, so now we're friends?

SONYA

Yes. *(They drink and kiss each other)* I've been wanting to make it up
with you for so long, but I felt ashamed somehow. *(Cries)*

YELENA

So what are you crying for?

SONYA

Oh, nothing. I—I can't help it.

YELENA

There, there. *(Cries)* Oh, dear, I'm so silly, I'm crying, too. *(Pause)*
You're angry with me because you think I married your father for
selfish reasons. But please believe me, I swear I married him for love.
I fell in love with him because he was such a famous man. It was not

real love. It was all so insincere, so artificial, but, you see, it seemed real to me at the time. It's not my fault. And since our marriage you have never stopped accusing me with those clever, suspicious eyes of yours.

SONYA

Well, we've made it up now, so let's forget it.

YELENA

You mustn't look at people like that—it's not at all like you. One must trust people, or life becomes impossible.
   (Pause)

SONYA

Tell me honestly, as a friend—are you happy?

YELENA

No, I'm not.

SONYA

I knew that. One more question. Tell me frankly. Don't you wish your husband were young?

YELENA

What a child you are! Of course I do! *(Laughs)* Well, ask me another one—come on.

SONYA

Do you like the doctor?

YELENA

Yes, I like him very much.

SONYA *(Laughs)*

I have such a silly look on my face, haven't I? You see, he's gone, but I can still hear his voice and his footsteps, and I have only to look at the dark window and I see his face. Do let me tell you more about it. . . . But I can't speak so loud—I feel ashamed. Let's go to my room and talk there. Do you think I'm being silly? Tell me truly. Tell me something about him.

YELENA

What do you want me to tell you?

SONYA

Well, he's clever—he knows everything—he can do everything. . . . He's not only a doctor, he plants forests, too.

YELENA

It's not only a question of forests or medicine. My dear, don't you understand? It's his genius that matters! And do you know what that means? Courage, an independent mind, bold initiative . . . He plants a tree and already he's thinking what will be the result of it in a thousand years. Already he's dreaming of the happiness of humanity. . . . Such people are rare; one must love them. . . . He drinks and occasionally he is a little coarse, but what does that matter? A gifted man cannot keep himself entirely spotless in Russia. Just think what sort of life the doctor has! Muddy, impassable roads, frosts, blizzards, enormous distances, coarse, savage peasants, widespread poverty, diseases—how can you expect a man of forty to have kept himself sober and spotless working and struggling like that, day in, day out, and in such surroundings? *(Kisses her)* I wish you all the happiness in the world, my dear—you deserve it. *(Gets up)* As for me, I'm just a tiresome character—an episodic character. . . . In my music, in my husband's house, in all my love affairs—everywhere, in fact—I was only an episodic character. Come to think of it, Sonya, and I mean it seriously, I'm very, very unhappy. *(Paces up and down the stage in agitation)* There's no happiness for me in this world—none whatever! What are you laughing at?

SONYA *(Laughs, hiding her face)*

I'm so happy—so happy!

YELENA

I'd like to have some music. I'd like to play something.

SONYA

Yes, do! *(Embraces her)* I don't feel like going to bed. Please play!

YELENA

I will in a moment. Your father isn't asleep. Music irritates him when he is not well. Go and ask him if I may. If he agrees, I'll play. Go on.

SONYA

All right. *(Goes out)*
    (The watchman is knocking in the garden)

YELENA

I haven't played for ages. I'll play and cry, cry like a fool. *(In the window)* Is that you, Yefim?

VOICE OF WATCHMAN

Yes, ma'am, it's me.

YELENA

Don't knock, the master's ill.

VOICE OF WATCHMAN

All right, ma'am. I'll be on my way now. *(Whistles)* Here, good dog. Here, lad! Good dog!

  (Pause)

SONYA *(Returning)*

No!

ACT THREE

(Drawing room in SEREBRYAKOV's *house. Three doors: one on the right, one on the left, and one in the middle. Daytime.*

  VOYNITSKY *and* SONYA *seated, and* YELENA *pacing up and down the stage, deep in thought about something)*

VOYNITSKY

The Herr Professor has been so good as to express the wish that we should meet him in this room at one o'clock today. *(Looks at his watch)* It's a quarter to one. He wishes to make some communication to the world.

YELENA

I suppose it's some business matter.

VOYNITSKY

He has no business matters. All he does is write rubbish, grumble, and be jealous. Nothing else.

SONYA *(In a reproachful voice)*

Uncle!

VOYNITSKY

All right, all right, I'm sorry. *(Motioning toward* YELENA*)* Look at her: a sight for the gods! Walks about, swaying lazily. Very charming! Very!

YELENA

You sit there buzzing and buzzing all day long—aren't you sick of it? *(Miserably)* I'm bored to death. I don't know what to do.

SONYA *(Shrugging)*

There's plenty to do if you really wanted to.

YELENA

For instance?

SONYA

You could do some of the work on the estate. You could teach. You could take up nursing. Plenty of things you could do. When Father and you weren't here, Uncle Vanya and I used to go to the market and sell flour.

YELENA

I'm afraid I'm not much good at that sort of thing. And besides, it's not interesting. It's only in serious novels that people teach and nurse sick peasants. How on earth do you expect me to become a nurse or a teacher just like that?

SONYA

Well, and I just can't understand how one can refuse to go and teach the peasants. You wait. You'll soon be doing it yourself. *(Puts her arm around her)* Don't be bored, my dear. *(Laughing)* You're bored, you don't know what to do with yourself, and boredom and idleness are catching. Look: Uncle Vanya does nothing but follow you about like a shadow. I've left my work and come to talk to you. Oh, dear, I've grown lazy, and the worst of it is, I can't help it! Dr. Astrov used to come and see us very rarely before—once a month. It was difficult to coax him into coming. But now he's here every day. Neglects his forests and his patients. You must be a witch.

VOYNITSKY

Why are you in such a state? *(Eagerly)* Come, my dear, my precious one, be sensible! You have mermaid blood in your veins—well, then, be a mermaid! Let yourself go for once in your life: Fall head over ears in love with some water goblin, plunge headlong into the whirlpool with him, and leave the Herr Professor and all of us gasping with surprise.

YELENA *(Angrily)*

Leave me alone! How can you be so cruel? *(Is about to go out)*

VOYNITSKY *(Barring her way)*

Come, come, my sweet, forgive me. I'm sorry. *(Kisses her hand)* Peace.

YELENA

You must admit, you'd try the patience of a saint.

VOYNITSKY

As a sign of peace and harmony, I'll fetch you a bunch of roses. I gathered them for you this morning. Autumn roses: so sad and so lovely . . . *(Goes out)*

SONYA

Autumn roses: so sad and so lovely . . .
   (Both look out of the window)

YELENA

September already. How are we going to live through the winter here? *(Pause)* Where's the doctor?

SONYA

In Uncle Vanya's room. He's writing something. I'm glad Uncle Vanya has gone out. I want to talk to you.

YELENA

What about?

SONYA

What about? *(Lays her head on YELENA's bosom)*

YELENA

There—there. *(Stroking her head)* There. . . .

SONYA

I'm not beautiful!

YELENA

You have beautiful hair.

SONYA

No! *(Turning her head to have a look at herself in the looking glass)* No! When a woman is not good-looking, she's told: You've beautiful eyes, you've beautiful hair. I've loved him for six years. I love him more than my own mother. Every minute I can hear his voice, feel the touch of his hand. I keep looking at the door and waiting—expecting him to come in. And—well—you see, I always come running to you to talk about him. Now he's here every day, but he doesn't look at me—doesn't see me. Oh, I can't bear it! I have no hope—no hope at all! *(In despair)* Oh, God, give me strength. . . . I've been praying all night. . . . I often go up to him, begin talking to him, look into his eyes. . . . I've lost all my pride, I've lost control over my feelings. . . . I told Uncle Vanya yesterday that I loved him. Couldn't help myself. And all the servants know that I love him. Everybody knows.

YELENA

Does he?

SONYA

No. He doesn't notice me.

YELENA *(Pondering)*

He's a strange man. . . . Look, why not let me talk to him? I'll be very careful—just a hint. *(Pause)* Honestly, how much longer are you to remain uncertain? Please, let me. (SONYA *nods)* That's settled then. It won't be difficult to find out whether he loves you or not. Don't worry, darling. Don't be uneasy. I'll sound him out so discreetly that he won't even notice it. All we have to find out is—yes or no. *(Pause)* If it's no, then he'd better stop coming here. Don't you think so? (SONYA *nods)* It would be much better not to see him. It's no use putting it off; I shall question him right away. He promised to show me some maps. Go and tell him that I want to see him.

SONYA *(In violent agitation)*

You will tell me the whole truth, won't you?

YELENA

Yes, of course. I can't help thinking that truth, however unpalatable, is not so dreadful as uncertainty. You can rely on me, my dear.

SONYA

Yes, yes. . . . I'll tell him that you want to see his maps. *(Is going but stops at the door)* No, uncertainty is much better. . . . At least, there's hope. . . .

YELENA

What did you say?

SONYA

Nothing. *(Goes out)*

YELENA *(Alone)*

There's nothing worse than knowing somebody else's secret and being unable to help. *(Musing)* He's not in love with her—that's clear—but why shouldn't he marry her? She's not good-looking, but for a country doctor at his age she'll make a splendid wife. She's so intelligent, so kind, and so pure-minded. . . . No, no, that's not the point. *(Pause)* I understand the poor child. In the midst of so much desperate boredom, living among walking gray shadows instead of men and women, listening to vulgar talk of people whose only aim in life is to eat, drink, and sleep; and here's a man who is so unlike the others: handsome, interesting, fascinating—like a bright moon rising in the darkness. To fall under the spell of such a man, to forget oneself . . . I believe I'm a little in love with him myself. Yes, I certainly feel bored when he's not here. I find myself smiling when I think of him. That Uncle Vanya says I've mermaid blood in my veins. "Let yourself go for once in your life. . . ." Well, why not? Perhaps that's what I really ought to do. Oh, if I could fly away like a bird from you all, from your somnolent faces, from your talk—forget your very existence! But I'm timid, cowardly. . . . My conscience will not let me rest. . . . He comes here every day, and I can guess why he's here, and already I've got a guilty feeling. I'm ready to throw myself on my knees before Sonya and beg her to forgive me.

ASTROV *(Comes in with a map of the district)*

How do you do? *(Shakes hands with her)* You wanted to see my drawings?

YELENA

You promised yesterday to show me your work. Can you spare the time?

ASTROV

Yes, of course. *(Spreads the map on a card table and fastens it with drawing pins)* Where were you born?

YELENA *(Helping him)*

In Petersburg.

ASTROV

And where did you study?

YELENA

At the conservatoire.

ASTROV

I'm afraid you won't find this interesting.

YELENA

Why not? It's true I don't know anything about country life, but I've read a lot about it.

ASTROV

I have my own table in this house. In Vanya's room. When I'm thoroughly exhausted, to the point of stupor, I leave everything and run over here and amuse myself for an hour or two with this. Vanya and Sonya click away at their counting frame, and I sit beside them at my

table daubing—and I feel warm and cozy, and the cricket keeps singing.
. . . But I don't allow myself to indulge in this pleasant pastime too
often—only once a month. *(Pointing to the map)* Now, look here. This
is a picture of our district as it was fifty years ago. The dark and light
green show the forests: half of the whole area was covered with forest.
Where those red lines crisscross each other over the green, elks and
wild goats used to roam. . . . I show both the flora and the fauna here.
On this lake there were swans, geese, and ducks and, according to the
old people, "a power" of all sorts of birds, thousands of them, clouds
of them flying about. Besides the villages and hamlets, as you can see,
little settlements were dotted about here and there, small farms, hermitages of Old Believers, water mills. . . . There were lots of cattle and
horses. It's all shown in blue. Now, for instance, in this small administrative area, comprising only a few farmsteads, there's a thick smudge
of blue: There were whole droves of horses here, and every homestead
had on the average three horses. *(Pause)* Now look lower down. That's
what the district was like twenty-five years ago. There was only a third
of the area under timber. There are no wild goats, but there are still
some elk left. The blue and green colors are paler. And so on. Now
let's have a look at the third section. This is the map of the district as
it is now. There are still bits of green here and there, but only in small
patches. The elk, the swans, and the wood grouse have disappeared.
There's no trace left of the old settlements and farms and hermitages
and water mills. It is, as a matter of fact, a picture of gradual and
unmistakable degeneration, which, I suppose, will be complete in another ten or fifteen years. You may say this shows the influence of
civilization, that the old life must naturally give way to the new. Well,
I admit that if there were high roads and railways on the site of these
ruined forests, if factories, workshops, and schools were built there,
the common people would be healthier, better off, and more intelligent.
But there's nothing of the kind here! There are still the same swamps
and mosquitoes, the same impassable roads, the same poverty, typhus,
diphtheria, and the same outbreaks of fire. It is, I'm afraid, a case of
degeneration as a result of too severe a struggle for existence. A degeneration caused by apathy, ignorance, and the complete absence of
a sense of responsibility. The sort of thing a cold, hungry, and sick
man does to save what is left of his life and to keep his children alive
when he clutches instinctively and unconsciously at anything that will
warm him and relieve his hunger, and destroys everything without
thinking of the future. Nearly everything has been destroyed already,
but nothing has yet been created to take its place. *(Coldly)* I can see
from your face that this doesn't interest you.

YELENA

I'm afraid I understand so little about it.

ASTROV

There's nothing to understand. You're simply not interested.

YELENA

To tell the truth, I was thinking of something else. I'm sorry. I ought to put you through a little interrogation, and I'm not quite sure how to begin.

ASTROV

An interrogation?

YELENA

Yes, an interrogation, but—a rather harmless one. Let's sit down. *(They sit down)* It concerns a certain young lady. We will talk like honest people, like good friends, without beating about the bush. We'll have our talk and then forget all about it. Agreed?

ASTROV

Agreed.

YELENA

What I want to talk to you about is my stepdaughter, Sonya. Do you like her?

ASTROV

Yes, I think highly of her.

YELENA

But do you like her as a woman?

ASTROV *(After a short pause)*

No.

YELENA

A few words more and I've done. You've noticed nothing?

ASTROV

No.

YELENA *(Taking him by the hand)*

You don't love her. I can see it from your eyes. She's terribly unhappy. Please understand that and—stop coming here.

ASTROV *(Gets up)*

I'm afraid I'm too old for this sort of thing. I have no time for it, anyway. *(Shrugging)* When could I . . . ? *(He looks embarrassed)*

YELENA

Oh, dear, what an unpleasant conversation! I'm shaking all over just as though I'd been dragging a ton weight. Well, thank goodness, that's over. Let's forget it just as though we'd never spoken about it, and please go away. You're an intelligent man. You'll understand. *(Pause)* Goodness, I'm hot all over.

ASTROV

If you'd told me that two or three months ago, I might perhaps have considered it, but now . . . *(Shrugs)* But if she's unhappy, then of course . . . There's one thing I can't understand, though. What made you undertake this interrogation? *(Looks into her eyes and shakes a finger at her)* You're a sly one!

YELENA

What do you mean?

ASTROV *(Laughing)*

A sly one! Suppose Sonya is unhappy. I'm quite ready to admit it, but what did you want this interrogation for? *(Not letting her speak, eagerly)* Please don't look so surprised. You know perfectly well why I'm here every day. Why I am here and who brings me here. You know that perfectly well. You sweet little beast of prey, don't look at me like that! I'm an old hand at this sort of game.

YELENA *(Bewildered)*

Beast of prey? I don't know what you're talking about.

ASTROV

A beautiful, furry little beast of prey. . . . You must have your victims. Here I've dropped everything and done nothing for a whole month. I'm mad with desire for you, and you're awfully pleased about it—awfully! Well, I'm conquered. You knew that even before your interrogation. *(Folding his arms and bowing his head)* I surrender. Come and eat me up!

YELENA

You're crazy!

ASTROV *(Laughs through his teeth)*

And you are—afraid. . . .

YELENA

Oh, I'm much better and more honorable than you think, I assure you!
(Tries to go out)

ASTROV *(Barring her way)*

I'm going away today. I won't come here again, but—*(Takes her hand
and looks around)* tell me: Where can we meet? Where? Tell me quickly.
Someone may come in. Tell me quickly. *(Passionately)* Oh, you're so
beautiful, so lovely. . . . One kiss. . . . Let me just kiss your fragrant
hair. . . .

YELENA

I assure you—

ASTROV *(Not letting her speak)*

Why assure me? There's no need. No need of unnecessary
words. . . . Oh, how beautiful you are! What lovely hands! *(Kisses her
hands)*

YELENA

That's enough—go away, please. *(Takes her hands away)* You're forgetting yourself.

ASTROV

But tell me, tell me, where shall we meet tomorrow? *(Puts his hand
around her waist)* Darling, you see it's inevitable. We must meet.
      (He kisses her; at that moment VOYNITSKY *enters with a bunch of
roses and stops dead at the door)*

YELENA *(Not seeing* VOYNITSKY*)*

For pity's sake let me go. . . . *(Puts her head on* ASTROV's *chest)* No!
(Tries to go out)

ASTROV *(Holding her back by the waist)*

Come to the plantation tomorrow—at two o'clock. . . . Yes? Yes?
Darling, you will come, won't you?

YELENA *(Seeing* VOYNITSKY*)*

Let me go! *(In great confusion goes to the window)* This is awful!

VOYNITSKY *(Puts down the bunch of flowers on a chair; agitatedly
wipes his face and his neck with his handkerchief)*
It's all right—yes—it's quite all right. . . .

ASTROV *(Trying to brazen it out)*

Not a bad day today, my dear sir. A bit cloudy in the morning, looked
like rain, but it's nice and sunny now. . . . To be quite fair, we haven't

had such a bad autumn this year—the winter rye isn't too bad at all. *(Rolls up the map)* There's one thing, though: The days are drawing in. . . . *(Goes out)*

YELENA *(Goes quickly up to* VOYNITSKY*)*

You must see to it; you must do your utmost to arrange that my husband and I leave here today. Do you hear? Today!

VOYNITSKY *(Wiping his face)*

What? Why, yes, of course. . . . I saw it all, Helen, all. . . .

YELENA *(Tensely)*

You understand? I must get away from here today—today! *(Enter* SEREBRYAKOV, SONYA, TELEGIN, *and* MARINA*)*

TELEGIN

I'm afraid, sir, I am not feeling very well myself. Been out of sorts for the last two days. My head's not quite—

SEREBRYAKOV

Where are the others? I hate this house. It's a sort of labyrinth. Twenty-six huge rooms, people are all over the place, and you can never find anyone you want. *(Rings)* Ask my mother-in-law and my wife to come here.

YELENA

I am here.

SEREBRYAKOV

Please sit down, everybody.

SONYA *(going up to* YELENA, *impatiently)*

Well, what did he say?

YELENA

I'll tell you later.

SONYA

You're trembling? You're agitated? *(Looks searchingly at her)* I see. . . . He said he won't come here again. . . . Yes? *(Pause)* Tell me—yes?

(YELENA nods)

SEREBRYAKOV *(To* TELEGIN*)*

I don't mind ill health so much—after all, one can't help that, can one?—what I can't stand is the way people live in the country. I have a feeling as though I've dropped off the earth and landed on a strange planet. Sit down, please, all of you. Sonya! *(SONYA does not hear him; she stands with her head bowed sorrowfully)* Sonya! *(Pause)* She doesn't hear. *(To MARINA)* You, too, Nurse, sit down. *(The nurse sits down, knitting a sock)* Now, if you please, suspend, as it were, your ears on the nail of attention. *(Laughs)*

VOYNITSKY *(Agitated)*
You don't want me here, do you? Do you mind if I go?

SEREBRYAKOV
Yes, it's you I want here most of all.

VOYNITSKY
What do you want with me, sir?

SEREBRYAKOV
Sir? Why are you so cross? *(Pause)* If I'm to blame for anything I did to you, then I'm deeply sorry.

VOYNITSKY
Drop that tone. Let's get down to business. . . . What do you want?
   (Enter MARIA VOYNITSKY)

SEREBRYAKOV
Ah, here's Mother-in-law at last. Now I can begin. *(Pause)* I have invited you here, ladies and gentlemen, to announce that the government inspector is about to pay us a visit.* However, this is no time for joking. This is a serious matter. I've invited you here to ask for your help and advice, and knowing your unfailing kindness, I feel sure that I shall receive both. I am a scholar; I have spent all my life among books and have always been a stranger to practical affairs. I cannot dispense with the assistance of people who've had practical experience of business, and I beg you, Ivan, you, Mr. Telegin, and you, Mother-in-law—er— You see, what I'm driving at is that *manet omnes una nox;* I mean, that we are all in God's hands. . . . I'm old and ill, and so I think that the time has come when I ought to settle my worldly affairs in so far as they concern my family. My life's over, I'm not thinking of myself. But I have a young wife and an unmarried daughter. *(Pause)* I'm afraid I cannot possibly go on living in the country. We are not made for country life. On the other hand, to live in town on the income we derive from this estate is impossible. If, for instance, we were to sell the woods, it's just an emergency measure that cannot be repeated

---

* A jocular allusion to the famous last scene in Gogol's comedy *The Inspector General.*

every year. We have, therefore, to look for some means that would ensure us a permanent and more or less stable income. I have thought of one such scheme, and I shall be glad to submit it for your consideration. Leaving aside the details, I shall give you a general idea of it. Our estate returns on average not more than two percent of its capital value. I propose to sell it. By investing the money in gilt-edged securities, we should get from four to five percent. I think there might be even a surplus of a few thousand, which will enable us to buy a small country house in Finland.

VOYNITSKY

One moment. . . . I think my ears must be deceiving me. Repeat what you've said.

SEREBRYAKOV

Invest the money in gilt-edged securities and use the surplus to buy a small country house in Finland.

VOYNITSKY

Never mind Finland. There was something else you said.

SEREBRYAKOV

I propose to sell the estate.

VOYNITSKY

Yes, that's it. You're going to sell the estate. That's rich! An excellent idea! And how do you propose to dispose of me and my old mother and Sonya here?

SEREBRYAKOV

We shall discuss it all in good time. You don't expect me to settle everything at once, do you?

VOYNITSKY

One moment. It seems to me that up to now I haven't shown a grain of common sense. Up to now I've been fool enough to believe that the estate belonged to Sonya. My father bought this estate as a dowry for my sister. Up to now I've been so naive as to believe that our laws were not made in Turkey and that the estate passed from my sister to Sonya.

SEREBRYAKOV

Yes, the estate belongs to Sonya. I'm not disputing it. Without Sonya's consent I shouldn't dream of selling it. Besides, I'm proposing to do it for Sonya's benefit.

VOYNITSKY

It's beyond everything—beyond everything! Either I've gone stark staring mad, or—

MARIA

Don't contradict Aleksandr, Jean. Believe me, he knows much better than you or me what's good and what isn't.

VOYNITSKY

No, he doesn't! Give me some water, please. *(Drinks water)* Say what you like, what you like!

SEREBRYAKOV

I don't understand why you're so upset. I don't say that my plan is ideal. If all of you think it's no good, I will not insist on it.
  (Pause)

TELEGIN *(Looking embarrassed)*

I've always had a great reverence for learning, sir, and if I may say so, my feelings for it have a certain family connection. You see, sir, my brother's wife's brother, Konstantin Lacedaemonov, as you perhaps know, is an M.A.

VOYNITSKY

Just a moment, Waffles, we're discussing business. Wait a little—later. . . . *(To* SEREBRYAKOV*)* Just ask him. The estate was bought from his uncle.

SEREBRYAKOV

Why should I ask him? Whatever for?

VOYNITSKY

The estate was bought at the prices current at the time for ninety-five thousand. My father paid only seventy thousand and twenty-five thousand remained on mortgage. Now, listen . . . this estate would not have been bought if I hadn't given up my share in the inheritance in favor of my sister, whom I loved dearly. What's more, for ten years I've worked like a horse and paid off all the mortgage.

SEREBRYAKOV

I'm sorry I ever started this discussion.

VOYNITSKY

The estate is clear of debt and is in good order thanks only to my own personal exertions. And now, when I'm beginning to get old, I'm to be kicked out of it!

SEREBRYAKOV
I don't see what you're getting at.

VOYNITSKY
I've been managing this estate for twenty-five years. I've worked and
sent you the money like a most conscientious agent, and not once during
all that time has it occurred to you to thank me. All that time—both
when I was young and now—I've received from you five hundred rubles
a year in salary, a mere pittance! And not once did it occur to you to
add a ruble to it!

SEREBRYAKOV
My dear fellow, how was I to know? I'm not a practical man and I
don't understand anything about these things. You could have increased
your salary by as much as you pleased.

VOYNITSKY
You mean, why didn't I steal? Why don't you all despise me because
I didn't steal? That would be only fair, and I shouldn't have been a
pauper now!

MARIA *(Sternly)*
Jean!

TELEGIN
Vanya, my dear chap, don't—don't—I'm trembling all over. . . . Why
spoil good relations? *(Kisses him)* Please, don't.

VOYNITSKY
For twenty-five years I sat like a mole within these four walls with this
mother of mine. All our thoughts and feelings belonged to you alone.
By day we talked about you and your work. We were proud of you.
We uttered your name with reverence. We wasted our nights reading
books and periodicals for which I have now the utmost contempt!

TELEGIN
Don't, Vanya, don't. . . . I can't stand it.

SEREBRYAKOV *(Angrily)*
What is it you want?

VOYNITSKY
We looked upon you as a being of a higher order, and we knew your
articles by heart. . . . But now my eyes are opened. I see it all. You
write about art, but you don't understand a thing about art. All those

works of yours that I used to love aren't worth a brass farthing! You've humbugged us!

SEREBRYAKOV
Won't any one of you stop him? I—I'm going!

YELENA
Be silent, Vanya! I insist. Do you hear?

VOYNITSKY
I won't be silent! *(Stopping in front of* SEREBRYAKOV *and barring his way)* Wait, I haven't finished! You've ruined my life! I haven't lived! I haven't lived at all! Thanks to you I've wasted, destroyed, the best years of my life! You're my worst enemy!

TELEGIN
I can't stand it—I can't.... I'm going.... *(Goes out in great agitation)*

SEREBRYAKOV
What do you want from me? And what right have you to talk to me like this? Nonentity! If the estate is yours, take it! I don't want it!

YELENA
I shall run away from this hell this very minute! *(Screams)* I can't stand it any longer!

VOYNITSKY
My life's ruined! I'm gifted, I'm intelligent, I have courage. . . . If I had lived a normal life, I might have been a Schopenhauer, a Dostoyevsky—but I'm talking nonsense! I'm going mad. Mother, I'm in despair! Mother!

MARIA *(Sternly)*
Do as Aleksandr tells you!

SONYA *(Kneels before* MARINA *and clings to her)*
Darling Nanny! Darling Nanny!

VOYNITSKY
Mother, what am I to do? Oh, never mind, don't tell me! I know myself what I must do. *(To* SEREBRYAKOV*)* You will not forget me in a hurry! *(Goes out through middle door)*
  *(*MARIA *follows him)*

SEREBRYAKOV
This is really going a bit too far! Take that lunatic away! I can't live under the same roof as he. He's always there *(Points to the middle*

door), almost beside me. . . . Let him move into the village or to the cottage on the grounds, or I will move myself, but stay in the same house as he, I cannot!

YELENA *(To her husband)*
We're leaving this place today! We must make all the arrangements at once.

SEREBRYAKOV
An utter nonentity!

SONYA *(On her knees, turns to her father, talking excitedly)*
You must be charitable, Father! Uncle Vanya and I are so unhappy! *(Restraining her despair)* One must be charitable! Remember how, when you were younger, Uncle Vanya and Granny sat up all night translating books for you, copying your papers—they used to do it every night, every night! Uncle Vanya and I worked without a moment's rest, afraid to spend a penny on ourselves, and sent it all to you. . . . We earned our keep! I'm sorry, I seem to be saying it all wrong, but you must understand us, Father. One must be charitable!

YELENA *(Agitatedly, to her husband)*
For heaven's sake, Aleksandr, go and talk it over with him. . . . I beg you.

SEREBRYAKOV
Very well, I'll have a talk with him. I'm not accusing him of anything, and I'm not angry. But you must admit that, to say the least, his behavior is extraordinary. Very well, I'll go to him. *(Goes out through middle door)*

YELENA
Be gentle with him. Try to calm him. *(Follows him)*

SONYA *(Clinging to nurse)*
Darling Nanny! Darling Nanny!

MARINA
Don't worry, child. The ganders will gaggle and get tired of it. Gaggle and—get tired of it.

SONYA
Darling Nanny!

MARINA *(Stroking her head)*
You're trembling as though you were out in the frost. There, there, my orphan child, the Lord's merciful. A cup of lime tea or raspberry tea,

and it will pass. . . . Don't grieve, child. . . . *(Looking at the middle door, angrily)* What a row these ganders make, drat 'em! *(A shot behind the scenes; a shriek is heard from* YELENA; SONYA *shudders)* Oh, drat 'em!

SEREBRYAKOV *(Runs staggering in, looking terrified)*
Stop him! Stop him! He's gone mad!
*(*YELENA *and* VOYNITSKY *struggle in the doorway)*

YELENA *(Trying to snatch the revolver away from him)*
Give it to me! Give it to me, I tell you!

VOYNITSKY
Let go of me, Helen! Let go of me! *(Freeing himself, runs in and looks for* SEREBRYAKOV*)* Where is he? Ah, there he is! *(Fires at him)* Bang! *(Pause)* Missed him! Missed him again! *(Furiously)* Oh, damn, damn, damn! *(Bangs revolver on the floor and sinks exhausted into a chair)*
*(*SEREBRYAKOV *is stunned;* YELENA *leans against the wall, almost fainting)*

YELENA
Take me away from here! Take me away—kill me. . . . I can't stay here. . . . I can't!

VOYNITSKY *(In despair)*
Oh, what am I doing! What am I doing!

SONYA *(Softly)*
Darling Nanny! Darling Nanny!

ACT FOUR

VOYNITSKY'S *room; it is his bedroom as well as the estate office. At the window, a large table with account books and all sorts of papers, a bureau, cupboards, scales. A smaller table for* ASTROV *with paints and drawing materials; beside it, a portfolio. A cage with a starling in it. On the wall, a map of Africa, apparently of no use to anyone. An enormous sofa covered with American cloth. On the left, a door leading to the inner rooms; on the right, a door leading into the hall; near the door on the right, a doormat for the peasants to wipe their feet on.*

An autumn evening. All is quiet. TELEGIN *and* MARINA *sit facing each other, winding wool.*

TELEGIN

You'd better hurry up, Marina, or they'll soon be calling us to say good-bye. The carriage has already been ordered.

MARINA *(Trying to wind more rapidly)*

There's not much more of it left.

TELEGIN

They're going to Kharkov. They're going to live there.

MARINA

So much the better.

TELEGIN

Got scared. Helen keeps saying, "I won't stay here another hour—let's go—let's go at once. In Kharkov," she says, "we'll have a good look around and then send for our things." They're not taking many things with them. So it seems, Marina, they're not going to stay here. No, they're not. A divine dispensation of Providence.

MARINA

So much the better. All that row this morning, shooting and God knows what—the disgrace of it!

TELEGIN

Yes, a subject worthy of the brush of Ayvazovsky.

MARINA

Never seen the like of it before. *(Pause)* We'll live again as we used to do in the old days. Tea at eight o'clock in the morning, dinner at one, and sit down to supper in the evening. Everything as it should be, like other folk, like good Christians. *(With a sigh)* Haven't tasted noodles for a long time, sinner that I am.

TELEGIN

Aye, it's a very long time since we've had noodles for dinner. *(Pause)* A long time. As I was walking through the village this morning, Marina, the shopkeeper shouted after me, "Hey, you, sponger!" It made me feel bad, I can tell you.

MARINA

You shouldn't take any notice of that, dear. We're all spongers in the sight of God. You, Sonya, the master—none of us sits about doing nothing. We all work hard, we do. All of us. Where is Sonya?

TELEGIN

In the garden. Still going around with the doctor looking for Vanya.
They're afraid he may lay hands on himself.

MARINA

And where's his pistol?

TELEGIN (*In a whisper*)

I've hidden it in the cellar!

MARINA (*With a smile*)

Such goings-on!
    (VOYNITSKY *and* ASTROV *come in from outside*)

VOYNITSKY

Leave me alone. (*To* MARINA *and* TELEGIN) And you, too, please go.
Can't I be left alone for a single hour? I hate being kept under
observation.

TELEGIN

I'll go at once, Vanya. (*Goes out on tiptoe*)

MARINA

Look at the gander: ga-ga-ga! (*Gathers her wool and goes out*)

VOYNITSKY

Won't you go?

ASTROV

With the greatest of pleasure. I ought to have gone long ago, but I tell
you again, I won't go till you give me back what you took from me.

VOYNITSKY

I took nothing from you.

ASTROV

Seriously, don't detain me. I ought to have gone hours ago.

VOYNITSKY

I tell you, I took nothing from you.
    (*Both sit down*)

ASTROV

No? Well, I'll give you a little longer, and I hope you won't mind too
much if I have to use force then. We'll tie you up and search you. I'm
quite serious about it, I tell you.

VOYNITSKY

As you please! *(Pause)* To have made such a fool of myself: fired twice and missed him! That I shall never forgive myself!

ASTROV

If you're so keen on shooting people, why don't you go and shoot yourself?

VOYNITSKY *(Shrugs)*

Here I make an attempt to commit muder, and no one thinks of arresting me and putting me on trial. Which, of course, can only mean that I'm regarded as a madman. *(With a bitter laugh)* It is I who am mad but not those who hide their stupidity, their mediocrity, and their flagrant heartlessness under the mask of a professor, a learned pundit. Those who marry old men and then deceive them under the eyes of everyone are not mad—oh, no! I saw you kissing her! I saw!

ASTROV

Yes, I did kiss her, and be damned to you!

VOYNITSKY *(Glancing at the door)*

No, it's the earth that's mad to let such people as you go on living on it.

ASTROV

That's a damned silly thing to say.

VOYNITSKY

Well, I'm mad, I'm not responsible for my actions, so I have a right to say damned silly things.

ASTROV

That's an old trick. You're not mad. You're just a crank. A damned fool. Before, I used to regard every crank as a mental case, as abnormal, but now I've come to the conclusion that it is the normal condition of a man to be a crank. You're quite normal.

VOYNITSKY *(Buries his face in his hands)*

Oh, the shame of it! Oh, if only you knew how ashamed I am! No pain can be compared with this acute feeling of shame. *(Miserably)* It's unbearable! *(Bends over the table)* What am I to do? What am I to do?

ASTROV

Nothing.

VOYNITSKY

Give me something! Oh, God! I'm forty-seven; if I live to be sixty, I have another thirteen years. It's devilishly long! How can I live through those thirteen years? What shall I do? What shall I fill them with? You see *(Squeezing* ASTROV'*s hand convulsively)*, you see, if only you could live what is left of your life in some new way. Wake up on a still, sunny morning and feel that you've begun your life all over again, that all your past was forgotten, vanished like a puff of smoke. *(Weeps)* To begin a new life. . . . Tell me how to begin it—what to begin it with.

ASTROV *(With vexation)*

Oh, you and your new life! A new life indeed! My dear fellow, our position—yours and mine—is hopeless.

VOYNITSKY

Are you sure?

ASTROV

I'm quite sure of it.

VOYNITSKY

Give me something. . . . *(Pointing to his heart)* I've a burning pain here.

ASTROV *(Shouts angrily)*

Stop it! *(Softening)* Those who will live a hundred or two hundred years after us and who will despise us for living such damned stupid, such insipid lives, will perhaps discover a way of being happy. But as for us . . . there's only one hope left for you and me, one hope only. The hope that when we are at rest in our graves, we may, perhaps, be visited by visions that will not be unpleasant. *(With a sigh)* Yes, old man, in the whole of this district there were only two decent, intelligent men, you and I. But in the course of some ten years this humdrum, this rotten life has worn us down. Its foul vapors have poisoned our blood, and we've become just as vulgar as the rest. *(Eagerly)* But don't you try to put me off! Give me what you took from me.

VOYNITSKY

I took nothing from you.

ASTROV

Yes, you did. You took a bottle of morphia out of my traveling medicine case. *(Pause)* Look here, if you've really made up your mind to make an end of yourself, why don't you go into the woods and blow your brains out? But you must give me back my morphia or else people will

start talking, putting two and two together, and end up by saying that
I gave it to you. . . . It will be quite enough if I have to do your
postmortem. You don't suppose I shall enjoy that, do you?
   (Enter SONYA*)*

VOYNITSKY

Leave me alone.

ASTROV *(To* SONYA*)*

Your uncle has filched a bottle of morphia from my medicine case, and
he refuses to give it back. Tell him that it's—well, not very clever.
Besides, I'm in a hurry. I ought to be going.

SONYA

Uncle Vanya, did you take the morphia?
   (Pause)

ASTROV

He did. I'm certain of it.

SONYA

Give it back. Why do you frighten us? *(Tenderly)* Give it back, Uncle
Vanya! I may be just as unhappy as you, but I don't give way to despair.
I can bear it and I shall go on bearing it until my life comes to its
natural end. You must bear it, too. *(Pause)* Give it back! *(Kisses his
hands)* Darling Uncle, give it back! *(Cries)* You are kind; you will have
pity on us and give it back, won't you? Bear up, Uncle! Bear up!

VOYNITSKY *(Takes the bottle out of the table drawer and gives it to*
ASTROV*)*
Here, take it! *(To* SONYA*)* I must set to work at once, I must do some-
thing immediately, or I can't bear it—I can't. . . .

SONYA

Yes, yes, work. As soon as we've seen them off, we shall sit down to
work. *(Nervously sorting out the papers on the table)* We've let everything go. . . .

ASTROV *(Puts the bottle into his medicine case and tightens the straps)*
Now I can set off.

YELENA *(Enters)*

Vanya, are you here? We're leaving now. Go to Aleksandr. He wants
to say something to you.

SONYA

Go, Uncle Vanya. *(Takes* VOYNITSKY *by the arm)* Let's go. Father and you must make it up. It must be done.

(SONYA *and* VOYNITSKY *go out)*

YELENA

I'm going away. *(Gives* ASTROV *her hand)* Good-bye!

ASTROV

So soon?

YELENA

The carriage is at the door.

ASTROV

Good-bye.

YELENA

You promised me today that you'd go away.

ASTROV

I haven't forgotten. I'm just going. *(Pause)* Frightened? *(Takes her hand)* Is it so terrible?

YELENA

Yes.

ASTROV

Why not stay? What do you say? And tomorrow on the plantation . . .

YELENA

No. . . . It's all settled. . . . And I look at you so bravely because it is settled. . . . There's only one thing I'd like to ask you: Think well of me. Yes, I'd like you to respect me.

ASTROV

Oh, blast! *(Makes a gesture of impatience)* Do stay. Please! You must realize that there's nothing in the world you can do, that you've no aim in life, that you've nothing to occupy your mind, and that sooner or later your feelings will get the better of you—that's inevitable. So don't you think it had better be here in the country and not in Kharkov or somewhere in Kursk? It's more poetical, at all events. And the autumn here is beautiful. There's the plantation and the half-ruined country houses Turgenev was so fond of describing.

YELENA

How absurd you are! I'm angry with you, but—I shall remember you
with pleasure all the same. You're an interesting, an original man. We
shall never meet again, so—why conceal it? I was a little in love with
you—that's quite true. So let's shake hands and part friends. Don't
think too badly of me.

ASTROV *(Pressing her hand)*

Yes, I suppose you'd better go. *(Musingly)* I believe you're a good,
warmhearted person, and yet there seems to be something peculiar
about you, something that is part of your very nature. The moment
you come here with your husband, all of us, instead of going on with
our work, instead of doing something, creating something, leave everything and do nothing all the summer except attend to you and your
husband's gout. You and your husband have infected us all with your
idleness. I became infatuated with you and have done nothing for a
whole month, and all the time people have been ill and the peasants
have been grazing their herds in my newly planted woods. And so,
wherever you and your husband go, you bring ruin and destruction in
your wake. . . . I'm joking, of course, but all the same it's—it's strange,
and I'm quite sure that if you had stayed here much longer, the devastation would have been enormous. I should have been done for,
but—you, too, would not have gotten off scot free. Well, go. *Finita la
commedia!*

YELENA *(Takes a pencil from his table and hides it quickly)*

I shall keep this pencil to remember you by.

ASTROV

It's all so strange. . . . We've met and, suddenly, for some unknown
reason, we shall never see each other again. Everything in the world is
like that. . . . But while there's no one here, before Uncle Vanya comes
in with his bunch of flowers, let me—kiss you. . . . A farewell kiss.
. . . Yes? *(Kisses her on the cheek)* Well—that's the end of that.

YELENA

I wish you all the happiness in the world. *(Looking around)* Oh, I don't
care! For once in my life! *(Embraces him impulsively and both at once
draw quickly away from each other)* I must go.

ASTROV

Hurry up and go. If the carriage is ready, you'd better set off.

YELENA

I think they're coming.
(Both listen)

ASTROV

Finita!
(Enter SEREBRYAKOV, VOYNITSKY, MARIA VOYNITSKY *with a book,* TELEGIN, *and* SONYA*)*

SEREBRYAKOV *(To* VOYNITSKY*)*

Let bygones be bygones. After all that has happened, during these few hours I've been through so much and I've thought over so much that I believe I could write a whole treatise on the art of living for the benefit of posterity. I gladly accept your apologies and I apologize myself. Good-bye.
*(*SEREBRYAKOV *and* VOYNITSKY *kiss each other three times)*

VOYNITSKY

You will receive the same amount you received before, regularly in the future. Everything will be as it used to be.
*(*YELENA *embraces* SONYA*)*

SEREBRYAKOV *(Kisses* MARIA VOYNITSKY'*s hand)*

Mother-in-law . . .

MARIA

Do have your photograph taken again, Aleksandr, and send it to me. You know how dear you are to me.

TELEGIN

Good-bye, sir. Don't forget us!

SEREBRYAKOV *(Kissing his daughter)*

Good-bye. . . . Good-bye, everyone! *(Shaking hands with* ASTROV*)* Thank you for the pleasure of your company. I respect your way of looking at things, your enthusiasms, your impulses, but please permit an old man like me to add just one single observation to my farewell: We must work, ladies and gentlemen, we must work! Good-bye!
*(*SEREBRYAKOV *goes out, followed by* MARIA VOYNITSKY *and* SONYA*)*

VOYNITSKY *(Kisses* YELENA'*s hand warmly)*

Good-bye. . . . Forgive me. . . . We shall never meet again. . . .

YELENA *(Deeply moved)*

Good-bye, my dear. *(Kisses him on the head and goes out)*

ASTROV *(To* TELEGIN*)*

Tell them, Waffles, to bring my carriage around, too.

TELEGIN

Certainly, my dear fellow. *(Goes out. Only* ASTROV *and* VOYNITSKY *remain)*

ASTROV *(Collects his paints from the table and puts them away in his suitcase)*
Why don't you go and see them off?

VOYNITSKY

Let them go. I—I can't. . . . I'm sick at heart. . . . I must get to work quickly. Do something—anything. . . . To work, to work! *(Rummages among the papers on the table)*
    (Pause; the sound of harness bells can be heard)

ASTROV

They've gone. The professor must be jolly glad, I shouldn't wonder. You won't get him to come here again for all the tea in China.

MARINA *(Comes in)*

They've gone. *(Sits down in an easy chair and knits her sock)*

SONYA *(Comes in)*

They've gone. *(Wipes her eyes)* I hope they'll be all right. *(To her uncle)* Well, Uncle Vanya, let's do something. . . .

VOYNITSKY

Work, work . . .

SONYA

It seems ages since we sat at this table together. *(Lights the lamp on the table)* I don't think there's any ink. . . . *(Takes the inkstand, goes to the cupboard, and fills it with ink)* I can't help feeling sad now that they've gone.

MARIA *(Comes in slowly)*

They've gone! *(Sits down and becomes absorbed in her pamphlet)*

SONYA *(Sits down at the table and turns the pages of the account book)*
First of all, Uncle Vanya, let's make up the accounts. We've neglected them terribly. Today someone sent for his account again. Let's start. You do one account and I another.

VOYNITSKY (*Writes*)

To the account of . . . Mr. . . .
 (*Both write in silence*)

MARINA (*Yawns*)

I'm ready for bye-byes. . . .

ASTROV

Silence. The pens scratch and the cricket sings. Warm, cozy. . . . No,
I don't want to go. . . . (*The sound of harness bells is heard*) There's
my carriage. . . . Well, my friends, all that's left for me to do is to say
good-bye to you, say good-bye to my table, and—be off! (*Puts away
maps in portfolio*)

MARINA

What's the hurry? Sit down.

ASTROV

Sorry, Nanny, I can't.

VOYNITSKY (*Writes*)

Balance from previous account two rubles, seventy-five kopecks. . . .
 (*Enter* LABORER)

LABORER

Your carriage is waiting, Doctor.

ASTROV

I know. (*Hands him the medicine case, the suitcase, and the portfolio*)
Take these, and mind, don't crush the portfolio.

LABORER

Very good, sir. (*Goes out*)

ASTROV

Well, that's that. (*Goes to say good-bye*)

SONYA

When shall we see you again?

ASTROV

Not before next summer, I'm afraid. Hardly in the winter. Naturally,
if anything should happen, you'll let me know and I'll come. (*Shakes
hands*) Thank you for your hospitality and for your kindness, for everything, in fact. (*Goes up to the nurse and kisses her on the head*) Good-
bye, old woman.

MARINA

You're not going without tea?

ASTROV

I don't want any, Nanny.

MARINA

You'll have a glass of vodka, though, won't you?

ASTROV *(Hesitantly)*

Thank you. Perhaps I will. . . . *(MARINA goes out. Pause)* My trace horse is limping a bit. I noticed it yesterday when Petrushka was taking it to water.

VOYNITSKY

You must change its shoes.

ASTROV

I suppose I'd better call at the blacksmith's in Rozhdestveny. Yes, I'll have to, it seems. *(Goes up to the map of Africa and looks at it)* I expect down there in Africa the heat must be simply terrific now. Terrific!

VOYNITSKY

I expect so.

MARINA *(Comes back with a tray on which there is a glass of vodka and a piece of bread)*
Here you are! *(ASTROV drinks the vodka)* To your health, dear. *(Makes a low bow)* Have some bread with it.

ASTROV

No, thank you, I like it as it is. Well, good-bye all! *(To MARINA)* Don't bother to see me off, Nanny. There's no need.
    (He goes out; SONYA follows him with a candle to see him off; MARINA sits down in her easy chair)

VOYNITSKY *(Writes)*

February the second: linseed oil, twenty pounds. . . . February the sixteenth: linseed oil again, twenty pounds. . . . Buckwheat meal . . .
    (Pause. The sound of harness bells is heard)

MARINA

He's gone.
    (Pause)

SONYA *(Comes back, puts candle on table)*
He's gone. . . .

VOYNITSKY *(Counts on the abacus and writes)*
Total: fifteen—twenty-five . . .
(SONYA sits down and writes)

MARINA *(Yawns)*
Mercy on us. . . .
(TELEGIN comes in on tiptoe, sits down near the door, and softly tunes the guitar)

VOYNITSKY *(To SONYA, passing his hand over her hair)*
My child, I'm so unhappy! Oh, if only you knew how unhappy I am!

SONYA
It can't be helped, we must go on living however unhappy we are! *(Pause)* We shall go on living, Uncle Vanya. We shall live through a long, long round of days and dreary evenings; we shall bear with patience the trials that fate has in store for us; we shall work without resting for others now and in our old age, and when our time comes, we shall die without complaining; and there, beyond the grave, we shall say that we have wept and suffered, that we had a hard, bitter struggle; and God will have pity on us, and you and I, Uncle dear, will see a new life, a bright, lovely, and happy life; and we shall rejoice and shall look back with a deep feeling of tenderness and a smile upon our present sufferings and tribulations, and—and we shall rest. . . . I believe that, Uncle, fervently, passionately believe it! *(TELEGIN plays softly on the guitar)* We shall rest! We shall hear the angels; we shall see all heaven bright with many stars, shining like diamonds; we shall see all our sufferings and all earthly evil dissolve in mercy that will fill the whole world, and our life will be peaceful, tender, and sweet as a caress. I believe that, I do, I believe it. *Wipes away his tears with her handkerchief)* Poor, poor, Uncle Vanya, you are crying. . . . *(Through tears)* You knew no happiness in your life, but wait, Uncle Vanya, wait. . . . We shall rest. . . . *(Embraces him)* We shall rest! *(TELEGIN plays softly; MARIA VOYNITSKY writes on the margin of her pamphlet; MARINA knits her sock)* We shall rest!
(The curtain descends slowly)

(1899)

MIKHAIL SALTYKOV-SHCHEDRIN

MIKHAIL SALTYKOV-SHCHEDRIN (1826–1889) wrote predominantly in the satirical vein; he is considered the greatest Russian satirist after Gogol. (Saltykov was his real name; he assumed Shchedrin as his nom de plume.) He served with success in many branches of the imperial civil service, in a variety of posts, in many different towns, and even rose to the position of vice governor of a province. Yet paradoxically, he also wrote scathing satires. In the late 1860s he was finally asked to resign because of his writings against the regime, and then devoted himself to literature and journalism. He became recognized as one of the leaders of the radical movement, but he also was involved in internal quarrels within the editorial staffs of particular journals and newspapers. In 1864 he was engaged in a bitter journalistic battle with Dostoyevsky, whose Notes from Underground *he greatly resented; Dostoyevsky naturally repaid him with a scathing attack of his own.*

Saltykov's Provincial Sketches *(1856–1857),* History of a Town *(1869–1870), and* Old Times in Poshekhonie *(1887–1889) humorously chronicle stupidity, mediocrity, and corruption. His best-known work,* The Golovlyovs *(1872–1876), is the story of the progressive moral, physical, and economic disintegration of a family. The indictments of this novel are unrelieved by any ray of light. Among the several unforgettable but depressing characters, Porfiry, or Yudushka the Bloodsucker, as he is nicknamed, stands out. He is one in the world's gallery of great hypocrites and misers, worthy to stand beside Molière's Miser and Tartuffe, Pushkin's Avaricious Knight, and Shakespeare's Shylock. Yudushka's simpering pieties and his relentless drive to dominate and crush his relatives are presented most powerfully.*

Saltykov's fables and fairy tales are outstanding nineteenth-century Russian examples of "Aesopian language," political criticism disguised under outwardly harmless, naive storytelling. They have humor as well as satirical bite. "How One Peasant Fed Two Generals" (1869) is one of the best known of Saltykov's stories. It combines the fantastic and the simple, the realistic and the exaggerated. The fable borrows many turns of phrase from Russian folk tales. In capsule form it comically pillories the parasitical life of the bureaucracy and at the same time may be quietly suggesting to the peasants that they are bound by ropes of their own making. It is a tiny allegory of the relationship between social classes in Russia, but its whimsicality does not detract from the pointedness of the satire.

THE STORY OF HOW ONE RUSSIAN PEASANT
FED TWO GENERALS

Once upon a time there lived two generals, and because both of them were flighty, so suddenly, for neither this reason nor that, they found themselves on an uninhabited island.

Both generals had worked all their lives in some kind of registratic 11 office. That is where they had been born, were brought up, and ha:t grown old. As a result they understood nothing. They did not even know any words, except for: "Yours truly, with my deepest respect."

The office was found to be unnecessary and was abolished. The two generals were dismissed. Finding themselves unemployed, they went to live in Petersburg, on Podyacheskaya Street, in separate apartments; each had his cook and received a pension. But suddenly they found themselves on an uninhabited island. They woke up and found that they were both lying under the same blanket. At first of course they understood nothing and talked as if nothing had happened to them.

"I had a strange dream, Your Excellency," one general said. "It looked as if I was living on an uninhabited island. . . ." He said this and jumped up. The second general also jumped up.

"Goodness me! What is all this! Where are we!" both of them shouted with a strange voice.

And they pinched each other, to see if such a thing had happened to them not in a dream but in reality. But no matter how much they tried to convince themselves that it was only a dream, they had to accept the sad reality.

To one side of them was the sea, on the other side a small patch of land, behind which stretched the same boundless sea. The generals started crying, the first time since the registration office had been closed.

They examined each other and saw that they we were wearing nightshirts, and each had a medal hanging around his neck.

"Coffee would hit the spot right now!" one general said, but then remembered what kind of a mishap had happened with them and cried a second time.

"What are we going to do?" he said through his tears. "If we were to write a report now, what use would it be?"

The second general said, "I have an idea. You, Your Excellency, go east, and I will go west, and in the evening we will meet right here again. Maybe we'll find something."

They looked to see where east and west were. They remembered their chief had once said: "If you want to find the east, stand with your eyes to the north, and what you are looking for will be on your right-hand side." They started looking for the north, stood this way and that, tried all the directions, but because all their lives they had worked in the registration office, they found nothing.

"Here is an idea, Your Excellency. You go to the right and I will go left. That will be better," one general said, who, besides the registration office, had also worked in the School of Military Cantonists as teacher of calligraphy and therefore was more intelligent.

No sooner said than done. One general went to the right and he saw trees and on the trees there grew fruit. The general wanted to get at least one apple, but all the apples were hanging so high that one had to climb up. He tried to climb, but it didn't work. He only tore his shirt. The general came to a stream, and saw there were fish in it, like in the fish pond on the Fontanka, swarming and swarming.

"If we could get a fish and take it back to Podyacheskaya Street!" the general thought, and his appetite showed on his face.

The general went into the woods, and grouse were whistling, woodcocks were calling, and hares were running around.

"Lord, so much food, so much food," the general said, and felt he was beginning to feel sick.

There was nothing to be done. He had to return empty-handed to the place they had agreed on. He came there, and the other general was already waiting for him.

"Well, Your Excellency, have you caught anything?" "I found an old copy of the *Moscow News*, nothing else." The two generals again lay down to sleep, but they could not go to sleep on an empty stomach. They worried about who would collect their pension for them, and they recalled the fruit, fish, grouse, woodcocks, and hares they had seen in the course of the day.

"Who would have thought, Your Excellency, that human food in its original form flies, swims, and grows on trees?" one general said.

"Yes", the other general answered, "I confess that before now I thought that rolls were born in the same shape and form in which they serve them in the morning with our coffee."

"It must be that if for example someone wants to eat grouse, he must first catch it, kill it, pluck the feathers, and roast it. . . . Only how is one to do all that?"

"How is one to do all that?" the other general repeated like an echo.

They fell silent and again tried to sleep. But hunger chased away sleep. Grouse, turkeys, suckling pigs flashed before their eyes, juicy, light pink, with cucumbers, pickles, and other kinds of salad.

"I would eat my own boots," one general said.

"Gloves are also tasty if they are worn thin," the other general said with a sigh.

Suddenly both generals looked at one another. An evil fire burned in their eyes. Their teeth chattered, they growled from deep in their chests. They crawled slowly toward each other and suddenly became frenzied. Tatters were flying about, there was squealing and moaning. The general who had been a teacher of calligraphy had bitten off his colleague's medal ribbon and had immediately swallowed it. But the sight of blood seemed to return them to reason.

"May the Christian God help us," both of them said at the same time. "We are going to eat each other up!"

"How did we get here? Who is the evildoer who played this trick on us?"

"Your Excellency, we must distract ourselves with some kind of conversation, or we are going to have a murder here," one general said.

"You begin," the other general answered. "Why, for example, do you think, why does the sun first rise and then set, and not the other way around?"

"You are a strange man, Your Excellency. You know that even you first of all get up, then go to the office, you write there, and only after that you go to sleep."

"But why not this kind of a turnaround: first I go to sleep, I dream various dreams, and only after that I get up?"

"Hm—yes. . . . But I must admit that when I worked at the office,

I always thought this way: now it is morning, and after that it will be noon, and after that they will serve me my supper—and it will be time to sleep!"

But the mention of supper threw both of them into dejection and cut the conversation off in its very beginning.

"I heard a doctor say that a human being can nourish himself for a long time on his own juices," one general began again.

"How is that?"

"This way. One's own juices in some way produce other juices. those juices in turn produce more juices, and so forth, until finally th juices stop altogether."

"And then what?"

"Then one must eat some food."

"Phooey."

In a word, no matter what the generals began to talk about, the conversation always came down to something reminding them of eating, and that excited their appetite even more. They agreed to stop talking, and remembered the copy of the *Moscow News* that they had found. They started reading it eagerly.

"Yesterday," one general read out with an excited voice, "a gala banquet was given at the home of the honored head of our ancient capital. One hundred guests were served with amazing luxury. It was as if the gifts of all countries held a rendezvous at this enchanted feast. There was 'Sheksinian gold sterlet,'* and pheasant, the inhabitant of the forests of the Caucasus, and strawberries, so rare in February in our northern—"

"Oh, Lord! Your Excellency, can't you find some other subject?" the other general shouted in despair, and took the newspaper away from his colleague and read the following: "A report from Tula: yesterday a sturgeon was caught in the river Ula, an event which even the oldest inhabitants do not remember having ever happened before, all the more so because the police officer B. was found and identified inside the sturgeon. The local club organized a feast. The cause for this celebration was brought in on a huge wooden dish, garnished with little cucumbers, and holding greenery in its mouth. Dr. P., who was the master of ceremonies, took pains to assure that all guests should receive their portion. There were many different kinds of fanciful dressing."

"Excuse me, Your Excellency, you, too, do not seem to be very careful about your choice of reading matter," the first general inter-

* A quotation from a poem by Gavrila Derzhavin (1743–1816). It is the opening line of his poem "Invitation to Dinner."

rupted, and picked up the newspaper himself. He read: "A report from Vyatka: an old-time local resident invented the following original manner of preparing the fish soup *ukha:* take a live eelpout, and flog it; its liver will become enlarged as a result of its feeling the pain, and then . . ."

The generals bowed their heads. Whatever they might look at, it all spoke of food. Their own thoughts played them false, because no matter how hard they drove away pictures of beefsteaks, their imagination pushed them back by force. Suddenly the general who had been a calligraphy teacher got an inspiration.

"What if we found ourselves a peasant, Your Excellency?" he said cheerfully.

"You mean a peasant?"

"Yes, simply a peasant . . . the kind of peasant that peasants usually are. He would serve us rolls and catch grouse and fish, too."

"Hm, a peasant. But where will we find one, this peasant, when there aren't any?"

"What do you mean, there aren't any? Peasants are everywhere One must only look for one. He is probably hiding somewhere, too lazy to work."

This thought cheered up the generals so much that they jumped up like a jack-in-the-box and started looking for a peasant. For a long time they wandered around the island without any success, but in the end, the sharp smell of coarse bread and of a rank sheepskin put them on the right track. Under a tree, a huge man lay sleeping, belly up, with his hands under his head. He was shirking work most insolently. There were no bounds to the indignation of the generals.

"So you are sleeping, you lazybones!" Both of them fell upon him. "You don't care in the least that for the second day in a row, two generals have been starving to death! Up and get to work right away!"

The man got up; he could see the generals were severe. He would have liked to give them the slip, but they seized him and held him firmly.

And he began to do things for them.

First he climbed a tree and picked each general ten of the ripest apples, and for himself he took one apple, a green one. Then he dug around in the ground and pulled up potatoes; then he took two pieces of wood and rubbed one against the other, and started a flame. Then he made a snare out of his own hair and caught a grouse. Finally he made a fire and cooked so much food of various kinds that the generals even wondered whether they shouldn't give a little portion of it to the idler himself.

The generals contemplated the peasant's efforts, and their hearts beat cheerfully. They had already forgotten that the day before they had almost died of hunger, and they thought: how nice it is to be a general—you're all right anywhere!

"Do you have everything you need, generals?" the lazybones-peasant asked them.

"Yes, dear friend, we see how diligent you are," the generals answered.

"Will you allow me to take a rest now?"

"Rest, friend, but first make a rope."

The peasant picked some wild hemp, soaked it in water, beat it, kneaded it, and toward evening, there was a rope. With this rope the generals tied the peasant to a tree, so he would not run away, and they themselves lay down to sleep.

A day passed, then another. The peasant became so clever that he even made soup in his hands. Our generals became cheerful, fat, white-complexioned, and their stomachs were full. They said that here they were getting their bed and board, and meanwhile in Petersburg their pensions were piling up and piling up.

"What do you think, Your Excellency, was there really a Tower of Babel, or was it just a story, only a parable?" one general said to the other after they had had breakfast.

"I think, Your Excellency, that it really existed, because how else could you explain why there exist different languages in the world?"

"So there must have been a flood, too?"

"There was a flood, too, because if not, how could you explain the existence of antediluvian animals? All the more so because in the *Moscow News* it says that—"

"Let us read a little in the *Moscow News*."

They found a copy, sat down in the shade, and read it from the first page to the last, how people ate in Moscow, how they ate in Tula, in Penza, in Ryazan, and everything was all right, they did not feel sick.

Time passed, and the generals became bored. More and more often they mentioned the cooks they left behind in Petersburg and they even cried a little, on the sly.

"What is going on at Podyacheskaya Street now, Your Excellency?" one general asked the other.

"Don't even ask, Your Excellency. I feel so sad," the other general answered.

"It is nice here, it really is, what is there to say, but still, you know. One does get a little homesick. And I miss my uniform, too."

"And how one misses it. Especially the fourth-class uniform, you look at the embroidery, you become dizzy."

And they started to get after the peasant. "Get us back to Podyacheskaya Street." And what a surprise, it turned out the peasant knew Podyacheskaya Street, he had been there, it was like in a fairy tale.

"We are generals from Podyacheskaya Street," the general said happily.

"And me, maybe you saw me: a man hanging outside of a house, in a box on a rope, and he paints the wall, or walks on the roof, just like a fly: that man, that is me!" the peasant answered. And the peasant began to think how he could make the generals happy, because they had taken pity on him, the idler, and were not above accepting his disgusting peasant services. And he built a ship, or if not a ship, then at least the kind of a boat in which one could row right up to Podyacheskaya Street.

"Look out, you scoundrel, don't drown us," the generals said to him when they saw the boat rocking in the waves.

"Don't worry, generals, I have sailed in boats before," the peasant answered, and got ready to leave. He took soft swan down and made them beds inside the little boat. Having made their beds, he put the generals in them, crossed himself, and pushed off. How afraid the generals were while they were sailing through storms and various kinds of winds, how they cursed the peasant for his fecklessness—you can't describe it with a pen or tell it in a tale. But the peasant rowed and rowed and fed herring to the generals.

Finally they reached the Neva and the famous Catherine Canal, and even the Great Podyacheskaya Street! The cooks clapped their hands when they saw how their generals had grown fat, white-complexioned, and cheerful! The generals drank a lot of coffee, ate buns, and dressed in their uniforms. They drove to the treasury and raked in so much money—you can't tell it in a tale or write it with a pen.

But they did not forget the peasant. They sent him a glass of vodka and a silver ruble. Peasant, go and have a good time!

(1869)

MAKSIM GORKY

MAKSIM GORKY (1868–1936) chose his last name, which means "The Bitter One" in Russian, as a pen name to suggest the bitterness of his attitude toward czarist society—his real name was Aleksey Peshkov. Gorky was one of the first Russian authors not born into the middle class or the gentry. Born in the town of Nizhni Novgorod on the Volga, the son of an upholsterer, he became an orphan at an early age and was brought up in squalor. He knew life as a laborer in a variety of jobs and as a vagabond. He worked on Volga riverboats and wandered in various parts of Russia. Gorky became a Marxist at an early age, joined the Social Democratic (later Bolshevik) party, and participated in revolutionary movements before 1917.

He wrote stories that caught the attention of established writers and that quickly made him a popular success as well. These works were of two clearly distinguishable kinds: rather sentimental, romantic tales and crass naturalistic stories. His play The Lower Depths *(1902) presented a collection of hopeless derelicts languishing in a slum flophouse. Staged by Stanislavsky in the Moscow Art Theater, it was a landmark of naturalistic theater. Gorky's novel* The Mother, *actually written in the Adirondacks in 1906 while Gorky was visiting the United States in order to raise money for anticzarist causes, has been called the first Russian proletarian novel, and it set the pattern for innumerable later propagandistic works with a proworker, anticapitalistic thrust, in Russia and elsewhere. Other plays and stories by Gorky also enjoyed remarkable success all over the world. His autobiography is unsurpassed as a gripping literary achievement and as a window into the life of working-class Russia. Gorky's reminiscences of famous authors (such as Leo Tolstoy and Leonid Andreyev) are also engrossing literary masterpieces and can be recommended to anyone interested in Russia, while his multivolume novels, such as* Klim Samghin *(late 1920s), which the Soviet regime forced on millions of schoolboys and schoolgirls, were monumentally boring.*

After the Bolshevik Revolution of 1917, Gorky vacillated in his attitude toward the government. He left the country in 1921. However, he returned permanently in 1929 and participated in Stalinist literary politics. His return was a great feather in the cap of the Soviet rulers. During his years in the USSR as a privileged writer acclaimed and glorified by the regime, he shut his eyes to the lot of prisoners in Soviet labor camps. He lent his prestige to inhuman exploitation of millions of people and allowed himself to be used as an argument against critics of the Soviet Union. Gorky died in 1936 under still unexplained circumstances. (Émigrés conjectured that he was killed on Stalin's orders.) After his death, the regime exploited the apparent support of the late writer to the utmost.

Gorky was a self-educated man of immense, perhaps naive faith in the power of education to transform humanity, with a crudely utilitarian view of the function of literature, but with tremendous talent and power that came to fruition in only a small number of works. Among them, his story "Twenty-Six Men and One Girl" (1899) presents a stark picture of life among the wretched bakery workers. The subterranean place of work is expressive of the inhuman conditions under which they labored. Gorky depicts their lives simply and directly. Their worship of the young girl as one ray of beauty in the men's dark existence is an example of Gorky's penchant to romanticize his positive ideals. D. S. Mirsky, the brilliant Russian critic who returned to the Soviet Union from emigration in England and met his death in a Soviet prison camp, described the tale in his History of Russian Literature:

> The story is cruelly realistic. But it is traversed by such a powerful current of poetry, by such a convincing faith in beauty and freedom and in the essential nobility of man, and at the same time it is told with such precision and necessity, that it can hardly be refused the name of a masterpiece. It places Gorky—the young Gorky—among the true classics of our literature.

TWENTY-SIX MEN AND ONE GIRL

We were twenty-six men, twenty-six living machines boxed up in a dark hole of a basement, where from morning till night we kneaded dough, making pretzels and biscuits. The windows of our basement looked out on a hole lined with bricks that were green with slime. The windows, on the outside, were closely grated, and no ray of sunshine could reach us through the panes, which were plastered with meal. Our boss had fenced off the windows to prevent any of his bread from going to beggars or to those of our mates who were out of work and starving—our boss called us a bunch of crooks and gave us tainted tripe for dinner instead of meat.

Life was stuffy in that crowded dungeon, beneath a low-hanging ceiling covered with soot and cobwebs. Life was hard and sickening within those thick walls smudged with dirt stains and mildew. We got up at five in the morning, heavy from not enough sleep, and at six, dull and listless, we sat down at the table to make pretzels and cracknels out of the dough that our mates had prepared while we were sleeping. And the livelong day, from early morning till ten at night, some of us sat at the table shaping the stiff dough and swaying our bodies to fight numbness, while others were mixing flour and water. And all day long the simmering water in the caldron where the pretzels were cooking gurgled drearily and sadly, and the baker's shovel clattered angrily and swiftly on the hearthstone as it flung slippery cooked pieces of dough onto the hot bricks. From morning till night the wood burned in the oven, and the ruddy glow of the flames flickered on the bakery walls, as though in silent mockery. The huge oven resembled the ugly head of some fantastic monster thrust up from under the floor, its gaping jaws ablaze with glowing fire, breathing heat at us, and watching our ceaseless toil through two sunken air holes over its forehead. These two hollows were like eyes—the pitiless impassive eyes of a monster; they stared at us balefully, as though weary with looking at slaves of whom nothing human could be expected, and whom they despised with the cold contempt of wisdom.

Day in, day out, amid the meal dust and the grime that we brought in on our feet from the yard, in the smelly stuffiness of the hot basement, we kneaded dough and shaped pretzels, which were sprinkled with our sweat, and we hated our work with a fierce hatred, and never ate what our hands had made, preferring black rye bread to pretzels. Sitting at a long table facing one another—nine men on each side—we worked our hands and fingers mechanically through the long hours, and had grown so accustomed to our work that we no longer watched our movements. And we had grown so accustomed to one another that each of us knew every furrow on his mates' faces. We had nothing to talk about, we were used to that, and were silent all the time—unless we swore, for there is always something one can swear at a man for, especially one's mate. But we seldom swore at each other—is a man to blame if he is half dead, if he is like a stone image, if all his senses are blunted by the crushing burden of toil? Silence is awful and irksome only to those who have said all there is to say; but to people whose words are still unspoken, silence is natural and easy. Sometimes we sang, and this is how our song would start: during the work somebody would suddenly heave a sigh, like a weary horse, and begin softly to sing one of those long-drawn songs whose mournful tender melody always lightens the heavy burden of the singer's heart. One of the men would sing while the rest listened in silence to the lonely song, and it would flag and fade away beneath the oppressive basement ceiling like the dying flames of a campfire in the steppe on a wet autumn night, when the gray sky overhangs the earth like a roof of lead. Then another singer would join the first, and the two voices would float drearily and softly in the stuffy heat of our crowded pen. Then suddenly, several voices at once would join in—and the song would be lashed up like a wave, growing stronger and louder, and seeming to break down the dank, heavy walls of our prison.

Now all twenty-six would be singing; loud voices, brought to harmony by long practice, fill the workshop; the song is cramped for space; it buffets the stone walls, moaning and weeping, and stirs the heart with a gentle prickly pain, reopening old wounds and wakening anguish in the soul. The singers draw deep heavy sighs; one will suddenly break off and sit listening for a long time to his mates, then his voice will mingle again with the general chorus. Another will cry out dismally, "Ah!" singing with closed eyes, and maybe he sees the broad torrent of sound as a road running far out, a wide road bathed in brilliant sunshine and he himself walking along it. . . .

The flames in the oven still flicker, the baker's shovel still scrapes on the brick, the water in the caldron still bubbles and gurgles, the firelight on the wall still quivers in silent laughter. And we chant out, through words that are not our own, the dull ache within us, the gnawing grief of living men deprived of the sun, the grief of slaves. And so we lived, twenty-six men, in the basement of a big stone building, and the burden of life was so heavy that one would think the three stories of the house were built on our shoulders.

———

Apart from our songs there was something else that we loved and cherished, something that perhaps filled the place of the sun for us. On the first floor of our building there was a gold embroidery workshop, and there, among many girl hands, lived sixteen-year-old Tanya, a housemaid. Every morning a pink face with blue merry eyes would be pressed to the pane of the little window cut into the door of our workshop, and a sweet ringing voice would call out to us:

"Hullo, prisoners. Give us some pretzels!"

We would all turn our heads to the sound of that clear voice and look kindly and joyfully at the pure girlish face that smiled at us so sweetly. We loved to see the nose flattened against the glass, the little white teeth glistening from under rosy lips parted in a smile. We would rush to open the door for her, jostling one another, and there she would be, so chirpy and charming, holding out her apron, standing before us with her head cocked and face radiant. A thick long braid of chestnut hair hung over her shoulder on her breast. Grimy, coarse, ugly men, we looked up at her—the threshold rose four steps above the floor— looked up at her with raised heads and wished her good morning, and our words of greeting were special words, found only for her. When we spoke to her our voices were softer, our joking lighter. Everything we had for her was special. The baker drew out of the oven a shovelful of the crustiest browned pretzels and shot them adroitly into Tanya's apron.

"Mind the boss doesn't catch you!" we would warn her. She laughed roguishly and cried merrily:

"Bye-bye, prisoners," and would vanish in a twinkling like a little mouse.

And that would be all. . . . But long after she had gone we talked about her—we said the same things we had said yesterday and the day before, because she, and we, and everything around us were the same as they had been yesterday and the day before. It is very painful and hard for a man to live and have nothing change around him. If it doesn't kill the soul in him, the longer he lives the more painful does the immobility of things surrounding him become. We always talked about women in a way that sometimes made us feel disgusted with ourselves and with our coarse shameless talk. That is not surprising, since the women we knew probably did not deserve to be talked about in any other way. But about Tanya we never said a bad word. None of us ever dared to touch her with his hand and she never heard a loose joke from any of us. Perhaps it was because she never stayed long—she would flash before our gaze like a star falling from the heavens and vanish. Or perhaps because she was small and so very beautiful, and everything that is beautiful inspires respect, even with rough men. Moreover, though drudgery was turning us into dumb oxen, we were still human beings, and like all human beings, could not live without an object of worship. Finer than she there was nobody about us, and nobody else took notice of us men living in the basement, though there were dozens of tenants in the house. And finally—probably this was the main reason—we regarded her as something that belonged to us, something that owed its existence to our pretzels. We made it our duty to give her hot pretzels, and this became our daily sacrifice to the idol, almost a sacred rite, that endeared her to us more and more every day. Besides pretzels, we gave Tanya a good deal of advice—to dress warmly, not to run too fast up the stairs, not to carry heavy bundles of firewood. She listened to our counsels with a smile, retorted with a laugh, and never obeyed them, but we did not take offense—we were content to show our solicitude for her.

Often she asked us to do things for her. For example, she would ask us to open a refractory door in the cellar or chop some wood, and we would do these things for her and anything else she asked gladly, with a peculiar pride.

But when one of us asked her to mend his only shirt, she sniffed scornfully and said, "The idea! Not likely!"

We had a good laugh at the silly fellow's expense, and never again asked her to do anything. We loved her—and there all is said. A man always wants to foist his love on somebody or other, though it frequently oppresses, sometimes sullies, and may even poison the life of a fellow creature, for in loving he does not respect the object of his love. We had to love Tanya, for there was no one else we could love.

At times one of us would suddenly start arguing: "What's the idea, making such a fuss over the kid? What's there so wonderful about her anyway?"

We'd brusquely silence the fellow who spoke like that—we had to have something we could love; we had found it, and loved it, and what we twenty-six loved went for each of us, it was our holy of holies, and anybody who went against us in this was our enemy. We loved, perhaps, what was not really good, but then there were twenty-six of us, and we therefore wanted the object of our adoration to be held sacred by others.

Our love is no less onerous than hate . . . and that, perhaps, is why some stiff-necked people claim that our hate is more flattering than love. But why do they not shun us if that is so?

———

Besides the pretzel bakery our boss had a bun bakery. It was situated in the same building, and only a wall divided it from our hole. The bun bakers, of whom there were four, held themselves aloof from us, however. They considered their work to be cleaner than ours, and themselves, therefore, better men; they never visited our workshop, and treated us with mocking scorn whenever they ran into us in the yard. We did not visit them, either—the boss banned such visits for fear that we would steal buns. We hated the bun bakers, because we envied them—their work was easier than ours, they got better pay, they were fed better, they had a roomy airy workshop, and they were all so clean and healthy, and therefore so odious. We, on the other hand, were all a yellow gray-faced lot; three of us were ill with syphilis, some were scabby, and one was crippled by rheumatism. On holidays and Sundays they used to dress up in suits and creaky high boots, two of them possessed accordions, and all used to go out for a stroll in the park, while we were clothed in filthy tatters, with rags or bast shoes on our feet, and the police wouldn't let us into the park—now, could we love those bun bakers?

One day we learned that their head baker had taken to drink, that the boss had fired him and taken on another man in his place, and that the new man was an ex-soldier who went about in a satin waistcoat and owned a watch on a gold chain. We were curious to have a look at that dandy, and kept running out into the yard one after another in the hope of seeing him.

But he came to our workshop himself. Kicking open the door, he stood in the doorway, smiling, and said to us:

"Hullo! How are you, boys!"

The frosty air rushing through the door in a smoky cloud eddied around his feet, while he stood in the doorway looking down at us, his large yellow teeth glinting from under his fair swaggering mustache. His waistcoat was indeed unique—a blue affair, embroidered with flowers, and all glittering, with buttons made from some kind of red stone. The chain was there, too.

He was a handsome fellow, was that soldier—tall, strong, with ruddy cheeks and big light-colored eyes that had a nice look in them —a kind, clean look. On his head he wore a white stiffly starched cap, and from under an immaculately clean apron peeped the pointed toes of a highly polished pair of fashionable boots.

Our head baker asked him politely to close the door. He complied unhurriedly and began questioning us about the boss. We fell over each other to tell him that the boss was a skinflint, a crook, a scoundrel, and a tormentor—the things we told him about the boss couldn't possibly be put in writing here. The soldier listened, twitching his mustache and regarding us with that clear, gentle look of his.

"You've a lot of girls around here," he suddenly said.

Some of us laughed politely, others pulled sugary faces, and someone informed the soldier that there were nine girls about the place.

"Use 'em?" asked the soldier with a wink.

Again we laughed, a rather subdued, embarrassed laugh. Many of us would have liked to make the soldier believe they were as gay sparks as he was, but they couldn't do it. None of us could. Somebody confessed as much, saying quietly:

"Them's not for us. . . ."

"N'yes, you're miles out of it," the soldier said with conviction, looking us over narrowly. "You're not—er—up to the mark. . . . Ain't got the character . . . the right stuff, you know, the looks. Looks is what a woman likes about a man. Give her a regular body . . . everything just so. And then, of course, she likes a bit o' muscle. Likes an arm to be an arm, this kind o' stuff."

The soldier pulled his right hand out of his pocket with the sleeve rolled back to the elbow, and held it up for us to see. He had a strong white arm covered with shining golden hairs.

"The leg, chest, everything must be hard. And then a man's got to be dressed right, well turned out, you know. Take me, now—the women just fall over themselves. Mind you, I don't go after them or tempt 'em—they just hang around my neck five at a time."

He sat down on a sack of flour and told us at great length how the women loved him and how dashingly he treated them. Then he took his leave, and when the door closed behind him with a squeak, we sat on in a long silence, musing on him and his stories. Then suddenly everybody spoke up at once, and it transpired that we had all taken a liking to him. Such a nice, simple fellow, the way he had come in, sat down, and chatted. Nobody ever came to see us, nobody talked to us like that, friendly like. And we kept on talking about him and his future success with the seamstresses, who, on meeting us in the yard, either steered clear of us with a grimace of distaste, or bore straight down on us as if we were not there at all. And we only admired them, in the yard or when they passed our window, wearing their cute little hats and fur coats in the winter, and flowery hats with bright-colored parasols in the summer. Among ourselves, however, we talked about these girls in a way that, had they heard us, would have made them mad with shame and indignation.

"I hope he doesn't . . . er, have a go at our Tanya," the head baker said suddenly in a tone of anxiety.

We were all struck dumb by this statement. We had somehow forgotten about Tanya—the soldier had blotted her out, as it were, with his large handsome figure. A noisy argument broke out: some said that Tanya would have none of him, some asserted that she would be unable to resist the soldier's charms, and others proposed to break the fellow's bones for him should he start making passes at Tanya. Finally, all decided to keep a watch on the soldier and Tanya, and to warn the kid against him. That put a stop to the argument.

About a month passed. The soldier baked buns, went out with the seamstresses, often dropped in to see us, but never said anything about his conquests—all he did was to twirl his mustache and lick his chops.

Tanya came every morning for her pretzels and was as gay, sweet, and gentle as ever. We tried to broach the subject of the soldier with her—she called him a "pop-eyed dummy" and other funny names, and that set our minds at rest. We were proud of our little girl when we saw how the seamstresses clung to the soldier. Tanya's attitude toward him bucked us all up, and under her influence, as it were, we ourselves began to treat him with scorn. We loved her more than ever and greeted her more gladly and kindly in the mornings.

One day, however, the soldier dropped in on us a little the worse for drink. He sat down and started to laugh, and when we asked him what was tickling him, he said:

"Two of 'em have had a fight over me—Lida and Grusha. The things they did to each other! It was a real scream, ha-ha! One of 'em grabbed the other by the hair, dragged her into the passage all over the floor, and then got on top of her. Ha-ha-ha! Scratched each other's mugs, tore their clothes. Did I laugh! Why can't these females have a straight fight? Why do they scratch, eh?"

He sat on a bench, looking so clean, healthy, and cheerful, laughing without a stop. We said nothing. Somehow he was odious to us this time.

"Why am I such a lucky devil with the girls? It's a scream! Why, I just give a wink and the trick's done!"

He raised his white hands covered with shining hairs and brought them down on his knees with a slap. He surveyed us with a look of pleased surprise, as though himself genuinely astonished at the good luck he enjoyed with the ladies. His plump ruddy face shone with smug pleasure and he kept passing his tongue over his lips.

Our head baker angrily rattled his shovel on the hearth and suddenly said sarcastically:

"It's no great fun felling little fir trees—I'd like to see what you'd do with a pine!"

"Eh, what? Were you talking to me?" the soldier queried.

"Yes, you."

"What did you say?"

"Never mind. . . . Let it be."

"Here, hold on! What's it all about? What d'you mean—pine?"

Our baker did not reply. His shovel moved swiftly in the oven, tossing in boiled pretzels and shooting the baked ones onto the floor, where boys sat threading them on bast strings. He seemed to have forgotten the soldier. But the latter suddenly got all worked up. He rose to his feet and stepped up to the oven, exposing himself to the imminent danger of being struck in the chest by the shovel handle, which whisked spasmodically in the air.

"Look here—what d'you mean? That's an insult. Why, there isn't a girl that could resist me! No, sir! And here are you, letting out hints against me."

Indeed, he appeared to be genuinely offended. Evidently the sole source of his self-respect was his ability to seduce women; this ability, perhaps, was the only human attribute he could boast, the only thing that made him feel a human being.

There are people for whom the main thing in life is some sickness of the soul or the flesh. It fills all their lives, it is what they live for. While suffering from it, they nourish themselves on it. They complain to people about it, and in this manner command the interest of their fellow creatures. They exact a toll of sympathy from people, and this is the only thing in life they have. Deprive them of that sickness, cure them of it, and they will be utterly miserable, because they will lose the sole sustenance of their life and become empty husks. Sometimes a man's life is so poor that he is perforce obliged to cultivate a vice and thrive on it. One might say that people are often addicted to vice through sheer boredom.

The soldier was stung to the quick. He bore down on our baker, whining:

"No, you tell me—who is it?"

"Want me to tell you?" the baker said, turning on him suddenly.

"Yes!"

"Do you know Tanya?"

"Well?"

"Well, there you are! See what you can do there."

"Me?"

"Yes, you."

"Her? Easy as pie!"

"We'll see!"

"You'll see! Ha-a!"

"Why, she'll—"

"It won't take a month!"

"You're cocky, soldier, aren't you?"

"Two weeks, I'll show you! Who did you say? Tanya? Pshaw!"

"Come on, get out. You're in the way!"

"Two weeks, and the trick's done! Ugh, you!"

"Get out!"

The baker flew into a sudden rage and brandished his shovel. The soldier recoiled in amazement, then regarded us all for a while in silence, muttered grimly "All right!" and went out.

We had listened to this exchange in silence, deeply interested. But when the soldier left we all broke out into loud and excited argument. Somebody cried out to the baker:

"That's a bad business you've started, Pavel!"

"Get on with your work!" snapped the baker.

We realized that the soldier's vanity had been pricked and that Tanya was in danger. And yet, while aware of this, we were all seized with a burning pleasurable curiosity as to what would be the outcome of it. Would Tanya hold her own against the soldier? We voiced the conviction almost unanimously:

"Tanya? She'll hold her ground! She isn't easy game, not her!"

We were terribly keen on putting our idol to the test. We tried our hardest to convince each other that our idol was a staunch idol and would stand up to this test. We even started wondering whether we had goaded the soldier sufficiently, fearing that he would forget the wager and that we would have to give some more pricks to his conceit. From now on, a new exciting interest had been added to our lives, something we had never known before. We argued among ourselves for days on end; somehow, we all seemed to have grown cleverer, we spoke better and more. It was as if we were playing a game with the devil, the stake on our side being Tanya. And when we learned from the bun bakers that their soldier had "made a dead set for Tanya," our excitement rose to fever pitch and life became such a thrilling experience that we did not even notice how the boss had taken advantage of this to throw in an extra fourteen poods* of dough daily. We didn't even seem to tire of the work. Tanya's name was on our

* A *pood* was equal to thirty-six pounds.

lips all day long. We looked forward to her morning visits with a peculiar impatience. At times we fancied that when she came in to see us it would be a different Tanya, not the one we had always known.

We told her nothing about the wager, though.

We never asked her any questions and treated her in the same good-natured affectionate manner. But something new had crept into our attitude, something that was alien to our former feelings for Tanya—and that new element was keen curiosity, keen and cold as a blade of steel.

"Boys! Time's up today!" the baker said one morning as he began work.

We were well aware of it without being reminded. Yet we all started.

"You watch her. She'll soon come in," the baker suggested. Someone exclaimed ruefully: "It's not a thing the eye can catch."

And again a noisy lively argument sprang up. Today, at length, we would know how clean and incontaminate was the vessel to which we had trusted all the best that was in us. That morning it dawned on us for the first time that we were gambling for high stakes, that this test of our idol might destroy it for us altogether. All these days we had been hearing that the soldier had been doggedly pursuing Tanya with his attentions, but for some reason none of us asked her what she thought about him. She continued regularly to call on us every morning for her pretzels and was always her usual self.

That day, too, we soon heard her voice:

"Hullo, prisoners! I've come. . . ."

We hastened to let her in, and when she came in we greeted her, contrary to custom, with silence. We looked hard at her and were at a loss what to say to her, what to ask her. We stood before her, a silent sullen crowd. She was obviously surprised at the unusual reception, and suddenly we saw her turn pale and disturbed. In a choky voice she asked:

"Why are you all so . . . strange?"

"What about yourself?" the baker said in a grim tone, his eyes fixed on her face.

"What about me?"

"Nothing."

"Well, give me the pretzels, quick."

Never before had she shown any signs of hurry.

"Plenty of time," the baker retorted without stirring, his eyes still glued on her face.

Abruptly she turned and disappeared through the door.

The baker picked up his shovel, and turning to the oven, let fall calmly:

"Well, she's fixed! He's done it, the scoundrel!"

We shambled back to the table like a herd of jostling sheep, sat down, and silently and apathetically set to our work. Presently someone said:

"Maybe she hasn't—"

"Shut up! Enough of that!" the baker shouted.

We all knew him for a clever man, cleverer than any of us. And that shout of his told us that he was convinced of the soldier's victory. We felt sad and perturbed.

At twelve o'clock—the lunch hour—the soldier came in. He was, as always, clean and spruce, and—as always—looked us straight in the face. We felt too ill at ease to look at him.

"Well, gentlemen, d'you want me to show you what a soldier can do?" he said with a proud sneer. "You just go out into the passageway and peep through the cracks. Get me?"

We trooped out into the passageway, and falling over each other, pressed our faces to the chinks in the wooden wall looking onto the yard. We did not have to wait long. Presently Tanya crossed the yard with a hurried step and an anxious look, skipping over puddles of thawed snow and mud. She disappeared through the door of the cellar. After a while the soldier sauntered past whistling, and he, too, went in. His hands were thrust into his pockets and he twitched his mustache.

It was raining and we saw the drops falling into the puddles, which puckered up at the impact. It was a gray wet day—a very bleak day. Snow still lay on the roofs, while the ground was covered with dark patches of slush. On the roofs, too, the snow was covered with a brownish coating of dirt. It was cold and uncomfortable, waiting in that passage.

The first to come out of that cellar was the soldier. He walked leisurely across the yard, twitching his mustache, his hands deep in his pockets—much the same as usual.

Then Tanya came out. Her eyes . . . her eyes shone with joy and happiness, and her lips smiled. And she walked as though in a dream, swaying, with unsteady gait. . . .

It was more than we could stand. We all made a sudden dash for the door, burst into the yard, and began yelling and whistling at her in a fierce, loud, savage uproar.

She started when she saw us and stood stock-still, her feet in a dirty puddle. We surrounded her and cursed her with a sort of malicious glee, pouring out a torrent of profanity and obscene taunts.

We did it unhurriedly, slowly, seeing that she had no means of escape from the circle around her, and that we could jeer at her to our heart's content. Surprisingly enough, we did not hit her. She stood among us, turning her head from side to side, listening to our insults. And we, more and more fiercely and furiously, flung at her the dirt and poison of our wrath.

Her face drained of life. Her blue eyes, which a moment before had looked so happy, were dilated, her breath came in gasps, and her lips quivered.

And we, standing around her, were wreaking our vengeance upon her—for she had robbed us. She had belonged to us, we had spent our best feelings on her, and though that best was a mere beggar's pittance, we were twenty-six and she was one, and there was no pain we could inflict that was fit to meet her guilt. How we insulted her! She said not a word, but stared at us with wild eyes, trembling in all her body.

We guffawed, we howled, we snarled. Other people came up. One of us pulled the sleeve of Tanya's blouse.

Suddenly her eyes blazed. She raised her hands in a slow gesture to straighten her hair, and said loudly but calmly, straight into our faces:

"Oh, you miserable prisoners!"

And she bore straight down on us, just as if we had not been there, had not stood in her path. Indeed, that is why none of us proved to be in her path.

When she was clear of our circle she added just as loudly, without turning around, in a tone of scorn and pride:

"Oh, you filthy swine. You beasts." And she departed—straight, beautiful, and proud.

We were left standing in the middle of the yard amid the mud, under the rain and a gray sky that had no sun in it.

Then we, too, walked in silence back into our damp stone hole. As before, the sun never looked in at us through our windows, and Tanya never came again.

(1899)

VLADIMIR SOLOVYOV

THE END OF THE NINETEENTH CENTURY saw a rebirth of Russian interest in religious philosophy and mysticism. This reaction against the dominant materialism and positivism of the mainstream Russian intelligentsia culminated in the writings of a group of writers who included, besides Solovyov, Constantine Leontiev, Nicholas Strakhov, Vasily Rozanov, Nicholas Fyodorov, Nicholas Berdyaev, Leo Shestov, S. L. Frank, Nicholas Lossky, Viacheslav Ivanov, Dmitri Merezhkovsky, and others. Some of them emigrated after the Bolshevik Revolution of 1917 and continued to write, chiefly in Paris.

Vladimir Solovyov (1853–1900) was the grandson of a priest and the son of a historian and professor at Moscow University. He had a vision of a beautiful woman, Sofya, when he was nine, and again on two later occasions in his life. While studying in the British Museum in London in 1875, he had a second vision of Sofya, who spoke to him and told him to go to Egypt. He did so, and saw a third vision of Sofya in the desert. He was aware these visions were hallucinations, yet attributed elaborate meaning to them. Sofya became the feminine principle of love and reconciliation. Sofya was the symbol for the ground of the divinely created world—almost like the fourth person of the Trinity.

Solovyov's first university dissertation was entitled "The Crisis of Western Philosophy: Against the Positivists" and the second, "A Criticism of Abstract Principles." He taught at Moscow University, and later at St. Petersburg University. He published his book Godmanhood, consisting of his university lectures, in 1878. Voluminous works of philosophy, religion, moral inquiry, and many essays followed. The depersonalization of man was to be overcome through striving to transform man into a divine human being; at the end of history, a true community (sobornost) was to be created and an existential union with God achieved.

Solovyov based his ethics on a philosophy of love. He sought a total unity, and created an original synthesis of pantheism with Christianity. He met and was influenced by Dostoyevsky, and exerted great influence on the Russian symbolist writers of the turn of the century, such as Aleksandr Blok and Andrey Bely. He was also an important poet and master in the genre of letter writing. His last work, the pessimistic and apocalyptic War, Progress, and the End of History, *was a study of the nature of evil that concluded that evil will be overcome only with the end of the world. After the fall of communism in Russia, his work again emerged as a powerful force in the Russian intellectual scene of the 1990s.*

LECTURES ON GODMANHOOD

. . . Although man as phenomenon is a temporary, transitory fact, man as essence is necessarily eternal and all-embracing. What, then, is an ideal man? In order to be actual, such a being must be both one and many. Consequently, it is not merely the universal common essence of all human individuals, taken in abstraction from them. It is a universal, but also an individual, entity—an entity that actually contains all human individuals within itself. Every one of us, every single human being, is essentially and actually rooted in, and partakes of, the universal or absolute man.

Just as divine energies constitute the single, integral, absolutely universal, and absolutely individual organism of the living Logos, so all human elements constitute a similarly integral organism, both universal and individual, the necessary actualization and receptacle of the first—a universally human organism—as the eternal body of God and the eternal soul of the world. Since this latter organism, i.e., Sophia, in its eternal being, necessarily consists of a multiplicity of elements, constituting their real unity, each of the elements, as a necessary component part of eternal Godmanhood, must be recognized as *eternal* in the absolute, or ideal order.

Thus when we speak of the eternity of mankind, we make implicit reference to the eternity of each separate individual who constitutes mankind. Apart from such eternity, mankind itself would be an illusion. . . .

It is the abnormal attitude toward everything else, the exclusive self-assertion, or egoism, that dominates our practical life, even though we deny it in theory—the opposition of the self to all other selves, and the practical negation of the other selves—that constitutes the radical *evil* of our nature. It is characteristic of everything that lives, since every natural entity—every beast, insect, and blade of grass—separates itself in its own peculiar being from everything else, strives to be everything for itself, swallowing up or repelling what is other (whence arises external, material being). Therefore evil is a property common to all of nature. All of nature is, on the one hand, in its ideal content, its objective forms and laws, *a reflection of the totally-one idea*; but on the other hand, in its real, separated, and discordant existence, it is something alien and hostile to that idea, something wrong or evil, and that in two senses. For if egoism, i.e., the striving to set up one's exclusive "I" in the place of everything else, to eliminate everything else, is evil in the primary sense (moral evil), the fateful impossibility of actually enacting such egoism, i.e., the impossibility of actually being everything while yet remaining in one's own exclusiveness, is radical *suffering*. All other kinds of suffering are related to this radical suffering as special cases to a general law. Indeed, the common basis of all suffering, physical as well as moral, reduces to the dependence of the subject upon something other than and external to itself, some external fact that coerces and oppresses it. Such external dependence would obviously be impossible if the given subject existed in an inward and actual unity with all else, if it felt itself in all beings. . . .

It will be clear from what has been said that evil and suffering have an inner, subjective significance. They exist in us and for us, i.e., in and for every entity. They are *states* of individual entities. Evil is the state of tension of a will that asserts itself exclusively, denying every other. Suffering is the necessary reaction of the other against such a will, a reaction that the self-asserting entity undergoes involuntarily and inescapably, and that it experiences as suffering. Hence suffering, which constitutes one of the characteristic features of natural being, is an inevitable consequence of moral evil.

We have seen that the actual being of the natural world is something improper, wrong, or abnormal, insofar as it is opposed to the being of the divine world (as an absolute norm). But this opposition and, consequently, evil itself, is, as has just been shown, only a condition of individual entities and a certain relation that they bear to one another (namely, a negative relation). It is not an independent essence or specific principle. It is this world of which the Apostle says "the whole world lieth in wickedness" (1 John 5:19). But it is not some new world, absolutely distinct from the divine world and composed of specific essential elements of its own. It is simply a different, improper *inter-relation* of the very same elements that also constitute the being of the divine world.

The wrong or improper actuality of the natural world is the discordant and hostile *positing*, with respect to each other, of the very same elements that, in their normal relation, namely in their inner unity and harmony, comprise the divine world. For if God, as the absolute or all-perfect [being], contains in Himself all that is, all entities that are, there cannot be entities that have the ground of their being outside of God, or have substantial being apart from the divine world. Consequently, nature, in contradistinction to Deity, can only be a different positing or *permutation* of given essential elements that have their substantial being in the divine world.

Thus these two worlds differ from one another not in essence, but only in their [mode of] positing. One of them represents the unity of all that is, a positing in which each finds itself in all, and all in each. The other, in contrast, represents a positing of all that is, in which each, in itself or through its own will, asserts itself apart from the others and in opposition to them (evil), and thereby undergoes the external actuality of the others as opposed to its own will (suffering).

This raises a question: how can we explain this wrong or improper positing within the natural world, this exclusive self-assertion of [distinct] entities? . . .

All entities, in their primordial unity with Deity, form a single divine world, [divided] into three principal spheres, according to which of the three basic modes of being—substantial, intellectual (ideal), or sensuous (real)—predominates in them, or by which of the three divine acts (will, representation, feeling) they are principally determined. . . .

Entities as pure spirits, in the first sphere, where they exist in the immediate unity of divine will and love, have only potential existence. In the second sphere, although the multiple entities are separated out by the divine Logos as determinate objective forms, having a stable, determinate relation to one another, and thus receive a certain specificity or individuality, this is a purely ideal individuality, for the entire being of this sphere is determined by intellectual intuition or pure representation. But such an ideal individuation of elements is insufficient for the divine principle as unitary. It requires that the multiple entities should receive their own real individuality; for otherwise the energy of the divine unity or love would have no object upon which to manifest or disclose itself in its fullness. Therefore, the divine being cannot be content with the eternal contemplation of ideal essences. . . . It pauses with each of them separately . . . asserting and fixing the independent being [of each], so that each in turn may itself act upon the divine principle. . . .

The unity of the [third] sphere, produced by the divine Logos, appears for the first time as an actual, independent entity, capable of acting upon the divine principle. Only here does the object of divine action become an authentic, actual subject, and the action itself a genuine interaction. This second, produced, unity—in contrast to the primordial unity of the divine Logos—is, as we know, the soul of the world or ideal mankind (Sophia), which contains within itself and unites with itself all particular living entities or souls. As the realization of the divine principle, its image and likeness, archetypal mankind, or the world-soul, is at the same time all and one. It occupies a mediating position between the multiplicity of living entities that constitute the real content of its life, and the absolute unity of Deity that is the ideal principle and norm of its life. . . . The divine principle, which is present in [the world-soul] frees it from its creaturely nature, while this nature, in turn, makes it free with respect to Deity. . . .

Insofar as it takes the divine Logos into itself and is determined thereby, the world-soul is humanity, the divine humanity of Christ, the body of Christ, or Sophia. . . . Through it, God is manifested as a living force, active throughout creation, or as Holy Spirit. . . .

When the world-soul awakens the separate will within itself, thus isolating itself from the whole, the particular elements of the universal organism lose the common bond that they had known in the world-soul. Left to themselves, they are doomed to discordant, egoistic existence, the root of which is evil, and the fruit suffering. Thus all of creaturely existence is subjected to the vanity and bondage of decay, not by its own will, but by the will of the world-soul which—as the free and unitary principle of natural life—has subjugated it.

The natural world, having fallen away from divine unity, appears as a chaos of discordant elements. The multiplicity of disintegrated elements, alien and impenetrable to one another, finds its expression in real *space*, which is not limited to the form of extendedness. All being for another, all representation, has a "spatial" form; even the content of the inner, psychic world, as concretely represented,* appears extended or "spatial" in this sense, i.e., in a formal sense. But this is only an ideal space, and it posits no permanent or independent limits for our action. Real space, or externality, necessarily results from the

---

* For example, when we are dreaming we undoubtedly picture ourselves in a certain space; everything that happens in a dream, all the images and scenes of dream experience, are represented in spatial form.

disintegration and reciprocal alienation of all that exists, by virtue of which every entity finds in all other entities a permanent and coercive limit to its actions.

In the state of externality each singular entity, each element, is excluded or displaced by all the others. Resisting this external action, each element occupies a certain determinate space, which it attempts to retain exclusively for itself. In so doing, it displays the forces of inertia and impenetrability. The complex system of external forces, impulses, and motions resulting from such a mechanical interaction of elements comprises the world of *matter*. But this world is not a world of absolutely homogeneous elements. We know that each real element, each singular entity (atom), has its own particular individual essence (idea). In the divine order, all of these elements, positively supplementing one another, form a complete and harmonious organism. In the natural order this organism is actually disintegrated but retains its ideal unity as a hidden potency and tendency. The gradual actualization of this tendency, the gradual realization of ideal total-unity, is the meaning and goal of the cosmic process. Just as, in the divine order, the all *eternally* is an absolute organism, so, according to the law of natural being, the all gradually *becomes* such an organism through time. . . .

Thus the divine principle appears here (in the cosmic process) as the active energy of an absolute idea striving to realize or embody itself in a chaos of discordant elements. The divine principle thus has the same aim as the world-soul, namely, the incarnation of the divine idea, or the deification (*theosis*) of all that exists, by giving all that exists the form of an absolute organism. The difference is that the world-soul, as a passive force, a pure tendency, does not, primordially, know what to strive for, i.e., lacks the idea of total-unity; whereas the divine Logos as a positive principle, an active and formative energy, has the idea of total-unity within itself, and gives this idea to the world-soul as a determining form. . . .

But a question may arise at this point: Why does not the union of the divine principle with the world-soul, and the resultant generation of a universal organism as the incarnate divine idea (Sophia)—why do not this union and this generation take place at once, in a single act of divine creation? . . . The answer to this question is wholly contained in a single word, a word that expresses something without which neither God nor nature can be conceived: that word is "freedom." As a result of the world-soul's free act, the world that it had unified broke apart internally into a multitude of conflicting elements. That whole rebellious multitude must, by a long series of free acts, be reconciled to one another and to God; it must be reborn in the form of an absolute organism. . . .

In man the world-soul is inwardly united with the divine Logos in consciousness for the first time, as a pure form of total-unity. . . . In man nature grows beyond itself and passes (in consciousness) into the realm of absolute being. . . . Man is the natural mediator between God and material being, the carrier of the divine principle of total-unification into the multiplicity of natural elements; it is his task to order and organize the universe. . . .

Thus man is not limited to one principle. He has within himself, first, the elements of material being that bind him to the natural world; second, the ideal consciousness of total-unity, which binds him to God; and third, since he is not confined entirely either to the first or the second, he is a free self or "I," capable of determining himself with respect to the two aspects of his being—free to move one way or the other, to assert himself in one sphere or the other. In his ideal consciousness man bears the *image* of God. His absolute freedom from both idea and fact, the formal limitlessness of the human "I," is his *likeness* to God. Man not only has the same inner essence of life—total-unity—as God; he is also free to will to possess it in the way that God does, i.e., he may spontaneously will or desire to be like God. . . . In order to possess [the divine essence as something springing] from himself, and not merely from God, man asserts himself in separation from God, apart from God, and falls away or isolates himself from God in his own consciousness, just as the world-soul primordially isolated itself from God in its total being. . . .

The principle of evil, i.e., the exclusive self-assertion which had thrown all that exists back into primordial chaos—a principle externally dominated in the cosmic process—now emerges in a new form, as the free conscious act of an individual man. The new and emergent process has as its aim the inner, moral overcoming of this evil principle. . . .

Thus, in order that the divine principle should actually overcome man's evil will and life, it was necessary for it to appear to [man's] soul as a living, personal force, capable of penetrating the soul and taking possession of it. It was necessary that the divine Logos should not only act upon the soul from without, but should also be born within the soul, not merely limiting or illuminating it, but *regenerating* it. And since, in natural mankind, the soul is actual only in the multiplicity of individual souls, the actual union of the divine principle with the soul necessarily assumed an individual form, i.e., the divine Logos was born as an actual, individual, human being. . . .

The setting in which the divine principle assumed human form was determined by the national character of the Jews; but the time was determined by the general course of history. . . . And when outward truth-justice, the truth-justice of a people and a state, was actually concentrated in one living person—the Roman emperor, as a deified man—then divine truth-justice appeared, in the living person of God-made-man, as Jesus Christ. . . .

The proper or right relationship between nature and God in humanity, a relationship attained in the person of Jesus Christ as the spiritual center or head of all mankind, must be attained by all of mankind, as His body.

Mankind as reunited with its divine principle through the mediation of Jesus Christ is the *Church*. In the eternal, primordial world, ideal mankind is the body of the divine Logos. Similarly, in the world of natural becoming, the Church is the body of the Logos incarnate, i.e., historically individuated in the person of Jesus Christ, as God-man.

This body of Christ, which made its embryonic appearance in the form of the tiny communion of the first Christians, is growing and developing little by little, until at the end of time it will encompass all of mankind and all of nature in one universal divine-human organism. . . .

This revelation, this glory of the sons of God, which all of Creation awaits with hope, is the complete realization of the free, divine-human bond in mankind as a whole, in all spheres of man's life and activity. All of these spheres must be brought into harmonious divine-human unity, entering into that free theocracy in which the Universal Church will reach the full measure of Christ's stature. . . .

(1878)

SUGGESTIONS FOR FURTHER READING

Allen, Elizabeth Cheresh. *Beyond Realism: Turgenev's Poetics of Secular Salvation*. Stanford: Stanford University Press, 1992.

Bakhtin, Mikhail. *Problems of Dostoevsky's Poetic*. Edited by Caryl Emerson. Minneapolis: University of Minnesota Press, 1984.

Bayley, John. *Pushkin: A Comparative Commentary*. London: Cambridge University Press, 1971.

Bayley, John. *Tolstoy and the Novel*. London: Chatto and Windus, 1966.

Belknap, Robert. *The Genesis of 'The Brothers Karamazov.'* Evanston, IL: Northwestern University Press, 1991.

Berlin, Isaiah. *Russian Thinkers*. London: Hogarth Press, 1978. (Wise and lively essays on leading Russian literary and intellectual figures, including Tolstoy, Herzen, Belinsky, and Turgenev.)

Billington, James. *The Icon and the Axe*. New York: Knopf, 1966. (An interpretive history of Russia, imbued with warm sympathy for the Russian people.)

Bristol, Evelyn. *A History of Russian Poetry*. New York, Oxford: Oxford University Press, 1991.

Christian, R. F. *Tolstoy: A Critical Introduction*. London: Cambridge University Press, 1969.

Fanger, Donald. *The Creation of Nikolai Gogol*. Cambridge, MA: Harvard University Press, 1979.

Fanger, Donald. *Dostoevsky and Romantic Realism: A Study of Dostoevsky in relation to Balzac, Dickens, and Gogol*. Cambridge, MA: Harvard University Press, 1965.

Frank, Joseph. *Dostoevsky, The Seeds of Revolt; The Stir of Liberation; The Years of Ordeal*. Princeton, NJ: Princeton University Press. (The first three volumes of a massive, original biography still in progress.)

Frank, Joseph. *Through the Russian Prism: Essays on Literature and Cul-*

ture. Princeton, NJ: Princeton University Press, 1990. (Essays on Dostoevsky and other writers.)

Freeborn, Richard. *The Rise of the Russian Novel*. London: Cambridge University Press, 1973.

Gustafson, Richard F. *Leo Tolstoy: Resident and Stranger*. Princeton, NJ: Princeton University Press, 1986. (A biography and analysis of Tolstoy primarily as a religious or theological writer.)

Jackson, Robert Louis. *The Art of Dostoevsky: Deliriums and Nocturnes*. Princeton, NJ: Princeton University Press, 1981.

Jones, Malcolm. *Dostoevsky after Bakhtin: Readings on Dostoevsky's Fantastic Realism*. London: Cambridge University Press, 1990.

Karlinsky, Simon. *Anton Chekhov's Life and Thought: Selected Letters and Commentary*. Translated by Michael Henry Heim. Berkeley, Los Angeles: University of California Press, 1975. (The introductions and the letters themselves provide a readable, full, and original biography and assessment of Chekhov and his world.)

Lawrence, John. *A History of Russia*. Bloomington, IL: Meridian, 1978. (A short paperback, very readable, informative.)

Maguire, Robert A., ed. *Gogol from the Twentieth Century: Eleven Essays*. Princeton, NJ: Princeton University Press, 1974.

Malia, Martin. *Alexander Herzen and the Birth of Russian Socialism, 1812–1855*. Princeton, NJ: Princeton University Press, 1961. (A pioneering book that goes far beyond its title and discusses brilliantly the main intellectual and social currents of the period.)

Miller, Robin Feuer. *The Brothers Karamazov: Worlds of the Novel*. New York: Twayne, 1992. (A literate, readable, brilliant introduction to Dostoyevsky's art, from the 1990s perspective.)

Mirsky, D. S. *A History of Russian Literature*. New York: Vintage Russian Library, 1958. (Original, lively, full of opinion and ideas as well as factual information, the fundamental, basic history of Russian literature by an émigré who was a top-flight anglicized critic and scholar, returned to the Soviet Union, and perished in a Soviet camp.)

Mochulskii, Konstantin. *Dostoevsky: His Life and Work*. Princeton, NJ: Princeton University Press, 1967.

Morson, Gary Saul. *Hidden in Plain View: Narrative and Creative Potentials in War and Peace*. Stanford, CA: Stanford University Press, 1987.

Terras, Victor, ed. *Handbook of Russian Literature*. New Haven, CT: Yale University Press, 1985. (A one-volume encyclopedia of Russian culture, available in hardback and paperback; an indispensable companion for anybody interested in Russian culture.)

Terras, Victor. *A History of Russian Literature*. New Haven, CT: Yale University Press, 1991. (An informed, up-to-date, scholarly history.)

Terras, Victor. *A Karamazov Companion.* Madison, WI: University of Wisconsin Press, 1981.

Thompson, Ewa M., ed. *The Search for Self-Definition in Russian Literature.* Houston: Rice University Press, 1991. (An anthology of essays.)

Todd, William Mills, III, ed. *Fiction in the Age of Pushkin.* Cambridge, MA: Harvard University Press, 1986.

Todd, William Mills, III, ed. *Literature and Society in Imperial Russia, 1800–1914.* Stanford, CA: Stanford University Press, 1976. (Collection of essays on various writers.)

Walicki, Andrzej. *A History of Russian Thought.* Stanford, CA: Stanford University Press, 1979.

Wasiolek, Edward. *Dostoevsky: The Major Fiction.* Cambridge, MA: MIT Press, 1964.

Wasiolek, Edward. *Tolstoy's Major Fiction.* Chicago: University of Chicago Press, 1978.

Wilson, A. N. *Tolstoy.* New York: Norton, 1988. (A fine biography.)

Zeldin, Jesse. *Nikolai Gogol's Quest for Beauty.* Lawrence, KS: University Press of Kansas, 1978.

Zenkovskii, Vasilii Vasilevich. *A History of Russian Philosophy.* 2 vols. New York: Columbia University Press, 1953.

FOR THE BEST IN PAPERBACKS, LOOK FOR THE 🐧

In every corner of the world, on every subject under the sun, Penguin represents quality and variety—the very best in publishing today.

For complete information about books available from Penguin—including Penguin Classics, Penguin Compass, and Puffins—and how to order them, write to us at the appropriate address below. Please note that for copyright reasons the selection of books varies from country to country.

In the United States: Please write to *Penguin Group (USA), P.O. Box 12289 Dept. B, Newark, New Jersey 07101-5289* or call 1-800-788-6262.

In the United Kingdom: Please write to *Dept. EP, Penguin Books Ltd, Bath Road, Harmondsworth, West Drayton, Middlesex UB7 0DA.*

In Canada: Please write to *Penguin Books Canada Ltd, 90 Eglinton Avenue East, Suite 700, Toronto, Ontario M4P 2Y3.*

In Australia: Please write to *Penguin Books Australia Ltd, P.O. Box 257, Ringwood, Victoria 3134.*

In New Zealand: Please write to *Penguin Books (NZ) Ltd, Private Bag 102902, North Shore Mail Centre, Auckland 10.*

In India: Please write to *Penguin Books India Pvt Ltd, 11 Panchsheel Shopping Centre, Panchsheel Park, New Delhi 110 017.*

In the Netherlands: Please write to *Penguin Books Netherlands bv, Postbus 3507, NL-1001 AH Amsterdam.*

In Germany: Please write to *Penguin Books Deutschland GmbH, Metzlerstrasse 26, 60594 Frankfurt am Main.*

In Spain: Please write to *Penguin Books S. A., Bravo Murillo 19, 1° B, 28015 Madrid.*

In Italy: Please write to *Penguin Italia s.r.l., Via Benedetto Croce 2, 20094 Corsico, Milano.*

In France: Please write to *Penguin France, Le Carré Wilson, 62 rue Benjamin Baillaud, 31500 Toulouse.*

In Japan: Please write to *Penguin Books Japan Ltd, Kaneko Building, 2-3-25 Koraku, Bunkyo-Ku, Tokyo 112.*

In South Africa: Please write to *Penguin Books South Africa (Pty) Ltd, Private Bag X14, Parkview, 2122 Johannesburg.*